FOSTER DADE

EXPLORES

THE COSMOS

FOSTER DADE EXPLORES THE COSMOS

NASH JENKINS

THE OVERLOOK PRESS, NEW YORK

This edition first published in hardcover in 2023 by
The Overlook Press, an imprint of ABRAMS
195 Broadway, 9th floor
New York, NY 10007

Abrams books are available at special discounts when purchased in quantity for premiums and
promotions as well as fundraising or educational use. Special editions can also be created to
specification. For details, contact specialsales@abramsbooks.com or the address above.

Library of Congress Control Number: 2022948257

Printed and bound in the United States

1 3 5 7 9 10 8 6 4 2

ISBN: 978–1–4197–6476–9
eISBN: 978–1–64700–835–2

ABRAMS The Art of Books
195 Broadway, New York, NY 10007
abramsbooks.com

FOR MOM AND DAD,
FOR SOPHIE, SUSANNA, AND EUGENIA,

AND OF COURSE FOR SLOAN AND JULIE

The boy himself is at once too simple and too complex for us to make any final comment about him or his story. Perhaps the safest thing we can say about Holden is that he was born in the world not just strongly attracted to beauty but, almost, hopelessly impaled on it.
—J. D. Salinger, book jacket synopsis of *The Catcher in the Rye* (1st edition, Little, Brown and Co., 1951)

And the morning lasted all day
—The Dream Academy

CONTENTS

PREFACE

SEPTEMBER 2019

The facts of this case remain disputed. I should start by making that clear, and by emphasizing that the following account will not pretend to resolve certain historical uncertainties. What's important here—what illuminates and gives shape to the story I am preparing to tell—aren't the facts but the contours of their dispute. What follows is one topographical survey of these fault lines. In the decade that has passed since the events in question, the loose nebula of half-truths has unfurled under the mythmaking tendencies of time. Clarifying this nebula, I have learned, means only construing its shape; the half-truths are the fibers of its form, and so remain untouched. Acknowledging all of this has helped soothe the unavoidable truth: this is not, nor has it ever been, my story to tell.

They still talk about Foster Dade at Kennedy, though the names of the supporting cast have mostly been forgotten. This is true even of Annabeth Whittaker and Jack Albright. The story as it is told today is less about truth than allegory. I'm sympathetic to these distortions, and will confess that my motivation in pursuing this project is in many respects selfish. It's probably fair to say that no one else will take the time to curate and organize its pieces, but the simpler truth is that this story has haunted me for the better part of a decade. I suppose I hope that telling it honestly will shake the ghosts off, or at least allow me to understand why they continue to linger. "Honestly," it should be said, is not the same thing as "accurately."

The "Adderall ring" had been a misnomer on the media's part. One lanky towheaded child of divorce does not constitute a ring, no matter how many federal and state lines its distribution network might have crossed. Sheila Baxter, whom Kennedy had poached from Bear

Stearns as the school's communications director in 2005 precisely in anticipation of events like this, had successfully intimidated reporters in the weeks and months thereafter, and the articles that followed were bloated with toothless innuendo and clumsy pseudonyms. There were students who talked to the press on background, against an administrative fiat that carried threat of expulsion.

With no voices on the record to confirm or deny these whispered narrative details, the more principled institutions of the national and New York media—the *Times*, *Vanity Fair*—were bound ethically and legally to denature their reporting into broad, colorless parables on adolescent pharmaceutical abuse. Most of these outlets simply dropped the stories and moved on. In September 2010, the *Atlantic* published a long and strangely glib feature on the role of "study drugs" in these "pressure-cooker country clubs," but it made only a passing reference to the series of events at Kennedy that had precipitated it. Three months earlier, Gawker had posted direct excerpts of the Facebook chat that would become known across the constellation of northeastern boarding schools as "the Kennedy Thread." But even Gawker's editors had the sense to pixelate the names and tiny square profile pictures of the four students who'd written it. Those four, at that point—as their parents' lawyers made abundantly clear—still enjoyed the legal protection afforded to minors on matters of privacy.

I'll note here that my own place in this narrative is necessarily peripheral. When I arrived at Kennedy as a new sophomore in the fall of 2010, seven months had passed since Foster Dade had been expelled. The last of the more resolute reporters still sometimes appeared on the porch of Brennan House, where I lived, as if by standing there long enough they might absorb by osmosis the ambient unknowns. I first heard the earliest shards of Foster's story that October.

There is an untraceable magic to the boarding school ethos, to those hermetic little kingdoms illuminated by the sparkling mythological tendencies of adolescence. This is especially true at night, after 11:00 p.m. lights-out, when boys hustle noiselessly down the hallways into the bedroom of whoever's been ordained as the nocturnal host. (I was never ballsy or popular enough to be this person; when I showed up, I'd huddle in the corner under the window, enchanted but mostly silent.)

We were still proximate enough to the events surrounding Foster Dade's expulsion for the truth to be more or less intact, albeit the flexible truth of secondhand accounts. We were Second Years, in Kennedian parlance; my hallmates had been First Years during the events in question, cushioned from direct access to upperclassman politics. The boys a year ahead of us in Brennan tended to regard us with bored disinterest, but every so often a few would join us late at night, and when the conversation turned to the previous spring they seemed to revel in their relative authority. Yet their contributions only seemed to give new dimensional edges to the vastness of the vacancies around it, illuminating the widening chasm between us and this story's recession into the past.

I would spend my three years at Kennedy in the half-paralysis of my own vague sense of unbelonging, lacking that innate interior alchemy that would allow me to push myself from the ranks of the supporting cast. This was fine, I told myself at the time. I wrote a couple of news stories for the *Kennedian* and managed to avoid any controversy; I did well enough in my classes to get into a college that has subsequently crept its way into the *U.S. News & World Report*'s top thirteen. I did go to my five-year reunion this past May, however anxiously, and my classmates told me that I was doing interesting things, albeit with the loosely patronizing surprise reserved for those formerly deemed uninteresting. I am still bitter sometimes, but mostly I covet a wistfulness that was foreclosed to me.

And so I listened that first autumn in silence as mythology found shape in the chasms between and beyond its originating facts, and I began to privately curate what truths I could. The characters in question were at that point just two years above us, but I was wide-eyed enough to see them as somehow older and more transcendent than seventeen: their sex more profound; their travails cast in a certain unintelligible luster of romance. Whether the grim sadness that trailed over them was only the imagined consequence of the stories shared late at night seemed beside the point. I would watch that winter as Annabeth Whittaker and Porter Roth and Sofi Cohen wordlessly made their way into Vito's, the pizza parlor across the village main street beyond the campus gates, stepping into the yellow light from the cold Wednesday night. I looked for secrets in their faces, chapped and pink from the February wind. I looked for sadness in the way they unzipped their Canada Goose parkas and felt—or at least chose to feel—the wordless friction in the crowded restaurant shift slightly but palpably as they parted it.

As far as mythologies go, the broad strokes of this one aren't all that unique: Foster Dade had come from Baltimore to arrive on that green campus in the final days of the summer of 2008 and vanished in the same fashion eighteen months later. Jacqueline Franck, a very pretty girl from Greenwich the year above me, would later claim to others that he'd been back on campus the night before his class's graduation, the year after he was expelled; she suggested that this had been an attempt to see Annabeth Whittaker. More than a few others claimed on supposedly good authority that at that point he was living eight thousand miles away in Hong Kong with Jae-hyun An, possibly operating pseudonymously, the two of them expanding their commercial enterprise with the financial backing of a South Korean crime syndicate. Like I said: disparate, twisting half-truths. We'll get to them in time.

With practice, I've managed to refine how I explain my project's motivating logic to those who ask. In October 2018, I got an email from Caren Haas at *New York*. I was working as a freelancer, and she wanted to see if I'd be interested in contributing to a forthcoming retrospective issue on the previous two decades' noteworthy prep school scandals. "You went to Kennedy, right—wasn't something there?" she'd written. Two weeks after I'd replied with the links to the Gawker and *Atlantic* pieces, the Democrats retook the House, and Caren informed me apologetically that the feature had been upended by a twelve-page profile of a vivacious young progressive from the Bronx who'd ousted the ten-term incumbent in the primary. "Plus," she wrote, "your story seemed juicy, but we'd never get it past legal—too much there that's unproveable."

In this version of things, it was my effort to prove her wrong in the pages of another publication that led to this project's untenable metastasis. I tell this version because it is preferable to the truth, which is that my earliest notes on Foster's story predate this assignment by several years. (Two different therapists have politely but unnervingly raised their eyebrows when I've disclosed the magnitude of my investment, and from a clinical perspective I can't blame them, though it's worth noting that both therapeutic relationships ended shortly thereafter.) I first attempted to write some primordial draft of this story for an undergraduate nonfiction workshop, where I produced what was basically a tortured piece of postmodern memoir, lyricizing rumor and stylizing my own experiences at Kennedy as a proxy for Foster's.

But the real truth is that I set out on this project long before even then. I would return to my room in Brennan House late at night in my first months at Kennedy and watch the smear of headlights push down Eastminster Road beyond the Meadow, feeling the darkness for solidarity with the faceless lives who populated the whispered folklore. I'd been assigned to a small bedroom by the back stairs on Brennan's second floor, which looked out onto the House Master's parking space. The closet by the door was narrow but deep, and one night that winter, I noticed the small door at the base of its rear wall. It resisted my pull at first, its wood swollen by a century of humidity. Inside was a small space, as high and deep as a shoebox and maybe slightly wider, bisected by a shelflike pine plank. On it sat a purple and green SpaceMaker pencil box, similar to the one I'd had in elementary school. I picked it up, and in my BlackBerry's flashlight I saw its owner's name written in Sharpie along its edge. Time and friction had smeared and faded the ink, but I could discern the contoured shadows of the words *FOSTER DADE*.

Except for a broken stick of lead from a mechanical pencil, the plastic case was empty. Over the course of that year, though, other little pieces of flotsam would present themselves from the room's liminal niches: a Post-it note stuck to the back of a desk drawer with the blue ballpoint-ink words *PRIDE AND PREJUDICE PAPER DUE FRI.—FOOTNOTES!* bloated and smeared across the blotch of a water stain, the forgotten opaque cap to a tube of Old Spice deodorant along the dusty wall behind the bed; once, beneath the dresser, a Ziploc containing what looked like the chalky eggshell detritus of crumbled pills.

I find credence in the metaphor that avails itself here, however cute. Adolescence is an exercise in coveting what exists just beyond our grasp; it is this inaccessibility that sustains its magic. At sixteen, I saw in the mosaic of these arbitrary artifacts the spectral contours of a life that shimmered precisely in this evasiveness, gesturing to something I could ascertain only in voyeurism. It is here that the story I am about to tell finds both its motive and determining shape: in the collation of relics from forgotten edges; in the exclusion of things left behind. Explaining the account that follows as an overdue piece of journalism on a scandal—as an attempt to report the story that Sheila Baxter so meticulously rendered unreportable in 2010—forgives the basic peculiarity of its endeavor, and at times I've believed it myself. Sometimes, late at night, when I find myself clicking through photos of the alumni events I didn't attend, I'll pull out my old coffee-stained copy of *Still Life with Woodpecker* and blink at the last line: *It's never too late to have a happy childhood*. And perhaps safer if it isn't your own.

I will say that I have done my damndest to treat the facts at hand with as much fidelity as possible. I remain somewhat shocked by the availability of many of the relevant primary sources. PDF files of the *Kennedian* and even the so-called Kennedy thread can be found in unlikely corners of the internet, if you know where to look, or whom to ask. An equally surprising number of secondary characters were eager to testify; that nostalgia may have warped or prejudiced their recollections is itself instructive. Most critically, Foster Dade had deleted his Blogspot that fateful night in March 2010, but a cached version can be found in the annals of the Internet Archive's Wayback Machine. From these disparate pieces of evidence, I have patched the narrative holes in this story with my own theorizations. I can only tell you that I utilized this license as responsibly as I could.

This is the certainty with which I tell this story: the confident, fabricated truth we retroactively assign to the filmstrips of our youths. The earliest repositories of Annabeth Whittaker's now-quiet Facebook page exist today as they did almost a decade ago, when I first visited them late one October night in the darkness of my room at school. After Foster's expulsion, she spent the summer in digital self-exile, but was back online as she entered her last year at Kennedy. Under the earliest pull of the spell that would follow me through nearly ten years of twilights, I arrived at an album of photos she'd uploaded a year and a half earlier. There are times when I've returned to these pictures in adulthood, usually after midnight, when the watery May dawn in 2009 they capture seems to pause for a moment in its recession into history. Manhattan is still Manhattan, of course, purple and gilded and ethereal in the spill of spring mornings; the Brooklyn Bridge still rises up over the East River. It's against these colors of permanence that we find the three teenagers standing there upon the bridge's pedestrian promenade, their faces lilac with the first light of day. There is Jack Albright, the dark-headed boy, looking back to the camera with the solemnity he'd learned for photographs, and beyond him on the bridge is Annabeth Whittaker, tall and ponytailed, the indecipherable magic that certain boys at Kennedy would still describe years later palpable even in suspended animation.

And there, between them both, is the wheat-haired boy with wide eyes, standing in the clarity of the morning.

If there is a truth to be found in my reconstructions, it is in a fidelity to these images, I think. They deny us certitude in any literal sense, but in its absence we are left to regard the plays of light that dance in the space of what we cannot know. The expressions of those who populate the image betray no absolute confidences. What we have instead is the spill of magmatic silver that bled across the sky of a forgotten May morning, and the way Foster Dade looked up at it.

This is what I do know: Foster's story is still told at Kennedy, in the dark hours after midnight when adolescence is given a quality of magic and stories like his feel almost religious. Art Tierney is set to retire next year; they're renaming the tennis courts after him. A childless middle-aged couple lives in the house on Overland Road in Baltimore now, the wife a psychologist and the husband a professor of English at Johns Hopkins. Foster Dade's old bedroom is the husband's study. Annabeth Whittaker is engaged to be married.

And the last time I was in New York, on a blustery day two weeks before Christmas, I was sitting in J.G. Melon and saw Jack Albright walking by outside. On his arm was an upright blond Episcopal-looking girl in a quilted Barbour. He did not see me, and I watched him as he continued down Third Avenue. I briefly considered following him down the block. But I stayed put, and he disappeared into the ebbing tide of the crowd. There were questions—so many questions—but I knew already that he would not answer them. In the interest of preserving the mythological luster of this story, I feel they must remain unanswered. There is enough there otherwise.

PART I

Coming out of my cage
and I've been doing just fine

—The Killers

I.

http://www.fhd93.blogspot.com/2007/09/first-words
(Posted October 19, 2007)

Here's the thing: I'm telling myself that my life would be over if anyone
ever found this, but when I really think about it, I can't help but think that
maybe I secretly want it to be read. Not now or anytime soon, obviously.
Yeah, I'm writing this for myself—it feels good to put words to all the shit
in my head—but at the end of the day I'm telling a story. Maybe I think
that thirty, forty years from now, I'll have done something important
enough to make people want to read this sort of thing—like Anne Frank
or Susan Sontag or Hemingway. Probably shouldn't compare myself to
Anne Frank, but you get what I'm saying. See—there you go: "you." Is
that "you" myself? Do I believe I'm actually having a conversation with
this blog? Or am I imagining someone, somewhere far off and far away,
actually reading this stuff?

It's also possible that I'm not as interesting as I think I am. Every
published journal I've read starts with the writer describing themselves,
so: I am fourteen years old and I live in Baltimore. I am the youngest of
two children. My father moved out thirteen months ago. I play tennis and
I hate it but I'm actually decent. I read a lot. And maybe I'm telling you
(!) that I read a lot because I want to be seen as someone who reads a
lot. I've never kissed a girl. Max says Lanie Tinsley from Bryn Mawr is
"into me." (We stopped saying "likes you likes you" in seventh grade.) I
have no idea how to make out with a girl. I practiced once with myself
in the bathroom mirror. I kept opening my eyes to watch myself in the
reflection. I think I mostly wanted to see what it would look like to kiss
me. I live in fear of looking stupid. I should go to sleep.

II.

There are eighteen courts at the Roland Park Racquet Club in northern Baltimore, six hard and twelve chalky Har-Tru clay, and in the late afternoons in August they were almost always empty. So it was that summer. The junior tennis camps let out just after lunchtime, to keep the sunkissed nine-year-olds from getting overheated under the remorseless mid-Atlantic sun. By four o'clock or so, when systems of low pressure would knead tall purple storm clouds not far overhead, the suburban mothers who'd booked a court for an hour would use the impending rain as an excuse to stay home and start dinner early. This itself was an excuse to pour themselves an early glass of zinfandel and stand at the granite countertops in the coolness of their darkening kitchens. It did not always rain, and when it did, the rain was merciless but very short.

It was during those fading hours in the late summer of 2008 that Foster Dade biked the mile and a half north to the club to hit against the ball machine. He had done this every afternoon since the beginning of June, two weeks after the end of his ninth-grade year at the Gilman School. Some might venture that he found romance in the solitude of this ritual—he left his BlackBerry on his bed at home—but the less lyrical reality is that he was then truthfully able to tell his mother—and himself—that he had done something that day.

For the preceding two months, he had woken up at eleven o'clock in the morning, the tartan shades against his bedroom window drawn. Except on Tuesdays and Thursdays, when the housekeeper, Alice, would vacuum downstairs, the house was silent. His mother's work had her in Washington, and his sister, Maggie, was spending the summer before her sophomore year at Amherst in an Italian-language immersion program at some mercenary affiliate campus in Genoa where, at least per the Facebook photos, she was spending most of her time drinking lots of Italian wine and draped under the arms of brown Italian boys in V-necks.

This was fine. The small glass bowl that lived more or less permanently on Foster's bedside table was blue streaked conservatively with a pearly white; he'd bought it at a gas station off Route 50 on the

Eastern Shore the previous summer, three weeks after Scott, Maggie's then-boyfriend from Andover, had gotten him high for the first time at a party Maggie threw while their parents were away. "The kid's fucking *stoned*," Scott had crowed to the other eighteen-year-olds, all kids from St. Albans or Gilman or St. Andrew's whose grandparents also had old clapboard homes along the Chesapeake and its tributaries. Maggie had been livid—not that she and Scott would last beyond the coming Halloween, what with her hunched over her papers on Tennyson at Amherst and his being tempted by the more than a few girls at Duke who wanted to fuck a member of the lacrosse team—but the truth is that Foster loved it. "The interior jigsaw's missing piece" was a line he'd remembered reading somewhere. When he returned inland to Baltimore that August, about exactly a year prior to where this story begins, he'd found a dealer, a graduate student in philosophy at Hopkins four years into a dissertation on Deleuze and Hegel that had long ago lost its coherence; by September, around the first anniversary of the gruesome events preceding his parents' divorce, he was almost always high by noon, ninth-grade History be damned.

So it was this summer. He would wake up at eleven and spend the better part of an hour lying in stasis in his boxers, occasionally falling back into fitful ten-minute spurts of sleep but more often than not just watching the ceiling. His first significant movement each day was reaching to the bedside for the bowl, where there was usually enough left in it from the prior evening.

When the marijuana-induced agoraphobia subsided after the first half hour or so, he padded his way downstairs, pulling a can of black cherry Polar seltzer from the fridge as his breakfast. If Alice was there, he'd pull an old gray T-shirt on over his tanned torso before descending, giving her an amicably sheepish wave; if not, he'd venture out to the back patio in his J.Crew boxer shorts, seltzer in one hand and a book in the other. Not his phone: this was maybe a year and a half before his generation's pathological dependency hit its stride, and besides, he had no one to text anyway.

"The dude was always reading," Will Thierry recalled to me recently. This was true, maybe especially when Foster was stoned.

That summer he'd strolled through Bret Easton Ellis's entire early oeuvre, then made a pass at *Bright Lights, Big City* but found himself annoyed by the second-person voice. *Sabbath's Theater* by Roth; *A Million Little Pieces*, which he'd first surreptitiously pulled from his mother's bookshelf at twelve and been haunted by. By that August, he was onto an almost deliberately dry and eponymously titled biography of Martin Luther, the last on his summer reading list for Advanced European History at Kennedy, where he would start as a new sophomore in two days.

He read until he nodded off, or until it got too hot, and then he retreated inside to stand before the fridge and fork at the tub of chicken salad his mother had bought from Whole Foods. By this point he was high enough to be ravenous but mentally more or less grounded; things were just shrouded in that peculiar patina of late-stage highness that made the contours of life seem a little heavier. So he ate the chicken salad, sometimes but not always finishing the thing, then padded back upstairs to strip off his boxers and lie naked until the sun was low enough to pleasantly bike to the club.

"Don't you get bored of hitting against the ball machine?" Charlotte Dade—she was still legally Charlotte Dade then—had asked him the previous evening as she served him pad Thai. She did not know that Foster had hit his bowl for the second time that day fifteen minutes prior. "Why don't you get a friend to hit with you? I bet Max would."

Max was Max Frieholdt, a cynical boy with whom Foster smoked weed and listened to R.E.M. after school; to Foster's knowledge, he had never held a tennis racquet.

"He's been super busy this summer." Foster sighed. "And besides, I actually much prefer hitting on the machine. It's more consistent. Playing with a shitty player just makes you worse."

"Or—Perry Wilson? I saw Barbara at Pilates the other week; she says—"

"No," Foster said firmly, feeling a quickening tension in his stomach. "Not Perry."

And so when the sun was low and the shadows of the suburban streets were green he pulled on a pair of athletic shorts and white

Nike socks and climbed on his Trek, which sat on its kickstand in the now-vacant left side of the garage. It was a fifteen-minute ride, past the Georgian sterility of the Hopkins campus and beneath the centuries-old oaks that still draped themselves over Charles Street; over the creek that wound through Wyman Park and through the quiet streets graced by homes like his: colonial, brick, handsome and suburban and wealthy, with secrets behind their darkening windows.

He pulled into the club's long driveway, the clouds overhead pustular and dark; soon, the lifeguard, some hot teenager from Towson, would blow his or her whistle and instruct the younger children to get out of the pool as thunder rumbled over the trees.

The emptiness of the courts and the adjacent tennis club was the real reason he preferred to hit at this time of day. Like many medium-sized American cities with a contained enclave of money, Baltimore was a small town. Today, by the water cooler outside Court Eight, two women maybe a handful of years younger than his mother stood gossiping. Their outfits were interchangeable—black Wilson tennis skirts; white Nike tops—and so were the stances with which they conveyed themselves, the casually languid tilt of women who worried about very little. He recognized one of them: Marsha Brenner, a dark-haired, big-toothed woman whose daughter, Mary Katherine, was starting ninth grade at Bryn Mawr. He stared straight ahead as he passed them, the back of his neck prickling with heat.

"That's Jim and Charlotte's son," he heard the blond woman murmur loudly. Marsha Brenner's voice dropped to a cadence just north of a stage whisper. "Oh my gawd," she said. "You know, Don always, always said there was something weird about them. Especially Jim. He'd never sit with the other dads at the swim meets and have a beer. I guess it wasn't—*exotic* enough for him!" Her voice picked up a bit on these final syllables, and she brayed an unattractive laugh that she fruitlessly tried to stifle by clasping a hand to her mouth. She had a yellow sweatband on her wrist.

There had been moments like this over the preceding two years: when he'd passed just close enough to discern the words being said, to feel their moral contempt breaking against the poor disguise of sympathetic objectivity. He had never ascertained the precise extent of what people knew, though the basic fact of the infidelity seemed to be beyond dispute. "Dade's dad was a fucking skeeze," he had heard Richard Kleckner say at a party the prior spring as he and Max Frieholdt returned inside after smoking a joint on the back patio.

We can maybe attribute what happened on this August afternoon to the accumulated mass of these instances, or to his anxiety about his impending arrival at Kennedy, or to the strange internal tension that accompanies a weed comedown. What we know for sure is this: Foster quite literally spun around on his heels. He stared Marsha Brenner directly in the eyes.

"I have a question, Mrs. Brenner, and forgive my bluntness. What could possibly compel you to be such a fucking cunt?" He said this very plainly. "Is it because no one likes your daughter? And, like, in what moral universe do you get to pass comment on anyone's home life? Has Mr. Brenner finally stopped snorting coke in the Hopkins Club bathroom?"

Marsha Brenner looked as if she'd witnessed a shooting. He turned back on his heels and marched toward his court. As the balls spat themselves out of the corroded green tube in a popping staccato, one after the other, Foster returned their angry velocity with startling force, hot with rage, not caring if they cleared the net.

III.

Foster Dade's MacBook Pro/Music/iTunes/Playlists/summer (Created July 29, 2008)

Name	Time	Artist
Mr. Brightside	3:43	The Killers
Life in a Northern Town	4:19	The Dream Academy
Time to Pretend	4:21	MGMT
Send Me on My Way	4:23	Rusted Root
Fluorescent Adolescent	2:53	Arctic Monkeys
Your English Is Good	3:11	Tokyo Police Club

Bleeding Love	4:22	Leona Lewis
There She Goes	2:42	The La's
Paper Planes	3:25	M.I.A.
I Still Remember	4:21	Bloc Party
Shake It	3:00	Metro Station
Everywhere	3:47	Fleetwood Mac
American Boy (feat. Kanye West)	4:45	Estelle
Sleeping Lessons	3:57	The Shins
Hungry Like the Wolf	3:41	Duran Duran
Young Folks	4:36	Peter Bjorn and John
You Might Think	3:04	The Cars
Just Like Heaven	3:32	The Cure
King Without a Crown	3:42	Matisyahu
Hey Girl (Live)	8:13	O.A.R.
Buy U a Drank (Shawty Snappin')	3:48	T. Pain (feat. Yung Joc)

21 songs, 1.4 hours, 176.3 MB

IV.

Because Charlotte Harrison Dade was to have primary custody of the two children, and because she had contributed to the shared revenue stream that had facilitated its purchase and early mortgage payments, and because unlike Jim's, her family was in Baltimore, she had gotten the house. This was not something Jim had challenged. The circumstances of the divorce had left him with little ethical latitude to push back on much of anything, and besides, if the events precipitating the divorce had any subtext, it was that Jim Dade was inclined to make a new home elsewhere anyway.

The more affluent suburbs laid out along the mid-Atlantic are all roughly interchangeable in their beauty. And they are beautiful, despite themselves: the trees that line their streets either predate the roads themselves or were planted alongside them when they were first paved in the early twentieth century, and their boughs are thick and green, casting the roads into canals of heavy marvelous shadows. In Baltimore, lacrosse goals sit in the front lawns, their netting gray and mildewed and sloughing after springs of rain and summers of sun.

190 Overland Road and its neighbors sat on lawns that rose above the uphill street, their earth held back from the sidewalks by brick bulkheads thick with kudzu and vines. The house had been bought by the relative newlyweds Charlotte and Jim Dade in April 1989, when Charlotte was a trimester pregnant with their first child, Maggie.

"It's exactly what we're looking for," Charlotte had told the real estate agent. Their neighbors were surgical heads at Union Memorial, vice-presidents at Legg Mason, and tenured economics professors at Johns Hopkins, the manicured campus of which was a quarter mile away on the other side of St. Paul Street.

Jim and Charlotte had spent the first twenty months of their marriage in Washington, in a small two-bedroom across R Street from the Grenadian embassy. It would be a decade and a half before the city buckled under the millennial tidal wave of gentrification; even in Dupont Circle, the glass of shattered crack vials smeared against the sidewalks like silver sand. Charlotte had been the one to insist on the move to Baltimore, and Jim deferred to his wife with an indifference that would mark most of their major decisions—an indifference that would be brought up years later in hushed cocktail-party postmortems of their marriage.

Charlotte Dade's pewter Lexus RX was parked outside the garage when Foster pedaled into the driveway. The light was by then yellow— the storm clouds overhead had been pushed apart in time for the last of the sun to cast shadows in the street—and the air was pleasant. He threw his bike onto its kickstand and went up the front steps of the house, opening the mahogany door quietly. The alarm system beeped three times anyway.

Six months after her husband had left in the fall of 2006, Charlotte decided to go back to work. Foster's understanding of her job was only the foggy sum of its descriptive keywords (political consulting; media logistics), and sensed from her defensive curtness that there wasn't much more to it. He recognized that she operated in some outer electron shell of Maryland Democratic politics. He'd once found the news clippings in a shoebox in a forgotten attic corner: Bill Clinton, ruddy and darker-haired, glad-handing through the months ahead of the '92 election; behind him, in the faceless scrum of reporters and apparatchiks, Foster's mother, a mid-level press aide, her hair shorter, her midriff not yet swollen with the rise of her second pregnancy. She entered her second trimester just ahead of Election Day, and when the President-elect's deputies offered her a post in the Office of Information and Regulatory Affairs, it was her husband—then a young vice president at BB&T—who suggested her time would be better spent raising their children. The following April, as her former colleagues scrambled to minimize the fallout of Waco, she gave birth to their son, who fourteen years later would be prostrate on his bed in Baltimore tossing an old Penn ball up toward the ceiling as his father pulled his Tumi bags and squash racquets down to the foyer below.

"Don't you—don't you fucking *dare* blame me for your fucking failures," Jim had hissed. It was warm for a spring night; cicadas were screaming pleasantly in the trees. "You chose this—this *misery*, as you call it. You built this for yourself. If you were me, you would have *lived a lie*"—his tone here was violent in its shrill impersonation—"too, darling."

Charlotte's laugh was cruel and mirthless. "*Built* this? You fucking *forced* me!" she shrieked. It was around nine o'clock. "I asked for *none* of this! And while I—I—*subjected* myself to this, you were—living a fucking *lie*, waking up every morning and looking me and your children in the face and pretending to—to—to—to be a *man*!"

Foster passed through the dining room into the kitchen to see her standing at the island beneath the wide skylights, her MacBook open before her. A shadow fell against the glass of white wine in front of her.

"Hi, bug," she said, frowning at the email draft on her screen and pecking something on the keyboard.

"I should warn you," he said flatly, sliding his Babolat racquet onto the counter, "you may be getting a telephone call from a less-than-thrilled Marsha Brenner."

Charlotte looked up from the computer to her son, her brow bent inward. "Marsha—?"

Foster sighed. "I, uh—lost my temper. For totally justifiable reasons," he added as his mother's thin mouth twitched. "And to spare you her version I'll admit that I called her a very nasty word. And brought up her husband's coke habit."

Foster had always found his mother beautiful, albeit in an angular Protestant way that appealed to him only objectively, as fine art or real estate might. Like her son, she was tall, with the genetic blessing that kept her lean regardless of diet. Her thinness emphasized her nose's aquiline edge, and in middle age the whites of her eyes had become almost conspicuously white—watery and glossy with little clusters of pinkish veins in their corners. Her hair had always been blond, blonder than her son's, now faithfully reproduced by a stylist.

"Foster," she said finally, closing her eyes for a moment. An edge of tiredness caught in his mother's voice. "Again. Enough. Is this—a badge of honor for you?"

The edges of Foster's mouth turned up in a dry smile. "I mean, I'm proud of it." And then his guilt at his mother's expression spilled over into the indignation of rage. "But Mom—that fucking bitch, she"—his voice quavered—"she was talking about Dad."

He watched her hear this. After that first night two autumns earlier there'd been an unspoken embargo of sorts on conversation concerning his father, limited to only the most clerical negotiations of divorce. This silent emotional thicket was tended to by one Dr. Willem Apple, Psy.D., M.D., who kept a practice in a low-rise brick office suite a mile south of the Towson mall. They had not sought family therapy; the things left unsaid had calcified and filled the new emptiness of the house, suffocating those who entered.

Charlotte paused with her son's words, then reached for the bottle of chardonnay. "People are going to talk," she said finally, her voice more even now, betraying a sympathy. She took a sip. "Let them. That's zero excuse for what you did. I get that you're anxious, Foster, but really, now."

Foster looked down at the counter. His rage had collapsed in its rawness into a hollow specter of shame that crystallized the flash of vulnerability to which he'd subjected himself. "I reckon I should probably apologize, right?"

Charlotte pursed her lips and took another sip of her wine. Outside in the garden the shadows of dusk were falling. "Give her a call first thing tomorrow, before we get on the road," she said, after a moment.

The upstairs hallway was dark and still lined with photos: the four Dades in Park City in 2001 and Anguilla in 2003, a prepubescent Foster grinning in airport-shop sunglasses; a thirty-something Charlotte with an infant Maggie on her lap on the porch overlooking the Chesapeake. Foster slipped into his bedroom, and realized it stunk sweetly of unsmoked weed. The sweat was drying on him in the air-conditioning, and he was cold. Kicking off his sneakers and peeling the Nike ankle socks off with the toes of the opposite foot, he then stripped off his T-shirt and shoved his black Gilman School athletic shorts to the floor.

He appraised himself in the mirror on the back of his bedroom door. His blond hair had thickened and darkened in adolescence. He was lean, and his thighs were pale against his summer tan. He had the appearance of muscular tone without ever lifting weights: he did not count the twenty haphazard sit-ups he did at night, convinced that exercise done while stoned didn't count. His penis and testicles hung loose from the heat of the day; a few sparse wisps of hair rose in an uneven trail up to his belly button. The light of the afternoon was beginning to fade beyond the windows.

He briefly contemplated jerking off, but instead he went to his bed and opened the MacBook perched on his pillow. At the foot of the bed were the three clear Tupperware crates and a blue L.L.Bean duffel bag that contained the life he'd bring with him to Kennedy: clothes; five Mead spiral notebooks and assorted other school supplies; the tartan comforter set Charlotte had gotten at Pottery Barn; a caddy carrying Old Spice body wash and Head & Shoulders shampoo. An aluminum desk lamp sat atop the bins, its black cord draped over its spine; an R.E.M. poster was rolled loosely and bound with a red rubber band. A USB flash drive sat unopened in its cardboard packaging.

He turned to the Safari window open on his screen. He'd left it open to the page of a Facebook group with the heading KENNEDY CLASS OF 2011, which in a thrash of disgust at his own impertinence he had joined two weeks prior. Over the evenings since, he had scrolled numbly through the list of members, every so often clicking a name to open into a new tab. There was a masochism in this. For several hours at a time, he had clicked through what tranches of data were publicly available on these pages: photo albums, mostly, of dances and dormitory birthday parties and field trips to Philadelphia. Foster had surveyed the conglomerations of lives documented in these photographs, attempting to parse the social politics that configured them and struggling to envision a place within them that he might find for himself. These exercises in voyeurism left him sleepless and, when he was high, curiously short of breath.

With the same grip of nausea he clicked away from the group to Facebook's home page, but instead of studying the contents of his News Feed he flicked up to his bookmarks bar, where a little pixelated "B" sat between YouTube and CNN. The icon had no identifying label.

Foster had created his Blogspot the previous autumn. It was his journal—*the word "diary" is faggy,* he'd written once—and to the best of his knowledge he alone was privy to its existence. Its hyperlink was too remote and untrafficked to catch in Google's trawl; he double-checked this once every few weeks. He'd created the page only after confirming that Blogspot provided password protection as a security feature. That the password he'd selected—*Tennis1993FD!*—was the same that protected his Facebook and iChat accounts had seemed ultimately inconsequential: *I'm not paranoid enough to worry that anyone would be trying to access my stuff,* he'd written once, *if only because I doubt anyone would ever find me interesting enough. But still.*

V.
http://www.fhd93.blogspot.com/2008/08/leaving
(Posted August 21, 2008)

I lost my temper at the courts today. Overheard Mary Katherine Brenner's mom—who is really just the worst sort of flashy tennis-mom bitch—gossiping about M+D. Called her a cunt; jabbed at Donald Brenner's coke problem, which is honestly an open secret anyway. Max told me about it months ago. To be honest it felt wonderful. This was my first "explosion"—that's what Dr. Apple calls it—since the party at Kleckner's. Most people think of me as soft-spoken, I think, and I fulfill this expectation, but this means I need to release the pressure gauge every so often. So be it.

I'm very nearly packed. I feel everything and nothing. The problem here is that as aloof as I may present myself, I want very very badly to be liked, to have friends, to fall in love, to be happy. I have retreated from this impulse recently but I feel it gnawing at me, and I'm worried I'm going to look desperate at Kennedy. I do feel sometimes like I'm fundamentally incapable of fitting in anywhere—that something about me repulses people, even if they can't put their finger on exactly what.

It's been eleven weeks today since I spoke to Dad, if that conversation counts as speaking. I talked to Maggie on Facebook Chat the other day and she says he's in Boston—I get the impression that they talk.

Mom and I leave tomorrow morning. Still haven't put my shit in the car. We'll get to Jersey at like noon. I'm a little nauseated I think.

VI.

FROM: mpark09@kennedy.org
[Tuesday, September 2, 2008 at 01:16 PM EST]
TO: [LIST: TOURGUIDES_08_09]
CC: spaulson09@kennedy.org
SUBJECT: Notes on school history

Congratulations on your selection as a School Tour Guide. We—Minji Park '09 and Smith Paulson '09—are this year's Head Guides, and we've put together some useful historical background to help you guys out when you're giving tours. You really should know this stuff. Any questions, ask us or Ms. Tompkins in the Admissions Building (ptompkins@kennedy.org). Anyway:

- Kennedy School: founded 1810 in Eastminster, New Jersey, as the Eastminster Classical Academy by Rev. Josiah van Arsdale, a Presbyterian minister, to prepare boys for Princeton University (we're the sixth–oldest boarding school in the U.S.)
- 1881: John Charlton Kennedy (Class of 1818) dies and leaves his estate to Eastminster Classical Academy. Kennedy was a merchant who traded spices, tea, opium from China/South America. **NO RELATION TO THE POLITICAL KENNEDY FAMILY. YOU WILL BE ASKED THIS.** (JFK actually went to Choate. Make a joke about how they're one of our athletic rivals or something.)
- 1883: Eastminster Classical Academy renamed The Kennedy School. School redesigned with Kennedy's gift: House system, new campus. Frederick Law Olmsted: designed Central Park; designed Kennedy. (See printout in your tour guide packet titled "Olmsted's Campus." Email one of us if you lost it.)
- House System: based on British boarding schools. Six Houses on Meadow for Second/Third Year boys and four Houses along Ellipse for Second/Third Year girls. "Your House is your family while you're at Kennedy"—say something like that. Mention intramural House sports (Kennedy's House football league is older than NFL!)
- Today's campus: 750 acres. "Bigger than many small college campuses"—they like it when we point this out.

VII.

The most striking thing about the Kennedy School campus in late August is its impossible greenness. This is truest when summer comes late, when the gray chills of the mid-Atlantic winter hang low and wet through late May. It is a lush heat this far inland, its humidity unstirred by breezes off New Jersey's coastal bight, and Main Street is quiet. The middle-class families who live there year-round reserve their trips to Seaside Heights or Six Flags Great America for these hottest days. By summer's end, when students and their families arrive on the Kennedy grounds, the boughs overhead are fat and wet and seem to bridge in their reach, spangling the ground below with the wet silver light filtered through them.

All of this was a matter of design. Frederick Law Olmsted was a semi-retired and deeply bitter septuagenarian when the school's Victorian leadership approached him in the 1880s: it had taken a quarter century for Central Park to open to the public, a period marred and prolonged by Tammany-style politics and internecine ego clashes, during which Olmsted had suffered two nervous breakdowns and resigned from the project twice, only to return again. He agreed to the New Jersey project on the condition of complete creative control and left New York City for good.

He hadn't lost his touch. Over four years, he shipped in no fewer than three hundred species of tree from no fewer than four continents, which in the century that followed would form the canopy of shadows over the network of footpaths and hedgerows that sewed the campus together. From the muddy banks of the creek along the grounds' southeastern cusp, a pond was dredged; a garden bridge freighted in from Kyoto led to a willow-draped islet at its center. Buford Burroughs, the effete, portly Rutgers-educated bachelor who had been the assistant director of Kennedy's Bradford Library, had spent a heady summer in 1999 holed up with Olmsted's own topiarian notes and then self-published a chapbook called *The Trees of Kennedy*, which was something between a botanical study and a lyric poem.

Olmsted's campus took its shape around a large oblong lawn he simply called the Meadow, which in satellite photos looks like a rich green bubble blooming from the mouth of the marble gates on Eastminster Road. His architectural collaborators had eschewed the day's Jeffersonian and neo-Gothic styles for what was then a radical riff on Victorianism's geometric complexity, conveyed in heavy brick the color of rich torrefied earth. The Head Master's Residence, with many porches and a high solarium, stands sentry-like at the lawn's punctum, where inbound traffic begins its slow counterclockwise slide along the Meadow's driveway. Upper House thereafter is a handsome barge of a building that houses nearly all of the Fourth Year boys; beyond it stands Memorial Hall, turreted and high-windowed, its wide imperial stairs leading up beneath a corbeled portico to the English Department. Above its angular profile is the high belfry of the Kennedy chapel, its tall stained-glass windows clouded with age.

By the late 2010s, it was considered deeply uncool among Kennedians to publicly liken their house system to Harry Potter's, but this speaks only to the ready availability of the comparison. Along the remaining half-moon of the Meadow beyond the chapel stood the six elegant Victorian manors known as the Meadow Houses: the residences for Second and Third Year boys, each with its own flag and clandestine traditions and intramural athletic teams. These residences—Brennan, Donavan, Talmadge, Kellogg, Arsdale, and Ames Houses—looked less like dormitories than the homes of well-heeled classics professors. Dense ivy swallowed swaths of their exteriors. The trim on their bay windows and porch awnings was green and cream. Arsdale had a rounded tower; a trellised roof covered Donavan's second-floor terrace, which looked out upon the Meadow to the muted rhythm of traffic beyond the vine-swallowed gates.

Three weeks before he arrived on campus, Foster Dade had received a letter from the school informing him that he would be living in Brennan House. Enclosed in this letter was a smaller impersonal note from one Scott McCall, the history teacher who served as Brennan's House Master. "I want to emphasize that what's in the past is firmly in the past," the letter's final paragraph began. "We enter the new academic year facing forward, and Ms. Chissom"—Delia Chissom, the Assistant House Master—"and I are confident that 2008–2009 will be a sterling year for Brennan—and not just on the House football field!"

Foster thumbed the corner of that letter as his mother steered the Lexus off I-95 onto the exit for Princeton. He had been silent since they'd left the house that morning—he did not call Marsha Brenner, either, and his mother forgot to remind him—and had his iPod's earbuds in, though he was listening to no music. He had spent the better part of an hour the previous evening after getting high standing before the clothes still hanging there, fretting more than he would have liked to over what he would wear. He decided on a pair of coral-green Vineyard Vines shorts that his mother had gotten him and a gray T-shirt that said AMHERST in purple, but now in the car he began to suspect he looked too casual, sloppy even, and wondered if he could reach the button-downs hanging in the back seat.

"You know I'd be delighted to do my part in Baltimore," his mother was saying into her BlackBerry, steering the Lexus with her knee. With her free hand she cleaned her Dior sunglasses against her blouse's linen hem to desmudge the lens. "It's really whatever the Senator's folks think is best—just email me the options—but Meg, listen—I'm about to drop Foster off at school." She gave her son a compensatory smile. "Yep, I'll tell him. And I'll have those names tonight." She placed the BlackBerry in her cup holder and turned to her son. "Sorry, sweet," she said. Foster smiled thinly and turned to the window. He realized that the cupolaed brick sentry box beyond the intersection was Kennedy's distant southernmost gate, across from the barren oil-stained pavement of a Lukoil station. Foster remembered that in New Jersey it was illegal to pump one's own gas, and then wondered if he was going to throw up.

"Here we are," said Charlotte in a singsong voice.

With the body of archival evidence at our disposal and a responsible degree of interpretive license, certain conclusions avail themselves to us. Among them is the observation that Foster Dade arrived at Kennedy in the fall of 2008 still believing in a certain homeostatic happiness to adolescence. It found its composite form in a certain strain of late-millennium cinema—a cosmology of summertime, of hesitant first kisses on lakefront docks, of well-rounded casts and closed systems—and in its inaccessibility he both pined for it and resented it. He believed in its narrative elegance, and we can imagine that it seemed to dance before him on the vast expanse of the Meadow that day as his mother's Lexus turned into the driveway. *When I witness certain moments I believe I am a voyeur to memories being made, and it makes me sad*, he had written once on his Blogspot, and winced at its sincerity.

VIII.

Brennan House was geometrically the simplest of the Meadow Houses, an L-shaped structure formed by the union of harsh edges. Its length rose almost tomblike along the Meadow; beyond its front porch were the common room and parlor, a floor below the House Master's apartment. Four bedrooms occupied the façade's third floor, but the rest were clustered in the L's base, where a simple turret of bay windows looked out toward the library.

A thin man in his late thirties with thinning brown hair and wire-rimmed eyeglasses had greeted them when they walked into the house's foyer. Scott McCall had been hired by Kennedy's History Department ten years prior, after a two-year stint at Francis Parker in Chicago. He loved his job—his emphasis was post–World War II America—and was by all accounts good at it, and had the luxury of embracing it single-mindedly: he was the bookish son of an old Richmond tobacco family who had taken every history prize at the University of Virginia, been accepted to the doctoral program at Chicago, and instead chosen to get his M.Ed. at Penn.

"You must be Foster," he'd said warmly, standing at the foot of the grand oak staircase that led from the foyer to his apartment. "Welcome to Brennan, and to Kennedy." The house was surprisingly quiet, and McCall must have noticed Foster's eyes darting down the hallway to the bedrooms. "It's actually a pretty slow day—most of the guys moved in before the weekend, for preseason." *Preseason?* Foster wondered, suddenly queasy with the haunting sense of being on the outside. *Is this something I should have been told about?*

"One of the senior guys will help y'all with your stuff, but here, let me get you situated with your welcome packet," McCall said, licking his index finger and flipping through a red file folder. "Dade, Dade—ah"—he pulled a thick black packet that read *Kennedy* in glossy red lettering—"here you go. So in that you'll find your room key, your Student Handbook, the school directory, which has everyone's picture, some forms that I'll need your signature on, and your fob, which will get you into the House and certain academic buildings. You can put your cash for the school shop on there as well." Foster pulled out a piece of white plastic indistinguishable from a credit card. DADE,

FOSTER HARRISON, it read. D.O.B.: 04/19/1993, and below that, BRENNAN HOUSE, 2008–2009. In the upper right corner was the headshot his mother had taken in what had been his father's study. The narrowness of his eyes in the photo betrayed the weed he'd smoked an hour prior.

"Your room is on this floor," McCall continued. "Quite the cool setup, really: you've got a cozy little bedroom, but you'll share a small common room with another new sophomore, Jae. His plane from Seoul gets into New York tonight."

Foster's suspicion that McCall was being unduly charitable was confirmed as he pushed open the door to suite 102. Inside the barren common space within—itself no more than eight feet by eight—was a second door to the left, which gave way to Foster's room. The head of the twin bed that seemed to occupy most of the narrow space rested against the sill of a tall cobwebbed window that overlooked the curved row of girls' houses known as the Ellipse, built thirty years prior with the start of coeducation. His room—which he'd eventually learn was the smallest in Brennan House—was roughly the size of his mother's walk-in closet at home. This had been the first thing Charlotte observed out loud. And as he turned from the window, his mother burst into tears in her hands.

"Mom! Christ!" Foster exclaimed, looking in humiliation behind him to see if anyone had witnessed this.

"I know, I'm sorry, I'm sorry," she sniffled, smearing away a tear with her wrist. "I guess I just haven't had time to really process this, your leaving, and now we're here"—she gestured reflexively out to the narrow room—"and I'm going to worry about you all the time and just—miss you so much."

"Mom, I'm fine, really," Foster said in a grim facsimile of comfort. "You'll see me all the time. And I couldn't give less of a shit about the room, really. Less space for me to make a mess in." He managed a thin smile. He wanted very badly for her to leave.

Shortly after, Ollie Richardson, a tanned senior boy from New Canaan, arrived. Ollie was one of the house's three prefects—ambitious, well-liked seniors who decided to spend their final year hanging back along the Meadow or Ellipse instead of joining their classmates in Fourth Year housing, in a position that hybridized the duties of mentor, House Master's aide, and good cop. It looked good on college applications. Ollie, who wore a Ralph Lauren T-shirt and Rainbow sandals, had endeared himself to Charlotte, opening up to her at length as he confidently heaved the Tupperware bins from the Lexus. Ollie rowed crew with hopes it would get him into Brown. "How 'bout you, Foster?" he'd asked the seemingly sullen boy, once the Tupperware was placed on the bedroom's dusty industrial mauve carpet. "You think about what sports you're gonna play?

"Tennis, I guess, in the spring," he said, gesturing with a shrug to the Babolat bag slung over his shoulder. *Obviously*, he wanted to add. "I exchanged a couple of emails with the coach back when I applied, but we'll see."

Ollie Richardson gave an appreciative laugh that did not feel entirely organic. He was less than a week off Nantucket; later, Foster would find him on Facebook and click through three picturesque months of photographs, of oysters being shucked and Coors Lights being drunk.

"Oh, Tierney's great. The tennis coach. Insane, but brilliant. I'm in his Milton class this year," Ollie said, wiping his hands on his khaki shorts. The tattered inseam of the shorts exposed muscular thighs that were deeply tan until they were not.

"Oh—awesome," Foster said lamely, unsure what else to offer.

With Ollie's help, the heaving of things from the car took about half an hour, and the assembly of the room—Ollie had at this point cheerfully disappeared—an hour more. Charlotte busied herself with mom things: the organization of Foster's toiletries in the shower caddy atop his dresser, the making of his bed. Foster spent ten minutes staring at the wall, a sheet of 3M adhesive strips getting sweaty in his hand, deciding where the R.E.M. poster should hang. So narrow was the bedroom that the desk's chair—the same standard-issue dormitory pine as the dresser and the desk itself—had to be pushed under the desk at all times; it backed up almost immediately to the side of the bed.

By three o'clock Charlotte had extinguished her list of excuses to stick around. ("Are you sure there isn't anything you need that we can go get for you at Target?") She wept again when she embraced him. "I don't know why I'm so teary." She sniffled into his shoulder. She retreated, clasping Foster's shoulders and staring him in the face. "I'm so proud of you. I know the last two years have been—well, shitty"—she smiled ruefully—"and you've been such a champ."

"It's all good, Mom, really," he said. He felt the anxiety of vulnerability encroaching and felt himself step backwards. "Now go, before the Philly traffic gets you."

She smiled and hugged him one last time. "I love you, Fosty," she told him, before turning out the door. He did not walk her to her car, though he knew he should have. And then after an appropriate tally of seconds had passed, he knew that she was gone. The yellow sunlight of the August midafternoon seemed to suspend itself in his window.

Years later, observers would differ on the exact circumstances of Foster Dade's early friendship with Jack Albright. These diverging accounts are unfortunately complicated by the attendant politics. But what we do know is that late into that first afternoon at Kennedy, as Foster lay supine upon his new comforter tossing an old tennis ball up toward the ceiling, there was a knock against his bedroom door.

"Yeah?" Foster asked a bit anxiously, sitting up quickly and running a hand through his hair, which he realized was thick with matted sweat. There wasn't an answer. He turned the knob gingerly.

By the time he'd entered high school, genetics and sports had left Jack Albright with the sort of body that seemed almost purposely constructed: its limbs long and defined, its torso broad and casklike. His brown hair had darkened and thickened with puberty; with every passing lacrosse season, the weight and contour of his helmet had inflected it with a parabolic swoop that curled up by his ears and turned gently across his forehead. Foster Dade wasn't *not* tall—he'd climbed just north of five feet eleven by the start of ninth grade and then to the best of his knowledge stopped growing—but the boy standing before his doorway had maybe three inches on him. It felt like more.

"You're the new sophomore?" the boy said, extending a browned arm. There was a quiet edge of theater to his masculine confidence. "Foster, right? Jack Albright. I'm in the tower room upstairs. You're from Baltimore?"

Foster arched his eyebrows slightly.

"It's on your door tag," he said, gesturing to the laminated index card with his elbow. The words KENNEDY LACROSSE across his gray T-shirt's chest rose against the press of his pecs.

"Oh," Foster said. "I figured they'd assigned you to watch after the new ones or something."

Jack grinned wickedly. "Hey, man, they don't trust me enough for that," he said. Foster watched the boy's eyes give an almost involuntary subatomic flick across the room—to the North Face fleece hanging on the hook by the closet door, to the Babolat racquet bag against the foot of his bed, to the BlackBerry charging by his pillow—and felt himself shift on the bed to obscure the R.E.M. poster that in his indecision he had let slide to the floor below his window. When Jack spoke again, his voice seemed to have accommodated a more organic benevolence. "So—stoked to be here, or what? Kennedy's honestly sick—and you seem, like, actually normal, which between you and me is great, 'cause Brennan is otherwise totally fucked this year. The older guys got into a bunch of trouble last spring, so the administration decided to stock the house with the lamest kids in our class, to give McCall a break or whatever. It's, like, two-thirds Korean now. But I'd already requested to be in Brennan, because my uncle and grandpa were in it and legacy counts, but all my friends ended up in Ames. Which fucking sucks but whatever."

Foster sensed that Jack Albright enjoyed the cadences of his own voice. "What happened last spring?" he asked.

"It's a long story," Jack replied breezily, with the air of someone comfortably aware of their information's privilege. "McCall says you play tennis?" He jerked his head down toward the Babolat bag on the floor.

From the objective perspective afforded by greater distance, Foster might have deemed this tall, muscular boy a prick—*ten years at Gil-*

man left me with a potentially unfair allergy to lacrosse players, he'd later write—and yet there was an aura of something to the boy in the doorway that had its own gravitational tug. Foster thought idly of his mother's descriptions of being in a room with Bill Clinton. He wanted to despise Jack Albright, and he wanted viscerally to be liked by him.

Foster's reply was broken by the sound of a girl's voice from the foyer down the hall. "Mister *Albright*!" the voice sang. "I've brought your *entourage* to see you!"

Jack cocked his head to the origin of the yelling. "Yo, give me a fucking *second*!" he yelled back amicably, then turned back to Foster. "Annabeth," he said self-evidently. "Whittaker. She's cool. And she's been dying to meet the new sophomores. You doing anything or you wanna come meet some chicks on the porch?"

Foster smiled wanly. "You're literally the one person I've met here, other than, like, McCall," he said. "My agenda's more or less open."

"Shake a leg, then," Jack said, already turning to head down the hallway.

If we were to locate a point of origin to the tragedy of the events that would eventually follow, we might find a compelling candidate in that afternoon at the end of August 2008, when Foster Dade saw Annabeth Whittaker standing in the Brennan House foyer. The girl at the foot of the House Master's staircase carried herself with the demonstrative confidence of someone indifferently aware of her own beauty. Her hair was haphazardly trussed in a thick plait that fell over her shoulder like a loose knot of challah; it seemed to carry the light of the afternoon that fell in a dusty sheet from the window over the stairs. She wore a loose white T-shirt that said DARTMOUTH in green and a pair of sunflower-colored athletic shorts. Her legs were brown, and a pinch of freckles fell over her nose, which sloped up gently near its point. It was clear she'd just worked out; she wore no makeup. She'd spent that summer on Martha's Vineyard, where more than a dozen men ten years her senior had slowed down in their Jeeps to gape dumbly at the woman in the bikini reading *Vanity Fair*, unaware that she was only fifteen.

"Everyone's on the porch but Sofi said you were back here, and it's fucking hot out there anyway," she said, pushing her tortoiseshell Wayfarers to her forehead. Her eyes were the first Foster had ever seen—or noticed, anyway—that could truthfully be described as green: pale and lucid like sea glass and flecked with ocher. "Schaefer had us run seven miles this morning, which I think would probably be legally actionable. Anyway"—she smiled with theatrical sweetness up at Jack Albright—"hi. Happy sophomore year. Who's this?" She jammed a thumb in Foster Dade's direction, a gesture that was somehow lovely.

"This," Jack said, "is Foster. Dade? He's new. Also in Brennan."

"Nice to meet you, Foster Dade," Annabeth said. "I'm Annabeth. Where do you hail from?"

Foster took her hand, feeling a storm inside him, and desperately hated himself for not looking in a mirror since he'd used the first-floor bathroom to splash water on his face two hours prior. "Hey," he said. "Baltimore." *I've spent the last hour thinking about all the clever hilarious things I could have said,* he would write on his Blogspot that night, *instead of sounding just . . . mentally damaged.*

But Annabeth continued to glow. "Maryland! Maryland's lovely. You play lacrosse?"

"He's a tennis player, apparently," Jack butted in. "So an outcast, basically."

Foster shrugged wanly. "Outcast. That's me." *Seriously, mentally damaged.*

"Come on, Dade, let's introduce you to the rest of the team," Jack said, wrapping an arm around Annabeth's waist. "Take me there, Whittaker."

They stepped out the front doors onto the porch, where the afternoon was dying and the light was warm. There was a tinge of possibility electrifying the final hours of summertime: the students on the Meadow's mown grass before them, some standing and some sprawled out on blankets, were tanned and taller after the three-month holiday, delighting in the thrill of their return.

Foster would have preferred to be out there in the waning light than up in the shadows of the Brennan House porch, where the band of teenagers perched on its brick walls opted instead for a vibe of performative boredom. There was a chasm between them and their peers below them on the lawn—a chasm between the earnestness of those in the grass embracing after months apart and the group appraising them from the porch. This, Foster knew, was what it was to be cool—perennially bored, sustained on a constant drip of irony.

There were nine of them sitting there, five boys and four girls. One of the girls, who had severe aquiline features and silken black hair, shrieked and ran to throw her arms around Jack's neck. "Jackie!" she screamed, jumping to throw her legs around his thighs. He spun her around theatrically, dipped her in his arms, and beamed. "Miss Cohen," he said. "It's been too long."

"Ah, the Lone Ranger, ladies and gentlemen," said one of the boys, a stocky, tanned kid with a crew cut and vaguely diabolical eyes, smiling. He was sitting on the brick half-wall on the far edge of the porch, his back against the green column. His was the sort of grin devoid of innocence; he seemed to leer. "What an honor it is for young Jack Albright to grace us with his presence, after he so cruelly sent his friends off to Ames House without the gift of his companionship."

"Hey, well, you can just go fuck yourself, Pretlow," Jack grinned good-naturedly, picking up a battered tennis ball discarded on the porch. "Especially when you have the audacity"—he lobbed the ball at the boy—"to colonize what is very much my porch." Annabeth beamed up at him, then out at the rest of them.

"And who do we have here?" the boy asked, jerking his head toward Foster, who suddenly felt conspicuous. There was a combativeness to the levity in his voice. "You new?"

"Oh, yeah," Foster said, extending an awkward wave at the group before him. "Foster. New sophomore."

"Foster," Annabeth said solemnly, sidling up to him with an air of theater, "is a tennis player from Baltimore. Everyone, this is Foster. Foster, this is everyone—Sofi"—the black-haired girl who had thrown herself on Albright waved cheerily—"Frances, Gracie, Porter, Freddie, Will, Mark, Pritchett, and"—pointing finally to the boy with wicked eyes—"Mason."

By the time I arrived at Kennedy two autumns later, this group of twelve—if we opt to include Foster, which we should, for reasons that will present themselves—had been cleaved to nine. The pallor of the events that whittled down this clique still hung over them with a certain luster of darkness. Listening in silence to those late-night conversations, I began to gather the snippets of what had happened. Because of this, or perhaps because of how impressionable I was in those early days, I dazzled at this contingency of souls through a certain clouded glass of romance.

In the beginning, there had been six. They coalesced in the first days of their freshman year with the magnificent ease that might have seemed impossible to those unacquainted with the humming social machinery of money and good family. Money and family, with their secret codes and electromagnetic pulses, unspool the thread interweaving the Eastern Seaboard like a string of summer lanterns. In this case: Annabeth Whittaker of Bedminster, New Jersey, had gone to Kent Place with a girl named Katie Corcoran, whose first cousin Frances Evans of Far Hills had also gotten into Kennedy. Frances had met Mason Pretlow of Alexandria, Virginia, at a handful of house parties on Nantucket that summer, when they were still learning to drink. Mason had an older sister at Deerfield; Lindsey Pretlow's best friend at school was one Celine Marin of East Seventy-Fourth Street and Park Avenue, who until Deerfield had gone to Brearley with Sofi Cohen since kindergarten. These were the connections made in the summer prior to their freshman year at Kennedy, plotting the footprint for a clique.

Sofi Cohen had been paired as a roommate with Gracie Smith of Chappaqua, New York, who years prior had been bunkmates at Camp Ravenwood with Porter Roth of Princeton, a day student. Across the recessed lawn in the First Year boys' residence, Mason Pretlow had been placed in the coveted triple suite with Jack Albright of Morristown and Pritchett Pierce of Manhattan—who'd loosely known Sofi

Cohen since sixth grade, when under the incipient spell of hormones he and his friends from Buckley had sought out the similarly insulated girls from Brearley and Spence—and in their first afternoon together they'd met Will Thierry of Winnetka, Illinois, whose older brother and sister had both graduated from Kennedy. Will Thierry's roommate was a beefy boy named Freddie Pieters, the son of a Kennedy alumnus who had made a fortune in derivatives trading and his Swiss wife, a former model. Freddie—Friedrich—was raised in Switzerland and had reportedly lost his virginity in his seventh-grade year at Zurich International School; in these two facts he was made exotic. And Mark Stetson, the son of two prominent Harvard-trained Black lawyers in San Francisco, who had spent the summer after eighth grade dancing in a regional tour of *Wicked*, was the sort of person born with the preternatural ability to dazzle them all.

Beyond the journalistic pop-psych paperbacks that come out every few years—the book that inspired *Mean Girls* comes to mind—there's an unfortunate dearth of sociological research on the contemporary American high school social taxonomy, and specifically on the caste we know as the "cool kids." There are common denominators, of course: the girls tend to be the prettiest, the guys athletic or handsome or both. But the generative forces are invisible, sublingual, to such an extent that those outside their merciful anointment are prone to diagnosing things in the language of conspiracy. But these are fourteen-year-olds, not Central American generals; they don't sit around in a huddle the night before the first morning of ninth grade and draft the fiat that'll impose their authority. Most of them—except for one or two somewhat diabolical girls—are generally oblivious to their position of privilege. The truth is that these groups retain their capital precisely and exclusively because the rest of the system chooses to inflate it.

So it had been the prior year. The rest of Kennedy's Class of 2011 had watched with a bitter, codifying awe as this junta claimed its new dominion. The upperclassmen had taken note, too: by October, the junior boys in Brennan and Davenport Houses were friending Annabeth and Frances on Facebook, making the most of the Poke function or commenting on their photos with coyly ironic affection.

Come Thanksgiving, these boys were sidling up to the girls at the Saturday night dances and, in more than one instance, taking them silently by the hand and leading them out into the chilly night before eleven o'clock check-in. (The freshman boys did not seem to mind so much: if anything, they took pride in the fact that their female compatriots were so clearly valued by the market, and found solace in the knowledge that their own time would come once they were older.) As their first winter at Kennedy hardened the earth and leached color from the silver skies, the group began absconding on certain weekends to Sofi's apartment in the city, where Mr. and Mrs. Cohen chose to ignore the handles of Smirnoff they'd pulled from their duffels.

"You play tennis, hm?" the boy named Pritchett asked Foster, peering up at him. He was imposingly Anglican: well over six feet tall, with an edged jawline and an elegant shag of wheat-colored curls. He wore pink chino shorts and a loose black T-shirt that read ST. BARTH'S, FRENCH WEST INDIES. "Let's hit sometime. I'm not great or anything, but I can hit."

"Shut the fuck up," Sofi cooed. She looked up at Foster. "He's great. Trust me. Remember that day in East Hampton? You kicked my ass."

"Hold on—*we* kicked your ass," Mason Pretlow said. "Don't rewrite history." Mason was stout, with the tannish pink shadow that follows acne in late-adolescent remission; his eyes were pale and unkind and flashed with a manic glint in moments of mirth.

"That was a fun day," the girl named Gracie said lazily. She was sitting on the left end of the porch's wall, her back against the house, her arms up on the stone. Her expression was at once passive and flinty; something about her made Foster uneasy, as if her presence meant inherently that he was not welcome. Her beauty was patrician—the sort that appeals to older athletic-types of unmitigated but uninspired libido, who had subconsciously taken to heart the American conflation of athletic fatlessness with beauty. Gracie's breasts were small but pert, the torso beneath them tan and firmly flat with the feminine muscularity that follows the intensive abdominal exercises innocuously recommended by not entirely benevolent mothers. The white Jack Rogers sandals on her feet were scuffed and the silver bracelet on her wrist was expensive. "We went to Tripp's that night, right?"

"No, that was the next night," Annabeth said sagely.

"We were at mine!" squealed the blond girl named Frances, who had a kind face and was both beautiful and, Foster would learn, legendarily stupid. "When Freddie puked in my parents' bathroom and clogged the toilet."

Jack Albright sprung up into a strange rictus and gave what Foster assumed was a very bad impression of a Swiss accent. "Ah, Miss Evans, Mister Evans—I am so sorry, I ate the bad fish for my lunch, and I am so very sick."

The porch cracked up. "Ah, fuck you," Freddie Pieters said. His accent was perhaps Canadian. And then they all proceeded to relitigate the wildest moments of the previous three months, nearly all of which transpired while drunk at their beach houses on Long Island and Nantucket and Rhode Island. Foster felt something palpable and vulgar in his superfluousness and after a couple of privately excruciating minutes he cleared his throat. "Hey, I need to go finish unpacking some things," he said, his face burning. "Great to meet you guys, though, really."

Those sitting murmured their *good to meet you too*. "Dade, I'll see you later, all right?" Albright said, clasping a hand on his shoulder. And then Annabeth turned and smiled at him almost expectantly. "So good to meet you," she said. The world stopped spinning. "I'll see you all the time, I'm sure."

IX.

Given the paucity of relevant sociological insight, the corollary question of how certain adolescent cliques find their nominal leaders leaves itself to speculation. One hypothesis: there's a brand of confidence that's so inherent to its possessor—so ostensibly devoid of the complexes and underlying insecurities that so often fuel swagger—that it's endearing, as hard as one might try to despise it. The Japanese call this *shibui* (渋い). George Clooney has it; when he wore a collared shirt, Anthony Bourdain did.

The only people who sincerely loathed Jack Albright were the ones who envied him. They did their best to reduce him to a caricature, which in any other case would be easy: he wore pastel chino shorts from the Vineyard Vines catalogue; his topmost dresser drawer was a rainbow of mesh lacrosse pinnies accumulated over seven years of clinics and tournaments. His unchecked adolescent virility was still eagerly learning about itself. In the late August evenings at the beginning of freshman year, he'd bring his stick out onto the lawn, cradling it mindlessly and without a ball as he politicked. He brought his Bose portable speakers into the bathroom and pumped Lil Wayne while he showered, angling them out the window, inviting his classmates to know his taste and possibly imagine him naked.

But he defied caricature—this much was clear within a matter of weeks as a First Year, when reports began to emerge in the English and History Departments of this vivacious boy who in Debra Sassoon's First Year Humanities section had written perhaps the term's best paper on *Lord of the Flies*. In early October he declared his candidacy for the Class of 2011's representative to the Student Council; he would ultimately run unopposed. That spring, at the annual First Year award ceremony he'd received not only the History Department Prize and the Student Athlete Award—he and Mason Pretlow had been the only freshmen to make varsity lacrosse—but also the William Noyes Whiting '43 Prize, given annually to "the boy and the girl whose scholarship, athleticism, citizenship, and goodwill best embody the traits of the model Kennedian."

The female recipient was Carly Wu-Saunders, a formidable day student and the daughter of two Princeton professors, who as a freshman had taken Advanced Spoken Latin and earned the second-chair oboe seat in the New Jersey All-State Symphony Orchestra. But her runner-up, according to reliable sources, had been one Annabeth Whittaker, whose case had been argued with particular fervor by several middle-aged men in the History and Math Departments. Their problematic biases aside, she had been a compelling choice. Like Jack Albright, she defied the obvious avenues to caricature. The quieter, homelier girls in their class loathed her because she was not only attractive but viciously bright, and more critically humble about both. She participated with eloquent enthusiasm around every seminar table. On quiet Sunday afternoons in spring, she took to a far corner of the Yard, as the sunken lawn between the First Year boys' and girls' dormitories was known, and leaned up against the vine-dressed brick wall with her book: *The Bonfire of the Vanities* in April; *Slouching Towards Bethlehem* and *American Psycho* in May.

More than anything else, though, she was kind. This was noteworthy not because of the kindness itself but because of the harsh juxtaposition it offered. In other words: she was kind, and the company she kept was decidedly not. With the possible exception of Gracie Smith, her friends were not outwardly cruel, but they saw little incentive to extend themselves beyond the confines of their world to embrace their fellow classmates. But Annabeth Whittaker was, in the words of the biology teacher and varsity field hockey coach Pam Sutt, a "bona fide team player." When she passed you on campus she said hello to you. More than one awkward boy in the class of 2011 misinterpreted her kindness for romantic affection, to inevitable heartbreak.

She carried a certain happy indifference to—or maybe an honest ignorance of—the ease with which she navigated the world. When upperclassmen boys led her from the Saturday dances, she turned and shrugged at her friends behind her with a grin that seemed to say: *Isn't this funny.* The daughter of a dutiful alumnus—Skip Whittaker, Class of 1980—she sincerely loved Kennedy, and comported herself as if every day there was a new treat, every classmate and teacher a character worth esteeming.

There's a girl here, Foster wrote on his Blogspot his first night at Kennedy, and I'm staggered by how perfect she is. It's tough to explain, but something inside of me shifted the minute I saw her, and I've been obsessing ever since, in a way I never have with anyone else. Her name is Annabeth. She seems to like me but I'm afraid to do anything, as if I have a beautiful, carefully crafted diorama of the world and making one minor adjustment could send the entire thing crumbling.

Foster's window was open when he returned to his room that night. Against the desk lamp's orange light, the mesh of the screen was heavy with years of gnats and detritus. He felt his phone buzzing in his pocket for the first time since he'd gotten to Kennedy in the afternoon. *Mom,* the white screen of the BlackBerry read. His stomach suddenly tight, he envisioned the nausea of that conversation: he found himself thinking of those books of prewritten summer camp form letters, given by piti-able mothers to their dull sons to fill out in their cabins during weekly letter-writing time. (My favorite activity is _____.) He let it hum up against his voicemail, and then the phone was silent and dark.

Beyond his window, the lampposts along the driveway spilled their glow upon the shadowed borders of the night, which was heavy with the pleasant drone of cicadas and bullfrogs. He pulled off his T-shirt and then his shorts, wondering distantly if someone outside could see him. Foster slept in his boxers, even when he jerked off in the moments before sleep. The insomnia of certain nights that summer suddenly seemed quaint, and he thought with intense longing of their vacancy: when, if midnight came and the tendrils of sleep hadn't pulled him downward, he'd reached down to his dick and rolled it in his fingers with a gentle absentmindedness until it began to stiffen.

But that night, the first of the 557 nights that would bridge Foster Dade's time at Kennedy, the idea of masturbating was obscene in its prior innocence. Instead, he opened his MacBook, thinking briefly and apathetically of a *Time* article in Dr. Apple's waiting room about the correlation between screen glow and sleeplessness. The brightness of the screen was violent as it awoke to his open Blogspot. He clicked back to an empty draft. And when he closed his computer afterward, the night held a new quietude; the last distant voices outside had receded long before.

The amicable hand Jack Albright had extended to Foster on the day of his arrival would withdraw so quickly that Foster wondered if he'd fabricated the encounter. He'd bent down to tie his shoe in the Brennan foyer on his first Friday morning at Kennedy when Jack bounded down the stairs. "Hey, man, what's good?" Jack had called as he moved toward the door, not once tapering his speed, not waiting for a reply. "Sick, man," Foster had muttered bitterly to the tongue of his white Adidas.

He had trudged alone that morning to his assigned seat in the back of the Manning Arts Center for the year's inaugural School Meeting. Kennedy's website had informed him that the building had been a gift of Mr. and Mrs. Wilson W. Manning '53 of Morristown in the early 1970s, whose grandson John Manning Albright was a proud member of the Class of 2011. This seemed to explain the unrestrained bravado with which Jack preened about onstage during the Student Council's welcome skit, for which he had volunteered to play the citric-lipped Head Master Pauline Ross. He wore a brown Paul McCartney wig and a thick rope of costume pearls over a green taffeta dress; even Mrs. Ross herself, who for all her administrative and interpersonal shortcomings could play along when she needed to, chuckled appreciatively as the auditorium screamed him on. "Gah, even in drag he's so fucking *hot*," a curly-haired girl in the row ahead of Foster had whispered loudly to her neighbor. That night, Foster had watched from the shadows of the Brennan parlor as Jack held court beneath the moth-spangled porchlight. Annabeth's laugh—a full, magnanimous laugh—was the loudest of all. With a lurch of nausea Foster went back to his room to begin his response paper on the Huguenots for Advanced European History, but found himself only blinking at his MacBook's screen. Through the many walls between them he could hear the baritone of Jack's voice.

"He was clearly so far up his own ass, but like—it worked for him," Georgina Pruett, who had been the Third Year Representative on the Student Council that year, told me in Washington a couple of months ago. "The only ones who disliked him were the ones who wanted to be him. He wasn't a nice guy or a shitty guy, per se—he was a performer, and so I guess his merits really rested in his capacity to engross us. Does that make sense?"

X.

For at least a generation, since the earnest bourgeois solemnity of *Dead Poets Society* collapsed into the lazy salaciousness of *Gossip Girl*, American cinema and television have dutifully imagined boarding school as the domain of fuckups. (The fuckups themselves in these portraits are themselves the sum of cliches: cokeheads, sluts, petty criminals, et al.) The truth on its face is more banal.

We can crudely organize the population of a school like Kennedy—or Choate, or St. George's, or any other first- or second-tier boarding school north of D.C.—into certain categories in a broader taxonomy.

Let's start with a group I'll call the Haves, for simplicity's sake. The Haves are those teenagers who go off to school simply because they hail from circumstances of affluence—and/or analogous geographies; towns like Darien, Conn. or Locust Valley, N.Y.—in which doing so is simply standard practice. Their fathers went to boarding school; perhaps their mothers did too. Within similar tax brackets, we have those from less patrician origins and more cerebrally inclined households—suburban Jews; the children of psychiatrists, economists, nerdy dot-com startup mavens, et al.—who see the top boarding schools as express lanes to Yale or Stanford. (In Kennedy's case, it's the day students who overwhelmingly sustain this demographic, hailing from the academic enclave of Princeton or incommensurately Chinese- and Indian-American towns like Edison or West Windsor.)

At first glance, we see little cohesion among them; indeed, the Haves operate within their own smaller taxonomies of power, defined by the prosaic metrics of adolescent social capital, which perhaps unjustly always come down to sex. (No one is going to pretend that the varsity lacrosse captain and the Executive Editor of the *Kennedian* operate on the same rung of the venereal food chain.) What unites the Haves is something more impalpable, legible by comparison with the shape of those who covet it. (The Have-Nots, as it were.) We find it in the quietest cadences of their movement through these worlds; in the way they comprehend deep in their marrow that these places are constructed essentially for them. The Haves very quickly gravitate toward those who share this instinct, like stray moons falling into orbit.

Confidence always compounds itself, and in time, the Haves in their easy navigational elegance are the leading players in their spellbinding production: the editors and star writers on the *Kennedian* or the *Rubrum*, Kennedy's literary magazine; the admissions office's Head Tour Guides; those who go onstage at School Meeting on Fridays and lean insouciantly against the podium to tell their eight hundred peers to come out to the lacrosse game against St. Paul's the next afternoon, concluding with a wry in-joke that only their fellow Haves possess the contextual knowledge to understand.

And there, silent and invisible in the darkness of the auditorium, are the Have-Nots, deafened by the incomprehensibility of their class-mates' laughter. They too are a diversely multicellular group, even if no one takes the time to contemplate it. This subpopulation is mostly white or Asian-American. With certain exceptions, those Kennedians of African-American or Hispanic heritage—many of whom were brought to Kennedy from places like the Bronx by nonprofit fellowship groups by virtue of their seventh-grade scores on the ERB or Iowa tests—tend to hang together, building their own rich and complex biomes within this vaster foreign frontier; ditto the rich South Koreans, except with more cigarette-smoking. We could say that what unites the Have-Nots is simply the inverse of what unites the Haves—the inverse of that unlearned ease—and this wouldn't be wrong, but it elides something more primal. The closest synonym would be naïveté.

In almost all these cases, the Have-Nots arrive in these worlds on their own. They are the bright, earnest sons and daughters of elec-tricians in Dayton or car salesmen in Altoona: maybe they'd read *A Separate Peace* in eighth grade; maybe a sympathetic guidance coun-selor nudged them. They almost certainly don't watch *Gossip Girl*, but perhaps they've seen *Dead Poets Society*. They have no contem-porary point of reference to argue against the assumption that these institutions are utopian: a kingdom where effusive chitchat prefers topics like Shakespeare and Tolkien over crushes and shopping malls. In other words, the traits for which they'd been ostracized or ignored in their public middle schools are instead celebrated at a place like Kennedy. To their parents, the notion of prep school holds a cultural and socioeconomic foreignness on par with Mediterranean holidays and evenings at the opera, but when they see their child's face renewed with the same light that the bullies of late childhood had fought so hard to stamp out, and when they read the four-page letter detailing the terms of the full financial aid package their child had applied for with the help of that guidance counselor, they relent.

It would be several weeks after their arrival on campus before the Have-Nots realized their parents' skepticism may have been something other than mere ignorance. It's then that, for the first time in their lives—even for those with the most merciless bullies back home—they come to truly know shame. Its incendiary light is grotesque in what it illuminates: the cheap shapelessness of the blouse they'd spent the summer saving up for; the expression of disgust upon the face of the pretty blond girl with whom they'd tried to strike up conversation after class. They realize with growing distress that intellect here is a weak currency, largely by virtue of its oversupply, and that their own bullish entry into the market in fact amounted to showing up on the Nasdaq floor with fistfuls of Guinean francs or Vietnamese dong. What qualified as brilliance in their home school district is not only devalued but deprived of basic fungibility. When it comes to academic success at a school like Kennedy, all the raw intelligence in the world can't buy the esoteric knowledge and rhetorical training provided by $25,000-a-year East Coast middle schools. They retreat abruptly into the shadows, burning with silent humiliation, loathing themselves for being naïve enough to assume they were welcome.

In a purely socioeconomic sense, Foster Dade belonged very plainly to the Haves. Jim Dade, whose own parents had come to North Carolina from New York, had gone to Andover after Charlotte Country Day. Maggie Dade had gone to Andover because their father had, and because Baltimore bored her; at fourteen she'd begun to cultivate the weary erudition that at Amherst would captivate lacrosse players and poetry professors alike.

Even before the divorce, Foster's relationship with his father was sanitarily distant. "I don't know if you'd be able to keep up at Andover," Jim had said. It was only a year later, in the wake of what happened, that Foster found himself wondering otherwise. Late one summer night, he had gotten stoned in his backyard and realized with a fit of terror that the walls of his world were closing in. "I think I want to maybe think about going away next year," he told his mother the following morning. Charlotte, herself still disoriented, nodded with understanding, however dazed.

Two months after that, on a cool Saturday morning in September, he climbed on his bike and rode to Hopkins to sit for the Secondary School Admission Test, the boarding school analogue of the SAT. Thirty minutes into it, beneath the fluorescence of the university athletic center, Foster realized he was still residually high from the night before, and resigned himself to the untenability of the fantasy he'd fleetingly nursed. When the results arrived via email two weeks later, he had missed out only one question out of two hundred and six. "I'm not going to fucking Andover," he told his mother that night.

And so on a sunny Thursday morning in April, Charlotte Dade—who was not yet fully undazed—and her son got in the Lexus and set out north on I-95 to visit the two schools to which he'd been admitted: first the six hours up to western Massachusetts to Deerfield, and then, on the way home, central Jersey, for Kennedy.

It rained hard on Deerfield the day he visited, and it was unseasonably cold for spring, even for New England. His tour guide, a vacuous redheaded girl named Pacey, did not bother concealing her displeasure at the task. "No," Foster told Charlotte firmly when they were back in the Lexus. They stopped in Amherst to have lunch with Maggie, who had been dumped the previous evening; the experience was even less pleasant than the tour. He was the type to believe in omens, and wondered if this was one. But when he arrived at Kennedy, the world seemed to have moved almost imperceptibly on its axis. It was one of the first truly warm days that spring, and he stared with something close to wonder as he was shown around campus by a Columbia-bound senior named Greer LeVerrier. *At risk of seeming vapid: everyone seemed happy*, he would write on his Blogspot that evening. *Now I get what people talk about when they talk about "gut feelings."* The boys and girls around him wore coral colors and Ray-Bans and seemed to outstretch themselves to the sun.

He'd spent the drive home to Baltimore in silence. For several weeks he allowed the glass bowl on his dresser to accumulate a thin patina of dust; the Hopkins philosophy student texted him twice to make sure he was still living in Baltimore. He allowed himself to touch the romance that had made him a very sensitive child and a maudlin,

vaguely poetic early teenager. He spent those evenings running, up
through Hopkins and along the wooded rises of Roland Park, listening
to the National and Coldplay and New Order. It was under a warm
April dusk that he set out in his Asics and ran six miles, and when he
got home, he found his mother in the kitchen and told her he'd made
up his mind. She cried for a moment, and he briefly thought he might
too, and then she ordered them a pizza.

Foster had overslept. Against the sickly morning light, he blinked this
realization into clarity, then threw himself upright in a panic, pulling
the pair of crumpled khakis up from the floor to his feet. He squeezed
a chickpea-sized bead of Colgate onto his index finger and scrubbed
it around his mouth as he hobbled out the front doors of Brennan,
still fastening his belt.

The twelve sets of eyes around the mahogany table turned to him
in unison as he pushed open the old white door. He had come to experience even the most mundane public gestures as acts of humiliation,
burning with shame as he clumsily spread cream cheese on his bagel
in the Dining Center or walked alone into the science building across
from the library; this was almost nonviable in its misery.

"Whoa-ah," the white-haired man at the table's far end barked
merrily. His face was flushed and thin, his fingers spindly as he clasped
them together. "Ladies and gentlemen—Exhibit A! As I was saying—if
I can heave my ancient self to the tennis court at six in the morning
on Tuesdays, you can pull your hands out of your boxer shorts and
cross the ten yards to my classroom in the far-too-generous ten-minute
window between classes. Tardiness! I won't allow it."

Around the table, a few tittered. Foster's intestines seized when he
realized he was looking at Annabeth Whittaker. She grinned at him
wildly. "You're late!" she mouthed with a certain theater. She wore
a loose plaid shirt.

"So," the teacher, whose name was Dr. Tierney, gestured widely
across the table. "Sit."

The chair's legs screamed against the hard floor as Foster pulled
it out.

"Anyway!" Tierney bellowed happily. "Second Year English exists because of this school's well-intentioned pedagogical architects, who see an opportunity for a grand survey of contemporary English literature that will suit you for the department's upper-level seminars before your theory-heavy undergraduate curriculum Cloroxes it all away."

"But!" he went on. "All that really means"—his eyes danced with light—"is that I have to teach you a specific list of books." He rapped his fingertips against a printed syllabus and grinned mischievously. "Beyond that—interpretive license. You! Our tardy friend! What's your name!"

"I'm, uh, Foster Dade—"

"Dade! Ah! The tennis player!" Foster felt a modest rush of satisfaction at this. "Tell us, then, Dade: What, in your mind, is the function of literature?"

Foster felt twelve sets of eyes, among them Annabeth's, turn to him in unison. "I mean—to capture the world in a way that's, I guess—beautiful?" He felt himself blush at this word and noticed a pale boy with small dark eyes study him from the end of the table. "Though I guess that's a little simplistic—"

Tierney grinned wildly. "Not bad!" he roared. "Not bad. Yes. There is beauty in the world and literature is how you bottle it. It is not horribly complicated or beyond your comprehension, despite what some of my well-intentioned colleagues might insist. So!" He slapped his palms on the wooden table, holding forth before his charges, who looked up at him, startled. "We will not gather in this room to look for hidden symbols or Freudian runes. I do not care what a yellow hat stands for! We've got one objective: to figure out what is being said and why. Our first book"—he picked up a battered paperback on the stack of papers before him—"is Fitzgerald's *Gatsby*. And don't you dare roll your eyes. This"—he thudded the book, clenched in his grip, into the air like a heartbeat—"is what it's all about. Find me a prettier packet of words and I'll give you my job. *Gatsby*!" He brandished the book again. "If you do not weep while reading it, I will not have done my job."

Arthur—Art—Tierney had come to Kennedy in 1988 after a decade as an editor at Time-Life Books, where with a doctorate in British literature from NYU he'd found refuge from the creeping tide of Der-ridean high theory. Sometime in this pre-Kennedian stretch his wife, Sonia, had died of cancer. Tierney's classroom was at the far corner of Memorial Hall's second floor, and on fall mornings the high ceiling carried a bright dusty light. Like all of Kennedy's classrooms, its desks had been replaced nearly a century before with one long mahogany table with thirteen sturdy chairs around its perimeter in an appeal to Socratic knowledge-building.

Later that day, Tierney sat in the Dining Center, an awful alien structure, a low hangar of turd-colored brick and opaque green glass that was a blight on an otherwise pastoral campus. Chip Mitchener, who had returned to his alma mater as a lacrosse coach and college counselor a few years after graduating from Trinity, was speaking to Tierney about the first senior of the year breaking down in the airy second-floor office during an advisory session. She was Seon-chu Lee, a cellist from Seoul, who wore a Brown hoodie every day because she wanted to go there. "That's got to be a record," Mitchener said through a mouth full of pasta salad. But Tierney was watching the blond boy from his Second Year English seminar across the Center's atrium.

Foster did not feel Tierney's eyes on him as he held his glass to the lemonade spigot. He was watching as Jack Albright and Pritchett Pierce stood at the salad bar, pantomiming something before two Third Year girls, whose hair seemed to catch the murky light as they tossed their heads back and laughed.

By late September the mornings held the earliest chill of autumn. Foster found himself waking each morning with the first pink light of dawn. The cedar waxwings sang their song in the trees and Grady Yates, a baby-faced Spanish teacher in his early thirties, padded by Foster's window, concluding his morning jog with a heavy-breathed stop in front of Perry House. There was a meager safety in the hour's solitude, and as the rest of Kennedy still slept Foster allowed himself to ask the question he was otherwise too ashamed to ask, which was whether he had made a mistake.

When his morning erection dispelled itself, he would take the tan towel from the back of his desk chair and move noiselessly to the bathroom down the hall. He forced himself to stand for a moment beneath the icy shower before it warmed. Around him the water bounced and slid down the white tile walls. Occasionally he jerked off, concluding always with a thrash of shame, but most days he simply stared upward and let the water fall onto his face as the birds sang outside.

Some afternoons Foster found himself running. There was a sudden press of life across campus as classes ended, toward the Field House and the playing fields and musical rehearsal at the Manning Arts Center, and when its bodies had receded in their transit he stepped out from Brennan in his weathered blue Asics and set out for where they were not. By mistake he had once found himself veering up to the varsity soccer field, and upon seeing Jack Albright, Mason Pretlow, and Pritchett Pierce lining up for shooting drills he had quite literally thrown himself into a bramble to avoid being seen. He learned to calibrate his routes accordingly.

He'd find himself back at Brennan, panting and briefly liberated, pulling his key card from his back pocket, slipping himself into the rare quietude of the House. Sometimes Jae, his suitemate, was home too, for reasons unclear. This was fine.

Jae-hyun An had showed up at Kennedy the evening after the rest of the student body that August. He had no good explanation for Scott McCall or anyone else for his tardiness. He arrived at the doors of Brennan in a black Suburban with tinted windows, the sort reserved for high-level Washington motorcades since the Bush years, accompanied by a Korean man in a suit with a crew cut and a square jaw. This was not the driver, who continued to sit behind the tinted glass, staring straight ahead. The man in the suit carried Jae's matching black bags inside; Jae, who wore a tall-collared vicar's shirt buttoned all the way up, walked alongside him, holding a leather attaché case.

He wore oversized, black-rimmed glasses and had the side-sheared haircut that would fall into vogue with American neofascists eight years later. The difference was that Jae's had a conspicuous lock that had been dyed blond. "I am Jae or Philip," Jae or Philip said to Foster as the man in the suit began to unpack his things. Foster, who had been tossing the Penn ball with himself on his bed when he heard Jae enter, smiled. "I like Jae," he said.

And he did. Like Foster, Jae seemed unclear as to what he was doing there; the two were similar in their reclusive passivity. This became an unspoken language of fraternity between them; because of Jae's limited English, they almost never interacted directly.

One evening in the second week of the year, Scott Hung, a Korean-American boy in Foster's year who lived on the third floor, told him over dinner in the Brennan dining pod that Jae was famous. "His dad is basically the George Clooney of South Korean cinema—he plays presidents in war movies and stuff," Scott said. Jae himself had not eaten a meal in the Dining Center since he arrived on campus, instead ordering sushi from a delivery place on Nassau Street in Princeton, which he consumed alone in his bedroom.

On these evenings, Foster would close his bedroom door and sit before the glow of his MacBook. With a perfunctory half-heartedness he would make stabs at his schoolwork, which had not ceased to stagger him in its quantity: a four-page document-based analysis of the Treaty of Westphalia; a three-page reading response on *The Yellow Wallpaper*; lab reports for chemistry and problem sets for Algebra II; study guides for coming tests on all of the above. But in his desolation the work seemed to assume an untenable mass. Instead, he would scroll idly through his Facebook News Feed, appraising the happiness of lives to which he was not privy; when the pang of this became too intense, he would click to Jetman, indifferent to his rocket-propelled avatar's steady rhythm of collisions with the barriers along his path, or to YouTube. Once, for unknown reasons that deeply distressed him, he was watching a *Family Guy* clip of Peter Griffin and his friends singing "Don't Stop Believing" when he found himself crying. At other times, he had an impulse to read: not his texts for school or the books that had accumulated on his shelf over the summer (*The World According to Garp*, *White Noise*) but the novels that he had cherished in those last fervent years before adolescence: *Walk Two Moons*; *The View from Saturday*; in particular *Stargirl*, which he'd read seven times in fourth grade after bringing it home from the Scholastic book fair at school.

Certain nights, just after lights-out at eleven, Foster's BlackBerry would hum softly with a message from Harris Adelstein, an aloof but affable Third Year from Manhattan, telling him to come chill. There within in Adelstein's second floor room he would find a small gaggle of lethargic Third Years—always Andrew O'Donnell, a sullen boy from Seattle's affluent suburbs who spent study hall downloading rap mixtapes—and ensconced in their cozy ranks would be Jack Albright, holding forth in the same hollow cadences Foster had heard on that first afternoon, very much at home.

In the sixteen months since Facebook had opened its design interface to third-party application designers, Honesty Box had become the second-most-installed app among the platform's thirteen-to-eighteen-year-old user base, trailing closely behind Jetman. One night that fall, Foster had sat in Harris Adelstein's room and listened in silence as Jack opened Andrew O'Donnell's MacBook and clicked to the application's page on Facebook, where, several nights before, the boys had commenced an anonymous dialogue with an attractive First Year girl named Jacqueline Franck. Its message bubbles were the pale medicinal pink and blue of birth announcements. "I want to motorboat your tits," Jack read aloud as he typed, drawing out each syllable in performed contemplation, "because they are huge."

These nighttime meetings sustained the most prolonged encounters between Foster Dade and Jack Albright. (Foster would install the app to his own Facebook account the following day, though its inbox would remain empty for several months.) On these occasions, as the boys around them laughed their goading laughs, Jack's eyes would meet Foster's in a fleeting and sardonic sort of salutation. Something in Jack's gaze would force Foster to hear the artifice in his own laughter, as if Jack had heard it first. There was a quantum tension in these moments, discernible only to the two of them; to the others, Jack missed no beats, and as he carried on in his rehearsal of testosteronal verve, Foster would slide himself silently down to Adelstein's ratty couch, for all intents and purposes not there. *When Jack does talk to me, it feels like he's not being friendly as much as . . . marking his territory*, Foster would write bitterly on his Blogspot that fall.

"The thing is, we actually did like him," Harris Adelstein would later tell me. "When he did talk, he was usually dry and witty. But we could never figure out if he didn't like us or if he was just shy or unhappy. He always seemed like he was waiting for permission to speak—especially around Albright."

And so we can imagine Foster's surprise—a surprise that was at once enthralling and deeply skeptical—when, on a Saturday afternoon in mid-October, his MacBook emitted the endearing little tubular whoop that marked the arrival of a message on iChat. He was prostrate on his bed. His window was half-open; outside, campus was filling with the round golden light of autumn's nearing zenith. They still had Saturday morning classes at Kennedy then, and that morning, Foster had gotten his first paper, on *Gatsby*, back from Tierney, with a B+ scrawled in green ink across the top. *You're smarter than this*, Tierney had written.

Foster pulled his MacBook from his desk. He hit the spacebar to clear the screensaver and saw not a new message but a query box: *albreezy43 wants to send you a message. Do you accept?* It was Jack Albright.

> **albreezy43:** yo
> **albreezy43:** u going to the dance tonight
> **albreezy43:** ?

Foster blinked and wondered if this was a prank, with Mason Pretlow and Gracie Smith sitting next to Jack on the other end, snickering cruelly.

> **fosterd419:** not rly sure
> **fosterd419:** worth going?

A moment passed.

albreezy43: fuck yea bittchhhh
albreezy43: first dance of the year
albreezy43: lotsa pent up hormones
albreezy43: lol
albreezy43: anyway come chill with us before in Ames
albreezy43: annabeth wants u there

Foster's stomach lurched and then wrapped around itself.

fosterd419: whittaker?
albreezy92: duh lol
albreezy92: she's obsessed
fosterd419: flattered
fosterd419: but yeah cool
fosterd419: just lmk the plan

annabeth wants u there. annabeth wants u there. she's obsessed. obsessed. Foster kept this chat window open for the remainder of the waning afternoon, returning to it like a talisman every few minutes. *I'm going to my first Kennedy dance tonight*, he wrote on his Blogspot. *No idea what to expect. I'm really only going for Annabeth. I feel good, for once.*

XI.

Foster Dade's MacBook Pro/Music/iTunes/Playlists/fitting in (Created October 3, 2008)

Name	Time	Artist
Love Lockdown	4:30	Kanye West
The General	4:07	Dispatch
A Milli	3:41	Lil Wayne
Play Your Part (Pt. 2)	3:25	Girl Talk
A-Punk	2:18	Vampire Weekend
Oxford Comma	3:16	Vampire Weekend

Call on Me (Radio Mix)	2:51	Eric Prydz
party_someday_strokes_vs_notorious _big.mp3	4:23	www.MashupCentral.com FREE HITS
What a Feeling (feat. Dominico)	6:48	Peter Luts
Let It Rock (feat. Lil Wayne)	3:51	Kevin Rudolf
Homecoming (feat. Chris Martin)	3:24	Kanye West
Champion	2:48	Kanye West
Live Your Life (feat. Rihanna)	5:39	T.I.
paper_planes_kid_cudi_freestyle.mp3	1:51	DATPIFF DOWNLOAD HOTTEST TRACKS FREE http://www.datpiff.com NEW MUSIC EVERY DAY!
Paranoid (feat. Mr. Hudson)	4:38	Kanye West
The World Is Mine (F*** Me I'm Famous Edit)	6:04	David Guetta

16 songs, 1.1 hours, 137.2 MB

XII.

**http://www.fhd93.blogspot.com/2008/09/lil-wayne-etc
(Posted September 29, 2008)**

I've never met white people who like rap so much. It's everywhere. I wake up in the morning and I hear some mixtape echoing in the bathroom while Andrew O'Donnell showers. I'll be on Facebook after study hall and see that Mason Pretlow just shared some Lil Wayne YouTube music video to Freddie Pieters' wall. (Mason and Freddie are roommates in Ames. You'd think there'd be easier ways to communicate. You know, like turning around in your desk chair to the person five feet away from you. This leads me to conclude that Mr. Pretlow isn't actually interested in communicating with his dear roommate at all: he's more interested in whichever hot First Year girl he and his buds friended on Facebook might happen to see the post, be impressed by his cool taste, stalk his Wall-to-Wall with Freddie and see all their inside jokes and pics of their fun summer adventures, etc. But maybe I'm being mean.) I feel like Jack is constantly listening to Kanye West. When we're in O'Donnell's room or another Third Year's room at night, he makes a point of knowing/enjoying all the random mixtape rappers O'Donnell plays, but I never hear him listening to that stuff when he's alone. Kanye is rap too, but it's different. Whiter. Does that make sense?

I've been making a playlist on iTunes to keep track of all the songs I've been hearing since I got here. A lot of it is the stuff that was starting to come on the radio at the end of summer. A lot of of it is, yes, rap, especially Lil Wayne, who I secretly think is really annoying. Some of it is older electro/dance stuff (I dunno what you'd actually call the genre)—the sort of thing I've always secretly found so catchy but what most guys I grew up with would call gay. (For some reason, on the Kennedy WiFi network, you can access other people's iTunes libraries if they're set to "shared"; mine is, because everyone's is, but thank God for the option to reset a song's play count: when I got here, "Believe" by Cher was toward the top of my Top 25 Most Played auto-playlist.) From watching everyone else, I've learned that there's a way to enjoy stuff like that—the stuff you're not supposed to like. The trick is to pretend you're listening to it because of how much you hate it. It's the same thing with how Jack and the older guys sometimes "ironically" watch Gossip Girl in the common room. At School Meeting last week, to advertise the big game against Mercersburg, the boys' varsity soccer team did this suggestive dance in ridiculous spandex outfits to "Call on Me" by Eric Prydz. I later learned they were just copying the music video, which is set in an aerobics class, except this time it was athletic dudes and not hot girls. And that's why it was supposed to be funny. I spent the entire time watching Jack. What I noticed is that he seemed to be genuinely loving it. So did the other guys too, I guess. But I saw something in him (in how much he seemed to be having fun) that I see to a lesser degree in his normal social interactions—it's something that seems to set him apart, something that draws people to him (girls romantically and guys socially). I couldn't help but think that if he wasn't so athletic, people would call him gay. I think that's why the whole thing kind of pissed me off. I tried to picture a world where I could be up there doing it with them, and be confident about it, and not be mocked, and I couldn't.

XIII.

Six months nearly to the day had passed since the last Saturday night dance at Kennedy, though Anne-Marie Cline would spend that week in October grumbling to her colleagues in the History Department that it hadn't been long enough. The dance in question had been the first held after spring break, when the days are finally longer and hormones high, and she had been its faculty supervisor. On typical Saturdays, this was a tedious but largely effortless job. She sat in a far corner with her Kindle, every now and again scowling down at it whenever a hip-hop song began to chafe against the speakers.

And then the vomiting started. Mrs. Cline had been lost in *The Devil in the White City* when she heard the shriek of some nameless First Year girl. There in the horror of the thrashing strobe lights were the tortured figures of what looked like two dozen Second and Third Year boys: not so much drunk as anesthetized, dark strings of purple onto the shoes and ankles by their feet. In the hours thereafter, eleven were taken to St. Francis Hospital in Trenton to have their stomachs pumped; ten others spent the night in the campus infirmary. The school would learn that three Third Year boys attempted to make moonshine in a discarded Gatorade water cooler in the basement of Brennan House. Bryan Harris, the project leader, was expelled, and Theresa Daniels, the Dean of Students, decreed that all dances were canceled until further notice.

It was only several weeks into the following academic year that the new Student Council's Vice-President of Social Life, a Fourth Year squash player named Nate Fitzsimmons, managed to persuade Mrs. Daniels that (i) "Hoochgate," as Dr. Tierney had taken to calling it, had been a Murphy's Law sort of exception to a norm that (ii) going forward would be jealously guarded. "It's not gonna be a free-for-all," he told her in her office a week and a half before the dance hosted by Kellogg House. Nate Fitzsimmons is currently in his second year at Northwestern Law, but that Theresa Daniels finally acquiesced speaks less to his rhetorical talents than to her own understanding that certain concessions must sometimes be made in the service of her own political viability.

Kellogg House's social chair that year was a Third Year named Will Bartholomew, a mousy, acne-pocked kid from St. Louis who had fallen in with the House's baseball and football players by virtue of his populist wit and his own origins as a geographic outlier. By the fall of 2008, Bartholomew's iTunes library was seven thousand songs deep, of which he was proud and intensely territorial. He spent no fewer than four hours constructing the playlist for the dance, a surreal blend of early-'90s Europop, the sort of mass-market Motown you hear at Bar Mitzvah receptions, and a sufficient concentration of that autumn's pop hits. "The Good Life" by Kanye West and T-Pain; "Low" by Flo Rida. "With You" by Chris Brown did not make the cut: there was no prommish slow-dancing at Kennedy dances; indeed, there was no desire for it.

Sex at boarding school is primarily an assemblage of its euphemisms. The responsible constraints are chiefly logistical: there are no drunken house parties on campus where inhibitions curl away; no upstairs guest bedrooms with locked doors. Many of even the most socially adroit Kennedians do not lose their virginities until college. What they do is *hook up*, fervently and with an ancient political ritualism that distinguishes it from the general carnal explorations of adolescence. Sex sometimes seems beside the point. There's a quaintness to the time-tested formula of its pairings. Roommates play ambassadorial roles, relaying declarations of interest and facilitating a dinner at Vito's the night before a Saturday night dance—less a group date than an exploratory committee. Beneath the spin of lights the following evening, the boy himself will leave the orbit of his male comrades' cluster and shift toward hers; the other girls will grin slyly as he finds her. And then they move together and begin to dance—if we can call grinding dancing—and at a certain point, five songs in maybe, the boy wordlessly takes the girl's hand and leads her out into the night.

Foster Dade's first glimpse of these rites came on the evening of the first dance, just after dinner, when he ran into Harris Adelstein in Brennan's first-floor bathroom. Harris's hair was wet, a blue towel wrapped incautiously around his waist. There were still suds of body wash in the dark hairs that rose from beneath the towel up to his belly button. "You gonna get lucky tonight, Foster Dade?" he asked, inspecting a pimple in the mirror over the sink.

Foster blushed, feeling his clumsiness in the banter of male adolescence. "Ah—prolly not," he managed.

"Who've you got your eye on?"

Foster blushed. "I dunno, there are a few cute girls—Annabeth Whittaker, maybe?" he said finally.

At that moment, the door swung open and in came Andrew O'Donnell, also toweled. "Andrew, our friend Foster Dade here has his eyes on one Annabeth Whittaker," Harris said. His tone was not unkind, but Foster blushed again.

Andrew grinned. "Whoo-ee," he said. "You've got your work cut out for you, bud. Godspeed."

Jack Albright was sitting on the wall of the porch, watching dusk fall on the empty Meadow. He wore a pair of pink chino shorts and a mesh pinnie that said MORRISTOWN LAX, with a low neck that betrayed his few sparse chest hairs. "Shall we?"

They set out through the evening's chill. Already in the late afternoons they could smell the burning of leaves from nearby farms. Foster had worn a Ralph Lauren blue-and-white striped rugby shirt with an old pair of jeans; he suddenly felt overdressed.

The double bedroom shared that year by Mason Pretlow and Pritchett Pierce was in one of Ames House's far catacombs, with two windows that looked out over Eastminster Road. Foster and Jack were the last to arrive. In addition to the boys in Ames—Pritchett and Mason, Will Thierry, Freddie Pieters, and Mark Stetson—were Annabeth Whittaker and her friends, there with the conditional blessing of the Duty Master downstairs: "Door halfway open," Mr. Byrd had said.

"Oh, hello!" Annabeth said grandly as they entered. Foster stuck up a hand in a self-conscious wave. "So glad you're joining us!" She turned to Jack. "Mister Albright," she said with jesting solemnity. She wore jean shorts and a loose white cotton T-shirt through which the contours of her bra were visible.

"Hey, man, what's good," Pritchett Pierce said to Foster, grinning and extending a hand. Foster liked Pritchett, with whom he had

Advanced European History; he was comfortable enough in his own self to liaise with those outside the silent strictures of social politics. He was, Foster had gathered, from one of those old Protestant Manhattan families that were by then an endangered species; his wealth and stature were most palpable in his apparent ignorance to it.

"Welcome to the dungeon," said the handsome and soft-spoken Will Thierry. ("He's our babysitter," Sofi Cohen had said that first night on the porch.) He sat on one of the two twin beds along the walls between the windows, beneath a poster for that summer's *Step Brothers* and another for the NANTUCKET JULY REGATTA, 1968. A pair of dirty boxer shorts had been kicked haphazardly beneath the opposite bed, where Mason Pretlow sat. His cordial nod to Foster seemed bored. The window behind the bed was cracked, and a chill broke against the room's bodily warmth.

"Hey, gimme," Jack said to Sofi, grabbing the plastic water bottle from her hand and taking a theatrical swill. The bottle crinkled as he did.

"You drink, Foster?" Sofi asked him. Her eyes were heavy with mascara.

"I don't *not* drink," Foster shrugged, knowing this was the only answer. "Didn't realize kids did it on campus, though."

The rest of the room laughed. "Oh, honey," Mark Stetson, the lithe Black boy, said, lounging on the bed and flopping his head in Will Thierry's lap. "There is so much to teach you."

Annabeth handed Foster her bottle. "Don't be bashful," she said, smiling at him, her eyes crinkling. "Go crazy."

Foster paused for a moment, then, feeling eyes on him expectantly, took a hefty swig. It was vodka, and not good vodka; Smirnoff at best. He fought back his cough and wiped his mouth, letting himself smile with the vodka's warmth. "Been a minute."

"Where'd you get the booze?" Pritchett asked Annabeth, his brow skeptical.

"Oh, J.T. picked it up for me in Princeton," Annabeth said airily. J.T., Foster would later learn, was J.T.—John Thomas—Ricciardelli, a Fourth Year day student from the solidly middle-class Ewing Township, just north of Trenton. J.T., who in 2005 had won both Most Popular

and Best All-Around in Gilmore J. Fisher Middle School's eighth grade
yearbook, had been happily oblivious to his own socioeconomic circumstances until he arrived at Kennedy that fall. He had been recruited
for football, and because of his athletic talent and looks, he'd found
himself absorbed into the Class of 2009's male patriciate. His new
social status belied the fact that he was rather sensitive, inarticulate,
and deeply insecure: about his height (five foot eight) and how his
blonder, leaner friends at Kennedy spoke a language whose cadences
he came to appreciate but whose exact meaning he could never quite
grasp—of debutante balls and ferries to the Vineyard. J.T.'s mother
would never fully understand precisely *why* her youngest son needed
the salmon-colored pants and Sperry Top-Siders from the premium
outlet mall in Jackson—his old jeans and sneakers still fit just fine—or
why he had seemed to fight against tears of humiliated anger when
she'd idly commented on how expensive they were; back at school the
following Monday, no one had the nerve to tell him he looked vaguely
silly in both. Of all the beautiful girls at Kennedy, only Annabeth
Whittaker two years below him seemed oblivious to the background
these desperate efforts betrayed, which is perhaps why he persuaded
his older brother to buy her liquor in exchange for a peck on the cheek.

Foster's mind was beginning to swoon with the vodka's confidence
when he delivered a modest impersonation of Tierney that elicited
especially loud laughs from Pritchett, Sofi, and Frances. *Sometimes
it feels like they* do *like me*, he would write on his Blogspot. "Foster
is the literal star of our English class," Annabeth was saying. "Tierney's absolutely obsessed." Foster's soul beamed, and then he felt his
BlackBerry buzzing in his pocket. He pulled it out; the number was
unfamiliar but began with 609, the local area code.

"Hello?" he said, stepping out into the hallway. Through the closed
door he heard Kanye West's *Graduation* from the tinny speakers of
Mason's MacBook.

"Foster? It's Mr. McCall. Uh, listen, it's eight thirty-five, and first
check-in was at eight. I'm happy to give you the benefit of the doubt
this time, but if you're on campus, it would please me to see you with
my own eyes in the next ten minutes."

"Shit," Foster said out loud. He stepped back into Pritchett and Mason's room with a sheepish, half-buzzed grin. "I fucking forgot to check in," he said.

"Make haste, sire!" Annabeth cried. He noticed Mason Pretlow and Gracie Smith making eye contact; as he turned to go, he thought he heard one of them snigger.

He had sprinted across the Meadow under the blue night while unwrapping a piece of peppermint Orbit from the pack in his jeans pocket. The Brennan common room was empty when he swung open the door and stumbled in, but in the adjacent parlor, Mr. McCall was reading a copy of *The Week*.

"I'm choosing to assume this was a onetime mistake," McCall smiled, reaching for his clipboard to mark Foster's presence. "But next time, it'll unfortunately have to be a detention."

Foster breathed his apologies and turned to head back outside.

"Oh, and Foster?" McCall said, peering up at him over his magazine. "I should ask—how are you doing? Everything's going okay?" There was something genuine in his expression, and Foster felt the strange impulse to cry.

"I'm great, Mr. McCall," he said, swallowing. "Learning curve and all that, but really—things are great."

Ames House was strangely silent when he returned. A blond boy sat in an armchair in the common room, his right leg in a cast propped up on a coffee table. "Hey," Foster said. "You seen Mason and Pritchett and those guys—they still upstairs?"

"They left like five minutes ago," the boy said, not taking his eyes away from *SportsCenter* on the flat screen before him.

To be unhappy on the periphery of something is to see it with a suddenly grotesque clarity. So it was that night. Foster had a momentary inclination to simply go back to Brennan and allow himself the cry that had been lodged in his chest, and then he forced himself to believe there'd been a misunderstanding. So he made his way alone through the darkness, past the Head Master's house and the Fourth Year girls' dorms and into the airy atrium of the music building.

"Hot N Cold" by Katy Perry was playing. The percussive bass of the subwoofer inside the concert hall was beating itself against the high windows. The heat of the bodies inside had spilled out from the hall; Foster thought idly of a greenhouse.

They were congregated toward the dance floor's center, a tight copse of life within and oblivious to the wider twisting field of bodies. *It hadn't been a mistake*, he heard in his head. He winced at the potential humiliation of making his way to them in the middle of the dance, bobbing on their periphery like an earnest child, pretending not to notice as they shut him out. He instead gravitated to the shadows beneath the far wall where a couple making out next to him did not note his presence. This was where he'd remain.

Foster's buzz had worn off. His eyes were fixated on Annabeth's head bobbing deep in the thicket of the dance floor. Sofi Cohen and Frances Evans were sidling playfully up to two similarly thick-chested boys. Gracie Smith was already dancing intimately with a boy named Walls Watson, who had been in Brennan and was friends with Ollie Richardson. They looked very close to making out. Porter Roth, Foster noticed, looked somewhat uncomfortable; she kept straining her neck, as if she was looking for someone. And then he realized that Mason Pretlow, in a cluster with the Ames boys maybe ten feet away, was watching her too, and moments thereafter he veered insidiously toward her and put his hands around her waist. Annabeth was both present and not; she knew the word to every song, and she at once provided the center of gravity while simultaneously somehow seeming detached from it, above it all. The light danced in the concert hall's tall windows, which were clouded with the fog of bodies. Will Bartholomew's playlist had moved to "Good Life" by Kanye West and T-Pain, and those boys who did not have their hands on a blue-jeaned waist gathered in ad hoc thrusting huddles and bellowed along. Their yells seemed to reserve a particularly happy vehemence for lyrics containing the n-word.

The cool air of the night greeted Foster kindly when he exited the music building not long thereafter, his feet carrying him listlessly back toward Brennan House. Under the lampposts over the campus driveways he could make out the silhouettes of students moving through the evening: some returning to their dorms; others, hand in hand, creeping to the athletic fields. (Postmortems would be conducted over brunch in the Dining Center the following morning—a sad sophomore girl would have given head to a Fourth Year baseball player, and at least one Second Year boy—someone like Mason Pretlow or Freddie Pieters—would have successfully persuaded some pretty First Year to administer her first handjob. Jack Albright, Foster would learn from the Third Years, had convinced one Jacqueline Franck of Greenwich, Connecticut, to leave the dance with him, to unconfirmed ends.)

He shut the door of his and Jae's antechamber and was already unbuttoning his jeans when his nostrils flared. He smelled pot.

It had been just north of eight weeks since Foster had been high. Amid the bleakness of everything else, he'd been proud of this, circumstantial as it was. He knocked hesitantly on Jae's door.

"Yo, Jae, it's just me," Foster said softly against Jae's panicked clamor.

There was a pause, and then the door cracked open. Jae was wearing a pair of skinny gray sweatpants and a matching hoodie, and his eyes were glassy, almost cartoonishly red.

Foster grinned. "I didn't realize you blazed, man."

Jae looked confused. Behind him on the windowsill Foster could see a little silver pipe. "Blaze?"

Foster grinned wider. "Smoked weed, dude."

Jae smiled. "Oh, yes," he said. "First time in bedroom tonight."

"Well—reckon you'd want to share?"

Jae let Foster into his room, which was identical to his but far sparser. The sheets on the bed were black. On his school-issued dresser was a magnum of Grey Goose, about two-thirds full. Foster laughed out loud. "Get the fuck out, Jae. I never knew you liked to chill." He jabbed his elbow in the direction of the bottle.

Jae's eyes widened, childlike. "Oh. Yes, brought from, erm, duty-free at airport. McCall never comes in here."

Foster took the bottle and pulled from it, realizing that his moments in Ames earlier had, on a purely physiological level, been quite nice. Jae took his little pewter grinder and dumped fresh weed into the bowl. "Here," he said, handing Foster the bowl and the lighter. Foster took. His rip was long, mostly to chase out the taste of the vodka, and he spluttered.

"Jesus, Jae," he said, laughing again and wiping his mouth. "This—this is some potent shit. Who are you getting this from?"

"New York City," Jae said sagely.

For a short and blissful moment there was a mercy in being high again. He lay back on his bed in the darkness, his earbuds stifling the happy noises of life outside. He'd recently found himself beholden to a new, sadder playlist—Damien Rice and Bright Eyes; Joy Division; once again *The Joshua Tree*—and he let the music envelop him. He thought idly of the Fruit Gushers in the Tupperware bin beneath his bed and blinked his dry eyes at the ceiling.

Foster was among the small fraction of people for whom marijuana was a purely psychoactive substance. Instead of tugging him toward sleep, it pulled his mind into coasting, recursive feedback loops, and on the best days it allowed him to grin at the rhythmic poetry of his own life. He'd spent the summer's evenings on Wikipedia, careening from topic to topic: pro-democracy activism in Hong Kong; apocalyptic terrorist cults in southern Japan; the town of Leland, North Carolina (pop. 9,301). He let it push his cerebral weathervane while absorbing almost none of it.

And other times these loops closed in on themselves. It was a little after midnight when he finally found himself blinking down to his BlackBerry, and without warning the very fact of the time startled him—what had felt like ten minutes of silent stasis had in fact been close to an hour. He pulled the headphones from his ears with a sickened, violent tug. And then he heard the distant raucous voices of Jack Albright and the Third Years somewhere upstairs.

His body was suddenly very hot. With a jerk that frightened him in its spasticity he sat up and shoved his window open, seeking in the cool air outside a respite that did not come. The tinny sound of U2 crackled from the earbuds now limp on his chest. There was something unctuous and carnal to the moonlit clouds pushing in over the shadowed rise of the library; they seemed bulbous with a glow that called to mind the color of Mr. McCall's thinning russet hair. This realization strangely sickened him, and suddenly he tasted the warm vodka of four hours earlier. He reached for the wastebasket under his desk to prepare himself for vomiting, and as he did, he heard a shrill distant laugh that sounded frighteningly like Annabeth Whittaker's. *You fucking loser; they're laughing at you.* He felt his throat seize.

When he was ten years old a neighbor's father had died of a sudden heart attack while driving up Charles Street. Foster's brain began to loop the audio of Charlotte Dade reciting to Jim the symptoms of cardiac arrest: *tightness of chest, shortness of breath, numbness in arm, sense of dislocation.* "I think I might be dying," Foster said out loud, his voice taut with arrested respiration. The greasy warm light of the room began to churn itself around the periphery of his vision. The bed felt gelatinous beneath him. He vaguely thought he might shit himself. "Jae," he said weakly out to nobody, before darkness.

XIV.

October became November. Seemingly overnight, the boughs of Olmsted's three hundred species burgeoned into fits of orange and red, concealing the upper windows of the Meadow Houses in endearing autumnal shadows in the afternoons. The bells of the chapel broke the chilly mornings as students made their way to breakfast in hooded sweatshirts and Bean boots, the freezing earth crunching beneath their feet, their breaths hanging in the air in front of them. After House football practice, boys returned to their common rooms with the flush of exercise in cold weather, the late afternoon sky hanging gray and low over their heads. The distant cornfields seemed to carry secrets.

Though he didn't yet have a name for them, Foster's second panic attack had come nine days after his first. He had been sitting in Anne-Marie Cline's mahogany-walled classroom when he found himself preoccupied by the ambient humming of the lamp overhead. The fluorescent whine seemed to intensify before he realized it was all he could hear. As if separated by a wall of water he heard Mrs. Cline ask him something—*what did she say?*—about the Industrial Revolution in Flanders. His brain felt diffused. "Um, I reckon I'll need to pass on this one," he thought he said. In his head his voice sounded like a bleat. Across the oval table Pritchett Pierce looked at him strangely. Foster found himself convinced that his father had died.

He'd made it to the restroom just as his throat seemed to close up. His panic over this compounded itself. *This is where I'm going to die fuck please I can't die I'm so young I thought there'd be lifeaheadofme—*

"I just feel feverish," he told the attending nurse in the infirmary's foyer. He had left his books on Mrs. Cline's seminar table. His claustrophobia had loosened, leaving him simply depleted. The nurse looked at him skeptically through large pink eyeglasses but showed him to a bed in the day ward.

Foster would remember his first term at Kennedy in the confines of these isolated events—schizophrenically discordant moments strung together by a single silk of profound loneliness. In the days that followed these episodes, the psychological nausea that had precipitated them receded, but in its absence his mind felt barren, like a cold beach after a storm. In this space a hollow fugue began to assemble itself from the misery of his first weeks. Getting out of bed to shower suddenly seemed a herculean task. Those in his classes during these months recall a boy who was regularly tardy and almost always silent; those who passed him on campus passively registered a boy who looked very sad.

The first Tuesday of that month was Election Day. Obama would win the mock election conducted by the Student Council in the Dining Center foyer that week, but with a turnout of 33 percent, the data was inconclusive. *An observation: no one here—no one cool at least—cares about politics*, Foster had written on his Blogspot that week. *Caring is uncool, apparently.*

In his early adolescence, Foster had passively absorbed his mother's anti-Bush fervor, but in the spring of 2007 she'd stuck a Clinton sticker on the Lexus. His attachment to the Illinois Senator was his own. As the primaries approached, he spent idle hours before YouTube, transfixed by the 2004 convention speech and the many electric town halls. He'd found out about volunteering while scrolling through Facebook, and six weeks before the Maryland primary, Foster had biked through the cold to a student center on the far edge of the Johns Hopkins campus, where the local Democratic Party had set up a canvassing office. With a sheepishness that soon acquiesced to its more primal excitement, he spent a dozen weeknight evenings going door-to-door in the cold with Hopkins professors and stay-at-home mothers three times his age, who told them they loved his gumption.

And so on Election Night that November he had carried himself to the Kennedy Field House, where the Student Council had arranged a viewing party. He did this despite the labor of doing so. He had brought this effusive electricity to Kennedy only to feel it wither into a shameful husk in his self-conscious solitude. In mid-September, he'd spent a humiliated evening on his own Facebook page, deleting every enthralled post from the prior year about hope and change. If going to watch the election was an appeal to something bygone, it was enervated and perfunctory, made possible only by the bitter nihilism that had germinated in its place. *Why the fuck not. Who the fuck cares.*

The Student Council had hauled an enormous projection screen to the head of the Field House track, flanked by clustered hemorrhoids of red, white, and blue balloons. It was a massive structure, the Field House, built in the heyday of the Cold War's professionalization of youth athletics. The ceiling, thirty feet overhead, was a gable of old opaque glass, like the hull of some great glassine ark, capsized into a Stygian sea of cloudy light. Stepping in from the night to the arena's edge, Foster contemplated the mass of people beneath its rise and realized with violent relief that Jack and Mason were not there. The crowd was compact but earnest, its faces foreign. They cheered as the looming figure of Wolf Blitzer onscreen called New Mexico and Iowa for Obama; they groaned when McCain won Mississippi.

Suddenly he felt a tap on his shoulder. He turned around to face a grinning Annabeth Whittaker. Her hair was in a loose ponytail; Obama stared nobly out from the button fastened against the rise of her chest.

"Hi, stranger!" she said cheerily, then pointed up at the screen. "Isn't this so—unbelievable?" Her eyes were bright.

Foster did his best to summon a cavalier grin. "History in the making and all that."

"Like, I hate to admit it, because I sound like a fawning fangirl, but I'm obsessed with him." Her eyes met Foster's, and he thought he saw her blush. "I—actually did some volunteer work for Obama over the summer. Dad was pissed. Not that it was worth anything—'cause North Jersey's been as Republican as you get for, like, forty years—but still, it's nice to be able to say that I helped."

"I did too." Foster flushed, then let himself smile. "I—don't admit that much here. I'm kind of convinced everyone is a Republican."

"My idiot friends claim to be," Annabeth said. "Not Jack—though he won't admit it to Mason and Pritchett. Technically we're not anything until we can vote. But yeah, no takers for this tonight. I dragged Gracie but—oh, speak of the devil."

As if on cue, Gracie Smith's brunette head appeared in the crowd, approaching them. Her face held its normal mélange of boredom and contempt. "I'm getting out of here," she told Annabeth. "Come?" She did not acknowledge Foster.

Annabeth was fixated on the screen; South Dakota had just been called for McCain. "Nah, I'd rather witness history," she said, squinting at the images and smiling. There was a candent light to the sound of Foster's words in her voice. "What's more important?"

"Jack says they're all up on the Brennan porch, so maybe there, or maybe to meet Walls if he texts me."

"Suit yourself," Annabeth said.

Gracie shrugged and disappeared. Annabeth grinned magically at Foster, and they turned back to CNN.

The Associated Press called the election for Barack Obama shortly after eleven o'clock, as the Field House crowd dispersed into the night ahead of check-in. Foster and Annabeth were walking up toward the Ellipse when they heard the spare cheers from the nearby common rooms' warm light. Annabeth's mouth fell open. With a violent whoop she threw her arms around Foster's neck. "Obama!" she shrieked happily into the cold night. She was wearing a green Patagonia fleece that was maybe two sizes too big; it fell to her knees and her hands were inside its sleeves.

"Yeah—pretty . . . unreal," Foster said, looking up at the crystalline stars of the cold November night. For the first time in several months, he let himself feel the thrall of things.

"Ugh, I wish my friends had come," Annabeth said. The Ellipse Houses glowed like distant trawlers. "They can be such . . . downers. Too cool, I guess."

Foster stepped to avoid a long tectonic crack in the driveway's pavement.

"What's Jack's deal?" he asked finally, and then burned with regret.

Annabeth frowned. "Jack?" she said. "I think I might know what you mean, but I'll ask you to elaborate."

"It's just that—he can be a nice guy, but it's like—so inconsistent, and I think your friends hate me, and—I just can't tell if he wants to be my friend," Foster finished lamely.

Annabeth looked up at the night. "That's just Jack," she said evenly. "Listen, the dude is great, but he very well may be nuts. He answers to himself and no one else, and sometimes, yeah, it's like he's not really there. His friends call him the Lone Ranger—and fuck Mason Pretlow, by the way," Annabeth said. Foster had not mentioned Mason by name. "He's an unhappy person. And sometimes I think maybe Jack is too."

Foster pondered this. "Don't tell him I asked," he said finally. "I don't wanna seem, y'know—desperate."

Annabeth smiled at him. The lightfall from the streetlamps overhead seemed to catch itself against her face in the darkness.

"Of course," she said. "Listen—I'm so glad we got to hang out. Don't be a stranger. Seriously! None of us bite."

She hugged him without waiting for his response, then pirouetted with a smile and disappeared into the orange glow of the house. Foster continued on home, half-contented and confused.

Annabeth Whittaker had been right about something—Tierney did seem to like him. *I've always been good at intellectualizing my problems, or at least channeling my problems into intellectualism—a defense mechanism, I guess*, he'd written on his Blogspot on an afternoon in ninth grade. It was on a Thursday in mid-November when Foster's passivity finally collapsed at last.

"It's incredibly violent in its treatment of women," Rosalie Haddish, a day student from Princeton with a round, combative face, said of *The Great Gatsby* in Tierney's class one morning the week following the election. "Look at everything Gatsby does—all of it is to reduce Daisy to a sex object. Not just the characters—Fitzgerald himself too."

Foster heard himself groan. The class was silent. "It would appear that Mr. Dade has a counterpoint," Tierney said evenly from the head of the table, his spindly fingers clasped together.

Foster felt twelve sets of eyes on him.

"I actually think the precise opposite is true. Look at Gatsby's attachment to Daisy—it is quite literally everything *but* sexual. In fact it's maybe explicitly *de*sexualized. Tom, sure—a misogynist and a creep; no argument there. But—Fitzgerald? How? Where?"

Rosalie looked affronted. "Have you seen how the novel portrays women? They're all idiots. That's not sexist to you?"

Foster laughed hollowly. "*Everyone* is an idiot. Nick pretty much says that outright. That's—" and he felt himself pick up his paperback and thrash it against the table, his voice fevering "—that's the point! Listen, I'm sorry, this is embarrassing." He felt Annabeth's wide eyes dilate on him.

"Excuse me, Doctor Tierney," Rosalie said, sliding her books into her satchel. "I do not deserve this." The door slammed behind her. The class seemed to struggle to comprehend what had just transpired. At one end of the table Freddie Pieters snickered. Finally Foster forced himself to look at Tierney.

"This," Tierney said, his face a carnival, "is *damn* good. Not that, of course"—he raised his battered copy of *Gatsby* and flapped it in the direction of the door, then looked to Freddie—"and Pieters, go see if you can find Miss Haddish—but the spirit of things. Dade!" He turned his bright eyes to Foster, who wasn't sure if he had breathed. "He *speaks*!"

XV.

What distinguished Foster Dade's third panic attack that term was his resignation to it. He and Jae had smoked together several nights a week since that first dance. It was a happy exercise in the lesson of forgotten afternoons in Max Frieholdt's rec room in Baltimore: that it is perilously easy to be friends with someone when you're both stoned. The jokes are funnier, the music prettier, but more critically there is an impermeable wax wall around those cortices of the brain that manufacture certain interpersonal affects, and in another high person, the crude signals of these curtailed circuitries—what might strike someone sober as disinterest or vapidity—find a compatible pair. So it was with Foster and Jae, a boy whose English was still competent at best. Together they blinked at the new clarity of the strange world they had joined together, and let themselves laugh.

The Saturday night before Thanksgiving break was the night of Kennedy's Homecoming Dance. Annabeth Whittaker was going with Pritchett Pierce. This was a platonic arrangement, designed to allow Pritchett to avoid inviting Sally Pinelli, a large-chested First Year he'd spent the fall aloofly hooking up with. (Jack Albright was taking his own freshman, Jacqueline Franck, the implications of which he dismissed with a literal wave of his arm. "Why the fuck not," he said on the Brennan porch after check-in the night he asked her.) Foster had inferred all of this from his silent place on the periphery of things, taking grim comfort in the knowledge that Annabeth wouldn't be ushered out to the golf course by some lecherous Fourth Year lacrosse player.

He was to spend the evening alone in his room in Brennan. Jae would be serving detention in Memorial Hall's upstairs lecture hall, and before he had set out into the darkness with his little leather knapsack, they had hit the bowl together. Strange Korean pop was playing from Jae's MacBook. Jae paused at one point and gestured to his window. Lorin Parsons, a stout English teacher and one of two lesbians on the faculty, was walking back from the Dining Center in a large brown jacket. Something about this sent Jae into gales of giddy laughter, and so Foster cracked up too.

He spent several hours after Jae's departure on his bed, staring at but not watching episodes of *The Office*. Other than Ms. Chissom, who was spending her evening on duty knitting a thick hat in the common room, Brennan House was empty. On his desk was the academic memo he'd received from Señora Willis after failing to submit the week's listening comprehension exercise. "I wish I could say this is an isolated incident, but the truth is that Foster's performance this semester suggests an entrenched attitude of indifference towards this class," Sra. Willis had written.

As the thickness of the weed congealed, a conspiracy began to gel in his mind, rolling certain phrases over in his mind like fat stones. *I have no friends. I have no friends and I cannot talk to my family and I think maybe there is something innate to me that makes this the case. I am an allergen; I am hideous; I am acutely defective.* He let the incontrovertibility of this realization fall over him like a blanket of iron mail. The evening slid away from beneath the fetid lights of his bedroom. He accepted that he might be losing his mind: in eight out of ten panic attacks, this is the precipitating thought. He reached out to the plaster wall to confirm its palpability, as if aboard a sinking ferry, his chest cage-like. Eventually the world returned somewhat to focus. An emptiness replaced the tumult. His window was open, and a cold wind flapped against the drawn shade. He put his face into his pillow and wept.

Winter was threatening itself in those final days before break: girls' wet hair began to freeze on the way to breakfast, and boys zipped their North Face fleeces up to their chins, their breaths billowing before them as they crossed the frost-hardened Meadow. Foster had returned to Baltimore on an early-evening Amtrak beneath an indigo sky. He'd watched the yellow lights of the mid-Atlantic spill past the Northeast Regional's cold windows, thinking of Sofi Cohen's apartment on the Upper East Side, where at that moment Annabeth and Jack and Mason and Gracie were stumbling into the living room, buzzed on Miller Lite and the giddiness of a holiday, blasting Lil Wayne from the Cohens' Bose speakers.

The familiarity of the Baltimore night was vaguely anesthetic as Charlotte's Lexus joined the hush of yellow headlights pouring up Charles Street. "My baby," she'd murmured into his neck as she embraced him, sniffing back a tear.

Overland Road was quiet and black, and in the Dades' home only the downstairs living room light was on. Maggie had extended her stay in Genoa through the autumn term. "Hey, Mom," he said, still unable to meet her eyes. "I'm actually feeling kind of crappy—there was something going around school. I'm gonna shower and chill for a bit, then let's maybe have dinner?"

Charlotte looked briefly crestfallen. "Of course, bug," she said.

His bedroom was as he'd left it. Atop his pillow was a handwritten note left by his mother that read WELCOME HOME, FOSTER! He swallowed the lump of tears growing in his throat. In his dresser, beneath discarded underwear from a bygone age—J.Crew boxers a size too small, a faded pair of white Hanes briefs—was the blue-and-white glass bowl, still half-packed. There was a lighter atop the dresser. With an earnestness that surprised him, he held it to his lips, flicked the lighter, and inhaled.

"I think—I think I might want to see Dr. Apple again," Foster told his mother over dinner. Her face tensed with what looked like worry, but to his relief she did not probe further. The night outside their windows was cold and dark with the clarity of early winter.

"Of course," she said finally. "I'll give him a call first thing."

Dr. Willem G. Apple had established his private practice in Baltimore in the early 1990s, his office off of Northern Parkway sparse of windows, which looked out to a forested ridge and availed little light. Its odd sadness seemed to suit him. He was in his early sixties when Foster Dade arrived as his patient, though for at least a decade he'd sought to veil this by dyeing his thick helmet of hair a shade of burnt apricot. It vaguely resembled a stage wig. He wore heavy turtleneck sweaters and thick, bulbous eyeglasses that occupied much of his face and seemed to date to at least the late Carter years. His office's beige walls held his diplomas—B.A. from Tufts, Psy.D. and M.D. from Hopkins—and an unsettling watercolor of a court jester.

In 1999 he'd brought on a partner, a daffy woman in her early fifties, to handle the side of the juvenile practice that was more behavioral than cognitive: toy-guided therapy for autistics; preliminary dialogues with victims of molestation; those with behavioral deficiencies that eluded singular diagnosis. Dr. Apple dealt with the real work: depressive teens with expressed ideation; middle-aged businessmen who privately fantasized about driving their Acura into a concrete barrier beneath the Jones Falls Expressway; lethally bulimic girls from Hopkins or Towson whose cases were above student health's paygrade but didn't yet warrant hospitalization. But the overwhelming share of his patients were women between the ages of forty and fifty-five. They appeared in his office in their Nike tennis skirts after dropping their children at Gilman or Bryn Mawr, claiming they felt so helpless and constantly frightened that they were physically ill, and that they'd heard good things about Xanax.

Whether Dr. Apple was good at his job seems like a rather meaningless question, given what unfolded. Statistically, he retained patients, and just as we don't expect cardiac surgeons to, say, light candles to the intricacies of the heart, our psychologists don't necessarily need to possess the traits we generally associate with empathy or emotional intelligence. It's all machinery; why be sentimental in dealing with it.

The cruder truth is that he gave those tennis moms their Xanax. It wasn't quite malpractice, per se: his Hippocratic philosophy was simply to err on the side of prescribing, with minimal preliminary or diagnostic inquiry. Call it a matter of expedience, which is what it was for the patients. As a psychologist with a medical degree, he was a one-stop shop: his patients could spend the better part of an hour with Dr. Apple and leave his office with a thin square of periwinkle-blue paper. For those with ADD and ADHD, amphetamine derivatives (Adderall, Vyvanse); for the depressed and anxious, SSRIs (Lexapro, Celexa, Prozac, et al.), often with a side course of a benzodiazepine or related sedative (Xanax, Ativan, Valium, Klonopin), the latter nominally to be taken before bed. CVS would fill it within an hour, usually.

Charlotte Dade had made her first appointment with Dr. Apple in May 2007. "It's easy—he'll give you anything," Harriet Farmer, whose husband was conducting a very conspicuous affair with a tennis coach at the club, had told her one evening after book club, Charlotte's first public endeavor since the events of the prior fall. They were reading *A Million Little Pieces*.

She described Dr. Apple as her therapist, and perhaps it was in the service of this euphemistic self-deception that three months later, in the wake of her divorce, she contacted him for an appointment for her fourteen-year-old son, so that he could "talk to a sympathetic

third party about everything that's been going on." The few fragments of Foster's medical records I was able to obtain indicate that he
attended four sessions between September 2007 and January 2008.
"I don't want him taking anything," Charlotte had told Dr. Apple
gently but firmly. "Just therapy." Those initial sessions would be
remembered as therapeutically unproductive at best. *He kept asking
about the most intimate details of the divorce, and specifically the shit
Dad did*, Foster had written on his Blogspot in the winter of ninth
grade. *As in: "Did you know any of these individuals personally"
and "Did you ever witness their interactions." The worst was that
he kept referring to Dad as precisely that, as in: "Did Dad ever try
to engage with you sexually."*

The doctor was as Foster remembered him, though today there was
inexplicably a small bandage just below his right eye. He peered at
Foster curiously through his thick glasses.

"Your mother says you have some things on your mind," Dr.
Apple had said.

And there in the unnervingly dark office Foster found himself
speaking with the openness he had denied himself for three months.
"I'm not so much sad as scared and hopeless, like I've—I dunno—been
taken from a decently lit road and dumped in some forest." Dr. Apple
scribbled something down on his legal pad. "And it's come to a head
lately—I've been panicking and thinking I've been going crazy, and I
guess basically I want you to tell me that isn't the case."

Dr. Apple seemed to consider this. "It seems evident to me that
you have clinical anxiety," he said, then paused to blow his nose in a
handkerchief from his pocket. The noise was goose-like. "Delusions
of insanity are common in anxiety attacks. And depression and anxiety are often coterminal. To me, you are suffering from both." There
was a pause as Foster contemplated these words. In their damnation
they liberated him.

"And you mentioned something about obsessions," Dr. Apple
continued. "Care to say more?"

"Yeah," he said after a pause. "I guess I've been having what you'd
call"—here he found himself blushing—"invasive thoughts." He had

spent several evenings quietly scrolling through psychology discussion forums, scribbling an improvised glossary on a Post-it.

Dr. Apple's poker face shifted slightly in its rictus. "Can I ask you to elaborate."

Foster's face reddened further. "Yeah, they're, erm—kind of sexual."

"Violently sexual?" Dr. Apple asked.

"Not really, uh—just, like, sexual scenarios showing up in my head when I don't want them to; nothing crazy," Foster muttered ineloquently, staring hard at his Adidas.

"Hm," Dr. Apple said. "I see."

These thoughts had amounted to the most acute instruments of torture. They occurred to him while masturbating, specifically in the moments immediately preceding orgasm, when the frenzied brain latches on to those mental images most likely to push one over the edge. They were violent hijackings, grotesque and guilt-inducing. One night several weeks prior, jerking off beneath the dark quiet of his comforter after lights out, his mind pivoted swiftly and without warning to the imagined nude bodies of Delia Chissom and Anne-Marie Cline. In horror, Foster attempted to tack his psychic sailboat about, but it was too late: he felt a sphincteric clench and then he came, his face seizing then slackening with sensation and disgust. The following morning in Cline's class, he found himself burning with shame and unable to bring his eyes to meet her face. The less arbitrary intrusions were no less menacing. On more than one occasion, he had been nearing climax when he found himself thinking with startling vividness of Jack Albright. At times in these visions Foster witnessed his own humiliation: Jack stripping him before some faceless crowd and pushing him to his knees; Jack sodomizing him as Gracie Smith and Mason Pretlow watched and jeered.

"Usually just, like . . . having sex with people I don't want to have sex with," Foster said to Dr. Apple finally. An evasive explanation, but not dishonest.

"I think we should have a conversation about medication," Dr. Apple said, mercifully. "What you are describing to me sounds quite a lot like what we call major depressive disorder and both generalized anxiety disorder and panic disorder. The lack of motivation and optimism is the depression, and so are the obsessive thoughts. The social worry is the anxiety; the panic attacks are, well, the panic. Are you familiar with SSRIs?"

"Just a little bit from the internet—they keep serotonin from getting sucked back into the brain, right?"

"More or less," Dr. Apple said. "And serotonin is one of the happiness neurotransmitters. Now, there are some excellent drugs in this category that have good results with both depression and anxiety." He pursed his lips. "I am going to suggest you begin a course of Lexapro, or escitalopram, which isn't as sluggish as some of the others. Let's start with ten milligrams every morning."

He pursed his lips again. "I should say that these take some time to start working. Three or four weeks, usually. And there can be some unpleasant side effects before they kick in."

"Like what?" Foster asked.

"Well," Dr. Apple said, pursing his lips. "Nausea, maybe vomiting, perhaps diarrhea. Something that people describe as 'brain fog'—they compare it to sleepwalking. And your anxiety might also spike before it settles down," he added as an afterthought.

Foster squinted. "So, like—basically I'm to suffer for a month before I know if these things even work," he said.

"We tend to see good results," Dr. Apple said. "But in the event that the anxiety spike isn't bearable, I'm going to give you eight tablets of Xanax—just a small dose, half a milligram. Save these for when you feel a panic attack coming on. It should help."

There was a bluster to the afternoon that intimated an early snow flurry as Foster threw his bike against the side of the garage. The house was empty and still as he climbed the stairs, tearing apart the CVS bag's white paper husk as he went. With his door closed, he sat at his desk and held the two pill bottles out against the desk lamp's glow, like a jeweler with a curious stone.

Though GlaxoSmithKline's sales reps had started pushing sexier and more pharmacodynamically complex drugs in recent years, most American psychiatrists still agreed at this point that SSRIs—then entering their second decade on the United States and Canadian pharmaceutical markets—remained the most effective treatment in most cases of major and atypical depressive disorder. The supplementary consensus was that escitalopram (Lexapro) was one of the better ones. "Cleaner," in the patois of pharmacology. Unlike fluoxetine (Prozac) and paroxetine (Paxil), the first-gen SSRIs whose introduction otherwise brought about the greatest paradigm shift in Western mental health since Nelly Bly infiltrated New England's rat-infested asylums a century prior, Lexapro's efficacy as an anti-anxiety drug did not come with pronounced sluggishness. Though the data is marginal, male patients also reported both a diminished frequency of erectile dysfunction and ejaculatory inhibition on Lexapro. (This was a cruel, even counterproductive irony of the drug's earlier siblings: you'd finally be confident enough to go out and meet girls, only to then realize you were incapable of getting hard and/or orgasming.)

The thirty Lexapro capsules were the eggshell white of a suburban powder room. "Start tomorrow morning," Dr. Apple had told him, but Foster figured why wait. He tapped a pill out onto his palm, and after a contemplative pause swallowed it without water.

"And please, only take the Xanax if it feels absolutely necessary," Dr. Apple had said.

Foster blinked at the second bottle. "They're fucking wild," Max Frieholdt had told him once, after stealing two Ativans from his insomniac mother. "Like you're floating on clouds."

"Let me try one, then," Foster had said. Frieholdt refused. "I wouldn't trust you on these things, Dade."

In the decade that has passed since Foster's expulsion from Kennedy, recreational benzodiazepine abuse has skyrocketed among a certain subset of affluent millennials with a fervor that would fascinate sociologists and gravely frighten everyone else. Its epicenters are the fraternities of schools like UNC and Penn, where Xanax and its anxiolytic neighbors are known simply as bars. To be high on benzos is to be "barred out." Only the most seriously panic-disordered—the adults whose agoraphobia keeps them from leaving home—warrant a prescription for two milligrams of Xanax, the strongest in Pfizer's benzodiazepinal arsenal. It was the crumbled moondust of these oblong Tetris bricks that I would find forgotten in a Ziploc beneath the dresser in my room on the second floor of Brennan House.

But the half-milligram pills that occupied that initial CVS bottle were little footballs of chalky peach, benign-looking as Tylenol. "It's just a small dose," Dr. Apple had said. So that November afternoon, Foster took two. He stood in front of his mirror for a moment, studying the light of his eyes. He had the hokey but not entirely inaccurate thought that he had just commenced a new chapter.

He was draped over the couch in the downstairs den when it hit him. His father's *Economist* still arrived weekly, and he was staring at an indecipherable piece on the housing market. He had vaguely understood that the nation was facing its worst financial crisis in a century. Mellie Jakes, a Third Year girl from New York who captained the swim team, had been heard sobbing in a Memorial Hall bathroom the day after the sinking of Lehman Brothers, where her father had worked for twenty years, but for the rest of Kennedy it was insignificant in its abstraction, an odd and inscrutable flicker beyond the dense prism of their bubble.

"Adjustable-rate mortgage," Foster heard himself say out loud. The house was empty. The text before him was suddenly only a series of geometric rhythms. It was just before five in the evening but through the den's bay windows the last harvest-light of the November afternoon seemed to hold physical heft. The house felt womb-like. He realized he was smiling stupidly. "Well, gee whiz," he said.

This was how Charlotte found him when she returned home forty-five minutes later, holding a Whole Foods bag carrying a rotisserie chicken and an asparagus salad. "I got us some dinner," she sang cheerfully. "How was your visit with Dr. Apple?"

"Really just fabulous, Mama." It was a sort of purr. His motor faculties seemed to be returning, but his smile had only widened. Clouds indeed. He was less alert to the drug's precise physical sensation than to the fact that for the first time in many months, he was at ease. The emotional latitude made him gregarious. He thought about who to text. Jae, maybe.

Or: Annabeth Whittaker. He'd gotten her number in October, for
a study group for their English class that had never come to fruition;
some nights, in bed in Brennan, he would thumb to her contact in
his BlackBerry and marvel at her name alone, at those ten digits led
by North Jersey's 973 area code: as if anything unique to her, even
something as banal as a phone number, was somehow splendid. Yes—
Annabeth Whittaker. They were friends, right?

It took him thirty seconds to unearth his phone from the folds of
the couch. The blue glow of its screen was suddenly nice.

"hi there. Happy early thanksgiving," he thumbed onto the message screen.

And such is the dreamlike state of the Xanax user's early forays—
things flow with an effortlessness never before bequeathed to the
dysfunction of the anxious mind. There's a Buddhism to it: allow
things to move like water and they will. Maybe a minute had
passed before Foster's BlackBerry buzzed on his chest, its little red
beacon blinking.

> oh hello stranger
> what a pleasant surprise!

She didn't text in caps—that was cool! She was so fucking cool!
we might imagine he thought, his stomach twirling like a summer
eddy. *Oh what do I say to that—*

"Come get a plate, sweetheart," Charlotte called from the
kitchen. Foster put the phone on the couch—*rather than fretting
about it, I'll let it be for a second*, his newly unanxious mind
concluded—and moseyed into the next room. He suddenly realized
that his legs wobbled.

Those who've used Xanax recreationally describe a spectatorial
experience. The world simply seems to happen to you, a filmstrip
produced previously and at low production value, and if you've taken
enough it just fades to darkness altogether. So it was that night. The
following morning, when Foster woke up after an eleven-hour sleep,
he realized he could remember virtually nothing after getting up from
the couch. He had a wispy recollection of sitting at the table with his

mother, forking asparagus into his mouth, but he could not say what they discussed or what happened thereafter.

Another thing Xanax users will tell you: sometimes the high imprints a pleasant afterglow onto the following morning, but more often than not your liver has done its metabolic work; your dopamine supply sucked, you're left feeling hollow and somewhat scared. It took Foster a couple of minutes to get his bearings, to realize his phone was absent from his nightstand, and to remember, with a jolt that pierced the haze, that he had texted Annabeth Whittaker. Downstairs, the house was empty again, and quiet. His phone was where he had left it, wedged between two cushions in the couch. To his sublime grace he saw that there'd been no further correspondence. *But—still one text—what if she told Jack and Gracie and*—his face became hot.

And then he was upstairs before the mirror in his bathroom, in which he looked ill. In his hand was the amber bottle of Xanax. Six of the tablets remained. The blissful surrender they'd brought the prior evening frightened him in its completeness. He thought back to the persuasive elegance of their spell, and against the rancid banality of the new day's sobriety it seemed to reveal a wickedness. He uncapped the lid, and with a certain finality turned to pour them into the toilet. Then he paused.

The addictive brain is an addictive brain well before its first contact with the object of addiction. Most recovery coaches with training in cognitive science will tell you this—that addiction is pure biology—and that in the autobiographical postmortems they hear in their work at 12 Step–oriented rehabs, certain details from the addicts' preaddicted lives tend to recur with predictable frequency. A precocious affinity for spicy food is one. An equally precocious ability to rationalize anything is another.

Foster stood with the pill bottle over the toilet. *They're for panic attacks, and I have panic attacks, and the panic attacks are fucking miserable.* After another pause, he slid two of the peach footballs from the bottle with his index finger and tucked them into a pocket of his leather toilet kit by the sink. Then he poured those that remained into the bowl. They slid from the porcelain down into the water of the basin, which made them seem larger, a distorted rupture of color against white, disappearing as the toilet flushed.

XVI.

There is an ethereal magic to the two weeks at Kennedy between the Thanksgiving and Christmas holidays. House Masters string ribbons of holly along the grand banisters up to their apartments. Winter arrives with little ambivalence in the students' late-November absence: the branches over the Meadow are barren; the sun sets by five. Vito's regularly reports its highest sales—seemingly everyone, from the lacrosse players and their groupies with their standard booths to the most faceless supernumeraries of the background, gather there in the dark hours before check-in, fogging its windows with their life.

Even the teachers seemed to operate with a devil-may-care verve. Little got done in the one week of classes before the term's exams. "Aw, hell," Anne-Marie Cline said one morning, waving away a thirty-page reading assignment at the end of one class. "It won't be on the final." Even the prospect of those tests and papers shimmered with the liturgical spell of all of Kennedy's constituent rituals: students huddled together in sweatpants in the library, where over pad Thai and dumplings ordered in from Princeton they quizzed one another on the Stamp Act and the function of cellular mitochondria, finding coziness in what was shared.

The two remaining Xanax pills were tucked deep inside Foster's suitcase when he returned to campus, and in his backpack was the bottle of Lexapro, which he longed desperately to flush as well. "There can be some unpleasant side effects before they kick in," Dr. Apple had said. *Fuck that*, Foster had written on his Blogspot the night of Thanksgiving, his mind wetly diffuse with the glasses of red wine his mother had consolingly poured him at the dining room table, which she had laid out for the two of them with a festive meticulousness that made him sad. He had found a second unopened bottle of malbec and smuggled it up to his bedroom. *Give me the panic attacks and the loneliness. This is the worst I've ever felt. I almost want to take a Xanax to just take me out of it.* He had tried smoking, but the ensuing high had frightened him, a dissociative press of panicked distortions. He had tried to watch *Forgetting Sarah Marshall*, but the flickering images made him want to vomit.

He would later struggle to recall the particulars of those two weeks back at school. What Dr. Apple had described as brain fog was a febrile stupor; twice he got lost on the way to class. The diagnosis of depression had intensified his misery by validating it, sending him deeper into the shadows of himself. He chose not to study in the library—he feared making eye contact with Annabeth Whittaker, who had commandeered a glass-doored study carrel on the second floor for her friends. Instead, he sat beneath the musky glow of the desk lamp in his room, struggling and failing to focus on the open binders before him.

Three of the five term-end reports he would receive over Christmas break would curtly endorse Mrs. Cline's belief that he "failed to meet his own potential and certain basic expectations." During his hourlong European History exam, the press of the fugue had effaced even the most basic details of the Revolutions of 1848—*Was it Berlin? Budapest?*—and he left five of the examination blue book's fifteen pages blank. He awoke with a start on the morning of his Spanish final after a limited and unpleasant sleep to realize it had started an hour earlier. His head spinning with shame and panic as he sprinted across campus, he apologized to Sra. Willis, who handed him the test with a gaze of contempt and pity.

I am starting to believe I am acutely defective, he wrote on the Thursday evening before the final day of exams.

Foster had spent dinnertime in his room, working in misery to finish his final paper for Tierney. The thesis he'd crafted with minor pride a month earlier—that Jay Gatsby's class insecurity was equally a crisis of masculinity shared by Nick Carraway, whose opaque encounter with the aesthete Mr. McKee implied his homosexuality—now defied conclusion or basic coherence, so with a lurch of defeat he opened his MacBook to his Blogspot.

I realize now I've been too proud to think about leaving Kennedy—calling it quits and cutting my losses and going back to Gilman, or maybe one of the hipper magnet schools. But pride is less important than my sanity. I'm not using that word lightly. I think I'm losing it. But maybe I should be glad that I'm at least contemplating leaving, i.e. making myself happier. Maybe the meds are working. Ha.

Brennan House was empty—Jae had curiously disappeared three days earlier, exams apparently be damned—and outside his window the night was quiet. Students would be moving into the warmth of the chapel for Lessons and Carols, the Yuletide service held each year on the last night of the term, a final relic of now-secular Kennedy's Episcopalian beginnings. A genteel old member of the Math Department named Edward Abernathy would sing "O Holy Night" at service's end. Eight hundred Kennedians would sit rapt at his sonorous voice in the orange shine of the chapel candelabras, rich with the glow of those moments that distilled the ephemeral wonder of Kennedy. And Foster was alone.

He pulled on his fleece and stepped out into the biting air. Beyond the porch, the windowlight of distant common rooms danced out over the blackness of the Meadow. Despite everything, it did feel like Christmas. Foster shoved his hands into the pockets of his corduroys and stepped down toward the frozen lawn. From inside the brightly lit chapel he heard the stifled music of "O Little Town of Bethlehem."

He made his way to the center of the lawn and looked up. The moonless sky was crystalline with the spread of the cosmos, unsullied by the hazy glow of far cities. Somewhere many hundreds of miles above that lawn, a satellite glided elegantly through the expansive blackness, its beacon a slowly oscillating globe of red. Later, he would not know if what he felt in that moment was only the retrospective spill of what happened next, but it was something akin to wonder: a certain mesmerized melancholy that made his loneliness seem suddenly profound, beautiful even. He blinked.

"Fancy seeing you here."

Annabeth Whittaker wore an oversized cable-knit sweater that appeared to belong to a larger man—her father, Foster hoped optimistically. Her cheeks were pink in the cold and her eyes were bright and kind.

"Oh—h-hey," Foster said. He found his breath. "Not one for carols, are you?"

Annabeth's smile was vaguely sad. "I went last year. I'll go next year. Gracie and France and Mason wanted to pregame it, but I felt weird getting drunk for something like that, and besides I've still got Tierney's paper. And I like being alone outside at night, especially in the winter."

Foster smiled. "Me too, actually."

"I haven't seen you in forever," Annabeth said. "And you texted me! Over Thanksgiving! And then you didn't respond to mine! Some might call you an unreliable friend, Mister Dade."

"Congratulations," Foster said dryly. "You're the first person to consider me a friend here."

Annabeth laughed. "Well, you're awfully good at hiding yourself, aren't you?"

"I do my best work in the shadows."

Annabeth laughed again. And then, somehow, Foster found himself telling her everything: about smoking late at night with Jae; about the catastrophe of his final exams; about Dr. Apple and the Xanax that had impelled him to text her, which made her laugh even harder.

"Lexapro's for amateurs," she said. "Wellbutrin and Celexa for me. A year and a half now. You'll get out of the funk soon. And then things start to be okay." Foster realized that the two of them had started walking, leaving the Meadow and heading down the long lawn that spilled down to the Dining Center. The library was empty, glowing like a ghostly cruise liner at sea. As they crossed the barren football field to the shore of the frozen pond, Annabeth was telling him about herself, about her two older brothers: Mark, the golden child who'd played lacrosse at Hotchkiss and Dartmouth and now worked on Wall Street, and brooding, clever Charlie, who'd recently been reprimanded at USC for cocaine possession. "You remind me of him, actually," Annabeth said. About her father, who made his money moving other peoples' around and whom she believed sincerely hated her mother. About Gracie Smith, nominally her best friend. "She's just, like, so passive-aggressive, and it kills me. It fucking kills me. I swear we're all insane." About Mason Pretlow and Porter Roth, who had been unhappily hooking up for several months.

"And all of this is just bullshit. The hookups. The way nothing lasts. We do these things because it's expected of us, and my theory is that we're all miserable but either too afraid or incapable of realizing it, because we're doing what we're supposed to be doing."

"H-have you been hooking up with anyone?" Foster bravely put forward.

Annabeth waved this question off with a brush of her hand. They were walking around the back of the field house, with the lights of the Ellipse Houses burning on the distant end of the parking lot. "Last year, yeah—Harris Adelstein for, like, a day and a half in the spring, but he was so bad at kissing that I couldn't even sustain it for the sake of appearances." She chuckled darkly. "So of course he tells everyone I'm a whore. Or a tease. Whatever. But nah, not since."

Foster took this information and held it inside himself. "At least people are interested," he said, with equal darkness. He found himself at ease around her, despite his recognizing the sacredness of this encounter. "I haven't so much as kissed anyone in, like, nearly a year." Annabeth arched her eyebrows. "A long and tedious story."

"I've got time," she said.

"You don't, actually," he replied, gesturing up at the lit windows of Hewitt House, her dormitory. They heard the distant murmuring of exalted voices: Lessons and Carols had ended, and students were returning home.

"Well," Annabeth smiled. "You make for a fine alternative to Yuletide church, sir."

"The pleasure was mine," Foster said.

She looked at him curiously. "Don't be a stranger, all right? I feel like we have a lot more to talk about." And before he could respond, she hugged him, and maybe—he would never be quite sure—gave him the gentlest kiss on the far recess of his cheek, near his ear. "Merry Christmas, Foster Dade."

The cosmos overhead was as elegant as it had been an hour before, woven of white filament and spooled out across the sky. Foster stared up at it as he walked back to Brennan, realizing that he was smiling as stupidly as he'd been when he took the Xanax. A group of four passed him—Jack Albright, Mason Pretlow, Sofi Cohen, and Gracie Smith. He grinned. "What's up, guys."

"How goes it, Dade," Jack said, sticking up a wave; the rest murmured hello. Foster did not break his gait. He kept smiling.

XVII.

In the popular mythology of Foster Dade, the end of the fall term of 2008 would later emerge as a pivotal, even primal moment precipitating the events of the fifteen months that followed. Those more intimately acquainted with the narrative would later fail to agree precisely as to why. Some would say that the Lexapro finally started working. Others would point to it as the start of his friendship with Annabeth Whittaker, and consequently Jack Albright. Others still would say that these two hypotheses were inextricably connected.

The only consensus was that something was different about Foster Dade when he returned to Kennedy in January. "Y'know, he would frame us as these, like, malicious *shunners*, but the truth is that he was kind of a ghost in his first months there," Sofi Cohen told me several months ago. We were sitting at a bar in the East Village, near the apartment she shared with a sorority sister from Cornell; she was working in marketing and happy as a clam, bemused by and seemingly enjoying the opportunity to indulge the ancient drama of adolescence. She sipped her vodka soda. "We weren't, like, ignoring him. But that spring, he'd changed—he was happier, more animated, more of a person. Insane, obviously—just, like, obsessed with Annabeth and we all knew it—but I liked him, at least, even before all the Adderall stuff." She looked up at me. "I never liked him just because of the Adderall."

Foster's end-of-term results had arrived in Baltimore three days after he did. Invigorated by his walk that final evening, he had stayed up past midnight finishing his final *Gatsby* paper; Tierney had given him an A. "I do sense sometimes, though," Tierney wrote in his term-end report, "that Foster believes certain rules don't apply to him. I would advise him that this is not the case." Both Mrs. Cline and Señora had given him B-minuses, their attending notes harmonious in their vague disappointment.

"The good news is I think the meds are working," Foster said with a feigned smile. "The bad news is they were really shitty at the worst time."

Dr. Apple did not smile. "Foster, I'm wondering if this is about more than just the anxiety and depression," he said. "I'm wondering if you might struggle to concentrate. Do you struggle to concentrate?"

"Well—sure," Foster said. The question seemed dumb.

"Do you find yourself starting tasks only to fail to complete them?" Foster nodded.

"I'd like to give you something that will mend those difficulties. It's called Adderall, and it's very effective, but I don't want you taking it every day—just when studying for tests and during the tests themselves. I think this could do wonders for your self-esteem."

But the periwinkle prescription would remain in his pocket until after Christmas. Pharmaceutical aid seemed suddenly less urgent: in the days after he returned home, he began to feel somehow buoyant, his thoughts liberated from their febrile knots. The sparseness of the Baltimore winter seemed tranquil and pretty. He found himself genuinely happy to be in his mother's company: he took the garbage out unprompted; they went to see a matinee of *Doubt* at the Charles Theater downtown, happily arguing in the car afterward whether Philip Seymour Hoffman's Father Flynn had done it.

It seems likely that the Lexapro was indeed finally effectuating. But the more salient fact is that not a day passed over that three-week holiday when Foster did not talk to Annabeth Whittaker. Late on his first night home, he was upstairs in his bedroom, contemplating browsing pornography, when an iChat notification box appeared on his screen with a little whoop. *awhitty93 wants to send you a message. Do you accept?*

Without a pause he pressed the enter key. A little gray box unfurled onto the glow of his screen. The smooth bubbles that contained each message within it were an iridescent pink.

> **awhitty93:** oh hello there
> **awhitty93:** it's annabeth

awhitty93: got your sn from albright
awhitty93: get home ok?

Foster's heart churned a fast little beat.

fosterd419: top of tho oovning
fosterd419: evening***
fosterd419: i did
fosterd419: how's nj??

Surprisingly few millennials who used iChat as a platform for AOL Instant Messenger as adolescents are aware that the software quietly but diligently archived their forgotten conversations, and that in all likelihood these chats still exist in a folder somewhere on their high school MacBooks. Together these records collate an oddly comprehensive catalogue of one's teenage social biography, both mortifying and nostalgic in its preservation of certain emotional and historical cadences. When I obtained access to the laptop Foster Dade used during this period, I found these folders intact. There's a great deal of banality to his early conversations with Annabeth Whittaker—so it goes with both archival work and digital correspondence—but what's salient is how very long they are.

By the second week of the holiday, they were video chatting. It was two days after Christmas, and he had been sitting with his mother in the living room, watching an old episode of *Saturday Night Live* on TiVo when a tinny ringing sound came from his MacBook, open and neglected on the coffee table. "What's that?" Charlotte said to nobody. Foster picked up his computer. *awhitty93 is calling. Do you accept?*

Foster shot up from the couch and darted up the stairs. "Foster?" his mother called. Once he shut the bedroom door, he looked at his webcam reflection in the video window, brushed a hand through his hair, and pressed "Accept."

Annabeth was sitting in what looked like an oak-paneled study. Behind her was a tall window that caught the smudged reflections of

Christmas lights on the opposite side of the room. Her hair was wet and lank and she wore an oversized T-shirt that said VAMPIRE WEEKEND.

"I'm bored and want to kill my family," she said. "Talk to me."

So he did. He listened as she told him about her mother's mother, who at Christmas dinner had said some unseemly things about the "homos" and the new president. He told her about his end-of-term reports and Dr. Apple, the Hopkins grad student he was still buying weed from, the ad hoc Christmas he and his mother constructed for themselves—Maggie was still in Italy, his father simply not there (though he elided the details), so they ordered General Tso's chicken and pork dumplings for lunch the following morning. Forty-five minutes passed. An hour more, an hour fifteen. It was nearly one in the morning; Annabeth had relocated from her father's study to her bedroom, the walls of which were pale pink. He wondered what her bed felt like.

"Congratulations," she said at quarter past one. "You are exceedingly good at keeping me up past my bedtime."

Foster grinned. "I have my talents."

"I need to sleep," she said. "Mom wants to take me into the city tomorrow to shop."

"Be nice to your mother," Foster said. "Sweetest of dreams, Miss Whittaker."

"You have the same, Mister Dade." In the screen Annabeth beamed and waved merrily, and then exited the video chat; the window froze on this image, and Foster was so enthralled that he almost screenshotted it.

For the first night since he'd gotten home, he did not entertain the thought of either getting high or jerking off. He fell asleep soundly.

He was sitting at the kitchen counter the night before New Year's Eve when Annabeth called. He was home alone and residually a bit high; his mother was at dinner downtown with a man she knew from her days in Washington. There was an empty bowl of Chubby Hubby in front of him and he was not wearing a T-shirt; he decided, with a sweep of audacity, not to put one on. He clicked accept.

He was startled to see not just Annabeth Whittaker's face but Jack Albright's; the window was cleaved in two, like an open book, their respective video boxes next to each other. Foster briefly wondered if this was an ambush.

"We're having an argument and we need an objective opinion," Annabeth said excitedly.

There was happy mischief in Jack Albright's grin. "We're debating whether Tierney smokes pot."

Foster's stomach eased. "Oh, God, one hundred percent," Foster said, grinning back.

"See?" Jack said to Annabeth.

"He does not get high," Annabeth insisted. "He's, like, sixty, and a teacher! You guys are stereotyping."

"Yeah, but, like, the thing about stereotypes is—"

"That they're often true," Jack finished. He was wearing an emerald-green lacrosse pinnie and his thick brown hair was matted and askew. He had on eyeglasses, the sort of unsightly wire-rimmed ones kept as a spare after the adolescent transition to contact lenses.

"Precisely," Foster said, confused and exhilarated and not entirely convinced they weren't setting him up for something. "Let's look at the facts: yes, he's 'like, sixty,' which means he was twenty in the late sixties, and the dude was so clearly a hippie. He went to NYU. He studied Milton!"

"Oh yeah, *Paradise Lost*, right up there with *Harold and Kumar*." Annabeth grinned conspiratorially; there was something electric about the innocence of the delight she found in her own cleverness. "Keep trying."

"And, like, look at just how rumpled he is, and how scattered, and for fuck's sake, have you heard him talk in class? He's all over the map!" There was an entreating facility to Jack's voice that Foster had not heard before, liberated from the heft of its normal baritone.

"I think he's brilliant," Annabeth said, sincerity interlacing her playful defensiveness.

"So do I!" Foster said. "Brilliant people smoke weed. I smoke weed." He grinned.

Annabeth addressed Jack. "Foster gets stoned with his Korean roommate."

Jack burst out laughing. "Get the fuck out. Jae? Where was my invitation?"

"Well, you stopped visiting our suite after, like, the first day of school, so," Foster said, happy to enjoy the boldness he heard in his voice. He found himself contemplating the bareness of Jack's chest above the pinnie's low neck.

Jack laughed again. "Well, I expect you to smoke me up back at school."

That night in late December 2008—that video chat, the three of them sitting alone in their homes in Bedminster and Morristown and Baltimore—marked the beginning of a curious, doomed, and briefly beautiful friendship. I should emphasize here that some of the more nuanced facts of it remain opaque. In the years that followed, Jack Albright would speak very little of Foster Dade; those few who could grasp at the full extent of the reasons—Mark Stetson, namely—also knew better than to bring it up. And so we are left to speculate about certain things.

In the two decades since its servers first whirred to life in Northern California, the Internet Archive's Wayback Machine has catalogued more than five hundred billion webpages from across the wide cosmos of the internet. Like the cathedral-size telescopes that discern the garbled radio waves of stars and nebulae from unseen reaches of deep space, the Wayback Machine collates a useful but fundamentally incomplete microcosm of an ultimately unknowable whole. More simply: the program is designed to comprehend websites strictly through the magnitude of cookies amassed by visitor traffic. When a site hums with activity, the Machine follows the bristle of data and catalogues the page as it appears in that moment. As with the unreached expanses of ocean floor or the farthest corners of the universe, there is something awesome and sad about realizing the finitude of this collective data, and in turn the vastness of what defies it: the irretrievable recesses of cyberspace where pioneers once spoke into an empty, uncolonized void.

There is exactly one transcription of http://www.fhd93.blogspot.com on the Wayback Machine, dated to March 9, 2010, the same day the page's contents disappeared from Blogspot's servers. I accessed this file several years before I began this project in earnest; it is this version that informed my first attempts at reconstructing Foster's story. It took me a long time to come to terms with the necessary imperfection of these attempts: to accept that certain gaps and paucities in the archive were a condition of and not a navigable hindrance to the story I sought to tell. I expended a good deal of my early bandwidth trying to redress these deficiencies, pursuing the one more conversation or one more tranche of data that would answer the unanswered. This was particularly true of Foster Dade's Blogspot, whose historical omissions then struck me as more salient than its inclusions. Given the arbitrariness of some of these exclusions, I suspected that the blog—narratively a single object but structurally a catalogue of several hundred discrete posts, each with its own hyperlink—had been parsed and dissevered by the Wayback Machine's exclusionary triage, a digital fishing net meant to snare big game but let minnows and shrimp slide free.

It was in the service of this hypothesis that I'd requested the PDF from Sofi Cohen. Several hours after I left Sofi at the bar in the East Village, my phone dinged with a Gmail notification. "as promised," the subject line read. Sofi was the curious sort of millennial who continued to use her undergraduate email address for personal correspondence several years after graduation, and next to sofi.cohen7@cornell.edu was a little iconographic paper clip.

"i'm honestly shocked i still have this tbh," her email read. "it was deep in the folder of stuff from my old computers. next to all my shitty college app essays hah." Then there was a line break, and I heard in it a hesitant pause. Below her subsequent line was the attached file, titled *lol.pdf*.

"for the record, i never shared this with anyone and never read most of it. it was fucked up what they did."

And yet I opened a document textually identical to the file I already had saved on my computer. There was a certain shimmer of historical verisimilitude to opening this one, sure—the minor thrill of handling an original artifact after too much time staring at mimeographs—but my unanswered questions remained almost insistently unanswered. There are notably few entries from Foster Dade's first winter at Kennedy that chronicle anything other than the rote facts of the friendship that began to metabolize in that video chat at the end of December 2008: *Went to Vitos with Jack and Annabeth; we split a pint of Cherry Garcia* (1/9/2009); *Spent study hall watching* Cast Away *with Jack on the huge monitor he brought back after Christmas* (1/30/2009). We might venture that for Foster, the prospect of contemplating the deeper shape of things perhaps threatened to shatter the chassis in which their filaments were preserved. In any case, such things are transitive; without this insight, the question of what would happen later requires that we acquiesce to the same uncertainty.

"Jack never said anything bad about Foster when Foster was new—not that I remember, at least," Sofi Cohen would tell me in our subsequent conversation. "In fact, I remember him going out of his way to be nice to him—inviting him to tag along to dances, whatever. It's not Jack's fault that wasn't enough for him."

XVIII.

Foster had returned to Kennedy on the Northeast Regional, watching the green light of winter dance on the Chesapeake's tributaries as the train rattled across their bridges. The sun was setting as the cab from Trenton pulled into the Meadow, pulling columns of faint ruby up against the cold sky. Foster ate a late dinner alone in the silent Dining Center and returned to his room, listening as Brennan and the grounds beyond it murmured with the happy intermittence of returning life. He'd been shifting sleeplessly in bed when he felt his BlackBerry hum against the mattress in the dark.

> Jack Albright [11:14:20PM]: yoooooooo
> Jack Albright [11:14:24PM]: got back mad late
> Jack Albright [11:14:27PM]: come thru

He'd pulled on a T-shirt and walked deliberately to keep the floorboards from creaking underfoot. Jack's room had been dark except for the convulsive spill of his MacBook's screensaver, which danced across the idle shapes of Harris Adelstein and Andrew O'Donnell on the floor.

"Happy New Year," Jack had said, grinning mischievously up at Foster through the silver shadows. "Shall we blaze?"

So they did. "Jae, huh, I had no idea the kid was such a stoner." Harris had laughed when Foster arrived in Jack's room with the contraband he'd borrowed from his roommate. "Like, weird Korean royalty, yes, but who knew he was blazing every night."

"Who knew *you* were blazing every night?" Andrew said, looking at Foster. Foster had grinned sheepishly.

In the weeks that followed, this would take the shape of ritual. They would pass Jae's bowl among themselves by the open far window, exhaling the smoke out into the cold night, delighted by the absurdity of being high, spasming in silent laughter. Foster spent an evening in a cruelly accurate impression of Head Master Pauline Ross, "just, like, so transparently a lesbian."

And then Harris and Andrew would go to bed, and Foster and Jack would be alone. Foster had been uneasy on those first nights: his paranoia would flicker with the echo of Jack's detachment in the fall, pressing him to see a conspiracy in whatever had changed. But the emotional cortices of the brain are elastic and quickly resilient, particularly when it comes to insulation against pain. Our most delicate emotional pirouettes remain at their core animalistic; all anguish seems primal in its threat. We survive as a species in the quick construction of certain bulwarks.

This is to say that Foster Dade eventually found himself coming to trust the thick-haired boy with whom he sat late into the January night, eating Pringles and working their way through Bo Burnham's YouTube oeuvre. Those who found themselves in Jack Albright's company in these years would later describe a marvelous sense of being let in on a secret. The music of these unspoken disclosures had frightened Foster at first in the vulnerability they seemed to invite. When we consider everything that happened later, we might find some credence in these residual anxieties, but with each successive evening they receded against the tide of these sparkling confidences.

"All they really seem to give a shit about is goofing off and talking shit about people and hyping themselves up to the freshman girls," Jack said sullenly one night. "Mason and Freddie the most. Try talking to them about books or music or movies and they'll call you a fag."

They made a small home together in this lament. Certain nights, they found themselves delighting in a common nostalgia, in its ability to converge and interlink their otherwise disjoined childhoods. They litigated the plots of episodes of *Hey Arnold!* and *Boy Meets World* and compared notes on the sexual innuendoes they'd eventually discerned in *SpongeBob SquarePants*; they confessed that they'd both enthusiastically attended all *Harry Potter* midnight book release parties at their local Barnes and Noble beginning with *Goblet of Fire* in the summer after second grade. One night, they found themselves sitting before Jack's laptop watching *Monsters, Inc.* They disclosed their first spontaneous experiences of masturbation: Foster to an illustration of a nude woman performing an at-home breast exam in a Red Cross family medical guidebook; Jack to a topless actress in a pirated copy of *EuroTrip* he'd downloaded from LimeWire. They traced these pasts to how they found beauty in the present: Jack obsessed over the Coen Brothers and Chuck Palahniuk; Foster lent him his old earmarked copy of David Foster Wallace's essays and insisted late one night that Jack was missing a crucial component of his soul because he had never gotten into R.E.M.

"This is actually, like, fucking beautiful," Jack said quietly, when Foster put on "Nightswimming." He'd pinched a small dark nugget of Skoal from the tin on his desk and tucked it into his bottom lip, then passed it to Foster.

"It's the prettiest song ever written, no joke," Foster said, his voice solemn. He saw Jack smiling.

"I'm sorry for being kind of an aloof dick in the fall," Jack said finally. "I wasn't, like, actively trying to not be your friend. I just had a lot going on."

"Oh," Foster said, surprised and happy. "It's cool. Really."

"You seem to have hit your stride," Mr. McCall told Foster one evening at check-in in the second week of January, handing him a laudatory academic memo from Dr. Tierney. "Keep it up, eh?"

He began to feel a happy purposefulness to his own motion. During study hall, he found himself vigorously poring over his readings for English and European History; in class the next day, he sat before the seminar table with his pages of notes and held forth, hearing cadences in his voice he had forgotten. "I think we should return to Rosalie's point," he said one morning in Tierney's class. They were reading *Hamlet*. "The maternal conflict is clearly the engine of the plot, more so than politics or anything else, and I think she's onto something." A flustered Rosalie Haddish looked surprised and pleased. Across the table, Annabeth arched her eyebrows at him and smiled. Tierney had been so pleased that he issued the memo to both McCall and Foster's mother. *Nothing wrong with a temper, but Foster's clearly at his smartest when he wants to engage his interlocutors, and today he did so beautifully. Bravo.*

In the summer of 2017, the Bradford Library's archivists set to work digitizing the century and a half of laminated back issues of the *Kennedian* that by then occupied three dozen file crates in the library's temperature-controlled basement archives. Art Tierney—who would remain the paper's faculty advisor until his retirement three years later—ultimately forced the newspaper's editorial staff to spend their Sundays assisting with the clerical labor, but even then, it would take just shy of six months to catalogue the details of the 90,000 articles that comprise the resulting digital archive. We have the option to search these records by author's last name, and so it's within a vast transhistorical sprawl of forgotten stories—*M. H. Davenport '98, "Greek Lecture by Mr. Havens" (Vol. XVIII, No. 21, May 9, 1897); E. Dahlstrom '42, "Dr. Kirby Addresses School in Chapel at Outbreak of War" (Vol. LXII, No. 13, December 12, 1941); P. J. D'Amico '86, "Pranksters Vandalize Squash Courts" (Vol. CIV, No. 6, October 30, 1983)*—that we find *F. H. Dade '11, "Kennedy's America Isn't Obama's America. Where's the Disconnect?" (Vol. CXXVIII, No. 16, January 23, 2009).*

The opinions editor that year was a pale, wiry Fourth Year named Neil Probst, who would go to Harvard that fall. "We've had a lot of school pieces lately, and we need some national pieces," Neil was saying before the weekly editorial meeting in the third week in January.

Foster leaned against a back wall of the newspaper's windowless office in the basement of Fenster Hall. He had showed up alone and on a whim. The staff writers in the dingy office were the ambitious academic ones from his classes: Rosalie Haddish and her friend Jenny Xiu, who also edited the yearbook; Noah Baum, a tall, sardonic Jewish boy whose parents taught at Princeton; Raj Chakravarty, who in his second week at Kennedy had privately decreed to become the Class of 2011's valedictorian.

"So," Neil Probst was saying, idly bouncing a threadbare tennis ball that lived in the office. "I'm thinking maybe something on Obama"—the inauguration had been two mornings prior—"and whether he'll live up to the promise of his campaign, especially when the economy's in the toilet. Any takers?"

Rosalie Haddish shot up her hand, and so did Foster Dade. Neil's eyes passed Rosalie's hand and met Foster's. "You're new." Foster felt the eyes of the room turn to him.

"Yeah, hey," he said. "Foster Dade." He enjoyed his surge of confidence. "I think it's an interesting idea, but I'm not so sure tons of people really care what a sixteen-year-old has to say on the subject unless he has a relevant perspective. Maybe"—he gazed upward in thought—"we write about what his presidency means for people like us, Kennedy students, and maybe appraise whether we're sufficiently attuned to what's happening in Washington and the rest of the country."

Neil looked at him quizzically for a moment. "I like it," he said finally. "Nice thinking. Can I get eight hundred words by Monday?"

The first proper snow that year came on the third Thursday in January. What had begun on sanguine meteorologists' radar screens as an amorphous tuft of motion over the mid-Atlantic had by dinnertime on Wednesday burgeoned low over central Jersey in fat copper clouds. The downstairs windows of the Houses along the Meadow danced blue against the yellowing darkness with the light of the Weather Channel on the common room televisions inside, its forecasters penitent.

"That's it," Jack said, standing shirtless before the window of his room on the second floor of Brennan, watching dime-sized flakes dance against the lampposts' tents of light. "I'm calling it." Even in the faint light Foster could see the slight contours of his abdominals. "No class tomorrow. No fucking chance."

Foster was sitting on the floor of Jack's room, his back against the wall below a poster for the film *Fargo*. Andrew O'Donnell was clicking a green Bic lighter, trying to ignite the half-charred node of ground weed in the bowl of Jae's silver pipe. They were all pleasantly stoned as the barren earth of the lawn below them whitened and swelled.

Foster woke the next morning groggy from the weed to find that a foot of snow had fallen on Kennedy. His BlackBerry blinked with the email from Head Master Ross: classes were canceled; day students shouldn't drive to campus. He pulled on a pair of jeans and a thick gray turtleneck and tugged his old L.L.Bean duck boots over his heels.

His footsteps were the first in the new snow that morning. It wasn't yet seven o'clock; most had woken up an hour earlier to check for Ross's email and then promptly rolled back to sleep. Fat flakes still fell, shrouding the campus in a curious silence. He stepped down from the Brennan porch, the accumulation meeting the tops of his boots, and proceeded along the long lawn toward the Dining Center. His mouth was still dry from the prior night's weed, so he reached down, picked up a handful of crystalline snow, and ate it. It tasted good.

The Dining Center's front doors strained against the bluster of the wind, and inside it too was silent. He walked upstairs and had poured himself a cup of coffee when he saw Art Tierney sitting in the front dining pod, who caught his gaze. "Morning, Dr. Tierney." Foster grinned, walking toward him.

"My boy," he said, his mouth full of scrambled egg. "This tempest, hey!"

"I'd say I'm sorry to miss your class, but I'll be spending most of the day working on your paper, so."

Tierney waved a hand absentmindedly. He had a fleck of egg in his unshaved white stubble. "Enjoy the day—you deserve a bit of a holiday for yourself," he said.

Foster blushed. "Yeah—I've been working hard lately," he said.

"I'm not talking about schoolwork. You're good at schoolwork. I'm talking about Kennedy, which can do a real number on the uninitiated spirit."

Foster blushed harder. "I guess I'm not sure what you mean."

Tierney appeared lost in thought. "What I mean," he said, "is that you have weathered storms, and it's nice to see you sailing out of them. A choppy voyage is good for the soul."

Foster felt vaguely touched. "I appreciate it, Dr. Tierney, thanks."

"Cherish your day off, Dade," Tierney said, returning to the eggs.

People began to trickle in, in sweatpants and jackets and gloves, bringing the grassy smell of melting ice. "I stopped by your room but you'd disappeared," Jack Albright said, grinning as he strutted into the Brennan pod, clutching a toasted bagel. He was wearing an old Barbour jacket and had a blue tartan scarf knotted around his neck; his cheeks were still warm and bright from the cold. "What did I say? What the fuck did I say? I fucking called it!"

"You called it."

"Technically snowball fights are forbidden, because last year Pritchett nearly lost an eye, but I'm sure that won't stop anyone," Jack said.

It was eleven or so by the time they left to return to Brennan. The snow was falling heavier still; guiding their return was only the dim burning of the distant lampposts through the shifting sheet of white in front of them. Pritchett Pierce and Will Thierry had joined them in the dining hall and were insisting that they build an igloo in the Meadow. Foster felt a muted envy: *Imagine being comfortable enough in your social station at a place like this to happily do something like build a fucking igloo and not give a shit about what anyone thinks*, he wrote on his Blogspot later that night.

"We're damsels in distress!" a familiar voice cried. Annabeth was clomping her way through the snow alongside Sofi Cohen, Frances

Evans, and Gracie Smith. She wore a long Patagonia down jacket that fell to her knees. Her face glowed pink from the cold as she beamed; there were tiny icicles in her eyebrows.

"It," she said as she approached them, "is fucking cold. Why anyone opts to live north of like Richmond I will never know."

"There's your Duke admissions essay right there," Pritchett chirped.

"I've never seen it like this," Gracie observed, looking around at the accumulation.

"Wanna put money on a second day off tomorrow?" Pritchett said.

"Fifty bucks," said Jack.

"You don't have fifty bucks."

A scrum of beefy Kellogg boys had indeed commenced a snowball fight on the expanse of the Meadow, and within half an hour it seemed that half the school had joined in. Snowball fights had always vaguely agitated Foster, prodding his deep ambivalence over conflict and its vulnerabilities. He huddled along the sidelines with Sofi and Annabeth, watching as Jack assumed the posture of a Napoleonic general directing his troops into Siberia. The snow was falling harder still. Will Bartholomew, who had set up his speakers in his upstairs window in Kellogg to blast Swedish House Mafia out over the Meadow before joining the fray, looked up only to be hit directly in the face by an icy snowball; he howled with rage and then threw himself on top of the Third Year from Talmadge House who had thrown it.

"As much as I love both male brutality and hypothermia, I am hungry," Annabeth said finally. "Vito's." Behind them, the frumpy silhouette of Theresa Daniels, the calculus teacher then in her third year as Dean of Students, emerged through the bluster of falling snow in her pink down jacket. "Enough!" she shouted over the din. "Enough! No more! Will Bartholomew and Evan Siegel!"—she pointed at the boy who'd thrown the ice ball at Bartholomew— "come with me now!"

The pizzeria was empty except for three high school girls from the town, who wore green eye shadow and cheap windbreakers. They stared at Foster as he entered with Annabeth.

"So, your first Kennedy snow day," Annabeth said, pulling off her jacket. "It's kind of magical, isn't it?"

The snow would fall with a new gentleness as the afternoon carried on. Only later would Foster do the math and realize that by the time the others showed up, he and Annabeth had been in the booth for just shy of four hours. *I don't remember the last time someone has made me laugh so much, or the last time I've made* someone else *laugh so much*, he wrote that winter.

"I'm starving," Jack announced to no one and everyone as he stepped inside. "Make room, make room." A group of pretty First Year girls sitting by the Ben and Jerry's cooler giggled. Outside, homebound cars were making their wet chafe up Eastminster Road, the last falling flakes dancing in the spill of their headlights.

"A bloodbath," Pritchett Pierce exhaled, pulling his Barbour jacket from his shoulders. He wore a canary-yellow sweatshirt with a yacht club's pink insignia stitched upon the breast. The tan of Christmas in Mustique was now a pale but healthy khaki. His curly hair danced with snow from the preceding battle. "Absolutely historical."

The others came soon: Porter Roth and Will Thierry and Sofi Cohen; Gracie Smith and then Freddie Pieters and Mark Stetson. The scowling Mason Pretlow. "I'm feeling magnanimous," Jack said, standing with a flourish. "Orders? My treat."

"Your dad's treat," Will Thierry corrected. "Slice of Brooklyn, slice of buffalo." Foster liked Will; to his knowledge there was no one in the Class of 2011 who didn't. His confidence was unassuming in its basic kindness; fifteen months later, when he would run for student body president, he would win with nearly 80 percent of the vote.

"It's the fucking thought that counts, and watch it, Thierry," Jack said, pointing at him with a wicked grin as he walked backwards towards the counter.

It was with a gymnastic elegance that he brought over the heavy mosaic of paper plates, the slices upon them overlapping and besmirching the paper with grease. "So Foster," Annabeth said, plucking an errant pepperoni, "was the one who just, like, obliterated Rosalie Haddish in Tierney's class that one time."

"Oh ga-a-a-a-wd, that girl fucking s-u-u-u-u-cks," Mark Stetson murmured, spreading his hands to the ceiling. He was a small boy, compact and muscular in the way younger male dancers are, but he moved with an emboldened splendor under which size seemed immaterial. Foster had once spent an evening scrolling down Mark Stetson's Facebook wall, where below a photo album from his four weeks at a Catskills theater camp he found a cluster of watermarked images saved from an event photographer's website. There was Mark, standing next to his lawyer parents, turned to the then-Senator Obama, his ashen exhaustion from the long Democratic primary briefly effaced by his obvious delight at the fourteen-year-old raconteur before him.

"And of course all the teachers fucking *love* her," Mark continued, rolling his wide eyes in time with the cadences of his words, "because she's, like—politically sensitive?"

"And the thing is, it's all a ruse," Foster said, hoping his voice was bored. "It's so disingenuous—like, are you really a good, attuned person if you're only good and attuned in order to get into Princeton?" Even Gracie Smith seemed to chuckle.

He did not allow himself to look toward Mason Pretlow in such moments, fearing the confirmation of the scowl or sneer that seemed to radiate its heat from across the table. *Of course I'm maybe just imagining things*, Foster had written on his Blogspot two weeks after returning to Kennedy after Christmas, *but he somehow seems even more hostile to me now now* (sic) *that Jack and I are closer. Maybe he's just jealous. Admittedly there's a part of me that would like that.*

It was with this new resolve that Foster had allowed himself to simply delete the message he had received on Honesty Box on a Thursday night at the end of January. He had returned from brushing his teeth just before lights-out when he saw the little red notification icon that had appeared in the corner of his Facebook page. No messages had arrived in his Honesty Box inbox in the four months since he'd linked his profile to the app, and with a minor spasm of thrill and dread he'd clicked on the notification.

are you into dudes?

Of course it had to have been Mason, Foster would write there-after, *who manages to call someone a faggot in every other sentence. I wish I could say it didn't bother me at all.* But after a momentary twinge of an otherwise forgotten nausea, he had willed himself to click the little trash can icon alongside the message, and gave it little thought thereafter.

At several points during dinner that night at Vito's, Foster caught Porter Roth glancing at him. He knew little about her, other than that she was a very intelligent day student from Princeton whose father was some sort of nationally celebrated economist. Something in her silence implied an anxious attunement to the politics of things. She was pretty, Foster thought, with gentle auburn hair that fell neatly over her shoulders and a small pouting mouth. Glancing at her hands, he noticed that she bit her nails. Mason Pretlow's arm was draped indifferently along the spine of the booth seat behind her. ("They're, like, sort of together, but it's ridiculous," Annabeth had said over video chat. "She can't stand him, but she's too passive to do any-thing about it, and to the best of my knowledge he's been hooking up with some freshman but is too lazy to end things with Porter." "I can neither confirm nor deny," Jack had said in a mock solemnity.)

Foster studied her as the conversation turned to a party Mason Pretlow and his Potomac friends had thrown at his parents' house a month earlier. "These fucking townie sluts showed up—I'm pretty sure one of them shat in my parents' toilet and didn't flush," he was saying. Only Foster seemed to notice Porter wince.

"Speaking of townie sluts," Gracie murmured, tilting her head almost imperceptibly to the door, where a cluster of First Year girls were unzipping their jackets. Jack gave an indifferent nod to Jacqueline Franck; Pritchett sank himself low in his seat and studied his plate as Sally Pinelli, whom he had glumly accepted he was dating, looked expectantly toward the booth. With them was a heavy-lidded girl named Kaitlyn Sanders. Foster knew her only as the sum of rumors overhead in the Dining Center and the Brennan showers: that she had blown not one but two Third Years on the baseball team after the Kellogg House dance; that she'd come to Kennedy after a series of nude photos she'd taken on her Motorola Razr had spread like brushfire across multiple middle schools in Wilmington, Delaware.

"Oh God, that girl is trash," Gracie said, sucking the last of her Diet Coke from her straw.

"Oh, be nice," Annabeth said.

"I heard she blew Jake Atkinson in the bathroom during Homecoming," Sofi Cohen said absentmindedly.

"Confirm," Jack and Pritchett said in unison.

Foster studied the girl as she moved toward the counter, noticing her eyes cast around the restaurant. Her chest was heavy beneath her sweatshirt. He contemplated Gracie's and Sofi's words as he watched her, sensing in her furtive glances a passively desperate unease. He felt strangely sad.

"Enough pot-stirring," Annabeth said finally. He briefly felt her eyes on him. "I want to watch *Gossip Girl*."

As they shifted from the booth, Foster noticed the pallid, dark-eyed boy from his fall term English class, who was sitting at an inconspicuous table by the ice cream coolers at the back of the restaurant. ("The bitch seats," Freddie had fumed once when the group found itself there one night that fall, looking murderously up at the First Year boy whose backpack had slid his plate of fries to the sticky floor.) His name, Foster knew, was Blake Mancetti.

The *New Second Year Welcome Lunch!*—or so it had been called in the invitation email from Mrs. Tompkins in the admissions office—had been held on the first Thursday of the fall term. There were seventeen of them in total that year, all of whom showed up in the windowless dining room on the Dining Center's ground floor with the forlorn expressions of those increasingly accustomed to being lost. Foster had been the last to arrive: only ten minutes into the lunch period had his nagging sense of a forgotten-about commitment finally disclosed itself, and with a face hot from both humiliation and his frantic run from Brennan he had entered the dining room to interrupt the panel of bored Fourth Years conscripted by the admissions office as they introduced themselves. After serving himself a plate of chicken piccata—feeling the acid of what he imagined as two dozen pairs of eyes on him and attempting valiantly not to vomit—he had taken the empty seat closest to the buffet, across from an olive-skinned boy whose name tag identified him as *Blake M. (Arsdale House)*. He wore the tag on the breast of a pink tattersall Ralph Lauren button-down that was tucked into canary-yellow khaki shorts; the crispness of both suggested they'd been removed from their tissue-paper sheaths that morning. He had cut his chicken breast into tidy symmetrical pieces, and Foster watched as he sporadically nudged them around his plate with his fork and knife; the plate would still be full when he brought it to the service window at the end of the hour. Every few minutes, Foster caught Blake glancing up at him, discerning something either accusatory or frightened or both in his eyes.

Foster slid from the booth in Vito's after Jack, and as he stood to collect his empty plate, he saw Blake looking in their direction with the same inscrutable gaze. His eyes twitched to Jack as Jack dunked his empty cup into the garbage, and Foster got the curious sense that Blake had been watching them for some time. There was an intensity to his attention that broke only when his eyes met Foster's: here again Foster found himself thinking of a cornered animal. He thought again of his own isolation in those first weeks of the year, of the unrelenting weight of his own conspicuousness, and he felt a sudden spasm of gratitude for where he'd sat, at Jack's side.

XIX.

Foster Dade's MacBook Pro/Music/iTunes/Playlists/insomnia, wistful, sleep
(Created January 3, 2009)

Name	Time	Artist
The District Sleeps Alone Tonight	4:44	The Postal Service
Crash into Me	5:16	Dave Matthews Band
Signs	4:39	Bloc Party
Street Lights	3:09	Kanye West

Ready 2 Wear	3:41	Felix da Housecat
Black Balloon	4:10	Goo Goo Dolls
Wake Up	5:35	Arcade Fire
Swing, Swing	3:53	The All–American Rejects
Nightswimming	4:18	R.E.M.
Screaming Infidelities	3:46	Dashboard Confessional
1979	4:26	Smashing Pumpkins
This Modern Love	4:25	Bloc Party
With or Without You	4:56	U2
Round Here	5:31	Counting Crows
'Til Kingdom Come	4:11	Coldplay
Fake Empire	3:25	The National
Apartment Story	3:33	The National
No Woman, No Cry (Live 1975)	7:08	Bob Marley & The Wailers
Gypsy	4:25	Fleetwood Mac
Brick	4:31	Ben Folds Five

20 songs, 1.5 hours, 161.9 MB

XX.

The rest of the winter term passed with the forgettable frozen monotony that enshrouds those dark months. The darkness of the mid-Atlantic winter has that amnesiac tendency: later, with the lucidity of summertime, Kennedians think back to the winter term and find themselves with only a sort of composite vignette, of the cruelly premature sunsets and the biting pain of passing beneath them en route to dinner, lit by the syrupy orange orbs of lamppost light that spill and bristle against the icy earth underfoot, rendering motion briefly tangible in the form of shadows.

So it was for Foster Dade that winter: an eight-week stretch of sameness, of one long trudge through the icy snow to the dining hall. Later, reflections upon this monotony were penetrated only by glimpses of the evenings after dinner, when he, Jack, and Annabeth would decamp to a private study room of the library, collectively getting very little work done.

There was one event in the winter of 2009 that threatened to upend that winter's frigid stasis in the narrative of Foster's memory; conveniently, it is an event that has some bearing on my project here. In the last week of February, Mark Stetson came out of the closet.

For the sake of historical context, it's maybe worthwhile to note just how drastically things have changed since that February. We'll leave it to the next generation's cultural historians to debate the precipitating factors—the Obama judiciary's dismantling of the Defense of Marriage Act; the coeval commodification of so-called identity politics by the content farmers at BuzzFeed et al.—and simply observe that this was uniquely true at Kennedy. All the early institutional pretenses to "diversity and inclusion" taking shape in those years could not efface the anxious politics of masculinity that percolate in such contained adolescent ecosystems, a politics that finds its potency in the ever-present threat of shame.

By the winter of 2009, there were three openly gay students at Kennedy. Two of them—a Fourth Year named Evan Linton, who enthusiastically held bit parts in the Terpsichorian Society's forgettable seasonal stage productions, and one Rich Spitz, a nearly anonymous greasy-haired day student from Cranbury who came to campus only for class, spending his free afternoons smoking Marlboro Reds on Nassau Street with eye-shadowed friends in leather from Princeton High—were peripheral to the point of irrelevance. The third, an almost deliberately flamboyant half-Filipino senior named Carlton Magdalan, had come out to his posse of girls in Perry House as a Second Year and since then wielded his identity like a cudgel.

For reasons that might later present themselves as obvious, it's fruitful to note here that until five months before Foster Dade arrived at Kennedy, the number of out students had been four. Scott Lansing "Tripp" Altridge III had been from Manhattan, where in his eighth-grade year at St. Bernard's he had come out with a vocality that felt nihilistic in its fortissimo: *I wonder what I'm going to fucking do next*, he seemed to say. He had carried that spiritual banner to Kennedy, worn it like a bedazzled caftan, and because the larger ethos of Kennedy functioned as a marketplace of social capital, where individuals are commodified and accordingly appraised in the service of the place's self-perpetuating colorful romance, he had thrived.

What ultimately endeared him to the boys atop the social taxonomy was alcohol and drugs. Fourteen-year-old boys are deeply and reflexively suspicious of flamboyance, and it was only when Mellie Jakes and Kendall MacPherson informed them of the veritable minibar on the floor of Tripp's closet in the First Year dormitory that they came around. In the curious alchemy of these things, he eventually became one of them, a fabulous aesthetic outlier who quickly embraced the protective value of laughing at himself, and who never quite let go of the association between these friendships and the half-empty bottles of Smirnoff and Jose Cuervo on the floor of his closet beneath the sag of his old St. Bernard's sweatpants.

By the fall of Second Year, this apothecary had expanded to include cocaine, which this group had started doing that summer at Tripp's parents' place in Water Mill. (I should note that Tripp's social alchemy might have been foreclosed altogether had he not been very wealthy.) They did a lot of cocaine that year—Tripp more than all of them, snorting it not only before dances and on weekend trips to the city but during study hall, alone in his room in Talmadge House, and sometimes on Saturday afternoons. Never quite forgetting his male friends' suspicion in those early weeks a year prior, he flaunted his sexual orientation by rendering it an almost delicious joke, anyone's game; the matter of sex itself was addressed in the most oblique of references. Tripp seemed to don the ambiguity as one more radiant, enticing layer. The rumors that he had blown an ostensibly straight Fourth Year on the ice hockey team out behind the ice rink's rattling heating units one January night never quite got the chance to materialize, though they were of course true.

All of this had lasted until the fateful Saturday night in the spring of 2008 during the ill-fated moonshine incident at the final dance of the year. Bryan Harris, the baseball player who'd spearheaded the bootleg operation, had watched *The Sopranos* with the other boys in Brennan that winter, and we might conclude that it lent inspiration for his final desperate attempt at self-protection, when through tears he betrayed Tripp Altridge and the contents of his bedroom closet to Dean of Students Theresa Daniels.

But a place like Kennedy breeds enough sycophants, and there's little administrative appetite for informants who themselves have flouted a half-dozen school rules in one endeavor. Six hours after Bryan Harris had been told to start packing his things, Talmadge House Master knocked on Tripp Altridge's door and asked its uncharacteristically affectless occupant to follow him to Theresa Daniels's office. He had not returned, and the boys along the Meadow, several of whom were themselves somberly awaiting arraignment, watched from their windows as Tripp's mother, a pale woman whose anorexic build and poorly cropped black hair suggested the enervation of neuroses, stonily moved her son's belonging in plastic Tupperware bins to the rented Tahoe parked outside.

Tripp Altridge would acquire the wraith-like mythological persistence that Foster Dade would come to occupy roughly two years later, a legacy reified and sadly spangled by both absence and the circumstances that had occasioned it. So it was that the number of openly gay students at Kennedy became three, until a cold night in February 2009.

Earlier that evening, exiting the downstairs bathroom in the Dining Center, Foster had watched from afar as Pritchett Pierce and Mason Pretlow addressed Jack by the front doors with expressions of strange consternation, which Jack's own then assumed. Mason was the first to notice Foster as he approached, and the sudden chilling was palpable.

"Enough," Mason said, conspicuously jerking his head in Foster's direction. Pritchett gave Foster a congenial nod and something of a sad smile, which Foster appreciated, understanding that he was not welcome.

"We'll talk there," Jack said to them, and the two turned to exit. Mason did not acknowledge Foster. Jack turned to him when they were gone. "Listen, I need to tend to something with these guys in Ames," he said. "It's kind of urgent. Can you tell Chissom that I'm over there stuck in a test prep session? I'll have the duty master send her a note." The measured formality of his tone, and the air of secrecy of the prior encounter, seemed to foreclose an invitation to any questions on Foster's part, and Foster felt the acute melancholy nausea of outsiderness from his first few weeks at Kennedy returning. *I sometimes feel like I'm walking a tightrope with these people*, Foster wrote on his Blogspot at one point that spring, in a rare moment of the self-reflective clarity that one tends to avoid in periods when things seem to be working out against all odds. *There's this sense that I should feel lucky to be in their company, and so I'm neurotically obsessed about not, like, overstaying my welcome or whatever.*

Annabeth's regular iChat to meet her in the library had assuaged this isolation. She sat beneath the warm light next to Sofi Cohen, whose dark brown hair had been carelessly twisted into a sloppy bun. Foster liked Sofi: like Will Thierry and Pritchett Pierce, and to a certain extent the vacuously kind Frances Evans, she interacted with Foster with an affable warmth that carried neither the circumspection or bored formality that Foster sensed when he tried to make conversation with, say, Mason or Gracie or Freddie.

"You'll be my biggest hero if you have snacks," Sofi said to him with a comic despair as he entered.

"Thought you were dieting, Cohen," Annabeth said, not looking up from her own notes.

Sofi lobbed a highlighter at her.

An hour had passed when the lithe figure of Gracie Smith appeared in the glass of the room's door. She wore an oversized Princeton Lacrosse sweatshirt and leggings.

"You guys," she said, closing the door behind her but not shutting it. "Urgent."

She cast a furtive look at Foster. "He can stay, Gracie," Sofi said. "Don't be a bitch." Gracie paused, then shut the door behind her.

"Mark just came out. As, like, gay."

"What!" Annabeth and Sofi proclaimed together. Foster said nothing.

Gracie gave Foster another suspicious glance. "Pritchett just told me. He got all the guys together in his room in Ames and told them. He'd been shut up in there since classes."

"I noticed he wasn't at track," Annabeth said. "Shit. Gay. Mark?"

Foster wondered if Gracie had chosen her words deliberately— what *all the guys* made evident was that he was not one of them.

"Gay," Gracie repeated. "He says he's always known."

"Well," Sofi said, appearing contemplative. "It suddenly kind of makes sense. The flamboyance and everything. Never trying to get with girls."

"I always assumed that was because he was Black," Annabeth said objectively. She then amended herself: "It's very Caucasian, the hookup scene."

"It also tends to require that you like vagina," Gracie said.

"Well, good for him!" Annabeth said. "We should text him and tell him we love him."

"Oh my god, guys," Sofi said. "We get to have a gay friend!"

Foster was quiet. Sofi was right: it made sense. Mark Stetson had been in his Honors European History section in the fall term, and one of Foster's earliest lasting observations in those first weeks had been of the effortlessness with which Mark insinuated himself into life. It was not unlike Jack's in its controlled effervescence—one that seemed to ride the cadences of the situation at hand, to illuminate its edges without transgressing them.

Those more credentialed than I to pass judgment on these things say that Mark Stetson was a breathtakingly good actor, even then. Since its founding in the late 1800s, the Terp—the Terpisochorean Society, Kennedy's august old dramatic club—had provided a sort of Bridesheadian alibi to more than a century of patrician queer impulses, realized or otherwise; it offered its constituents something more than a chance to act. For this reason, Mark Stetson's membership in the Terp was perfunctory: in both theater and life, he'd built for himself a commonwealth of greener pastures. The orthodox Terpies resented him for this, and for his talent. Cynicism is envy's best salve, and there were many Kennedians who chose to read Mark's skill in theater as only the stylized shape of a deeper disingenuousness. He was a good actor, the bitter argument went, because to act is to embody a lie, requiring the very emotional equipment with which Mark charmed Anne-Marie Cline out of her irritation when he forgot his European History homework. It would only be much later, with the luxury of knowledge then still inconceivable, that Foster Dade would realize that precisely in his performed elegance, Mark Stetson was one of the few honest people he'd ever known. In that moment, though, sitting there silently in the library under the thickness of Gracie's news, all Foster understood was that he coveted it.

On a cool spring morning thirteen years later, I would meet Mark Stetson in a coffee shop in the East Village. For the sake of historical clarity, I should note that as I write this, three and a half years have passed since I first sat down to collect and intensively organize this story's pieces. (The barren fruit of my earlier slapdash attempts warrants no note.) Had certain global epidemiological happenings not cleared my calendar, I suspect it would have taken longer. The pieces themselves would come to sit in high, unbalanced towers of reams and gigabytes on my laptop's desktop and most of my apartment's flat surfaces. Even now, I still sometimes roll over in bed to feel a forgotten printed email crinkle beneath me. I once found one in my freezer. This unruly archive amassed itself by the logic in which its components appeared, which is to say capriciously, giving formal shape only to the convoluted social networks that had led me from one source of information to another. In more than a few cases, several years separated two interviews devoted to reconstructing a single forgotten afternoon.

Mark Stetson would be one of my final conversations, for the simple reason that he was perpetually overbooked. After several months of spastic back-and-forthing, we agreed to meet at a coffee shop on the Bowery. It was one of several in a lower Manhattan chain, trendy in the irritatingly derivative way that has prospered in this decade alongside and for Instagram. Edison bulbs hung from long ropes over narrow pine tables; the speakers overhead played the Chainsmokers.

Mark was late. He had, like his mother, gone on to Yale, moving between the Dramat playhouse and the Scroll and Key tomb in a radiant network of affluent internationals and jaded Manhattanites. Afterward, he'd moved to the city to act, and to no one's surprise he managed to find work. Of the four productions in which he's since appeared, three have received write-ups in the *Times* Theater section;

of these three, two have reserved a paragraph of special regard for—in the words of the more recent column—the "astonishing young man who wears his awesome talents with the happy nonchalance of a Zara model." The morning we met, he'd been up on the Columbia campus, where the last episode of his four-episode arc on *Billions* was preparing to wrap.

He hadn't aged, really, though while the dazzling edge of his charisma remained intact and legible, it seemed blunted by a new disenchantment: fleeting and philosophical and couched in wit, yes, but disenchantment all the same. I'd heard from someone—I couldn't remember exactly who; maybe Eloise McClatchy—that there'd been a bad breakup not long before, though in retrospect this seems too convenient an explanation for something less measurable.

We spoke for a few minutes about his Kennedy friends. Weekends on Long Island allowed his path to cross with Pritchett Pierce's and Sofi Cohen's in those first summers after undergrad, in the crush of Southampton Social or out at Surf Lodge in Montauk. Of all of them, he had remained in closest contact with Gracie Smith and Frances Evans. He told me this disinterestedly, dispelling the restraints of geography or politics with a solipsistic shrug.

"Will and I get coffee sometimes. But God, I don't think I saw Mason or Freddie once between the Five-Year and the Ten, and I haven't seen them since." The Class of 2011's tenth reunion had been held nine months prior, over a rainy and unseasonably cool weekend in May. "But, like, no serious love lost. Once I got to college I realized you could go a day without your alleged best friends making jokes about you sucking their dicks."

"See much of Annabeth?"

Mark laughed, beautifully. "Well," he said. "I'm invited to the wedding. Which surprised me, by the way, but whatever. Sofi and Gracie and Frances—they keep up with her. She's maybe moving to London, apparently. But, like, different lives now, as they say."

"What about Jack?"

And in the flippant twitch of Mark's smile I again saw the sadness. He was silent for a moment. "He's around."

"There's a girl."

"Yeah. Whatever. No comment."

I took a sip of my coffee through the hole in its disposable lid, only to realize it was empty, though the beat this gesture offered was fortunate. The last dregs were milky and cold. A police car screamed outside.

"But this is about Foster, right?" Mark asked, after the silence.

"Hence these questions."

There was another pause. "And I assume you know where that story ends?"

I crumpled up the khaki-colored paper napkin on the wooden table between us. "I haven't really decided yet."

Jack's bedroom door was closed when Foster approached it. A late freeze had rendered the softening earth intransigent again, and as he had returned from the library, pulling his scarf up over his chin and mouth, he had let himself be taken by the rhythm of its crunch beneath his feet. Delia Chissom had smiled at him airily as he waved to her upon entering; she was reading *Three Cups of Tea* and wore a caftan.

Foster hesitated, and then knocked on the door at the end of the second-floor hallway. Jack typically kept his door ajar during study hall, as if the thought of shutting himself off from the sheer potential of activity outside was distressing. Roughly once a week the evening duty master would kindly ask him to turn down his Lil Wayne. But tonight the space on the other side of the door was soundless, and the door itself was not only shut but locked.

"Yeah, one sec," Foster heard Jack say when he knocked, and after a brief shuffle on the other side, the handle clicked. Foster paused again, and when he did finally open the door, Jack was back at his desk, his face cast pale in the light of his MacBook. The cleft below his lower lip was heavy with a wad of wintergreen Skoal.

"McCall would castrate you if he knew you were locking your door," Foster smiled. "Might think the golden boy was up to no good."

Jack jerked his head in Foster's direction but did not look away from the screen. "Yeah," Jack said absently. "Just trying to do this paper for Larson's class." Foster's angle askew from the screen gave it a distorting halation, but he made out a Word document open, blank and white except for what looked like the beginning of an incomplete sentence. He felt uncomfortable.

"So," he said finally, "Mark."

"What about him."

"Well—are you surprised?" Foster found himself straining to fabricate the usual sense of casual levity, but he felt uncomfortable, or more aptly unwelcome. Jack's hair was wet from a shower, but he had not bothered to style it to its typical capillary swoop.

"I mean, not really." Jack clacked out a short string of words on his keyboard with almost aggressive force. He held the Dining Center mug on his desk to his lips and let a thick string of brown tobacco spit fall into it. "The theater thing and everything."

"How'd everyone take it?" Foster delivered this question awkwardly, reminding him as it did of his absence from the Everyone to which he referred.

"I dunno," Jack said. "Fine. It's whatever. I just don't want him to make a big deal out of it. Be gay or whatever, but spare me the details."

He had not looked at Foster since he had entered the room. Foster felt aware of his own presence standing there on the faded green carpet. The vague realization that he had been impelled there by some half-conscious motive did not elucidate what, precisely, that motive was, only that it now felt shameful in its rebuff. He looked at Jack, whose face now seemed closer to the screen, the svelte contours of his nose and chin casting the rest of it in translucent shadows. The screen's light was the color of spun candy. There was a wideness to Jack's eyes that Foster had never noticed before, and they were cistern-like in the chalky glow. It was only in his eyes that Foster suddenly understood that Jack Albright looked very young, which is to say frightened.

"Yeah," Foster said. "I get that." Another pause. "I'll let you work, though."

"Yeah, sorry, man," Jack said, finally looking up at Foster with a wan, forced smile, then returning to the papers shuffled on his desk before the laptop. "Just under the wire. We'll talk tomorrow."

Jack's room stayed silent after Foster shut its door. He listened there for a moment, unsure of what he was hoping to possibly hear. When he turned to walk down the hall to his own room, he heard the click of the lock on the handle behind him. In the darkness of his room, he felt in his gut what was either loneliness or fear: the sort made more frightening by the absence of a lucid object.

The radiator in Foster's suite was whistling airily when he flipped on the overhead lights, which suddenly felt too bright. He opened his dresser's top drawer and reached in to parse the chaotic sea of boxer shorts until he found the red sock. He pulled it out and shook it gently. The four pills fell and bounced just barely on the wood with little quick staccatos: the two peach footballs of Xanax and the canary-yellow Klonopin discs he had found in a bottle in his mother's medicine cabinet on the last night of Christmas break. He took one of the Xanax and placed it on the back of his tongue. A half-empty bottle of grape Gatorade was on his desk, left there from the prior evening; he opened it and chased the bitter tablet with the lukewarm juice. He stood there for a moment, and then undressed. The plaid Gap boxers he was wearing were old, riding up high and tight on his pale thighs after three years of wash cycles. He reached for the light switch and turned it off, then pulled his boxers down too.

The Xanax began to encroach upon him as Foster put himself beneath his tartan comforter, and as the pill's warmth insinuated itself, he reached for his BlackBerry, which spilled a sphere of ghostlike white light into the peripheral darkness.

His last text from Jack had come six hours earlier, after Jack's track practice—*going to dinner now*. With a soporific thumb Foster typed out two words: *You okay?* He pressed send, and imagined the message casting itself out into the cold ether of the night, dancing briefly with the red light of a cell tower rising high above the winter fields before falling back to earth. He imagined the screen of Jack's iPhone illuminating suddenly with a gentle vibration. He imagined the candent network of souls with secrets, alone in the warmth of their spaces as the silent rush of the world swirled unabated out in the dark winter night, these little glowing technologies reifying their loneliness by constellating it to the rest of life, like satellites or the blips of light that mark ships far on distant horizons.

He fell asleep without realizing it with his phone on his chest, waiting for the blinking light of a returned message that didn't come.

XXI.

Spring came reluctantly to the mid-Atlantic that year. Kennedy's spring break spanned three weeks across the bulk of March: Charlotte Dade would spend them in London, on a trip organized by an old tennis friend in one of the awkwardly transparent gestures of sympathy bestowed upon the recently and dramatically divorced. The fact of Foster's isolation was fine.

"Bug, this is completely on me," Charlotte had told him over the phone four evenings before his scheduled train south. He had stood in his bedroom in Brennan in a pair of Patagonia gym shorts, having just submitted his final paper for Advanced Euro to Mrs. Cline ("Speech, Press, and Truth in the Napoleonic Age").

"Mom, it's fine; I really don't—"

"But!" Her voice had the hollow timbre of speakerphone; Foster heard the opening and closing of drawers. "Your sister will be back on her break for a few days! And," she said, her voice now closer, "I've made you an appointment with Dr. Apple, on the sixteenth."

He spent his final days before break in the frenetic stretch of final exams. Finals removed Kennedians from their mundane routines, and in the days after Mark Stetson came out of the closet, Foster saw Jack only once. The Second Years took their English exam on a side court in the Field House. Foster had left the building surprised by the strut in his walk—the exam's three essay questions had all concerned *Hamlet*, which Foster had read four times—before seeing Jack's familiar red boathouse jacket many yards ahead, the black words KENNEDY LACROSSE stark against it.

"Yo!" Foster called. Jack turned as Foster jogged up to him, gambling a casual grin. The events of three nights prior had turned in

Foster's head like a strange stone; he had both fretted Jack's frigidity as a personal affront and understood, if subconsciously, that other currents pulsated through this tension.

Jack looked not angry or irritated but eminently distracted. "Yo," he said. "Good test."

"I rocked it, I think," Foster said happily. "You going back to the House? When are you getting out of here?"

"Oh, uh—" Jack turned around and looked up the path that ran from the Field House parking lot alongside the Dining Center to the girls' houses. "Leaving in a bit, but, eh, need to"—he looked around again—"grab something in the Dining Center. Left it there."

He furrowed his brow. "You good, man?"

Jack blinked twice and looked away. "Yeah, dude, no worries. Go, I'll see you back at the House in a bit."

But if Jack returned to Brennan House imminently thereafter, Foster did not see him, and when he went upstairs to Jack's room before leaving for the train station he found it empty, the suitcase typically at the foot of the bed now gone.

Foster had spent his first week and a half at home in solitude. He woke at nine against the muted light of the morning, idly fondling his tenuous erection and waiting for the accumulation of weak sunlight to pull him from the bed before swallowing his Lexapro with a palmful of water from the bathroom sink. Mist hung thinly over the yard outside. Some days, he biked to the club to hit against the ball machine, early enough in the day to minimize the risk of interaction with others. "If you're rusty, you'll need to deoxidize," Art Tierney, who coached boys' tennis, had said in an email to the prospective varsity players a week before the break. And he was: his serve was limper than he remembered, his returns to the ball machine's steady ordnance perfunctory and uncalibrated. He found himself indifferent to this.

Maggie Dade landed in Baltimore on a Wednesday. Foster sat in the kitchen, rolling himself a slender joint with the last crumbs of weed from the jar in his bedside table. He did not see the headlights of her taxi, or hear the garage's side door open.

"Well, well," his sister said. He looked up spasmodically, startled, and slid a nearby copy of *Vanity Fair* over his assembly station, sending dried flakes of weed across the marble. Maggie's smile was not unwarm.

"Hey, Mags," Foster said sheepishly.

Maggie and Foster Dade had the sort of unspoken committed partnership you'll find in two-sibling families. This is especially salient in families of divorce. Even in the most stable of homes, the presence of a single Other in early childhood lends itself to a certain subconscious fantasy of mutual defense, in which the abstractly menacing authority—the symbolic gestalt of Mom and Dad—can be assuaged by finding a bond with the closest thing the child has to an assumed sympathizer. All small children are afraid of their parents, though in the vast majority of cases this fact is conveniently repressed by, say, kindergarten. Maggie had been four when Foster was born, enough of a temporal distance to preclude the most violent squabbling you'll see in siblings closer in age. But what really mattered here was shared disposition. Like the dying elderly and certain intelligent breeds of dog, young children are almost clairvoyantly perceptive to the affective energies of things; at some point, perhaps sensing in their home the quiet tension of broken emotional circuitry, both Maggie and Foster had retreated inward, finding respite in themselves.

By early adolescence, this had materialized in Maggie Dade in an aura of cool, one admittedly aided by the fact of her beauty. At Bryn Mawr and then Andover, she not so much navigated her world as let herself be carried through it in an unconsciously understated *petit battement*. She wore sweaters that looked old and dark jeans and kept her hair—the same thin pale yellow as her mother's—knotted in a terse bun; when she spoke in class, which she did rarely, her words cut through the cotton of uncertain adolescent musings that hung over the seminar tables after their voices trailed off. She kissed boys and later slept with them but said very little about it, which made her unthreatening to girls. Those who saw her reticence as a personal insult said she was a bitch, which she took as neither an affront nor a commendation, as others would. At Amherst three different boys had likened her to Gwyneth Paltrow's Margot Tenenbaum.

"Smoking marijuana in our dear parents' house," Maggie said, resting her canvas bag against the kitchen island. "Quite the rebel you've become."

"Our dear mother's house," Foster said, letting Maggie bend over to give him a crisp kiss on his cheek.

Maggie had returned from Amherst on the closest thing to a pleasant evening Baltimore saw that month, and as they sat on the terrace's recliners with the joint, the last of the day's sun—still the oversaturated orange of winter sunsets—had seeped through the clouds, helping the illusion of spring. Maggie had pulled a bottle of merlot from the wine locker and poured it into two mugs.

"Are you as miserable as I was in my first year at Andover," Maggie said, taking a curt drag of the hand-rolled cigarette and dispassionately exhaling its smoke up in a tidy band up toward the night.

"No—I mean—yeah, sometimes," Foster said, taking the joint from her thin fingers. "I was. I have friends now, I think. But"—he took a hit, one that was too big; he felt the cannabis fill him and knew he was flirting with the dread that accompanies being too stoned—"like, sometimes I feel like I'm speaking an entirely different language. Or operating on an entirely different frequency. Than everyone around me, I mean. Whichever metaphor works."

Maggie waved this observation away. High, Foster suddenly and unwillingly recalled the family vacation to Anguilla in maybe 2006, when he was thirteen and still flooded with the disorienting hormones of early puberty, when they'd shared a room and he'd feigned sleep in order to watch her dress after an evening shower. Her thong had been black lace, her breasts small and white.

"That's boarding school," she said. "No one is real. And if you're indeed hanging out with the lacrosse boys, you've got no one to blame but yourself. It's wild the extent to which they're all sociopaths." She seemed to contemplate this for a second. "And they'll mostly grow out of it. But, yes, sociopaths. In part because they're rewarded for it. Or perhaps no one recognizes it as such. When no one's real, the collective lens is weird."

The last of the syrupy sun was falling into the barren branches of the yard's peripheral trees; it suddenly made Foster vaguely queasy.

Behind them, the automatic floodlights above the kitchen doors came on, dancing off the blackness of the cold swimming pool.

"But," Maggie said, lifting her mug of wine to her lips, "there's this girl, you say?"

Foster blushed, not wanting to talk about it. Annabeth was in St. Barth's with her parents and her brother, Charlie, for spring break; at night, he found himself flipping in his phone to the last text she'd sent him before taking off from Newark. ("gtg taking off pray we don't crash x_x")

"She's, like, a friend, but I dunno, maybe it's more," Foster said, not looking at his sister. "Smart as fuck, though, and funny and real—not like her friends. Her friends—her friends are cunts."

Maggie smiled. "My advice would be to proceed with extreme caution," she said. "The 'smart' ones, the 'real' ones, in those cliques—you'd be surprised how fine they ultimately are with just being another member of the oligarchy. They aren't going to give up what they've got, even if they wouldn't admit it."

Foster said nothing. And then Maggie's BlackBerry, forgotten on the small glass table between them, started to buzz. "Oh, fuck," she said, looking at it. "It's Dad."

A whippoorwill sang plaintively from a far-off yard. "I'm not here," Foster said, looking intensely at the darkening surface waters of the swimming pool.

Maggie didn't seem to hear him.

"Hi, Daddy," she said with a sad smile. Foster found himself thinking about the crude, frustrating depiction of telephone calls in film and television. *Why does the person talking only take a second or two between saying things?* reads one entry from June 2004 in the red spiral notebook he kept in the final analog pre-Blogspot days. *It's like they're not actually talking to someone. It doesn't seem real.*

"Yeah, we're both here," Maggie was saying. "Finals exhausted me, but it's nice to be home. I'm fully intent on sleeping in."

A pause.

"Yeah, you too. I'd like that," Maggie said, her smile sadder now. "Yeah, he is. Do you want to talk to him?"

Foster felt again how stoned he was, his soma flinching with heat with the imminent flares of anxiety. *No*, he mouthed at his sister, hoping his eyes conveyed his urgency. *I'm too fucking stoned.*

"Yeah, I'll put him on," Maggie said into the phone. *Sorry*, she mouthed back. "Yeah, I love you too, Daddy." She extended the phone to Foster. The glow of its screen was gentle in the darkness.

Fuck you, Foster mouthed at Maggie, who shrugged regretfully. A moment passed and he took the phone, placing it to his ear. He felt himself stand.

"Hello," Foster said, his voice heavy and affectless.

"Hey, buddy," the voice on the other end said, stilted with a tentative appeal to gentleness. "It's been a minute."

Foster felt himself turn away from his sister and approach the glass door. "Yeah," he said to his father. "Been busy."

He opened the door to the kitchen, bright with yellow light, and stepped inside. The air-conditioned air felt prickly. "I believe it," Jim Dade said. "I'd love to hear everything about school."

"I've been there for seven months now," Foster said, refusing to situate his eyes on any point in the gleaming room. "Suddenly interested?"

A pause on the other end. "I wanted to give you your room, bud."

"And Mom couldn't have filled you in? Or have you not summoned the balls to apologize to her yet?"

In a different moment, before things happened, Foster knew his father would have instinctively blanched in anger at this, with the vein that arced beneath his thinning brown hair becoming tumescent—it's not just a cliché, this phenomenon. For Jim Dade, rage was a silent, seething detachment, a moving atmosphere of unspoken hatred. *Hey, buddy*: there is a reason Foster flinched at this line. Jim's thinning hair had always been sparser and darker than his son's. They had been in Anguilla for the week after Christmas when Foster, then eight years old and happily brown from the Caribbean sun, had climbed into the villa's shower after his father to rinse the salt from his body before dinner. He noticed the spare black strings that had veneered themselves in sloppy wet twists to the white porcelain.

"Daddy's going bald," Foster had cheerfully announced to his family as he emerged from the bathroom with wet hair, an oversized white towel wrapped just below the sternum of his sinewy juvenile body. The paranoid modesty of early pubescence was still four years away. The shower's hot water had elicited the day's sunburn, which was the color of mottled roses. Charlotte had cackled at this, her laugh liberated and sharpened by the chardonnay she drank from a vacationware plastic glass.

"You are losing your hair, Daddy," Maggie, then twelve and with the earliest budding of breasts making unsightly contours in her tank top, said thoughtfully. Charlotte cackled again.

"Should we see if they sell Rogaine over the counter here?" she crowed, holding her wine. But the seeming joviality of Maggie's and Charlotte's comments only slid across the surface of a darker heaviness, like droplets of oil on still water. Jim sat on the couch perpendicular to his wife's, holding a martini. He was closest in the room to Foster, though his back was to his son, facing the glass doors looking out over the beach. Foster's announcement had recalibrated the atmospheric dimensions of the room between the poles of father and son, with the still tension of the thunderheads that were growing out over the bay beyond their living room.

"Hey, buddy," Jim had said, the calmness of his voice straining beneath the vitriol it lashed down. Children, like certain animals, can sense the incipience of violence.

"Sorry, Dad, I just saw—"

Jim shifted to face his son. His rising hairline revealed the shapeless artery that crossed his right temple, like a thin collapsed sausage. The exposed peripheries of his scalp were red from the sun; his eyes were dark. With a violent intimation of a smile, he reached out for the knot of his son's towel and snatched the cloth away.

"Like father, like son," he said, pointing at the hairless white space above Foster's penis, which the boy had instinctively clasped with two hands, his knees buckling and his torso bending inward to conceal his nakedness.

"Jim!" Charlotte had cried. Maggie was silent.

"Oh, come on," Jim had said, lobbing the towel in the direction of his son's midsection, not looking at him. "We're just goofing off."

A fact of human evolution: the intensity of the worst humiliations precludes the clarity of memory-making. Foster would look back on that event perhaps only three or four times across the remainder of his life, with the masochistic temerity of a boy holding his fingers to a scalding stove; indeed, it was nearly a decade before the event even availed itself to his memory. Jim's hair continued to thin, and at tennis matches Foster would look to the stands and locate the baldness of his father's head in the white sodium of the lights overhead. ("He really outdid you," Jim told Foster on one drive home, after a match with a wiry Indian boy whose game was one of stoic determination. "And a guy who spends all his time studying for the spelling bee, too. Eesh.")

"Listen, buddy," Jim said now, and Foster could hear the old strains of violence, but then his father paused. "I'm not trying to fight with you. I don't like what's happened, and I—I want to make it right." Another pause. "And I resent this attitude you're taking against me."

Because he was stoned, Foster's fury became thick in its abstraction, dense without making its emotional edge legible. Foster slammed his sister's phone on its face against the marble countertop.

"Jesus, Foster!" Maggie cried. Foster blinked, rudderless. He turned the phone over. A rhizomatic crack split the blackened screen like a river delta. Smaller fractures from the longer fissure gave the illusion of eddies and islets in the splintered shards of synthetic glass they fragmented. Foster impulsively thumbed one from its bed, revealing the patchwork grid of flat copper circuitry beneath it.

"Fucking stop it," Maggie said, snatching the phone and holding down the red telephone key. The extant screen came to white life, but the fracture smeared its pixelated coastline with a miasma of illegible colors. Foster could barely discern the digital clock that presided above the BlackBerry's home screen; it was either 8:46 or 9:46 in the evening.

"You made me talk to him," he muttered, not looking at his sister.

In the winter months that had ensued since their last meeting, Dr. Apple had apparently set out to grow a beard. The result was grotesque: it wasn't so much a dearth of follicles as the sickliness of what they produced that gave the psychiatrist's tanned fleshy face the appearance of a long-rotten vegetable; the pale, oddly reddish fibers seemed less to grow from his face than on it. He wore the same oversized plastic eyeglasses, now primarily associated with the dated eggheadedness of the late millennium's pedophilic serial killers.

"So—the Lexapro," Dr. Apple said from across the plastic faux-mahogany surface of his desk, looking down at the contents of a manila file folder with an inadvertently eerie half-smile. The repugnant growth of hair around the corners of his mouth seemed to move with it, taking almost sentient form. "How's that working out."

"Uh—I think fine," Foster said. "But"—and he had rehearsed this in his head on the bicycle ride uptown that morning—"I'm still kind of panicky sometimes, and I've used up all the Xanax you gave me. Which I think proved really helpful, even though"—and this was the line whose edge of guilelessness he had turned over in his mind most cautiously—"I don't love the way it makes me feel always, like groggy."

Dr. Apple nodded to himself. "So I'll give you more Xanax"—Foster's gut lurched with the triumph of a successful deceit—"and maybe we should up your Lexapro to twenty milligrams, or perhaps move you to another SSRI more efficacious for anxiety—Celexa, maybe."

"Okay," Foster said evenly.

"And what about the Adderall?"

"Well—I actually never tried it," Foster said. This was honest. He had filled the prescription at CVS in the final days of Christmas break, and back home he had watched the tide of chalky peach disks slide against the amber against his bedroom's desk lamp before placing the bottle on the dresser. Later, in the throes of the Lexapro-sanctioned renaissance that radiated well beyond his schoolwork—he thought of sitting in the booth at Vito's with Annabeth and Jack, snow falling wonderfully against the umbrella of the streetlights outside—the Adderall's nameless promise seemed less urgent, and the bottle had gathered dust.

But Dr. Apple frowned at this news. "Has your academic performance continued to suffer?"

"Um—I mean, I feel less distracted by my anxiety, so I've been able to focus," Foster said. "I haven't gotten my winter quarter grades back, though. But my housemaster at Kennedy says other teachers have commented on my improvements." (This was true: Scott McCall had pulled Foster aside one evening at check-in three weeks prior and told him how much Mrs. Cline had enjoyed his midterm paper, and to "keep trucking on.")

Dr. Apple frowned again. "What about your emotions—do you feel impulsive or volatile, like you can't keep your feelings to yourself?"

Foster paused, thinking about Maggie's BlackBerry screen. "You're fucking paying for this," she had said to him, opening the door to his bedroom an hour after he hit the phone against the countertop, before slamming the door behind her and leaving the residually stoned boy alone prostrate atop his bed. She had been chilly to him that morning, but despite her silence made them both coffee.

"Uh—actually, yeah, I've been kind of temperamental," Foster said. "Not angry or anything, at least not all the time, but—yeah, I get pissed off."

Dr. Apple looked up across the desk. *Everything in his office is a variation on the ugliest shade of brown*, Foster wrote on his Blogspot that night. *Or orange, when it's plastic. It's like he never left 1983.* "You see, Foster," Dr. Apple said. He spoke with the patronizing pretense to concern you witness in physicians who fail to see teenagers and young adults as anything other than physically larger children. "That's more a symptom of ADHD than anything. And I'm not thrilled that you didn't try taking the Adderall at my advice, but I wonder if a more rigorous treatment regimen might be worthwhile."

"More rigorous?" Foster asked, feeling his impatience stir. The events of the prior evening had cast over him a patina of guilt; his psychiatrist's words now affirmed Foster's suspicion that his temperamental constitution was somehow defective. "And—since when do I officially have ADHD?"

"Well, there's a very new drug called Vyvanse," Dr. Apple said, ignoring the second question. "The FDA just approved it a couple of months ago. It's like Adderall, but it works longer, throughout the day, and it isn't as pronounced. I'm wondering if we might want to try it out."

My biggest fear isn't just becoming a cliché, but the fact that I'm weirdly okay with it, his blog entry that evening read. More than okay— it's like I subconsciously believe that being a fucked-up, medicated teenager somehow makes me interesting. Even when I acknowledge that this is a gross mindset, I'm still stuck with the mindset itself. I'm not a jock or conventionally hot; it's like the only worthwhile person- ality that fits is the personality of the poorly adjusted druggie misfit in therapy. I wonder if I would care as much if I wasn't so hung up on making Annabeth think I'm cool. God, I fucking hate that word. And I hate that I care about it.

"Yeah, sure," Foster heard himself saying to Dr. Apple. "Let's give it a whirl."

XXII.

In a marriage of her family's secularism and her own vanity, Sofi Cohen had declined to have a Bat Mitzvah. "I grew up in New York," she explained to me later. "Even at Brearley there was, like, one every other week in seventh grade, and that's not even counting the kids from other schools. Why just be a number?" Donald Cohen, who in 1977 had been among the first of the Jews to graduate from Kennedy, was a senior litigator at Skadden, Arps, Slate, Meagher & Flom whose adoration of his only daughter was in many respects an exercise in narcissistic projection. He reveled in the prosecutorial vigor he ascribed to her; in July 2005, when twelve-year-old Sofi assaulted Don and Rhona Cohen over a summer dinner in Southampton with a meticulous case for a Sweet Sixteen party as an alternative to a ceremony "that's really only about the after-party anyway," he had clasped his hands with paternal vim and promised his wife that he would explain away the heresy to her parents in Palm Beach.

She was sharp, her father was right about that, and almost three years to the date after her opening argument she emailed her parents a Word document listing feasible weekends the following spring when her city friends and school friends and camp friends could convene in Manhattan at one of the seventeen venues she enumerated in detail *cf*. Sofi turned sixteen in the first week of spring break in 2009, and ultimately opted for a celebration in the weeks thereafter, when the warming spring would permit her to wear the sheer pink Givenchy dress she had selected for herself at Bergdorf Goodman. *APRIL 18*, she had sent in two separate groups on BlackBerry Messenger that December—Annabeth, Frances, Gracie, and Porter comprising one; "brearley bitchez" being the other. *got dad to rent out a lounge in nolita—the whole thing I.e. dont have to worry About id. obvs wont be serving booze but we can pregame HARDDDDD.*

When journalists in the subsequent years would attempt to piece together the story of Foster Dade's enterprise, the narratives they produced would conspicuously fail to identify any concrete point of origin, as if Foster had simply arrived at Kennedy with his pharmaceutical operation already fully matured. This is to say that the events of April 18, 2009, eluded them. In fairness to the reporters in question, the significance of these events also seemed to escape those who'd participated in them. When I met Sofi recently, over drinks in the East Village, her surprise seemed sincere.

"Oh my God, was that when?" Sofi exclaimed. In the years since she'd left Cornell, quadweekly morning sessions at Barry's Bootcamp and the Bryant Park Equinox had resolved the illusion of thickness imposed by her large breasts; she sat before me looking almost deliberately svelte, her keratin-glossed hair sleek and at last chemically deprived of the frizz she had spent hours punishing with a comb before a mirror in the second-floor bathroom of Hewitt House. "Jesus. I mean, we were all so fucked up that night, and I had, like, bigger fish to fry, keeping my parents distracted and everyone happy, but wow!" Her place in the mythology seemed to delight her.

The embossed invitation had arrived in Foster's campus mailbox in the final week of the winter quarter. He had spent those early months of his friendship with Annabeth and Jack—and with the rest of them only by association—deeply uncertain of its stability; when Gracie or

Mark made passing references to "Sofi's party," a nausea had erupted in him. *I'd actually be pretty crushed if I didn't get an invite, I won't lie,* he wrote on his Blogspot on March 2, 2009. *It shouldn't matter but it does.*

He kept his triumphalism at receiving the invitation, which he pulled from its envelope in the mailroom to find gilded letters stenciled into pale rose stock (*MR. AND MRS. DONALD COHEN OF MANHATTAN WARMLY INVITE YOU TO A SWEET SIXTEEN CELEBRATION FOR THEIR DAUGHTER, SOFI . . .*), to himself. This proved to be the prudent decision, because by nightfall, he had ascertained that Sofi had invited not only Foster but roughly half of their class and a third of the class above. "Dude," he heard the pimply Will Bartholomew telling his baseball teammate in line for the salad bar at dinner, "everyone's gonna be so fucked up. No curfew. Think about how sloppy the chicks will be."

"They're gonna need something stronger than booze if they're gonna get with your nasty ass."

Don Cohen's allegiance to his high school alma mater had taken the form of pronounced fiscal generosity, and in February of that year, shortly before invitations went out, he concluded a visit to Kennedy's development office with a stop by the chambers of Theresa Daniels, Dean of Students. Since her appointment to the office two years prior, Daniels had redoubled and fine-tuned the deanship's disciplinary mandate with a cold autocratic gusto, but even she knew where the buck stopped at Kennedy, and Don Cohen's visit to the development office had been financially productive and made known to her. So she listened with tight lips as he persuaded her to allow him to hire a charter bus to pick up the partygoers at Kennedy on the Saturday afternoon of the party and return them to campus from Manhattan upon its conclusion later that evening, well beyond the night's ordained eleven o'clock check-in. "And of course Rhona and I won't tolerate any drinking, or any other . . . nonsense," he told her, with the sharkish charisma that he had recently brought to the federal courthouse in lower Manhattan, to argue for British Petroleum's exculpation in the oil spill that decimated the Gulf of Mexico.

The coach would accommodate only sixty-three adolescents; Sofi had invited roughly eighty-five from Kennedy. She denies it today, but this seems less a faulty counting job than a strategic machination—one, the cynical argument would go, that undermined Sofi's apparent social benevolence. Kennedians from New York City could utilize their Away Weekend privileges to spend the night with their parents uptown, and invite their friends to stay with them. It was a boon on a practical level—they could get fucked up without the worry of their bleary-eyed housemaster catching vodka on their breaths upon their 2:00 a.m. return—but it is also difficult to ignore the political optics, whereby the Haves once again seemed in possession of a unique code inaccessible and inscrutable to the Have-Nots. The Have-Nots, with their awkward makeup smeared or their Old Navy khakis wrinkled, would climb back into the bus's cramped seats to marvel, sober, at how cool their night in the Big Apple had been, watching the ember-like glow of Newark's oil refineries passing them on the Turnpike. The Haves' nights, meanwhile, would just be starting, privileged to something that affirmed their placement over the pitiable masses.

This is both an allegory and an account of what happened that night.

Foster had spent the two and a half weeks of spring break thinking more than he would have liked of Sofi's party. With a certain interpretive license, we might rephrase this to say that he was thinking of Jack. He had returned to Kennedy on the northbound Amtrak on the afternoon before the start of spring term classes. The unseasonable chilliness left him uneasy, and so did the timidity of the early spring light, which was nearly gone from the colorless sky, now dark, when he opened the door to his suite in Brennan. "Yo, Jae," he called in the direction of his roommate's door, before opening his own and switching on the desk lamp. The smallness of his room made him feel sorry for himself. He had not spoken to Jack or Annabeth since the start of break, which after Maggie's departure for Amherst he had spent in the grim quietude of the house. He had glumly lobbed his L.L.Bean duffel bag onto the foot of his bed when he felt a body entering behind him.

"Hello, hello!"

It wasn't Jae but Jack, whose windburned complexion made him seem taller. His hair seemed longer, too, pushed back from his forehead and hardened with dried sweat. He wore sweatpants and his lacrosse jacket, his face flushed with the heady glow. He had spent spring break in Deer Valley, and he returned to Kennedy with the chapped glow of a ski tan, his eyes bright within the pale rings of skin that his goggles had occluded from the alpine sun.

"Just got done with our last preseason practice," Jack said, gesturing to the lacrosse stick he'd propped against the wall outside Foster's door. A Kennedian more veteran than Foster would know that the members of the lacrosse team kept the entirety of their gear in their designated locker room on the Field House's second floor—a gift from a former midfielder who'd launched a hedge fund—and that those players who carried their sticks with them around campus, cradling imaginary balls as they walked from class to lunch, were doing so for reasons of show. "I've been here since fucking Tuesday, out there dawn 'til sunset." He gestured in the direction of the lacrosse pitch, a stark square of meticulously maintained Astroturf, beyond the darkening shadows of the lawn overlooking the pond. "Long fucking time, bud!"

He threw his arms around Foster. "Nice to see you too, Albright," Foster said, smiling inside.

They'd walked to Vito's soon thereafter, and Foster had quietly delighted in a normalcy that felt effervescent in its return. "You should have come to the city!" Pritchett Pierce told him, picking up a curly fry. "I did fuck all. Slept and jerked off."

Gracie Smith lobbed a crouton at him. "Gross." She sat immediately next to Foster, who realized this was the closest he'd been physically to her; he slid himself uncomfortably against the wall.

"Pritchett spent a month in London last summer, and now he thinks it's okay to say things like 'fuck all' and 'bloke,' " Annabeth explained, teasing him with her smile. The sunshine of St. Barth's hadn't graced her as much as infused her very aura, her radiance like the warmth itself.

"Hey, I'm technically British," Pritchett said through a mouthful of mushed fry.

"Doesn't a statute of limitations apply if your family came over on the *Mayflower*?" asked Jack, who had pulled a chair to the head of the booth.

"You tell me. Yours did too."

"True," Jack said thoughtfully, reaching over and taking a fry. Foster felt at ease again; Gracie's iciness alone somehow seemed less maleficent without its masculine foil in Mason Pretlow's scowling contempt. *He's an unhappy person*, Annabeth's refrain echoed. *And sometimes I think maybe Jack is too.*

"Oh!" Pritchett slapped his wide palms onto the booth's green vinyl surface. "Speaking of the city, by the way. Sofi's party. Stay with me." He looked to Jack and then to Foster. "My parents are cool with it. Mason and Freddie and Will are, too."

"And I'm being forced to stay with the girls now that the boys know I'm a *homo*," Mark said as he sat down with his pizza, singing the last word.

"I told you, Stetson—you can stay with me if you agree to suck all of our dicks." There was an amicable mischief in Pritchett's grin.

"Careful what you wish for."

"Where are the boys, by the way." Gracie's bored monotone tended to preclude the inflection of the question mark.

"With their hoes," Pritchett said. Gracie threw another crouton at him, which he deflected with the back of his hand. "Well, no, Will's studying, natch, but Freddie's with that random freshman from the last dance, Laura whatever—"

"Lauren," Annabeth corrected. "Lauren Brewer."

"Lauren Brewer, and Mason's off persuading Porter to surrender her virginity."

"They're still hooking up?" Foster asked.

Gracie snorted. "What you don't know," she said softly to his left, "could fill a book."

Foster blushed, ashamed of what he now felt to be his empty presumption of camaraderie. Annabeth frowned at her. "It's a weird thing," she said, shrugging. "Porter likes him but won't admit it, and Mason—well, I don't know that Mason's capable of liking anyone, but he keeps doing it, for whatever reason."

"Whatever. Anyway"—Pritchett waved away Annabeth's words impatiently—"city. Sofi's party. My place. Train up Saturday after classes. Train back Sunday. Booze. Night on the town. Girls stay with Sofi. Boys with me." He grinned mischievously at Gracie. "Officially, at least."

"Color me there," Jack said, grinning.

"Yeah, totally," Foster said. *We're cool again*, he would write later that night. *Whatever was plaguing Jack before break seems to have resolved, and I don't think it had to do with me.*

The six boys had claimed the two rows of facing seats at the end of the double-decker car's lower level, which was quiet for a Saturday. Jack pulled an old Dasani bottle from his backpack, its contents the color of bad frying oil.

"What the fuck," Pritchett said, "is that?"

"Vodka. And Arnold Palmer." With a grin, Jack unscrewed the cap and took a pull from the bottle, grimacing as he swallowed. "I brought it back from break. In the event of an emergency." He handed the bottle to Foster, who consciously took a longer pull than Jack's. He felt the old somatic warmth crawling through him, and at once a tension dissipated; the afternoon, which held the sun behind its clouds, seemed somehow more mirthful.

"Maybe don't hog it," Mason said, reaching for the bottle without looking him in the eyes.

Jack took the final draining swig as the train pulled out of New Brunswick. The boys were buzzed but not quite drunk. The symphony of their mirth—Jack impersonating the adenoidal Rosalie Haddish mid-coitus; Freddie regaling them with the tale of an alleged threesome with two Swiss models in a Zermatt steam room—drew the irritated side-glances of a tired-looking couple four rows forward. It was the flow of the lukewarm booze, but also the ecstatic thrill that is the boarding school student's night in the city. Of course, this itself is only a very bourgeois subgenre of a more universal thing—those dizzy flights of euphoria that lift certain various newnesses of adolescence, when the whole world has a shimmer of possibility and we are all our own main characters. Foster realized he was grinning. He sat next to Jack against the window, watching New Jersey take new forms as the gray afternoon light commenced its earliest diminuendo.

The hazy glow of the Empire State Building was distinguishing itself over Secaucus's tepid wetlands as Foster felt his phone buzz twice against his side. He pulled it from his jacket pocket to see two BlackBerry Messenger notifications from Annabeth. He frantically thumbed in his password, 0419, which was his birthday, which was the following day.

> **ALW [04:17PM]:** omg hi
> **ALW [04:18PM]:** where the hell are you

Foster could feel Jack's eyes casting over the little screen. "Flirty flirty," Jack sang.

> **foster d [04:19PM]:** On the train yo
> **foster d [04:19PM]:** Nealry in the city
> **foster d [04:20PM]:** Nearly***
> **foster d [04:20PM]:** What about y'all. At Sofi's yet?

A pause.

> **ALW [04:22PM]:** yeah yeah, already drinking lolz. lets meet before the party???

The heat of the vodka still in his nerves, Foster felt brave.

> **foster d [04:24PM]:** For sure.
> **foster d [04:25PM]:** I know it's Sofi's night but I hope you brought me a birthday present . . .

The subsequent pause seemed to fill the shaking railcar, which was approaching its slide down into the long tunnel across the Hudson. Then the BlackBerry buzzed within Foster's hand, which he realized was clammy.

ALW [04:28PM]: i guess you'll have to wait and see :)

Like the expanse of Midtown Manhattan above them, the gray fluorescent catacombs of Penn Station already teemed that decade with the sensorium of a dying empire in denial. Beneath its low dirty ceilings, the anonymous masses of labor pushed along to their transits, a shifting hive of faces pallid and tired. A Macedonian tourist had vomited beneath the cerulean sign of the Hudson Books on the upper concourse; navigating the countercurrent of outbound commuters, the boys sidestepped the South Asian employee who was covering the carroty spill of sick with an old *Wall Street Journal*. The clotted noise from the hapless intercom system overhead announced a delay on the northbound train somewhere, sometime.

"It's really fucking depressing, isn't it," Jack was saying as they stepped from the chute-like escalator to Penn Station's main concourse, pivoting to avoid a pink-haired woman with a faceless infant against her chest. "The greatest city in the world, and this is your introduction to it."

"The airports aren't any better," Pritchett said evenly, looking straight ahead. For those who grew up above Fifty-Ninth Street, as Pritchett had, their New York City tends to be a sanitized one. Their imperviousness to the homeless schizophrenic's wails or the Pepsi bottles of urine along the sidewalks when they go shopping for slacks with their mother in Midtown finds sustenance in the safe knowledge of the uptown refuges to which at day's end they will retreat.

They shoved themselves into two taxis beneath the neon climbs of Midtown. Going north on Park, Foster watched the broken red numbers of the meter climb upward, and tried to remember the balance on his Bank of America debit card. Beyond the windows, the dirty glow resolved itself into the statelier geometry of the East Side along Central Park.

Pritchett had nonchalantly slid a silver American Express through the mounted credit card console as the cab pulled to the curb on East Seventy-Third, and it was with the same indifference that he'd helped himself to a bottle of red wine and a handle of George Dickel from the butler pantry off his parents' kitchen upstairs.

He held the bottles before the boys in his bedroom with his arms outstretched. "Oh, let's fucking *go!*" Jack had hooted. Mr. and Mrs. Pierce did not seem to mind, nor did they seem especially interested in the flock of teenage boys their youngest son had ushered off the elevator into their foyer earlier that afternoon. Catharine Pierce was the first person Foster had met whom he could describe truthfully as bony. her coiffed hair, the artificial hay yellow of middle-aged women, seemed too large for her emaciated head, which seemed to wobble on a body lost beneath a muumuu-like shawl. The darting of her eyes was nervous.

"Your father's sleeping," Mrs. Pierce had said to her auburn-headed son, whose affable insouciance suddenly seemed somehow sad. It wasn't yet eight o'clock.

"Mom, you know everyone but Foster, so this is Foster Dade. Foster, this is my mom."

Mrs. Pierce seemed repulsed by the hand that Foster outstretched toward her, finally taking it not with a shake but a brief clasp. Foster heard Mason, behind him on the elevator, stifle a snort, and his face burned.

"Thanks for having us, Mrs. Pierce," Foster said determinedly. "It's really nice to be here."

Mrs. Pierce appeared in that moment to not understand English, smiling thinly at her son's friend before turning—teetering—back into the home. The Pierces' apartment occupied half of the top floor of a twelve-floor building between Park and Madison. The Manhattan bourgeoisie is a hermetic entity, and Foster had little idea of what to expect of one of its homes: he'd thought of Patrick Bateman's minimalist gallery-like space in *American Psycho*, but stepping into the Pierces' apartment he remembered *Metropolitan*, which he had watched with Maggie two summers prior. In terms of aesthetic taste, the apartment was not drastically different from his parents' own colonial in Baltimore: old oriental rugs along hardwood floors; oak moldings that were elegantly unostentatious; along the walls, family photos within silver frames that only an affluent buyer of such accoutrements would recognize as expensive.

Pritchett's bedroom was the last off of a long hall; across from it were the undisturbed rooms of his older brother, who was a freshman at Princeton, and sister, two years above him at Harvard. "Okay," Pritchett said, opening these two doors. "Um—Freddie and Mason, you take Everett's. Will, you can sleep on my floor, or in the bed with me, no homo, and Albright and Dade"—Pritchett opened the last door—"y'all share Cecily's."

The light of the day was graying as they gathered in Pritchett's child-hood bedroom, and the dark windows danced with the orange sodium of the streetlights and headlamps twelve stories below. They were passing the whiskey and merlot among themselves, young enough to not mind the sickly discord of the two spirits in their stomachs. Foster had chosen carefully a green J.Crew sweater over an old plaid Brooks Brothers oxford; he worried his jeans looked too pedestrian. It was a quarter past eight.

"God," Jack murmured, standing before Pritchett's mirror. "I look fucking great." He studiously buttoned his periwinkle Vineyard Vines oxford, and after a moment of pensive thought, he unfastened two buttons below his Adam's apple.

"*Miami Vice*." Foster smiled.

"Be careful, or you might get Mark coming after you tonight," said Freddie Pieters, who wore a silken black button-down over dark jeans.

"Where is Mark, anyway?" Mason asked, without interest. He was lying flat on the flannel duvet over Pritchett's bed; his hand stretched beneath the waistband of his chinos, fondling his testicles both idly and conspicuously.

"He's getting ready with"—here Jack inflected an effete lilt, throwing his hand out with a loose wrist—"the *girls*."

"Well, he's one of them now," Mason said, shifting his hand within his boxer shorts.

"Oh, come on," Will Thierry said, examining a pimple on his chin in the reflection of his phone's black screen. "Don't be a dick about that."

"If Mark ends up back here he can—well, he can decidedly have the floor," Pritchett replied.

"I'm just saying," Mason began. "Be queer or whatever. But don't, like, impose it on me." *I think you're flattering yourself a bit*, Foster wanted to say, looking with incipient disdain at the pug-faced boy who seemed for whatever reason to despise him. Foster knew from a slapdash archive of gossip that among them only Freddie and Mason were no longer virgins. Mason engaged his world with a silent leer, and his own sexual mythos flourished secondhand, stylized by the dark veneer of dubious facticity. He had purportedly received his first blowjob in seventh grade, from a ninth grader at Potomac, and lost his virginity to her best friend the summer thereafter. Months prior, Foster had overheard Harris Adelstein telling Andrew O'Donnell that "the Pretlow kid" kept two Post-it notes in his desk drawer in Ames House: one on which he enumerated the "five or six" virginities he had taken; another naming those girls he deemed "worthy targets."

"Let's all support each other's unique journeys," Jack said in an uncanny impersonation of Delia Chissom. "You have any luck yet, Pierce?"

Pritchett remained engrossed in the shirts hanging in his closet, now turning their breast pockets inside out. "I swear, it's in here somewhere," he muttered. "There's no way it could have—"

"What are you looking for?" Foster asked with attempted casualness.

"Coke," Jack said simply.

"Cocaine," Freddie cooed.

"The devil's dandruff," Pritchett said, turning to his friends from his hapless search. "My brother gave me a baggie over Christmas. I bet the fucking maid took it."

"You do blow, Dade?" Mason asked from his bored recline.

Foster blushed. "Eh—nah," he said. "I mean, haven't tried it." Then, quickly: "I fuck with other stuff—weed and a little Xanax."

"Badass," Mason dripped.

"Dade is low-key Brennan's biggest stoner," Jack said, putting an arm around Foster's shoulder.

"I have some, actually, in my backpack," Foster said, ashamed of the desperation in his voice. *It's like I subconsciously believe that*

being a fucked-up, medicated teenager somehow makes me interesting.
"If we want to blaze."

"Ask me at three a.m.," Freddie said. "But, fuck, if we're going to be out late—we need something to pump us up. If not blow then we need to score Adderall or something."

"I have Adderall."

The five boys all turned to Foster.

"You do?" Jack asked, with surprise.

"Yeah—Adderall and this other thing, longer lasting. Vyvanse. I'm, like, prescribed."

"You are?"

"I've actually never used it, but—yeah, my psychiatrist in Baltimore says I have ADHD." Foster resented the cadence of authority he heard edge into the words *my psychiatrist.*

"Since when have you been fucking prescribed Adderall?" Jack crowed. "You've been holding out on us, Dade."

Foster grinned what felt like a bashful grin.

By then, it was fairly evident that Foster Dade's physiochemical relationship with substances was already in the gestational stages of its grim trajectory. The mentally typical teenage boy, no matter how curious or sad, does not steal benzodiazepines from his mother's medicine cabinet, at least not more than once, and while some do embark on a touristic affair with solitary and daily weed smoking, the unsustainability of this practice—the consequent anxiety, ennui, and general feeling of cellular queasiness—manifests itself quickly; this is why so many high school stoners abandon the stuff altogether by the end of adolescence. So we might wonder why the temptation of curiosity had not inclined him to try the ADHD medication, but less so why he filled the prescription that he remained unconvinced—embarrassed, even—he needed.

"ADHD" is a synonym for "fuckup." I'm fucked up, but I'm not a fuckup, he had written on his Blogspot over break. *And I'm smart. That's my one thing: I'm smart. I can do my work when I want. I don't need to be treated as an intellectual defective.*

"Beggars can't be choosers," Mason said, sitting up. For what may have been the first time, he looked Foster in the eyes. "Do you have the long-release capsule things or the little powdery pills?"

"Both," Foster reiterated. Then, with more bravery than it should have required: "Experienced in the stuff, are you?"

"Younger sister used to have it. We'd do it at parties in middle school." Mason had returned to neglecting Foster's gaze. "Y'can crush the fast-acting pills into powder and snort them like lines."

"You down, bro?" Freddie was looking at Foster.

"You guys are animals," Will Thierry said, taking a sip from what was still his first cup of wine, poured into one of the Pierces' coffee mugs.

"Little Willie thinks he won't be student body president if he doesn't live by the Boy Scout code."

"Fuck off."

"Dare you to have more than a single beer tonight, Will."

"Two-Sip Thierry."

"Suck my dick."

"Too bad Mark's not here," Mason sneered.

"So," Jack said, turning to Foster, who was still under his arm. He smelled like Old Spice. "Down to spare a few?"

"Fuck it," Foster said. "Let's."

The stillness of the night in Cecily Pierce's bedroom hiccupped with the glide of taxi lights passing below as Foster stepped inside to where he'd left his backpack. As he dug through it past pencils and folded boxer shorts for the plastic vial of Adderall, the discordant *Nachtmusik* of the city rose up from the streets and avenues to press almost incidentally against the windows. In the darkness Foster could not make out the contours of the bedroom, but that itself brought the space the strange comfort he found in it: the sense that he was safe, that he belonged. He felt the sense of the cosmos turning slowly overhead, and the warmth the world seemed to be proferring. It made him sad, and when he felt his hand clasp the Adderall bottle—slightly smaller than the Vyvanse's—he had the urge to cry. But he blinked and forgot it.

It seems fair to say that Foster would have been far more inclined to try the pills if he had known how good they made him feel. Both Adderall and Vyvanse are variations on the same neurochemical fantasia; in layman's terms, they're stimulants. Uppers. Speed. The *DSM* first included Attention Deficit Disorder among its recognized diagnoses in its third edition, published in 1980—replacing *DSM* II's "Hyperkinetic Reaction of Childhood"—and for a decade and a half thereafter, the market for medical treatment of the condition was monopolized by methylphenidate, which we know as Ritalin. It was in February 1996 that the FDA's Center for Drug Evaluation and Research gave Shire the nod to manufacture amphetamine salts under the brand name Adderall.

By the end of the Clinton administration, Ritalin prescriptions were mostly being reserved for small children and adults with histories of substance abuse: two demographics united in their acute vulnerability to the sway of the newer alternative. The vast majority of patients with ADHD or its nonhyperactive sibling were being prescribed Adderall: first in the basic, quick-acting amphetamine salt form, which was rebranded as Adderall IR (Immediate Release) upon the introduction in 2001 of the longer-lasting Extended Release (XR) capsules. Per one industry study, nine of the ten patients whose doctors had transitioned them from Ritalin to Adderall during this period claimed emphatically to be happy about it.

It's not really that difficult to understand why. Contrary to the hefty promises in the advertisements taken out in *Time* and *Home & Garden* during the Reagan years, a ten-milligram Ritalin pill is basically comparable in efficacy and duration to a Big Gulp of iced coffee. As far as accelerators of the nervous system go, Ritalin is crude oil; you'll feel your heart racing more than anything. Amphetamines, on the contrary, are a symphony. Whereas Ritalin simply keeps your brain's neurotransmitters alight and moving, Adderall drops a *Deepwater Horizon*–caliber oil rig on your prefrontal cortex, for two to fourteen hours mining its recesses for lodes of dopamine and norepinephrine that otherwise lie dormant.

And in this time you fucking prosper. You do not defy the metaphysical gravity that grounds mere mortals as much as you operate just beyond the topographical constraints of its laws. Like an an astronaut on his first trip to low earth orbit, your unbridgeable proximity to what you've escaped allows you to observe in its cartographies an organizing shimmer of light, one unknowable in the immersive mundanity of lower altitudes. The slate is wiped clean and wider than ever; indeed, the slate is suddenly a gorgeous thing.

The epidemic of Adderall abuse among America's undergraduates and young professionals is now one of those apocryphal motifs of neoliberal precarity, sustained by regular headlines in the *Huffington Post*, but what these fretful reports fail to understand is: yes, people take Adderall to get their work done, but more important, it makes doing that work *fun*. Fun in the way a carnival ride is fun, which is to say—palpably. The esoteric article on, say, Belgian talk radio's role in the Rwandan genocide not only makes immediate sense but reveals its hidden poetry. You start to write, and an idea that deserves maybe a sentence becomes the most elegant page you've ever conjured. The people who populate your mundane world suddenly illuminate it. You tend to send a lot of Facebook messages, or texts, their effusiveness choreographed to the suddenly revelatory electronic music throbbing through your headphones. In its waning twilight, the mind wanders to sex, but as Foster Dade and one other boy in that room would learn firsthand, about half of the men who take it find it uniquely difficult to achieve an erection under its influence. It hardly matters—for a little while, nothing does.

Mason crushed three pills on the flat navy surface of Pritchett's 2001 Buckley School yearbook. He used his Kennedy student identification card to do so, licking the patina of orange from his expressionless photograph on the card's face. "Who's got a bill," he said as he cut the anthill of dull fluorescent powder with the card's edge into five log-like lines.

He took a twenty Freddie handed him and rolled it into a straw, holding it over the leather surface with a prospector's scrutiny, before finally looking up at Foster. "Where are my manners," he said dryly, extending the book and the bill in his direction.

For half a moment Foster's worry was that he'd drop the yearbook or, thinking of *Annie Hall*, disperse its chalky orange ridges into the air of the room with a sneeze. Instead he felt its weight taken by his nervous arm, and the gazes of the boys—could they have been called friends, at that moment?—filling the lamplit ether of the bedroom. He thought for another brief moment about those inflection points when stretches of life end and begin, and then he held the rolled twenty to the second-largest of the orange lines.

"Either hold the yearbook or hold my nostril," he said in Jack's direction. Freddie laughed, but not cruelly, and Jack stepped over and took the edges of the yearbook in his hands, as if it was proffered. Hunched, Foster glanced up at him, their eyes meeting with a certainty with which they hadn't before, pressed his left nostril, and inhaled.

First, the numbness of his palate; the bitterness of the drip against his throat, from where the Adderall had stuck and slurried with saliva. Less than a moment after, though: the awakening, it seemed, of every nervous fiber in him, demonstrated most palpably in the concerted widening of his eyes against the light. His heart ticked up its pace and thrust itself against his chest, but this was incidental to the bigger picture—the quickening not only of his corporeal being but of life itself.

"Well, fucking shit," he said, grinning at Jack and then to Will and Freddie and Pritchett and then Mason, whose aura of menace had dissipated.

Freddie and Pritchett laughed appreciatively. Will's pursed lips betrayed a slight smile.

"Lemme see it," Mason said, and Jack extended the yearbook toward him. What remained of Foster's line was the peachy shadow of its residue; Mason slid his index finger over it and rubbed it against his top gum. "Bill, please," he said to Foster. He snorted the thickest of the remaining lines quickly, and after a moment looked up at them with his Cheshire Cat grin, its menacing mirth even wider now.

"Let's fucking go."

Jack suggested they crush two more of Foster's Adderalls onto the yearbook for a second round—"just little baby lines; why the fuck not"—and convinced Foster to bring four to Sofi's party. "The girls would fucking love you if you could hook them up, and worst-case scenario, we just take them ourselves if it wears off," Jack said, grinding his palm against his nostril and inspecting it for wet orange residue. The Adderall ignited something in all of them, but in Jack particularly so. The magisterial brio with which he propelled himself through the world—the blasting Lil Wayne not into the bathroom but out its windows when he showered; the self-conscious confidence with which he performed at weekly School Meetings   seemed to find in the drug a sustenance for its calibrated tempo.

They had not so much stumbled as tromped out the brass-framed doors of the Pierce's building—"This shit sobers you up," Jack complained happily, tucking a bottle of wine into the breast of his North Face before leaving—and turned to the corner of the southbound avenue.

Pritchett and the other assumed the role of flagging down taxis—this was long before the domination of the city's traffic by Uber and Lyft—leaving Jack and Foster hanging back from the corner of Seventy-Third and Lexington.

"I fucking love you, man," Jack said suddenly to Foster. "I'm so fucking glad you came to Kennedy."

Foster looked at him. He was startled by the euphoria the drug provoked in him, by the pathos it liberated. Jack's eyes seemed to actually glow; there was a sadness and a beauty in his upturned mouth that Foster had not recognized before, and he wanted to embrace him. Instead he grinned.

"I love you too, Jack."

And so the city found the quickening luster it assumed for Foster Dade on that night. The world in its candent orbit seemed to lean into Manhattan, these vectors converging at these six boys, who pulled the tug of cosmic gravity with them as their taxis pushed downtown through the traffic along Lexington. Will and Jack and Foster took one taxi, with Jack in the middle and Foster watching the city transpire through the smudged window. But it was not just the city but the tension of Jack's thigh against his, the fibers of their khakis chafing together with little shifts, the heat of the two bodies melding. Foster did not have the words for the strange muted crackle he sensed in Jack; it was intelligible only as the wattage that seemed to spill between them from a wonderfully ersatz circuitry. There would be time for

the words to come to them, with all the attendant pain, or perhaps
they wouldn't. Foster would turn sixteen in three hours.

"I got soul, but I'm not a soldier!" Jack Albright screamed, throwing his arms out unto the night. The red beacons across the bridges
spanning the East River pulsed their glow out into the nothingness,
casting a sad elegy for the inscrutable darkness of Brooklyn. The city
around them ebbed with the hush of a forgotten whisper; the matrix
of streetlights gave the illusion of a cocoon, or a womb.

"About fucking *time*!" Annabeth screamed from the corner as they
pulled themselves out of the taxi. In the chemical ecstasy of the evening, Annabeth's beauty seemed to spindle out from her and into
Foster's heart, which pumped fast and freely. Her dress was the blue
of dusty bottle glass. It stopped below her shoulders, which were
naked despite the coolness of the spring evening, and her hair hung
down over them with what looked like the beginning of a curl; in
the dirty neon effluent of the bodega behind her, it seemed to capture
the light itself. Foster could not remember if he had seen her in eye
shadow before.

"We got, uh, held up," Jack said with a purposely mischievous
grin, tapping the tip of his index finger to the side of his nostril.

"Blow?" Gracie Smith, who stood to Annabeth's side, next to Porter Roth, asked dubiously. She, too, looked stunning, Foster conceded.
He noticed the flat tautness of her chest and pictured some unnamed
lacrosse player from the year above ogling it animalistically as he
undressed her in some placeless darkened bedroom.

"Adderall," said Pritchett, now out of the taxi that had pulled up
behind theirs. "Courtesy of Mister Dade."

Annabeth looked at Foster quizzically.

"Yeah—I'm, like, prescribed, actually."

Annabeth's brow furrowed further for a moment, and in it Foster
sensed a curious thrall of loosely erotic power—the thrall of disclosing
a certain secret, and with it the fact of the secrecy itself.

"So does this mean you boys are going to, like, be up breaking
shit until six in the morning," Gracie intoned flatly.

"Feel free to join us," Jack grinned.

"I brought a few extra," Foster said, touching the spot on his chest where the Ziploc containing the pills sat, feeling the plastic whisper.

"My idea," said Jack.

Foster noticed that Porter Roth, whom he had never really taken the time to contemplate, looked vaguely uncomfortable. She was pretty, Foster had acknowledged before; unlike her friends, Porter's prettiness seemed to correspond with what he could only articulate as her verisimilitude. Where the others seemed to capture in their erotic form the ethereal, foreign luster of Kennedy, Porter, meanwhile, seemed merely true, a real person. Foster found himself wondering if she was happy, and then felt his brain stifle in shame the interior question that followed, which was what her underwear looked like.

"Sup," Mason said, appearing next to Foster. His taunting grin had calcified a bit upon seeing Porter, whose discomfort Foster now realized may have not exclusively concerned the casual talk of prescription drug abuse. *Mason's off persuading Porter to surrender her virginity*, he remembered Pritchett saying.

"Francie's inside with Sofi, who's of course drinking every sip of the spotlight," Annabeth said, thumbing at the purple neon ocher that emanated from a doorway halfway down the block. Foster realized from the effusive lilt in her voice that she was somewhere approximating drunk. "We came outside to meet y'all. And to drink more."

Foster now saw that Gracie was holding a Dasani bottle of her own, its contents the translucent backwashy pink of rosewater.

"Vodka and like a splash of Crystal Light," Annabeth explained, taking the bottle and sipping from it. It left her lips wet as she smiled.

"The Cohens are kind of being Nazis about booze in there," Gracie said. "Part of their whole deal with the school in getting this party to be okayed."

"What's the ethical status of calling Jewish people Nazis?" Foster wondered aloud. When he made these sorts of comments, their wry levity was often lost within the heft of their candor; since coming to Kennedy, he had come to subdue them, but tonight, with the Adderall's mirthful confidence, that inhibition had dissipated.

Gracie pursed her lips at him, but Porter and Will laughed. "A decided no-no," Annabeth said, stepping forward to put her arms around Foster. "Hi, by the way," she whispered into his ear. He felt the contour of the Dasani bottle in her hand against his hip and, in a spat of horror and delight, the earliest quickenings of an erection within his boxer shorts despite the amphetamine's thrall, and then she pulled away. "So—Adderall? Sharing the wealth tonight?"

"We've got three," Jack said, stepping in to hug Annabeth himself. "Probably can't get away with snorting it, but let's just break 'em up and swallow it, yeah?"

The twenty-milligram Adderall pills were debossed with the shape of a cross that partitioned the disk into even segments. Taking the Ziploc from his pocket, Foster tapped them into Jack's outstretched palm. Jack gave a look of theatrical concentration and snapped each of the three pills into quarters. "Two for you," he said, pinching up two of the orange little nuggets and giving them to Annabeth. "And two for—who wants?"

Pritchett and Gracie picked one of the quarters from Jack's palm; Mason and Freddie each took two. "I deserve plaudits for my generosity," Foster said, taking two for himself, feeling his fingertips against what he realized was the clamminess of Jack's hand, pink and soft.

"You're a real mensch, Dade," Jack said.

"Y'all, let's make haste," Will Thierry said, jerking his head at the boulder-like bouncer who stood in the bath of the purple light in the club's doorway down the block. He seemed to be assessing them, Foster thought, but this might have just been the Adderall.

"Well then," Annabeth said, holding up the two segments pinched between her fingers, like a seasoned jeweler with familiar stones. "Cheers. To friendship," she said squarely at Foster with a smile that carried her own secrets, and then placed the pills on her tongue.

"Wait," Jack said. "We've still got this wine!"

"No thank you," Pritchett said. "I'm in fact making it a goal not to vomit into a urinal this evening."

"Suit yourself," Jack said, handing the bottle to Gracie. She took a demure sip—*Is she pathologically incapable of enjoying things, or is that just what she wants everyone to believe?* Foster would write fatefully on his Blogspot months later—and handed the bottle to Mason. It remained closer to full than not by the time it reached Foster and Jack.

"Shall we?" Jack twinkled, and Foster felt himself grin. He realized in that moment how drunk he already was and did not care. He watched the bubbles gurgle within the darkened green glass as Jack turned it upward and sucked down its contents.

"Pfaaaah," Jack said, wiping the purple from his mouth. "Do your worst, Dade."

Feeling the eyes of his friends on him—again, were they his friends? Tonight he could pretend so—Foster took the bottle, just under half of its contents still there, and closed his eyes. He emptied it, and in a fit of rare pique he flung the green bottle like a grenade into the adjacent alley, where to his delight it rattled soundly into an open cardboard box. He felt himself grin again.

Foster would recall only swathes of Sofi Cohen's sixteenth birthday party and the hours thereafter. The gaudy club was crowded—it was strange, as if the motley milieu of the Dining Center during Monday lunches had simply transposed itself here. Will Bartholomew and his baseball friends, dressed in starched button-downs from Ralph Lauren factory stores, were dancing the Soulja Boy with the self-conscious irony demanded of a dance that had passed its cultural moment a year prior. A group of bookish girls from Wilson House stood in a compact huddle to displace their anxiety, their hair pressed and sheened with a conspicuous deliberation. Fourth Year boys on the lacrosse team stood by the bar, their bored pulls from the flasks in their jackets only half-discreet. One of them, J. T. Ricciardelli, stuck up a hand in an awkward wave to Annabeth. His Top-Siders looked, as they always did, revealingly unbeaten. "Sad," Foster heard Gracie mutter behind him as Annabeth beamed.

Foster watched as Jack and the boys tumbled themselves onto the dance floor with the innate knowledge that space would clear for them. That's where Sofi Cohen was, radiating the anxious confidence of one enjoying her position at the center of gravity but attuned to its tenuousness. (Don and Rhona Cohen stood off by the bathrooms, surveying the scene with a sort of aloof contentment at their daughter's temporary celebrity.) The party swiftly became only an effluence of purple light and the distant thump of music, as if it were playing underwater.

The moments that preserved themselves in his memory did so with what felt then like arbitrary motive. At one point, Foster looked across the club and saw Blake Mancetti, standing next to two unnamed boys from Arsdale House. He realized that Blake was looking in their direction. Again Foster discerned an intensity in his dark eyes: Blake seemed to be gazing toward him and Jack with something that Foster's mind registered as an inexplicable rictus of anxiety or hurt.

At some point, a fourth covert disk of Adderall sang out in the lure of its secret excess, and before leaving the nightclub hours—was it hours?—later, Foster swallowed all but a quarter of it. It was on the corner of East Second and the Bowery that Foster returned to the world, like a deep-sea diver opening his eyes before breaching the sun-speckled surface, into a scene of light and color slowly gaining clarity. They'd left the party, he realized. There was the charter bus the Cohens had rented; there were the tired faces of the Have-Nots shadowed behind the tinted windows in nighttime. And there Foster stood on the other side of a real or imagined barrier, with Annabeth, Jack, and the rest. Freddie Pieters had somehow acquired a cigarette. "Fuckin' hell," he murmured, fumbling with the light.

Soon Foster felt himself receding into lower Manhattan's dirty nebula of light, navigated by the automated shuffling of his own feet. He realized that Sofi Cohen was now with them, and she had not bothered to wipe the streaks of mascara from her cheeks, where it dried like the oxidized streaks on old limestone.

Suddenly they seemed to be in someone's apartment. Foster did not know Manhattan enough to know that they were on the Lower East Side, not far from where they had left. A Basquiat print hung in its frame over the television next to which Foster found himself sitting. Gracie Smith sat on the couch, her dress hiked high up her brown thighs, and next to her was a sallow boy with thin black hair, who was focused with surgical intensity on slicing the lines of what must have been cocaine on the glass coffee table.

"It's one in the morning and I'm not going to be out until dawn," someone—it was Jack Albright—said from somewhere behind Foster. Drunk as he was, Foster noticed the leer in the eyes of the black-haired boy, who looked up from the coke. Only later would Foster learn that he was Tripp Altridge, the boy who had been expelled from Kennedy the prior spring.

"Oh, you know you want to stay."

Before Foster could turn to Jack, Sofi Cohen emerged from a doorway leading to what must have been the bathroom, a tired-looking Porter Roth behind her. "Fuck you!" Sofi wailed at Annabeth Whittaker, who Foster realized with a lurch was sitting next to him, their legs very nearly touching. Porter sighed and shot her a frustrated look. It was the least passive gesture Foster had seen her summon.

Next to him, Annabeth exhaled. "Anyone want to hit the road."

"Me," Jack said. Foster looked to him. The early jubilance in Jack's expression had hardened. *Unhappy* wasn't quite the word for it, for there was the intimation of a violence there too, one that Foster had sensed before.

"I'd—I'd stroll," Foster thought he heard himself say.

"Take my spare key," said Pritchett, who emerged with Mason and Frances from an adjoining room. They brought with them the wooly heft of marijuana smoke. "Don't you dare lose it."

And then Foster realized he was standing and making his way to the door, and Jack was saying something under his breath like *need to get the fuck out of here* when Tripp spoke again, firmly now and directly to him.

"Oh, come on now, Jackie—thought you wanted to get coked up."

A moment, a pause. "I'm gonna text you in like fifteen," he said to Foster and Annabeth, avoiding their stares. "And then we can meet up."

And then Foster and Annabeth were out on the street. There was more clarity now, in the cool of the night. Annabeth's hair was unkempt in its fall over her shoulders, and she was more beautiful for it. The street on which they stood was wide, with trucks passing by in silent heft. Annabeth turned to face Foster and put her hands on his shoulders.

"We're going on an adventure."

If she was particularly drunk, it did not blunt the earnestness of these words and her stare up at Foster, which danced with a delight in her own mischievousness. Foster allowed himself to hold his own gaze in its communion with hers; in his own residual intoxication, the instinct to turn his eyes away—the sudden fear of what this communion would betray if prolonged—approached but then flitted away, and for what felt like the first time Foster appreciated the roundness of Annabeth's eyes, bright and wide with incredulity, as if nothing in the world they observed could escape her predisposition to wonder.

"I love adventures," Foster said finally. "Oh, and—wait—"

He found himself reaching into his pocket for his wallet, probing his fingertips within it until he found the last fragmented quarter-moons of Adderall. "I smuggled some cargo," Foster said with a consciously sheepish grin as he held the chalky pill pieces before Annabeth. She burst out laughing.

"You fucking asshole," she said. "Who knew you were such a fuckup." Her fingers grazing his palm, she took a fragment and placed it on her tongue. Foster did the same.

"I'm sucking on it," Annabeth said through a tight mouth, "like it's candy, except it tastes like absolute bitter shit."

They set forth into the night, their motion constellating the spills of fluorescent ether that hung out from the Lower East Side's bodegas and smoke shops.

"I needed to get the fuck out of there," Annabeth said. "Sofi's low-key hammered and is furious with me for God knows what—*making the party about me*, or some shit."

"Do girls actually like being friends with each other? Because it seems like it's just, like—mutual hatred with a social purpose, or something."

Annabeth snorted. "I hate girls," she responded. "In fact"—she stopped in her stride, then reached to adjust the strap of her chalk-colored heel—"I kind of hate everyone."

"Not me," Foster blurted, looking to her for a moment. "You don't hate me." They were walking south now, past the shuttered grocery stores of Chinatown, toward the phosphorescent amber haze colored by the glow of Wall Street's skyscrapers.

"Not you," Annabeth said, and Foster realized that she had taken her hand in his. It seemed she was going to cry. "You're my best friend."

And then with her free hand she reached into the handbag that Foster had not realized was hanging at her side. It emerged with the shape of something square and flat. With a sudden marvelous bewilderment Foster saw that she bit the corner of her lower lip before sliding the object beneath his arm. It was a CD jewel case, the sort sold with the accompanying disks in packs of fifty at Office Depot, and in the mercurial light of the bridge's spires overhead he looked down to the words she had written in Sharpie on the CD's silvery face. *A Musical Education for F. H. Dade on the Occasion of His Sixteenth Birthday, 4/19/2009 (Feat. Erudite Commentary from the Author).*

"Happy birthday, Foster Dade."

And once again, his eyes caught hers with that rare locking clutch—the one that engenders a mutual magnetism, the one that precedes a kiss. Later, he would not remember the words he said to her in that moment when he finally looked up, only that there was suddenly a clarity that had not existed before. His fear of her inaccessibility had vacated itself. She looked at him with a curiousness. The spasm of vulnerability was fiercer this time, and he felt himself look away, but when he did, he did not feel her hand slip away from his. With his thumb he stroked its edge. *Even though we didn't kiss, the world was for a brief moment all right*, he later wrote. *I don't know what I feel but I've never felt it before. I want to feel it forever.*

Then he felt his BlackBerry's hum against his thigh. "Must be Jack," he said to no one in particular, hating himself for the readiness with which he pulled it from his pocket.

> **Jack Albright [02:34:03AM]:** Yo
> **Jack Albright [02:34:07AM]:** I bounced let's get the fuck out of here
> **Jack Albright [02:34:14AM]:** Meet me at Delancey and Essex and lets get a taxi

"So, uh"—and Foster heard the sheepishness in his voice chafe against the ethereal spell of the preceding hour—"Jack wants to get a cab and call it a night."

Annabeth's brow creased. "Absolutely not," she said. "Nonsense. Give me that."

She pulled the BlackBerry from Foster's hand, scrolling up to Jack's contact page and pressing the keypad's green button before holding it to her ear. She grinned magnanimously at Foster as he heard the muffled burble of Jack's voice against her ear.

"Don't '*sup*' me, Jack Albright. We're on an adventure. Be at Canal and Mott in ten minutes or I'm telling everyone that you listen to the *Mamma Mia!* soundtrack while writing papers."

Jack was clutching a bottle of red wine as he stepped out of the taxi. "Keep it," he mumbled to the driver as he thrust a bill through the open window. He stumbled a bit as he stepped up onto the sidewalk and seemed briefly taken aback by their presence, as if encountering them by chance.

"Dade," he said, after taking a pull from the bottle, "you got any more Addy."

"Only if you're sharing that wine." The segment of the pill Foster had swallowed had begun to metabolize, sheening the luster of his drunkenness with its edge of confidence; the distressed discontent in Jack's voice and expression seemed only an aberrant rhythm in the vaster symphony of things. Their eyes met as Jack thrust the bottle of wine toward him. Foster felt the Adderall's sympathy concentrate itself in his gaze, and something in Jack then seemed to soften.

"We're delighted you could join us, Mister Albright," Annabeth said, taking the bottle from Foster and tilting it in salutation toward Jack before bringing it to her lips. It mottled the edges of her mouth, which widened into a smile.

"So I've got another quarter of a pill and then just, like, some detritus," Foster said, holding his wallet out to Jack. "Go crazy."

Jack fished the last segment from the leather pocket and then ran his finger within its creases. He contemplated the crust of peachy dust on his fingertip and then sucked it for a moment, and after closing his eyes and taking a pull from the bottle of wine he looked at them and grinned.

"You've saved me."

I don't know how far we walked, or even for how long. All I know is that everything prior to it—the train to the city, pregaming at Pritchett's, Sofi's party itself, that kid's apartment after (I think his name is Tripp)—now seems like only a basically irrelevant preamble to what the night really was. The Adderall helped, obviously—it pulled me out of my blackout and gave me the stamina to walk across Manhattan when I'd been drinking for nine hours and hadn't slept in basically twenty-four—but it wasn't the Adderall that made it what it was.

We talked about everything. We ended up way downtown, where Annabeth flirted her way into getting us a bottle of shitty champagne from a little convenience store: we drank it right by Ground Zero and spent forty-five minutes talking about 9/11. That sounds more macabre than it was. We'd all been in third grade when it happened; I told them about being brought in from PE then led to the auditorium to watch CNN. It's hard to explain, but there was something weirdly intimate and wistful in talking about it together: in realizing that eight-year-old me and eight-year-old Annabeth and eight-year-old Jack had shared something so significant long before our lives would ever converge. (Relatedly: it turns out we all read *The Curious Incident of the Dog in the Night-Time* within four weeks of each other when we were in eighth grade.) We talked about where we wanted to go to college (Annabeth: Columbia or Brown or Dartmouth; Jack: Princeton or Harvard; me: Yale or UChicago or even maybe Hopkins), and we talked about our sexual experience: which in my case is limited to Lanie Tinsley kind of sort of trying to give me a handjob in Max Frieholdt's rec room when we were both really drunk two Halloweens ago. In any other context—if it had been Jack and Mason and not Jack and Annabeth, for example—I would have been embarrassed by it, and I would have almost certainly exaggerated. But something happened as we walked that hasn't happened since certain sleepovers in middle school: the rest of the world ceased to exist. It was just the three of us, and then the night all around us.

I told them about Mom and Dad's divorce. Not the actual specifics—I don't think I'll ever tell anyone the most vivid details, for like ten different reasons. But I told them about Dad cheating, and I told them about how it all came out into the open. I hadn't planned on telling anyone anything. They'd known my parents were divorced, obviously, but they'd never asked for any details—probably only out of politeness, but whatever. But as we walked, I realized that I wanted them to know. I don't know why—I could blame the alcohol or drugs or whatever, but I'd know deep down that it wouldn't be the truth.

I think I'd always imagined that I could tell Annabeth, but when I finally forced myself to look up at them, it was Jack who looked like he was going to cry.

They had begun walking north out of Tribeca's tangle of narrow streets when Foster remembered the joint in his shirt's breast pocket. The night that had enclosed them in their transit had not yet lifted its caul, but its darkness had commenced its slow retreat; the hazy spill of the stoplights up ahead seemed smudged and chalk-like in the weakening contrast.

"Dade, you're literally a force of nature," Jack said as Foster reached beneath his sweater's neck and withdrew the slender cigarette from his pocket, where it had crimped against the press of Annabeth's CD. Jack had untucked his periwinkle oxford and rolled its sleeves up past his elbows. With a spectacular upward lurch of the bottle he had taken the last of the champagne before lobbing it down a dark street, where it had bumped along the cobblestones without shattering before rolling sedately against the curb. "You're basically Willy Wonka."

"If we get arrested for smoking pot, you guys get to be the ones to call Skip and Diane Whittaker and tell them." But there was a wickedness to Annabeth's grin as she said this, and as they approached the corner she turned to them and stopped. "I have an idea."

And with a sudden verve of purposefulness she turned right and crossed Broadway, keeping several paces ahead of Foster and Jack. In the sepia shadows of the streetlights overhead Foster saw that she seemed to be diligently suppressing a smile, yet it betrayed more delight than her grin.

"Where the fuck we going, Whittaker," Jack called.

"It's a surprise."

They followed her east, and every so often she turned to them with the same silent smile, her eyes bright with a new conspiratorial intensity. "How is it possible that she's been wearing fucking heels this entire time," Jack muttered, then grinned at Foster. He pushed a hand through his thick hair, still matted into wayward Einsteinian tufts by the sweat of dancing: a relic of a stretch of hours that otherwise seemed to occupy a different calendar altogether. The events of the earlier evening had fallen away like a rocket shedding its boosters; the silent weight of whatever had encumbered Jack then had been left behind to a more terrestrial orbit.

It was only when Annabeth stopped and turned again to face them that Foster realized the sky overhead had begun to gray. The boys blinked at her. She bit her bottom lip to restrain her grin, and with a wonderfully infantile happiness she pointed behind her beyond the plaza in which they stood.

"Bridge," she said simply.

Behind her rose the earthen limestone towers of the Brooklyn Bridge. Their silhouette stood dark against the earliest palings of morning. In the residual darkness, its rise up over the river could be discerned only in the smear of yellow headlights that spilled over its distant crest. Like a child presenting a piece of artwork, Annabeth beamed.

The sky began to elucidate itself as the three of them set out up the slow rise before them. They were silent as the streets began to fall below them, and only as they approached the foot of the bridge's wooden promenade did Annabeth turn to Foster. Far below, the traffic moving up the FDR seemed unbound by inertia as it moved along the river's edge.

"Joint," she said with the same directness.

Letting the joint hang limply from his lips, Foster found the lighter forgotten in a crease of his pants pocket, but then took the joint in the same fingers and held them both out toward Jack and Annabeth. Annabeth only smiled and shook her head.

"You do the honors," Jack said.

The weed was clean in its pungency as it broke against the morning, and Foster let the mass of its smoke take shape within the contours of his chest before exhaling. A jogger cast them a disdainful look as she pattered past.

"Admirable," Foster grinned, passing the joint to Annabeth.

She seemed to contemplate it as she took a hit, and exhaled with what felt like the same plaintive silence; the smoke met the sky's cobalt light in a stream that was at once untempered and elegant. As she extended it to Jack, she reached in her bag for her phone. She stared down at it as she scrolled, and as the music began to play, she turned and set out up the bridge's footpath.

Annabeth clutched her BlackBerry as LCD Soundsystem played. (*this is maybe the prettiest song ever written*, she'd messaged him on iChat late one night over spring break below the link to the music video for "All My Friends.") Far to the east, beyond the rooftops of Brooklyn, the sun seemed to have broken the soft seal of the horizon over the Atlantic. The bands of cloud that ridged the sky were the first to betray its light, reddening against the stone-colored dawn. The city was behind them now. Annabeth reached down and undid the straps of her shoes and picked them up. She dragged their heels against the percussive grate of the walkway's fence as she walked and then slid them into the bag on her arm.

She paused for a moment, and as Foster came to her side he realized that she was crying. She studied him and then Jack, and with the same silence she took both of their hands in hers and began to run. Foster felt the subdued throbs of the BlackBerry against his palm and hers with the beats of the music from its speakers as they moved out over the river. *In my memory, she was laughing as we ran, or maybe Jack was, or maybe we all were*, Foster would write. *All I really know is that we were running together, the three of us, and her hand was in mine.*

Only at the bridge's apogee did Annabeth stop. The stone towers were now radiant with the ember-light of the sun, and in it Foster could see the dark beads of mascara that hung to Annabeth's eyelashes, wet from tears that had etched sandy paths down the makeup on her cheeks. Once again her face was childlike, this time in the innocence of what it seemed to expect.

"I feel—like everything and nothing," she whispered. "I feel so young."

"You're so lame," Jack murmured. But Foster saw too that there was a brightness to his eyes as he turned toward the morning. And he turned that line over in his head—a line that seemed to be spun with the silver intractability of the stars receding far overhead. He thought fleetingly of those that had smeared against the boundless glass of sky over Kennedy on the night of Lessons and Carols, spanning it in long diffuse creeks of firmament. Their crystalline wonder had transposed itself in the kaleidoscopic light of the spring morning. Its solitude was the same. He extended his fingers and found Annabeth's: stroking them for a moment, taking them in his, and then letting them go. Then hers found his again, taking his hand and clutching it gently. He turned to see them both standing there in the pink light of morning.

"Everything and nothing," he murmured.

XXIII. (Interlude, or Interruption)

There is no universal half-life for the mythologies that constitute the idea of Kennedy. We could say somewhat tautologically that it comes down to the myth in question, but this isn't entirely sufficient. The perseverance of these stories ultimately speaks less to their content than to the function it serves. As sociological artifacts, they're most valuable not as an illustration of the past they address but as a sort of psychological imaging of the present. Their individual threads interweave into a vaster tapestry, and while it's easy to get distracted by the radiance of its colors or the complexity of its patterning, the thing that's really important here—the thing that gives these aesthetic distractions their radiance, ironically—is the tapestry's broader topography. It gives shape to the idea of Kennedy itself. Its contours shift with the evolutions of history; its threads are pulled and replaced to accommodate this. Certain stories stick around longer than others, and no matter how much their fibers fray or pill or split, the only really germane thing is the structure they sustain.

I tell this particular story with the conviction that it gestures to something more universal, or more aptly something to which I belong. My early attempts to patch its holes with the narratives of my own time at Kennedy were graceless but in an important respect indistinguishable from the pages you are reading here, at least in their motivating logic. If I had to parcel this project in the Trojan horse of, say, cultural sociology, I might say that it's my attempt to comprehend the adolescent predisposition to mythology: how coveting the spell of others' stories allows us to find faith in what our own might become, and keep going.

I find small comfort in the knowledge that I'm not utterly alone. I'd suspect here that a reader arrived at these pages having some vague acquaintance with the story in question. "No one else wants to read six hundred pages about rich white kids behaving badly," Sofi Cohen told me the night we met for drinks. She had her own motives, presumably—it had been her parents who'd been the first to hire lawyers in the immediate aftermath of the events of the spring of 2010, and when we spoke I sensed a carefulness to not jeopardize the thoroughness of the job Don and Rhona had paid good money for—but there's also a basic truth in this, one that's independent of and more universal than the cultural appetites Sofi's comment acknowledged. We seek in certain narratives a prismatic image of our own. *It's weird, but when I used to read Harry Potter, I pictured Number Four Privet Drive as our house in Baltimore, and Hogwarts as the old building at Gilman*, fourteen-year-old Foster Dade had written in one of his first Blogspot entries. *It's one reason I've never liked the movies—they kill the sense that the story belongs to me and me alone.*

XXIV.

"Dade, you were fucking blitzed," Jason Stearns said.

"Three sheets to the wind, as they say," followed Noah Baum.

"Obliterated."

"Obliter-*Dade*d."

"B-plus at best."

It was the Tuesday after Sofi's party. Spring was finally pressing itself through the last gossamer screen of the stubborn winter. It was among the first days when the members of the Kennedy varsity boys' tennis team found they did not need to pull their Patagonia fleeces back on after practice; the sun, however muddled its glow, was in fact warm as it spilled itself fitfully through the clouds.

Of all the anxieties in his first year that give shape to this story, the news that Foster wasn't as stellar a tennis player at Kennedy as he had been in Baltimore did not rank particularly high. "By the skin of your teeth," Art Tierney, who'd coached the varsity boys' squad for two decades by then, told him at the end of tryouts after spring break, though he'd clapped his gangly white hand on Foster's shoulder. Three other Second Years had made varsity. As a doubles pair, Jason Stearns and Noah Baum operated like silent tuning forks in a chess-like match of attrition. (They shared a double on the third floor of Arsdale House and since the first week of their First Year had moved inseparably together across campus, comic foils in a politically indifferent double act.) Raj Chakravarty brought to the court a violent chutzpah that hours of calculus homework and *Kennedian* article-writing both stifled and incubated. Foster liked them, with their enviably cavalier bookishness, and he liked Tierney. Tierney, who padded out to the courts in knee-length khakis and a faded white Kennedy polo after his First Year English seminar let out, swinging his ancient old Wilson like a baton, his thighs white in the sun. "I'm telling you, Baum, when I see you decline to move to the ball, what crosses my mind are AXE THOUGHTS!" he'd bellow.

"You're a gem when you decide to run, Dade," Tierney had told him approvingly that Tuesday afternoon after Sofi Cohen's birthday party.

Jason Stearns grinned at him once Tierney's gangly frame was far enough down the path toward the dining hall. "Too bad you're still sweating vodka."

"Whiskey, actually," Foster smiled meekly. "And I'm not proud of it."

Noah Baum feigned a swoon. "My stars, are you to tell me that flowers as delicate as Gracie Smith and Annabeth Whittaker are—whiskey drinkers?"

Jason smirked. "I'd have guessed gin."

"Why's that?"

"My grandmother says gin makes you mean."

"So Gracie Smith drinks it with breakfast is what you're saying."

Foster grinned as they laughed. *It's not that their jokes themselves are funny,* he wrote that night, *but the ease with which they tell them. They're, like, comfortable in their skins or whatever, and I guess it's up to me to figure out why I find that so endearing. In a different universe they'd be my best friends.*

Sunday's hangover had followed Foster into the week. The persisting cloudiness of his synapses fermented into anxiety. *What did I do or say in those hours I can't remember, and is my brain going to be like this forever,* he'd written on Sunday night, after the silent trip south from Penn Station aboard New Jersey Transit. Pritchett and Mason and Freddie had fallen asleep, lulled by the womb-like pulsing of the metal passenger car along its tracks; Jack, sitting across from Foster, was awake but wordless, staring down at the paperback copy of *Freakonomics* he balanced on his knee. He did not seem to have turned the page he'd opened it to, and as the train passed New Brunswick he let it close limply on his lap and turned to stare out the smudged window, the sound of Kanye West bursting in tinny little presses from his iPhone's earbuds. *I still sometimes find myself worrying more often than not that he secretly hates me,* Foster would write that evening.

Foster's fugue lingered on Tuesday, and at lunchtime he found himself back in his room, tapping an Adderall into his palm. Its minor verve got him through tennis, but exercise accelerates the metabolization of amphetamine, and by the end of practice his interior architecture threatened a new hollowness—its edges rough, its ether nauseous.

After practice, Jason and Noah carried on toward the Dining Center and Foster retreated into Brennan. The house was quiet as he stepped into his room, but still he shut the door gently behind him.

He wiped the cooling sweat from his face with the gray Kennedy Athletics T-shirt as he pulled it over his head. He slid his shorts to his ankles and kicked them in the direction of the mesh laundry basket in the corner. He stood there naked for a moment, taking inventory of the darkening shadows accumulating there in the late afternoon, and through the bleakness the towel hanging on the hook across the room seemed irretrievably distant. He stood there for a moment longer, more conscious than he might have been otherwise of the fact of his nudity, and finally he felt himself sit down on his desk chair and reach for his MacBook.

When Theresa Daniels's tenure as Dean of Students came to its ignominious end just under a year later, the three years she spent in the office would perhaps unfairly be remembered only through the pall of the events that immediately precipitated her departure. ("Like Carter and Iran," Scott McCall would later observe wryly to Art Tierney over steaks during one of their several ad hoc postmortems of that spring's events.) Given the entrenchment of this legacy, it is odd to contemplate the fact that her appointment to the job in the spring of 2007 had been an occasion of relative optimism for a student body that eventually came to revile her.

We could make the case that this trajectory was inevitable. For whatever auxiliary responsibilities may crop up, the Dean of Students's function is first and foremost disciplinary. All adolescents are inclined to anarchy, but this is uniquely true at a school like Kennedy, where intelligence and privilege together find a warrant in an institutional culture explicitly programmed to—and this is in the Student Handbook—"foster intellectual inquiry, public engagement, and open expression." Liberty is only as good as the tyranny it counterposes, and in the Dean of Students, a particularly eloquent adolescent caricature of fascism finds human form. Success at the job lies in one's ability to weather the inevitable mutinous storms.

The early cynics would say that it was with an eye toward her own long-term political viability that, in the second month of her deanship, Theresa Daniels decreed to restore internet access to Kennedy's Houses during the hours of study hall. The policy it reversed had been in place since the first year of the new millennium, when the increasing prevalence of personal laptops on campus hadn't yet corrected an early misconception of the World Wide Web as nothing more than a bazaar of pornography and felonious contraband. In 2001, this simply meant limited access to AOL Instant Messenger and Flash sites like eBaum's World, but as the decade progressed, Kennedy's students—whose friends at Taft and Andover kept asking why they hadn't yet signed up for Facebook—came to imagine the data embargo as a symbol of a deeper and more insidious authoritarianism. "The Berlin Firewall," one editorial in the *Kennedian* sniped in early 2006, "has ushered in a new era of political distrust among Kennedians, who see it as an infantilizing effort by a shortsighted administration that claims to care for our intellectual livelihood."

This exercise in defiance rustled something latent in Kennedy's student body, and when Theresa Daniels finally announced the embargo's end a month before the start of the 2007–2008 academic year, the cynics welcomed it as little more than the partial return of inalienable rights that had been wrongfully stripped from them. The Information Services office would still, after all, shut down the campus network after lights-out at 11:15; perhaps more saliently, the liberalization fiat had not shortened the list of websites and services blacklisted by Kennedy's servers. For sixteen- and seventeen-year-olds at the end of the first decade of the twenty-first century, two categories within that list were salient: (i) peer-to-peer file-sharing sites—ThePirateBay and BitTorrent being the most prominent two in those years, though LimeWire had stubbornly held on—and (ii) pornography.

"Trust me—that's why in five years you'll all have iPhones," Jack Albright had said several weeks prior, shifting his legs to recline across the length of Harris Adelstein's couch without looking away from his phone. "Don't hate me for being ahead of the curve. Here—look at that *resolution*, baby!" With a diabolical grin, he had proceeded to hold his phone out toward the room. Occupying the screen were the spread naked buttocks of a dark-skinned girl perched in a squat over a glass cup held by a female acquaintance. Her sphincter gave a little twitching pulse, and then she began to defecate into the glass. Only after Harris had physically seized Jack's phone—at which point the two women had begun to make out with mouths full of shit—had Jack finally stopped laughing.

Over the preceding weeks, this had become a sort of hobby. They would be sitting at dinner in the Dining Center or at a table upstairs in the library and Jack would suddenly hold up his phone to reveal a video of a large-breasted middle-aged woman fellating two men at once or a girl sliding a cucumber into her rectum, howling until someone snatched his phone away. He seemed to revel in the opacity of the line between pornographic and sensational.

I always get uncomfortable with stuff like that, just because I've never found sex funny *the way that other guys do. I've also never found professional porn appealing at all—the girls just look unhealthy and cheap and sad,* Foster would write one night after returning from Vito's, where two horrified First Year girls in an adjacent booth had glimpsed the Japanese woman being spanked with a wooden paddle on the screen of Jack's phone, *but in this case there was the awkward fact that . . . I actually found the video kind of hot.*

Foster's uniqueness in this respect is uncertain. Until the iPhone assumed its monopoly over the consumer market several years later, there were two dominant approaches to negotiating Kennedy's online pornography moratorium. The BlackBerry's internet browser was crude but functional, and if you had retrieved a male Kennedian's phone from his bedside while he slept, there you would find terms like *creampie* or *slut gangbanged* or *college girl anal* among its most recent Web searches. Others, disinterested in masturbating to low-resolution videos on a business-card-size screen, found themselves subconsciously broadening their libidinal horizons. Had they less faith in their firewall's efficacy, members of Kennedy's Information Services office would have studied the activity on the school's servers and observed a minor but nonnegligible surge in traffic to the artwork-sharing website DeviantArt coming from male residences between the hours of 9:00 and 11:00. What had begun as a platform for fan art and amateur graphic design had by the late 2000s also become a repository for forms and genres of erotic content too recondite to snag in Kennedy's content filters: artfully softcore illustrations, certain schools of fetish art, fantasy-driven erotic fiction. It was with a certain horror that Foster had discovered his receptiveness to the latter.

He paused for a moment as he sat naked at his desk, listening to gauge the perfectness of Brennan House's silence. He opened his laptop with one hand and took his penis in the other. It was cold and taut with the bloodlessness of the Adderall's vasoconstrictive vise, and for several minutes he jerked it spasmodically. It was only when he numbly opened his Chrome browser and clicked to DeviantArt that he felt it find something approximating fullness.

He had been both horrified and anthropologically fascinated to discover the internet's rich catalogue of Harry Potter erotic fanfiction while browsing the internet one summer afternoon in middle school, in between the releases of *Half-Blood Prince* and *Deathly Hallows*. The very premise had left him vaguely affronted—he thought of the Gryffindor robes from five Halloweens past in the attic—and it was a thrash of self-loathing shame when several years later, suddenly confronted by a dearth of pornographic variety as a Second Year at Kennedy, he found himself reading it. On this particular afternoon, perhaps impelled by the Adderall comedown's spiritual despair, he arrived at a story with the alliterative title "Hermione's Humiliation." Its pairing of Hermione Granger and Severus Snape honored what he bleakly knew to be a trope of the genre, and he found himself struggling to picture anyone other than Alan Rickman as the one derobing Hermione to punish her for her academic immodesty.

And yet Foster felt his penis stiffen as he scrolled down the text, as a nude Hermoine bent over Snape's desk for spankings by an enchanted riding crop. He paused momentarily on lines that emphasized her shame. He shifted naked against the chair, the tips of his toes chafing against the carpet underfoot as they curled. It was only when he arrived at Snape levitating a broomstick handle-first in the direction of Hermione's vagina that he suddenly recoiled at the grotesquerie of the entire enterprise, and with a spastic jerk he slapped his laptop shut. Against the new darkness of the room, he knew that his orgasm was nearer than he'd realized, and instead of feeling his dick soften in his hand, he found his mind reeling around almost arbitrarily for something to affix itself to. He thought suddenly of Annabeth standing as Hermione had, naked and debased. The spasmodic rhythm of his hand quickened just as the sick thrash of guilt burned inside him, and as his buttocks clenched and his orgasm approached, he found himself imagining Jack standing before him, his naked penis palpable in the vividity of his thoughts. Before he could dispel the image in his mind, his eyes wrenched shut and he ejaculated. He felt his semen spill over his edge of his hand. After a moment, he reached down almost rhythmically for the T-shirt he'd removed minutes before. After wiping his hand and dick he dropped the shirt to the floor and sat there in the darkening shadows of the afternoon.

It was a little after nine when Foster heard the knock. He was sitting at his desk; the copy of *Death of a Salesman* he was to read for Tierney by Friday was neglected atop his stack of Mead spiral notebooks. In his apathy, Foster had surrendered himself to the milky glow of his MacBook's screen, idly scrolling down Facebook and only vaguely consuming the disjointed narrative of data that spilled before him.

Annabeth Whittaker uploaded seven new photos to the album <u>round deux</u>. He clicked on the first thumbnail above this bulletin. It was a grainy shot, captured via her BlackBerry's three-megapixel camera, of Gracie and Frances as they walked down a Manhattan sidewalk before Sofi's party. Their backs were to the camera but their heads were turned back to Annabeth, laughing together at some secret joke. Annabeth had not tagged—and indeed may not have noticed— Porter Roth, who stood farther down the sidewalk, waiting for her friends, half-concealed by the low-resolution night. Foster had seen these already but tapped through them again dully with his right arrow key: Annabeth and Frances in the mirror of the nightclub bathroom, cast ghostly in its purple light; Mason and Jack and Pritchett, mugging before the camera on the dance floor; Sofi and Gracie on an Upper East Side corner, in the daylight of the morning after the party, the malaise of their hangovers filtered into something wearily cosmopolitan by the muted composition of the cell phone camera. That Foster was in none of them was not lost on him. He clicked out of the window and scrolled idly down his News Feed. Will Bartholomew and Evan Siegel joined the group <u>KELLOGG HAUS 08–09</u>. Mark Stetson, Harris Adelstein, Jack Albright, and 18 other friends are attending the event <u>KENNEDY LAX VS. DEERFIELD LET'S F***IN GOOOO</u>. Porter Roth joined the group <u>"not my daughter, you bitch!": molly weasley appreciation society</u>. Then there was the knock—four abbreviated raps, quick and yet somehow hostile.

"Yeah," Foster called, quickly closing Safari and clicking to Word's minimized icon so that *honors_euro_study_guide.docx* spilled out to occupy the screen.

The door opened, and there was Jack, and behind him stood Mason Pretlow.

"Can we come in?"

"Yeah, yeah, for sure," Foster said. Jack and Mason closed the door quietly behind them, and within the confines of Foster's small room they seemed to loom. The two boys were dressed in the conspicuously cavalier athletic gear they'd accumulated over years of summer leagues and private clinics and out-of-state championship tournaments, with hair uncombed and vaguely deadened by the industrial shampoo-soap from the dispensers lining the walls of the communal showers. Both wore sweatpants; neither had on underwear underneath. (*I always wonder if that's intentional*, Foster had once written.) The letters across the chest of Mason's fluorescent blue mesh pinnie had sloughed away in the wash. His arms were naked, tanned, and thick; within the rise of his sweatpants, his penis seemed fat and heavy.

"Not happy to see me, Dade?"

"More surprised to see you in Brennan during study hall." In the psychic twilight of the lingering Adderall comedown, Foster found he did not have the confidence to look at Mason directly; he reached down to his naked foot and picked at the nail on his big toe.

"We were just in the lib with Annabeth and some people, and Chissom said he could pop by for a moment," Jack said. There was something intentional about his ease. At some point, he had pulled the drawstring from the hood of his sweatshirt (2006 TRI-STATE ALL-STARS) and cut away its metal ringlets, allowing the holes to fray and open. "She thinks he's borrowing my Euro notes. But we actually had something we wanted to talk to you about."

Foster's mind jumped to the weight of Annabeth's hand in his on the Brooklyn Bridge, and the sparkle of friction he had felt between her and Jack in certain moments, when she threw her head back and screamed a laugh at the jokes Foster had always found heavy. He thought, as he had more than once in the days since Sofi's party, about the silent things he might have betrayed in those hours his blackout prohibited him from remembering.

"Yeah," he said, his voice hollower than he would have liked. "What's good."

"So"—Jack looked at Mason, who gave a stiff half-nod—"we were telling some of the guys on the team about your Addy prescription, and how chill it was that you let us take some at Sofi's this weekend. And Brent Rivenbark"—an affable, erotically magnetic Third Year "with balls as big as fucking apples, I shit you not," Foster had once heard Jack saying—"was telling us about how his summer team back in Boston used to take it before they'd play. And, y'know, we have a decent shot at actually taking Mid-Atlantics this year, and so we"—he jerked a thumb to Mason—"got started talking, and—"

"We think you should enter the market," Mason interjected.

"Enter the market," Foster repeated.

"What we're saying is"—Jack looked down at Foster with a searching, earnest face—"it would be, like, a miraculously good deed if you could let us buy some of your Adderalls. It would just be for us and some of the lax guys. For games, and then maybe a few for, like, before dances and exams."

"You'd be the fucking hero of the lacrosse team," Mason said. Foster was not sure if he imagined the mocking bite in these words.

"It's just like"—Jack anxiously shoved a hand into the front of his sweatpants, where Foster felt his eyes go—"this is the year when colleges are gonna start looking at me and Mason, and, like—we can't afford to ever not be on. And normally I wouldn't even think about this, but, like, you're a friend and I feel like, with tennis and everything, you kind of understand where—"

"Think you've made your point, Albright," Mason said.

Mason was certainly not north of five-eight, but he had the aggressively compact build of someone who'd spent his early adolescence trailing his two older brothers to the gym. His brown hair was curly, almost nappy, but he cut it short and it hugged his head close, like half-cooked instant ramen that had been laid there soggy and left to dry.

The date of the short entry posted to Foster's Blogspot the following day allows us to affirm that this was the night of April 21, 2009, though the short collection of sentences therein only alludes gesturally to the specifics of the encounter itself. *I wish I could say that I was cool about it, that I sounded like I was the one holding the cards. That's the me I want to be; I'm him on my best days, when everything aligns, but I realize that the truth is that I'm hardwired to be a pussy. I'm embarrassed to even write that. Fuck.*

"Yeah," Foster said. "Sure. No problem."

"Are you—sure?" Jack asked. Their eyes met, with the same illegible intensity Foster had felt standing in Pritchett's bedroom three nights prior, the lines of Adderall enumerated on the surface of the yearbook. "We'll pay you, obviously, that goes without saying, but I don't want to, like, force—"

"He said yeah, Jack."

"I wouldn't even be asking if you hadn't said yourself that you don't ever take it, but, like, of course—"

"Yeah. It's cool. I'm down. How many do you need?"

It was only in the startling relief that passed over Jack's face at Foster's words that Foster finally realized the desperation that had proceeded it. *It was weird how badly he seemed to need it*, his Blogspot read. He held out a curved hand for Mason to slap, which Mason did with an aggravated intensity. "Yeah. Fuck yeah. Dade, seriously, I can't th—"

"Let's start with twenty," Mason said. Foster saw that he was looking over to the dresser on the other side of the doorframe, where the three orange bottles—Adderall, Vyvanse, and Lexapro—sat urn-like next to the cup holding Foster's toothbrush.

"If you can spare that many."

"I can spare that many," Foster said, intending a tone of casual experience. "My doctor gave me ninety, and the only ones I've used were on Saturday and then one today. And then there's also this other thing I have, Vyvanse, which is apparently similar but takes longer to wear off, if—"

"The Addy's fine," Mason said brusquely. "Twenty Addies. We'll let you know if we need more or want to try that other—thing." Before Foster could respond, he reached over to the dresser and picked up the closest bottle. Foster realized with a start that it was his Lexapro.

"Escit—escitalo . . . pram," Mason said, furrowing his brow at the label. "Take once daily each morning for depression and anxiety." He looked at Foster with taunting inquisition. "What, not happy to be here, Dade?"

Foster felt himself flush and opened his mouth, hoping it would conjure a retort that was suave.

"Fuck you, Mason," Jack said first. He pulled the bottle from Mason's meaty hand and placed it back on the dresser, looking to the other two. "The orange ones, yeah?"

"Yeah," Foster said, hoping he did not betray his gratitude.

"So—twenty," Jack said. Foster could feel the menace of Mason's stare. "Wanna say—ten bucks a pill? So—two hundred bucks?"

Foster blinked. He thought of the savings account in his name at Bank of America, quietly heavy with years of birthday checks, and the checking account whose red plastic debit card he used at Vito's and the student shop. ("It was never about money for him, I don't think," Pritchett Pierce told me recently. "Like—we heard about all the stuff with his parents' divorce, in the end, but he wasn't on scholarship, and, like, we were sixteen and at boarding school. What would he need that sort of cash for? So, no. I don't think he was doing it for the money. Which kind of makes it a lot more interesting, but I'm no therapist.")

"That's chill," Foster said.

"And if this becomes a regular thing," Jack said, "You'll make serious fucking bank." His voice had calmed, but there was an eagerness with which he twisted the cap of the bottle open. Turning his head anxiously in the direction of the closed door, he poured a pile of the little disks into his palm and placed the open bottle onto the desk behind him.

"Serious fucking bank," Mason intoned, as Jack plucked up pill after pill and handed them to him, Jack's mouth silently forming the shape of the numbers he counted off. The empty Ziploc bag that Mason pulled from the pocket of his sweatpants was suspiciously ready. Mason grinned at no one in particular and sealed it with his thick fingers before cramming it into his pocket.

"And"—Foster looked up at them—"do you think this will be a regular thing?" He was not sure what he wanted the answer to be.

"We can talk about that later, if you're up for it," Jack said quickly. "But in the event that it does—"

"It goes without fucking saying that this stays between us."

"What—what he said," Jack said lamely.

Less passive now, Foster found himself wanting very badly to punch the contoured outline of Mason's genitals. "Yeah, sorry, was planning on having lunch with Theresa Daniels to fill her in on my entrepreneurial pursuit." He forced himself to look Mason directly in the eyes. "Maybe a Facebook status, too."

Mason's nostril twitched. "I'm saying don't go fucking giggling about this with the girls, as much as you enjoy being their little gal pal."

"Relax, dude." It was unclear whom Jack was addressing. He looked to Mason. "Dade's chill. He gets it. But seriously"—he turned then to Foster—"like, I think we all know how fucked we'd be. Pretty sure that drug dealing tends to trump the two-strike rule."

Drug dealing. Foster turned the sickly words over in his head. The flash of nauseous anxiety would be his most palpable emotion that evening, but it abated.

"Trust me," he said wanly. "I get it."

Jack smiled at him. "We'll have your cash tomorrow. Gotta settle up with the boys on the team who want it." He paused. "Mason's gotta bounce, and I need to do some work, but—you're a fucking hero, Dade. Really.

The smile Foster returned was thin and sadder than he meant, but Jack had already turned to follow Mason out. Foster had his hand within the waistband of the old Patagonia athletic shorts he had pulled on from a heap of clothes on his floor after his shower, idly holding his penis. He sat like that for an indefinite period, until he heard from somewhere in the house Delia Chissom's singsong lilt: "Ten minutes until lights-out!"

He was shifting upward to pull off his clothes when another knock came on his door, lighter and gentler than the one before. "It's open," he said, pulling his hand from his shorts.

It was Jack. His hair was wet and hung dark against his forehead.

"Run out already? Foster smiled, tilting his shoulder in the direction of the pill bottle open on his desk.

Jack grinned. "Don't put it past me." There was something melancholy to his smile when he wasn't around his friends, and again Foster sensed the nameless thing he'd felt in the lock between their eyes. "Listen—I just wanted to say: thanks for hooking us up."

"It's no biggie."

"And yo"—he paused again—"fuck Mason, too. He's a dick. Don't take it personally."

"Hard not to."

"You're a saint, Dade, and everyone knows it. And, like, just so you know, about your other pills"—Jack appeared to be searching for his words, and finally resorted to jerking his head in the direction of the Lexapro bottle on the dresser—"I get it. I've, like—had a doctor tell me I should try that stuff out."

Foster looked at Jack quizzically, and found himself replaying the night that Mark Stetson had come out, when Jack sat despondently at his desk, his face pallid in his MacBook's light.

"Yeah, you know—I get really fucking stressed about school and lax and everything," Jack said, breaking his eyes away from Foster's and looking off in the direction of the closet. "I'm fine, of course, but, like—I can talk about that stuff if you ever want to."

Foster felt the quiet energy of ten things at once. He looked at Jack and managed a smile. "For sure, dude. Of course."

"Bedtime, gents!" Delia Chissom leaned her head into the ante-room behind Jack, her long brown hair tangled into a pleat.

"On it, Ms. Chissom." Jack looked at Foster again. "Anyway," he said, patting his hand awkwardly against the doorframe. "You're a superstar. Cash tomorrow. Mum's the word."

Foster shrugged indifferently. "All good, Jack."

I am writing this on a night more than ten years later, and I imagine that several hundred miles away, among those dark fields of rural New Jersey that stretch beyond the intractable glow of Manhattan and the muted constellation of refinery towers' red beacons, the teenagers who now occupy those dormitories do so no differently, with the same wordless belief in the magic of the rituals of their lives. They were kindergarteners, if that, at this moment in Foster Dade's story. They fill the spaces shaped by the shadows of those of us who preceded them. It is the presence of our nameless ghosts that inculcates this magic, just as for us it had been the ghosts of those who came before us, who fleshed out the legitimacy of the drama we believed we occupied.

And on this night, when his lights were out and he lay beneath his comforter, Foster stared up into the darkness, finding the contours of shadows that were not there. His phone sat next to him on the mattress. He found himself hoping it would buzz, but it remained silent and black.

XXV.

Foster Dade's MacBook Pro/Music/iTunes/Playlists/early spring. (Created April 13, 2009)

Name	Time	Artist
Sleepyhead	2:55	Passion Pit
Lisztomania_Phoenix_SNL_04_04_09_	3:44	YouTubeAudioDwnld.mp3
Cuddle Fuddle	4:33	Passion Pit
Favourite Colour	2:37	Tokyo Police Club
I Love College	4:01	Asher Roth

CHIDDYBANG_OppositeOfAdults.mp3	3:15	MashupCentralDotCom
Float On	3:28	Modest Mouse
IDreamedADream_SusanBoyleBritainsGotTalent	5:49	YouTubeAudioDwnld.mp3
Ottoman	4:02	Vampire Weekend
She's So High	3:44	Tal Bachman
5 Years Time	3:55	Noah and the Whale
Death and All His Friends	6:19	Coldplay
That Was a Crazy Game of Poker (Live)	8:43	O.A.R.
Life in Technicolor	2:29	Coldplay
Walcott	3:42	Vampire Weekend
N.A.S.A.	4:27	Futurecop!
Age of Consent	5:15	New Order
She Moves in Her Own Way	2:49	The Kooks
Heard 'Em Say (feat. Adam Levine)	3:23	Kanye West
This Charming Man	2:43	The Smiths
Dreams	4:31	The Cranberries
Kids	5:02	MGMT

22 songs, 1.6 hours, 190.4 MB

XXVI.

On a Thursday morning in the second week of May 2009, Brent Rivenbark woke up in his room on the third floor of Kellogg House to the chime of a Facebook Chat message arriving on the MacBook he'd left open on his desk. It was from his older brother Scott, then a sophomore midfielder on the lacrosse team at Haverford, and it contained only a link to a YouTube video.

The video had been published to YouTube two days prior. It was titled "The Ultimate Lax Bro," and Brent's first thought was that the boy in it looked vaguely familiar, before realizing that he simply resembled a paler postpubescent version of his Second Year teammate Jack Albright: the same thick dark hair coifed by the enclosure of a lacrosse helmet; the same baritone insouciance. (The coral-colored shorts and mesh pinnie very well may have been Albright's, but they could have also been anyone's.) Brent watched the video twice before

clicking back to Facebook and finding Albright's profile. "yo it's you,"
he typed above the link he pasted on Jack's wall, before turning to
where Carter Macksey, his roommate, snored beneath his comforter.
"Yo, Macks. Wake the fuck up and watch this."

By the start of practice that afternoon after classes, the video had
been shared across the Facebook Walls of no fewer than sixteen members of the Kennedy varsity lacrosse team. During practice that day,
Chip Mitchener, who had returned to his alma mater twenty years prior
to coach lacrosse after leading Trinity College's team to two consecutive
national titles, would blow his whistle and shout at his players to "quit
sucking each other's cocks and get their heads out of their assholes" after
a third shooting drill collapsed into a series of dueling impersonations
of the video. "We have fucking *Deerfield* on Saturday and you're out
here prancing around like a gaggle of bitches!" Mitchener yelled from
the sidelines. "If you're enjoying yourself so much, Albright, why don't
you get the fuck off my field and go join the fags at theater practice!"

"Yes sir, coach. I mean—no sir."

"The Ultimate Lax Bro" acquaints the viewer with a gregariously
vacuous young man named Brantford Winstonworth—the titular
Bro—who plays midfield on the club lacrosse team of an unspecified
New England liberal arts college. Winstonworth moves across his
campus with the nonchalance of a young man whose grandfather's
name adorns half its buildings, sloppily cradling his lacrosse stick
while sharing his athletic and sartorial wisdom.

A decade later, the six-minute video has amassed just shy of three
million views on YouTube. There are not three million lacrosse players in the world: indeed, a slim majority of those teenagers along the
Northeast Corridor who would post the video's link to Facebook in
the spring of 2009 did not play the sport. To them, it was an overdue
lampoon of the passive vulgarity of the boys in coral-colored shorts
who moved across their high school campuses with a self-fulfilling
air of authority, whose social capital—or so these viewers chose to
tell themselves—would after graduation suffer the precipitous collapse that they knew from AP Economics always follows periods of
grotesque overvaluation. But no one loved the video as much as the
lacrosse players themselves.

There is always a narcissism in self-recognition, of course, and even the most trenchant satires thus never quite sting as they're meant to. (For curious evolutionary reasons, teenage boys tend to prefer watching films and television shows they've already seen; of the titles populating this communal shortlist at Kennedy in the spring of 2009—*Old School, V for Vendetta, Almost Famous, Step Brothers*, with occasional nostalgic returns to *Napoleon Dynamite*—Mary Harron's 2001 adaptation of *American Psycho* was among the most watched, and almost certainly the most quoted, at least among the boys whose fathers could have been among its characters.) There's a case to be made that the members of Kennedy's varsity lacrosse team would have no longer needed Foster Dade's pregame Adderall to play against Deerfield that May Saturday after "The Ultimate Lax Bro" appeared on YouTube. It was their *Triumph of the Will*, eliciting a warlike, even libidinal thrall of which Riefenstahl would be jealous. (If all of this seems too serious a psychocultural exegesis, my only response is that one cannot overstate the certitude with which these boys believed in the mythic imperiousness of their own egos.)

And of the thirty-two players on Kennedy's varsity lacrosse team that year, none seemed to revel in the video's narcissistic verve more than Jack Albright. On the Friday morning before the Deerfield game, Foster Dade awoke to the sound of Jack's manic bellows pushing through the stucco walls of Brennan House. "This one is my *morning spoon*!" The shout was followed by the unmistakable sound of the lacrosse ball's dense rubber being heaved hard against a carpeted floor. "I use this one to just toss around in the backyard with my *buddies*!" The heavy thwack again, followed by the softer sound of the ball bouncing waywardly down the stairs from the second floor.

"Shut the *fuck up, Albright*!" Harris Adelstein yelled.

"I will literally pay you money to never quote that video again," Gracie Smith said over the lunch table that day, not looking up from her BlackBerry as she thumbed out a text.

"I think the correct nomenclature for this work of art is actually 'film,'" Jack said with what appeared in the light to be an actual gleam in his eye. "And besides, I don't need your money, because"—he looked across the table and locked eyes with Mason—"*I'm very affluent,*" they said together, dropping their voices two octaves.

A spasm of murder crossed Gracie's face as Annabeth hooted with laughter.

"Your boyfriend was quoting it in the locker room all day yesterday, for what it's worth," Mason said with an even smile. "It managed to keep our eyes off his enormous johnson in the shower."

"Fuck you, Mason."

"So—boyfriend now, huh, Smith?" Jack asked, grinning.

"Not by a mile."

"Yeah—haven't you heard, Albright? You can fuck someone who isn't your boyfriend. It's the twenty-first century, man, get with it."

"Boys, come *on,*" Annabeth moaned, as Gracie glowered at Mason and Jack. Her mouth twitched as if on the precipice of opening, and then raged out of the glass-windowed dining room.

"It her time of the month or something?"

"Yes, actually, but also fuck you." But Sofi Cohen's lips twitched with a smile as she spoke.

The prior Sunday, Annabeth had confessed to Foster that Gracie had, on some unspecified Saturday night in the preceding weeks, surrendered her virginity to John Stillwell, a surly, taciturn Fourth Year from Vermont who would be playing at Duke that fall. "Do you think he talks more during sex?" Foster wondered aloud, the image of the two of them in the baseball dugouts or atop a seminar table in Memorial Hall—Gracie, flat-chested and tanned and stoic even in coitus, flexing her face not to show the winces of pain; John, thick and boulder-like and muscular, thrusting atop her with the abandon of one utterly at home in his unquestionable heterosexuality—passing by his thoughts and then fleeting. Annabeth laughed at this, loudly. They'd been the only two left in the Dining Center at the end of brunch, and only when an elderly employee in a hairnet had finally rapped on the window of Brennan's dining pod with a bottle of Windex had they set out into the afternoon. "Honors Euro can wait," Annabeth had said decisively, pulling off her old Lake Placid crewneck and briefly exposing the flatness of her stomach. "It's fucking beautiful. We're walking." They'd moved along the Field House's driveway and then down the length of the soccer fields, Annabeth bounding ahead to do a cartwheel in the wet grass. At the fields' end she'd kicked through the deadened vines to the vast, harvestless expanse of the cornfields. "*I love summertime!*" Annabeth had bellowed out over the deadened plain. It had been four in the afternoon by the time they'd emerged from the far woods to the stretch of golf course before the girls' Houses.

We walked around the fields maybe eight times without either of us realizing it, Foster wrote that night. The clichés, Jesus, they're true: I lose track of time when I'm with her. Am I stupid to even wonder that she might feel it too? She told me that Gracie Smith fucked John Stillwell, and also mentioned that she's still a virgin, which I knew, but it was nice to hear. "I know it's dumb, but I want my first time to be special," she told me. I told her I did, too. I didn't have the nerve to see if eye contact was a possibility in that moment. We went to Vito's after and sat for another hour. It all felt so easy. I mean, god, fuck, I was awkward and probably borderline autistic. I wonder how other guys know if/when to make a move. Maybe I'll get Annabeth drunk sometime. Dream big.

Clouds had hung obstinately over Kennedy the week that followed, and on the Friday night before the Deerfield game they relented with a short, angry storm. Foster had fallen asleep happily with the wind straining against his windows, the rain dispersing the light of the streetlamps below into banded smears of amber, and when he awoke on Saturday morning the clouds were gone, and the sky an even cleaner blue.

There was an electricity to the movement of bodies to and from classes that morning. It had begun to hum a week prior, when the varsity lacrosse team had returned from Connecticut just after midnight after beating Groton in double overtime; along the Meadow and Ellipse, their classmates had awoken to their triumphant bellows. By midweek, even the frailest and most allergy-prone Kennedians knew that the coming Saturday's game against Deerfield would either guarantee or quickly truncate what would become the team's first undefeated season in just over a decade. Few students gave much thought to the sport proper—by virtue of the game's historical and geographical peripherality, the ratio of current or former lacrosse players to lacrosse enthusiasts isn't quite one-to-one but close enough—but as the week grew warmer and the players' cross-campus whoops grew louder, the game amassed the heft of those events that bedazzled and sustained the wordless mythology of Kennedy: the more raucous school meetings; certain dances. Will Bartholomew, the pimpled Third Year who found in his enormous iTunes library a substitute for a personality, had been enlisted to DJ from the sidelines. Kendall MacPherson, the varsity girls' captain that year, had volunteered her team to preen and sashay outside the Dining Center at lunchtime on the Saturday of the game, brandishing Sharpied poster boards and screaming with unfettered delight whenever one of the male players left lunch for their locker room in the Field House.

"It's like they're going to war," Jason Stearns had muttered loudly to Foster as they approached the Dining Center after leaving Cline's Honors European History. "Look at their fucking scowls. Jesus."

But Foster had been watching Annabeth, who stood in a white T-shirt and a pair of short red Nike athletic shorts and whooped especially loudly when Jack Albright, Mason Pretlow, and a severe-looking First Year whose name Foster did not know walked through the building's glass doors. "Crack some *skulls*, Albright!" Annabeth shouted, kicking a browned leg skyward in a deft impersonation of a cheerleader. *I think she's funny because she borders on irony without being insufferable about it*, Foster wrote once. As he had when she had cartwheeled down the soccer field, Foster watched with shameful intentness as the fringe of the shorts slid with her leg's upward movement, exposing the curve of her thigh where her buttocks began their contours. He thought fleetingly that apart from incidental post-shower encounters with his sister in their mutual prepubescence, he had never seen a vagina.

Jack blew her a kiss, and as he turned toward the stairs down to the Field House door, Foster watched as Kendall MacPherson leaned over and quietly said something to Annabeth with a prurient smile. Annabeth squawked with laughter and pretended to slap Kendall across the face, and then, Foster noticed, her smile did not wane.

Foster had met her on the brick stoop of Hewitt House at half past two. *All of our friends will be at the game, but she asked me to walk over with her, alone,* he'd written after lunch while prostrate on his bed. The air was heavy with its warmth, humming with the distant roar of a lawn mower tending to the golf course beyond the other side of the girls' Houses. The grounds felt still: most were already making their way beyond the Dining Center toward the Astroturfed lacrosse field; those who weren't—a scant handful of the most book-ish day student types, mostly—sat hunched over textbooks in the air-conditioned recesses of the library or had had their mothers pick them up after their last morning class.

"And approaching on the right we have Foster Dade, who breaks Maryland records as the one white kid from Baltimore to never pick up a lacrosse stick," Annabeth said in a deep baritone into an invisible microphone in her fist, then beamed at him.

"I'm a disgrace to my countrymen," he said, grinning back.

"I think you just like being a contrarian."

"I think you just like making fun of me."

"'Cause I'm so *good* at it."

They moved with the last stragglers beyond the Field House toward the wooded rise of Chauncey Field. Of all of Kennedy's collegiate-caliber athletic complexes, none approached the dignified professional-ism of the park-sized expanse of clean Astroturf that had been carved into the campus' highest hill twelve years earlier: a gift from the Class of 1971's MacIntyre "Mac" Chauncey, who had captained the team at Princeton before setting up the highest-earning hedge fund on the West Coast and who had been given a platinum-lacquered shovel for the groundbreaking ceremony in the summer of 1997. The industrial sodium lights that rose above the high bleachers along the three fields gave the Astroturf an extraterrestrial luster; during night games, students in the front booths at Vito's could look in the direction of the Meadow and see the silhouette of the chapel's belfry discerning itself against the chalky pallor of the lights three-quarters of a mile away. A long concrete embankment fifteen feet high held back the earth below the hill's upper slope; here, a vast LED scoreboard paced between live footage of games and brief biographies of their players, either grinning or scowling—preference varies by player—in Athletic Department headshots now seven feet tall.

Foster could hear the hoarse bark of Chip Mitchener's yells before they approached the gravel path to the field. "Is he just, like—always unhappy?" Foster asked wildly.

The *Kennedian* would later estimate that seven hundred people turned out to Chauncey Field for the Kennedy-Deerfield game. Mitchener would strike the reader as uncharacteristically effusive in this article, quoted as saying "it was the biggest crowd I've seen in twenty years, and the boys just want to say thanks for the support." As Annabeth and Foster stepped up the narrow path to the stadium, the crowds were spilling onto its grassy banks from the dangerously crowded stands. The vaguest sonic contours and rhythmic bassline of Empire of the Sun's "Walking on a Dream" could be discerned from Main Street half a mile to the northwest, billowing from the stadium loudspeakers that hung with the lamps on their silver poles. Beneath them, Will Bartholomew hunched intently over his MacBook on a grainy-plastic folding table, his pale face in a furrow of concentration.

Foster and Annabeth found their group on a central row in the center box of bleachers, which Sofi and Porter and Mark had seized by showing up to the field an hour earlier. The two pushed their way apologetically between the legs of ambiently annoyed spectators to where they sat: Sofi and Porter and Mark; Gracie and Pritchett and Freddie and Will. The latter three boys rowed crew, and had the afternoon off ahead of a race against a gaggle of Philadelphia private schools the following day. Mark and Porter shifted away from the sole open space of bleacher between them, on which Sofi had sat her wallet.

"About damn time," Sofi said to them, her eyes still scanning the green pack of Deerfield players returning to their bench from warmups. "Had to nearly fight like eight people to keep these. We've made enemies."

"We owe you the world and more," Annabeth said, sliding in against Mark.

"He's gay but doesn't realize it yet," Mark said, pointing in the direction of a Deerfield player, indiscernible from the rest. "I grew up with him and I just know it."

"How good's your gaydar, Mark?" Pritchett asked, turning out toward him two seats down. He gave Foster an amicable nod and grinned.

"Never been wrong yet."

Foster awkwardly sat between Annabeth and Porter. His buttocks felt hot and shameful as the girls shifted in profitless courtesy. "Sorry I'm obliterating whatever space you had," he said to Porter Roth, who was wearing jeans despite the warmth.

She grinned awkwardly. "It's all part of the fun."

He could feel the palpability of both her thighs and Annabeth's against his, the naked skin of Annabeth's legs rubbing against the leg of his shorts. He noticed again, as he had in a recent shower, that the dark hairs climbing his lower legs were thickening, and in that moment he was glad for it. Forcing himself to look away from where Annabeth's exposed thigh met his, he found his eyes on the natural crease in the zipper of Porter's jeans. Annabeth had told him that Mason had recently done what Porter had not been able to bring herself to do and ended the pseudo-relationship that had spanned months out of bored convenience. "She won't let him fuck her," Jack had told him on the floor of Andrew O'Donnell's room in Brennan after lights-out, a recent Lil Wayne mixtape trickling quietly from the speakers. "He says he fingered her a bunch, to no avail. He keeps claiming her pussy is—sometimes less than rosy, if you catch my drift, but that's precisely the sort of shit Mason lies about out of spite."

Foster, for whom such sexual explorations were still more or less an academic matter, found himself put off by the crude expectations boys his age expressed: that vaginas be waxed bald and odorless; that a certain submissive svelteness of body was more important than breast size. ("She has small tits because she's *skinny*," Mason had said with irritated confusion on the train to Manhattan weeks prior, when the conversation had turned to the sexual appeal of their female friends and Foster had commented on Gracie Smith's flat-chestedness.) Out of a vague puritanical shame he looked away to the field. His anxieties had always mitigated the fear that seemed to plague other boys his age: that he would find himself getting an erection simply from the presence of an attractive girl.

The starting lineups were taking their places along the geometrical turf. Today, the midfielder taking the face-off was Jack Albright. That Albright was just a Second Year was not lost on Larry Goldenberg, Kennedy's gruff, squat Director of Athletics, who sat above the stands in the commentators' box to interrupt the flow of Bartholomew's playlist with abrupt little observations adjoining the data on the scoreboard's digital screen. "He's young, but he's fast, with impressive ball-handling skills that make it clear that he's a mature player—yep, he's the right one for this today," Goldenberg was saying.

Before hunching down before the opposing Deerfield player, Jack had looked toward the stands and given what was unmistakably a grin, wide and confident, from under the black bars of his helmet's face mask. Foster did not join his row in its eruption in that moment. "Let's goddamn go, Albright!" Freddie Pieters hollered, pumping his fist toward the blue sky. "I love you, Jack Albright!" Sofi Cohen screamed. "I love you ten times more!" Annabeth screamed in return.

The whistle blew. The scrum of midfielders enclosed on the skirmishing pair within their circle, in the aid of a ball cast wayward in the struggle, but this was unnecessary: within seconds the red-jerseyed form of Jack Albright pushed from the throng and sprinted in the direction of the goal beneath Will Bartholomew's perch. "That's Albright with the ball after a picture-perfect face-off," Goldenberg was saying, "and he's just swimming by those Deerfield defenders, thanks to a pretty check by defensive midfielder Mason Pretlow, who typically stands with the defensive line but is versatile enough to run with the midfield—and there's Albright—and *there's the first point of the game, ten seconds in*! Watch Albright, ladies and gentlemen—just sixteen and already a hurricane!"

The stands around Foster erupted; his eardrums throbbed. Jack ran back from the goal toward the field's center, stick above his head, the pantomime of warlike seriousness he typically wore during games briefly subdued. "*Do I get chicks? Yes,*" he roared, to both his teammates and their audience, shifting his vocal octaves to summon Brantford Winstonworth. "*Do I play lacrosse? Yes. Do I get chicks because I play lacrosse? No. I'm very affluent.*"

The aluminum bleachers seemed to strain beneath the crowd's noise. Foster felt vaguely claustrophobic.

"Keep your head on straight, Albright!" Mitchener was yelling from the bench on the field's opposing side, but there was a glint of excited mirth there. "Don't get cocky; keep your focus!"

"God, he's such a fucking ham," Pritchett said as the players lined up for a second face-off. Foster was not sure if Pritchett by then knew what he did: that Jack and more than a few of the teammates around him had broken Foster's Adderall into chalky orange halves in the Field House locker room before walking out to the field. Though he may have been imagining things, Foster believed he could feel the edge to Jack's kinesis on the field.

Two and a half weeks had passed since he and Mason had stood in Foster's room during study hall. Foster had returned to Brennan the following afternoon to find an unmarked white postal envelope slid unceremoniously through his bedroom door, fat with crumpled twenties, tens, and fives. There had been no comment of the transaction to Foster since—Mason Pretlow had returned to his usual stance of aloofly contemptuous disdain—but when he'd passed members of the varsity boys' lacrosse team on campus, a much higher number of them than usual gave him the cursory nods that pass for amicable acknowledgment in teenage males.

"He loves an audience," Annabeth said admiringly. "Hey," she said, turning to Gracie and Porter, "where's France?"

"Crying in the library," Gracie said simply, watching the players grind their cleats into the vivid floor of the polyurethane field.

"She bombed another math test," Porter said solemnly, "and Cantrell told her today that that means academic probation. I dunno if it's official, but still"—Porter, a famously meticulous student, seemed to shudder slightly—"I feel horrible for her."

Annabeth frowned. "I'll text her." And then she turned back to the game. "Get in his business, Albright!" she yelled.

Foster made it six minutes into the second quarter. *It's honestly staggering how miserable I am when I'm forced to watch sports*, he'd written once. The game before him was nothing more than a random spat of motion. He considered making further conversation with Porter Roth, who was similarly quiet, but found himself too nervous to do so. It was a mundane sort of nervousness, but nervousness all the same.

White clouds were beginning to sit over the trees at the stadium's far end when Foster finally found the grit to rise. "Hate to be lame," he said, looking to Annabeth and then Pritchett and Will, his most certain social allies on the bench, "but I actually need to go finish that paper for Cline. Library's less distracting when no one's in it."

"Aw, but it's such a stellar game!" Annabeth's pout up at him seemed both genuine and somehow erotic.

He shrugged, ignoring the aggrieved rictus of the North Jersey father three rows behind him. "You're blockin' the game!"

"But of course," Annabeth smiled. "Baltimore's prodigal son."

He smiled back, hitting Pritchett's and Will's fists with his own as they extended them out in his ungraceful shuffle past. From the speakers overhead came the machine chafe of Passion Pit's "Sleepyhead," which in the weeks since spring break had come to occupy the hundred or so more avant-garde iTunes libraries on the Kennedy network. And then he descended the bleachers and made his way down the gravel path.

Foster let himself revel in the quietude of the empty campus as he crossed it. The sounds of the game behind him distorted themselves and faded into an ambient smother as he rounded the trees below the trail from the stadium. Two Third Years were making out on the empty football stands that descended from the rear terrace of the science building.

There wasn't a paper for Cline; he'd submitted his op-ed for the next week's *Kennedian*, picking apart Kennedy's requirement that all students attend one campus religious service of their choosing per term, the night before. He was going back to Brennan, to enjoy the solitude of the empty house and perhaps jerk off, but as he approached the library he remembered the email he'd received that morning from its lost and found, informing him that he'd left his Spanish textbook in the reading room the night before.

The library was empty. The slap of his Rainbow flip-flops against the marble floor climbed in their echo up to the eaves of the building's tall-windowed atrium. He had retrieved his textbook from the indifferent library attendant in the lost and found office on the second floor and turned back down the alley alongside the book stacks when he collided with a girl exiting their narrow lanes. "Oh, shit, whoops," he said. And then, looking at her, he realized it was Frances Evans, and that she had indeed been crying.

By the spring of 2009, no fewer than ten boys in the Third and Fourth Years—broad-shouldered baseball- and lacrosse-playing boys—had harbored serious, persisting, schoolboy-sappy crushes on Frances Evans of Far Hills, New Jersey. The earliest of these dated to the evening in her first weeks at Kennedy when she and Annabeth Whittaker had sauntered over to the Meadow in tank tops and Soffe shorts. Of the small cabal of beautiful girls that had magnetically cohered in the First Year girls' dormitory that September, Frances was, popular opinion held, the one most commonly understood to be Hot. Tousled streaks of summer blond ran through her beechwood-colored hair, even in the winter; her breasts were fat and pert, and her smile—and this is where we see the pathos and innocence of those boys' fixations, in their attention to her smile—seemed to economize the joy of whatever moment prompted it, widening and natural and white. She claimed she did not know that she led these boys on purposefully. "They're my *friends*," she'd protest. She would carry on six or seven conversations on BlackBerry Messenger with any of them in any month, and they would message her ceaselessly; as her phone buzzed behind her on her bed, she would be removing her bra before her MacBook's camera, delighting in the awestruck stupor of the sophomore Bucknell University midfielder she had nominally been dating since they met on Nantucket the prior summer, where he had taken her virginity.

And Foster understood it, in that moment, noting that even with her hair tousled and the skin below her eyes red and puffed, with boogers of mascara clinging to her cheeks, Frances was very pretty. That she looked deeply embarrassed to have been seen in the present state was only more endearing. This did not make the moment less awkward.

"Hey, France." He had never called her France before.

"H-hey, Foster." Frances sniffled. "Shouldn't you be at the game."

"Not a sports guy." He shrugged with a half-smile. Then, lamely: "Are—are you okay?"

Frances searched his face, and for half a moment she seemed suspicious, perhaps angry. And then she burst into tears and collapsed into Foster's body, her sobs like squeals in the chest of his Gilman T-shirt.

He stood there for several seconds, very much startled and also suddenly sympathetic to those baseball boys who craned their necks for her in the stands at their games. Then, not knowing what else to do, he put his arms around her back slowly and gave it several pats.

"Hey—hey—it's okay," he said. "What's going on?"

She kept her face against his chest for a moment longer, but the squealing sobs subsided, and then she separated and looked up at him, her cheeks glossy.

She sniffed again, with the congested sound of snot returning upward. This too was attractive. "It's stupid, I'm sorry. I'm so embarrassed," she said, trying to smile. "It's just that"—she looked about to sob again—"I'm just so fucking stupid, and I know I shouldn't be here, and I wish I'd known that when I applied but now I might have to leave because of it, and I only applied because my mom made me, because her brothers went here, and she already thinks I'm dumb to begin with, and—" Her face was quivering; her eyes were red and her voice heavy with mucus.

"Hey," Foster said, and his warmth was sincere. "Slow down. What's really up?"

She paused to control the incipient tears, then swallowed. "It's math. And chemistry too. English and history kind of but mostly math and chem. It's just that, like"—she swallowed again, then sniffed again—"I just can't make my head understand it. I look at the page and it's just numbers and symbols and I just can't. And my teachers are nice but they mostly just feel bad for me. And I failed another test which meant that they had to tell Cantrell and then Cantrell had to send an email to my parents, and my mom, my mom—"

She began sobbing again, this time into her arm, as if hoping to hide herself. *You're dumb, Frances; you're just dumb*, her mother had said once when her daughter returned home from seventh grade to find her drunk in the kitchen, the year before she went to her first AA meeting in Far Hills.

"Hey," Foster said again. "It's all right."

She looked up at him, wiping a string of snot onto the arm of the yellow cable-knit sweater. "Easy for you to say," she sniffed. "You're a genius, Annabeth is always telling me."

Foster's stomach quietly swooped, though it was not lost on him that Frances's voice had formed a sniveling tone of mild contempt around Annabeth's name. His face apparently betrayed this.

"It's just that, like," Frances said, "She's so fucking *smart*"—the same tone again—"and always makes a point of letting us know that she got another A-plus or that another teacher called her brilliant, and, like, I'm her roommate, and she knows I struggle with the school stuff, and sometimes I feel like she's, like, doing this on purpose."

The fullness of the comment made Foster wonder if this was true, but he swiped the thought away. "Hey, let's talk about this," he said. "Ignore Annabeth and ignore your mom. Listen. Chem is fucking stupidly hard—I barely get it either, and while I appreciate the thought that I'm a genius, I don't get A's in it, for the record."

She seemed to search his face again, this time with something resembling a very sad form of hope. "You don't?"

"Hell no. You should see my grades from fall term. Hardly genius material. And you know"—he paused for a beat—"have you ever thought that maybe you have ADD, or been tested for it? Because like, I have it, apparently, and it kind of does explain a lot." He realized he had never said this out loud to anyone before, the plain fact of his diagnosis.

Her face soured. "My mom says she doesn't believe in it. So she won't pay for the test. And they won't do it in the counseling center here, because kids just want the drugs." Now she paused. "But wait, Foster—" (He later wondered if she knew that her quizzical look was profoundly endearing, and if she'd made a point to say his name.) "Freddie mentioned to me the other day—is it true you're selling Adderall?"

"Freddie told you that." With unpleasant clarity he pictured Chip Mitchener or Mr. McCall finding the Ziploc of little broken pills in Mason's lacrosse bag or on Jack's desk.

Half a look of worry flashed over her face, alert to her error. But she stayed composed. "No, no, don't worry—I think Mason mentioned it to some of the Ames boys, but that's all. And Freddie told me just this week. I don't think anyone else knows."

Foster was silent. "Yeah," he said finally. "I have Adderall. And—this stuff called Vyvanse too. I don't ever really take it. I gave some to the lacrosse guys but I think that was, like, a onetime thing."

Frances sniffed again. "Yeah, I get it," she said. "I get it. But, like"—her face searched his once more, its intention evident now—"so, I have a makeup test for Algebra Two, but I have to get above a C-plus or I'm put on academic probation, and, like—I mean, if you think I might have ADD, I wonder if—"

"You're wondering if you could have some Adderall." He would later despise himself for how cool he believed in the moment his smile to be. *It's like I subconsciously believe that being a fucked- up, medicated teenager somehow makes me interesting.*

Frances nodded, with a silent eagerness that was both childlike and erotic. "Yeah," she said hoarsely. "How much for it?"

And he would later despise himself for the way he would just begin talking, suspending the anxiety that so regularly paralyzed him as if the conditions of this Faustian self-bargain suddenly permitted him to do so, as if the adrenaline of what felt like this moment's possibility allowed him to finally trounce it. *Cool. God, I fucking hate that word. And I hate that I care about it.*

"Yeah," he said. "It's fine. Totally fine. I get it. So—the lacrosse guys paid ten dollars a pill. My advice for you would be to split them in two and take half. Or if you want, you can try the other one, Vyvanse, too. Apparently it lasts longer. So I'd say ten dollars a pill, and I don't know how many you want, but I wanna let you have two or three for free, since, y'know, like I said, I get it."

The words just came. The ease of their flow accelerated as Frances Evans's face brightened with them; when Foster finally shut up, she was beaming.

"Ten bucks is fine, totally fine," she said. "Jeez, Foster, you're amazing. You're so nice. Thank you." He felt himself blushing. "So—you said take half of the Adderall, and how long will that be good for?"

"For me, about four hours, but maybe longer for you, because you're smaller."

The flash of confusion on Frances's face suggested that she did not comprehend what Foster had thought was a rather self-evident inference of human metabolic function. "I gotcha," she said. "And what about the other one, the Vy—Vyvern?"

"Yeah, the Vyvanse," Foster answered, careful not to sound as if he was correcting her. "So, my doctor says it's 'smoother' than the Adderall, whatever that means, and that it'll keep you focused for longer. I actually haven't tried it, but honestly, I probably should—finals and all."

Frances nodded. "So—what if I bought, like, four of the Adderalls, which I'll split in half, and then—two of the other thing? Just to try it?"

"Then I'd say you owe me forty dollars, because two are on me."

She beamed again and threw her arms around him.

"God, jeez, Foster. Wow. Wanna just text me when you have them and I can come by Brennan or something?"

"Yeah, that works," Foster said. And then he heard, from a quarter mile beyond Chauncey Field, the muted roar of seven hundred Kennedians on their feet, screaming their throats raw. "Listen, I need to bounce. But I'll holler in a little while or else tomorrow, is that cool?"

"Totally." Frances was still beaming. "Amazing. God." She looked at him. "Annabeth has been so right about you, you know. You're just wonderful."

XXVII.

http://www.fhd93.blogspot.com/05_09/days_of_sunshine
(Posted May 15, 2009)

Recenty [*sic*] I feel just . . . taller. My back is straighter. I want to smile
more. I don't know what it is. Maybe I'm just nostalgic because this
strange fucking year is already almost over. And maybe that's why I'm
being reckless. But maybe that's also why the sun seems to be shining
warmer and brighter. I'm in love with her and I think maybe I'm in love
with life again.

XXVIIIa.

Among the attempts to excavate truth from the apocryphal rubble
more than a year later, only the particularly dogged reporter for the
New York Times managed to pin an ID to the party involved in Foster
Dade's second transaction. In deference to both his editor's legal skit-
tishness and the courtesies of journalistic ethics, that reporter—who
like many in his industry later relocated to Washington to cover the
Trump administration—made the two calls to politely request confirmation of what a deep-background source had texted him from a
New Jersey area code that morning. This was a Tuesday afternoon in
November 2010; the story was slated for seven columns at the front
of New York/Region that Friday. He would ultimately leave two
voicemails. Kennedy's Communications Director, Sheila Baxter, the
indefatigable former crisis-PR exec whose political-but-nevertheless-
friendly patience with this reporter had expired quickly, had stopped
returning his calls three weeks prior; like many by the early 2010s,
the Watson and Marjorie Evans he'd found listed in Far Hills assumed
most calls to their landline were from telemarketers, and let them ring
until the answering machine broadcast its transcription to the kitchen.

The following morning, the reporter's otherwise dormant fax
machine whirred to life twice in a span of fifteen minutes. Lawyers
still use fax machines, even at Sullivan and Cromwell, which would
be representing both Kennedy's Board of Trustees and one Frances
G. Evans in the twin defamation suits that would land on the *Times*'s
Midtown stoop with an infrastructure-shaking thump should the paper

choose to print "names of unrelated persons in a manner intended to damage another's character and/or reputation." The letters were almost interchangeable, written with the calm atonality that attends the confidence of the ruin they threaten, but these were two discrete cases. Kennedy was defending not its former student but itself.

But while Frances Evans's name was effaced from these accounts, their narratives commenced with this Saturday afternoon in the second week of May. Which is to say: it is at this juncture that subsequent details will begin to align with whatever version of this story you may have encountered elsewhere—in the *Times* or the *Atlantic* or *Vanity Fair* or even Gawker. In these tellings, the story spans those ten months from May 2009 until its culmination early the following spring, with only digressive, scene-building regard for whatever may have preceded this window. It did not help that at the time of their writing, almost all the characters in question had been told that talking to the press was grounds for "exceptional disciplinary action": Kennedyese for immediate expulsion, two-strike system be damned. Others, of course, simply could not be reached.

After that afternoon with a sobbing Frances Evans in the library, it all seemed to happen all at once. All at once, and by the time he could really stop and think about it, his first year at Kennedy was over. But if we try to assign those nebulous last weeks to some narrative structure, we would start by noting that Foster returned to Brennan from the library and locked his bedroom door, then pulled out the two pill bottles. He tapped out four of the peach-colored Adderalls onto the cover of the notebook on his desk and then opened the second bottle. He had noticed then, watching the Vyvanse capsule wobble and roll across the lamplit desktop, that the blue-and-white pills were oddly elegant. He picked one up with his index finger and thumb, holding it to the light as their ethereal jeweler might. He thought he could hear the silent rattle of the micronized chemical salts within it.

He wondered why he hadn't tried them. Without giving a visible amount of conscious thought to the matter, he placed the capsule on his tongue and swallowed.

Feeling no different twenty minutes later, he walked in his bare feet to the water fountain down the hall when he heard Brennan's front doors open, bringing with them a wave of triumphant bellows. From the mob of Third Years ensconcing him, Jack Albright looked up at Foster Dade with a manic grin. "*Dude*," Jack yelled, breaking from the pack. His hair was hard with sweat; he was still wearing his elbow pads. He threw his arms around Foster. "I reek but whatever. Dude," he said, quieter now, "You saved . . . the . . . fucking . . . day. The Addy. I was fucking superman. You saw, right? You were there?"

"I saw," Foster lied, grinning amicably. "I thought Goldenberg was going to ejaculate in his Dockers in the commentator's box."

"They're gonna rename the stadium after you one day if I have any input on the matter," Jack said, clasping Foster's shoulder. "Dude. Let's celebrate. Talmadge dance tonight." His voice fell an octave. "Freddie and Pritchett have booze. Let's do it right. I'm not gonna have a comedown from the Addy, am I?"

Foster thought about the pill he had swallowed and the fiery kinship between them early on that night in the city. *I fucking love you, man. I'm so fucking glad you came to Kennedy.* "Well," Foster said, looking at Jack. "You know that other stuff I have? That's like Adderall but longer and apparently better? I just took one"—he grinned—"if you wanna join me and stave off the comedown."

"You *dog*," Jack crowed in delight. "Fuck yes. Hook me up."

The Talmadge House dance was the last of the year. Classes the following week would be muted by the double ennui that precedes final exams and the promise of summer beyond it; teachers would attempt to conduct review sessions and then invariably surrender to the fidgets and wayward stares before them. Scott McCall had sent an email to the boys in Brennan and their parents, instructing them on where to park their Suburbans and Lexuses on the Friday after exams for move-out day, with a postscript for those lucky underclassmen who'd been asked to the following night's Fourth Year Prom. Things were ending.

"Shit always gets weird at the last dance," Andrew O'Donnell had told Foster while shaving what stubble he had from his pale face one morning that week, a white towel wrapped haphazardly around his bony waist.

Immediate-release Adderall is akin in intensity and duration to a more empathetic, more cerebral cocaine; Vyvanse takes this jagged spike of neurological activity and smooths it into a long elegant wave: not so much rolling over its consumers as carrying them up along their gorgeous tidal sweep. This is what psychiatrists mean when they call the drug "smoother" than its cruder amphetaminic predecessors. Adderall is the harsh crash of the cymbal and Vyvanse is the long, pensive jazz solo on the clarinet, seamless and endless and beautiful.

"I, like, don't think it's working," Foster said to Jack as they crossed the Meadow from Brennan for Mason and Freddie's room in Ames. Jack's hair was wet from his shower.

"Mason has more of your Addy if nothing happens," Jack said. The sun was setting; the blue sky seemed to carry the gold interwoven in its fabric. "We can just snort it."

Indeed Mason and Pritchett and Freddie were doing exactly just that when they arrived in Ames, Swedish House Mafia straining the capacity of Freddie's speakers. Framing the square on Freddie's desk on which the lines had been cut was a small collection of plastic Coke Zero bottles of varied fullness. "Rum and Coke," Freddie grinned to Jack and Foster, handing them a bottle. Foster clutched it and took a generous pull, and to his happy surprise he realized that the flat rancid syrup somehow did not repulse him as it might have. Jack had leaned in toward the Adderall, but Foster grabbed his wrist.

"Wait," he said. "I think it's starting to come on. Maybe wait and see."

"What's coming on?" Freddie asked eagerly.

And it was. A warmth was spanning the strange intimacy Foster began feeling in that space, a space occupied with people who in clearer-headed moments had provoked in him a quiet and unassailable discomfort for the preceding nine months. He had felt a shadow of this security in Pritchett's bedroom in Manhattan the prior month, but this was gentler, less ragged, seemingly more authentic. A moment

later, Jack—his metabolism accelerated by an afternoon of exercise—
turned to Foster.

"Yeah," Jack said, with a slow grin. "I feel it."

"Feel *what*?" Freddie whined, lobbing a mechanical pencil at him.

"We took the other ADD med I have—Vyvanse," Foster said,
exploring this new confidence. "About an hour ago. And—it seems
to be doing its job."

"What, none for us?" Mason asked, looking at Foster, but even
he seemed kinder.

"You plebs are stuck with the spoils," Jack said, theatrically
extending his hand toward the crumbled orange chalk on the surface
of Freddie's desk. "In due time, maybe. We've taken it upon ourselves
to inaugurate it."

"Well, technically, Frances Evans was the first."

The boys looked at him with confused brows. Foster, grinning as
the Vyvanse began to rise over him like some shimmering majestic
cloak, found himself just talking.

"Well, someone"—he jerked his head at Freddie and Mason with
a conspiratorial smile, enjoying this confidence—"let our prior business transaction slip, and I found her sobbing in the library about her
substandard scholastic performance, and, well," he grinned wider, "I
guess I took pity."

"You gave it to her?" Pritchett asked.

"I sold it to her. Same rate applied."

"Dude, Dade," Freddie said excitedly, turning up from the line
he had just inhaled. Freckles of orange dust clung to his nostril's
periphery. "This is, like—a business opportunity. With finals next
week, and the SAT next year—you could be the king of the school.
Fuck, I'll singlehandedly keep you in business."

Foster smirked. "Come by my office sometime."

To the deep chagrin of the Kellogg House social rep Will Bartholomew,
a large faction of students would note in the days thereafter that Talmadge had put on the best dance of their time at Kennedy to date.
The cards were always stacked in the event's favor, of course, coming
not only at the end of the year, with the flirtatious imminence of sum-

mer, but also mere hours after the most explosive lacrosse victory in recent memory, but the successful execution of the venue does deserve its credit. From the edge of the Meadow by the darkened Memorial Hall, the strings of lights a hundred yards away gave the illusion of a cruise ship out on the horizon of a warm estival sea, its orange miasma spilling into the settling twilight. Foster had the sudden urge to sprint toward it, feeling his pace quicken, and apparently so did Jack, who bounded forward and then turned to face the boys behind him.

"*Weeeee . . . are the champiooooons . . . my frieeeeends,*" he bellowed in song, shutting his eyes and throwing his arms up into the coming night.

"You're so fucking lame, man," Freddie Pieters called out, but he, too, was grinning.

Mark Stetson and Will Thierry had joined them for the walk to the dance, Jack bounding before them to the distorted sways of the music coming from the lamplit distance. "You boys are certainly enjoying yourselves tonight," Mark said, craning his neck to parse the small mob of tall First Year boys crossing the grass ahead of them.

"Looking for someone, Mark?" Pritchett grinned.

"I would put fifty dollars on the odds that Matt Dawson is a fag, and I intend to follow this hunch to its logical conclusion," Mark said, still scanning the broad-shouldered mob.

"Matt Dawson from lacrosse? You fucking wish," Mason crowed.

"You'd be surprised, Pretlow," Mark said with a smile.

The plot of earth beneath the strings of lights was already crowded with bodies, frenetic with the excited pulse of imminent summertime. This was still the era of the mash-up; throbbing from the sound system was a pastiche of Pitbull's "I Know You Want Me" and Coldplay's "Viva la Vida," which surprisingly worked. The boys arrived on the fringe of the dance and took it in. "Let's fucking go, shall we," Jack said with a magisterial grin.

Foster did not black out that night—the stimulus of the Vyvanse guaranteed that—but his subsequent recollections were nebulous, spilled with the effluent glow of the string lamps and the sway of the shadows they cast. He would remember the music clearly. "DONT-TRUSTME" by 3OH!3, beloved by Annabeth and her posse the prior summer in Nantucket and Southampton, was on when Foster saw those girls weave themselves into the dance floor; Beyoncé's "Sweet Dreams" played as he watched J. T. Ricciardelli wander up to Annabeth awkwardly, flanked by the brawn of his friends, and put his hands around her waist. She turned to see who had done so, and when she saw it was J.T., whose affections she had deftly dodged for more than twelve months, she smiled warmly and leaned in to whisper something in his ear, sidling herself from behind up into his groin and waist. Foster was delighted by the absence of any jealousy, and under the incandescent lift of the Vyvanse, he moved with the boys to where a group of First Year girls danced at the center of the floor.

Pritchett Pierce had spent the better part of the winter and spring terms abstrusely involved with a First Year from the Philadelphia Main Line named Sally Pinelli. The pairing, in Pritchett's account, was deeply ambivalent and mostly physical, less a relationship than a sustained series of somewhat sullen evening encounters in unlocked classrooms and dark baseball dugouts. The daughter of an orthopedic surgeon whose face grinned down from billboards over I-295 and the Schuylkill Expressway (*PREFERRED SURGEON OF THE PHILLY FLYERS!*), she was a very pretty girl with large breasts and wide hazel eyes, and also clever and coarsely funny in the way that the daughters of affluent Italian-Americans only a generation removed from the ethnic lower middle class tend to be. Under different circumstances, Pritchett, who was also clever and cynically observant in a way Foster felt was underappreciated, might have liked Sally quite a lot, though of course she had given up any effort at demonstrating her charms months earlier. Sally's unrequited infatuation with this tall, taciturn Manhattanite was the unromantic sort that blossoms, diseasedly, only in the void of the other's disinterest. It was a dynamic born of logistical and political convenience. The sex itself—or sexual contact, in this case; both were still virgins in the spring of 2009—is almost incidental. It was out of duty to this political self-perpetuation that Sally Pinelli morosely found Pritchett beneath the string lights.

For the first time in his first year at Kennedy, Foster's inhibitions seemed to have dissipated, burning off into the night as he danced, both self-reflexively and passionately, with an equivalently spirited Jack. Mason, Freddie, Will, Pritchett, Mark: they danced too, but they formed the orbiting electrons to Jack and Foster's atomic center. Even Mason seemed to have forgotten his resting contempt. Those around the boys laughed appreciatively, their usual disdain for the cabal's perceived arrogance tempered by the commanding force of Jack, whose charisma made him well-liked, and Foster, who remained even then a sort of enigma. Foster and Jack gyrated and spasmed with each palpable beat of "Sandstorm," the infectious electronic track familiar to anyone who frequented a sporting event or mainstream nightclub in the same era. Their eyes were wrenched shut, sweat dripping happily from their faces. Occasionally they opened their eyes to meet in a mutual lock, and then their dancing would assume a sort of frenetic, dialectical pantomime. *It was—really just fucking fun*, Foster would write the next day.

It was not Sally but two of her own cohort who penetrated this cluster and thrust themselves between its constituents. The first was one Bettina Scott of Darien, blond and tanned and sprite-like. The second was Kaitlyn Sanders. *Speaking of townie sluts*, Gracie had said that winter night at Vito's, as if commenting on the weather.

With a certitude and confidence that was both contrived and persuasive, Bettina and Kaitlyn thrust themselves into the center of the cluster where Foster and Jack were dancing. Noticing this, Jack grinned, taking Bettina's hand and spinning her beneath his and then pulling her in. Foster froze for a moment, attempting a mental calculus that would inform him how to convincingly emulate Jack's carnal ease, but this was unnecessary: Kaitlyn sidled up in front of him with a suggestive half-smile, placing her hand on his hip.

"Hi," she said, and then pulled him even closer, moving her hips against his. He felt her dark hair against his cheeks. "Foster, right?"

"Y-yeah," Foster stammered, his voice lost to the music. "Kaitlyn, yeah?"

"Yeah," she murmured as she pulled her mouth close to his ear. She knew what she was doing; despite both his sexual anxiety and the Vyvanse, he felt a warmth trespassing into his penis. Her hips seemed to convey heat and he felt his hands gingerly grasp her waist; she took them in hers and moved them down to the face of her thighs. Foster looked past her hair to lock eyes with Jack, who was ensconced identically against the nimbler Bettina. Jack grinned, and Foster felt himself grinning back. That the motions of this dancing were in Foster's head contrived and infertile did not preclude his knowledge that it did not matter: this—dragging one's groin in short jerky spasms against a First Year's ass and silently acknowledging the venal triumph in the wordless language of masculine friendship—is what one did when they belonged. He allowed himself to revel in it, even if he did not.

And then there on the far end of the dance floor, along the parking lot abutting Gregory House, were Annabeth and Gracie and Porter and Frances, each of them involved in a liaison of their own. Their boys were Fourth Years, all lacrosse or hockey players, high on the dissociative thrall of their final weeks in this kingdom with which they'd pressed themselves with impunity toward the girls. Annabeth seemed lost in the moment as she swayed herself against J. T. Ricciardelli. *Look at me*, he thought with summoned intensity. And then, impossibly, she did, and their eyes locked. Annabeth looked at Foster and then to the girl thrusting against his groin. Her expression was hard to discern, but it felt like surprise. And then, in a turn of kismet that seemed almost too spectacular through the perceptive prism of the Vyvanse, Kaitlyn turned her head toward Foster's.

"Want to get out of here?" she purred. In the spill of the lights Foster noticed a small clump of foundation against her cheek, the color of unripe peach flesh.

"Y-yeah," Foster heard himself say, looking away from Annabeth while keeping himself in her peripheral vision. He felt Kaitlyn's clammy hand take his. Another rhythm of kismet: the path along which Kaitlyn led him from the dance floor took them immediately by the corner where Annabeth and her friends danced. (That this may have been a deliberate and impetuous calculation on Kaitlyn's part did not dispel its flicker of munificence.)

Foster felt his female friends' eyes follow him as he moved. Sofi and Frances cast him playful grins as they moved within the grasp of their respective boys; Gracie did not bother to contain her disgust. Porter Roth was awkwardly attempting to seem at ease under the meaty clutch of an ice hockey player named Jeremy Brevard. To her left was Annabeth grinding against J.T. *She seems to be able to find happiness in anything, any situation*, Foster had written on his Blogspot one night that winter. *I don't know if it's authentic, but if not, it's an impressive skill, and I think it's why so many people are drawn to her.* Her mouth was caught in an elusive half smile; her eyes seemed to be closed, until they opened wider as Foster passed, her delicate eyebrows arching upward. Kaitlyn Sanders seemed to deliberately brush by her as she led them from the dance, but Annabeth looked not at her but at Foster. Her lips opened in a small O of what again seemed like surprise. *Of course I want to believe that she was jealous*, Foster would write the following afternoon. *And I shouldn't delude myself. But, like—she didn't seem, like, delighted to see it.*

Foster felt himself try to arch his own eyebrows and offer what he hoped was a sly grin, but Kaitlyn had pulled him through the throng before he could see how Annabeth received this. He chose to believe what he thought he felt, which was the burn of her eyes following him as he stepped out toward the darkness.

Even the most incredible rumors have a point of origin in the truth. This is purely an epistemological point; morally, I'll note, there's not really a conceivable defense for the fever with which stories had percolated around Kaitlyn Sanders since approximately the time she bought her first bra. The nude cell phone photos, blowjobs, more than one alleged threesome—the truth of these allegations is ultimately less interesting here than their genesis. It offers a study in the oldest Puritan ritual, which weaponizes the conveniently vast edicts of sexual morality to punish those whose sins are on their own terms less actionable. For the other middle school girls at Wilmington Friends, where she arrived on scholarship in sixth grade, Kaitlyn Sanders's cardinal transgression was not promiscuity but presumption. A baffled and hurt twelve-year-old Kaitlyn had not understood why the girls at her new school looked at her the way they did, or why, after she spent her savings at the Ralph Lauren factory store on the pinks and greens they favored, their vicious laughter followed her down the hallway as she retreated to the bathroom to sob. (Her mother, an office administrator for a periodontist in Hockessin, would return home that night and find the shirts in the bottom of the kitchen garbage.)

Unwanted by those of her own gender, Kaitlyn turned instead to the attention of boys. She taught herself to apply eye shadow before her mirror and saved up her money for push-up bras; in seventh grade, she began walking alone on Friday nights to parties hosted by the ninth-grade boys who'd affably asked her for her number or screen name. The expressions on girls' faces never softened, but suddenly their lacerations cut shallower. It was a sophomore in the upper school named Kyle Dupree who told her over AOL Instant Messenger that she was beautiful, late on a December night in her eighth grade year, and with these words those early scars closed over. He said it again in a text message the following night, and then he asked her if her phone had a camera.

And so we return here to the sociological fact of the matter: there's always truth to be found in gossip. When, just over two years after Kaitlyn arrived at Wilmington Friends, the photos of the naked teenager in the dirty mirror—clutching her right breast in one hand and her already-démodé Motorola in another—spread like a flu virus across cell phones throughout Wilmington's and suburban Philadelphia's private schools, it seemed to be incontrovertible evidence affirming the worst of the rumors, and even Kaitlyn herself seemed to concede defeat, returning home from the school-ordered counseling session to google financial aid packages at various northeastern boarding schools.

Foster was jarred by how quickly things proceeded after Kaitlyn led him from the dance into the darkness. He was only beginning to mentally articulate some form of small talk when, beneath the awning of the Moyer History Building, she turned to him and thrust her mouth on his, her tongue vast, wet, and intrusive. As they had on the dance floor, the procedure felt to Foster something like a performance, or at least less authentically libidinal than he imagined sexual encounters to be. Which is to say he was not hard. Kaitlyn pulled away and stepped up onto the narrow brick veranda that ran along the front of Moyer, pushing Foster against one of its stone columns. She smiled at him with what he thought she imagined to be a suggestive smile, and the thought occurred to him that he had only met this person forty-five minutes prior. She took his hand and rather forcefully shoved it up the white tank top she wore.

"You like that?" Kaitlyn murmured as she leaned in and nibbled his earlobe. He was again aware of his loins' stillness. They had been kissing for maybe two minutes, his hand idly stroking the contours of her bra, when he realized that more than anything he was bored. Perhaps Kaitlyn sensed this too, because she then pulled away and, after taking a glance around her to ensure that the darkness sufficiently shrouded them from any potential passersby, she looked at Foster with a sickly gaze and pulled her tank top over her head. She let it slide down her leg to the concrete at their feet. Her bra was purple and spangled with a leopard-print pattern. Foster found himself thinking, to no small degree of distress, of Matilda Wormwood's gaudy mother Zinnia (Rhea Perlman) in Danny DeVito's 1996 adaptation of the Roald Dahl novel. And then Kaitlyn unhooked the bra and let it fall dumbly to the ground.

In the meager darkness Foster could not discern the details of her breasts, beyond the fact that they were large. In the absence of his arousal he found himself only bewildered by the situation, by the foreignness of the contours of the shadows before him. He wanted very much to not be there. "You like that," Kaitlyn said again.

The twin prospects of offending her and humiliating himself distressed him equally, so he closed his eyes and, thinking wildly of a Pornhub clip he'd once seen, bent down to put her areola in his mouth. In the darkness he did not know if it was in fact her nipple that he was sucking. He probed it with the tip of his tongue and felt the dull protrusion of the nipple itself.

Kaitlyn emitted a moan that even in his sexual inexperience Foster understood as only a bad imitation of pornography. She took his head in her hands and pulled it back upright, and with the same stare look of erotic magnanimity, she reached down to his waist and pulled the leather tongue of his belt through its buckle. That she did so without breaking eye contact was one of the things that made the rumors seem credible. He stood there catatonic. She pulled his jeans to his ankles—he realized now she was crouched on her knees—and the force tugged the elastic waist of his boxer shorts—J.Crew, blue and patterned with yellow tennis balls—down several inches, exposing the whiteness of his flesh beneath and the highest perimeter of his pubic hair. Positioned before him as if prostrating herself, Kaitlyn looked up at Foster through the heavy darkness of her eye makeup. And then she pulled his boxers down as well.

Because of both the Vyvanse and his stress, his dick was not only flaccid but shorter and thinner than usual. The first expression that spasmed across Kaitlyn's face was less one of disappointment than surprise, but she seemed to catch herself and correct it, and before Foster could offer any version of a humiliating apology she had taken his now-nimble penis in her fingers and opened her mouth onto it. His curiosity briefly trumped his mortification, and he looked down to see the top of her head rocking back and forth against his naked waist as she attempted to slurp life into him. For a moment, the taboo of the scenario—one in which he was nude and exposed from the waist down in public; one in which, in a more ideal fantasy, Kaitlyn Sanders would be absent—threatened to stir the blood in his groin. He thought he felt the earliest twitch of an incipient erection, and considered allowing himself to close his eyes and escape into his most prurient fantasies, as if he were simply masturbating. Just as he was going to turn his head back and let his eyelids shut, Kaitlyn gazed up at him while frenetically sucking his lifeless dick. There was an odd, contrived look in her eyes, and Foster realized that even then she was attempting to pantomime the practiced gestures she believed to be seductive or coquettish. Foster was now not only humiliated but also sad.

This went on for a minute before Kaitlyn finally pulled her mouth away. She looked up at him again and wiped the accumulation of saliva from her mouth.

"Um—maybe it's nearly time for check-in," she said, embarrassedly.

Foster felt his face burn once more, and blinked out toward the darkness of the night. The muffled bass thumps of the dance from beyond Gregory House seemed to have faded. "Yeah, hey, this isn't typical for me," he said, forcing a sheepish smile. "So, like, I took my ADD meds before the dance, and I guess I didn't think I'd be leaving with anyone, because they're, just, like—a boner killer."

To his great relief Kaitlyn stood up, wiping her mouth again. He leaned down to pull up his boxers and then his jeans, cognizant of how his buttocks flexed and spread as he bent. She squinted at him curiously while leaning down to pick up her bra.

"Adderall?" she asked, pulling the bra's purple cups up under her breasts.

"Vyvanse, actually," he said, and found that his confidence had returned now that they were clothed. "And it sucks, because nothing's worse than hooking up with a hot girl and not being able to get hard." He realized how foreign he sounded to himself as he said this.

"Wait," Kaitlyn said, pulling her tank top over her head. To another wave of relief Foster realized they had wordlessly commenced the short walk to the First Year Houses. Shouts peppered the night; in the distance, silhouettes passed through faraway lampposts' tents of light. The dance was over. "I heard about all the lacrosse guys getting Adderall to take before their games. Was that you?"

"Y-yeah, it was," Foster said, grateful that they had escaped the awkward misery of the preceding twenty minutes with some pretense to normalcy. In his relief, the words simply seemed to come. "I kind of sell to people, and Jack—Jack Albright—he's a good friend—we're in Brennan together—and he got me to do a wholesale thing with the team."

They passed the darkened windows of the art studios and arrived beneath the shadow of the cupolaed Fenster Hall, which stood solemnly at the head of the Yard. The long First Year Houses flanking it glowed in the warm night. Foster considered taking Kaitlyn's hand in his, before refusing himself the perpetuation of the farce.

"Well," Kaitlyn said, with a slyness that now seemed less contrived, "if you're interested in doing some more business, my friends and I would love to get some before finals."

"I think I could handle that," Foster said, both grateful for and loathing the edge of machismo confidence in his voice.

They were at the door of Kaitlyn's dormitory. From inside the foyer came the noise of the First Year girls gathering in the common room for check-in. As he entered his number and BlackBerry Messenger PIN into her contacts, he observed that the silver casing of her BlackBerry Pearl—the company's smallest, least expensive model—was pecked with dents and scratches, as if she'd bought it used. He found himself sad again, but did not know why.

"Yeah," Kaitlyn smiled gently. "I'll text you. Um . . ." Half a moment passed. "It was—nice to meet you."

"Yeah. You too. Maybe—we can hang out again," he said, knowing that this would never occur, and indeed that neither of them wished it to. But she smiled, and after another pause leaned in and gave him a quick peck on the lips. And then she turned and went inside her dorm.

XXVIIIb.

"Sanders! You—*dog*!"

Jack took a triumphant pull from the bottle of whiskey and handed it to Foster. It was shortly after midnight in Andrew O'Donnell's room. This, the Third Years' last regular-order Saturday night in Brennan House, demanded commemoration—Harris Adelstein had gone to the third-floor utility closet and retrieved the handle of Jack Daniel's he'd hidden above its ceiling tiles in the fallout of the prior spring's moonshine debacle—and they had invited Jack and Foster along once it was learned they had sexual exploits to recount. Jack had bounded into Brennan five minutes after eleven o'clock, bowing munificently to a bemused Mr. McCall, who peered up at him through his eyeglasses.

"Forgive me, good sir, and issue a detention if you deem it necessary," Jack had said, bowing low enough to graze his fingertips on the common room's oriental carpet.

"You're lucky I'm feeling generous tonight, Mr. Albright," McCall had said.

"I'm in love," Jack now declared to the audience of his housemates. "Scott. Bettina Scott. Where has this woman *been*? Thank God

Jacqueline had detention—though I just remembered on the walk back that they're roommates; whoops." There was a whimsy to his grin, magnetic in its ebullient earnestness.

"You get your dick touched, Jackie?" Andrew O'Donnell smirked, scrolling through his iTunes library.

"Indeed I did," Jack said, grinning. "And thanks to Mr. Dade's pharmaceutical services here I was unable to achieve orgasm, but my God, if I've ever had a better futile blowjob I couldn't tell you when." Then he turned to Foster, grinning wider. "You should have warned me. I don't think she believed me when I said it was the meds."

"I don't think Kaitlyn"—her name sounded awkward and foreign in his mouth—"did either." Foster grinned back. "Talk about a shitshow."

"Are her tits as nice as they seem?" Danny Clements, a rower from Los Angeles, asked.

"If your only concern is size, then yeah," Foster said, taking a pull from the bottle of whiskey.

"What other concern is there?" Harris Adelstein remarked.

"Like all good Jewish boys, Mr. Adelstein's perspective is skewed by his people's tendency to be heavy in the chest," Jack said, lobbing a nearby sock at Harris, and Foster found himself envying his subtle bravado.

"So—Bettina Scott." Foster turned to Jack, eager to pivot the conversation elsewhere. "That gonna be a thing?"

Jack shrugged as if the question were inane. "End of the year—who knows. But"—he took the bottle of Jack Daniel's and took three generous swallows—"my *God* I'd love to spend some more time with that bod."

It was shortly after two when the boys wandered off to their rooms. Foster had swallowed enough whiskey to mitigate what persisted of the Vyvanse. He had left his phone charging on his pillow after check-in; its red light was blinking in the darkness when he opened his door. He pulled off his shirt, kicked his shorts and boxers under the desk, and as he slid himself beneath his comforter he pressed the sleek sugarcube-shaped directional button below the BlackBerry's screen to wake it. The little blue BlackBerry Messenger icon sat below the digital clock—2:17am—with a red flag like a postage stamp in its corner. He thumbed in his passcode and scrolled to the app.

> **Kaitykins xo** has added your PIN from her contacts.
> Two new BBMs from **kaitykins xo**!
> Four BBMs from **ALW**!

His encounter with Kaitlyn Sanders already seemed to belong to a different, distant calendar. That she had contacted him helped quiet the anxious flicker that had recurred in his mind since leaving her at the First Year Houses, of his flaccid penis and her perplexed face before it.

> **kaitykins xo [11:49:02PM]:** it was great meeting u tonightt ☺
> **kaitykins xo [11:49:05PM]:** lmk about the aderall! two
> of my friends would love some too if that's ok

He tried to summon the masculine insouciance he had feigned in the twilight of the night's humiliation, pausing for a moment with his thumb on the keyboard before finally typing.

> **foster d [02:18:14AM]:** Hey sorry i've been drinking with
> some of the Brennan guys and didn't have my phone
> **foster d [02:18:19AM]:** For sure. Wanna meet me in the
> lib tmrw afternoon? I have adderall and vyvanse (longer
> lasting, better imo); $10 per pill

Foster was only mildly disquieted by the cruel satisfaction that came with tacitly correcting her spelling. He thumbed to Annabeth's messages, with an accompanying rush in his stomach that had been absent when opening Kaitlyn's.

> **ALW [12:37:35AM]:** fun night?

There was, he noticed, a margin between the first message's time-stamp and those that followed it.

ALW [01:02:46AM]: i was hoping we'd walk home together after lolz
ALW [01:02:51AM]: for what it's worth i think you can do better than kaitlyn sanders hahah
ALW [01:02:58AM]: but i hooked up with jt ricciardelli tonight so who am i to talk
ALW [01:03:01AM]: he asked me to prom
ALW [01:03:05AM]: look out world

He stared at this line of messages for a moment. The screen's spectral glow cast lines of shadows like receding tides on the bedspread before his chest. He could not remember a message from Annabeth to which he had not responded immediately and earnestly. He thought about the occasions when those responses had received no reply, when every few minutes he would look away from his reading assignments to thumb to BlackBerry Messenger in the hope that *ALW is typing* would pulse onto the conversation's header. *i was hoping we'd walk home together after lolz.* He paused, and then locked his phone. In the resultant darkness he placed the BlackBerry next to his head and turned over onto his side.

The stupor of the fading Jack Daniel's allowed him to drift off nearly seamlessly. He fell into that fugue state of dull colors that immediately precedes sleep, when vignettes of that day's spare subconscious memories—the runners-up for the coming night's dreams, maybe—weave together to create a very surreal, dully satisfying film. The darkened naked arms of the trees along the football field; Tierney's voice booming out over his classroom's oval table; a soothsayer, for some reason. The buzzing of his phone.

The buzzing of his phone—three quick spasms into the mattress near his head. It didn't always, but that night it stirred him. He wrested himself up from the curling tentacles of sleep; suddenly, in fact, he realized he was not tired: as he reached for his phone he thought of Annabeth, insomniac and restless across the darkness in Hewitt House, more bothered than she'd expected to be by Foster's silence. The screen was bright; the clock atop it said 2:43am. It seemed strange that only half an hour had passed.

But the notification was not from BlackBerry Messenger but the SMS text inbox, with its little low-resolution yellow envelope spangled with four-pixel red stars. He knew of only one person who ever contacted him who did not have a BlackBerry. "Trust me," that person had once said over lunch in the Dining Center. "In five years you'll all have iPhones. Don't hate me for being ahead of the curve."

Jack Albright [02:42:31AM]: yo
Jack Albright [02:42:36AM]: you awake?
Jack Albright [02:42:40AM]: come chill

We can speculate as to why this particular invitation impelled him. Perhaps it was the crackle of what felt like sincerely intimate friendship he had sensed at the dance and on only a handful of instances prior. Or, more aptly, the gulfs of distance and suspicion in or against which these instances sat, like threads of sunlight in a gray sky, rare and dazzling and cruel. Perhaps, subconsciously, he had read something quiet and unarticulated in any of these moments, sunlight or gray. He pulled himself from bed and found the boxer shorts he had worn that evening. That he left the room wearing nothing else is of little significance: among boarding school boys there is an anxious unspoken contract of ritual heteronormativity designed to regulate and constrain the frightening currents of their unusual proximity to one another; the ability to blithely hang out in your underwear and make no fuss about it is among its edicts.

The perennial brightness of the hallways' lights—a stipulation of New Jersey fire code—made the house's silence strange and uncanny. Foster pressed his feet silently against the stairs, fearing their usual creak, and held his breath as he passed the upstairs door to the McCall family's apartment. He tapped on Jack's door at the end of the hall with only a graze of his knuckles. "Yo," came the enunciated murmur from the other side, and Foster opened the door.

The sagging loveseat on which Jack sat had been left behind by a resident of Brennan two decades earlier; neither he nor the room's subsequent residents had ever been bothered to try to maneuver it out the door. His desk stood against the opposite wall, and on it was the thirty-inch Apple monitor he'd brought from his parents' attic after spring break. A cord ran from its base across the carpet to Jack's laptop, which was perched open on his knees. He was bathed in the blue glow of the monitor's screen; the room was otherwise dark. He, too, was in his boxer shorts. Their seersucker legs were bunched up beneath his thighs, which were pale and hairless. He turned to the doorway, and in his grin Foster could detect something that felt like both chutzpah and nervousness. "I got past the firewall."

"The—internet firewall?" Foster closed the door behind him and sat himself on the loveseat's arm, propping his feet on the open seat cushion and facing Jack. He was careful to position his thighs as to keep the legs of his boxers from sagging open. (A condition of the aforementioned edict involves unspoken boundaries of physical distance.) Even with that space between them he caught the heavy musk of whiskey that seemed to emanate not from Jack's breath but Jack himself. Jack grinned again, more impishly this time.

"Yessir," he said. "Huynh"—a silent Vietnamese Third Year who had ended up in Brennan largely by accident—"figured it out for me."

Now Foster grinned. "No more iPhone porn, then?" What was left of his tiredness had dissipated. In response Jack clicked a Safari window that was minimized in the screen's bottom-right corner. It filled the monitor with the frozen image of two naked women, one blond and one ambiguously Eurasian. The latter had buried her face into the rear end of the blonde, who crouched on all fours and had turned her head toward the ceiling with a contrived grimace of rapture. Foster found himself thinking fleetingly of Kaitlyn Sanders. A tattoo of what was either a rose or a boa constrictor climbed up the blonde's thigh.

"Is she—eating her ass?" Foster asked, furrowing his brow.

"Maybe her pussy," Jack said, turning to the screen with a child's wonder. "Hard to tell. She's moaning like it's her pussy. Here"—he patted the cushion next to him—"stay awhile."

As Foster slid onto the seat, careful to preserve a gully in the sagging cushion between himself and Jack, Jack clicked the play button on the dashboard along the bottom of the video window. The blonde resumed her ecstatic yawps, thrusting her ass into her colleague's face. The Eurasian carried on diligently, then reached up to slap the blonde's naked buttock. The blonde screamed.

"Jesus Christ," Foster said. "You've gotta admire her dedication."

As the video played, they sat in a silence that to Foster felt palpable. And then Jack spoke.

"Dude," Jack said. He seemed to turn toward Foster but did not meet his eyes. "I'm gonna say something and you'd better not fucking judge me."

Foster felt a strange lurching in his stomach. It was not a bad sensation. "Do your worst."

"I didn't get to bust earlier, with Bettina, 'cause of the Addy or whatever it was. And now I'm, like, really fucking horny." Jack had turned back to the screen, fixated upon it almost clinically. He seemed to be speaking to the naked women before them. "Would it be, like . . . super gay if we jerked off to this?"

The lurch redoubled. Foster had been forcing himself to disregard Jack's near-nudity, and especially what he saw now to be a shifting form in the pleat of Jack's boxers. He realized, now, that his own penis was quickening in his underwear.

"Nah," Foster said, finally and quietly. "Not, like, super gay— you're not trying to jerk me off or anything."

"No, I'm not," Jack said firmly. "I'm not a fag. I'd be doing this if you weren't here. Just pretend we're in different rooms."

"Yeah," Foster said, praying Jack did not catch the strange hinge in his voice. "Why not. Boarding school memories and all that."

Foster would not record the events that followed on the pages of his Blogspot or anywhere else. The account that follows is not entirely speculative: many years later, some version of what happened that night would percolate in the form of whispered hearsay, however muted and hollowed out by time. I proceed with the caveat that appends this entire story, which is that certain truths find sustenance beyond fact.

Foster found himself watching as Jack shifted his boxer shorts down his thighs, lifting himself slightly off the faded cushion to do so. Foster's first observation was that Jack's dick was bigger than his own, though not by a significant margin. They shared the similarly faded contours of a circumcision scar. Time had lapsed since he'd last trimmed his pubic hair; its bristle was lighter than Foster's, a burnt copper darker than the hair on Jack's head.

Foster found himself following suit with trepidation. Again staring intently at the video on the monitor, Jack was stroking his dick with aggressive rhythm, his brow furrowed in agitated concentration. Foster began to stroke, and while in his nervousness his penis had softened, but he felt it quickening within his grasp. *Just pretend we're in different rooms.* "Oh, yes, bitch, lick that cunt!" the blond woman in the video moaned, thrusting her rear into the dark-haired woman's face with more frenetic urgency now. But Foster found his attentions not on the crudeness of the monitor's scene but on what he could follow in his peripheral vision—the shadowed blur of Jack's hydraulically spastic arm; what seemed to be his other hand idly stroking his hairless chest.

"Oh, fuck yeah," Foster heard Jack murmur. He realized that though neither of them had shifted in their seat, their naked knees were no longer parallel but turned inward, toward the other. There were maybe four inches between them. In his mounting arousal, Foster's fear assumed a luster of excited purpose. He grabbed at it, and found himself turning his leg even closer to Jack's, and slid himself maybe half an inch in his direction. Jack continued to stroke his penis, but his eyes turned to catch the gesture. He said nothing, and then after a moment his own knee turned toward Foster's. Now they grazed. In a moment that seemed to consume lifetimes and strain against the freight of its psychic capital, Foster watched as Jack took his penis with his left hand, liberating his right, which then reached toward Foster's naked thigh.

Jack's hand seemed to approach with the concerted trepidation of a docking aircraft carrier. What felt like its contact with the coolness of skin may have only been the hot bristle of their silence's palpability. For a moment, Foster thought he braced to shift his weight to accept the touch of contact, but in this infinitesimal choreography Jack's hand had suddenly moved away; in the motion's parabolic tidiness, it was uncertain that it had ever been there at all. When Jack finally spoke, there was a catch in his voice that echoed Foster's own, borne not of his arousal but something deeper and less triumphant.

"We shouldn't," Jack said quietly, looking at neither the screen nor Foster. "We're—"

"We're not gay," Foster finished, pulling his hand away neither slowly nor quickly. "Yeah."

"It's cool," Jack said, turning back to the screen with a newer intensity. What may have been thirty seconds or three minutes lapsed in silence; even Jack's intensifying breaths seemed to have quieted. And then:

"Oh, shit," Jack said. He closed his eyes, and Foster turned to watch as he cast his head back. His eyes were wrenched shut; his mouth had fallen open in a little silent gasp. "I'm gonna—I'm busting—oh, *fuck*."

In the taut periphery of his vision, Foster watched the semen spilling from the tip of Jack's penis onto his fingers as he came. It was copious and milky. And then Foster felt his own accumulating intensity approach its threshold. The porn on the screen had ended several long moments earlier; the video box was grayed out and held the circular icon offering the viewer the option to watch it again. Foster watched Jack's body release its tension, his face slack but his mouth still open, and then Foster's buttocks clenched beneath him in time with the curling of his toes and he had his own orgasm, intense and splendid and followed immediately—before it was even over, actually—with the tide of shame.

"Shit," Foster said finally. He held his hand up to the light of the screen. His semen webbed the spaces between his fingers, its thick strands breaking as he spread them. Jack had pulled a box of Kleenex from the floor and was wiping his dick and hand in silence. The motion with which he then extended the box in Foster's direction was a cursory jerk. Foster took a tissue and wiped himself off, then crumpled it into a lopsided ball within the clench of his fist. He could feel what he took to be Jack's hardened unease, and the shame redoubled.

"Uh, things we should never talk about again," Foster finally said, in a stab at exoneration. "This." He did not look at Jack, staring instead at the foot of the desk across from him. The screen of the monitor had collapsed into the MacBook's screensaver; its twisting belts of cosmic color spilled afterglows that shifted upon the darkness of the room.

"Obviously." Jack's voice was strained.

"It's no big deal," Foster said, hoping to believe it.

"Yeah," Jack said. "Just one of those things."

It was three thirty when Foster returned to his lightless bedroom. As he opened its door, he realized the crumpled Kleenex was still within a fist he had not unclenched. He held it in the darkness like some sort of primordial seed pod, oblong and bristly, and the shame returned with a new intensity. He reached into the fullness of the iron-webbed wastebasket beneath his desk and shoved it deep beneath the strata of papers and empty water bottles and pencil shavings.

It is difficult to say if things actually changed between both boys that night, but we should also consider the possibility that this is the wrong question altogether. Or perhaps: not wrong so much as naïve. I reached out to Jack Albright via iMessage this past summer three months after I followed him on Instagram. My hesitation in doing so—the result of anxiety, I'll admit—was a journalistic miscalculation: by that point I had contacted many of his friends and spoken to several of them; whether they blithely mentioned this in passing or extended him a more concerting warning is unclear. It was a quiet Friday night in July; his Instagram story showed that he was in Montauk. The lights that hang over the back courtyard of Ruschmeyer's are not unlike the ones that spanned the perimeter of the Talmadge House dance a decade prior. He was with boys I did not know, friends from Princeton, I gathered, but in the dizzying video snippet of the crowd around the cornhole platforms I caught the unmistakably silver eyes of Freddie Pieters, who had gained thirty pounds at Wesleyan and now worked for a boutique private equity shop in the city. And then there was the girl, the blonde whom I would later see on Jack Albright's arm as they disappeared into the December press of Third Avenue. In the photo she was kissing his cheek; his eyes were closed and his tongue was out. Mark Stetson had been surprisingly blasé about forwarding me his contact, but it had sat in my phone until that approaching midnight.

Hey Jack, I typed, and identified myself. I had used variations on the same two sentences to approach his friends in the preceding months, and I typed them out here, but then before pressing send I wrote a third that I had not before.

I'm writing a story about everything that happened with Foster Dade at Kennedy. I'm wondering if you'd be willing to talk, either on the record or on background (meaning I don't use your name). I get the sense you're a bigger part of this story than most realize.

Though he would continue to post to his Instagram that evening, it was not until the following afternoon that my phone vibrated with his response. It came in two parts; both were short.

> lmao
> fuck you

Foster used his BlackBerry's flashlight to sift through his sock drawer. It had been many weeks since he had taken Dr. Apple's Xanax; indeed, it had been many weeks since he had felt compelled to. He found the bottle and pulled out two of the little tablets. He swallowed them without water, feeling their chalky edges stick in his throat, and put himself back into his bed. And there he remained sleeplessly, his mind a hum of empty but noxious static. He began to count his blinks. Eventually dawn came, the watery yellow light bleeding through the cream-colored blind pulled down over his window. The birds in Kennedy's old trees began to happily confess. He heard a shower running down the hall. When sleep finally fell over him, it was fitful, and morning was already there.

PART II

And I haven't felt so alive
In years

—Depeche Mode

I.

Like most public relations professionals trained in the subfield of corporate crisis communications, Sheila Baxter made sense of the world in the language of what anyone else would call paranoia. This is why she was good at her job.

As a psychological endeavor, crisis comms is not dissimilar to the United States Navy's most clandestine Special Operations work. Both require a fluency of anticipation—the ability to envision the present as the sum of all the worst-case scenarios that haunt the immediate horizon, and to mitigate them before their potential is realized, *Minority Report*–style. The required psychic recalibration displaces the pleasant banality of the world and understands it instead as a Rube Goldberg death machine whose gears and levers—what was once understood as life's mere metaphysical furniture—must be monitored and adjusted to preempt the catastrophes of the final piston's turn. These eschatological neuroses aren't easily left at the office at five o'clock, and these individuals eventually realize their own fundamental discord with the rest of the world. There is no such thing as a simple trip to the grocery store for the retired Navy SEAL; there is no such thing as an innocent or unblemished person in the eyes of the crisis comms executive. Friends start to keep their distance. The divorce rate in both professions is roughly six times higher than the national average. Convinced of the impossibility of fate or kismet, these professionals tend to either shun religion or immerse themselves desperately within it.

It was its own minor feat of clairvoyance that Pauline Ross's first major administrative move at Kennedy was to poach Sheila Baxter away from Bear Stearns to serve as the school's Director of Communications. It is in the definitional nature of clairvoyance to seem preposterous until it suddenly does not. Kennedy's Board of Trustees had the sense to steel itself after announcing Ross's selection as the school's eleventh Head Master in the spring of 2003, but even then the backlash defied expectations. The aggrieved bloc of Old Kennedians who confederated in opposition to her hiring never acknowledged the operative misogyny outright; indeed, they never had to: even those who championed her appointment—Kennedy's financial officers; a few older Second Wave feminists on the faculty—had to acknowledge that her résumé lacked any reference to secondary education. The school would desperately market her appointment as a historical step in a progressive direction, but this was of course not entirely honest.

Like the private universities to which they proudly matriculate their graduates, American boarding schools are for all intents and purposes investment funds. This is a necessity of magnitude. Infrastructurally, these institutions are small city-states, with autonomous utility grids and labor forces and in Kennedy's case its own zip code; tuition revenue accounts for only a fraction of the necessary annual operating budget. To ensure the requisite liquidity, these schools depend on (i) their endowments, allocated across medium-risk investment portfolios, and (ii) fundraising drives, the largest of which might follow a decade of preparation and generate sums surpassing the GDP of certain Caribbean countries. But even by these standards, it is difficult to overstate the magnitude of the Kennedy School's Bicentennial Campaign.

In a phone call from Martha's Vineyard during the summer of 2001, J. Edward McDermott conveyed to the Board that the forthcoming academic year would be his twenty-seventh and last as Kennedy's tenth Head Master. A cheery, bow-tied son of old Providence money whose ecclesiastical respect for boarding school's spiritual idea dated to his own days at Deerfield, Neddy—even his students called him Neddy—had weathered the storms of coeducation and progressivism as an arbiter of compromise and public-facing wisdom. His impending retirement allowed the Board to indulge a new unsavory truth: for what was already shaping up to be the largest fundraising effort in secondary school history, Kennedy needed as its figurehead not an educator but an executive.

Kennedy would not turn two hundred until 2010, so it is a testament to the Campaign's ambition and scale that within six months of McDermott's announcement, the Trustees had already commenced off-record salary negotiations with Pauline Ross, who would be the first Kennedy Head Master with an M.B.A. (Harvard Business School '94). A square-jawed, short-haired woman in her mid-forties, she was then in her eleventh year as one of the most ruthless portfolio managers in the quietly merciless sphere of American nonprofit organizations. What Pauline Ross lacked in cultural familiarity she provided in a form of socioeconomic meteorology. PDFs of the mock prospectus she drafted for her job interview still circulate among envious development officers along the Northeast Corridor. In early 2002, bomb-sniffing dogs still patrolled the New Jersey Transit platform at Princeton Junction. The markets were bad and would get worse; over the subsequent fiscal year, alumni donations would drop by nearly 35 percent. In a geopolitical moment focused with pathological singularity on the Middle East, Pauline Ross surveyed the rubble of the Asian financial crisis and saw the looming economic reality that all but the most stoic Sinologists would fail to consider until it was too late. *Kennedy's current recruitment and fundraising efforts in South Korea, Hong Kong, and Singapore are overdue for replication in mainland China,* she wrote in the prospectus that landed her the job, *which as a potential source of high-volume donations remains largely untapped.*

It was in the service of this multinational project that Pauline Ross sought out Sheila Baxter as Kennedy's Director of Communications, a job that until that point existed mostly to oversee the biannual publication of Kennedy's alumni magazine. Within a year of Baxter's arrival, *The Old Blue* had become the responsibility of a twenty-seven-year-old assistant, and Baxter settled into a role that was chiefly preemptive: as seven-figure donations came in from China's metastasizing, potentially overvalued, and ethically ambiguous economy, she worked to vet the legal hygiene of the funds that would go to a new baseball stadium or music building. Faculty members who had been petitioning for new lab equipment or research software saw the new

Comms Director's Audi parked outside Alumni Hall and muttered bitterly about broken priorities.

And yet here too Ross would prove to be almost supernaturally prescient. Sheila Baxter would spend thirteen years at Kennedy, and no other service in that time justified her salary like her response to the events of March 2010. In the hours before a tsunami reaches the coast, certain tropical birds have been reported to fly inland, their squawks guttural and violent; for reasons that baffle ornithologists and seismologists alike, they begin their tortured flight shortly before the first seismometers' needles twitch. With the privilege of retrospect, faculty members at Kennedy would say that they had felt a subtle shift in their students' collective energy prior to the events in question, but it was only Sheila Baxter who arrived in Dean of Students Theresa Daniels's office that afternoon with a strategic response file already two dozen pages long. Within eight months, it would contain more than four hundred.

There are two reasons that so many crisis communications experts came to the field from careers in journalism. The first is obviously money. The second is that crisis comms requires skills that are essentially reportorial. What Sheila Baxter knew—what she had learned over a decade at the *Boston Globe* and another at Bear Stearns—is that controlling a narrative demands an encyclopedic mastery of its content. This is why she was good at her job. When the staggering magnitude of this story began to present itself and the reporters from the *Times* and *Vanity Fair* began to call, Baxter was able to insist persuasively and threateningly to the contrary, with a menacing authority over the emerging narrative's contingencies.

Barring some future subpoena-happy legal embroilment, we won't ever know the full extent of what Sheila Baxter's files contained. Certain educated guesses seem justified, sure. Jack Albright had provided Theresa Daniels with the documents that almost certainly sustained its early pages, though the exact constitution of this dossier has never been independently verified. Sources familiar with the events of early March 2010 confirm that when she drove with Mrs. Daniels and the Hewitt House Master, Roberta Cantrell, to the home of Hannah Phelps-Berkowitz's parents in Princeton Junction, she did so with her

Sony voice recorder in her handbag. We can surmise that a transcript of that conversation exists.

We can certify the existence of only two records within that otherwise unknowable archive. The first, of course, belongs to the many files obtained by Jack Albright, a document that in and of itself was preliminary and heavily circumstantial as a piece of potentially admissible evidence. The second, one of a dozen confidential memos addressed to the ad hoc intra-administrative circle that found its shape in the wake of these events, is less evidentiary than meta-evidentiary, but this affords its own insights. What follows is excerpted from that document.

[ENCRYPTED MESSAGE]
FROM: sbaxter@kennedy.org
[Saturday, April 29, 2010 at 09:44 AM EST]
TO: pross@kennedy.org; tdaniels@kennedy.org,
smccall@kennedy.org, mdaughtry@kennedy.org
CC: bbradshaw@sullivanandcromwell.com;
dbassett@sullivanandcromwell.com
SUBJECT: FD CASE—UPDATE APR 29

All:

I write to update you on recent developments related to our last correspondence dated April 17 and the meeting of April 21 that followed.

The *Atlantic* will publish its story in its September issue. This news follows the phone call of April 24 between me, Kennedy's lawyers at S&C (copied), and the publication's in-house counsel and the following call of April 25 between the aforementioned parties and the story's editor (Sam Jeffries). The *Atlantic* has confirmed that the story will not identify Kennedy by name in relation to any alleged events, nor will it identify any members of the school's administration, faculty, or student body. Kennedy has made it clear that it reserves the right for final review, to ascertain the appropriateness of any pseudonyms or descriptions used by the writer (Eliana Pollack). When I receive a draft of the piece, I will let you know.

Our primary objectives as laid out in the first meeting and subsequent correspondence of March 11 remain (1) to prevent or at least minimize all publicity relating to the case of Foster Dade (FD) and (2) to preempt judicatory action by any persons or agencies beyond the Kennedy School's internal judiciary apparatuses and procedures.

As of April 27, Woodberry Forest School has concluded its own internal investigation into the matter addressed in our last correspondence. Three students who were receiving shipments from FD have been expelled. Woodberry Dean of Stud. Ralph Beauchamp informed me yesterday that any alleged connection to Kennedy/FD will not be investigated further.

Kennedy mailroom director Ken Burress has now provided me with the mailroom's record of all incoming packages addressed to FD (Mailbox #263) between 09/01/2008 and 04/20/2010. I have narrowed this record's window of concern to between 09/15/2009 and 03/17/2010. Within this window 14 parcels arrived for FD from one Alexei Kuznetsov in Hong Kong SAR sent via Hong Kong Post. The final parcel obviously arrived after his departure from Kennedy. I am investigating this matter and am consulting with S&C's partners in both Hong Kong and Beijing (mainland China) on relevant questions re: international and Chinese law. Two other parcels arrived for FD in this window, sent via USPS and postmarked in Baltimore. They appear to have been sent by FD's mother and warrant no additional concern.

II.
Foster Dade's MacBook Pro/Music/iTunes/Playlists/summer 09 (Created June 1, 2009)

Name	Time	Artist
1901	3:13	Phoenix
Truth	2:53	Chiddy Bang
Sweet Disposition	3:50	The Temper Trap
Can't Hardly Wait	3:08	The Replacements
Little Secrets	3:59	Passion Pit
I Don't Like Mondays	4:19	The Boomtown Rats
Invisible Touch	3:28	Genesis
Knock You Down (feat. Kanye West & Ne-Yo)	5:26	Keri Hilson
But Not Tonight	4:15	Depeche Mode
Waking Up in Vegas	3:19	Katy Perry

Play Your Part (Pt. 2)	3:25	Girl Talk
Friday I'm in Love	3:34	The Cure
Body Language	3:42	Jesse McCartney (feat. T–Pain)
Take On Me	3:45	a–ha
Short Skirt/Long Jacket	3:24	Cake
Young Americans	5:14	David Bowie
Cruel to Be Kind	3:30	Nick Lowe
Panic	2:21	The Smiths
I Know It's Over	5:49	The Smiths
Catch My Disease	4:14	Ben Lee
Good Girls Go Bad (feat. Leighton Meester)	3:16	Cobra Starship
RoboCop	4:34	Kanye West
Flying Horses	5:27	Dispatch

23 songs, 1.8 hours, 207.1 MB

III.

Foster had woken up a little after one o'clock on the Sunday afternoon following the Talmadge House dance. The sleep that had finally come with morning's grayness had been fitful, suffused with the unpleasant sunlight that insisted itself through his blinds. It was with a sudden nausea that the prior evening's events in Jack's room returned to him. For reasons inarticulable to himself, he felt an impulse to apologize, and was arranging the words in his uncomfortable head when he felt his phone's stifled buzz against the mattress.

> **frances evans [01:12:44PM]:** foster!
> **frances evans [01:12:48PM]:** thank u so much for the conversation yesterday u made me feel so much better
> **frances evans [01:12:59PM]:** do u think i could get the aderal/other thing today? i have the $ and will be in the lib!!!!

Kaitlyn Sanders had also been waiting for him on the library's front stairs with Bettina Scott, both in leggings and long ponytails. With a nauseous pain he imagined them laughing in the First Year girls' residence about his flaccid penis, but then Kaitlyn smiled warmly, almost treacly, and Foster's panic pulsed into quiet bravado as he handed her pills he'd wrapped in a Kleenex. "Four Adderall, four Vyvanse," he said, taking the wad of bills from Kaitlyn and feeling her fingers' graze. "Just holler if you need more."

He found Frances in an upstairs study room, sitting at its round table with Sofi, Gracie, and Annabeth. He tapped on the glass door's mahogany frame, grinning at Sofi and Frances as they looked up.

"Delivery," he said wryly, stepping inside. He could feel Annabeth's eyes on him and forced himself to resist their pull.

"You're a hero, Foster," Frances squealed, unwrapping the parcel. "And I hope you don't mind, but Gracie"—she jerked her shoulder toward Gracie, who had not looked up from her MacBook—"told John that you were selling this stuff, and I think he told Brent Rivenbark, and he and some of the Third Years might want some for finals, if that's okay."

"Totally okay," Foster said, not knowing if it was. "Just give him my number, or Jack can." He contemplated Gracie's indifferent silence and felt a certain satisfaction in this knowledge, then resented himself for it.

He had been halfway down the narrow hallway along the stacks when he heard Annabeth's call.

"Hey."

He could not diagnose the look on her face. She seemed to falter as she approached. "Want to—go for a walk?"

He allowed himself a genuine smile. "Yeah."

Later, when Foster Dade sought to comprehend the violence of what eventually followed, he would find himself thinking about this afternoon. To his distress he could only summon its fragments: vignettes colored by the honey-milk of the setting May sun. They walked, as they had taken to doing, beyond the Field House toward the expanse of the cornfields. The sun seemed to jump in Annabeth's hair. She was strangely quiet, and even when she spoke there was a constraint to her words.

"So you finally made Mr. Ricciardelli's dreams come true," Foster had said as they approached the head of the soccer fields. Their expanse seemed limitless, the thatch of woods at their far end an ethereal boundary.

Annabeth snorted mildly. "It seemed cruel not to finally just relent. Tedious, truthfully," she added. "But prom will be—fine. Sofi and Frances are going, and I think Porter's gonna get asked by that oaf Jeremy on the ice hockey team, poor girl."

Foster felt lighter at her ambivalence, but said nothing.

"So—was Kaitlyn Sanders as wild as they say she is?" Annabeth asked finally.

"She—gave me head." Foster decided this was not technically a lie. He watched Annabeth's face, but it remained stoic. "And then she persuaded me to sell her and her friends my Adderall."

At this Annabeth's mouth twitched. "Foster," she said, and there was a palpability to his name that Foster wanted to reach out and hold. "You need to be careful. With the lacrosse guys, that was ballsy enough. But you don't want it getting around that you're, like, literally dealing drugs."

It would be months before the costume of glib indifference Foster had discovered through these transactions began to fray. "Relax," he said. "I know my limits. This is isolated, I swear." Annabeth remained quiet as they walked on under the fading light of the day.

So he would not tell her when, over the subsequent eight days, his phone began to hum with new regularity: Freddie Pieters, Bettina Scott, the Third Year Brent Rivenbark and two of his friends in Kellogg House. On the last Thursday of classes, he received a Facebook message from the attractive Third Year Kendall MacPherson. just two or three pills, i'm so fucked for next week!

With each transaction, Foster arranged to meet the inquiring party in the small study room he and Jack and Pritchett had colonized with their MacBooks and water bottles in the week ahead of finals. Nothing in Jack's demeanor indicated that the events of that late Saturday night had ever transpired. He would smile knowingly—amicably—when Brent Rivenbark or Kendall MacPherson darkened the study room's glass door and Foster reached into his backpack for the twin Ziplocs of pills. At night, back in Brennan, Foster nested the loose wad of tens and twenties in a purple-and-green plastic SpaceMaker pencil box he'd last used in fifth grade.

He himself had consumed the Vyvanse during his exams and in the days preceding them. The new user whose neurotransmitters have not yet acclimatized tends to describe a heady, almost physically happy cocoon of concentration; later, he would recall the final days of his first year at Kennedy and see only his MacBook and notebooks before him, the periphery held at bay by the drug's chemistry and the Passion Pit throbbing in his headphones. He received A's even in Chemistry and Algebra II. "You took my breath away," Tierney had told him outside Memorial Hall on the morning Charlotte Harrison was to pick him up. (She was, as of a month prior, once again Charlotte Harrison.) The old teacher clasped his spindly white hand in Foster's with triumph. "I've never read a final paper so gorgeous. I want you around my table next year."

And then it had been over. "It's not goodbye," Jack had said grandly on the Brennan House porch, throwing his arms around Foster in an affable hug. "I'll see you. Come up to the Hamptons a few days early." And then Foster had watched him as he retreated across campus to the Field House, feeling the imminence of certain thoughts that never came. He had returned to his room to find Jae and his matching black luggage flanked by the same silent, besuited Korean man who had accompanied him to Kennedy nine months prior.

"Jae!"

"I leave for Korea now," Jae said sedately, and Foster felt a surge of guilt. Jae, he understood, had assumed an imperious position amid the not-insignificant cabal of Korean students at Kennedy—who because of both the language barrier and a more chauvinistic suspicion happily kept to themselves—but Foster liked his quasi-roommate, and was embarrassed to concede that their nights together with Jae's bowl had become less frequent as Foster's loneliness had waned.

"Dude," Foster said, hugging him. "Safe travels. Let's stay in touch this summer."

"I will be in Hong Kong," Jae said. "My father is filming new movie there. You can come visit."

"I'd love that, buddy," Foster said, both touched and knowing that this would likely never happen. "Just hit me up whenever."

It was only when Charlotte Harrison had parked the Lexus along Brennan's rear driveway that he heard Annabeth Whittaker shriek. "i want to meet your mom," she'd messaged him that morning.

"Mom, this is Annabeth," Foster said with an embarrassed grin after Annabeth had danced over to them. She wore the same yellow Nike athletic shorts she had worn on that distant August afternoon, when his heart had first thrashed in his chest. "Annabeth, my mom."

"It's so good to finally meet you, Ms. Harrison," Annabeth said, ignoring Charlotte's outstretched hand and hugging her instead. Foster silently loved her for her social grace. (He had watched his mother's lips purse that morning when Scott McCall had addressed her as Mrs. Dade.) "I've heard so much about you. Was the drive from Baltimore terrible?"

And with a gloriously dumbstruck silence Foster watched his mother and Annabeth laugh together for many minutes, until Annabeth then turned to him.

"Hey," she said, and her eyes glistened with what seemed almost wistful. And then she threw her arms around him, and he felt her kiss him on the cheek. "Adirondacks. This summer. I'm not letting you say no."

"Yeah, absolutely," Foster said, after finding his hollow voice. "We'll talk."

"We'll definitely talk." And then she hugged him again, and after saying goodbye to Charlotte she bounded off in the direction of Hewitt House.

"She's a keeper," Charlotte said, watching her disappear.

Foster had returned to Baltimore under the verdant regency that bridges spring and summer in the mid-Atlantic, when life erupts with a yawp ahead of the heat to come. The boughs of the oaks over the city's affluent northern streets are suddenly heavy and fat, under which the ethereal hours preceding dusk become at once green and purple and gray. Secrets seem to occupy these shadows, which had found harbor in the silent house on Overland Road. Foster had spent those first weeks between a lounge chair by the pool and the cool recesses of the quiet house, with *Me Talk Pretty One Day* under his arm and his BlackBerry in his pocket. The gram of old weed he'd found in his underwear drawer was brittle and crumbling, but smokeable.

By three, when the shadows began to fall, he found himself walking. The heat of summer was still threatening only in the chafes of distant thunder. He would cross University Parkway and move along the manicured quadrangles of the Johns Hopkins campus, citadel-like in their languid vacancy. The cool silence was strange but not unpleasant, and Foster took inventory of it, an exercise facilitated by the nub of Xanax he'd begun slipping under his tongue after lunchtime each afternoon. He'd found the prescription bottle in his mother's medicine cabinet while looking for toothpaste his second evening home; that night, prostrate on his bed, he'd swallowed the segmented tab while watching *Saturday Night Live* clips on YouTube and woken up thirteen hours later against the sickly light of late morning, his MacBook's screensaver twisting blithely on the screen beside him.

"You're going to need to find something to do," Charlotte had told him during his second week home from Kennedy. "You've been sleeping 'til noon every day. It isn't healthy."

"How do you know I've been sleeping 'til noon if you haven't been home?" Foster asked, sipping his coffee and grimacing at its tepidity. He had not heard her come in late the night before, nor had he inquired further when she'd left six evenings prior for the 5:03 Acela to Manhattan. ("It's work, sweetie, I'm so sorry," she'd said, to his silent relief.)

"Well," Charlotte said, nodding toward the clock above the oven. It was shortly after eleven. "And Alice came to clean twice and said you were in bed when she got here." She pulled a container of Fage yogurt from the fridge. "And don't get defensive. I'm only worried you're going to get anxious and unhappy if you don't have structure."

"I'm seeing Doctor Apple this afternoon," Foster said. "That's structure."

"That's psychiatry."

"Maybe he'll prescribe me something for structure."

He suspected, sometimes, that his mother knew far more than she vocalized, though the ethics of this selective withholding were as elusive as the maternal sorcery by which she acquired her data. With a spasm of pride that recoiled into a sickly guilt, Foster found himself thinking of the two amber pill bottles atop his dresser upstairs. They were very nearly empty.

The shadows that filled Dr. Apple's office were darkening with the retreat of the afternoon. The psychiatrist looked to his client with a self-satisfied smile, his fingers arched cathedral-like to meet his thick chin. He did not know that Foster Dade had spent the bike ride up York Road rehearsing some version of these lines in his head.

"And I should have taken your advice—I think I was just nervous about starting another medication, but I did just amazingly well on my exams, and felt, like—felt like my best self."

"Yes, I'm hearing similarly good things about Vyvanse, good," Dr. Apple said. "And your anxiety has not rebounded? Or might we consider an increase in your Lexapro?"

"No, my anxiety's fine," Foster said. This was true, more or less. Months had passed since the lurch of tension in his chest that had precipitated the prior autumn's panic attacks, and we tend to appraise the severity of our psychic ailments only through their most palpably somatic symptoms. "But I've noticed"—and this, too, he had practiced—"that if I take the Vyvanse in the morning with breakfast, it tends to wear off by early afternoon. And this isn't great if I have homework or studying to do in the evening. But I was reading online"—he assumed the practiced look of earnest curiosity—"that some people get prescribed what I think they call an Adderall . . . *booster?* . . . that gets them through the rest of the day."

Dr. Apple gave his sickly smile and nodded. It may or may not warrant noting that as of late 2019, the name APPLE, DONALD G, MD remains listed in the Maryland Board of Physicians' database of licensed practitioners, his Hippocratic integrity unquestioned.

"I've seen success with the booster," Dr. Apple said through his ill smile. "We might also want to consider an uptick in the Vyvanse dosage. So what I can do"—and Foster was startled by his relief that Dr. Apple did not ask him the obvious question, of his old Adderall's whereabouts—"is write you another prescription for the immediate-release Adderall: twenty milligrams, again, but you should break it up into quarters and take five in the afternoons. And I'll also write you a prescription for Vyvanse at sixty milligrams. If the booster doesn't seem to be working"—and here he licked his finger and turned to a blank page of his prescription pad—"you can fill the new Vyvanse and try that."

"That would be marvelous."

And in the idle moments of those first weeks of summer Foster found himself missing Annabeth with an intensity he knew was undeserved. Through nothing but her own precocious charms—her parents were Republicans—she had secured a part-time internship in the office of Newark's Democratic mayor, Cory Booker, whom she told Foster was the next Obama. "I'm just sorting mail and making copies, but I swear," she'd told him in a video chat one night, after Jack and Sofi had left their four-way call to go to sleep, "he's going to be president one day. He has that electricity."

They would talk until one or two in the morning, sometimes three. Annabeth was always the one to end the call, and when she did, Foster would stare again at his iChat contact list, waiting for the small green orb to the left of Annabeth's screen name to fill with the yellow tint that indicated idleness. Some nights it did not. Once, several moments after she bid him good night, he realized—with a dread he'd thought he'd escaped—that her camera icon had gone gray, and so had Jack Albright's. *lol*, he typed into the chat box after a moment, before deleting it and shutting his MacBook with a slap.

When the calls ended, Foster would turn off the lamp and masturbate. Sometimes he opened Safari and went to YouPorn—always after logging out of iChat, his mind briefly tensing with the thought of somehow inadvertently sending Annabeth the link to *Teen hottie spycam shower masturbate orgasm SHAVED*. Some nights he closed his computer and slid it to the floor below his bed instead thinking about Annabeth. The vividness of these moments burned with the shame of transgression, and they made him despise himself, with a fervor that left his penis soft in his hand. Other times—more frequently than he would have enjoyed—in the moments before climax, he saw the screen-lit silhouette of Jack Albright on the upstairs couch in Brennan.

IV.
http://www.fhd93.blogspot.com/06_09/food_for_thought
(Posted June 29, 2009)

I sometimes wonder if we design our own suffering without realizing it. This probably isn't as profound of an insight as I think it is. But I was reading on Wikipedia about personality disorders today—don't ask me why—and I kept coming across the phrase "self-sabotaging tendencies." Tierney also told me I should try reading some Freud this summer, after I did my Death of a Salesman paper on Willy Loman's depression, and lo and behold I came across his name. Freud's name, I mean. Not Willy Loman's. Or Tierney's. Here I quote Wikipedia, which we're never supposed to do, of course:

> In 1895, Freud and Ferenczi turned their attention to the wounds of childhood trauma. They noticed that children who were raised in an unhealthy environment were more often the ones to act out and take part in self-destructive behavior.

There was a time when I was maybe thirteen or so—before the divorce—when I very much liked the idea of myself as a victim of a toxic or even abusive home. I'm (a little) older now, and I realize now that there's actually a reason to find truth in this statement, but at thirteen it was purely a figment of melodrama/narcissism. I felt "misunderstood" or whatever; that's it. I still do, of course, but I no longer think it's as interesting a fact as I used to. The point I think I'm trying to get at: I used to imagine myself as, like, a character in a dramatic narrative. So, two questions:

1. If this narrative only existed because I saw myself as a character in it, is it logical to conclude that the narrative itself—climax and all—is my own invention?

2. I'm using the past tense here, but what if I shouldn't?

V.

June became July, and the infrastructure of July collapsed under its heat. Across the transmission signals of Z104.3—*Baltimore's Number One Hit Music Station!*—Blair Waldorf from *Gossip Girl* sang that she was a good girl who'd gone bad, her voice throbbing against the windows of air-conditioned Suburbans ferrying wet-haired children from swim team practice. Lawn sprinklers cast rainbows in the golden humid air. In the afternoon thunderstorms hung in plum-colored skies over the Inner Harbor. A body, the sixth that year, was found in its waters, his waterlogged flesh chafing against a barnacled piling near the Bubba Gump Shrimp Co. A lunchtime diner had spotted it; her Forrest's Favorite Coconut Shrimp was on the house.

It had been Charlotte who pushed her son to book a flight to Hong Kong. He had been staring idly at YouTube on an afternoon in early July (SCHIZOPHRENIC MAN RECORDS PSYCHOTIC EPISODE—AUDITORY HALLUCINATIONS!) when a pleasant chime sounded from a minimized window. He clicked it and Facebook spilled open from his MacBook's dock to occupy the screen.

> **Phillip Jae-hyun An 안재현 [03:16PM]:** I am drink GRAY
> GOOSE ha ha
> **Phillip Jae-hyun An 안재현 [03:16PM]:** It is 4 in morning in SEOUL
> **Phillip Jae-hyun An 안재현 [03:17PM]:** I fly to HONG KONG
> tomorrow
> **Phillip Jae-hyun An 안재현 [03:17PM]:** We will have good time
> ~~ HK has good night clubs and my cousin who lives there can
> get Drugs ~

"let me ask my mom!" Foster had written, with no serious intention of doing so.

It was only when Charlotte inquired into the whereabouts of a pill bottle from her medicine cabinet while preparing a salad that Foster introduced the topic in desperation, thinking of the broken Klonopins in his bedside drawer and the empty bottle he'd hidden in an old winter boot. It was a warm evening in early July, and the lights of the swimming pool outside danced in yellow smudges off the twilit house. "I think it's a wonderful opportunity," she'd said, shaking the final globs of dressing from a Briannas bottle onto a spinach salad. "What a nice friend you must have been to that boy—Joe?"

"Jae," Foster muttered, not looking up from the copy of *Harper's* he was reading. His mother's enthusiasm bemused him. *She wants to get me out of the house, I think*, he wrote the evening he booked his ticket. By mid-July, she had spent a collective sixteen days at home in Baltimore that summer. *She says it's work—I never ask further— but I'm 90% sure she's dating someone in New York. Whatever, I guess—I'll go get high in Asia with Jae.*

And as the dusk outside the window darkened into night, he found himself on Expedia, charging $1,364.72 to the credit card she had shoved at him across the breakfast table with a flamboyant finality. *Your trip has been confirmed!* He then clicked over to the adjacent tab, where Jae's messages were waiting. He paused for a moment.

> **Foster Dade [10:14PM]:** I'm coming. just booked my tickets.

He looked to the list of his friends that rose from the browser's bottom-right edge to see Annabeth Whittaker's name. He clicked on it. The last message there had been from her, in May. (*hey hey my phone is dead but I just got to the lib, come through*)

> **Foster Dade [10:21PM]:** true life: i'm flying to fucking hong kong next week to see jae.

He hit enter, and suddenly the absurdity of the message amused him. He opened Wikipedia and typed *hong kong* into the search bar, and then he laughed.

VI.

Clifford Chance (Hong Kong)
27th Floor, Jardine House
One Connaught Place
Hong Kong (SAR)
Tel +85228258888
Fax +85228258800

FROM: Mr. Kenneth Brayton-Dalrymple

RE: Defamation of Character—for Libel and/or Slander

TO: Mr.

New York City, NY 10

@gmail.com

( ) -

CC: Mr. Douglas Martin (Litigation: Clifford Chance NY), Ms. Cynthia Lap-sut Chen (Clifford Chance HK), Mr. Han-gyeol Kim (Edwin) (Kim & Chang: Seoul)

Tuesday, September 3, 2019

Dear Mr. ,
I am writing on behalf of my client, AN JAE-HYUN (PHILLIP AN) (the "CLIENT"), in response to your inquiry dated Friday, August 9, 2019, and containing the subject line "Your relationship with Foster Dade" (the "EMAIL"). The EMAIL pertains to a journalistic piece you are writing ("the STORY") which discusses the CLIENT in relation to the individual mentioned in its subject line, Mr. Foster Dade (the "INDIVIDUAL"). It has come to our attention that the STORY contains historically inaccurate descriptions of events that untruthfully implicate the CLIENT and cause malicious damage to his personal and professional character.

Under the laws in the state of New York, it is unlawful for an individual to make deliberate statements that intend to harm a person's reputation without factual evidence or based on hearsay.

The defamatory statements in the STORY relate to the following queries sent by you in the EMAIL:

I. "I'm specifically wondering about the trip Foster took in July 2009 to visit you in Hong Kong, where you were spending the summer break while your dad was filming a movie. Can you tell me about that trip? Did you two participate in any illegal activities: namely buying/consuming drugs? (Also: Can you confirm that Foster did cocaine for the first time in Hong Kong?)"

II. "After Foster was expelled, Kennedy traced the shipments of pharmaceutical drugs he was receiving to an address in Hong Kong. Based on certain things he said on his Blogspot page, it seems like you may have had a part in helping him secure those drugs. Are you willing to say more about this? Happy to take your answers off the record—meaning I won't say that they came from you."

III. "It's never been quite clear what you were expelled for. Are you comfortable sharing? More specifically: Were you covering for Foster in any way?"

Our CLIENT categorically denies any connection to the INDIVIDUAL implied in the above queries or elsewhere in the STORY.

Mr. An lives in Seoul, where he is a successful music producer. After his departure from the Kennedy School in January 2010, he attended Virginia Episcopal School (Lynchburg, VA) before matriculating to New York University (New York City, NY). He has lived in Seoul since 2014. His departure from the Kennedy School in January 2010 related to academic matters.

<u>**You are hereby directed to CEASE AND DESIST ALL DEFAMATION OF THE CLIENT'S CHARACTER AND REPUTATION. If you do not comply with this letter, or publish a version of the STORY that contains defamatory statements about the CLIENT, legal action will be commenced against you.**</u>

Please respond within ten (10) days to acknowledge receipt of this letter and confirm that you have complied with the directive for immediate cessation of defamation.

Sincerely,
Ken Brayton-Dalrymple, Esq.
Litigation and Dispute Resolution, Clifford Chance

VII.

There is an elegant precarity to the apartment towers that rise aspen-like from the middle slopes of Victoria Peak, where Hong Kong's thrust of commerce and light ends its uphill climb. Like the forged iron *chevaux de frise* that lined the beaches at Normandy, the collective rise of these buildings stands at angular odds with the earthen ground they demarcate, their garrison of thin stakes along the hillside bulwarking the city below. The older buildings—those built in the final decades of British rule, when the port colony's fidelity to the Thatcherite project made it a useful node in the spreading global matrix of neoliberal finance—are stucco dyed in hues of pale coral, which at sunset catches in the blue steel and silver glass of their newer neighbors. The elegance of these towers exists specifically in the implausibility of their errant rise: they are imposing and strange only through the setting they contravene. There is a stillness to their geometry, codified in the litany of public ordinances posted along the streets and manicured parks below. The atmosphere of enclosure hushes the city. Belowground, the metro's trains arrive at clean station platforms quietly and on time, before sliding away again with a gentle hydraulic whoosh.

Foster Dade would remember his eleven days in Hong Kong only in amnesiac refractions of this silence. The worst cases of jet lag are less like exhaustion than minor psychosis, its vague sense of unreality flirting with dissociation. But there was also the Xanax, and the sleeping medication he bought on his first evening from a small pharmacy below Jae's building. It came in a cardboard box that read

ZOLPIDEM TARTRATE—10 mg, which he learned from Google was generic Ambien at its highest administered dose; that first night, he pressed two of the tablets from their blister sheet and swallowed them.

There was also the fact that he and Jae had been stoned each day from the time they woke up until they fell asleep. This ritual had commenced promptly upon Foster's arrival at the apartment on Conduit Road. It was not yet eight thirty in the morning; he had landed no more than an hour earlier. With befuddled arithmetic he realized it had been fewer than twenty hours since his mother had driven him to Baltimore-Washington International. He had taken the first Xanax on the half-hour U.S. Airways Express flight to JFK and two more as the Cathay Pacific 777 pushed back from the Jetway and began its slow climb over the Arctic. He had watched the orange lights of Queens and New Jersey slide below him, thinking of Annabeth and Kennedy and then nothing at all. When he awoke—had he slept?—many hours later, *Revolutionary Road* was playing on the small screen before him; he did not remember starting it.

The driver Jae had promised was standing in the baggage claim's atrium. He wore a black suit and held a sign that said Mr. DADE FUSTER. From the black leather back seat of a Mercedes-Benz sedan, he watched the approaching skyline. A tunnel beneath the harbor; the climb of the road up the Peak, enclosed by mossy walls that since the colonial years had contained the knotted banyan roots in the rainy season. And then they were in an elevator, he and the driver who held his L.L.Bean duffel and who had said exactly nothing in the hour since they'd met, trusting that the sheepish white teenager who'd moseyed awkwardly up to him at baggage claim had indeed been Mr. DADE FUSTER. Jae's apartment was on the fifty-first floor, the building's highest, and when the doors slid open, there he was, in silk pajama pants and no shirt, clutching a bottle of Grey Goose by its neck. Behind him, through a glass door within a long wall of windows, was a wide terrace, and below were the many hundreds of skyscrapers that distinguish Hong Kong as the densest city in the world. The terrace rose above their spires, looking out to the harborfront and the hills of Kowloon beyond that, steepening in their northward reach to the vastness of mainland China. On the glass coffee table before Jae was his leather attaché case opened to present the several dozen containers of marijuana within it.

They smoked. Each day insinuated itself into the next. Each morning they awoke shortly before noon and lit the bong that stood by the patio's door, exhaling their smoke out over the city, and then they looked at each other and laughed and set out in Hong Kong. They wandered down the staircased alleys of Sai Ying Pun where keymakers and tailors sat hunched, their faces shadowed by naked lightbulbs overhead. They passed through the wealthy foreign arrondissements of Sheung Wan and SoHo, where arguments in French sounded from the coffee shops that occupied what had once been Chinese apothecaries. They boarded a double-decker streetcar on Des Voeux Road and sat at the front of the upper deck, lurching eastward through the steel canyons of Central and Admiralty; they disembarked in Wan Chai beneath the darkened neon signs that hung out over the press of Hennessy Road, advertising bars with names like Tropicana and the San Francisco that promised LIVE NUDE GIRLS and EXOTIC DANCING. Tired Filipina women loitered out front in cutoff jean shorts and bikini tops, extending a hand toward the boys and singing solicitations of *free sex shows with drink, you like the girls?* Every so often the discharge drip of an air-conditioning unit in some apartment high overhead would hit their heads, and as the days wore on and the marijuana took its psychic toll Foster would find himself shuddering.

Foster never met Jae's father, for reasons unclear and unquestioned. Every morning, an Indonesian woman would appear in the kitchen, wordlessly disposing of the liquor bottles and marijuana crumbs on the marble island before disappearing. It was several days before he realized that the woman lived there with Jae, retreating to some closet-like chamber beyond the kitchen. The only other human presence in the apartment came late one dark afternoon. Foster emerged from his room after a sleepless nap and found Jae sitting on the living room's leather sofa across from a man in black leather. The resemblance between them startled Foster. They shared a smallness in build and the same wide upturned nose. The man's age was ambiguous. He was hunched over the edge of the glass coffee table. Foster looked at the table and saw four thin rows of pearl-colored powder.

Jae looked up at Foster. "Coc*aaaaaine*," he said. He angled his head in the direction of the other couch. "This is my cousin, Dong-woo."

With this disclosure the man now seemed younger. His shoulders sagged with the jaded surliness of privileged men in their early twenties. He continued to furrow the cocaine into lines, tapping the card against the glass to dispel the powder hanging to it.

"Hey, Dong-woo," Foster said, still looking at the cocaine, feeling the incipient gastric lurch that precedes a spell of anxiety. "Foster. I go to school with Jae."

Dong-woo still did not look up.

"No English," Jae said with the hesitantly self-assured grin that came in moments of relative confidence in his language skills. He looked to Dong-woo and said something in quick Korean. Dong-woo grunted. He held a small plastic straw to his nostril, and with little fanfare he moved it along the fattest line, which disappeared as he did. He grunted again and then at last looked up, giving Foster a jerking nod, extending the straw in his direction.

In a different moment, or a different mindset, Foster might have felt a stab of something sad or half-profound in this moment. Instead, he thought of nothing but the gesture he prepared to complete. The skies outside the high windows had blackened with a summer storm that had not yet broken into rainfall. Far below, bankers and accountants were fumbling with umbrellas toward metro stations. The silver lights that tesselate the rise of the city's skyscrapers had begun their rhythmic spasms against the darkness of the late afternoon; their dance snagged the corner of Foster's vision as he held the straw to the coffee table. He closed his eyes—he was not sure why—and after a cautious pause, with his fingertip against his opposing nostril, he inhaled.

There was a moment of suspension, and then Foster felt a certain palpable twitch to his chest that he had not felt before, and with the intensity of impulse he felt himself both smile broadly and stand up from the couch. He looked at Jae, whose face was mesmerized and delighted.

"Hey," he said. "Wow. Fuck."

It started to rain.

"What we can do," the blond Russian said, "is provide you with product. It is easy to ship. Don't worry. Bank transfers—also easy. Jae's friend, I'll be nice—no need for wholesale."

He stared at Foster, idly tapping the residue of cocaine from his credit card against Jae's coffee table. Foster seemed to remember that his name was Alexei.

It was well after midnight. Hours had passed since the first lines of cocaine that afternoon. After those lines there'd been vodka, tall shots taken straight from Jae's magnum of Grey Goose that seemed almost magically to replenish itself each morning. The fourth line of coke thereafter had threatened the panic attack that had been gestating within Foster's cannabis-worn psyche over the prior day, and so as evening fell, he'd retreated to his bedroom and taken a Xanax from the bottle Dr. Apple had refilled after their most recent visit. His third drink soon thereafter brought the night's first lapse in memory.

He was not sure how or when they'd left for the nightclub in which he emerged from his blackout. He was perched between Jae and Dong-woo at a small table slick with melting ice from the champagne bucket at its center, each thrash of strobe light smelting the edges of the water's spill. At some point they had been joined in their vinyl-seated booth by a pale young man who didn't seem much older than Dong-woo, or for that matter Foster and Jae. His blond hair was cropped short and his face was soft and quizzical; in demeanor and presentation he resembled a European tourist in Times Square. He wore a Barcelona soccer jersey and black cargo pants; his aviator eyeglasses were lensless and in his right ear were three silver studs. Jae had introduced Alexei only as his cousin's business partner; Alexei had told Foster that he worked in finance.

My cousin who lives there can get Drugs, Jae had told him on Facebook Chat. This would prove to be something of an understatement.

Back in Baltimore several weeks later, Foster would spend an evening reading on Wikipedia about South Korean organized crime: its origins in the turmoil that followed war; its creeping transnational metastasis across East and Southeast Asia, rising like Whac-A-Mole gophers in Bangkok and Hong Kong and Tokyo; its strategic but tenuous alliances with the triads in Hong Kong and the yakuza in Japan and the Russian mafia's envoys southeast of Lake Baikal.

The nature of Dong-woo's role within this network was never clarified. Jae spent the evening by his cousin's side, their faces reddening and eyes growing glassy. Every so often Jae would turn to his cousin and mutter something in Korean, to which Dong-woo would grunt or nod or make a sort of conciliatory fricative sound. Dong-woo, Foster realized, was gruff and taciturn even in his native language. But he found himself observing Jae in those moments, and saw someone unfamiliar and more flamboyant than the catatonic boy who had moved into his suite in Brennan House the previous fall. There was an enthusiastic, almost manic modulation in Jae's spoken Korean that seemed to borrow Japanese's songlike melodies and the emotive caws of Cantonese. Jae brought forth his words with a gesticulatory sweep, as if his hands, too, had been liberated from the repressive constraints of English. Alexei, significantly less churlish and mute than Dong-woo, spoke surprisingly competent Korean, and when Jae talked, the Russian seemed not only to listen but to find himself ensnared by the teenager's words.

At several points Foster had felt Alexei's eyes on him from across the table. The club was vast, and in the steadfastness of its rhythm, the throb of the music felt somehow distant, its heft absorbed and dispersed by the blue twist of bodies before them. And so Alexei did not have to shout to be heard, and in subsequent recollections Foster would hear in his words a conversational and almost indifferent easiness.

"Jae says you're selling phets at your school," Alexei had said, just as two Eastern European girls in slip-like polyester dresses approached their table with another magnum of Grey Goose. Sparklers erupted from its mouth; Foster thought vaguely of the long vase of decorative reeds in his mother's bedroom.

"Phets?"

"Amphetamines. Your Adderall, your Vyvanse."

Foster realized that he had been twisting and shredding a cocktail napkin in his hand. "In—a manner of speaking."

"I do not know the meaning of that."

"Uh—sort of, I mean," Foster said, studying the soft-faced Russian. Jae appeared to be nodding off next to him; his body seemed to have slid down the couch into Alexei's torso, and his black-haired head threatened to lurch over onto the Russian's shoulder. "Some friends. But—people keep asking if I'm gonna keep doing it. So, yeah, I guess I do."

He was sober enough to feel himself straighten up at this; in the cocaine's thrall, he saw the new clarity of a Foster Dade manufactured by these words' truth. He suddenly pictured Annabeth telling her friends from Peck about her brilliant, profound best friend, about a desire that in this vision denied all refutability. The dance of the sparklers' light in Jae's and Alexei's faces made them appear unreal. Jae's face was red and his expression euphoric, and after brandishing the sparklers in imitation of a warlock, he'd thrust a full tumbler of the vodka into Foster's hand. Foster had taken it, and then he blacked out again.

And then they were back at Jae's apartment. It was unclear how much time had passed, or how or when they'd left the club; when he found it in his wallet two days later, Foster would not know how he acquired the empty plastic baggie of cocaine, only that it at least in part accounted for the evening's subsequent lucidity. It was well after midnight. Foster was sitting on the couch; he realized he had a rose-colored Hong Kong banknote rolled between his fingers, and that there was a tear in the sleeve of his oxford shirt. Dong-woo had disappeared into the kitchen. Across the coffee table, Jae sat next to his cousin's business partner, his face slack and absent. There was a fervor to Alexei's gaze.

"But, wait." Foster was furrowing his brow with his eyes closed, trying to assemble the details as they passed him. "I don't understand how this happens. Are you like—robbing a pharmacy?"

Dong-woo frowned with a certain menace. The Russian turned his head in his direction and said something quietly in Korean, then looked back to Foster.

"No," he said stoically. "Illegal in Asia anyway, as medication, phets. Guangzhou." With a jerk of his head he arced his eyebrows in the direction of the high windows, toward the northern reaches of Hong Kong and the cities of the Chinese mainland beyond it. Foster was not sure when or what exactly Jae told Dong-woo about the Adderall. *He can help you with your drugs,* he recalled Jae saying cryptically early in the evening. Alexei looked back to the table and unsentimentally did another line of coke. "Major pharmaceutical manufacturing center. Major. We"—he now cocked his head at Dong-woo—"have connections. Access to inventory."

"And you have both? Vyvanse too?"

Nod.

"Adderall immediate release and extended release?"

Nod.

A pause. "Xanax?"

Nod, coy smile. Foster realized that Dong-woo had returned to the living room, and in his hand he held a Ziploc bag of white pills. Alexei said something to Dong-woo, who jerked his head in a nod. Then Alexei reached for the bag and held it out before Foster, his coy smile wider and more confident.

"We got Oxy too." The tablets' chalky reside had left the bag filmy and opaque; Foster thought idly of frosted glass. "You want?"

"Oxy, like—OxyClean?"

"OxyContin." Alexei pulled three pills from the bag and tucked one into his mouth, chasing it with a swig of Grey Goose. "Painkiller."

"Like Xanax?"

"Like if Xanax was warm bath. Here."

Alexei handed one to Foster and then turned to Jae, whose body was now limp against his. With the two fingers that held the last pill, he gently pulled Jae's lower lip down from his mouth and slipped it inside. Jae gave a gurgling little moan and seemed to smile. Alexei kept his finger pressed against Jae's lip for a moment. With a certain helplessness Jae's smile seemed to widen, and Alexei took the Grey Goose bottle and held it to the boy's mouth. Clear trickles of vodka dribbled down from its corners onto his shirt, and then Jae swallowed. Alexei extended the bottle in Foster's direction, looking at him with a solicitousness that made Foster's face flush and impulsively turn away. He felt himself take the bottle and put the pill in his mouth, shuddering as the vodka followed it down his throat.

"So," Alexei said, smiling at Foster, revealing his teeth for the first time. They seemed broken and cleaved by a chisel. "What's it going to be."

Beyond these negotiations, certain events that night do permit their admission to the record. Their evidence is no more or less tenuous than any of the archival material that gives shape to this story, but we should note two caveats. The first is that (i) even more than his Blogspot—which bears no explicit mention of this particular occurrence—the final paper Foster Dade wrote for Dr. Art Tierney's winter term Third Year English is both a central motif of the legend still told today and an operative engine of its uncertainties and half-truths. Unlike the Blogspot, the paper is understood to be a lost document. It exists in the contemporary mythology purely as a plot point. There is a narcissism to storytelling, and in this material absence, those who tell this one accordingly fail to consider how the paper determined the first contours of a legend they have inherited and mistaken for their own. It was only upon finally acquiring it that I learned of what happened in Hong Kong that night. Though the richness of the relevant archives and databases has allowed me to cross-check many of the paper's assertions, there are instances where no supplementary records exist, and this is one of them.

There is also the problem that (ii) the events of that forgotten night in Asia in July 2009 passed under the perceptive effluence of Foster Dade's first encounter with narcotic opioids. The OxyContin came on insidiously but quickly, presumably as he and Alexei agreed to the final logistics. It was in the blissful catatonia that followed that he allowed himself to spectate what happened.

At some point thereafter, Alexei had turned toward Jae and was murmuring words in Korean into the catatonic boy's ear. Occasionally Jae's eyelids would flutter in response, but his body twitched only fleetingly as Alexei began to slide his hands up Jae's black V-neck T-shirt. Jae made another gurgling moan, and Alexei pulled another

OxyContin from the bag on the coffee table and slid it into Jae's mouth before moving his hands down to unbutton the boy's jeans. With slow atrophic labor Alexei tugged the waistband down Jae's thighs, then returned his hand to Jae's groin and slid his fingers beneath the elastic of his briefs. With a lifeless wobble Jae's penis flopped out above the waistband, taut under the liquor and cocaine's vasoconstrictive seize. What Foster noticed, before Alexei shifted his weight on the couch and brought his mouth to Jae's dick, was the band of redness that ran along its circumference below the head. Unlike Foster's circumcision scar, faded to a fleshy pink by the passage of years, Jae's incision was precisely that: a recent wound, not the tan of his skin but the rust-brown of the vascularity beneath.

(Later, late at night in his childhood bedroom eight thousand miles away, Foster would find himself reading a paper written by two Japanese sociologists with the simple title "Male Circumcision: A South Korean Perspective," which detailed the postnatal practice's arrival in the country with the U.S. Army's postwar occupation and subsequent absorption by Confucian coming-of-age rituals; in contemporary South Korea, Foster learned, boys are circumcised not at birth but near the onset of puberty.)

It was with a nauseous sort of curiosity that Foster watched Jae's penis stir and stiffen as Alexei's mouth moved along it. Each time the Russian's head rose, Foster would see the yellow light of the room catch the sanguinary scar of Jae's circumcision. Alexei's saliva gave the scar the slick appearance of a fresh wound: as if Jae's foreskin lay discarded in his bedroom's bathtub, the white porcelain around it flecked by coins of blood. Unable to do much more, Foster found himself following the tempo of Alexei's motion, metronomic under the OxyContin's thickness. The lights of Hong Kong blinked and fluttered into the periphery of his vision. He let himself turn to their benevolent smear in the dark windows for a protracted moment, and when he looked back, he saw that Jae was no longer sitting but bent crudely over the seat of the couch, his knees on the floor below. His buttocks were hairless and pale.

Alexei was standing next to him, his cargo pants at his ankles, his penis pulled through the fly of his copper-colored briefs. It was large, uncircumcised, and erect, purple and organ-like. He pressed the head against the cleft of Jae's left buttock, and then he turned to Foster. His grin was not unkind; it seemed to imply that the two of them were sharing a private joke. Then Alexei turned his back to Foster. From Jae's motionless form against the couch Foster heard an enfeebled, indifferent moan. Then with a jerk and shift Alexei's hips buckled and he began to thrust.

Sometime many hours later, Foster emerged from sleep to the strange sensation of dampness against his face. Not quite awake, he tongued the corner of his mouth and felt a mealy clump that clung there. He realized it was vomit. In the sickly half-light of Hong Kong that came in through the closed curtains, he saw that what had soaked into his pillow and the mattress below it was a rich, earthen brown. The absorptive pull of the fabric's fibers had left behind small beige lumps and a beach of fine particulate grit, colorless but discernible. He realized that a clod of the khaki something was stuck between his gum and lower lip; with a shudder he dislodged it with his tongue. He realized that he was naked.

He went unsteadily to the bathroom. The mirror was wide and high, occupying the wall above the sink within a trim of clean fluorescent light. As he turned on the sink to wash his face, he caught the peripheral edge of his naked reflection in the glass. He recoiled with a violent spasm, as if assaulted. Something about the coarse fact of himself broke the dam of a sickening rage he had known before but forgotten. With an animalistic blindness he craved his own destruction. He turned on the shower. It was a wide cubicle of clean white tile within a high sheet of glass; its door swung out on a silent hinge. He pictured with the same violent delight the door swinging shut on his skull, the svelte edge crushing it against the cusp of the glass wall with the brutal elegance of a jeweler's hammer against a Fabergé egg. With savage force he shoved his hand through his hair and snagged his fingers in the vomit's matted tangles, breaking apart the brittle strands that had hardened together. He stepped into the shower and let it scald him.

He felt his hand take his penis. Like his reflection in the mirror, the idea of looking at it for some reason repelled him, a reflex he later came to half-understand as an almost infantile fear. The same self-loathing dread returned before the crude dopamine motors of arousal began slowly to churn. With a lucidity and crudeness that he had previously refused the vision, he found himself thinking of Annabeth, of her own humiliation and debasement, piss and shame and brokenness. He saw her bent over a couch with her asshole shamefully exposed; he pictured his hard penis against the cusp of her buttock. Then he realized the smoothness of her butt was Jae's, and he was Alexei, and Alexei was watching him from the opposing couch, grinning the same grin. And at the thought of himself thrusting into Jae's resistance he felt his knees bend and his toes curl and his orgasm spasm through all of his body.

He stood there for a moment. The shower's falling water swept the seminal fluid from his fingers and into its dilutive stream down to the drain, leaving behind the white clods of sperm that seemed to curdle and tighten against his hand. With a convulsive jerk he flung his hand away as if he'd touched dry ice, and the knotted strings of white hit the tile wall before sliding down. The nausea came suddenly. He cocked his head forward and vomited. Thin tethers of the same brown refuse fell to the tile floor and were pulled toward the drain, and Foster closed his eyes and heaved until nothing came out.

When he would finally emerge from the shower after what could have been an hour, he would not notice that his laptop was open on the table next to his bed, its Safari browser still displaying the Blogspot post he did not remember writing nine hours prior. He would remain in his room until twilight, emerging to find Jae lighting the bong on the terrace overlooking Hong Kong. He would join him resolutely, and Jae would say nothing, as he always did. And though the subsequent four days before Foster's return flight to JFK would pass precisely as those preceding it had—stoned and lethargic and meandering—he would realize much later that he had not once looked Jae directly in the eyes after that night: not only in their remaining time in Hong Kong but back at Kennedy that fall as well.

He would later understand also that the nausea never fully subsided in the months that followed. But there, for a delicate, ethereal instant after the heaving slowed, there was a brief spell of almost cosmic vacancy. It was a humming, vacuum-like blackness, and under the quantum physics of the galaxy it contained, he was for the first time in his life fleetingly but unequivocally not there. This itself was more bath-like and euphoric than the OxyContin had been. And then he opened his eyes. The tile of the shower seemed so white. He sat with his back against the wall, and as the water fell around his naked body, he began to sob.

It was startlingly easy to locate Alexei Kuznetsov a decade later—Jae's Facebook page led me to Dong-woo's, whose friends list was publicly searchable—and though he eventually went silent, his responses on Facebook Messenger up until then were curt but sufficient enough for reconstructing the night of July 23, 2009, from the evidence I'd already amassed. With respect to the letter I received following my email to Jae, certain details refuse us the possibility of speculative reproduction. With our evidence, we know only what happened before and what happened after. We cannot say with certainty that Foster Dade and Alexei Kuznetsov agreed to the specific terms of any transaction, but we do know that once a month over the autumn and winter that followed, padded parcels arrived in the Kennedy School mailroom from Hong Kong, and that in this period Foster Dade also received a regular supply of the white plastic jars in which pharmaceutical manufacturers distribute inventory to America's pharmacies. We do not know how quantities were determined ahead of each monthly shipment, but we know that months later, one *ALEXEI♞✈HONG KONG☙ 8* was found among Foster Dade's fifty-four contacts on BlackBerry Messenger, immediately above the dormant *Annabeth W.*—the final iteration of her display name before she finally traded in for an iPhone in her first October after Kennedy—and that their correspondence had been erased.

We know that in the final months of 2009, Bank of America registered no high-volume activity on the checking account Charlotte Harrison had set up for her son in the summer of 2008. We cannot say for sure that Jae-hyun An drunkenly offered to facilitate certain transactions through his own financial accounts, but we do know that between the start of the 2009–2010 academic year and Jae's expulsion from Kennedy in the third week after Christmas break, Brennan House's sign-out log sheets have PHILLIP AN leaving campus on eight separate Wednesday afternoons, each time filling the space under DESTINATION with BANK. Harris Adelstein, who would spend that year as one of Brennan's three Prefects, later confirmed that these cryptic errands came up during those final disciplinary proceedings; earlier that same week, three pills had been found in a Ziploc in the Donavan House common room. We don't know how this circumstantial suspicion factored into Jae's expulsion—the case for dismissal on grounds of academic performance was pretty much open and closed—but we know for sure that it found no answers during those interrogative dialogues in Alumni Hall. Silent 'til the end, Jae-hyun An kept his mouth shut.

VIII.
http://www.fhd93.blogspot.com/2009/08
(Posted August 1, 2009)

There is this sense I get sometimes where what's happening in the present feels somehow—I dunno—preordained. It's hard to describe, and I dunno if I'm doing a good job of it. Maybe "preordained" isn't the right word. It's like: I'll have this weird, intense feeling inside me, but I won't realize that I've had it until there's some encounter (usually with a person) that gives it a physical shape. When you meet someone and it seems like you've known them forever, or, like . . . in a past life. Ugh, that sounds stupid. But what I'm talking about is real. It's almost like I'm haunted by ghosts from my own future. Or maybe they're from the past, and real, and it's actually the encounter that's bullshit—my brain trying to tether these ghosts to something credible in the real world. Like I'm trying to take the things that are foreign or distant or unexplainable and make sense of them by shaping them to fit a place within a longer story.

I got back to America three days ago.

IX.

"Qi? Are you fucking kidding?"

"Try me."

"You're fucking with me."

"Qi. Chinese, originally. The Confucian term for the life force innate to all things."

"We're not playing in Chinese."

"No, we're not. *Official Scrabble Players Dictionary*, fourth edition. Merriam-Webster before that. Triple word score, so"— Annabeth Whittaker slid the wooden tile away from the square in the board's upper-right corner—"eleven times three. That's thirty-three. All you, Dade."

Foster frowned as he recorded the score, the tip of the ballpoint pen stalling briefly on a grain of something beneath the page. "I don't think I've ever lost before."

Annabeth shrugged. "Good. This'll keep you from getting complacent."

It was mid-afternoon, and the heavy clouds that had hung over the Adirondacks since Foster's arrival three days prior seemed lower now, more bilious, darkening the still surface of the lake beyond the living room's cathedral windows. The plump bulbs of the chandelier overhead, a ring of wrought iron suspended from the high pine ceiling by two heavy nautical ropes, were illuminated only to their dimmest. The cocoon made by the enclosing shadows carried a certain spell they'd decided against breaking.

It had taken Foster eight hours to get to Lake Placid from Baltimore. Jim Dade had bequeathed the 2001 Acura SUV to a newly licensed Maggie two years before the divorce, and so it would stay in the garage on Overland Road after the lawyers' sequestration of assets. Maggie had decided in the summer before her first term at Amherst that the turd-colored carpool hearse (her words) impugned an incipient personal aesthetic, and so in the garage it had remained, metaphorical in its forlorn silence. Its tank was still half-full when Foster left Baltimore that morning, pushing north against the traffic of I-95. With the windows open in the summer day he found himself singing aloud for the first time in many years, Passion Pit and Phoenix and U2 straining against the Acura's tired sound system. He let his arm out the window to surf the pockets of wet mountain air, feeling the temperature fall as he climbed beneath heavy boughs of fir and hemlock, catching the wind before it slipped through the net of his open fingers. As he passed, he unplugged his iPod from the iTrip FM transmitter he'd bought at Best Buy a summer prior and reached into the backpack on the passenger seat for the CD case Annabeth had given him in Manhattan four months earlier.

It's been a really long fucking time since I've been so excited about a stretch of weeks to come, he'd written on his Blogspot the night after he returned from Hong Kong. I didn't think Annabeth was serious about having me up to Lake Placid, but she called me yesterday when I landed and told me that they were heading there today, and that I should join. Just us.

So: the Adirondacks for four nights, and then I'm heading straight from there to the Hamptons. Everyone's going to be there—Sofi is apparently gonna have a huge party. Most of the guys are staying at Pritchett's, but Jack's family is renting a house out there for August, so I'm gonna get there two days before everyone else and chill with him before the crowd shows up. It'll be great to see everyone, but I'm honestly most stoked about Lake Placid. Annabeth. "I've missed you," she told me on vid chat. She's missed me.

And there she had been. She stood on the home's front porch in an oversized Dartmouth crewneck, frowning passively down at her BlackBerry. With the first crunch of the Acura's tires on the gravel, her head sprang up and she took flight. The page Foster had printed from MapQuest the previous night was creased and open on his lap. Her stride was long and parabolic; her legs were brown with the glow of summer. Her millet-colored hair was assembled in a wide, lazy plait that bounced as she ran. She threw herself around him.

"You *bastard*," she murmured, before pulling away to beam at him. "I've been so bored without you."

The Whittakers' house was built upon a valley's lower cleft, a retreat of dark wood and silver stone with tall windows that caught the

light of the sky over the lake beyond it. The house gave dutiful form
to the shadowed cloistering of the mountains that rose over the lake
beyond it, rising in a tessellation of narrow staircases and discrete tiers
to bedrooms that emphasized their separation. Charlie Whittaker's
resin-streaked bowl still sat on the windowsill when Foster deposited
his bag atop the bed's flannel comforter. Beyond the window, a pair of
kayaks wobbled lazily against the Whittakers' pier on the darkness of
the lake. The stairs led down to the kitchen, where Annabeth waited
for him at the foot of the waning afternoon.

"It's a misnomer, actually, Lake Placid," Annabeth said, balancing
along the old bulkhead that enclosed the beach's rocky bank. The
lake slapped against the bloated wood as Foster followed on the grass
alongside her. "This"—she pointed out to the dark water—"is not
Lake Placid. It's Mirror Lake. Lake Placid"—she gestured toward the
front yard—"is over there, on the other side of the street. We take
the boat out there, because it's deeper and much bigger and there's
incredible cliff jumping—let's do that, by the way—but, like, the entire
town is built on a lie." She grinned at Foster.

"*Placid* is an endearing word, though."

"I mean, like, definitionally, yeah," Annabeth said. "But *placid*
just makes me hear *flaccid*. *Tranquil*, *halcyon*—there are plenty of
less icky synonyms."

"Maybe you should get your mind out of the gutter, Whittaker,"
Foster smiled.

"You first, Mister Dade." She beamed at him and jumped from the
bulkhead to a wide stone buried in the grassy hillside. "Don't want
Skipper to worry about leaving us alone together."

Foster would later remember those four days as only a formless
vignette of these moments. The constituent memories were peripatetic
and dancing in a color that defied chronology, heavy with their insistent solitude. He would not recall on which day they had mounted
the Whittakers' old beach cruisers and pedaled along the footpath
that circled Mirror Lake, or on which night they had hauled old wine
boxes to the fire pit by the lake. Instead, he remembered the way
Annabeth's legs had risen and fallen with the bike's pedals, and how
her ponytail bounced as she rode, the wind rippling against the lake.

He remembered the sparks and embers of cardboard that danced up to the night as Annabeth mirthfully sprayed the bottle of Kingsford lighter fluid at the burgeoning flames, her face colored by firelight, and the cool glass of Charlie's bowl against his lips as he took in the smoke of the weed he'd brought from Baltimore. He remembered the warm glow of the kitchen and the pleasant swell of the cabernet they had stolen from the Whittakers' wine cooler, how they passed the green bottle between themselves as the pasta bubbled on the stove.

"I learned this from *The Sopranos*," Annabeth had said proudly, tilting the colander over the simmering Bolognese pot and letting the pasta slide into it. "You cook the pasta for a minute or two in the sauce, and it actually absorbs the sauce, rather than having the sauce just sit on top of it."

He did not know if it was during that night's Scrabble game or one of the other six when he noticed their knees touching. At this, he felt his penis twitch and begin to stiffen in his sweatpants, and he had resisted the hormonal urge to reach beneath the table and lay his hand on her thigh. Later, alone upstairs in bed, he'd thought briefly of masturbating, letting his hand move down beneath the waistband of his boxers and taking the idle weight of his penis in his fingers. He then thought suddenly of Annabeth asleep in her bed down the hall, and he recoiled at the shame of his audacity. He did not know if it was the following morning that he awoke to the sound of Belle and Sebastian playing in the kitchen downstairs, where he found her in a loose Duran Duran T-shirt making chocolate chip pancakes on the stovetop griddle, a streak of batter across her cheek.

From its initial airing in January 2001 through its culmination in a Hollywood feature film two and a half years later, *Lizzie McGuire* enjoyed consistent acclaim from those early-career critics tasked with reviewing the otherwise lobotomized slog of children's programming. The series was an unprecedented triumph for the Disney Channel, which after years of languishing on premium cable as a sort of passive repository for Disney's intellectual property had observed Nickelodeon and Cartoon Network's late-millennium chokehold on the 2–11 and 12–17 key demographics and risen belatedly to the challenge. For critics long stupefied by the canned laugh tracks of *Full House* and the lobotomizing plotless flashes that comprise the Cartoon Network's entire lineup, *Lizzie* marked a stylistic and dramatic revolution in the infantilized space of preteen television. It was ambitious in both its postmodern formal conceits (an animated Hilary Duff popping in to relay her titular character's inner monologues) and narrative concerns (anorexia, Reform Judaism).

The Disney Channel had joined Comcast's basic cable lineup in Baltimore in the winter before Foster Dade's eighth birthday. His social life up to that point had been a serious of tedious, alienating playdates spent staring with blank boredom at *Dexter's Lab* or *Rocket Power*. (He had the grim sense that these boys arrived in front of their television sets upon returning home from school and did not move until the following morning.) In preschool he'd enjoyed the cerebral verve of *The Magic School Bus* and the suburban social dramas of *Arthur*, but finding no close analogues in the sea of grade-school-aged programming, he'd indifferently relinquished control of the remote to his sister and returned to his books, until the Friday evening he walked into the playroom and found her watching *Zenon: Girl of the 21st Century*.

He'd come to appreciate the network's prime-time lineup—reruns of *Boy Meets World*; original films like *Get a Clue* and *The Color of Friendship*—but nothing captured Foster's emotional attention as fully as *Lizzie*. Its maturity entranced him, and so did its most primary dramatic throughline: the intimate friendship between Lizzie and her bookish, socially indifferent neighbor David Gordon ("Gordo").

It wasn't particularly original, of course. Like Jim Halpert and Pam Beesly in the years to come, like Sam and Diane before *Frasier*, what illuminated Lizzie and Gordo's friendship was the latter's profound unrequited love for the former. *Lizzie McGuire* ran for only two seasons, but the movie that concluded the series—the second-biggest theatrical earner its opening weekend in May 2003, trailing behind *X2: X-Men United*—brought Lizzie and Gordo's relationship to what Foster would come to understand as its logical, necessary conclusion.

He was ten that summer, and on a stormy June afternoon his mother had taken him and his sister to the AMC megaplex at Towson Commons. Maggie spent those two hours sighing huffily at the gimmickier dialogue, having graduated to *Law & Order* around the time of her fourteenth birthday. Her brother did not notice. He watched the lights of the Trevi Fountain dance upon Lizzie's face in the movie's final scene as she leaned in to kiss Gordo beneath the Roman night, crouching slightly to meet his lips, realizing that she'd been in love all along. And as the credits rolled and the sconces lining the theater walls awoke with nudging light, ten-year-old Foster Dade did not move, transfixed in perfect silence, staring out at the screen, for the first time in ten years flattened by the sense that the world could be understood.

And so we can perhaps understand why one afternoon would clarify its precise location within Foster Dade's otherwise nebulous sunsmear of memories of that week in August 2009. In the weeks and months that followed, he would return to it with desperation. A Blogspot entry written in its immediate aftermath exists, but we might venture that Foster's initial comprehension of that afternoon is less salient than this subsequent reshaping—the new edges it found as he turned it talisman-like in the palm of his mind, with each turn hoping in vain to elucidate the certainty and meaning that had ultimately been effaced by the events that followed.

It was the afternoon before Foster was to leave for the Hamptons. He and Annabeth had returned from town with sandwiches and ate them on the dock, where a tethered canoe bumped happily against an algaed piling. The edgeless sheet of yellow sky overhead was thickening and finding form, binding into towers of cloud that hung low over the mountains. When she finished eating, Annabeth wiped the corner of her mouth with the sandwich's parchment paper.

"They never give us enough napkins." She reclined onto her back and lobbed the ball of foil overhead, catching it in front of her face. Vanessa Carlton was playing from the little speaker. "*Summer's all in bloom—summer's ending soon,*" Annabeth sang grandiloquently up to the hills. She pulled her yellow T-shirt over her head to reveal a cornflower-blue bikini top. "They say you can get tan even when it's cloudy—that the UV rays penetrate the clouds, or some shit." She grinned at Foster. "Worth a try."

Foster did the same, self-conscious not for the first time that week about his smooth but bulkless torso. There seemed to be a curious gravity to the space separating them—a sort of quantum tug that had felt more urgent as the week had carried on. From just beyond the woods nearest to the edge of the Whittakers' property there was the hush of a passing car.

"Hey," Foster said, breaking the stillness that had followed, "thanks for having me up here. I honestly"—he paused—"I honestly can't think of a better end to summer."

"Summer's not done, though. Despite what Vanessa says. I doubt my humble cabin will compare to the extravagances of *the Hamptons*."

"What's that guy's name—the *Fabulous Life* guy on VH1? Robin something?"

"Robin, uh—Leach. Robin Leach." She affected the same English courtier's accent. "*Lifestyles of the Rich and the Famous*."

"Well," Foster said, "this was better than whatever the next week will look like. No Mason Pretlow. My best friend." He heard his own spite.

"Mason's just—Mason," Annabeth said. "I don't think it's anything personal. He'd punch his own mother if he thought it complemented his masculinity. And besides—Jack invited you up there, not him."

Foster thought of the night two weeks prior when Jack had video-chatted him, breaking their two months of only irregular and superficial communication. There had been a small collection of nights over the summer when a new message from albreezy42 arrived—something like *what's good breh*, followed by a short and perfunctory exchange. These conversations were brief for the same reason that Foster had not initiated them. He had never stopped approaching their friendship as he would a sort of intricate glass ornament: dazzling but implacably unreal, its tenuous elegance inseparable from its fragility. Even the best days—those days when Jack was his most magnanimous and theatrical, when their high-fives culminated in a hearty embrace and clap on the back—only seemed to emphasize the risk of its shattering: its beauty seemed thoroughly conditional on its handling. And so

Foster placed it on some high mental shelf to foreclose the temptation of carelessness, despising it for the very reason he marveled at it.

"That's true," Foster said. "It'll be nice to see him."

"And then—we're *juniors*," Annabeth effused. "Sorry—*Third Years*. The big kids. Our social capital off the charts." She picked up a small ant that had crawled onto her shoulder and frowned at it. "You're free, little one," she said, flicking it gently down the dock.

"It's nice to be looking forward to the start of school," Foster admitted. "I was such a fucking wreck a year ago. You know I spent last summer, like, comprehensively stalking all of you on Facebook."

He had not admitted this anywhere beyond his Blogspot. He had joined the Kennedy Class of 2011 Facebook group with the lurch of panic, imagining an orchestra of ridicule in more private channels: *this earnest loser; he hasn't even started yet and he thinks he's one of us.* With this same panic he had clicked from profile to profile. He found the other semi-public Facebook groups to which his classmates belonged, ad hoc cloisters of loose belonging that emphasized his own emphatic alienation: *I Survived Cline's First Year Humanities*; *Kennedy Varsity Mudsliding*; *"Obstreperous!": The Art Tierney Appreciation Society*.

"I think that's adorable," Annabeth said. "You were nervous!"

"I was nervous," Foster confessed. "Scared shitless, honestly. And sometimes—sometimes I still am."

And then he felt Annabeth's hand take his.

"Well, for what it's worth, I think it's profoundly sweet. The way you worry and care. And if it's any consolation, I'm not sure I'd survive Kennedy without you there."

Foster's face was hot. "I don't think you realize how mutual that is."

With a lurch of courage he turned his head toward hers. She was already facing him. But as he began to navigate the heat of her smile, she sat up and then stood, pulling her hand away.

"Dare you to swim out with me."

Before he could respond, she had pulled her athletic shorts to her ankles, kicking them aside. She stuck her tongue out at him. "Don't be a pussy, Mister Dade."

With a pointed bounce from the dock's spongy wood she dove, her legs disappearing with a ghostly green slide beneath the dark water. She resurfaced maybe fifteen feet out, bobbing and grinning up toward where Foster stood. The clouds overhead had darkened and looked aggrieved. The light that passed through them was the color of wilted lilacs, the color of dusk. Annabeth pointed to where maybe thirty yards out a buoy bobbed with a lopsided shrug. "I'll race ya," she called, then dipped again beneath the water, her feet a fluttering pale shadow as they slid into the darkness.

And so Foster jumped. He felt himself drop down into the lake, his feet touching the beginnings of its cold lightless depths. The water smelled of old driftwood, like an earthy tea. He blinked against the muted light. Behind him the lake slapped against the dock, and between him and the buoy was Annabeth, treading water and beaming.

"You're *graceless*!" she called.

Foster grinned and slid back beneath the water, propelling himself with a breaststroke. He dared himself to open his eyes to the bottle-like darkness before returning to the surface. And then there was Annabeth, grinning, her breaths heavy and triumphant just beneath the surface, the white of her breasts shimmering ghostlike against the black depths below. They were close enough for Foster to feel the heavy push of the water she was treading. A chafe of thunder came from somewhere over the mountains, which now seemed to rise impossibly to enclose the lake in their shadows.

"I'm faster than you," Annabeth said. Loose strands of her hair clung wet along her cheek.

The drops of a gentle rain cast quiet rings on the water around them. Their fall against his face chilled the air with a lucid edge, and in its contrast the lake suddenly seemed warmer, insulating. He realized that their faces were closer now, and felt the kick of her knees graze his.

"It's—raining," Foster said dumbly.

"Yes," Annabeth smiled. "It would appear it is."

And then, beneath the shadow of the climb of the Adirondacks, with a suddenness that shimmered like starlight, she kissed him.

It was raining, and Annabeth Whittaker's lips met his: these are the facts that afford themselves to us. Beneath the water, he felt their bodies make contact, the mercurial chafe of their knees and legs in their mutual gesticulations and the gentle press of her breasts against his chest. His mouth had been gently agape when hers met it, and her lower lip took the space between his. It was there, full and heavy, and then as Foster reached up to place a hand on her cheek it was gone. The kiss had spanned only the suggestion of a moment. On more than one occasion in the months that followed, he would wonder without irony whether it had actually happened. He knew even as Annabeth pulled her lips away that this moment—irrespective of whatever moments might follow—would not be discussed between them, and that this wordless pact was the condition of its magic, the same magic that had left him spellbound in a cinema seat half a decade prior.

And so Annabeth pulled away, and their eyes met. In a moment even more infinitesimal than the kiss itself, her face was an archive of meanings, each negating the others. There was a dance of utter bewilderment, the expression of a child lost in a store. It effaced itself into something both plaintive and assured, even defiant, as if acknowledging some undisclosed inevitability. And then her lips twitched. Later, Foster would return to it, parsing it for artifice or a quaver of fidelity. But in the fleeting span of that moment, as the rain fell around them in bright shimmers on the lake, it was merely a smile.

"I'll race you back to the dock," she said. "Winner picks the movie tonight."

And then she arced herself down into the lake. She did not resurface for maybe half a minute, and when she did she was already halfway to the pier. She did not turn back.

X.

Foster Dade's MacBook Pro/iTunes/Playlists/cruise control (or: songs to sing along to)
(Created August 8, 2009)

Name	Time	Artist
Escape Me	4:17	Tiësto (feat. CC Sheffield)
Girls Just Want to Have Fun	3:58	Cyndi Lauper

Never Let You Go	3:57	Third Eye Blind
Heaven Must Be Missing an Angel	6:34	Tavares
Come On Eileen	4:47	Dexy's Midnight Runners
All These Things That I've Done	5:01	The Killers
Any Way You Want It	3:22	Journey
Daylight	2:51	Matt & Kim
You Can Call Me Al	4:40	Paul Simon
Shine_ft_HotBoys_DopeNewJams.net	5:03	Lil Wayne
When I Come Around	2:58	Green Day
Jessie's Girl	3:14	Rick Springfield
Heaven Is a Place on Earth	4:07	Belinda Carlisle
What Dreams Are Made Of	4:02	Hilary Duff
Send Me on My Way	4:23	Rusted Root
Believe	3:59	Cher
Down Under	3:42	Men at Work
Knowing Me, Knowing You	4:02	ABBA
Always on My Mind	3:58	Pet Shop Boys

20 songs, 1.4 hours, 166.8 MB

XI.

http://www.fhd93.blogspot.com/2009/08/hungover_summer _thoughts
(Posted August 13, 2009)

There's something both sad and beautiful about parties where you're the only one who doesn't know anyone. You're basically a trespasser, intruding upon something intimate and old and not yours. It used to just feel awkward, and when I'd try to fit in, to make people laugh, it would make things worse. But if I'm fucked up enough, simply keeping quiet and observing becomes its own sort of activity. You meet strangers who are only strangers by virtue of fate—who wouldn't be strangers if I'd gone to Choate or Taft, whose lives and complexities would populate/ illuminate my own. I imagine those alternative worlds sometimes, where I'd be drunk at some party and encounter Annabeth or Jack (or Frances or Gracie or Pritchett) as those strangers.

I think that's where I find the magic in observing from the outside: you know (from your own intimacy with those who aren't strangers) that those complexities are there. What's eerie is that their inaccessibility comes down to something as stupid and mundane as chance. I'll sit there, drunk or stoned or whatever, off to the side, and imagine the backstories to this thing I'm otherwise intruding upon: the friendships and the love and the sex. The accuracy of these stories isn't really the point, and I kind of know deep down that if I tried to actually learn the truth, it would be a lot less romantic than the story I'm telling myself. And I like romance. The point is that I think maybe I'm learning how to inhabit the outside of things and be okay with it.

XII.

The uneasiness had begun that morning as a wordless question. Foster had left Lake Placid shortly after breakfast. He'd stopped at a Sunoco station for gas just south of the town; as the tattooed cashier inside scanned his Red Bull and IceBreakers Sours, he studied his distended shape in the convex security mirror overhead, feeling the first muffled thrashes within his stomach. He'd reached into the cardboard display shelf for a dusty tube of cherry Tums, which he tore open with his teeth as he signed his debit card's receipt. He drove. As he rounded the northern edge of New York City and began to move up the unsentimental spine of Long Island, the unease began to insist itself, tauntingly.

The rain had already started to subside by the time Foster reached the dock the prior afternoon, though the sky over the dark enclosing mountains had lost its light. Inside, he'd pulled on sweatpants and a T-shirt and found Annabeth in the kitchen peering over a trifold red-and-green takeout menu. That night, they shared a margherita pizza and buffalo wings in front of *Silence of the Lambs* after finishing the last hour of *Fatal Attraction*; the previous evening, Annabeth had fallen asleep on the couch with her feet in his lap. "I saw some list online ranking Hannibal Lecter as, like, the evilest movie villain in all of cinema," she said at one point, her eyes wide in the television's blue light. "But, like—he's not the villain! The antihero, if anything."

She did not look away from the screen. "It's this weird bullshit moral absolutism—no complexity at all. Or maybe I'm just totally soulless and subconsciously think necrophilia is chill."

"You know Anthony Hopkins was their second choice," Foster heard himself say. "They initially tried to get Sean Connery."

He would not remember her response to this. At the far end of the couch, Annabeth had curled herself beneath a knitted blanked. Later, he would hate himself for his impotence, desperately opting to believe that he, and not the fact of the space between them, set the course for the events that followed, or did not follow. "I'm exhausted," Annabeth said when the movie ended. When Foster emerged from the bathroom after brushing his teeth, her bedroom door was closed.

He spent the first hours of the drive returning to the finality he heard in these words. *There's a weird element of masochism to my anxiety*, he'd written once. *When I'm anxious, I find that I* choose *to keep engaging the very thoughts that are* making *me anxious—kind of like scratching poison ivy.* It was only as he moved past Nassau County's low suburbs and through the yellow farms and fields that spread out along Long Island's foreland that he began to recognize that the sickly knot of ambiguity in his stomach had not complexified its tangles with thoughts of Annabeth; indeed, it seemed to have nothing to do with Annabeth at all. The afternoon was bright with sunlit brine as Montauk Highway turned to hug the coast. Each passing sign jeered at him: *Southampton 7*; *Amagansett 22*; *Montauk 34*. The sign that welcomed Foster to Southampton informed him that it was the oldest English settlement in the state of New York. He wished he had a Xanax.

It had been three months since he'd said goodbye to Jack Albright on the Brennan House porch. "I'll see you," Jack had said, embracing Foster. The tidy coda afforded by that farewell seemed to foreclose any subsequent litigation of the Saturday night several weeks before; divorced from their referent, these formless memories fermented into something unnamed, tinged with a fear that threatened to leach through the vessel enclosing them.

And then the seas were calmed. Jack was standing in the lush bright grass of his yard, shirtless and barefoot, spinning his lacrosse stick in his hands before an old goal that had sunk long canals into the wet earth. As Foster turned off Halsey Neck Lane and into the driveway, Jack cocked his naked arms and whipped the rubber ball into the corner of the net. The force of the shot precluded its bounce.

Foster gave the Acura's weary horn a gentle press, as if the press of the sound would wrest him from the lurching below his ribs. Jack turned. A brief startled shadow had crossed his face, but then he grinned, lobbing his lacrosse stick out into the yard like a javelin as he darted toward the car.

"You motherfucker." He laughed, pulling open the Acura's driver door and slapping Foster's chest. He reached over and undid the seat belt, which shrugged indifferently against Foster in its rising retreat. "Get the fuck out here."

Jack Albright seemed to have grown over the three months since the end of school. That Jack was shirtless rewarded the illusion: his chest and shoulders had widened and firmed, their contours brought into steeper contrast by the darkness of his tan. He was very tan. His hair seemed to have gone uncut since May; weeks of summer lacrosse clinics had further shaped its swoop within his helmet's contours. On his chin and below his jaw were the shadows of a stubble Foster had not seen before. Jack's skin was warm as he embraced Foster, the gentle glistening of the sweat on his neck and shoulders pressing into Foster's shirt. For a deliberately fleeting moment, Foster thought he could sense a firmness within the soft mesh of Jack's athletic shorts—not the harsh turgidity of an erection but the healthy fullness of adult genitals—and with a reflexive spasm of fear he felt his own waist twitch away.

"It's been a minute, Albright," Foster said, hoping the relief in his voice could be heard as a less qualified happiness. "I've missed you—no homo."

He regretted these last words, which had an unintended but inevitable weight, and thought he sensed a flash of terseness to Jack's lips, but then it was nothing.

"You bitch," Jack grinned. "You goddamn *recluse*. Let's have a fucking *legendary* week."

Annabeth had told Foster that he would like Jack's parents—"they're like Jack, if every day was one of his good days"—but the truth of this

prediction was less salient than the revelation of their sheer human-
ness. *There's something almost phenomenal (in the original sense of
the word) about people as vivid as Jack*, Foster would write. *It's hard
to imagine them coming from somewhere—I think I assumed he just
showed up on Earth one day fully formed, cradling a lacrosse stick.*
Yet it was in the mortal elegance of John and Melinda Albright's affa-
bility that their son's charisma finally made sense: its flamboyance was
nothing more than a bedazzled, congenital sort of confidence. They
moved through the world with the unconscious certitude of those
who've never known anything but the security of their own past and
posterity. John Albright had clapped Foster on the back and called
him "buddy"; Melinda had swatted away Foster's extended hand
and brought her tanned, Pilates-toned arms around him; at dinner,
they'd probed him with great interest on the state of the *Kennedian*
and the new museum developments along Baltimore's Inner Harbor.
If fourteen-year-old Parker Albright and thirteen-year-old Sally lacked
their older brother's gregarious swagger, they seemed to have at least
interpellated themselves within the same matrix of confidence that had
nourished it. "Don't drink the good beer, and don't you dare let your
sister convince you to give her one," Melinda had called as Foster
and Jack stepped out to the back terrace after dinner.

It had been dusk when they set out for Water Mill in the Albrights'
Yukon. The sky over the eastern end of Long Island was bluing in its
ocher, its sudden coolness betrayed by the chafe of crickets in distant
grasses. Jack seemed suddenly silent; the bottle of George Dickel he'd
pulled from his parents' bar clinked happily as it rolled on the floor
behind them.

"Tripp's having a party—figure we've got nothing else going on,"
he had said on the back terrace, looking down into a canvas cooler
to fish out two Michelobs from the melted ice. His foot was tapping
insistently against the stone. "I can probably get us some more blow
there, at least."

He fished his finger along the crease of the stamp-sized plastic
bag he'd pulled from his wallet. Foster had taken the smaller of the
two thin lines Jack had tapped out onto his Kennedy ID, and as its

bitter drip touched his throat he'd watched with fervent intensity as the glow of the pool lights spasmed across the tree limbs overhead.

"I've got my Addy, too," Foster said.

"Bring it. Maybe make a few bucks. Honestly, I'd rather have Adderall than shitty coke."

"I'm not sure I'd know the difference between shitty and—not shitty."

"Not shitty makes you want to hug the person next to you. Shitty makes you want to punch them in the face. If it's really shitty you're mostly just concerned that your heart is going to explode."

"How does this rank?"

"I've had worse. If it was better, I'd be inside shitting my brains out. Cocaine diarrhea is a legit thing."

"Kinda makes the anorexic coke whore stereotype a lot less endearing."

"Kinda makes Gracie Smith a lot less endearing."

Foster snorted. "That's fucked up."

"Not even. I have it on good authority that she spent most of freshman year taking laxatives to—maintain her figure. Maybe that's why she's such a coke fiend."

"Wait, so—" Foster said, aware of his own Adidas's drumbeats against the patio "—remind me who's gonna be there tonight?"

"Some older kids. Adelstein, maybe; maybe Mellie Jakes if she's out here. Probably randos." Jack was holding the filmy bag before the light of the pool, studying it fixedly.

"And it's—that guy Tripp's party? The one who was expelled?"

"Mhm." He did not look away from the bag as he flicked it to the patio. "Figure we don't have anything else going on," he said again, then ground the flattened bag against the stone with his sneaker's heel.

Several of those who were at Tripp Altridge's house that night in August 2009 say they recall the sad-looking boy who arrived with Jack Albright. Some claim they spoke to him, though they are unable to summon the memory of about exactly what. We know, of course, that the events that transpired in the seven months after that August evening reverberated far beyond the quiet Houses of Kennedy's campus: not only to its peer institutions but across the NESCACs and certain Ivies. And so we can understand why those who were there in Water Mill that evening might choose to believe that there, under the dark shawl of the Long Island night, their own stories intersected with something more plaintive and profound and shimmering.

The Altridges' home was bright when they arrived, its yellow light hanging a halo in the mist that had come in from the Atlantic. The birches that lined the long driveway passed white and phantom-like in the Yukon's headlights, and as the gravel beneath crunched beneath the braking wheels their beams caught the edges of the decals on the rear windshields before them: ST. PAUL'S, DARTMOUTH; GRO-TON, TRINITY, HARVARD. Jack parked behind a Nissan Xterra (HOTCHKISS; BUCKNELL).

"Shall we," Jack said evenly.

The boy who opened the door met them with the practiced ease of a seasoned if weary host. Tall and gaunt, with pomade-coiffed black hair atop his pale face, he held himself at a minor angle, his thin black jeans hugging low on his waist. His thin smile was purple with the stain of good wine.

"Well, well," the boy drawled, "Mister Midfielder. And a sidekick." He cast his head toward Foster, then returned his eyes to Jack. There was something taunting about his gaze.

"What's up, Tripp." There was an uncomfortable curtness in Jack's voice; Foster had a sudden memory of hearing Mason Pretlow in conversation with Mark Stetson.

"Well, *please* come in," the tall boy said, twirling in bare feet on the hardwood floor toward the light of the home behind him. "Very kind of you to bring liquor, too."

"We're outta blow." Jack's baritone seemed lower, hollower.

"Doubt that's an issue."

"I'm Foster, by the way."

The boy extended his hand: his fingers were long, his hands larger and more masculine than his affect. "Tripp. A fellow *Kennedian*?" He seemed to sing this last word. Foster nodded, both discomforted and entranced by the boy's solicitous show. "Me too, once upon a *time*," he sang again, retrieving a plastic cup of red wine from a bureau next to the foyer's wide staircase.

There had been something familiar about the boy, about the paleness of his face and the glibness of his leer.

"I've been in your apartment," Foster said suddenly, recalling the night of Sofi Cohen's birthday party. "Or we've been in the same apartment. We've met before."

"If you say so, darling," Tripp said. Jack was silent.

There is an alchemy to small parties in big houses, a gentle choreography of movement and dispersion across its rooms. Tripp had led them to a sort of solarium at the rear of the house, where he'd retrieved a fat emerald bottle and splashed it over plastic cups. "Absinthe," he said, taking a pull from the bottle. "The real shit. My mother's."

The last conversation Foster's memory would uniformly transcribe was with a large, jovial boy from Deerfield named Patterson Hughes. His heft and pink face made Foster think of an oversized toddler. Patterson had pulled a Saran-wrapped nugget of cocaine from the breast pocket of his Ralph Lauren oxford like a WASPy Santa Claus, spilling its contents with happy wantonness onto a wide book of Robert Rauschenberg's paintings. He partitioned it into fat little bunkers with his American Express Platinum card.

"Yo, Tripp!" he bellowed happily out toward the house. "Stop suckin' dick and come do a line!" He then looked at Foster with an invitingly boastful grin, as if looking for acclamation for his impertinence. "Let's fuckin' go, baby—you said your name's Farmer?"

Today, Patterson Hughes lives in Manhattan with his wife, a girl from Trinity, who is pregnant with their first child. Of the many individuals who declined to contribute their voices to this project's record, he was perhaps the most affable about it; given his purely functional significance to the narrative at hand, it would feel unseemly to diligently reinvent the specifics of his conversation on this night in August 2009. What we know is this: Foster Dade's distribution network would eventually constellate seventeen campuses across seven states; with the records at our disposal, we can identify this evening as its point of origin.

Trafficking in specificity here would also ascribe an undue coherence to an evening that for our purposes refuses one. Foster would remember returning downstairs from the bathroom and encountering Harris Adelstein coming through the front door with a case of Natural Light under his arm, but he would retain no recollection of the conversation they may or may not have had. Ditto with Mellie Jakes, a thin, horse-like girl from Manhattan a year above him in Hewitt House, who appeared at some point thereafter with a girl from Taft whose name Foster would subsequently learn was Elle O'Connor. He would remember screaming along to Jay Sean with the rest of the sweaty bodies in the solarium, his arm draped over Patterson's meaty shoulder, but he would not know if it was before then or after that he stumbled into an upstairs bedroom to find Jack and Tripp hunched over lines of cocaine laid out on the dresser. He would remember that Jack was the drunkest Foster had ever seen him. He had been leaning with his shoulder up against the wall, looking at Foster with an uncomprehending vacancy. Foster had then returned downstairs, hearing the door shut behind him. He would not remember seeing Jack thereafter.

It was mid-afternoon when Mark Stetson left me at the coffee shop on the Bowery. The eastern sky over Houston Street was beginning to yellow when I finally pulled my fleece over my shoulders and stepped out into the minor chill of the spring. I had sat at our table for what must have been an hour after he left; my laptop sat open but forgotten on the dense wood before me.

"I mean—it's fucking sad," Mark had said. "The whole thing. I liked Foster—honestly, as a person, all the teenage drama aside, I theoretically liked him more than I liked the others."

"Even Jack?"

"No comment means no comment." But again there was a sadness in his smile that betrayed the finality in his words. "Relitigating the past is overrated."

I walked without motive or destination until after nightfall, returning with minor stabs of nausea to the assault I chose to hear in these words. I thought about this as I walked across lower Manhattan, as aimlessly as Jack Albright and Annabeth Whittaker and Foster Dade had twelve springs prior, watching the silhouettes of NYU undergrads buying Juul pods through bodega doorways and couples my age stepping out from their buildings in Greenwich Village to meet their Ubers and go to dinner. Eventually I forced myself to conclude that it was my still-guilty conscience that had given Mark's words their imagined pointedness, and went home.

Still, I could not bring myself to work that night, and instead spent the evening staring at but not watching *The Sopranos*. I'd left my phone on my desk across the room, and it was only when I got up to rummage through my papers for a sheet of Nicorette that I saw Mark Stetson's name on my screen. We had been corresponding over private message on Instagram—"he literally hasn't replied to a text since college," Sofi Cohen had told me—and it was there that he'd messaged me an hour and a half earlier.

> **Mark Stetson (@markstet):** hey
> **Mark Stetson (@markstet):** got a sec

It was just before midnight when I found him sitting on a bench at the lower edge of Washington Square Park, his face indigo in his phone's ethereal light. It had been my idea to go for a walk. I'll confess that I was struck by the lyricism of the prospect, but in retrospect I'd sense that he'd been too, despite himself.

"I wouldn't be doing this if I wasn't still infatuated with the idea that my own life story is more poignant and important than it actually is," he said, and for the third time that day I'd felt the almost elegiac sadness in his smile. "Though I'm gonna tell myself it's all important to the whole Foster thing. Which isn't untrue, by the way."

He paused for a moment, then pulled his Juul from his track jacket's pocket. He exhaled its vapor in a thin stream that broke against the glow of the high stone arch in the middle of the square.

"And I'm just gonna trust my suspicion that you're the only person who'll end up hearing this," he said. "If this whole thing you're doing ends up going somewhere, we'll talk. But—no offense—for a story about a bunch of white prep school kids misbehaving, your timing is utter shit." He hit his Juul again and tilted it toward a BLACK LIVES MATTER sign taped inside a pizzeria window. "Not planned, I swear to God."

"You're my diversity hire."

"I think we both know that I'm much more than that."

I smiled what I hoped was an insouciant smile. "Jack told me to fuck off when I reached out to him."

There was something rueful in Mark's smirk. "At least you had the privilege of being told directly. I just became invisible." His Juul blinked stoically in his fingers. "And even then I never told anyone. Anything."

"More than you can say for Tripp Altridge."

"Yeah, well"—Mark took another drag on his Juul, then let its smoke spill from his nose—"Tripp Altridge is a fucking sociopath who ruins people for sport, and also a pathological liar, so there was no real damage done, fortunately for dear Jackie."

"Do you believe it? The Tripp stuff?"

We'd crossed Houston onto Wooster, moving without direction down the quiet alcoves of SoHo. The ridges of the cobblestones seemed to shift beneath our feet. "I wasn't there that night," Mark said, with a diffidence that refused my solicitation. His smile was defiant but not unkind. "And you're the one telling this story."

"You're the one who said you'd help." I said this with a compensatory smile.

The defiance in his coyness had also betrayed a more essential candor, and I found myself suddenly less abashed: as if the reticence of his smile had amounted to—if not a confession per se, then a tacit invitation.

"If I knew, yeah, I'd tell you," Mark took another long drag on his Juul and tilted his head back to let the vapor break against the haze of the night. He studied me for a moment. "But that's not why you're walking with me at one in the morning. And my narcissistic nostalgia draws the line at walking across Manhattan until sunrise. So."

"So tell me what there is to tell me."

Foster awoke against the harsh light of the following morning on a couch in a room he did not recognize. The house was silent; the room's surfaces were heavy with half-full cans of Bud Light. He was still drunk. With a shadow of the amorphous dread that follows intensive cocaine use, he eventually forced himself to stand up and step tentatively toward the house's foyer.

The Altridges' front door was ajar, welcoming the bright warmth of the morning. A spout of dread seized him when he saw the figure of the person standing out on the stoop, facing out toward the green lawn, and then he realized it was Jack, smoking a cigarette for what Foster suspected was the first time in his life.

"Yo," Foster said, his voice carrying the uncertainty with which he stepped toward the threshold.

Now Jack flinched. His face was pale with hangover and exhaustion, his eyes narrowed and dark. Something in his stance seemed to sag under an unseen weight.

"Let's go." The snap in Jack's voice had tripped on an enfeeblement Foster had not heard before.

The drive back to Southampton had been silent, and there Jack had ascended wordlessly to his upstairs bedroom. "Fucking hungover," he'd muttered, not looking back as he stepped up the stairs.

Foster spent the day on the poolside terrace with *Infinite Jest* open before him. There was a soporific pull to its sentences, and he let them tug him into spats of hungover sun-warmed half-sleep. It was Jack's voice that nudged him from his fugue late that afternoon. "I'm a new man," he yodeled, emerging from the house and lobbing an empty Gatorade bottle at his scowling sister's head. "Let's go to Pritchett's and get baked as shit."

And as they passed beneath the cooling evening up Montauk Highway, Jack had bellowed along with the heavy piano stomps of Kanye

West's "Homecoming," and with a relief Foster was too ashamed to comprehend he heard himself singing along. Twilight was extending its gossamer as they arrived at the house on Lily Pond Lane, where Davison Pierce, a textbook publisher who'd won the Greek prizes at both St. Paul's and Yale, had once poured gimlets for Willem de Kooning and Lillian Ross. "I'm sure he'd be very proud," his grandson had said, taking the gravity bong Mason Pretlow had carved from two empty Fresca two-liters with the crude utilitarianism of an Antietam surgeon. They all spent that evening implausibly high, even Will Thierry, whose stoned stupefaction at the betrayal of his own moral code delighted the others. As Freddie Pieters tapped shredded cheddar onto a plate of Tostitos, Mark Stetson had appeared in the kitchen doorway wearing a woman's wide-brimmed sunhat, and after pointing to him agape for a few moments, Will had joined the others in cracking up.

And then, sometime after midnight, while Will gawked with the same mirth at the sight of Jack Albright swimming breaststroke in circles in the Pierces' pool, Foster's BlackBerry hummed with a text message from a Connecticut area code. *Hey brother it's Patterson from Tripp's party lol things got sloppy but yo just wanted to say Im still interested in the aderal if your still willing to mail it Ill pay for shipping.* Then another, timestamped eleven minutes later: *And i have some buddies at Deerfield who r also interested fyi but no pressure man.*

XIII.

Sunlight was coming through the clouds as the Montauk Branch train slowed toward Southampton. Shrimpers off Montauk had waited out the morning's storms belowdecks, listening to the untroubled automated voice of the National Weather Service's Marine Forecast on its tired but steadfast frequencies. When light did break the rain, it was the color of millet. Twenty winters of groundwater's freeze had broken jagged cracks along the station's parking lot, leaching the asphalt's heat into thin spills of vapor against the rain-cooled air. BMWs and Mercedeses and Porsches idled with their hazards blinking.

"Honestly, we're too nice." Pritchett sighed, leaning against the hood of the copper Lexus. His light curls were denser than they'd been in spring, his Adam's apple more pronounced. "*We're expecting you to pick us up*—you'd think we were waiting for, I dunno, the Secretary of fucking State. Amagansett to Southampton isn't, like, a quick cruise down the road."

(Frances and Annabeth had called Jack from the Hudson News in Penn Station concourse late that morning. "Sofi's gonna be stuck at her cousin's fucking horse show out in, like, Patchogue." Foster heard Annabeth over speakerphone in the Albrights' bright kitchen. "You'll be our eternal saviors if you get us—we'll pay you in booze.")

"I don't mind the outing," Will said. "We weren't really doing anything else, anyway."

"Selfish bitches. Kinda insane that they still refuse to blow us."

The conspiratorial, caustic grin with which Mason Pretlow said this had always unsettled Foster in its provocation: *Ask me if I'm serious or not.* A young blond mother in tidy black athleticwear jerked her head at him in startled outrage, and Mason's simper only widened, his eyes locking with hers with predatorial audacity.

"It'll be nice to see them," Foster offered flatly, not looking at Mason.

The train was beginning its uncertain lurch away from the platform toward Bridgehampton when the girls emerged from the thick of disembarking passengers. Gracie Smith's grimace tensed as she stepped around a shih tzu that strained against its leash. "Fucking Jews and their miniature dogs," she grunted as she reached the Lexus. "The thing spent the last three hours fucking barking."

"It's really just delightful to see you, too, Miss Smith," Jack said, grinning at her.

"I sincerely thought she was going to chuck it out of the train at Islip."

Annabeth's voice seemed to constrict Foster's throat. She was wearing an old men's linen button-down and a pair of aviators that she pulled from her face as she appeared behind Gracie. She seemed somehow older than she had mere days earlier. "Gentlemen," she said, and with a widening smile she put her arms around them. When she reached Foster last he felt his shoulders spasm.

"Hey there, stranger," she said to him. She seemed to whisper this into his ear. Foster had not spoken of the kiss to Jack or anyone else: to acknowledge it with words threatened to shatter its preservation.

Porter Roth was the last of the girls to step down from the platform. "I was worried for a sec that I left my EpiPen on the train," she said to Frances. Realizing that the boys stood before her, she blushed, busying herself with the zipper of the burgundy Longchamp bag that hung by her side. She, too, hugged the boys, but they were perfunctory, nervous embraces. ("She's so fucking *awkward*," Foster remembered Mason once moaning bitterly.)

"Hey, Foster," she said as she reached him, her voice shy.

"What's going on, Porter," he said, grateful to look away from Annabeth.

"You guys, I need a *drink*," Frances moaned. "Can we just go get fucked up *now*?"

The Cohens' house was along the thin peninsular strand of beach stretching appendix-like below Southampton, dividing the brackish marshland of Shinnecock Bay from the cold seas of the North Atlantic. The home was one of the exercises in modernism that intersperse the old clapboard manors of Meadow Lane, standing wide and stout against the beachhead. They'd arrived to find Sofi draped theatrically along a chaise lounge by the pool. Her sunglasses were large and bug-like; Foster thought of Jackie Onassis. She wore a red bikini and held against her stomach a paperback copy of *Extremely Loud & Incredibly Close*, one hand clutching the top of its spine.

"A horse show, huh?" Pritchett hollered over the pool.

"Rain cut it short," Sofi shrugged with a flourish as she stood to receive them. "Hi, dolls," she said, kissing them one by one on the cheek. "I see the drive didn't kill you, Pritchett."

"Ugh, Sof, how could you," Foster heard Annabeth say. "I *hate* Jonathan Safran Foer."

"Me too," Foster said, truthfully, and he felt the nag of Mason's stare. "Pretentious drivel."

"You're both just anti-Semites," Sofi said.

"No, that's Gracie," Annabeth grinned. Gracie shrugged.

"And Pritchett," Pritchett said. Mason and Freddie cackled.

"You're lucky my dad isn't here."

"House to ourselves, hm?" Mark said, kicking his pink canvas Toms from his feet and pulling his shirt over his head.

"Aunt's Shabbat in Bridgehampton." Sofi nursed a sip from the can of seltzer by her chair. "Probably staying over. They're in denial about the fact that their little girl drinks." She removed her sunglasses and smiled. "So let's enjoy ourselves."

They were drunk by the time night fell, when the timer-programmed lights inside illuminated the Cohens' tall windows with a warmth that softened the home's hard brutalist edges. Pritchett and Freddie had dragged an inflatable raft into the pool and organized triangles of Solo cups on either end; after the third round of pong, Mason, reeling from defeat, threw himself belly-first upon it, and the beer bloomed up to the surface from the jettisoned cups in a smeary amber cloud.

"You fucking *asshole*!" Sofi screamed, emerging on the deck from a downstairs living room, clutching bottles of Jose Cuervo and Smirnoff in her fists. But she started laughing with the rest of them.

By ten thirty, or what felt like ten thirty, the raft was limp and deflated from a puncture of unknown provenance, its plastic carcass resting indifferently against the stairs down into the pool. Empty Solo cups bobbed on the water's surface. Earlier, when the last ribbon of orange rode the western horizon, Frances informed her audience that she was too lazy to change, pulling off her T-shirt and jumping into the water in her Nike shorts and bra. Foster found himself silently watching the night play out from a dark table at the pool's far end, near the foot of the path out to the dunes. Sitting at the pool's opposing edge with her feet in the water was Annabeth. *I realized I was unable to do anything other than just* watch *her. In a very meaningful sense, this has always been my problem.* So he'd looked on as the pool's watery olive light undulated lazily against her legs, studying the turns of her smile in its shadows. At one point, she looked up, and catching his eyes on her, she grinned at him before turning back to where Freddie and Frances treaded water before her.

He watched, also, as Jack and Mason retreated inside and returned again, emerging each time with a new stride of emphasis.

"Don't you boys dare leave cocaine in my mother's bathroom," Sofi said as they stepped out onto the patio with wide grins.

Foster watched as Annabeth sat up straighter. "You have coke?" she asked, turning to Jack.

"Surprised Gracie hasn't stocked you up for the next month. Hoarding it all for yourself?"

"Fuck you, Mason," Gracie said, but her smile's reflexive twitch suggested that she had already joined them on a journey inside.

No one noticed when Foster rose from the table and moved to Jack's Yukon in the Cohens' driveway. The night was suddenly cool, and he retrieved his old Gilman hoodie from the trunk. Pulling it on, he felt a thin bristling in its pocket, where he found half of a forgotten Adderall IR in a matted Ziploc. Its promised shock of confidence beckoned, so he placed the pill on his tongue and retrieved its crumbled orange detritus from the plastic with his fingertip. He was drunk enough to not mind the bitterness.

The house's downstairs hallways were quiet. Foster heard Pritchett's muffled yawp from the patio beyond its walls and let himself stand for a moment in the darkness. And then a door opened, and from the bright light of the powder room stepped Annabeth. She was frowning absently down at her BlackBerry as she thumbed out a message. The weight of her eyes suggested that she, too, was drunk.

"Yo," Foster said quietly from the darkness.

Annabeth's head shot up, startled. "Jesus," she said, darkening the screen of her phone and bringing it to her side. "You scared the shit out of me." And then she smiled, casually. "Hey. You've been MIA."

"Just—chilling," Foster said dumbly. "I like my me time."

They stood there for a moment in the darkness, their faces half-lit by the glow of the bathroom that spilled out from the doorway. Only Foster seemed to sense this pause or feel its weight. Had he taken the Adderall half an hour earlier, he knew, his words may have delivered themselves: *I want to kiss you again, Annabeth. I love you. I love you so much.*

"Well, go join the crowd," she said. For the first time, he heard in her default merriness its edge of aloofness. "Everyone's out there. Go talk to Porter—she hates parties like this."

And before Foster could respond, the shadow of Jack Albright appeared before them. He was shirtless, wet from the pool, and the flint of cocaine sharpened his expression of banal surprise.

"Oh, sup," he said. "The old squad. Where you been, Dade." He said this with his shoulders turned vaguely away from Foster, as if it would efface his presence.

"Jack and I were going to look for mixers upstairs," Annabeth said. "Wanna come?"

There was a hesitant, perfunctory flatness to these last words that cut through her cheerfulness. The same yawp came from outside, followed by Frances's pronounced squeal. "I do *not* want to see your balls, Mason Pretlow!"

"I guess I picked the right time to return to the scene," Foster heard himself say with a deadened grin, jerking his head in the vague direction of the pool, feeling his feet shuffle in the direction of the dark hallway's end. "Y'all go."

"Sure, no worries," Jack said vaguely. And then Annabeth was turning toward the narrow staircase that abutted the powder room door, and Jack shuffled dully past Foster toward her.

"We'll see you out there in a sec, Foster," Annabeth said with a strange note of something conciliatory in her voice as they headed upstairs. "Holy God, I'm fucked up." She said this as she disappeared above the landing; these words were meant for Jack.

In what may have been his only valuable remotely therapeutic insight ever, Foster would write late one night that October, Dr. Apple once told me that I intellectualize things to depersonalize them. To make them less painful. (Case in point: my awful atheism phase in eighth grade, a few months after Dad left, when I posted AIM away messages (I didn't have a MacBook/iChat yet) blindly quoting Richard Dawkins.) To indulge this psychological impulse once more—

Fatalism: the belief that all events are predetermined. Sometimes by God (e.g. John Calvin), but not always. Still, you can accept that X→Y

isn't a function of your individual agency and still analyze exactly how
X→Y—or, better yet, why X→Y1 rather than Y2.

There was a bottle of red wine, open but full, on a wicker table by
the door as Foster stepped back out onto the patio. No one in the pool
noticed him seize the bottle by its neck and take an aggressive pull, its
glass mouth sudden and hard against his lips. He turned toward the
pool's far end, where he'd left his Solo cup and the little Advil bottle
that contained his weed, and saw that his chair was no longer empty.

Porter Roth sat beneath the darkness of the canopy above, hugging
her knees to her chest and holding a beer between them as she sat.
For half a moment Foster began to halt, but with the same tempo of
warm determination he felt himself approach.

"Oh, shit, sorry—did I take your seat?" Porter rearranged her
legs to stand, embarrassed. "Sorry—I thought you'd gone inside with
Annabeth and Jack. Here, I'll—"

She began to rise, but Foster felt himself smile wanly at her. "You're
good," he said, declining himself into the chair next to hers. "Nah,
they're—I dunno what they're doing." He heard the flatness in his
words. "Not shotgunning beers in the pool." He tilted his head toward
the far end of the water, where Mason belched.

Porter giggled. "Determined avoidance is my strategy for engaging
Mason. I'm also just—bad at parties. They think I'm lame for not
doing coke, but god knows what the fuck that would look like."

Foster laughed. Porter was not drunk, but the dry dispassion Foster
heard in her voice was cloudless with liberation. She looked at him
with half a smile; he had not before noticed the pleasant fullness of
her lips.

"Wine?" he said, angling the neck of the bottle toward her. "I
don't have any cups, unfortunately, so I'm just—"

Porter took it from him and took an abrasive pull. "Yeck," she
said, wiping her mouth with a mild shudder, and then pulled from it
again. "Sorry, Sofi."

"She won't miss it."

The darkness guarded them from the light of the pool, where
Mason and Freddie were imploring Frances and Gracie to make out.

As five minutes became twenty-five or something beyond it, no one looked to the chairs where Porter and Foster sat together, ensconced in the shadows.

"Wait, are you genuinely making the argument that *The Life Aquatic* is better than *Rushmore*?"

"I never said that. I said that Wes Anderson didn't find his groove until *The Royal Tenenbaums*, and that—"

"You said that—"

"I know what I said." Porter took another pull of wine. "Though I'm mostly just stunned that someone here actually has taste in movies." She smiled coyly at Foster. "Even if it's bad taste."

"I take pride in my taste, thank you. And I'll grant you the satisfaction of knowing that I actually admire yours." He dropped his voice half an octave and jerked his head in the direction of the pool's other end. "Go ask Frances what her favorite Wes Anderson movie is."

Porter snorted, then leaned toward him conspiratorially. "You know what my dad asked me after she spent the night at my house this past spring? He asked me if Kennedy had started a special education program."

Foster grinned. "Your dad sounds funny."

"Accidentally. He's one to talk—he's brilliant but, like, exists on another planet socially. Comes with the territory of being a *celebrated economist*, I guess."

"Nice to have around if you ever need to balance your checkbook, though."

"Until I don't get into Harvard next year."

"Oh, come on."

"He's been writing them checks every year since he graduated. God, if I end up being a bad investment, he'll be so pissed." Porter's laugh was hollow.

"Surely he won't be *pissed*."

"Maybe not at me, no. At himself. I think he sees me as, like, his vanity project. Why do you think I'm going to be one of two Third Years in Multivariable Calc this year?"

"Who's the other?"

"Raj Chakravarty, of course." She rolled her eyes. "What about Mr. and Mrs. Dade—surely they're delighted with their little literary genius."

"Not if you call her Mrs. Dade. It was one of those divorces." Foster quietly flinched at his words, but found his composure. "*Ms. Harrison.*"

Porter frowned. "I didn't know your parents were divorced," she said. "I'm sorry—that sucks. Or"—the flicker of her old panicked self-consciousness briefly danced—"does it suck? Sorry, I'm shutting up. Honestly, I'm such a dork; I never know how to have these conversations."

Her spasm of vulnerability loosened something in Foster. He had realized relatively early after the divorce that the topic would lie mercifully dormant if he so wished, so mercifully dormant it remained, and yet something in Porter's attention—perhaps tinged only by the Adderall's magnanimity—conveyed an unspoken sense of concord.

"Don't be. You're fine," Foster said, waving away her apology. Then, quieter: "My dad was—is—a scumbag. I don't think much about it."

Porter's face seemed less dismayed than sad. "Still," she said, "I'm an asshole. If only because I'm sitting here bragging about taking Multivariable Calc."

Foster shrugged. "You're not. I'd honestly kill to be as good at math as you are. You should have seen my grades in Algebra Two."

"Well," Porter said, "I'd do anything to write the way you can write. I'd blow Art Tierney if it meant I didn't have to write another English paper."

She seemed to blush at her coarseness, but her embarrassment provoked in Foster what he would later understand to be the earliest stirs of arousal. "Well," he said, feeling himself cross his legs, "maybe we should join forces. You can do my Pre-Calc homework and I'll write your papers for you."

"It would mean you'd actually have to acknowledge my existence at school." It was the first time Foster had seen Porter grin.

"Wow, brutal!" Foster impersonated outrage, but he, too, felt himself grin. "You're the one who never talks to *me*! Whose existence do I acknowledge, by your standards, Porter Roth?"

Porter shifted her voice into a deadened baritone. "*Oh, Annabeth, you're such a genius, you're not like anyone else, I'm just a sad sensitive boy who hates sports and need someone like you to tell me how good my book collection is.*"

"I'm honestly flattered you think I have such a masculine voice."

"I wouldn't know," Porter said, taking the last sip of the wine. "You've never talked to me before tonight."

Their eyes met, their conversation breaking for the first time since he'd sat by her side. Her face was soft and honest, with a skepticism that seemed to imply some gesture of understanding. He had been ensnared by it in a way that conversations did not usually ensnare him.

"*Yo.*" From across the pool, Freddie's voice shattered the brief spell of solitude between them. There was a drunken vivacity to his voice, like the enthusiasm of a child's discovery. "Albright and Whittaker are getting it *on.*"

Because of the Adderall, I was almost fine in the moment—even happy for them, as if a pivotal scene in a play I was directing had gone off without a hitch. If I am the central character in my own story, I am also its producer and audience, and sometimes one role trumps the other. In this case, I was honoring the script I'd written.

Through the darkness, Foster continued to look at Porter, holding his expression still. He expected Porter's face to reveal a sense of vindication, as if to say: "*Bummed?*" But hers, too, remained constant with what seemed like the same fixed intent, as if trying to preserve the strange affective spiderweb they'd woven between themselves that now seemed tenuous and frail.

And with the same kicking lurch with which he'd seized the wine from the wicker table, he spoke.

"Do you—wanna go see the beach?"

A moment passed, and then Porter nodded, her mouth shifting into a half-smile of ambiguous meaning. As they walked in silence into the woozy spill of night, Porter moved alongside him, closer than they'd been on the patio. The sky was thick and amber with the glow of the towns beyond the silent bay, but despite this the cosmos sought to stage their pageant. Their most steadfast stars had pushed through the darkness to the east and north, nudging their attendant choirs to come along. Like teenagers at a dance, the stellar objects couched their timidity in close huddles. They were less stars than effluent smears of saltwater against the darkness. The fuzzy warm seed of Mars shrugged lazily just over the horizon. Below it, delimiting where dark ocean became sky, a trawler maybe ten miles offshore had laid its anchor for the night, its beacon burning out over the deepening seas.

They walked up along the high ridge of the dunes, sliding unseen into the dark sand. The noise of the party behind them faded into only the muffled husk of the music's beat, riding every so often with the distant suggestion of a voice. They were stepping down into the dip beyond a high bank when Foster felt their footfalls slow. He looked back at the Cohens' house, which seemed distant and far below them, ensconced in a warm halo of electric lamplight that rose over the wall of dune separating it. Its stucco walls danced with the mosaic shimmer of the illuminated pool. Occasional freckles of shadow against the glow indicated the movement of people otherwise impalpable.

"Do you think any of them would care if we got murdered out here."

Porter's voice was dry and flat, and Foster snorted. It was an honest laugh, and its authenticity felt lucid and clean inside him. They were close enough then that he could discern her grim and expectant face, as if the moment had been ordained by a long-mobilizing inevitability— something that had less to do with him or her or the two of them together than with a common vantage, metaphorized by the dark ridge of the dunes, both estranged and protected from the foreign glow of the far-off party. He cast himself into the sadness, and he kissed her, cupping her cheek in his hand.

She was an ambitious kisser. Her lips opened as they met his, her tongue reaching out and grasping in an improvised choreography that was at once blind and determined. Together their bodies moved down onto the sand, slowly and awkwardly in the service of keeping their mouths together. He shifted himself on top of her, feeling their collective weight slide down the slope that now guarded them from the night beyond it. The sea grass that grew in the dune's gully bent and broke beneath the weight of their feet. She was grasping his face and he was grasping hers. He felt her body squirm beneath his mass, and he broke his mouth away.

"You okay," he said. His voice sounded unfamiliar to himself. She nodded silently, vigorously. Foster grinned as his mouth returned to hers. He felt a fricative heat against his upper leg and realized it was nuzzled between hers. He panicked for a moment at the realization that his penis was soft from the Adderall and alcohol. He thought back to the house beyond the dunes, to the twin footsteps leaving him alone in the darkened downstairs hallway, and with a jihadist's rudderless gumption he took his hand and slid it up beneath the end of Porter's shirt. Her flinch at this intervention was one of purely neutral surprise. Her bra's wire was hard and committed, denying the possibility of breach, so he sent his fingers up over its crest. Her nipple, when he found it, was soft and felt almost delicately thin. He felt himself play with it, noting her responsive stirs and murmurs with an anthropological satisfaction.

This went on for many minutes. In their silence he realized how drunk he was. His panic subsided—he was intoxicated enough, he acknowledged, to speak honestly on the matter if he had to, and rehearsed the address in his head with the rhythms of their kissing: *I took an Adderall and I can't get hard on it.* But Porter's hands left his face only to clutch his back, and there they stayed. Every so often there was a static press of sound from the direction of the house, a laugh or a yell dissipating out into the silent night. The despair that would take its shape in the weeks and months thereafter still had its ethereal press of destiny, and their motion there in the dark dunes seemed to suspend its animation, benevolent in its surreal detachment.

And then he felt Porter shift beneath him. Slowly, she pulled her mouth back from his. Foster opened his eyes and let them adjust through the darkness to the strange shape of her face. She looked up at him with what seemed like a curious sort of sadness.

"I'm getting cold," he heard her say. "And it's got to be really fucking late."

In silence, they descended the footpath to the head of the Cohens' patio to see that things had carried on. There was Will and Freddie and Pritchett and Mason and Mark; there was Frances and Gracie and Sofi; they were together cast in the dancing light of the pool, tucked obliviously within the security of the dark night. Annabeth and Jack were not there.

"I've actually gotta pee," he said to her. "Gonna go back out to the beach, but I'll be back in a sec."

He felt Porter's eyes on him as he turned, refusing the questions they may or may not have asked. Much later, Foster would remember the final movements of that night only by the strange spell of impersonality that seemed to carry him out to the beach. He crossed back over the dunes and reached the foot of their rise. The stars were brighter now, more distinguished from their companions. The night carried out in all directions. He thought of what lay beyond their boundless distances: of the sleeping towns with streets bridged by lamplight, of the cars passing silently down highways and the anonymity of the lives within them. He looked south to where the dark stretch of Long Island bent inland with the Atlantic. He thought of Manhattan, of the strings and webs of lights that burned patiently over black water. He thought of the dark stretch of country that lay beyond it, of the yellow ghosts cast by oil refineries and freeways, and, where the stretch became darker, of Kennedy.

I tend to think the saddest and most desolate things are also the most beautiful, he would later write. I realize now that this is not a passive tendency. I plot my own sadness in the interest of this beauty. Whether this is a coping mechanism or what Dr. Apple calls "self-sabotage" I don't know. I am sad all the time and there is a magic to it.

He stood on the beach for a very long time, until the house behind him was silent and dark.

XIV.

http://www.fhd93.blogspot.com/2009/07/untitled_6
(Posted July 23, 2009)

It is five in the morning here in Hong Kong and I will not remember writing this.

I've realized I'm really good at listening. And by listening I mean: giving the impression that I care. Ethically the jury is out. Maybe the act of providing comfort is itself a noble or good thing, full stop, no matter what lies behind it. But I can't help but feel guilty about the fact that what I'm really feeling is only self-satisfaction at the illusion of my goodness.

I am a liar and I am violent. I deserve to be ruined for it. I already know firsthand my capacity to destroy others or to let them be destroyed. I have done this and I feel nothing.

This has always been true but I blame Kennedy. I think the thing about Kennedy is that it's never felt real. It's like a play whose set I've stumbled onto. I told myself over the last year not to read that as a sign of my happiness or lack thereof. This was bullshit, but I was right in the sense that it's about something more basic than happiness. It's about feeling real.

I don't know what "real" would look like, but I imagine it as feeling old and warm. I don't think any of this makes sense but bear with me. I'm super fucking fucked up. Alexy was right about the Oxicotin (sp?)—it's like a bath. (Mental note: find more.)

There's a voice in my head that says I don't need to sell drugs to be interesting. But it's not about being interesting. It's about justifying my presence. Which I have never been able to imagine—my presence I mean—as anything other than wretched, repulsive, an unwanted intrusion.

PART III

But it's just the price I pay
Destiny is calling me

—The Killers

I.

Foster Dade's MacBook Pro/Documents/personal files/untitled [Hidden Folder]/untitled.xls
(Date Created: September 24, 2009 at 11:41 PM)

NAME	SCHOOL	DATE	ITEM	QUANT	$$$$$
Frances Evans	Kennedy	25–Sep	Vyvanse 50mg	4	$40
Brent Rivenbark	Kennedy	25–Sep	Adderall XR 10mg	4	$28
Hannah Phelps–Berkowitz	Kennedy	27–Sep	Vyvanse 50mg	3	$30
			Adderall IR 20mg	2	$14
Jack Albright	Kennedy	27–Sep	Adderall IR 20mg	4	$28
Patterson Hughes	Deerfield	29–Sep	Vyvanse 50mg	10	$150
			Adderall IR 20mg	10	$90
			Adderall XR 10mg	5	$35
Freddie Pieters	Kennedy	1–Oct	Vyvanse 60mg	2	$24
Evan Wainwright	Choate	2–Oct	Vyvanse 60mg	7	$112
			Adderall IR 20mg	10	$90
Kendall MacPherson	Kennedy	3–Oct	Adderall IR 20mg	2	$14
Jacqueline Franck	Kennedy	3–Oct	Adderall XR 10mg	4	$28
Maddie Richardson	Deerfield	5–Oct	Adderall XR 10mg	5	$45
Hannah Phelps–Berkowitz	Kennedy	8–Oct	Adderall IR 20mg	3	$21
			Vyvanse 60mg	5	$60
			Adderall IR 20mg	4	$28
Jack Albright	Kennedy	10–Oct	Vyvanse 60mg	5	$60
			Adderall IR 20mg	15	$105

NAME	INST	DATE	ITEM	QUANT	$$$$$
Elle O'Connor	Taft	11–Oct	Adderall IR 10mg	10	$70
Tripp Altridge	NYC	11–Oct	Adderall XR 15mg	10	$135
			Vyvanse 60mg	4	$64
			Adderall IR 20mg	5	$44
Hannah Phelps–Berkowitz	Kennedy	12–Oct	Adderall IR 20mg	5	$35
				TOTAL	$1,390

INVENTORY:

VYVANSE 50mg ($10 Kennedy; $15 elsewhere)

VYVANSE 60mg ($12 K; $16 e)

ADDERALL XR 10mg ($7; $9)

ADDERALL IR 10mg ($5; $7)

ADDERALL IR 20mg ($7; $9)

II.

On January 26, 2006, a user named SailorMoonGurl94 registered her account on the forums of VirtualTeenTalk.org. Though such message boards remain surprisingly vibrant today—usually those dedicated to a niche hobby like astrophotography or a particularly esoteric fetish, in compensation for a paucity of informational resources elsewhere—aesthetically and culturally they remain artifacts of an earlier, quainter internet. In their hypertextual minimalism, what these forums preserve is both a logic and ethos of pseudonymity. Beyond the most cursory statistics (gender; birthday; time zone), the table of personal information on each user's account page is less biographical than metabiographical: the dates and times of the user's registration on and last visit to the site; the number of threads they'd started and posts they'd authored. With nothing more to offer, these data portraits perpetuated an illusion that for certain users became more literal: the pretense that these sites themselves were in fact the whole world.

The domain name VirtualTeenTalk.org was registered on a server in Barstow, California, on the third day of July 2000. Its first post appeared nine days later. "This is a place for us teens to talk, get to know each other, ask questions we're too embarrassed to ask, etc. ☺," VTT_Moderator wrote. By the time SailorMoonGurl94 registered her account five and a half years later, there were just north of two hundred thousand members. The site and its several dozen subforums were organized thematically: Teen Lifestyle (*Television and Movies*; *Sports*; *Music*; *Hobbies*) and General Discussion (*Introductions*; *School*; *Relationships*; *Life's Big Questions*; *Vent!*); Puberty 101 (*General*; *Girls Only!*; *Boys Only!*; *Sex*); Help and Advice (*Sexual Identity, Depression, Anxiety, and Mental Health*; *Abuse*; *Eating Disorders*; *Cutting and Self-Harm*; *Bullying*).

None of these regions was ever idle—the site's least active subforum, *Sports*, still boasts nearly 25,000 discrete posts—but it was the latter two categories that brought most users to VirtualTeenTalk. In many cases, it had been a purely utilitarian endeavor: some faceless adolescent had registered and posted their motivating query in Puberty 101—*Boys Only!* or Help and Advice—*Sexual Identity*; when answers came—and they always did come—the user took their epistemological solace and logged out forever. But the narrowness of these fact-finding missions belies a deeper motivating truth: that the internet has prospered because it offers one what the physical world cannot. And so many of these users, with usernames like *xxx_bLaCk_VeLvEt_xxx* and *you_killed_kenny_911*, would find themselves clicking around the site, to threads about *Kyle XY* or the forthcoming release of *Harry Potter and the Half-Blood Prince*, and see for the first time in their lives a space in which their own presence might not be an intrusion. (Of VirtualTeenTalk's forty-three subforums, Help and Advice—*Bullying* ranks among the most visited.)

The archives of VirtualTeenTalk.org suggests that the user Sailor-MoonGurl94 understood the site as her digital homestead: a base camp from which she could set out to the internet's more distant outposts with the warm knowledge that there were people waiting for her back home. SailorMoonGurl94's account page still exists on VirtualTeen-Talk.org today, desolate but very much there, and in its tidy stack of information we learn that between January 2005 and March 2010, she authored 4,023 posts across the site's four dozen subsections, the first of which can be found in Puberty 101—*Girls Only!*

So I think I had my first period 0__o and there isnt much blood
but it smells kind of weird . . . X__X . . . is this normal? Im too
embarrassed to talk to my mom about it LOL

The first person to reply was a user named lonelygirlinindiana.

yessssss it hapens to me too sometimes ahhh I hate my peiroid
it started last year and i want 2 die every time!!!! Sailormoongurl
(i LOVE <3 <3 sialor moon btw) send me a private messag!

In the weeks and months that followed, SailorMoonGurl94 would
return to VirtualTeenTalk every day. *this is the first time since 4th
grade that im not spending all my time on the computer playing :-p*,
she wrote on February 20, 2006, on a subforum dedicated to *The
Sims 2*. *BTW does anyone know how to get the mailbox cheat for
money?* Certain usernames would recur in her posts from this time,
dragonball_fan _10 and *CrazyMouse100* and *PhantomOfTheOpera
Luvr95*; scrolling through them chronologically provides a sort of
socioevolutionary history of SailorMoonGurl94's five and a half years
in this curious virtual nation, with its rifts and alliances and secrets.
We can say with some certainty that none of those exchanged lines of
text are more freighted than that initial reply from *lonelygirlinindiana*,
who recurs throughout that lengthy archive.

But the significance of that first reply goes beyond the digital confines of VirtualTeenTalk. Behind the interwoven ribbons of data that
gave SailorMoonGurl94 her incorporeal form, there was a corporeal
life. Our glides into the digital sea can wash away certain truths of our
sublunary existence, but others hang on stubbornly to the swimmer's
refracted edges. In this case there is one. On that day in January 2006,
three weeks shy of her thirteenth birthday, Hannah Phelps-Berkowitz
had made her first real friend.

For all its occasional flashes of richness, the extant biographical database on Hannah Phelps-Berkowitz—the living, breathing, nondigi-
tal human constrained by mortal flesh and the analog geometries of

Princeton Junction, New Jersey—provides little insight into how or why she ended up at Kennedy as a day student in the fall of 2008. We can place a certain stock in the most generic explanation: that her family—which is to say Hannah and her parents, Drs. Daniel Phelps and Rose Berkowitz—belonged to the sizable bloc of academic or academically striving families in neighboring Mercer County who see Kennedy's academic caliber and college matriculation stats as superior to those of the still nationally ranked Princeton High. (The financial investment is steep but high-yield: between 1998 and 2008, day students accounted for seven of Kennedy's ten annual valedictorians.) Still, our parcel of the relevant data is limited to the most cursory facts: that Daniel and Rose met and married as doctoral students at Princeton—he in the then-still-incipient field of computer science; she in mathematics—and that in the spring of 1994, a year after beginning tenure-track positions in their home departments, Rose gave birth to a daughter.

Some of those in Hannah's advisory group or First Year Humanities section would later claim to remember the strange muteness of the pale tall girl with braces—the nickname Weird Hannah that had followed her through Princeton's public school system mercifully did not come with her to Kennedy—but it is unclear if these memories emerged retroactively, a means of contextualizing what had followed. In the silence she brought with her to Kennedy, it was only in her physical existence that she made any notable impression on those who passed her on campus. Puberty had come early and aggressively. The five-foot-tall ten-year-old by the start of sixth grade was now just shy of six feet. She seemed to have inherited her trousers and turtlenecks from one of her parents, though it was unclear which; like her unkempt curls beneath her trilby hat and the rolling backpack that skidded and stumbled on the pavement behind her as she crossed campus, they existed only in colorless hues of beige.

Many day students at Kennedy do their best to simulate or vicariously absorb the school's residential experience. They pass their free time in the House to which they've been assigned; they stay on campus until study hall and sleep over on Saturdays after dances; Hannah Phelps-Berkowitz, meanwhile, arrived on campus each morning in her father's twenty-year-old Econoline van and left each day when classes let out at three, the vehicle spewing wet guttural chokes as it lurched out of the campus driveway.

Those who would later try to clarify the opacity of Hannah Phelps-Berkowitz's early time at Kennedy would find an unlikely source of marginal insight in Jacqueline Franck of Greenwich, Connecticut. It had been with a rictus of barely disguised horror that Jacqueline had learned she was to be lab partners with the ridiculous-looking day student with the rolling backpack. "She's an ogre—I swear, she smells like fucking lunch meat and vagina," she would moan to Sally Pinelli and Bettina Scott at lunch, staring murderously at Hannah as she scooped herself cottage cheese from the salad bar. For the subsequent nine months, she would successfully say no more than six words to Hannah, going so far as to ask Mr. Harding for her own fetal pig to dissect. That Hannah seemed to accept this impassively only sickened Jacqueline more.

Our account of her response to much later events is unfortunately flimsy. I somewhat nervously wrote and rewrote my only email to Jacqueline Franck—who after nearly a decade still existed in my head as the beautiful, contemptuous girl a year ahead of me who once muttered something violent after I took the last passionfruit Vitamin Water from the glass-doored fridges in the student shop—and received no response. So we are left with SailorMoonGurl94's digital imprint, which, either on VirtualTeenTalk or elsewhere, has never surfaced or been connected in any meaningful public way to its author. I offer this one archival document only in the service of the story we are telling.

VirtualTeenTalk Forums—General Discussion—School
BY: SailorMoonGurl94
August 19, 2009 / 10:41pm EST
RE: Frustrated x__x

So IDK if this belongs here or in Vent lol. I feel like alot of my posts recently have been venting . . . sry VTT frendz. (o˚∧˚o) Plz enjoy this happy bear as an apology ʕ•ᴥ•ʔ

So I start 10th grade in two weeks and Im really nervous. My high school is really really hard and intense and sometimes I think I don't fit in. I spend pretty much all day waiting to get home and log on to VTT. Ive started playing less Kingdom Hearts and more Sims 3, which is what I always did in middle school when I was bummed out. (*cries pathetically in Simlish*)

I was always rly good at school but my high school is HARD. Im pretty good at english and science but rly bad at math. I feel like the kids who do best at school at my school are also the kids who r good at everything else. I don't play sports and I don't have many friends IRL (*cries pathetically in Simlish again*).

So I have 2 questions . . . . . .

> 1. Does any1 have any tips for being the best student? I know Im smart but I get distracted really quickly (usually by someone here on VTT ;-]) and lose focus. Idk if any of u have read Flowers for Algernon but I kind of wish that there was some sort of surgery or medicine to make me a supergenius . . . . . . LOL.
> 2. I think I would do better at school if I fit in more. Do u guys remember my lab partner from 9th grade science that I talked about and asked for advice with? Does any1 have tips? Also I also realllllllyyyyyy reeeellllllly want a boyfriend . . . . . . LOL. Idk if I am pretty or not (x∩x) but I'm really nice And have a lot of interests.

n e way . . . . . . sry for complaining!!!! As always send me a PM or add me on Yahoo! Messenger if u want to talk

---

We know from the timestamps on the posts that follow that the replies came quickly, as they always did. One in particular warrants its reproduction here.

VirtualTeenTalk Forums—General Discussion—School

BY: lulz_commando_43
August 23, 2009 / 6:17pm PST
RE: Frustrated x__x

hey sailormoongurl—sry to hear ur having a tough time. Can't rly help u with the fitting in stuff. I'm pretty lame lol.

> *Does any1 have any tips for being the best student? I know Im smart but I get distracted really quickly (usually by someone here on VTT ;-]) and lose focus. Idk if any of u have read Flowers for Algernon but I kind of wish that there was some sort of surgery or medicine to make me a supergenius . . . . . . LOL*

well . . . have u heard of adderall? it's pretty much this. i take it for ADD and it legit makes me the smartest ''ve ever been. know ur a kingdom hearts player . . . adderall is also the only way i was able to beat sephiroth in KHII lulz. if u cant get a perscription ask around @ school.lots of ppl have it

> *Plz enjoy this happy bear as an apology ʕ•ᴥ•ʔ*

Nice 2 meet u happy bear no apology neccesary

III.

Foster was sitting beneath the vaulted ceiling of the library's reading room when the girl in the trilby appeared before him. It was around dinnertime, and the library was mostly empty, its silence punctuated every so often by the muffled shouts and laughter of the shadows leaving the Dining Center under the warm late September twilight.

"Pardon me."

Foster jerked his head upright. He had been staring dumbly at the white slate of an empty Word document, from which Tierney's latest English paper prompt taunted him. Standing uncomfortably close to the long table's opposite side was a tall girl he realized he had seen before. "Look at that girl's fucking *hat*," Jack Albright had sneered in the Dining Center two weeks prior, pointing out toward the salad bar. She was still wearing the trilby, which seemed to wobble atop the volume of her untamed curls.

"Uh—hi," Foster said, fleetingly expecting her to confront him.

"You are Foster Dade."

"I—am, yes." The girl's absence of expression unnerved him.

"I would like to buy Adderall from you, if you're selling it. I heard that you were."

Foster's discomfort flashed briefly with anxiety. "Uh—can I ask who you heard it from?"

The girl's eyeglasses were smudged, he realized. "I overheard three girls saying so outside our European History classroom. I can give you their names. It was Jacqueline Franck, Sally Pinelli, and—"

"Got it. Uh—yes. Sort of. Sometimes."

"I would like to buy Adderall from you," Hannah repeated.

Though Nazi military commanders gave their soldiers and pilots amphetamine compounds primarily as a means of combating battle fatigue, there was an upshot that became increasingly valuable as the war entered its agonizing later years: under the influence of such drugs, nothing is banal; indeed, things become lovely. After classes that afternoon, Foster had pulled apart the two gelatin segments of a blue-and-white 50-milligram Vyvanse and tapped its contents into the open Vitamin Water bottle on his desk. An oblong nugget of clumped white particulate had dropped dumbly in the water: it bobbed for a second before slowly tumbling down, its phosphorescent pieces breaking away in its fall like the deck chairs of a sunken ocean liner in its glide down to the ocean floor. He'd taken four swallows of the tincture as he walked to the library and then tucked a moist pinch of spearmint Skoal between his lower lip and gum; the nicotine buffed the medicine's residual sheen. As the girl in the trilby stood before him, he suddenly pictured her attempting to tame her curls with a straightening iron, and it made him sad.

"I can probably do that," Foster said, looking up at her. "But—uh—do I know you?"

"I'm Hannah Phelps-Berkowitz," the girl said. Though their eyes met, Foster had the curious sense that she was not in fact looking at him. "I have read your articles in the *Kennedian.*"

Foster was both amused and vaguely flattered. "Well, Hannah," he said, "it's nice to meet you. If you need it right now, I can sell you some immediate-release Adderall, and I also have Vyvanse, which works longer. Use the Adderall if you just have a few hours of studying. And if you want to sleep, take the Vyvanse before, like, two in the afternoon."

"All right."

"Uh, well," Foster said, concerned by the constancy of Hannah's empty expression and wanting very badly to spit the Skoal's accumulating saliva into the Deer Park bottle by his feet, "it's seven bucks each for the Adderall, and ten for the Vyvanse."

"All right."

Helpless, he bent down to his backpack, where he found a near-empty bottle of Vitamin Water. Hannah did not seem to notice as he unscrewed its top and let the rope of brown tobacco spit fall into it. The two amber pill bottles were on their sides in the pencil pouch. He looked up at her. "Sorry—how many did you say you wanted?"

"I would like two of the short-term pills and three of the long-term pills."

Except for two Korean girls whispering over a far table, the reading room was empty. From outside came another muffled laugh.

"So, let's see—three times ten is thirty, and two a—"

But Hannah had already placed a collection of weathered bills next to *Pride and Prejudice.* "Forty-four dollars," she said.

"You got it," Foster said, offering her what he thought was a cordial smile. Still her face stayed put as she placed the Post-it in a pocket within her corduroy jacket.

"Well—thanks for the business," Foster said. "It was nice to meet you."

With a small spasm Hannah simply turned. There was an urgency in her walk that seemed less emotional than erratically physiological. Then the trilby disappeared beyond the landing as she descended, the wheels of the backpack clacking loudly on the stone.

Foster turned back to the table before him and realized that his BlackBerry, forgotten, was blinking at him from beneath *Pride and Prejudice*. There was a yellow icon of an envelope, waiting with its grim inevitability. Foster exhaled.

> **Porter Roth [06:58:14PM]:** Hey. I just finished dinner. Wanna hang?

The cursor continued to blink at him from the Word document on his screen. Behind it was a sliver of the Outlook window he had clicked open earlier that afternoon.

FROM: atierney@kennedy.org
[Tuesday, September 29, 2009 at 05:17 PM EST]

TO: fdade11@kennedy.org (You); jstearns11@kennedy.org; bchung11@kennedy.org; rhaddish11@kennedy.org; proth11@kennedy.org; and 8 others [click for more]

SUBJECT: DON'T FORGET
——
PAPERS DUE TOMORROW START OF CLASS—STAPLE PLEASE—HAVE MERCY ON THE SOULS WHO FORGET BIBLIOGRAPHIES—TIERNEY
——
Dr. Arthur "Art" Tierney H'88 '92 '96 '02 '07
English Master on the William H. Summerland '46 Distinguished Teaching Chair
The Kennedy School

Foster looked in dismay at the words he had written on his MacBook's screen. He exhaled again and closed his eyes, then thumbed two messages in succession without looking.

Me [07:05:31PM]: hey

Me [07:05:31PM]: i'm still way way behind on the tierney paper :/

He felt grimly aware of his entrapment. His mouth twitched toward a frown.

Me [07:06:41PM]: but i can get away from it for a bit before check-in

Me [07:06:47PM]: sry my phone was being glitchy hence the delay between those texts ha

She was waiting for him at the foot of the chapel, where the driveway around the Meadow diverged into the lane leading to the Ellipse Houses. A group of the Second Year boys who had moved into Brennan a month earlier were on its porch with Jacqueline Franck and Sally Pinelli and the other new residents of Hewitt House, sitting up on the short brick wall that enclosed the porch's rise over the Meadow, their blitheness betraying the satisfaction of their visibility. "Get some, Dade!" one of the Second Years, a short sprightly boy from Glen Ridge named Nic Bergman, bellowed out as Foster passed. Foster extended an affable middle finger in the direction of the porch, the gesture of a thinly concealed self-satisfaction that was not in fact there.

Porter's hair was still wet from the shower she had taken after soccer practice. As she'd walked, her ponytail had slapped damp streaks on the back of her gray Harvard T-shirt. She waved to Foster with a self-aware shyness as he approached.

"He lives," she said. There was a contingency to her smile's affection, as there always was, as if straining against what it betrayed. She looked very pretty, Foster thought.

"Thank you for prying me from the lib. I think they might start charging me rent."

Their lips met gently and briefly. "Get *some*!" he heard Nic Bergman holler again, and as Foster pulled his mouth away he felt Porter's twitch into an embarrassed smile. He slid his hand into Porter's and the two began to walk.

Foster had left Southampton seven weeks earlier before the others rose for breakfast. He'd woken with the harsh light of dawn on a futon in the Cohens' living room, where Porter had positioned herself awkwardly next to him. Freddie Pieters snored violently on an adjacent couch, naked except for a pair of blue briefs. The sunlight over the ocean was white and colorless. Desperately careful not to stir Porter, he'd retrieved his North Face backpack at the edge of the living room and found his Advil bottle of weed empty but for crumbs on the kitchen island, next to the nectarine-colored glass bowl he knew to be Mason Pretlow's, still mockingly fat with ash. He was stepping toward the upstairs landing when he heard the press of a door opening down the hall.

Annabeth was wearing Jack's long T-shirt, which hung down past her naked thighs: MORRISTOWN SUMMER LACROSSE CLINIC 2006. The emotion on her face was something less ephemeral than surprise. He had the peculiar sense that she had heard him leaving.

"It looks good on you," Foster heard himself say, jerking his head toward the shirt.

There was a stoicism to her absence of reaction. *Foster*, he hoped for a splinter of a moment she might say, in preface to protest or confession. Instead, her eyes in the darkness were knowing and resigned and averting, and with a dry swallow she nodded slightly. He had turned away at her nod and headed purposefully down the stairs, waiting for a voice that did not come.

A vague, nameless nausea moved with him as he pulled away from the Cohens' back toward Southampton. It followed him to Baltimore and congealed around him in the days that followed: his mother would give a pleasant little yelp of surprise when he arrived home several hours ahead of his original plan, and he would give her a sad smile before disappearing with his duffel bag upstairs, where he would remain for most of the next week and a half.

There was only one other post on Foster's Blogspot from this time, four days after his return home, which discusses the events of August 14 only with respect to Porter Roth. *I think I may have made a fool of myself,* he wrote, *and I have no idea what's gonna happen back at school. We've texted a bit but not really. Can't tell*

*if she wants/expects us to continue hooking up. It's a complicated
prospect.*

Back at school, it had happened quickly, via an arithmetic compelled not by Foster or Porter but some impersonal inevitability. The
first dance of the school year had been held on the mezzanine behind
the science building, where they had found each other in the shadows
by the building's door. They'd stood together in silence and watched
the sweaty bodies below the ropes of light. An awkward exchange of
words carried them to the wide expanse of fields along the campus's
edge where the intramural House football teams played. He'd kissed
her or maybe she'd kissed him, and they lowered each other clumsily
to the cool grass below, where she reclined herself beneath him. He was
residually somewhat stoned—he and Jae had smoked after dinner—
but otherwise sober, and as the rush of headlights along Eastminster
Road slid along the grass through the gaps in the campus's iron fence,
Foster realized that his penis was stiffening. He was surprised at the
degree to which this delighted him.

They had met up again before check-in two nights later. Porter
was more confident than she'd been that Saturday, when their mutual
sobriety had seemed to jeer at them, and after he reached a tentative
hand up to the cusp of her bra, she had proceeded to simply pull
her shirt over her head and unclasp the bra's hook. Her breasts were
small but fuller than he'd anticipated, her nipples the pale fleshy color
of young cantaloupe, rising slightly from crests of cream-like skin.

"What," she'd said, noticing his eyes widen slightly, an edge of
insecurity returning to her voice.

"I just—didn't know—that it was okay for me to do that. I would
have done it," he added quickly.

He grew more comfortable with his own arousal over the weeks
that followed, and with this comfort, his arousal intensified, with
a vigor that again took him aback and thrilled him. (Dreading his
humiliation, he had been careful to abstain from taking Adderall on
those days when he and Porter would find each other at dusk.) Later
he would find a spot of dark dampness off to the side of his shorts' fly,
as small as a dime. Porter had on several nights placed a hand atop

Foster's thigh to finally find a taut rise of fabric above it, stroking its tented contours in a crude grasp.

He found solace in those other moments when Porter's startling boldness seemed to falter. Once or twice, he had reached his hand up through the legs of her shorts or beneath her dress and fumbled lamely at the lace-spangled elastic edges of her underwear. He realized in those first ventures that he had no idea what to do with a vagina. On one occasion he had slid his fingers beneath the elastic, and with a reflexive jerk she'd pulled her own hand from his cheek to clasp his wrist in prohibition. As his fingers retreated, he felt a sort of nucleated heat. It startled him in its anatomical foreignness.

Foster had come to appreciate how agreeable Porter was in her navigational exchanges with the world. What had once struck him as her diffidence or insecurity seemed to color what he now understood as an impatience with—even a contempt for—a territory and politics from which she felt acutely estranged. He found himself flattered by her willingness to disclose this, as if doing so exonerated him of the grievances in question. She was funny. In the evenings, when they walked out to the dusky edges of campus, he let her gripe about Gracie Smith, for whom she reserved a particular, almost principled disgust. Her vitriol was wonderfully alien in its honesty.

Foster had declined to ask her for the details of her prior involvement with Mason Pretlow, which she seemed uninterested in discussing; nor had Foster commented upon the fact that the contemptuousness with which Mason studied him seemed to have found a new violence. I hate how gratifying it is: not just walking with her to hook up at night but the fact that people see us—the fact that other people know, Foster would write later that fall. The fact that Mason sees me taking his ex to hook up. The fact that Jack knows. The fact that Annabeth knows. This has been particularly true ever since I got the office key from Mastoff— honestly, I'd be jealous too.

Three years after the Class of 2011 graduated, the accumulation of capital brought by Pauline Ross's Bicentennial Campaign allowed Kennedy to embark on a multimillion-dollar renovation of Fenster

Hall. "Like the Nazis invading Warsaw," Art Tierney would later remark of the armada of bulldozers that rolled through the main gates that June. No extant structure on Kennedy's campus had required structural attention more urgently. In the final years before the retrofit, faucets in the second-floor bathrooms would hiss and cough up a thick spray of something rust-colored before finally bringing water of some thin Afghan tea. St. Paul's had been trying to poach Madame Theroux from Kennedy's French Department for two years before the gorgeous mid-May afternoon when the building's southern portico collapsed as she left for the day, sending down the shower of worm-eaten wood and New Deal–era electrical wiring that missed her by several feet; the next morning, she put in her notice and began to search for apartments in New Hampshire.

The students on the editorial boards of Kennedy's three major student publications—the *Kennedian*, its weekly paper; *Farrago*, the yearbook; the school's literary magazine, *Rubrum*, published twice a term by the pensive students who usually went on to edit the *Yale Lit* and the *Harvard Review*—took a certain Calvinistic self-satisfaction in the bleakness of their offices, which were located in Fenster Hall's basement: an arrangement of low-ceilinged concrete bunkers illuminated only by dusty naked lightbulbs overhead. Atmospherically these spaces were improved only by the threadbare couches and old rugs dragged in over the decades by past editorial boards. It was there that the *Kennedian*'s editors had held the first writers' meeting of the academic year, on a warm Tuesday evening in the second week of classes.

"Don't get used to it," Sasha Burnell, the board's Editor-in-Chief, had said as she pulled a piece of buffalo chicken pizza from the row of grease-sodden Vito's boxes. "Food's free at the first one—it's how we entice you."

"Like a heroin dealer."

Sasha had rolled her eyes at Foster. Across the room, a forceful Second Year girl with long equine features named Eloise McClatchy laughed loudly. Foster had stood along the wall with the other Third Years: Raj Chakravarty, Rosalie Haddish, and Jenny Xiu; Jason Stearns and Noah Baum; all of whom had showed up in an anxious

effort to leave no stone unturned ahead of the editorial board elections five months away. Their initial suspicion of Foster had waned
with his fifth or sixth opinion piece; persuaded by his seriousness of
purpose, they'd decided they liked him, this harmless interloper from
the inscrutable upper social echelons. He'd left the office with them at
meeting's end, listening listlessly as they discussed the term's syllabi,
and as they moved toward the stairs he heard Andrew Mastoff's voice
say his name.

"So, uh," Mastoff, the spindly, self-deprecating squash player
from Westchester who'd succeeded Harvard-bound Neil Probst as
the *Kennedian*'s Opinions Editor, said. He looked pained, perhaps
constipated. "You're still good to do the piece on Major School Rule
Violations? By, like, Sunday?"

Foster smiled. "You can ask me what you really want to ask
me, Andrew."

Andrew's thin shoulders seemed to flinch. "I, uh," he said, not
meeting Foster's eyes, "I understand you sell Adderall."

"Sorta, yeah," Foster said, shifting noncommittally.

"Well—" Mastoff said, sensing Foster's unease, "I need to get my
SAT score up about a hundred points. Doctor Perry—she's my college
counselor—would be a lot more enthusiastic about Princeton—that's
the goal—if I cleared a 2250. And—I could use the help."

Foster was embarrassed to have found a certain satisfaction in these
nervous appeals, in the knowledge that these recitals of vulnerability
were written and staged purely for him. "I can hook you up," Foster
said, looking at Mastoff. "How many you think you'll need? It's ten
for the Vy—"

"Yeah, so, here's the thing." Mastoff seemed desperate to be elsewhere. "My parents are, like, frugal to the point of parental neglect.
We're Jews, after all." He managed a weak grin. "They give me enough
cash for, like, a slice of pizza at Vito's per week. Plain cheese pizza.
But I was thinking—" and here he seemed vaguely more confident
"—you're hooking up with Porter Roth, yeah?"

Foster was not sure if his blink was as pronounced as it felt.
"I—guess, yeah," he said finally.

"So, what I was thinking," Mastoff said, "was this. You give me Adderall, and I give you my spare key to the newspaper office. It's all yours when we're not working—everyone's single but Sasha, she's with that baseball oaf Edmonds, but I'm pretty sure she has a fetish for getting fucked on the golf course when it's still light out, so—"

Foster looked at him. "Are you—serious?"

"About Sasha's sex life?"

"About the office."

Mastoff was smiling, his gumption reawakened. The following day, Foster would meet him after dinner and slide the five parceled Adderall XRs into their handshake, and Mastoff had returned the small brass key. That Friday night, with the *Kennedian*'s new issue stacked high in the distribution boxes across campus, the office was empty, and Foster had taken Porter's hand and led her down into the basement. "I can't tell you what a treat it is," she'd murmured as they shifted themselves down through the darkness onto the office's sagging couch, "to take my bra off without Mrs. Cline walking her dog fifty feet away."

And on this night in late September, after leaving his prompt from Tierney still unaddressed on his laptop's screen in the library, Foster found himself walking with Porter once again in the direction of Fenster Hall. She idly stroked the edge of his hand with her thumb. The dusk broke every now and then with distant happy shouts.

"You know what," Porter said as they approached the door. "It's not gonna be warm for much longer. Let's walk and see where we end up. The office will be there this weekend."

"It will indeed," Foster said. They set out in the direction of the soccer fields.

"Or"—and Foster felt Porter slow a bit and turn her eyes to him—"we could go to my house. I'm not trying to bully you into meeting my parents—in a perfect world, you never would." She glanced at him with a momentary embarrassment at his silence, then looked away. "Just for a change of scenery, and, you know—an actual bed."

"Yeah," Foster said, suddenly aware of the sound of his voice's distance. He contemplated the fact that he was indeed very attracted to her. "Sorry, sorry—just distracted by this Tierney paper. I'd love to go to your house."

They passed between the First Year boys' residence and the low brick wall that enclosed the Yard. Down within its grassy recesses, the First Years were finding confidence in their emergent politics. They sat or sprawled beneath the dusk in the clusters of five or six that had assembled almost autonomously in those first weeks; the spans of grass separating them did not call out to be bridged. The girls with long legs gathered at the lawn's median had found one another immediately, as the beautiful ones always do.

"Kaitlyn Sanders is already thinking about how she's going to haze them when they're in Hewitt," Porter said, looking in the direction of the Yard.

"Nic Bergman is keeping a list of the ones he wants to hook up with. A literal list, codified in writing."

"Well, if he wants to look in the opposite direction age-wise, Frances actually thinks he's cute. Despite him being, like, barely five feet tall. You didn't hear that from me."

They turned left at the Yard's end and stepped down the grassy decline along the football field. Two nameless Second Years kissed frantically on a bench by the school pond, becoming one shape in the thickening dusk. Porter and Foster moved wordlessly up the steep wooded rise of the turf fields, and with the same silent correspondence their bodies turned together and their mouths met. The gravel shifted beneath their shoes as they moved together down to the metal bench of the bleachers.

There was something almost genial about the sexlessness of their hookup on the turf field bleachers, a sort of academic exercise in the simple mechanics of making out. Porter no longer briefly flinched as Foster's fingers found the shape of her nipple; he had come to expect the warmth of her breath against his neck as it slowed and thickened with his touch. Her athletic shorts revealed the lacy swath of her underwear, a lucid surprise of color. "The Adderall, sorry," he murmured into her ear when he felt her hand upon the upper reach of his thigh. For less than a moment, he thought he felt her tense at this; for all of her quiet impudence, she was sincere in her straightedgedness, and seemed committed to avoiding the topic of Foster's pharmaceutical enterprise altogether. But then she kissed him again, and he contemplated the pleasantness of her breast's gentle weight in his hand, and they carried on until Porter pulled away.

"You need to write your paper," she murmured. "Collect your stamina for this weekend."

There is a quiet beauty availed at the edges of the Kennedy campus on nights like this, under the final dusks of late summer. This is especially true in the twenty minutes or so before study hall, when silhouettes pass before the yellow light of the Houses along the Ellipse and Meadow; beyond them, over the distant cornfields, the hazy red lodestars of far cell towers illuminate and recede as if keeping time. The strange electric promise of a new year will dissipate into the banality of things by October with the approach of midterms' drudgery, but for a minute let's sit with it: it lingers, still, on nights like this, when the cool hush of dusk gives form to the nameless cocoon spanning those who pass beneath it. Beneath their porches' lamplit awnings, boys in Brennan and Talmadge Houses will disappear inside to procure their sweatshirts for the girls who've come by on their way back from Vito's. In the months that follow, some of them will fall in love with each other, or believe themselves to have fallen in love, which is the same thing.

And for a moment there it seemed perfect, the inaccessibility of it all, receding into the night before Foster as he walked in silence alongside Porter toward the Ellipse.

And then there was a laugh, loud and familiar and cruelly bright, from somewhere behind them.

Annabeth and Jack did not seem to have noticed them. They, too, were returning from the direction of the athletic fields: a week earlier, Foster had overheard Jack say that they'd found a little shelter below the tall, latticed timbers of the school ropes course. Jack was holding Annabeth's waist in his arm as they approached the hillside stair. Broken blades of grass still clung to their knees, which were scuffed with the shadow of earth.

"Hey," Foster heard himself say dully. In the darkness he could see Annabeth's brow twitch as her eyes registered the encounter.

"Well, well," she said. "Fancy seeing you two here." Annabeth was, Foster had come to realize, fluent in this style of pleasantness, one uncorrupted by and inoculated against the unpleasant facts of history or politics.

"We're just—strollin'," Jack said with a dumb, off-kilter grin, avoiding Foster's gaze.

"So that's what they're calling it these days," Porter said wryly. Her hand in Foster's felt suddenly thick and clumsy; he wished very palpably that she was not there.

"Just an evening constitutional," Annabeth said in a Hepburnish mid-Atlantic drawl. Foster stared rigorously out into the night. "You— finish your Tierney paper yet? I'm still struggling."

"Nah, lot to do still," he said, not meeting her eyes, but instead recording the dark shapes of the trees around the pond against the night.

"Gonna be late for check-in," Jack said, stirring slightly on the pebbled stair. "See you back at the House? Gotta drop her at the library."

"For sure," Foster said to the night.

And then they parted. Before the shadows took them, Foster saw Annabeth turn her face toward Jack's and then lean up and kiss him, placing a gentle hand on his cheek. Neither Porter nor Foster acknowledged this or the encounter preceding it, and as they walked toward the lights of Hewitt House, they did not speak.

IV.

http://www.fhd93.blogspot.com/2009/09/expectations
(Posted September 23, 2009)

I think at some point I'll learn not to trust my own expectations. It's almost as if believing in any given future is a curse: if you put your faith in it, if you spend your time imagining how it will look and feel when you're there, you're actually somehow foreclosing it. Foreclose: a good word. I'll take the SAT in January, and every time I come across a word that feels like an SAT vocab word, I write its definition on a Post-it note and stick it to the frame of the window next to my desk. I've been doing this for four weeks and my wall looks like the cabin in *A Beautiful Mind*. I'd be lying if I said I didn't enjoy that effect. I'll leave my door slightly open during study hall, so when Jack passes by and if he glances in, he'll see the room of someone too intellectually serious/formidable to waste his time giving a shit. Foreclose made the wall last week, thanks to David Foster Wallace's cruise ship essay, which Annabeth told me in Lake Placid I should reread. *Foreclose: to rule out or prevent a course of action.*

Side note: "Expectations" by Belle and Sebastian is a great song.

It was an idea of being a Third Year that excited me. It was the idea of confidence, a new invincibility, the idea of walking across campus in the sunshine of a new year without the miserable anxiety and self-loathing that defined my first term (and significant chunks of my second and third) last year. I've always daydreamed while running, and on my runs this summer I'd start picturing myself on the Brennan porch, flanked by Annabeth and Jack and also a newly inured (another Post-it) Gracie and Mason, blasting Passion Pit from my speakers and making them laugh. I cringe now when I think about it.

They were together pretty much from the first night we were all back. It felt almost predetermined, how quickly it happened, and I know (even though I wish I didn't) they must have spent the week and a half before school talking. Of course, Annabeth and I talked too, the way we did all summer. She iChatted me the night I got home ("did you survive the journey south") and I knew then that there would be no discussion of . . . well, any of it. For whatever reason, I chose—am continuing to choose—to respect these terms: to pretend that nothing in those ten days in August ever actually happened, to be an accessory to the FORECLOSURE (!) of any formerly possible contingency, so that she and I can carry on as normal, even though nothing is normal.

She BBMed me on the first Sunday morning back at school. It was still pretty early, 9 or so, and campus was quiet as we walked, the way we always walked. I'd hooked up with Porter the night before out of a certain hopelessness. She made sly passing comments about it and I blushed, the way I blushed when she made sly passing comments about Kaitlyn Sanders, as if confessing to it would shatter any possibility of a future where we're together. I took my cues from her: she did not bring up Jack, just like she never brought up J. T. Ricciardelli or any of the older guys she hooked up with last year. We have Tierney's class together again, with Porter. We've continued to walk on Sundays; I'm not sure if Jack knows. It'll start getting chilly very soon.

Unsurprisingly, the guys on the lacrosse team who were First Years last year ended up in Ames. They've basically become satellites to the group: particularly this kid named Chandler McDermott from North Jersey, who idolizes Jack and whom I'm annoyed to say is apparently quite bright, and this fucking lummox named Thomas Connelly, McDermott's shadow basically, whom I'm genuinely surprised doesn't get lost on his way back to the Meadow from dinner. If McDermott is smart, he's insecure about it, because he acts as dumb as Connelly, and I've always been uncomfortable around stupid guys. They tend to make the dumbest and most obvious jokes about sex, the kind that have always made me oddly uneasy. They also tend to not like me very much. Chandler idolizes Jack, but both of them *love* Mason.

And Mason—well, Mason hates me. Mason always hated me, but I always got the sense he knew this was (i) irrational and (ii) more or less at odds with popular opinion, or at least a vocal faction of the popular opinion. Unfortunately I've now given him grounds for his dislike. He never gave a shit about Porter, I know this for a fact, but you can not give a shit about someone and still be pissed when they stop pining for you and start hooking up with a person you already find loathsome. He used to be passive-aggressive; now he's just aggressive. This isn't really an exaggeration. His hatred is suddenly very physical. Last night we were at Vito's, getting ready to throw our shit away and leave, and as I stood up behind him he suddenly planted himself there as I rose, right into him. I dropped my plate and cup, and as I picked it up (I refused to meet his eyes) and turned toward the trash cans, I heard him laugh in my direction. It sounded like a bark.

I would like to believe that Jack was laughing at something else.

I'm not sure if Jack's coldness is the same aloofness he's always had, and if I'm only reading it as coldness because of everything else that's happened. But it feels new. He's been spending more of his free time—his non-Annabeth free time—in Ames. He does not invite me. Maybe his benevolence, which always felt conditional, has run out. Maybe he knows I've been in love for the last year with the girl who is now basically his girlfriend. Maybe he never liked me but had some reason to pretend otherwise last year.

Maybe I'm simply not as welcome as I'd thought, and I'm being punished for believing otherwise.

But—I have made $2,115 in the four weeks I've been back at school. The first shipment from Hong Kong got here yesterday. Pretty soon I imagine my pencil case won't be big enough.

V.

Foster Dade's MacBook Pro/Music/iTunes/Playlists/junior fall (Created October 18, 2009)

Name	Time	Artist
Starlight	4:00	Muse
So Lonely	4:49	The Police
Your Hand in Mine	8:17	Explosions in the Sky
Lost in the Supermarket	3:47	The Clash
Hounds of Love	3:03	Kate Bush
So Damn Lucky (Live)	6:52	Dave Matthews and Tim Reynolds
Perfect Situation	4:14	Weezer
Flavor of the Weak	3:09	American Hi-Fi
Strobe	10:33	deadmau5
Dancing with Myself	4:50	Billy Idol
Unchained Melody	3:38	The Righteous Brothers
Making Love Out of Nothing at All	5:42	Air Supply
I Will Be Here (Tiësto Remix)	3:26	Tiësto and Sneaky Sound System
Here on Earth	4:56	Tiësto
Expectations	3:34	Belle and Sebastian
Perfect Symmetry	5:12	Keane
Get Me Away from Here, I'm Dying	3:25	Belle and Sebastian
Linger	4:34	The Cranberries

Us	4:52	Regina Spektor
Blue Skies	4:08	Noah and the Whale
Moth's Wings	4:16	Passion Pit
White Houses	3:45	Vanessa Carlton
Swing, Swing	3:53	The All–American Rejects

23 songs, 1.9 hours, 201.2 MB

VI.

It was on the second-to-last day of my first year at Kennedy that I found a second Post-it left behind by my room's prior occupant. I had begun to halfheartedly organize the contents of my desk into shoebox-size Tupperware bins, and as I reached down beside it to unplug an extension cord, my wrist brushed a square of paper stuck to the wall below. *Lassitude (n): a state of physical or mental exhaustion; laziness.*

The seven advisors in the Office of College Counseling at Kennedy would not commence their formal relationship with the members of Kennedy's Class of 2011 until the following spring, and it was with a collective murmur of neurosis that the Third Years awoke on the first Monday of October to find an email from Valerie Wendell, the office's director, in their inboxes. *Please be advised that your classes on Saturday morning Oct 10 will be canceled for the PSAT, which will begin at 8:00 in the Field House.*

Foster would arrive in the classroom at the end of Memorial Hall's second-floor hallway after lunch the following Thursday to find Dr. Tierney at the head of the table clutching a pale blue booklet, his expression aggrieved. The cover read, *Test-Taking Strategies for the PSAT/NMSQT: A Guide for Teachers and Students: Critical Reading (2010 Edition).*

"So—today!" he barked, looking up to the faces of twelve bemused Third Years as they pulled their chairs up to the table. "My esteemed colleagues in the college counseling office have asked that we devote our class time this week to *synonyms and reading comprehension*! I pride myself on my diplomacy, so I did not tell them that the P-S-A-T," Tierney bellowed, spitting out each letter, "is a racket. Ditto the

Advanced Placement exams. The National *Merit* Scholarship—
a racket, and meaningless." He brandished the rolled booklet out
toward the table like a scythe. "*Larkin!*"

Johnny Larkin, a slight, forgettable boy from Ohio, looked up
with a start from the BlackBerry on his lap, where the little pixelated
BrickBreaker marble tumbled into the gutter below the screen's frame.

"What did you pay the College Board for the pleasure of sitting
for the PSAT?"

"Uh—fifteen bucks or something," Johnny said dumbly.

"Seventeen dollars," Rosalie Haddish corrected. "Billed to our
student accounts."

"And what is seventeen dollars times three million students? Mr.
Larkin, please." Tierney held up a hand to silence Rosalie.

"Uh—"

"Fifty-one million dollars?"

"Tell Ms. Whittaker thank you, Mr. Larkin." Annabeth smiled in
embarrassed pride and then grinned conspiratorially at Johnny, whose
face, Foster saw, quite literally went red. "Right-o," Tierney went on.
"The commodification of higher ed, boyos and girlies. You'll spend a
hundred bucks for each *A-P exam*"—again he spat each letter—"and
then fifteen hundred to apply to nine dozen schools each. And where
do your daddies' credit card payments go?" His students blinked. "To
the *executives*!" He seemed to be suspending himself above his chair's
cushioned seat, like some sort of crazed birdlike yogi.

(In places as insular as Kennedy, aesthetic genres emerge, and the
Tierney soliloquy was one. The school's more flamboyant satirists
offered different variations: Jack Albright's Tierney captured the
wild, frenzied gesticulations, the aria-like sweep of his extempora-
neous riffs; Jason Stearns's was more attuned to the rhetorical and
maxillofacial tics lost in Albright's more operatic rendition. Both
could mimic Tierney's most violently enthusiastic exclamations—
shit, man; *that's fuckin' jazz*; *he's fuckin' GOT it*—but only Stearns
could replicate the accompanying minor bulge of the old teacher's
watery eyes, though most agreed that Albright's lucid rasp was
tonally more accurate. Unlike the impressions of Dean of Students
Theresa Daniels, which were bitter and cathartic and usually kind

of misogynistic, there was nothing disrespectful about this. Even the most jaded of these Kennedians—even those who'd go on to become doctoral students in English, a demographic disproportionately populated by the bitterly self-pitying—would concede that Art Tierney was perhaps the smartest teacher they'd ever had. His discursive monologues lent themselves to impersonation not because they were laughable but because they were spectacular.)

I'd never admit this to Tierney, but the truth is that I actually love taking standardized tests, Foster would write on his Blogspot the following evening, after arranging his pencils and TI-84 graphing calculator in a Ziploc for the next morning. *I suppose it's mostly because I'm good at them. There's the thrill of quantified success, but also the satisfaction of their roteness. (Side note: no idea if "roteness" is a word. As in: the state of being rote.) It's like doing a bunch of push-ups when you're in good shape.*

He had pulled the Vyvanse from his backpack's side pocket as he left Brennan House the following morning. The October morning was brisk and still; the house was silent. A few minutes before, he had heard the clomp of Jack's sneakers on the foyer's wood floors as he descended the stairs, stepping out into the chill without him.

The Third Years had been seated alphabetically by last name across the Field House's North Court, where Buildings and Grounds had placed the desks after the previous evening's junior varsity volleyball game against Choate. Sofi Cohen had given Foster a theatrical little grimace and then a grin as she sat into the desk two before his, pulling her pencils and calculator from her black Longchamp tote. She'd spent half a minute arranging her four pencils into perfect linearity along the edge of the test booklet that Mrs. Cline had passed out from a stack within a thin plastic sheath.

Foster had given Sofi the ten-milligram Adderall XR *gratis* the evening before. "My parents are, like, weirdly intent on me becoming a National Merit Scholar," she'd said to him in the library. "Stupid as fuck. I told them to chill until the actual SAT. The only worthwhile thing about tomorrow is that it's a Saturday morning without classes."

"You should have had them call Tierney," Foster had said with a wan smile, gently flicking the drab apricot capsule toward her across the tabletop. "He'd set them straight."

He'd felt his own Vyvanse begin to kick in as Mrs. Cline slid the test booklet onto his desk. "You may begin," Ms. Cline had said indifferently from her seat at the white plastic folding table beneath the North Court's bleachers. She was reading a biography of Margaret Thatcher. Foster opened the booklet. The first of the test's four sections was Critical Reading.

> (1.) Although Mount Saint Helens has been more ———— over the years than any other volcano in the contiguous United States, its long dormancy before its 1980 eruption ———— its destructive nature.
>
> (A) astounding . . diffused
> (B) gaseous . . confirmed
> (C) explosive . . belied
> (D) anticipated . . predicted
> (E) volatile . . subdued

Foster lifted his pencil to the page. The graphite's stroke was clean and incisive as he circled (C) and darkened the corresponding bubble. He wondered if Mason Pretlow knew the word *belied*. He smiled to himself and then kept going.

"Math was totally fine, but I definitely fucked up the reading comp. But—whatever. I only care because I'm psycho. I swear those lights are like bagpipes after a while; I could barely focus."

The sun had burned through the gray morning. Porter was wearing a J.Crewish flannel, the sleeves of which she'd rolled up just below her elbows. Foster watched her bracelet, a thin twisted rope of pale gold, bounce as she gesticulated. He blinked against the sudden sunlight. At the start of the test's third hour, the hum of the industrial lights overhead—what we think of when we think of the sound of electricity—had begun to impress itself upon Foster, occupying the silence of the North Court. He'd thought idly of the declassified FBI and CIA reports from Waco and Abu Ghraib he'd spent a summer evening reading, which defined the immersion in unpleasant noise as psychological torture. In his periphery he'd watched as his classmates' arms moved metronomically across their own desks, their bodies sporadically shifting a bit in their seats as they did so. The gentle scratch of two hundred pencils moving diligently across paper seemed to thread the wool of the humming lights.

Of these two hundred bodies, at least two dozen had been metabolizing the pills he had sold them.

Foster and Porter had met each other at the Field House's edge, where Porter kissed him gently. They set out into the sunlight toward Hewitt House, where the black Audi was waiting. "You can throw your bag in the back," Porter said, and then gave him a self-conscious grimace as the trunk door rose on its slow automated hinge. This betrayal of her nervousness mollified his own. In the rearview mirror up ahead, he glimpsed a blond forehead.

"Hi, Mom," Porter said as she slid herself onto the passenger's seat. Her voice was affectless and seemed embarrassed, almost resentful.

"How was the *test*, Portie? Are you wiped out? And you"—she jerked her head in an awkward half-turn toward the back seat—"must be Foster!"

Mrs. Roth drove the way she spoke, flightily. Her voice was airy and vaguely distracted, but with edges of a wit that seemed subdued by a long stretch of inactivity. As they turned from the oak-shadowed gully of Eastminster Road and moved out through the wooded farmland of Hanover and then Mercer County, she chatted brightly about the extortionate prices at the new organic supermarket in Hamilton. Two decades of Princeton's cultural remove had not completely abridged the patrician Chicago roundness of her vowels. In an understated, dignified way, she was beautiful: her eyes, her daughter's eyes, were small but round and earnest. Her hair was lighter and straighter than Porter's. Foster found himself at ease with her, realizing he was parlaying her flightiness into his own wryly flamboyant charm. Up front, Porter was silent, staring out the window with a furrowed brow at the passing fields.

"I'm warning you," she had said the prior evening as they approached Hewitt House, "my mom is a psycho. She just, like— doesn't get me at all. Sometimes I think my dad genuinely prefers me to her. And I think she resents me for it."

It was a testament to Porter's perceptive intelligence that she allowed herself to speak openly to Foster on the matter of family. They had arrived at a mutually satisfying unspoken concordat here: Porter's honesty on the topic did not expect any sort of reciprocal candor from Foster; Foster's silence did not imply a discomfort or unwillingness to listen. On the contrary, he realized he rather enjoyed it. With time he had assembled a broad psychobiographical sketch of the Roth family.

That there was nearly a decade between her mother and her father seemed important in a vague allegorical sense. Lawrence had grown up on Chicago's North Shore, where the vast city gives way to the eighteen-mile strand of affluent suburbs laid out along Lake Michigan like a gilded necklace's broken chain. At stubbornly Episcopalian Groton, Lawrence succeeded as basically heritageless, safeguarded by both the absence of a *stein* or *berg* appending his surname and his reputation as a mordant and rather unsparing social pundit. His posture of aloof cockiness belied what his teachers at Groton had realized within a month of his arrival: that he was the smartest student they had ever taught.

With two 800s on his SAT he went to Princeton, finishing in three years and packing up his Mercedes-Benz 450SL—a graduation gift from his parents—to head the five hours north to Cambridge, where he'd been accepted not only to the doctoral program in Economics at MIT but to Harvard Law as well. A joint JD/PhD normally demands a decade of shuttling back and forth between intellectual and methodological foci; Lawrence finished in four and a half years. At twenty-four he authored the paper that would become his dissertation ("Consumer Choice as Jurisprudential Logic: A Normative Legal Analysis of Recent Market Trends," *Quarterly Journal of Economics*, vol. 97, no. 4, Dec. 1983), which upon its publication by Princeton University Press in October 1985 would explode like a skyrocket across—and indeed almost singlehandedly burn down the methodological and political barriers between—four different academic disciplines.

It was on a November afternoon in 1991 that twenty-three-year-old Susan Ketter appeared shyly in the doorway of Lawrence's office at the University of Chicago, where six years prior he'd arrived as the youngest tenure-track professor in the Economics Department's history. Several years later, their young daughter would quietly collate a mental portrait of this moment from the scant evidence on hand: a younger, darker-haired version of her father sitting beneath high shelves of books, peering up through thick eyeglasses to receive the quiet, curious girl standing before him. What danced in ten-year-old Porter's mind was the reverie of intellectual communion, crackling with friction of the econometric formulae that spilled down the pages across her father's crowded desk.

The plainer truth is that Dr. Lawrence Roth, PhD, slept with a student. A graduate student, but still. Susan Ketter had returned to her hometown the summer prior with her Barnard diploma to begin her MBA, brokering a private compromise between two parental inheritances: her stockbroker father's shrewd quantitative mind and her mother's aloofly bitter self-doubt. It was almost too perfect an emblem of this internal negotiation that Susan ended up dating and a year later marrying her behavioral econ professor. For Lawrence, at least, it was very nearly an ethical nonissue: he'd already been lured away by the department at Princeton, enticed by minimal teaching obligations and a rock-star salary by academia's standards. The money was purely an ego thing: Lawrence had begun cultivating his investment portfolio in his last year at Groton, and while we lack the hard numerical evidence to measure how his "clairvoyant insight into contemporary market economies"—the Nobel committee's words, when he was shortlisted in 2016—translated into annual dividends, we do know that when Lawrence and Susan Roth bought the twelve acres off Cherry Ridge Road in the summer of 1992, they did so in cash.

Lawrence was thirty-five when Porter was born the following January; two and a half years later came Harry. The three academic years that separated the Roth siblings weren't wide enough to keep Harry from the long shadow cast by his older sister. Porter was in third grade when Harry arrived at Princeton Day School, and when she'd pass the kindergarten classroom's open door, dutifully holding her bathroom pass out for any discerning teacher, Ms. Crenshaw would look at the braids bouncing by and exclaim, "Boys and girls, that's Harry Roth's big sister. She was the only one who came to kindergarten knowing how to read!" The kindergarteners would murmur little impressed kindergarten murmurs, and Harry Roth would think about how he did not yet know how to read, and about how at night their daddy would sit on the side of his sister's bed with Harry Potter or *From the Mixed-Up Files of Mrs. Basil E. Frankweiler* and sometimes forget to tuck him in, and he got sad.

Porter loved her father. She knew, too, that he loved her just as much, if not more. She also loved her mother and her little brother, but they felt incidental and at times inconvenient: unwitting intruders upon the little world she and her dad had built for themselves, a world of chess games and science projects and documentaries about outer space. She'd been four when he'd taught her chess at the little coffee table in his upstairs study, and for many years thereafter she would remember his delight at how quickly she'd learned. He never let her win, and she both hated and loved him for it. Much later in life, at sharehouses in Amagansett and Airbnbs in Park City, Porter would find an old chess set on some dusty low shelf, the box's cardboard edges broken and depressed beneath the weight of Scrabble and Risk and Cards Against Humanity, and she'd extend an invitation to whomever she was with, rolling her eyes self-consciously at her own nerdiness. Someone usually accepted—almost always a male—and with little fanfare or theater she would proceed to mate them in no more than twenty moves. On one such instance, she wondered aloud if she should have stuck with it.

Her career on New Jersey's junior chess circuit had lasted two years. Her game was consistent and basically mature, if a bit too restrained by formal training. (She never ascertained how or where her father had discovered Mr. N, the fat little man with a European accent who arrived in his minivan on Cherry Ridge Road every Thursday afternoon with Xeroxed pages from *Bobby Fischer Teaches Chess* and a Ziploc of chalky Hershey's Kisses.) What did her in was her neuroticism. It was only after a round robin tournament in Bergen County on the last Saturday of fifth grade—during which, after a defeat, she would excuse herself to the linoleum-tiled bathroom down the hall, lock the stall door, and vomit—that she told her father she wanted to try another activity the next year. Whether she only imagined Lawrence's intense disappointment is beside the point.

But there were other things for them to do together, and to Porter's delight, they did them. Like America's resumed westward expansion in the decades after the Civil War, the little two-man nation that Lawrence and Porter cohabitated didn't collapse under its early challenges but matured and broadened in the years that followed; like pioneers, they left its desiccated lands for new, more promising territories. In sixth grade, at his urging, she petitioned the Lower and Middle School Activities Director at school to create a Young Investors' Club. The request was noted but gently declined, citing the absence of an available advisor; that evening, the Director received a call at home from an irate Dr. Lawrence Roth, PhD, who berated him for suffocating a child's passions before offering to advise the club himself.

The club lasted for exactly a year. Not incidentally, its quiet demise coincided with Porter's tenuous emergence into puberty, when suddenly she found herself imagining Mark Swanson and Philip Bridgers laughing at her for loving something as nerdy as numbers. Lawrence felt her withdrawing, and was briefly confused by it, and from the wings Susan watched quietly, in anticipation. That summer, after sixth grade, Porter and her mother had spent a Wednesday at the Short Hills mall, where a young woman at Neiman Marcus had fitted Porter for her first bra. It had left Porter mortified—in no small part because she knew, and hadn't needed the saleswoman to tell her, that a bra's structural support wasn't quite what she needed yet—and after fuming in quiet humiliation across Nordstrom and Crate & Barrel, she had finally erupted on the drive home. In a dark sense, Susan got her wish: the silence of mutual incomprehension that had distanced mother and daughter since Porter had begun to speak had finally been shattered. What filled its chasm was suspicion, contempt, and acrimony, stoked in the years to come by the dueling hormones of puberty and menopause, and certainly not helped by the passive, vaguely amused indifference of its most intimate witness.

The twelve acres Lawrence Roth had bought occupied the face of a hill that rose up from a thin shallow creek, which delineated the Roth's property's southern edge. The bottom of its four stories was dug into the earth of a hill, bunker-like. According to Hanover County's publicly accessible property records, its primary standing structure was erected in 1993 and occupies 6,500 square feet, with three garages, a spa and steam shower, and a central vacuum system. Google Street View is useless here: the house itself sits half a mile in from Cherry Ridge Road, hidden from the property's edge by a thick bank of forest and a stone-pillared gate.

"We had no idea how fucking rich she was," Freddie Pieters told me recently. "Like, even for Kennedy."

It gestures to Freddie's point that at the end of her first year at Kennedy, when Porter Roth told her parents she'd prefer to board at school with her friends, their only hesitation—Lawrence's only hesitation—was the threat dormitory life posed to her academic performance. (For the 2008–2009 academic year, tuition and fees for Kennedy's boarders stood at $57,600—it has since risen with inflation, and according to a 2019 *Business Insider* listicle Kennedy is the most expensive high school in the United States—while its day students paid nearly $15,000 less.) Of the 612 boarding students listed in the following year's student directory, Porter Roth was the only one whose home address contained an adjacent zip code. While her housemates dumped their hampers into the grungy crimson bags issued by the school's contracted laundry service, Porter would bring hers each Sunday morning to the Audi waiting outside Hewitt, and would spend the day studying in her father's library while her socks and underwear swirled around the Miele washing machine downstairs, never shrunken or discolored or placed in a boy's bag by mistake. Annabeth Whittaker and Sofi Cohen sometimes tagged along, and the three girls would drink Diet Coke by the Roths' pool as Susan prepared them chips and salsa.

"Susan is sweet and basically saintlike, despite what Porter says," Annabeth had told Foster over video chat late one night early that summer. "Lawrence is maybe one of the twenty smartest people alive in America today but also—uh—intense. Not, like, sports father intense. Not an asshole. Just like—have you watched *Curb Your Enthusiasm?*" Foster had. "He's Larry David."

Dr. Roth was standing in front of the microwave when Porter and Foster entered the kitchen, which was wide and bright.

"Hi, Dad," Porter said. Lawrence did not respond. He seemed transfixed by whatever was gyrating within the yellow light of the microwave. Next to it on the counter, Foster saw, were two open slices of what looked like ciabatta atop a flattened nest of Saran wrap. Whatever he was doing did not seem to puzzle his daughter.

"Dad, this is Foster." Foster was suddenly self-conscious of his physical awkwardness, standing there dumbly three steps behind Porter in the kitchen's awning like Prince Philip trailing the Queen. Porter looked back at him apologetically; she seemed stressed. ("By the way—they don't know we're—together," Porter had told Foster the previous evening. "Easier for everyone that way.") Then the microwave's chime sounded, and from its door he pulled a dish containing what appeared through the glass's condensation to be a small pile of sliced deli turkey.

"From the student center," Dr. Roth said, wincing a bit and dropping the turkey from his fingers back into the dish. "Hot." He tilted the Pyrex and the turkey slid lamely onto the bread.

"Dad worries about bacteria on the meat." Porter said this apologetically, caught between amusement and embarrassment.

"Hello—Foster, right?" Dr. Roth's words were muffled by a mouthful of turkey and bread. He wiped his hand on the thigh of his khakis and extended it. "Needs mustard. Susie!" He looked past Foster toward the wide staircase past the entryway. "Where's that spicy mustard?" He shrugged with theatrical exasperation and gave Foster a conspiratorial grin.

The thing is—I actually really got a kick out of him, Foster wrote the evening he returned from the Roths' house. *I think he thought I was an idiot. But: it's rare to meet people who are vaguely interesting.* For all his eccentricity, there was something magnetic about Porter's father, and Foster found himself embarrassed at the intensity of his desire to be liked by him. It was some consolation that he detected something similar in Porter. They seemed to be auditioning together. Dr. Roth's face did not betray much emotion, but every so often the corner of his small mouth would give the insinuating shift of a smile; the edge of Porter's voice seemed to modulate itself with these twitches.

He and Porter spent the next hour following her father around the house, listening to Dr. Roth narrate. There was a childlike ebullience to his rehearsal that seemed to salvage it from narcissism or self-indulgence; plus, the things he exhibited were interesting, and he talked about them well. "I found this globe"—he turned it on its axis with the palm of his hand, and Foster watched the faded earthtone continents slide together—"at this little antique store in Budapest that I believe was owned by a former Nazi. Nice guy. Susan was stuck at the hotel with the worst diarrhea, and I tend to buy things when I'm alone and bored." The globe sat in the center of the Roths' library, which occupied two stories on the home's eastern end. A vast, deep oriental carpet spanned its dark wood floors; between the high windows were bookshelves that rose to the eaves of the second level, which was skirted by a balustraded balcony that ran from the upstairs door around the library's perimeter. *I remember hearing Gracie once describe Porter's house as tacky*, Foster would write, *but I kind of liked it. It feels like a place where smart people live, albeit smart people who like being seen as smart—which I get.* Every so often, Porter would roll her eyes affectionately at her father's performance, but at moments her excitement absorbed his. "I was such a little brat; I was the one who made him install the projector," she told Foster in the media room, smiling at her dad. On the room's walls hung framed posters for *Chinatown* and *Dr. Strangelove*. "But he was so obsessed he got one for the basement, too."

They were back in the kitchen when a sallow boy with dark hair appeared in its entrance. He was wearing a blazer and a necktie with red and blue stripes; his wet hair had been raked back against his head by what Foster instinctively knew to be a mother's aggressive comb. His face was young, with the awkward angularity of early pubescence, but he was nearly as tall as Foster, whom he looked at briefly with furtive, suspicious eyes.

"Mom says we're leaving in ten minutes and you need to get ready." He said this to his father without looking at anyone. His voice seemed to have not yet found a home in its recent deepening.

"Oh—shit. Yep. Wish she'd told me sooner. Thanks," said Dr. Roth, not looking at his son.

"Foster, this is Harry. Harry, Foster." Something in Porter had loosened with her brother's presence, as if the focus of the scrutiny she feared had shifted.

"Hey," Harry Roth muttered with a small jerking nod, his eyes still downward.

"Sup," Foster said. He heard his voice fall to a flat baritone. Eleven months of Lexapro had stifled most of the more jarring invasive thoughts, but he still found himself compulsively contemplating how others—other boys, more often than not—privately related to their own pubescence, and for a moment he idly wondered if Porter knew that her younger brother almost certainly masturbated once a day, if not more.

"Where are you guys going?" Porter asked.

"Bar Mitzvah," Dr. Roth said, absentmindedly scribbling something on a pad on the counter. "The Milstein kid."

"Ben?"

"He sucks," Harry muttered. "Smells horrible."

Foster and Porter both snorted at this.

"That's not very nice, Harry," Susan Roth said, emerging from upstairs. "It was very nice of him to invite us." She was wearing a blue dress and had put on lipstick. Foster was struck again by her beauty. Dr. Roth did not look up.

"Only 'cause he doesn't have any friends," Harry said, tugging at the knot of his tie.

"Neither do you." This wasn't Porter but their father. He was still jotting something on the pad. Foster chose optimistically to believe this had been a joke, though he noticed a certain tensing discomfort on Porter's face.

"Anyway—we're gonna go for a walk. You'll bring us back to school when you're home, yeah?"

Dr. Roth grunted. "Have a lovely time," his wife said absently. Harry said nothing.

Foster and Porter walked the wooded length of Cherry Ridge Road. It interwove the vast parcels of residential land that partitioned the hill's rise of earth like patchwork. Porter told him about the neighbors who lived within the high gates they passed. He watched his dark reflection distort azimuthally in the black orbs of security cameras that watched them from the gates' stone pillars. "Peter Watson—his parents started Stacy's, that pita chip company. Huge crush on him circa 2001. We used to play hide-and-seek in his backyard. *Five-seven-seven-five*—how fucked is it that I still remember their gate code. Marilyn Coudreaux—she went to Kennedy but was like seven years older; always thought she was so cool. Played field hockey at Yale."

The leaves were late to change that year, and that afternoon they were neither green nor yellow. In their ambivalence they deferred to the honey-spill of sunlight that made it through the boughs canopying the quiet street, speckling the pavement in wide streaks. Thinking back on it, Foster wouldn't know if he'd taken Porter's hand or if she'd taken his. He remembered only the strange, beautiful solitude of that afternoon as it retreated behind the woods. On several instances in the months that followed, he would return to it, and alone in his bed in Brennan House he would try to persuade himself that it had been merely a fiction, gilded by the autumn sunlight and the romantic nostalgia with which he pushed out the turpitude of his own life. Sometimes this effort would prove successful, but not always.

Their feet took them to the head of the Roths' driveway.

"Hey," Porter said, and he looked at her.

There was something new in her face then, made beautiful by the light of the day. He felt his own face return it, and its warmth frightened him. He found his mind jump toward Annabeth, but only in a lazy fizzle; she was suddenly distant and indecipherable, denuded of any prior halo. Porter's eyes were wide and brown. He moved the tips of his feet to hers and took her other hand. Their faces were close.

"I'm glad you came over," Porter murmured. He felt the hum of these words resonate in her chest, which was grazing his. The afternoon's stillness stirred with the whisper of traffic beyond the wooded valley. And then they were kissing. They were kissing in the way that at nine and eleven and thirteen Foster had always understood kissing: as something symphonic and encompassing, the dramatic climax before the credits roll. He had spent sleepless early-adolescent evenings imagining the chemical intensity of the love these kisses would consummate. Later, Foster would note his minor tinge of disappointment at something vaguely resembling anticlimax. Their passion did not swell with the bravissimo of some grand Viennese philharmonic. They were simply kissing.

It's weird, he'd write that night. On TV and in movies, I never think about those kisses as even incidentally sexual. Yet when I think about the intensity of the kiss today, I think mostly about how I only wanted to pull her close, tell her she's the most beautiful person alive, etc., *after* I got hard. It wasn't false or disingenuous, just—kind of crude. I was horny. I am choosing to believe for now that I haven't been misleading myself all this time, and that the thing I saw on TV and in movies exists in its own right, not only as some vulgar precursor to sex.

And then Porter moved her mouth from his, pulling herself closer to Foster's body. "Let's go inside," Porter murmured into his ear. Her words had a warmth and density he hadn't heard before. "I want to show you the basement."

They hadn't turned on the lights overhead when they'd come down, and the basement was darkening with the shadows of late afternoon. The percussive tumble of the dryer upstairs, muffled by the walls and floors enclosing them, insulated the silence of the empty house. Foster was suddenly aware of their isolation. Only in its absence did he now see the trepidation in those nighttime encounters at school: any privacy there, behind the *Kennedian* office's locked door or under the cover of night on the turf fields, was contingent, fragile. They began to kiss again and he felt as if he'd been cured of a stammer, and as he slid his hand up Porter's shirt to her breast he realized he was the hardest he'd been in a very long time. He slid himself on top of her on the couch and pressed his groin into hers. She withheld her face from his for a moment, only to then smile at him with a look of amusement. "Hey," she said, and she sat up a bit, then pulled her T-shirt up over her head and let it fall to the floor next to them. Her bra was pink with a fringe of lace; her breasts seemed somehow larger. He felt his dick spasm warm and tense against the inside of her thigh, and as he reached around her for the bra's clasp she pulled herself back again into the couch, stopping him. He felt himself try to press his body back into hers, but she withheld herself again.

"You first," she smiled, and he felt her hands meet his waist, gently lifting the hem of his shirt as they did. "Fair's fair."

Later, he would wince at his disinhibition that afternoon, beginning with the haste with which he pulled his shirt over his head. *It was like I was drunk*, he'd write. The insecurities that had abandoned him in the moment—about his absence of muscle; about the slight puffiness of his nipples—had receded almost tidally, pulled back from his psychic beach by the bewitching conjunction of some strange and looming lunar object. *Or, better yet: it was like I was under the Imperius Curse. Forgive the Harry Potter reference.*

Things had moved quickly. Foster sensed her hesitations dispersing into the effortless progression of things. He'd found himself placing his hand between her thighs, where the warmth he had felt before seemed to be radiating against the thick fabric of her jeans. She shifted amicably into his hand's presence, and at this he moved his fingers up toward her jeans' button. With his fingers against it, he pulled back from their kiss and looked at her. Her nod was subtle but deliberate. With thumb and forefinger, he clumsily shifted the button through the buttonhole and then undid her zipper. The jeans were still snug against her waist. With a frown she slid them down to her ankles and then shook them from her feet with a kick. "Fucking pants," she muttered. Then she looked up at Foster. They both seemed suddenly struck by her near-nudity, and for a moment Porter's eyes widened with something like fear, but then she smiled slyly.

"Come back," she said.

He wasn't sure which of them had undone his pants, or who finally pulled Porter's thong down to her knees. It seemed to have just happened, almost inevitably. They made out—"French kissing," it had been called in fifth grade—with an increasing fortitude and his penis ached and spasmed in its rigidity against her groin, and then at some point she was naked; he was in only his boxers, and then he was naked too.

"You're dripping," she said with a giggle. Foster looked down and realized with a horror muted by his arousal that his naked penis was jutting upward, and that she was right. Its swollen tip glistened. But there was no mirth in her giggle, only a girlish fascination and delight, and as she kissed him again he felt her take his penis in her hand. Her tugs were gentle but purposed. With an inadvertent spasm, he heard himself moan, a quiet glottal murmur that came from somewhere in his chest. The noise frightened him, and he halted briefly in the face of his vulnerability. Almost reflexively, his hand moved to just below her navel, then moved downward. He felt his eyes follow, and then despite himself he smiled.

Her vagina is . . . beautiful, he wrote that night. Maybe that's an exaggeration. By "beautiful," what I mean is—it's what I always envisioned a vagina looking like, even though I know from porn that there are all sorts of vaginas. (Side note: I'm saying "vagina" too much. But "pussy" makes me uncomfortable.) It's just, like, put together nicely. None of the weird hanging skin or whatever. The lips (side note: gross word) come together symmetrically. She was also perfectly shaved, which was kind of crazy, though I wouldn't have minded hair. Hair can be kind of hot. Not a popular opinion apparently but whatever. I feel like it's kind of pathetic that I'm so picky, though. Other guys just seem to get turned on by anything. Point being, though: today was a very big relief.

Porter's body tensed almost imperceptibly as Foster's fingers met the top of the cleft of skin. He was quietly grateful for this, and to extend the delay he looked up to meet her eyes. For the first time he noticed that her face was flushed.

"Two things," she said. Her voice was not only quiet but almost breathless. "One"—and here her eyes flicked away from his—"I think I really like you. I hate to admit it."

I kissed her and told her it's mutual. Which made her smile.

"And two," she said, leaning her face against his cheek, her lips meeting the corner of his, "I'm, like, really fucking turned on."

There was something to these words that seemed to come from someplace carnal within her. He thought of the soft-spoken girl diligently completing her calculus problem sets alone in the library, whose naked breasts were now against his chest, and he felt his penis spasm.

"What does it feel like? For girls, I mean."

She paused, then moved her eyes away from his.

"It feels kind of like"—she blushed—"really having to pee. Like you're about to pee your pants."

But something in her had shifted with this, and as she kissed him with a new aggression, he felt her take his hand and put it between her legs. He let her guide his fingers in coarse pulses against whatever it was she wanted him to touch. It went on like this for a minute or so. And then with a sudden burst of tenacity that he would later find himself baffled by, he pulled his hand away, and with a deliberate heavy shuffle he felt himself push his weight down the couch to bring his mouth to her vagina.

The urge just . . . kind of struck. And of course I was completely clueless once I got . . . down there. I just sort of went at it, like a dog drinking water out of a bowl. Ugh. What a gross description. She seemed kind of bemused by the whole thing, and despite the horror of it all I was still really really turned on.

And after another minute he looked up at her with a grimace of defeat. He realized his face was slick.

"I have no idea what the fuck I'm doing."

Her smile was at once amused and benevolent. "Try—refining the motion. Tiny scribbles, not big brushstrokes. And like—localize it. Here—"

She took his hand from her waist down to her vagina and pulled his index finger to a minor ridge along the slickness between her labia, wet and soft but nevertheless there. He extended his tongue again and found the small node, and with furrowed concentration he focused on flicking his tongue's tip against the spot.

It was with a marvelous sort of delight that he realized her physicality slowly began to change. He carried on, and as he did he felt the leather of the couch creak as she pulled her back up from against it, gently but perceptibly bringing her hips up toward the ceiling to meet Foster's face.

And then . . . she came. Holy shit. Or at least she said she did. But I've had a lot of orgasms, and if a girl's orgasm is anything like a guy's (and all the websites say it's sexist to say they're different), then either Porter is a tremendous actress or . . . she came.

Her breathing subsided after a moment, and with her hand against his neck she seemed to turn his head up toward her.

"Hi," Foster said, her face still between her legs. He grinned.

And so did she, and then they both began to laugh. And then he moved back up along the couch to where she was, and after she pulled her shirt from the ground and wiped the slickness from his face, she kissed him, still smiling as she did.

VII.

VirtualTeenTalk Forums—General Discussion—Chat
BY: SailorMoonGurl94
October 14, 2009 / 11:01pm EST
RE: Adderall

Has anyone Here ever taken Adderall or Vyvance? lulz_commando_43 u were completely right LOL. But I have a few questions

I have started taking it every day. Some days I will take two. I took one an hour ago so don't get mad if this post is too long ●~● I shouldn't have done it since it is so late at night but I don't have school tomorrow.

My Questions:

1. Is it normal to feel like you have superpowers on it? The first time I took it I felt like I could do anything, even talk to boys o__0 The boy who gives it to me is really cute and I wish I could ask him out! Anyway when I took it I did all of my homework for the whole week and then I finished crocheting the oven mitt I am giving my Mom for her birthday. I have always been really smart but this makes me feel like I am the smartest I have ever been. I do not do drugs or drink alcohol but this is medicine and I think I need it. Does it mean that I need it if I feel this way on it?

2. Does anyone know how to fall asleep after taking it? Sometimes I will take it and then I can't fall asleep until the next morning. Usually I just play The Sims or Kingdom Hearts heheh But then I'm super tired the next day. I love Adderall but I want to sleep!!!!! o__0

3. After you take two do you ever start to hear weird noises especially if you don't sleep?

Anyway thanks in advance and sorry if this doesn't make sense.

VIII.

Each House along the Meadow had its own process by which its soon-to-be Third Years chose their rooms for the next academic year. Both Talmadge and Donavan implemented a completely random lottery; cerebral Arsdale went by ranked GPA. Some intense House Master in Ames a quarter-century prior had devised a cumbersome and seemingly arbitrary algebraic formula that took into account each boy's academic, attendance, and disciplinary records to assign him a numerical ranking. Kellogg had for many years staged a sort of annual Battle of the Wits that was finally put to bed after its ping-pong tournament culminated in a scrappy but vicious fistfight; in lieu of a good alternative, it joined Brennan House in assigning room picks based on attendance record alone.

Of Brennan's twelve Second Years, Jack Albright and Foster Dade had received the seventh and eighth picks that May. "It's a fucking farce," Jack had muttered darkly. "Sorry the fucking Asians are like computationally incapable of even *considering* being late to class. Sorry that some of us have other things going on besides, like, *math*." He had said this privately to Foster and then spent the evening going from door to door in Brennan, giving Eric Shan and Alex Luo amicable high-fives ("Shan fucking *missed*") and telling them how happy his family would be if he had the third-floor tower suite that two of his relatives had previously inhabited. "I'm gonna make it so sick, with a TV and furniture and stuff, and we can all chill together there." Foster had listened from downstairs and been rather impressed to hear Alex Luo stand his ground. "But I want that room," Luo had said flatly, more perturbed than flattered by the sudden amicable appeals from a boy who had never once acknowledged his existence. It was unclear what followed, but the charm fell from Jack's voice, and at House Meeting the following evening, Mr. McCall had observed that for the first time on record, the largest and most pleasant room in Brennan had remained unclaimed until the seventh pick.

To the undiscerning observer, the room Foster chose as his own, located on the second floor between the back stairs and the House Master's apartment, was nothing to write home about. In more than one year previously it had been the penultimate room chosen, coming only before the repurposed laundry closet on the third floor to which perennially tardy Jae would be sentenced. It was a question of real estate. The muffled clomps of Bean boots and running shoes descending the back stairwell was musical compared with the noises of Mr. McCall's apartment. The oldest of his four sons was eight, the youngest nearly three. "Goblins," Foster had heard Anne-Marie Cline mutter to herself in the Dining Center at breakfast one morning while the McCall boys flung smeary chunks of cream cheese bagel across the carpet. By seven in the morning, Foster's room would hum with their muted thuds and squawks and wails.

It had been Andrew O'Donnell who told Foster about the room's closet. It was unclear who'd discovered the painted-over electrical box at its foot and chiseled through its edges, or when; all Andrew knew was that at least three of the room's subsequent occupants had used it to store weed. "Pretty sure there was a dude who sold it—that's what I think my sister said, at least," Andrew had said. "He either got expelled or died in a car crash; can't remember."

The following evening, Foster had looked down at the house blueprint Mr. McCall had printed out and written his name in the little square to the left of the ladder of stairs.

By early November, three parcels had come in from Hong Kong. They were no bigger than a child's shoebox, with Foster's name and campus address scrawled in faint blue ballpoint on the shipping label beneath the purple and teal insignia of the Hong Kong Post. The automated email from the mail room would usually come by mid-morning, but Foster would wait to retrieve it until the end of classes, when the Dining Center was quiet. He would feel its weight shift in his backpack as he walked back to Brennan, imagining he could hear the pills rattling within it. He would pause for a moment in the House's doorway, listening for the jangle of Chissom's bracelets or McCall's hearty stomps, and then he would go to his room and lock the door.

He'd bought the little plastic containers at the Target in North Baltimore a week before returning to school. They were the same ones his mother had used for packing trail mix or homemade applesauce in the school lunches of his childhood: little oblong boxes of cloudy plastic the size of Rubik's cubes, with translucent blue lids that snapped onto their rims. This is where he kept the pills. It had taken him half an hour to empty the first shipment's white bottles into these receptacles, though he'd passed those first five minutes gawking in disbelief at the sheer enormity of what was before him. When a bottle was emptied, he tossed it in a kitchen-sized garbage bag from the box beneath his bed, which he then double-knotted and shoved into the wastebasket below his desk, among its crumpled papers and ripped Post-It notes and empty Vitamin Water bottles.

The blue-lidded containers sat on the shelf inside the closet cupboard, and below it were the Ziploc bags and white envelopes in which he delivered his product: Ziplocs for protection; envelopes for discretion. Next to the envelopes was the old SpaceMaker pencil box. If he looked closely, he could see the faded shadow of his own name on its green-and-purple lid, written in Sharpie in third grade. The bills inside it were twenties and fives, mostly; his clients, who when it came to their parents' money were less generous than indifferent, preferred to round up rather than wait for change in crumpled singles. There was a handful of hundreds. Foster had initially tried to stack them within the box by denomination, but by mid-autumn their quantity defied organization. The box would reach its capacity every few weeks, serendipitously around the time Foster's BlackBerry would spasm with a message from *ALEXEI⚨✈HONG KONG☸ 8*.

On these nights, Foster would sort through the cash and put it in an envelope he then placed under his MacBook in a vain attempt to flatten its bulk. The following morning, he would wake to the sound of Jae's four little raps on the door. (*cash is ready*, Foster would message him the night prior.) That afternoon or the next one Jae would sign out in the logbook in Brennan's foyer and climb into a black taxi, and within eighteen hours of that Foster's phone would hum with a curt little thumbs-up emoticon from Alexei. And within a week of that the next shipment would arrive.

There have been three substantial renovations to Kennedy's website in the years since I've left, each orchestrated by Web designers whose hourly rate is competitive with Manhattan's white-shoe law firms. The basic skeleton tends to survive each overhaul—the tabs that line the site's masthead (ADMISSION, ABOUT, ACADEMICS, ATHLETICS, ARTS, CAMPUS AND RESIDENTIAL LIFE, GIVING) still exist in the order they did twelve years ago, though the seventh (DIVERSITY) appeared much more recently—but the genetic stuff within it evolves to accommodate the fluxes of history. There was no Sustainability Initiative to chronicle under the ABOUT tab ten years ago; the Lukoil station off Eastminster Road, cited for many years as a landmark for visitors inbound from the east, is now a Starbucks. Other revisions, in places like *Belonging to Our Community*, register something less tangible, more essential in the culture of the school and the world in which it awkwardly coexists.

But the text that occupies the page headed *In Loco Parentis* (under CAMPUS AND RESIDENTIAL LIFE) exists precisely as it did twelve years ago. Its two concise paragraphs are lyrical but clearly lawyered. "As a residential school, Kennedy offers opportunities for personal growth that simply don't exist at schools that empty out after the last class bell rings," it reads. "In such a setting, the faculty assumes certain roles otherwise fulfilled by parents, specifically with respect to discipline and related matters of individual and communal well-being. Our teachers and administrators take these duties very seriously, and are committed to building an environment that nourishes each student's potential for growth."

There are more than a few adolescent psychologists who've gone on record to disdain boarding school from a developmental perspective; fourteen, many of them say, is far too young to leave the parental kingdom. We can follow their logic without accepting its conclusion. Childhood is little more than the sustained belief in our parents' superhumanity, and if the prematurity of boarding school's emotional emancipation inflicts some subconscious trauma of abandonment, we might also suggest that the fourteen-year-old in question will instinctively seek a proxy for what was lost. It's through this psychological algebra that *in loco parentis* assumes its mandate. "Honestly, I was afraid to drink at school," Will Thierry told me recently, "only because I had this intense sense that the teachers somehow instinctively *knew.* In my mind, they let us get away with it to a certain point—maybe because they expect teenagers to fuck up sometimes and didn't want to ruin lives because of it. They only seemed to act on it when things got to a certain point."

Virtually every Kennedian to whom I spoke would say it was basically miraculous that Foster Dade did what he did for as long as he did it. Even with the archival records at our disposal, it's difficult if not altogether impossible to quantify just how many students at Kennedy knew before his expulsion that the tall fair-haired tennis player in Brennan was selling Adderall from his dorm room, although later, after everything that followed, everyone claimed to have at least heard something.

What we do know is that by the end of the autumn of 2009, Foster Dade was executing no fewer than twenty discrete transactions per week. Extant records confirm that his clientele came mostly but by no means largely from the intangible caste we've called the Haves. Claudia Wong, a Second Year in Perry House, was an inconspicuous oboist in the Kennedy Symphony Orchestra; Dante Smith, a day student in Foster's year, belonged to the eccentric but firmly ignored cast of characters who colonized the editorial offices of *The Rubrum,* Kennedy's literary magazine. These are just two examples. There also seems to be little harmony to how Foster's clients found themselves soliciting his services.

"I was roommates that year with T—— S—— in Talmadge, and I'm pretty sure he told me about it," one shared with me recently, speaking on the condition of anonymity. "But Foster was the year above me and we didn't run with that crowd at all, so who the fuck knows how T—— knew."

They almost always approached him via Facebook Chat, if only the first time. "He'd take a little while to respond sometimes, but when he did, he'd reply super quickly," another anonymous client told me. "I always assumed he was kind of weird, just because the whole *thing* was kind of weird—but then when you'd meet him he seemed really nice. He didn't say much, and he always seemed—I dunno—kind of sad. But nice."

There is a quiet stillness to the Bradford Library in the evenings around dinnertime, in that hour and a half leading up to eight o'clock check-in. It's one of those stretches of time in Kennedy's daily clockwork when the centers of human gravity shift most perceptibly. Congregations of bodies move from the Field House into the Dining Center, and in their concentration, the darkening stretches of campus beyond feel almost magically desolate, punctuated only by spare trickles of life drawn toward some remote satellite of burning light: the fogged glass of Vito's across Main Street or the distant glow of the music building, dark except for the high atrium windows of the concert hall, where members of the String Ensemble are warming up. Equilibrium will find itself again at check-in, when the library will fill again during study hall. It's in anticipation of that activity that the library finds its prior quietude, limned by the knowledge that, for a short and stellar stretch of time, the rest of the world is somewhere else, out there in the darkness.

It was in this hour and a half that they could find Foster Dade, alone in a glass-doored study carrel at the far end of the second floor. *You'll see me*, he'd write to them on Facebook Chat ahead of their first meeting. *north face jacket, macbook, blue nalgene bottle, by the music listening room upstairs.* On these nights, he would eat dinner by himself. He arrived at the Dining Center as it opened at five thirty, empty except for faculty families with small children. He would sometimes chat with these kids as their mothers ladled pot pie onto plates, or offer to help pour their iced tea. He ate quickly and in silence—always thanking the staff as he left, telling them how good it was—before heading out across the lawn to the library.

And there he would be: sitting alone at the carrel's round table, usually with his headphones in. Their knocks against the door's glass were always hesitant, even on return visits, and the smile he gave in response upon looking up was at once beckoning and inscrutable. There is a special genre of small talk that accompanies all drug deals, irrespective of the substance; years later, when buying coke or weed in off-campus fraternity houses or Kips Bay apartments, certain Kennedy alumni would feel themselves slide into that ritual of nervous vacuity and think fleetingly of the quiet boy who'd sold them Adderall a decade prior. Sometimes he would ask them what they were studying for; if he'd had the teacher before, he'd offer his own pithy little insight, understated but trenchant in its brevity. And then he'd reach into the backpack for an envelope folded in half, and with a cursory glance to the hallway along the bookshelves beyond the glass door he'd hand it across the table to its receiver. He simply accepted the money when it came, his expression pleasantly unchanged, and tucked it into some recess in his backpack before giving an affable but final smile and looking back to whatever was on his MacBook's screen. "He always seemed to be typing when I'd come in—as if he was always writing a paper, or an email," one client told me.

Certain procedural exceptions existed. By early November, the list of clients beyond Kennedy's campus had grown to just shy of three dozen. His original liaisons from that night in the Hamptons—Patterson Hughes at Deerfield; Elle O'Connor at Taft; Tripp Altridge—had not only followed up enthusiastically but taken the liberty of sharing news of his endeavor with their peers. Tales of the "Adderall guy at Kennedy" had slowly but incisively metastasized that autumn across the social network spanning the Northeast Corridor's private schools, a tangled matrix of mutual connections and shared histories forged in institutions designed with that purpose: the day schools, the sleepaway camps, the summer colonies. Every few days that term, Foster's Facebook Chat chimed with a new message from someone at Kent or Groton or Pingry, sometimes Woodberry

Forest or Virginia Episcopal. Once, oddly, a school in Wilmington, North Carolina, called Cape Fear Academy. There would always be at least four or five mutual friends among them—Gracie Smith and Pritchett Pierce recurred frequently, as did Jacqueline Franck— though this figure rose steadily as the weeks went on and his business expanded and Foster became without realizing it a nexus for the intersecting connections of a social web that a year before had confused and frightened him. It was Jae who would handle these off-campus shipments; there was a FedEx/Kinko's in the same Pennington strip mall as his bank.

There were those at Kennedy who by virtue of their social proximity to Foster did not go through the same Facebook Chat/library carrel rendezvous as the rest. Frances Evans and Freddie Pieters would remain regular customers until social politics made the necessary interactions too cumbersome. With the privilege of hindsight, it's difficult to look back upon that November and not see the starkness of that looming inevitability, but there were also still markers of normalcy. They'd be in the corner booth in Vito's, and as Porter or Sofi or Pritchett went to retrieve their slice of pizza or refill their Diet Coke, Foster would slide the folded envelope across the Formica tabletop, streaking it almost imperceptibly with the surface's grease.

And then there was the sole customer who came to Foster in his room in Brennan, who by November had become his most regular and high-volume client.

There were moments that autumn when others seemed to recognize that something palpable but nameless had shifted in Jack Albright. He had returned to school imperceptibly older than he'd been in Southampton a fortnight prior—his torso broader, his jaw fuller and darker with unshaved stubble. Several weeks into the term, Foster realized that what was different was the absence of a smile. He would later reject this observation as a trite and reductive summary of something vaster, but it was also simply true. Foster realized with a strange and embarrassing longing how much he had simply enjoyed watching Jack operate in the world the prior year. His spirited flamboyance had adhered to the controls of its own rhythms with the rigor of verse relayed in iambic pentameter, benevolent in its infectiousness. Though Foster recognized his own tendency to romanticize aspects of history incapable of arguing otherwise, he noted that Jack's previously inter-mittent spells of darkness now seemed somehow lyrical in hindsight, the necessary tonal variations in some grander symphonic project.

What was there now was anger. Jack Albright still emanated an intensity of energy as he moved through the world; he still blasted Lil Wayne from his Bose speakers when he showered. But something in his demeanor rendered the habit humorless and even violent, its bass and volume throbbing with spite. As if sleepwalking, he performed the rituals expected of him: he hustled in soccer practice and went with his friends to Vito's, but he no longer commanded their attention or sought the thrill of a captive audience. What was alarming about his laugh wasn't its diminished frequency but the uncanniness of its familiarity: its soaring ring was now hollow and metallic not with humor but with mirth. At a lunch once, a gangly Second Year boy in Donavan House had failed to apprehend the glass that separated his dining pod from the central mezzanine; when he dropped his tray, spilling fruit punch onto his white sneakers and sending a bowl of yogurt and granola sliding down the thigh of his pants, it had been Jack who laughed the loudest of anyone.

It was only the most combustible moments that seemed to register with those who surrounded him. *Pritchett and Will seemed genuinely bothered by the whole thing,* Foster wrote on his Blogspot early in November, *though they'd only ever address it as directly as guys ever address anything with other guys—which is to say not really at all. I'm sure they'd say it wasn't personal. But given some of the stuff that's happened, I still can't shake the sense that at the end of the day, it really has to do with me.*

yo were going to vitos, Jack texted him earlier that evening. Foster had been sitting in his carrel, staring at but not reading a packet of primary documents for the following morning's Honors United States History test ("The Townshend Acts of 1767: Three Perspectives"). In the envelope in his backpack were two ten-milligram Adderall IRs.

Marcie Capella, a quiet but sardonic girl in his year, had said she'd come by for them after her fencing practice.

Foster Dade [06:13:14PM]: nice when

Foster felt his thumbs consciously emulate the disinterest of Jack's absent punctuation. It had been two and a half weeks since their last exchange of messages. He continued to stare down at his screen in the moments that followed, and his face flushed with shame at the intensity with which he waited for some flicker of activity to indicate Jack's response. Several minutes passed.

Foster Dade [06:19:43PM]: ?

He strangely wanted to vomit. And then his phone hummed once within his clutch.

Jack Albright [6:21:33PM]: were here now

A pause.

Foster Dade [06:21:58PM]: kk coming

With a spasm of agitation, he clicked to Facebook and typed briskly to Marcie (*hey so sorry—something came up and i'm tied up for a bit, wanna meet during study hall*). He despised himself for the speed at which he crossed campus, the crystalline November night dancing on his still-hot face. He stared at his BlackBerry as he moved to distract himself from the fact of his anxiety, and as he passed the side door of Brennan he had to swerve to avoid colliding with Blake Mancetti, who seemed to be lingering there.

They were crowded around the booth when he got there: Jack, Mason, Pritchett, Mark, and Freddie; the Second Year Chandler McDermott; Gracie and Frances and Annabeth. Annabeth. Her smile was merciful as Foster entered; he briefly wanted to cry. He went to the glass counter and heard himself order a slice of Hawaiian, too distracted by the laughter coming from the far booth to register what it would cost him.

"I was gonna invite you myself, but my phone died," Annabeth was saying, suddenly beside him, her voice coming through the underwater silence. Something in his sternum quavered. The width of his smile was compulsive.

"Glad I'm just the afterthought."

She returned his grin. "I needed a thirty-second break from that zoo. And I've missed you."

Foster felt Jack's eyes on him as they returned to the booth, where Annabeth had pulled a chair next to her seat on the bench's end. Once or twice he felt the edge of his foot bump hers.

"Where's Roth, Dade," Freddie said through a mouth of meatball sub.

"Dinner in Princeton with her parents," Foster said. "Lawrence and Susan." He tried to say this with a note of observant irony. In his periphery he thought he saw Mason's eyes meet Chandler's.

"I'm telling Pedro he needs to bring the jukebox back," Annabeth was saying. "Still have no idea why they took it out. Probably speaks to how depressing our lives are here that I'm delighted by the prospect of a jukebox, but here we are."

"They took it out because Freddie fed it fifty dollars and made it play 'Take On Me' for twenty-four hours straight," Mark said, not looking up from his phone.

"Great fuckin' song," Freddie said absently. "What's your favorite band, Dade."

I think it was just Freddie being Freddie—he's totally out there, and if anything maybe he was trying to include me in a conversation he knew I wasn't part of. But part of me thinks he was targeting me. I probably only feel this way because of what happened after, but whatever.

"Oh, fuck, I dunno," Foster managed, trying to shove through the sudden fissure of anxiety that seemed exacerbated by Mason's and Chandler's taunting eyes. Mentally he desperately tried to leap to the field of his iTunes library upon his MacBook's screen. "Uh—the Smiths.

New Order. U2." (At this, both Mason and McDermott conspicuously snorted.) "The Cure. I've—I've been listening to a lot of the Police lately."

"What album."

Foster looked blankly at Jack, despising his face for reddening.

"What album," Jack said again. His face remained stoic, but there was a leer to his words, a viciousness to his eyes. "What album by the Police." He said these words slowly, as if belittling a child.

It was *Synchronicity*. Fucking *Synchronicity*. One fucking album title and my brain just couldn't do it.

"Uh, y—"

"Your iChat's set to show what you're listening to. I've seen 'Every Breath You Take' and 'So Lonely.' So—I guess you're talking about the *Greatest Hits* album?"

It did not matter that no one at that table beyond the two of them— save maybe Freddie and Annabeth—likely had any idea what they were talking about. *I'll admit it: I have the* Greatest Hits *album. And like it.* The taunting glint had gone from Jack's eyes; he was looking down at his phone in his lap, disinterested, even bored, as if his cruelty had been as rote and perfunctory as swatting a fly.

"Leave it to Albright to have a psychotic episode over something as unimportant as classic rock," Pritchett said. He was grinning, but Foster could tell from the silence that prefaced his words that he had recognized the antagonism in Jack's. "I swear, if you hadn't been athletic your parents would have tested you for autism years ago."

Jack shrugged, not looking up from his phone. He was slouched indifferently in the green plastic seat, his showered hair dampening his sweatshirt's hood.

"I need to get drunk very soon," Gracie said to no one in particular. She, too, had been fixated upon her phone's screen, and Foster was bleakly grateful that she seemed to have not been listening. In his desperation to affix his gaze elsewhere, he saw that from across the table Mark Stetson was studying him curiously.

"I thought you were gonna come to my house for the first weekend of Thanksgiving," Frances said. "Only my mom will be home. And then there's the Poinsettia Ball!"

"Can't," Gracie said. Her face twitched with an unintended smile at whatever BBM had just flashed upon her screen. "Grandparents are making me come into the city. Seeing a play or some shit. But yes, then there is the Poinsettia Ball. Good for you for remembering what month it is, France; that's a big step."

It was to his immense relief that Foster's own phone hummed against his thigh in that moment.

> **(717) 3██7██ [07:11:01PM]:** Hey Foster it's Marcie. Saw your Fb message. I have SAT tutoring at 8. Can you meet me beofre
> **(717) 3██7██ [07:11:09PM]:** before*

Something in his stomach loosened with strange relief. "Leaving us, Dade?" Pritchett asked as Foster folded his plate in half over the uneaten slice and stood.

"Yeah, alas," he said, in a voice he hoped was both sheepish and nonchalant. "Business obligation." There'd been no reason to share this, he knew, and he cringed as he felt his eyes glance to Gracie and then to Mason and Chandler and Jack and as he did. *It's about justifying my presence.*

"Yo, tell Chissom that I may be fifteen minutes late," Jack said without looking up from his phone. "Left something at the Field House."

"Yeah, no prob." Something kept Foster from meeting Jack's eyes, and as he walked back into campus he would wonder if he had only imagined the edge of embarrassed penitence in his words.

His eyes met Mark's, and Mark's smile there was something that looked strangely like compassion, or pity. And before Foster turned toward the door, Annabeth looked up at him and gave one of his jeans' belt loops a playful flick.

"Glad you came." There was something contemplative in her eyes. "You've been a recluse."

"Blame one Porter Roth." These words seemed to have organized themselves in his head, and he did not like how proud he was of them.

Something in Annabeth's face seemed to shift almost intangibly, but then her mouth turned up in a smile.

"Whatever you say." She stuck the tip of her tongue out at him.

Foster had bought himself the noise-canceling headphones on a cool Saturday afternoon in October, when Mr. McCall had taken a vanload of boys to MarketFair Mall ahead of the evening's Halloween dance. After lunch that day, he and Jae had headed out toward the cornfields, where they smoked Jae's bowl on a weather-worn bench in the fields' far woods. They'd giggled through the mall and gotten two chicken sandwiches each at Chick-Fil-A, and as they passed the Bose retailer Foster looked to Jae.

"Jae, we've made a lot of money," Foster had said finally.

"A lot of money," Jae said solemnly.

Foster had doled out the three hundred dollars in crumpled twenties and fifties. The headphones' oval ears were the size of ashtrays. "Can you hear me? Can you hear me?" Jae had yelled to Foster as the store's demo headphones pumped in the Bose-sanctioned Mahler symphony from the central console. Foster couldn't, and Jae had laughed so hard that he'd farted.

So he had not heard the knock on his door after returning from Vito's that night several weeks later, sitting at his desk with Passion Pit throbbing in his ears. It was only when Jack appeared in the doorway that he jerked himself upright and brought the headphones down around his neck.

"Fuck—shit, sorry," Foster said, straightening himself. "Totally spaced out."

"I knocked." There was something vaguely apologetic to Jack's words. The minor flush to his cheeks and the track jacket on his shoulders suggested he had only just returned to Brennan from the Field House, though he was empty-handed.

"Sorry, y'know"—Foster tapped the headphones' right ear with his finger—"noise-canceling."

"Yeah, dope," Jack said, neutrally. "Uh—"

"Vyvanse or Adderall."

"Uh—could I do both this time actually?"

Foster stood from his chair and moved to his closet, feeling Jack's gaze as he bent to preoccupy himself with the array of colored pills in the plastic containers before him.

"Here you are," he said, handing Jack the parceled Ziploc.

"You're a hero, Dade," he said, and there was a relief to Jack's smile that was at once familiar and estranged. The encounter at Vito's suddenly seemed detached by not only time but some deeper, intangible metaphysics. "Oh, uh—I'm out of cash. Tomorrow?"

"Yeah, man." Foster waved Jack's words away. "No worries."

He returned to his desk and placed his headphones back atop his head. But he did not press play on his keyboard, and through the earphones' sonic muffle he listened as Jack Albright moved up the stairs.

IX.

Foster would spend the first Saturday night of November in detention in Memorial Hall's lecture room. His excuses had left Ms. Sutt unmoved when he'd stumbled into Honors Biology twenty minutes late that Tuesday—"I guess I missed that page in the School Handbook, where it says tardies are excused whenever your phone's alarm forgets to go off"—but he had been unbothered and even curiously relieved to settle in along the lecture hall's back row. Donavan House was hosting a kickball round robin on the turf fields, four boys and four girls a team, and as Foster worked through his precalculus homework he listened indifferently to the distorted sounds of excitement that every now and again reached the heart of campus, rising up from the haze of sodium light tinging the night's edge.

Foster had returned to his room before eleven o'clock check-in. He was reclined on his bed staring at an episode of *Summer Heights High* on his MacBook when an acoustic muffle of activity pressed through his headphones. From downstairs, the competing bellows in which teenage boys confide shared enthusiasms was so loud that the panes of his windows briefly hummed. "Fuckin' *get it*, Albright,"

Nic Bergman was yelling. "Let's *goooo*." Foster couldn't remember a time when these expressions of testosteronal discharge did not leave him feeling alienated and more than vaguely annoyed—his own early attempts to participate had felt unnatural and somehow indicting—and he rolled his eyes and returned the earphone to his head. Jack Albright's prowess at kickball did not intrigue him.

He did not realize he had dozed off until he felt his pillow quiver with the vibration of his BlackBerry underneath. His light was still on and his MacBook was still hot against his stomach. Foster closed the computer and blinked his phone's screen into clarity. It was just after one in the morning.

> **ALW [01:02:58AM]:** i see your light from hewitt—are you up?
> **ALW [01:03:04AM]:** and if you are, can you call me? know it's late

He felt himself shift up on his bed with a sudden alertness.

> **foster d [01:06:11AM]:** Hey hey sorry—I sorta fell asleep while watching tv but just woke up and checked my phone
> **foster d [01:06:16AM]:** What's up? Is everything okay?

He held on to his phone, waiting for it to hum with her incoming call, and looked out the dark window toward Hewitt House. With twinge of guilt at his imagination's lucidity, he heard her anguished sobs as she hunched beneath the Bob Dylan poster over her bed on the third floor; he saw himself unlatching the laundry room window downstairs and sliding out into the darkness to meet her at the foot of the golf course, Major School Rules be damned; he felt his arms close around the form of her body as she wept into his shoulder. Then his phone hummed.

> **ALW [01:07:37PM]:** ack i didn't mean to wake you up! i'm sorry!!

No no you didn't you didn't I'm here, he hastened to write, before seeing that she was still typing.

> **ALW [01:07:42AM]:** plus i just realized how exhausted i am
> **ALW [01:07:43AM]:** lopl
> **ALW [01:07:44AM]:** lol*
> **ALW [01:07:47AM]:** but do you want to meet for coffee and go for a walk in the morning? early, before everyone's up. like 8
> **ALW [01:07:55AM]:** i just wanted to tell you that . . .
> **ALW [01:07:59AM]:** . . . jack and i had sex for the first time tonight.
> **ALW [01:08:04AM]:** and i know i'm so corny and lame but all i want to do is talk about it
> **ALW [01:08:06AM]:** lmao.

There was a perfection to the darkness outside the window.

> **foster d [01:09:46AM]:** oh fuck. wow. congratulations (is that the right thing to say to that? lol)
> **foster d [01:08:51AM]:** but yeah i'd love to walk. i'm going to porter's in the afternoon so 8 is good.

And so he'd pulled on his Amherst sweatpants and his Patagonia fleece and stepped out into the thin light of the morning that followed. He'd swallowed the sixty-milligram Vyvanse with a handful of water from the bathroom tap in Brennan, and the warmth of the caffeine nudged it from dormancy. Later, he thought back to the morning and winced at how, under the lisdexamfetamine's metabolic spell, he'd earnestly allowed himself to say the things he had been brought there to say, for how gorgeously he played the role for which he'd been cast. *If I hadn't taken the fucking Vyvanse I would have been a lot more honest*, he wrote that evening after returning from Porter's, *and less of a fucking . . . eunuch*. He asked questions that were compassionate in their specificity and concern, and their collated replies reconstructed the events of the prior evening with naturalistic rigor.

They—Annabeth and Jack—had decided to do it two evenings prior, in a phone call that spanned the duration of study hall. She had called him to apologize. At dinner Mason had apparently mocked the two of them for their failure to consummate things; Annabeth had been wounded by Jack's inadequate defense of their honor in the moment. "Then I was walking back to Hewitt by myself, still crying like— a Victorian widow, and I realized I was just completely overreacting— mostly, I realized, because I was sensitive about the topic, about the fact that we hadn't done it yet, which I took personally or saw as a failure on my part, which of course was self-indulgent and dumb. And he was, like, startlingly sweet, and just said he'd really wanted the first time to be special."

And so they had walked hand in hand on Saturday night to the turf fields to meet Gracie and Pritchett and the rest, and after an hour of irking their opponents with gregarious, indifferent play, their team—the other members of which had of course been apprised of the evening's agenda, the boys by Jack and the girls by Annabeth—had honorably resigned from the tournament. Pritchett and Freddie and Frances had whooped amicably after them as Jack and Annabeth left the fields once again hand in hand, disappearing from the ethereal snow of the stadium lights overhead into the autumn darkness toward the baseball fields' dugout, which is where it had happened.

"And like—it was mostly just fucking weird, and yes, it hurt, even though I knew it would, but, like"—and here she looked at Foster with a smile he had not seen before—"as, like, a theoretical thing, and as an emotional thing—I loved it."

That afternoon he was at Porter's house. Tierney had assigned them twelve to fifteen pages on *The Sound and the Fury* for the term's final paper, and they spent an hour sitting across from each other in silence at the Roths' kitchen table: Porter diligently typing out an outline and Foster catching up on the chapters he'd failed to finish reading for the previous week's classes. *Faulkner's 1929 novel is many things— a family drama, an elegy to the destitution of the post-Reconstruction South, a self-conscious variation on the Greek tragedy—but more than anything else it is a study in the recklessness of memory*, Tierney's prompt had read. *Your task: choose one thematic concern from* The Sound and the Fury *and tell me how it works within the novel's larger relationship to the past—or multiple pasts—it illustrates.*

"Imagine getting into Harvard and then killing yourself," Porter said aloud. "I like the name Quentin, though."

The afternoon beyond the windows was Gothic and gray: the earth was soft and wet with October leaves, their naked branches petrified neurons against the November-dark sky. The stillness of the kitchen trembled vaguely with the distant thudding slap of Susan Roth's feet against the whir of the treadmill in the home gym two floors above. Dr. Roth had left that morning for a conference at Penn. "I wouldn't say no to a break," Porter said, half-closing her laptop and looking up over it at Foster with coy eyes.

She locked the door of the basement guest bedroom behind them. Foster climaxed almost indifferently into her hand, his fingers pausing against her clitoris as his body tensed against the still-made bed. "I came really hard," he heard himself lie, and she smiled at him as she wiped her hand into a Kleenex from a bedside sleeve.

Porter hadn't turned on the lamps when they'd come in, and what little light still came through the small high window only pooled in thin ghostly blue on its recessed sill. They lay there naked and still for a little while, Foster's hand idly stroking her shoulder, until finally he heard himself say the words that in the preceding hours had nauseated him in their dreadful insistence.

"Have you ever thought about us—having sex?"

She turned her eyes up to him, and after searching his face through the shadowy darkness, she finally nodded her head against his chest.

"I never have," she whispered. "Had sex, I mean. Not thought about it."

"Me either." They'd known this, of course.

"But—yeah. Yeah. It seems like everyone else is. And I don't really make a big deal about these sorts of things, but still, I—trust you." With these last words she looked away out into the room. Only the starkest shadowed contours availed themselves in its darkness; a belt of cloudy puce marked the space below the door to the room's bathroom.

"Should we, like—think about when?" Foster said. "It feels cheap to just, like, do it."

"Yeah," Porter said. "What about—after the Homecoming Dance? That feels, I dunno, appropriate."

"What's that, two weekends away?"

"I'd say next weekend but I, uh—am on track to be getting my period."

"Then two weekends away it is." He resented the persuasiveness of the confidence in his voice.

"I've"—and here Porter paused—"been thinking about it for a while, actually. I just had no idea how to bring it up."

Foster blinked out into the darkness. "Same," he said finally, and then shifted his arm to hold her closer.

Only later would Foster contemplate the significance of the fact that, on that afternoon or in the two weeks that followed, they did not discuss what had transpired between Annabeth and Jack. There were moments when Porter would make references to their friends and then pause almost imperceptibly after Annabeth's name, her wide eyes appraising Foster's face for anything that might betray what lay beneath his determined reticence. There was a vulnerability in the subsequent silence, in which she seemed to hear a flicker of the very unspoken truths that impelled these gambits, and the enormity of what they had silently decreed to ignore was left once again to metastasize in its neglect. There's no record to suggest that Annabeth and Porter's friendship had suffered in any way, at least by the end of that academic term; on the contrary, there was soon a brief spell where their shared privileged knowledge of a certain mode of sexuality brought them closer together. (Gracie had lost her virginity the prior winter to the surly lacrosse player John Stillwell before he headed off to Duke; Frances the summer before that to some suntanned Deerfield boy on a couch at some party in Nantucket—but the steady sex of romantic relationships occupies its own category, with its own pre- and post-coital politics of engagement and its own catalogue of satisfactions.)

Counterfactuals are really only useful as rhetorical devices, but I don't think it's reckless to venture that if Jack Albright and Annabeth Whittaker had not lost their virginities to each other on the first Saturday night of November 2009, Foster Dade and Porter Roth would not have planned to follow suit after the Homecoming Dance two weeks later. If there's merit to this hypothesis, it would also provide some insight into the dread both Foster and Porter silently suffered in the two weeks ahead of the ordained date in question: a dread we associate less with exhibitions of mutual passion than with the closure of some financially existential business transaction. Fearing the unknown consequences of vocalizing this terror, they instead both remained silent.

It was just after seven thirty on the Saturday night of Homecoming when Foster had finally put the small glass bong on Jae's dresser and looked down to the clock on his BlackBerry. "Fuck," he'd said to Jae. "Can't I just go to detention with you."

They'd returned from the Dining Center to a Brennan bright and warm with getting-ready sounds: Kanye West and Lady Gaga and questions shouted down hallways against the warm fug of several running showers. Nic Bergman was standing in khakis and untucked oxford in Charlie Obermeier's doorway; Charlie, a pensive dark-haired pole vaulter from Pittsburgh, gave Foster a genial half-wave from behind him. "Yo, Dade, I stole a tie from you," Nic had said, holding up the green necktie Charlotte had bought Foster from Brooks Brothers for his Episcopal Confirmation four years prior. "Oh, can you tell Frances Evans I want to fuck her? Yo—*Albright*! Where you going, bitch?"

"Call me a bitch again, Bergman."

Foster turned his head and saw Jack standing with his back to them at the foyer's table, scribbling on the check-in clipboard. He hadn't looked back.

"You know I love you, Albright. And your hot girlfriend."

"I'm going to Ames to pregame—if McCall asks, that's where I am, but I wrote it down." With a tilt of his hand at his mouth Jack improvised drinking, then his eyes caught Foster in the shadows of the side entranceway. "Anyway—gotta bounce." And he'd turned on the heels of his loafers and disappeared out the front door toward the Meadow.

It was in a certain feeling of emptiness that Foster found himself following Jae upstairs to smoke, though the cluster of tension in his stomach told him not to. He was still too high as he tightened the knot of the pink Vineyard Vines necktie, its cheerful cerulean dolphins shifting beneath his clumsy fingers. His room was dark except for its desk lamp, and in its feeble warmth he stepped back and looked at himself in the mirror. *Send me a picture of yourself tonight!* Charlotte had texted him that afternoon, and as he contemplated what that photo would look like, he found himself thinking of Jack and Mason and the rest of them, taking shots of vodka from paper Dixie cups in Pritchett's room. There was a stain on his blazer's lapel that had the crusty silvery sheen of dried semen, and in the weed's myopic press he imagined Jack and Mason and Chandler seeing it and laughing. It had been four months since he'd had a haircut, and in its length his hair seemed fairer. He looked at himself and thought again of his mother, and to quell his impulse to cry he narrowed his gaze upon his reflected face and wondered what it looked like to Porter.

I first reached out to Porter Roth on Instagram, where I'd followed her two years before. She was the sort who posted infrequently, but her LinkedIn profile provided the broad biographical contours: I knew she'd worked for Facebook in Manhattan and then San Francisco after college, and that she'd returned east to do her MBA at MIT. It was against Sofi Cohen's counsel that I finally decided to approach her, and as always there was a wisdom in Sofi's words. My message to Porter remained read and unanswered for several days before I returned to see that she'd blocked me.

Still, certain germane details were retrievable elsewhere. Years after the night of Kennedy's Homecoming Dance in November 2009, at sorority dinners at Duke and in candlelit Manhattan bistros under the wine-drunk confessional impulse of third or fourth dates, Porter would tell the story of how she'd lost her virginity. She would laugh at the absurdity of the endeavor. "It was like we were planning a rocket launch," she'd say, and with each telling she'd get better at protecting these words from the weight of the very real pain that had once been their payload. It was many years before she began to realize that the pain of that night was not only distinct from the pain of the months that followed but also its originating wound. There was something to that first laceration beneath them that never perfectly closed. She would learn to live alongside its pain, and indeed with time she forgot it was there. But this is not the same thing as healing.

The prior spring, after mounting an unserious and mostly reactionary campaign for Student Council President in the vein of '96-vintage Ross Perot, Will Bartholomew had thrown his hat in the ring for the office of Vice-President of Social Life. To his great surprise, he'd won. He was to DJ the Homecoming Dance, and as dusk chilled the November night the distant throbs of Usher and Pitbull's "DJ Got Us Fallin' in Love" reached the Meadow from the tent erected along the House-league football fields.

"I hate this song.

"I *fucking* hate this song."

They had met along the Meadow's edge. "You look very nice," Porter said as they broke away from their kiss. In the sickness of his own panic, he did not recognize the nervousness of her grin. "I like your dolphins." She took his necktie in her hand and then let it fall back to his shirt.

"All right, Dade? Rothie?" Freddie said as they approached the edge of the lawn, clutching a SmartWater bottle of vodka. He was there in a silver bow tie alongside his date: a completely anomalous and almost implausibly sexy First Year girl from Shanghai named Xiaoyu Fu. Pritchett was approaching glumly with a very dour-looking Sally Pinelli, with whom he'd broken up and gotten back together twice since the start of the academic year. Freddie took a long sip from the plastic bottle and then handed it to Xiaoyu, who appeared to drain half its contents before wordlessly handing it to Foster. Foster took it and looked at Porter, who shrugged, and after he pulled from it, she took it and did the same. In the initial flood of its warmth the vodka seemed for a moment to promise the night some salvation. Approaching from the middle of the Meadow were the others, midnight shadows turning through the darkness, and then there they were, and there was Annabeth, her naked shoulders shivering above the slip of a crimson dress, lurching on Jack's arm and laughing at the absurdity of her own high heels.

"Hi, friends!" She waved cheerfully, and Foster could hear from the richness of her words that she, too, had been drinking. "Shall we dance?"

They moved to the warm gloaming of the distant tent and then beneath it, negotiating the motion of bodies on the ad hoc dance floor. The interlocking polyurethane tiles beneath their feet would grow dark and sticky with grime as the night went on: it was one of those things you noticed inadvertently then forgot, committing the image to the strange subconscious effluence that sustains the clearer picture of a memory.

Foster and Porter remained proximate and in the suspension of some sort of gentle but impenetrable orbital tug, turned toward each other even when their faces were not facing. He could not bring himself to meet her eyes directly, and every so often he'd disappear to the desolate refreshment table at the far end of the tent for the excuse to simply watch things transpire. The throng from which he'd broken did not seem to register his absence. Freddie and Xiaoyu had begun making out at the dance floor's center within perhaps five minutes of arriving, and now she had thrown her legs up around his body and let him lift her from the floor; inexplicably shoeless, she seemed to be gnawing at his face as she straddled him, and he seemed very pleased with himself. And Annabeth's arms had not left their lock around Jack's neck.

"Hey hey, Foster Dade!" It was Tierney, wearing some sort of wide-lapeled vomit-colored shirt, his hair somehow wilder than usual. Foster caught the strong and not unpleasant smell of cigar and felt himself grin at his teacher, briefly forgetting himself.

"Enjoying yourself, Dr. Tierney?"

The speakers along the dance floor suddenly spasmed with the loud farting chords of "Party in the U.S.A." by Miley Cyrus; as if bewitched into some glitter-spangled coven, what seemed like every girl present threw her head back and shrieked in unison, moving in harmony toward the center of the dance floor in a sort of manic horah.

Tierney was shouting something that sounded like a female student's name over the music.

"What?"

"Donna Summer!"

"Disco Donna Summer?"

"Fuck, *yes*, Dade, you've got it! *That's* music! Not this—snuff-porn audio track! Jeez!"

And with a violent grin Tierney moved past Foster onto the floor and began to dance a spastic little tarantella. Foster was happy to hear himself laugh.

"Hi."

Porter's makeup had been slightly perturbed, but in the drunken chalky light of the colored orbs overhead her beauty seemed at once boundless and irretrievably distant.

"Did you see Tierney."

"I thought for a second he might be drunk," Porter smiled, looking out at the floor, "but then I remembered he's just Tierney."

Will Bartholomew had transitioned into "Down" by Jay Sean and Lil Wayne and was swaying with the music, his eyes closed and his hands grasping upward with the beat. Minutes before, Theresa Daniels had stormed the dance floor with the fury of a Victorian preceptress and pulled Xiaoyu from Freddie, who was now grinding with Kaitlyn Sanders. They disappeared with the music into the oscillating puzzle of sweat-kissed bodies, and when its shape breathed outward again Foster saw Annabeth and Jack, their interlocked form shifting with the music's vaster rhythm, kissing as the light spilled around them, the edges of Annabeth's mouth turned up from Jack's in an unmistakable smile. And then Foster felt Porter take his hand.

There was a blissfully distended moment outside the door to the *Kennedian* office when he convinced itself that it would be taken—that a naked Sasha Burnell would look up from under the sweaty mass of some athlete and hiss at the two of them in the doorway to *get the fuck out*, and that, faced by the insurmountable disequilibrium of their carefully constructed plans' disruption, they would laugh and cut their losses and spend the rest of the evening alone in a booth at

Vito's, happily out of place in their rumpled formalwear, and commit to a rain check when the time felt right.

But of course the door opened with the push of his key onto only desolate blackness. As Porter shut it behind them, Foster was reminded of a recurring nightmare that had followed a fourth-grade evening by himself in front of ABC Family's *Scariest Places on Earth*, in which he was locked alone overnight in a crypt beneath an abandoned mental asylum.

The shuffle through the darkness to the old couch seemed newly dense with obstacles. He unzipped her dress and pulled it to the old concrete floor, and as they kissed with a new violence he stood there helplessly while she pulled the tie from his undone collar and unbuttoned his shirt. He took the odd curvature of her strapless bra in his hands and then moved them down to the edges of her underwear, which to his distress had already slid down from her waist to hang loosely along her thighs. The euphoric familiarity he'd forged with her body in the preceding weeks seemed to suddenly jeer at him from some distant dock as he drowned; as he cusped his hand between her legs, he met only the antagonism of what he felt to be its unfamiliar heat. She brought his body down with hers to the limp cushions of the sagging couch. Her bra seemed to fall off of its own accord, and as he felt his pants and boxers drop to his ankles, he was met with a shame he'd forgotten from those childhood moments of unwanted nudity.

"Yeah," she breathed as he began to bring his fingers against the ridge of her clitoris. The distant hoarseness of fear in her voice was something he would not hear until much later; in the moment, it was only a pornographic caricature of pleasure, and it disgraced him. With an almost biological impulsivity he took his fingers to his mouth and sucked them to moisten their edges.

Just as he did not remember the sickening trepidation that had followed him to the dance, he did not fully internalize Porter taking his index finger and guiding it inside her. She seemed to have registered his bewilderment through the silence. "This is my vagina," she said, with a desperation that sounded then only like contempt. The ingress was lower below her body than he'd ever contemplated, and the slickness that seemed to close around his finger seemed unnatural, almost implausible. He had positioned himself above her, supporting his weight with his forearm against the hard edge of the couch.

"Do you have—the condom," she whispered from below him, and with a seize of horror Foster realized that he did not know where her words came from; her face had been taken by the darkness, and like in the blindness-borne hallucinations suffered by those lost without light in black caves, he believed very sincerely for a moment that he was going mad.

"Yeah," he thought he heard himself say, and with another stab of shame at his own nudity he pressed himself up from the couch to find the lump of his wallet in the crumple of his pants below.

It had been Jack who'd given him the singular Trojan, sometime in early October's last spill of warmth, on an evening when, for the first time that fall, they'd found themselves alone together. The density of things unsaid or unknown had not yet reached the chafing mass it would assume as the term progressed. With the conspiratorial grin Foster hadn't seen since returning to school (and indeed hadn't seen since), Jack had opened his desk's bottom drawer and pulled out a blue box of thin cardboard. Its flimsy tabs had been opened at both ends, and a footlong sleeve of the flattened little vertebrae had fallen accordion-like to the floor. "CVS last week," Jack had grinned. He held the band of condoms at one end and let the rest collapse into his other palm, as if shuffling a deck of cards.

He found his wallet and pulled the condom from it in the darkness. The wrapper was the blue of a fifty-milligram Vyvanse's colored end; the white words TROJAN ENZ had chafed against his debit card's raised numbers. *When do condoms expire*, he had googled the previous evening before the internet shut off, and to his dismay he learned that he was fine.

He could feel the pull of Porter's expectation below him in the darkness. "Got it," he said, and under the cover of the lightless room he first reached down and felt his penis. He wasn't soft, but there was a reluctant slackness to his erection that frightened him. As if to nudge it to its duty, he felt himself reach down and cup a hand around Porter's breast.

"What are you doing."

He pulled his hand away from her skin as if it had corroded his fingerprints. "One sec," he said, and tried to pull a tear in the condom's wrapper in the darkness. It did not relent. Desperately, he held its edge to his teeth and tore it open, fishing the slick latex from its wound with his fingertip. He held it to the tip of his penis. "One sec," he said again. "I've—never done this before." And in a different moment he imagined that Porter would have laughed, but under the schizophrenia of the darkness she seemed to have become someone else. She was silent.

He was hard enough to unroll the lubricated condom down to the base of his penis, wincing for a moment as stray strands of his pubic hair snagged beneath its edge. "It's on," he muttered, and moved his knees back around Porter's legs. With a blind grasp he relocated the slick cusp of what she had shown him to be her vagina, and with his fingers as his guide he brought the end of the condom on his dick to it. He thought fleetingly again of the warmth of a booth at Vito's. In a desperate sense of ethical duty he brought his other hand to Porter's cheek and leaned down to kiss her.

"Are you—ready?" he asked, hating his voice.

"Yeah," Porter breathed, and before he could resume anything she spoke again. "Foster—I love you."

Neither of them would later remember how long the intercourse had lasted, or even where its temporal coordinates drew their boundaries. He hadn't been hard enough to get inside her, and only after several minutes of his desperate masturbation at the base of her vagina could he find himself able to slide his penis into an orifice that did not want it there. He had felt the torture of Porter's agony in her silence as he jerked himself off, and the note of triumph intended in the words that followed—"I'm ready"—had humiliated both of them in their hoarse lewdness. Panicked by the fickleness of his arousal, he had pressed himself into her before it could relent. There was a reflexiveness to both Porter's moan and her body's bend away from his that frightened him, and he held his waist stationary as she forced herself to return her hips toward his. "Are you okay," he'd said, moving his hand through the darkness for the familiar edge of a shoulder or cheek. "Does it hurt."

"No—no, it's fine, it's fine." Porter had said this through clenched teeth, but Foster's hips resumed their motion without registering their signals, and her exhalations with every subsequent thrust carried the involuntary heft of something that was not pleasure. And that went on for an unclarified number of minutes, a corrupted transaction between nothing more than two analogous zones of human flesh, before finally Foster's motions slowed to nothing and with a quiet but mortifying squelch he slid his penis out from inside her.

"I, uh—I think I'm too new at this to orgasm this time," he forced himself to say, and for the first time in many months his synapses prolapsed with the violent screams of self-destruction.

"It's okay, seriously," he heard Porter's voice say through the roar that wanted his self-immolation. "No worries. It's new." And despite the noise inside him he could discern the smallness of her voice, the distance of the person who spoke it. He pressed his body onto hers, and as his mouth found hers he felt in the sudden dryness of her lips the faint rigid tensing of a flinch.

They found their clothes through the darkness in silence; Foster would realize back at Brennan that he'd put his boxers back on inside out and backwards. "Shall we head back," one of them said to the other. The haunted emptiness of Fenster Hall seemed to scream with its desolation as they moved out into the basement and up the stairs.

There was still music coming from the tent across campus, though the dance had ended. Bartholomew had either put on "Baby" by Justin Bieber or relinquished control of his iTunes to some other member of the Student Council during clean-up duty. The clusters of bodies crossing the grounds to their Houses seemed to have carried the ethereal ember-light of the dance with them. It was the sort of night that got you drunk on friendship; like all adolescent drunkenness, it was unabashed and earnest and delightfully slapdash, nourished by the warmth of their happy juntas. The motion of their amber silhouettes brokered an accord between the contested territories where one tent of lamplight met its neighbor.

Boys with sweat-tangled hair and untied neckties moved in clusters of their own unconcerned noise; still flush from dancing and high on its endorphins, they let their shirts go unbuttoned, their hairless chests naked and defiant in the November chill. On the darkness of the lawn before the library, packs of girls broke the stillness of the cold night with shouts of spontaneous a cappella, Taylor Swift and Katy Perry. They marched barefoot across the frozen earth, clutching the high heels on which they'd wobbled alone before their bedroom mirrors in the hour before the dance in self-flagellation, mocked by the audacity of their faces and the datelessness to which they were now so mercifully indifferent. In the stillness just beyond their wake were the couples who had left the dance an hour earlier, spoking the vast geographical wheel of campus in their returns from its farthest edges. There was an almost imperceptible rhythmic distinction to each pair's passage beneath the darkness, encoded by the shared privacies of the previous hour. The girls wore their companions' blazers as wonderfully preposterous overcoats over their naked shoulders, and the boys shivered chivalrously, the knees of their khakis wet with the brown and green of the earth on which they'd ultimately been discarded.

And Foster envied all of them, envied the coyly smiling couples and the roving ad hoc fraternities in equal measure; he envied them with a lurch of sickness he hadn't felt in eleven months. He could not bring himself to look at Porter, and so he simply stared straight ahead, oblivious to the motion of his own feet.

"Library looks kind of eerie," he felt himself say stupidly.

"Yeah," he heard Porter say.

They reached the curb of the driveway in front of Hewitt House. From inside came the stifled sounds of girls checking in, a bright and happy noise. He found himself still desperate for a distraction, but did not let himself move his eyes to the common room windows and ascertain the faces that populated it.

"I think—it will be better when we try it again," he said finally. "The first time is supposed to be a shitshow, right."

He finally turned himself to Porter. She had not asked for his blazer—he had not thought to offer—and he could tell from the hunch of her shoulders and the rise of goose bumps along her arms below them that she was very cold. The scalloped edge of her bra had pushed itself up slightly over the top of her dress. And then he looked to her eyes and saw that they were vivid and bright, a child's eyes.

"Hey," he said suddenly, unable to withhold from his voice's concern the distress of the helplessness that suddenly pressed itself on him. "Hey. Are you okay?"

"It's nothing—it's really nothing," she said, and there was an odd, almost compulsive sincerity to her smile, and as she brushed her hand to her face to preempt it, the brightness in her eyes slid into a single plump tear that seemed to almost tumble in its fall to the stone path below. She smiled again, ruefully and desperately now, and wiped the back of her hand against her eye, where her mascara-clumped eyelashes shone with little ova of wetness.

Foster felt himself take both of her hands in his. "Hey," he said again, not knowing what else to say, feeling the insides of his torso contract and his chest skip, and then when he still did not know, he simply said: "Porter—I'm really sorry."

"No, it's nothing," she said again. She was not looking at him, and the smile was now only sad. "Sorry, just—it's nothing."

And there was a constriction in her voice that let him know that speaking was paining her, and this realization nourished the burn of the humiliation that had disoriented him in the darkness of the *Kennedian* office. *I'm really sorry*, she'd say to him in a text message shortly after midnight. *Objectively I know I was being crazy.* But the mortification would not quell itself with this, and even in the weeks that followed, its stain would remain tender and unsuppressed.

"Okay," Foster said, stupidly. "Seriously, I'm—really, really sorry."

She did not correct him then, and the halt of her silence let him know that she quietly understood this apology to be deserved and indeed necessary, even if she was too polite to acknowledge it as such, and his stomach spasmed again.

"You have exactly ninety seconds, McElwee," some distant duty master's voice rang out from the direction of Donavan House.

"Well, uh." Foster looked at Porter in surrender to this sudden finality, and with no superior alternatives he leaned in and kissed her. It was a perfunctory, passive kiss, and as his nose met her face he felt another tear fall and graze its edge.

"I'll text you when I'm back and checked in, yeah?" he said to her, repulsed at the contrivance of his voice, and she nodded and swallowed.

Her eyes were still wide and heavy with the light, and for a moment they met his, but whatever fleeting mutual disclosure this may have mercifully allowed disappeared as she turned and moved to the door of Hewitt House. It closed behind her, and she did not look back.

X.

VirtualTeenTalk Forums—General Discussion—Chat
BY: SailorMoonGurl94
December 17, 2009 / 3:44am EST
RE: Powers

Does anyone else ever think that telekeneses might be real? Sometimes I will be going through my day and I will suddenly think of something random, and then almost immediately it seems to happen. I believe it has to do with my mind. I have never told anyone else this before but I am a Genius. They tell me I'm not supposed to share this with anyone but I feel like my VTT friends are my family. I believe we knew each other in seven different past lives and have been brought here to the world for a purpose because of the powers we have. That is what my Genius tells me. The Genius is me but it is also William. I live near a very famous university (I won't say which because I have to protect my privacy. There are people who would hurt me if they know) where my parents are professors, but I was the one who gave them their Genius. That's why God made me live where I live, because Albert Einstein lived here, and he gave me his brain after he died. Again this is not something I am supposed to share but I love you VTT friends and I promise I will protect you when I begin to move the Weather. I did not protect Michael Jackson and this is why he died but I will protect you

XI.

http://www.fhd93.blogspot.com/2009/12/little-victories
(Posted December 11, 2009)

I can now proudly report that as of 12/2, I have successfully had sex. By this I mean I came inside Porter. Well, inside a condom inside Porter, but still. And it only took me a dozen tries.

I guess maybe I'm being too hard (ha) on myself. What does it mean to have "had sex"—i.e., what qualifies as doing so successfully? Is it still sex if there isn't an orgasm? Similarly: I am sort of sad about the fact that, in light of this confusion, I have no idea when I really lost my virginity. Was it the night of the homecoming dance when I first sort of got inside of Porter, or a few nights later, during finals, when I was able to stay hard enough for long enough to thrust for a couple of minutes? Thanks to my anxiety/general ineptitude, the only thing I can say with total surety is that I lost my virginity over a stretch of two and a half weeks, culminating in last Wednesday's triumph. I hate that I have to use words like "triumph" to describe something as biologically basic as ejaculating, but it felt like a triumph.

I am choosing not to think about Homecoming. I'd be lying if I said that something didn't change between Porter and me afterwards. We finally met up before check-in the next night. She told me it was okay, and that I was right, that the first time was always supposed to be weird. She looked like she'd been crying again.

I guess I always just pictured a different sort of weirdness. A weirdness that wasn't so . . . alienating. In my imagination, it would have been kind of like traveling to a foreign country and trying some crazy exotic food together. Sheep testicles, maybe. We'd laugh about how out of our depth we were and be brought even closer together by the shared strangeness. That's the thing: there was nothing shared. I guess I can't speak for her, but I've been trying not to think about why it was so miserable for me, or why it felt like such a horrible personal failing, like I was betraying something that I'd otherwise successfully managed to forget. I can't help but wonder if that's why I felt so alone—I was stranded with my own secrets.

After Homecoming, I made a conscious decision to stop jacking off. I knew from past trials how horny I get around the second or third day; when I finally touch my dick, it takes like five seconds to come. (Side note: I hate the spelling "cum"—it feels pornographic.) I figured the same principle would apply if my dick was inside a vagina. When we hooked up that week, I went down on her, making a point to prolong it so there wouldn't be time for her to return the favor.

Finally, one night, I was hard enough to try it again. I got out one of the condoms I'd gotten when Jae and I walked to get cigarettes and put it on, and I got inside her. It didn't feel good or bad; I was just sort of thrusting. For a moment it seemed like I was getting somewhere, and then out of nowhere, I found myself thinking of walking in on Nic Bergman taking a shit in Brennan with the stall door open that morning. It's like my brain was mocking me: I knew immediately that I wouldn't come. So I faked it. And because I wasn't in fact consumed by orgasmic pleasure, I could very much see that she had no idea I'd faked it, and I could very much see the relief in her face.

So I faked it again the next night, and every night we met up thereafter, and I returned to my vow of masturbatory celibacy or whatever over Thanksgiving. And finally: last Wednesday, in the *Kennedian* office, it happened. Having not had an orgasm in nearly two weeks, I found myself wanting her in a way that I hadn't since before Homecoming. When I went to put my dick inside her, I noticed that she was wetter than she'd been before—as if her body had picked up on my horniness (side note: I hate the word "horny" for the same reasons I hate "cum") and gotten turned on as a result. I guess because she was wetter, it suddenly felt better than it ever had: the heat was still kind of weird but it was also just insanely wonderful. When I was in middle school, I'd sometimes spit on my hand before jerking off, which I guess was gross but it also kind of felt incredible. It was like that multiplied by a hundred.

So we started . . . having sex, I guess. I don't think she liked it as much as me fingering or going down on her (side note: I take pride in the fact that I now know the difference between the clitoris and the vagina. I get the sense most other guys just shove their fingers inside and the girls are good sports about it) but there was something in her breathing I hadn't heard before. And all I could think about was how good it felt, and then I considered the fact that I was having sex; that my dick was inside a girl, a real girl with boobs that were naked in front of me and kind of bouncing as I thrusted. And then: I came. It came (ha) out of nowhere, and it was better/different than any orgasm I'd had before. The tip of my dick was so sensitive that the tingling almost . . . hurt.

I don't think she realized what had just happened. In other words: I don't think she realized that I'd been faking it until just then, which makes me feel both pathetic (for faking it) and guilty (for lying). I kind of collapsed on top of her and was like, "I just came."

"I know," she said, and she laughed, either at (what sounded to her like) the absurdity of the comment or at her relief over the fact of it. I made a point of letting her see the condom as I pulled it off my dick (whereas previously I'd clutched it in my fist until dropping it in the big garbage can by the door). I was weirdly proud of how much semen there was in it.

And instead of throwing away the torn condom wrapper, it's now in the little Tupperware where I keep important papers and good Academic Memos and stuff like that. Kind of a trophy, or a souvenir. Fucked-up but whatever.

That was a week and a half ago and we've had sex seven times since. I've come every time. On three occasions I've thought about Annabeth.

I'm reading back over all of this and I guess it's not entirely honest. The facts are correct, sure. But the truth is that I've been feeling as empty and bleak as I was last fall, when Dr. Apple first put me on Lexapro. Part of me believes the sex is nice.

Another part of me hates Porter.

"Hates" is maybe a strong word. "Resents" might be better. I wish I could really understand why. I wish I could know why I somehow feel lonelier than I ever have before. I used to always hear my mom telling Maggie that there shouldn't be sex without love, and maybe that's it. Maybe I don't love her, and I hate pretending otherwise. But it feels more complex than that. Maybe a part of me—a big part of me—resents her for resuscitating the anxiety and self-hatred and insecurity and misery that for a very long time I thought I'd killed for good. (This doesn't fully explain the anxiety, self-hatred, etc., but oh well.) I resent her for the way she cried the night of Homecoming. I resent her for the way she's sometimes silently seemed to resent me since then.

Annabeth and I have been spending time together, the way we did last year. I've told her about the Porter stuff, sort of. By "sort of" I mean: I've shared the emotional dynamic—the sense of mutual estrangement, etc.—without divulging any of the mortifying sexual specifics. (I choose to believe that I'm not the only mortified party, and that accordingly Porter's told her nothing.) She listens. She tells me that Porter is more insecure than anyone she knows and that I shouldn't take it to heart. "She's like Jack in that way," she said on a walk around the cornfields last Sunday—she didn't elaborate, and I was afraid to pry further at the risk of shattering the tenuous but wonderful thing I felt in that moment, which was my heart singing.

There's a week left before Christmas break, and then I'm going to the city for the Poinsettia Ball. Sofi is having the after-party. I'm staying at Pritchett's with the guys again. I'm embarrassed to think about how close I came to crying when he invited me. I'm choosing not to think about what Jack and Mason have to say on the matter. But maybe I've been overthinking the Jack thing—he's been a dick to everyone, and maybe I'm feeling it the most fiercely because he and I are the closest.

XII.

Of the 950 employees of the Midtown Grand Hyatt, nearly three dozen had been there since its Trump-backed renovation and subsequent reopening in 1980. A few had arrived fresh from the hotel administration programs in Ithaca and Lausanne to begin de facto apprenticeships in upper-tier mass-market hospitality; others had begun as desk attendants or dishwashers and worked their way up to managerial positions by sheer grit. Some had arrived as bartenders or bellhops and stayed bartenders or bellhops, and after three decades carried out their work with what struck guests as a monastic fealty to the four walls around them. These veterans' most valuable wisdom was in the fact that they knew this, and so they practiced their soft rabbinical smiles, the breasts of their uniform jackets fattened by fist-size wads of twenties.

In these three decades, this small league of old-timers had negotiated, executed, served, and cleaned up after more than four thousand events in the Empire State Ballroom, which occupied the entirety of the Grand Hyatt's third floor. It was roughly eight times the size of the hangars in which the National Transportation Safety Board reconstructs crashed jetliners; its occupancy limit of three thousand spoke mostly to the litigation-averse conservatism of the New York City fire code. It existed mostly for things like pharmaceutical shareholder meetings and medical association conferences—easy-to-execute, easy-to-cater affairs—but each December, the hotel's managers and staff began preparing the vast space for the Poinsettia Ball, with a grim resignation that with each passing year seemed to penetrate their collective soul a bit more deeply.

The day before the Poinsettia Ball, as several hundred adolescents at boarding schools across the northeast submitted their last preholiday assignments and double-checked their train reservations to Manhattan, the hotel's Food and Beverage Director held a refresher meeting with his bartenders on how to spot a counterfeit driver's license. This was an academic ritual: the teenagers would be drunk when they arrived, and they would be drunker when they left. Policies enumerated on the back of the invitation sent out over Thanksgiving—*no backpacks, large handbags, or any other large personal items; young ladies may carry one small purse*—proved both unenforceable and easily circum-navigable; the following morning, empty Vitamin Water and Diet Coke bottles would spill across the ballroom's vast ocean of floor. The ball chaperones' primary disciplinary task was to surveil the sea of intoxicated teenagers for the drunkest—the ones falling on their faces while dancing or vomiting into their hands—and to usher them out of the ballroom down to the taxi line on East Forty-Second. What happened to them next was beyond the chaperones' concern. This, of course, was precisely the point: to shift liability away from both the Hyatt and the Manhattan women's league that had orchestrated the event in the service of some ever-shifting philanthropical effort every Christmastime for half a century. By some spectacular miracle no teenager had ever turned up dead.

Early every November, one thousand invitations were printed on squares of card stock and sent out in prestamped envelopes to a thousand addresses, taken from a list curated by the daughters and nieces and adolescent family friends of the social league's members. In the days that followed, postal workers in towns like Andover, Massachusetts, and Wallingford, Connecticut, would take note of the identical envelopes that crowded the bins they set aside for the local boarding school, where students would spend that week rehearsing indifference as they checked their campus mailboxes. More than a few of them would ultimately find themselves doing their best not to cry before their empty slot, watching the thin girls with clearer skin apathetically slide their envelopes into expensive handbags.

Over Thanksgiving break, these girls would go with their mothers to the Neiman Marcus in Short Hills or the Saks boutique in Greenwich to try on dresses; the boys would drive to their parents' preferred formalwear shops and stand uncomfortably as old men in tweed suits fitted them for tuxes. These rituals brought the event into sudden imminence, and over iChat that week they would begin negotiating the evening's logistics. In the three weeks between Thanksgiving and the Poinsettia Ball, rumors of after-parties in some friend of a friend's Upper East Side apartment or at a Lower East Side bar metastasized to Gatsbyesque proportions before collapsing under their own untenable grandiloquence; in the end, almost everyone would wind up finishing the night alongside five or six of their school friends, drinking the last of the water-bottle vodka on some corner along Fifth Avenue or slipping a bottle of gin from the back of some Manhattan classmate's living room liquor cabinet.

Even still, many years later, they would look back on the night as nothing short of magnificent.

For Foster, the two and a half weeks between Thanksgiving and Christmas breaks that year were colored by a broken pastiche of his nighttime encounters with Porter. Everything else—the silvery chill that had hung over campus and occasionally burst into flurries; the bow-spangled garland along the House porches; the happy earnestness that even the teachers seemed to bring to class as the holiday approached—had been lost in the rigid alignment of this mosaic's pieces, taut with an anxiety that never really went away, only got more familiar. With a pang of longing he could not name, he found himself craving the lonely spell of those two and a half weeks the year before, which now seemed poignant in the press of their sadness. He found himself thinking of how beautiful the campus had once seemed in the clarity afforded by his past solitude, when being at Kennedy felt like he had intruded upon some magical, gorgeous secret to which he wasn't privy.

And sometimes, when he couldn't sleep, he would think about Annabeth finding him in the Meadow on the night of Lessons and Carols a year before. When everything was over, he would see that it was in that ephemeral moment, as the chapel behind them swelled with warm light and their breaths broke against the cold, that he'd come closest to grasping Kennedy's cosmic mystery without shattering it. Things had changed afterward: the loneliness had receded, but so too did the mystery itself. Its wonder had always been in its inscrutability, and in its retreat it left behind only the crude scientific-instrument data that had been obtained in its brief moment of proximity. The slow explication of this data over the months that followed would produce knowledge at the expense of radiance. In this sudden, short perihelion, the magic's gravitational tug had nudged him from the axes upon which he'd begun to learn to orbit its starlit field.

Like all minor adjustments in axial tilt, the consequences of this wobble were largely imperceptible. The deregulation of lunar rhythms softened its salty tides; sunlight was pulled up towards once-frigid northern latitudes, spilling new grasses and lichens across their rocky beaches. The silver flows of light in the aurorae overhead broke free from the poles and strung themselves out over the darkness of the plains below, but in their proliferation, they thinned. In the months after that night in December 2008, Foster Dade would sometimes recognize his new estrangement from the prior boreal magic. At certain moments, when the right electromagnetic tributaries aligned at the right geotemporal coordinates, Foster would feel the shimmer of that capricious beauty. But then it dispersed, and there was a new empty silence to his continued transits, their emotional gulf streams waveless and unlit by the explosions of starlight above.

"Sofi's parents aren't in the city—tbh I think it'll be cool if you stay there with me after the ball instead of going back to Pritchett's," Porter had texted him the night before the start of the holiday. "Wish you'd joined tonight by the way."

They were all going to Vito's for dinner, Porter and Jack and Annabeth and the rest of them, already changed into their chapel dress for Lessons and Carols. The pizzeria would be past capacity, as it always is on the last evening before a holiday, and Foster pictured them delighting in the effusive clamor of it all—in how, two and a half years on, they still reoriented a space's collective gravity when they entered it together.

But Foster would remain in his room, kneeling before his closet, pulling smooth capsules of Adderall XR one by one from the little Tupperware with his index finger and jotting their tally on the legal pad by his knee.

No addral this time, Alexei had said via BBM the week before, without elucidating. *Gave u Vivanc mg70 instead. Worth more but same price. Crazy shit. Also fifteen Oxy. Christmas Present* ☺☺ *Msg me when Jae sends $.* The parcel had arrived the day before Lessons and Carols. Seventy milligrams, he knew, was Vyvanse's highest denomination, and the idea of it had always frightened and fascinated him, for the same reason that the jugs of Everclear and Bacardi 151 had frightened and fascinated him when they'd been brought out at parties with the panache of some gimmicky but mesmerizing magic trick. There was something sedate about the staid blue-and-white capsuling of lower doses, calling to mind the steadfast, dignified image of a storied and well-managed national rail service, but the 70 mg was unlike any medicine Foster had seen before. The pills were cerulean on one end and the angry orange-red of a dystopian rust on the other. It was a visual crime, the pairing of these colors. The effect was violent, and almost aggressively cautionary in what it seemed to tell the patient. They invoked chemotherapy, or treatments for acute radiation sickness after a nuclear disaster: chemical treatments that by some violent utilitarian calculus would ravage and sicken the body in the interest of healing it. *Well, if you really want to get better . . .* they seemed to say, menacingly.

He'd only just begun sorting through his closet's small hidden chamber when he heard the knock on his bedroom door. He'd jerked upright so suddenly in his fear that the floor's coarse carpeting had

skinned his knee. "Yeah?" he'd called weakly, fleetingly imagining
Mr. McCall or Ms. Chissom or both standing out in the hall.

"Yo."

Jack was wearing his father's old Barbour jacket over his blazer
and tie for Lessons and Carols. It was a bit too large, the jacket, and
many seasons of sleet and cold rain had chafed its wax to a weathered
olive brown. Little pink seashells spangled the navy of the Vineyard
Vines tie he'd worn to Homecoming. His hair was still wet from the
shower, and his cheeks were rosy.

"Which do you want and how many." Foster hadn't intended his
voice's hollowness, and the candor of what it betrayed both gratified
and frightened him. For a moment, there was a bewilderment in Jack's
eyes. Foster felt his stomach clench, hating himself for pointing to the
very reckoning he had for three months so desperately craved. He
was not sure if he was only imagining that Jack feared it too, but in
any case he felt a profound gratitude for the response that ultimately
came, which was only sheepish.

"Uh, I'm not—I actually—" and here Jack looked down to the
thighs of his sweatpants. "We're all going to Vito's before Lessons and
Carols if you wanna come. Annabeth's here, downstairs."

"Ah, yeah, Porter texted me. But nah." There was still a distance
to Foster's voice, but he let its edges soften. "I've got a bunch of packing to do. Only remembered like ten minutes ago that we're leaving
tomorrow." He let himself grin. "Thank you, though."

Jack's face seemed to relax. "No worries, breh," he said, and
then he grinned too, and Foster chose then to pretend there was no
artifice in this nonchalance, to believe in the negation of the things
it negated. "We'll have a lotta time to chill this weekend. Poinsettia,
beetch." And then he turned to leave, but before Foster could close
the door, he halted.

"Oh, yo—since you, uh, mention it." There was a different, cheaper
artifice to his grin now; a new, self-serving sheepishness. "Could I
actually get, like—four or five of the Vyvanses? The sixties? For break.
SAT studying."

A pause.

"What would you say to seventy."

And when the grounds beyond his window were quiet, Foster and Jae stepped out into the night and to the edge of the golf course, and as they stood there in the darkness smoking the joint Jae had rolled, they heard the distant throb of the chapel organ. Foster passed back the joint and watched its faint glow dance up in Jae's face as he inhaled. The night was cold and still, and then against it came the thin but unmistakable sound of eight hundred voices joined in song.

They'd started drinking on the platform at Princeton Junction. As they stood before the automated ticket machine, each tide of cold wind that found credence in the openness of the station's vast parking lot brought one or two fat errant flakes that didn't fall as much as tumble across the late afternoon. "Well, since it's fucking freezing, and since we've survived the first half of Third Year mostly unscathed," Pritchett said grandly as the distant lights of the northbound 4:12 express pressed closer through the gray, reaching down into the duffel bag on the platform's cold concrete, "we might as well cut to the chase." He pulled out a virginal handle of Myers's dark rum, the provenance of which he proudly declined to disclose, and when Will Thierry finished its last half-sip with a bashful grin just before the train slowed to the platform at Rahway, Pritchett went back into his bag and retrieved another. Foster looked out the window with his hand in Porter's, watching the reflection of Annabeth's head on Jack's shoulder bend and ripple against the passing slide of New Jersey. When the bottle was passed to him, he took it and drank.

The dark afternoon collapsed prematurely into nighttime under the spell of their drunken movement across Manhattan. They kept drinking. They'd parted ways with the girls outside of Penn Station, all of them pale and luminescent in the silver-blue of lower Midtown, golden headlights shattering against the plastic protective bags that sheathed their tuxedoes and crinkled as they climbed into their taxis.

In their drunkenness, the Pierces' apartment seemed swollen with something as warm as candlelight. Pritchett's sister Cecily, who had finished her fall semester exams at Harvard the afternoon before, was sitting at the breakfast table overlooking the trickle of light along East Seventy-third, reading a novel by Junot Díaz, with a near-empty mug of tea to one side and what looked like a gin and tonic to the other. He would remember that they'd talked about Díaz (she found him pretentious; he liked the way he wrote about sadness), and about her own plans for the evening (drinks with old friends from Chapin; early bed). As her youngest brother and his friends gave their black bow ties a final fidget and prepared to set out into the night, she'd looked back to her book and smiled the learned and pleasantly patronizing smile of someone who had stood where they stood not long before.

The curious but essential truth of events like the Poinsettia Ball is that the event itself is incidental. By this I mean that these happenings function chiefly as a sort of orbital object, gravitationally dense in its spatial and temporal boundedness, around which a broader and more complex cosmos of activity takes shape. So it was for Foster Dade, who in the desolation of the days that followed would find himself returning in his mind to the dance in search of some suddenly salvaged memory: one that might emerge from the blackout and elucidate the calculus that had culminated in what happened afterward.

They found one another in the press of drunken bodies leaving the ballroom, in which there was then a frenetic and ambitious but ultimately evanescent flurry of unsuccessful strategizing: on the mezzanine, Frances had shrieked upon seeing a childhood friend from either Far Hills or Nantucket who'd said a Deerfield crew was heading to a Mexican bar on the Lower East Side; the girl had promised to text Frances and then promptly disappeared. Pritchett, who at some point had repurposed his untied bow tie as a headband, had spent the evening shouting cryptically about a Buckley friend at Hotchkiss named Steve Langford. "Stevie!" Pritchett shouted repeatedly into his BlackBerry as they idled along a stretch of Lexington. "Stevaay!" He was very drunk.

"I refuse to spend the next three hours walking around Midtown waiting for a plan to materialize," Mark said, sliding a Marlboro from a pack he'd pulled from his tuxedo jacket's pocket.

"Executive decision," Annabeth said, sticking her arm out to a westbound taxi on Forty-fifth. Foster realized she, too, was very drunk. "We're burning daylight. Back to Sof's."

"Right, because it's your house," Sofi muttered to Gracie. In her intoxication she said this loudly, in a sort of whine, but Annabeth either did not hear her or pretended she hadn't. An hour earlier, alone in the crush of bodies on the ballroom's dance floor, Foster had pulled the crumbling half-moon of Adderall IR from the breast pocket of his tux jacket and let it disintegrate under his tongue. They had moved from the Hyatt up Lexington in a wobbling sort of semicolon. Dotting the group behind them all were Jack and Mason. Something about their removed distance seemed deliberate and agitated, and when Foster glanced back Jack seemed to be leering. He realized he had not seen Jack and Annabeth exchange words since parting outside Penn Station many hours earlier.

"You okay?" Porter said, appearing suddenly at his side, sliding her arm through his.

"Oh—yeah, for sure," Foster said distractedly, watching Annabeth hail a second cab while pulling herself into the first. Porter seemed very far away; the idea of meeting her gaze seemed suddenly unpleasant. He was quiet in the taxi uptown, and next to him he felt her silent helplessness and bafflement as his hand hung limp in hers.

It wasn't yet midnight when they found themselves in Sofi's living room. The Cohens' apartment occupied the southern end of their building's thirty-first floor, where its expressionless sandstone rise narrowed into a steep ziggurat of duplexes and penthouses with views of the park a block west. It was a newer building, at least within the geological history of the Upper East Side's stoic residential canyons. With a small but expensive militia of interior designers, Rhona Cohen had waged war on the apartment's parquet-floored affectlessness when she and Donald had bought it in the late 1990s, replacing it with a more contemporary brutalism that reminded Foster of the perfunctory furnishings of a living room in a porn film. Sofi had disappeared and returned with two handles of Absolut and two of Jose Cuervo, clutching the vodka handles' necks and cradling the tequila like infant twins. With a drunken stumble she'd slid them onto the living area's vast glass coffee table, where Freddie was spilling a small hill of cocaine from what looked like a Saran wrap satchel he'd taken from his jacket pocket.

In the days and weeks that followed, in the private litigations that would ultimately dictate the course of the months thereafter, they would concede that they'd all been almost uniquely fucked up, in a way they hadn't been together since Sofi's house in the Hamptons that August. Though they lacked the words to articulate it, several of them seemed to understand that on this night there was something darker in their intoxication that hadn't been there in August, something uncomfortably close to a form of passive violence. If it was aggression, it lacked a referent or cause, until it didn't.

They'd been playing Cheers Governor with drams of tequila poured into plastic cups, kneeling around the glass table. Every few minutes, one of them would reach over to one of the coffee table books Sofi had beached at a far corner—*Portraits of the Promised Land: Israel at 50*; *The Shores of Long Island*—and with little pretension or fanfare do a small line of the cocaine Freddie had scraped onto their covers with an American Express card. Only Will Thierry would abstain. "I like that you don't do coke," Foster had told Porter once. "I mean, I wouldn't give a shit if you did, but I like that you don't do shit because other people are." She had returned from the bathroom with Sofi and Frances, her eyes glassy and red. Foster was not sure if he'd only invented the glower of spitefulness that burned fleetingly across her face as she took the rolled twenty from Gracie. "Welcome to the cool kids' club, Rothie," Freddie had said after cutting her a child-sized little line with the Amex, and when they'd all laughed afterward as she violently rubbed her nose with the palm of her hand, she grinned with self-conscious satis-faction, and then looked across their uncomfortably conspicuous distance to Foster, who was sitting on the other side of the expanse of glass. Her grin didn't falter, which made the darkness that then fell on her face more poignant, and Foster saw that her eyes were still rheumy and bright.

The plain fact is that I just don't like drinking games, Foster wrote in his first Blogspot entry after that night. *Never have. Not sure why. I think I'm just allergic to any sort of public competition unless it's something I know I'm good at. Point being: I always find an excuse to leave.*

The hallway from the kitchen to the small bedroom was long and dark enough to permit closing the door behind him. Foster exhaled and sat at the end of the bed. The Cohens' building rose higher than its neighbors, and beyond the room's wide window was only the hazy ocher of the urban night sky. The noise of the others came from down the hall, and there was an almost sickening powerlessness to his estrangement from it. He realized that his depression was back. It was in this dearth of hope that he reached into his jacket. Against a battered pack of Camel Blues Jae had left in his room many weeks earlier, he found the small Ziploc from which he'd taken the Adderall.

The pills in the small bag he'd found in Alexei's most recent shipment were white and nondescript little disks; they could have been aspirin, or Smarties. He had taken one from its bag, and in the light of his room's desk lamp he saw that its inscriptions had been worn down with what looked like either age or handling or both. He'd held the pill under the light and with his free hand pecked out its discernible characters into Google, which informed him that it was indeed *Oxycodone 10 mg, generic (Jiangsu Wuxi Pharmaceutical Co., China)*. He'd poured the little satchel into the Ziploc of brittle Valiums and Adderall IRs and Lunestas with which he traveled through the world.

Five months had passed since that night in Hong Kong, and in that time he'd thought about the merciful incapacitation of the pill Alexei had given him there in Jae's apartment. The arrival of the painkillers had frightened him in the blissfulness of its possibility. He sat there alone in the Cohens' guest bedroom and studied their shape for a moment, letting the bag sit limp in his open fingers. And then he heard the stifled noises of the far living room, its alienating choir sharpened by the lines of cocaine he'd done, and he felt himself open the bag and remove a single pill.

"We've moved on, Dade," Freddie said from his perch on the couch. "Never Have I Ever. Let's do it."

Even before he felt the spill of the Oxy, Foster realized that he was drunker than he'd been when he left his spot on the floor, and with a certain benumbed apathy he returned to it. He poured a loose splash of tequila into his cup and held his fingers up.

There was something banal about the depravity of the questions, as there almost always was. The secrets they invoked portrayed a vivid but shallow and sanitized sexuality, reduced to its mechanics and politics, its embarrassment impersonal. "Never have I ever—broken Parietals and snuck into someone's room to hook up." "Never have I ever hooked up with two people in the same night." (Gracie brought her finger down with a shrug of indifference.) "Never have I ever—come on someone's face, or had my face . . . come upon," Pritchett concluded philosophically. (Another finger for Gracie, who looked bored. Foster did not look at either Annabeth or Jack.)

After Pritchett was Jack. *The Shores of Long Island* had come to rest in a permanent home before him on the table, and there was a smear of white just below his nostril. His hair was leonine in its disarray. The surliness with which he'd left the dance had metastasized into something more ruthless under the spell of the cocaine. He was still silent, but there was a violence to it: every now and again, after taking a line, he'd train his eyes upon some cross-section of activity before him and smile derisively to himself, amused by what the fierceness of his eyes suggested to be the private reflexive sadism behind them. Annabeth was sitting on the couch to Foster's left, across from Jack, and she seemed consciously engrossed by whatever was not her boyfriend.

As they looked to Jack, he seemed to leer, as if impersonating Mason. "Huh," he said in a cruel impression of thoughtfulness, then ran a fingertip along the book before him and rubbed the coke's smeared residue against his gums. "Let's see." He looked suddenly at Annabeth, who was avoiding his eyes, and as he turned back to the group his smile widened with malice. "Never have I ever . . . had . . . a pregnancy scare"—and as Jack paused here for effect, Foster saw both Gracie's and Frances's pinkies twitch downward—"and had to take a fucking bus to Planned Parenthood . . . because a condom—dripped jizz on my stomach."

Foster understood from the palpability of the silence that followed that he alone lacked access to the meaning and magnitude of Jack's words. The boys looked away in embarrassment—except for Mason, who snorted. "Jack—" Will said tentatively. And then the silence broke.

"You fucking asshole."

This wasn't Annabeth but Porter. Jack seemed mildly taken aback by the fact of this aggression, and for a moment Foster thought he was going to train his malice on her, or him, but then the other girls came to her aid. "Really not cool, Albright," Gracie said, though her voice hadn't completely shaken its normal indifference.

"Don't fucking try me, Jack."

It may have simply been the edge of the coke, but there was a vehemence to Annabeth's words that Foster had not heard before. She rose to the sliding glass door to the apartment's terrace, managing to withhold her tears, though her eyes were starlike and clear with their weight. Jack gave a theatrical shrug and leaned down to do a small bump of coke. Mason cackled at this. Foster was staring up at Annabeth, and he wanted very badly for her to meet his gaze. But she only blinked, and before anyone could see her cry, she turned and stepped out into the terrace's darkness, closing the door behind her.

"Well," Mark said finally.

"Seriously, what the fuck is wrong with you, Jack," Sofi said. "In what fucking universe do you say that to someone."

He shrugged again, and then reached for his tequila.

Other than the necessarily imperfect account we find in Foster's subsequent private writings, the only useful record of that hour comes from Will Thierry, who was drunk by his own standards but would be still able to fill the gaps in his friends' recollections in the days that followed. A decade later I would be startled by both his ability and his curiously philosophical willingness to rehearse the events of that night as he'd witnessed them. We got there in our first meeting, which followed an hourlong phone call the week prior. (During that call, he'd mostly listened as I explained my project within an inch of its life, in what I retrospectively understand as an anxious attempt to convince not only him but myself of its merits.)

"The whole thing," he told me at the J.G. Melon near NYU, where he was a second-year law student, "was in hindsight just—really sad. Not sad as in pathetic—sad as in, well, sad."

As Will remembers it, the night had recovered thereafter, with a quickness that makes sense only if you've spent an evening with strong-willed people under the capricious influence of too much alcohol and too much cocaine. They'd responsibly gone back to Cheers Governor, and at some point—Will believes this was shortly after Foster rose from the coffee table—Sofi and Mark had the idea to make hot toddies at her parents' stove. The congregation would follow them to the stools around the white kitchen island, upon which Mason and Pritchett decided to play beer pong with red wine splashed into the Cohens' water glasses. The night had been flirting with languor and then sail-deflating crisis there on the couches, where refuse and spillage accumulated in a sort of metaphor before them on the coffee table, and the relocation to the kitchen seemingly restored things. In their reinvigoration, they either did not notice or did not care that Annabeth had not rejoined them. So they also gave negligible or no thought to how, early in the final round of the Cheers Governor redux, Foster Dade had stood from the floor and reached into his jacket.

"I'm gonna go have a cigarette."

"Cigs?" Freddie said eagerly, looking up at him and beginning to rise, but before Foster's regret could give shape to an excuse, Frances had grabbed his wrist and tugged him back down to her side. "No, you're going to mess me up if you go," she squealed plaintively. And Freddie shrugged with a self-satisfied resignation, grinning up at Foster and sitting back next to Frances, closer to her than he'd been before.

He was unsure of how much time had passed since Annabeth had closed the terrace door behind her. It may have been five minutes; it may have been two hours. He was beginning to feel the Oxy's gentle warmth spilling into the wider spell of his intoxication, and in the glow it brought, he oddly felt more sober. He sat there with it, and then he stood and reached for his jacket. Freddie had immersed himself back in the game, and no one else looked up as he opened the door and stepped out into the night.

She was standing at the terrace's southwestern edge, just beyond where it tucked around the corner of the building, guarded from the view of the living room doors and the light that spilled from them. There was a curious perfection to the darkness in which she stood. Her silhouette took its shape against the colored effluence of the Manhattan night, which smeared red and then green with the circadian rhythm of the stoplights thirty stories below. She was looking south toward Midtown. Foster paused for a moment at the edge of the yellow rectangle of light that fell onto the patio, pulling a Camel from the pack and hanging it from his lips before stepping out toward Annabeth.

"You've gotta appreciate the comedy of you taking a Hanover County bus."

She jerked her head toward him, startled. In what light there was he could see there were soft pale paths where tears had slid through her makeup. She pondered him for a moment as he stepped into her sluice of darkness, and then she began to laugh. It was the laugh Foster had heard that first night on the Brennan House porch, earnest and unabashed and almost conspiratorial, and as she laughed Foster realized that she was still crying. She looked at him again, this time with something that seemed childlike in its desperation, and as she turned away toward the darkness her shoulders began to shake. There was something to these shudders that seemed irreparably broken. With a strange lurch Foster understood that what he was seeing was something that few people in Annabeth Whittaker's life had. The city seemed still. Beyond the other end of the terrace, Central Park began the vastness of its sprawl. Then she looked back to him, more evenly now.

"I refuse on principle to ask you for one of those just because I'm upset," she said finally, jerking her chin toward his cigarette, "but if you're planning on actually lighting it, I would very much enjoy a drag."

The first inhale from the Camel seemed to stretch along the quiet majestic highways the Oxy was spanning within him, and suddenly its warmth was warmer, syncopating in a strange magic with the shimmer of the lights of Manhattan before them. He studied the cigarette in his fingers as he passed it to her.

"It's not even a big deal, all things considered," she said after exhaling a thin cone of smoke. "Pregnancy false alarm, whatever. It's just—the whole thing. Sex with him. It's like he hates me for it. I don't know. And he's on fucking Adderall all the time these days so a lot of the time he can't even get *hard*, and then he basically blames me for it, which, like, makes no sense, given that I know he's *on Adderall*." She seemed to realize the words she'd said only after she said them. "Don't repeat that—the thing about him getting hard. But I just, like—I don't know what I'm doing wrong. I don't know why he's so angry all the time. I just—"

And then she began crying again. Her sobs were noiseless, but she shook with wet, entropic jerks. Foster realized how little space there was between them.

"Hey," he said, and he felt himself bring his hand to her shoulder. After a moment her shaking slowed, and she reached up and felt his hand, as if contemplating its shape. She brought it down but held on to it by her waist.

"I'm so fucked up," she said finally, blinking tears free from her eyelashes and looking out toward the celestial mausoleum of the MetLife Building.

"Fucked-up drunk or fucked-up, like, psychologically."

"Both." With a wet sniff she rubbed her hand against her nose, and Foster thought unpleasantly of Porter doing her line of coke earlier, of the vulgarity of it. "I just think—I feel sometimes like I was designed poorly. I meant fucked up like drunk. But both."

"If it's any consolation, I go through life believing I'm fundamentally unable to connect with other human beings." He found himself willing his eyes to stay on hers, as if the freighted pull of his intoxication might reach her. By its miraculous logic it seemed to work. She looked to him.

"I felt that way until I met you."

He realized that his hand had slid more closely into hers.

"Me too," he managed to say.

"I was really hoping you'd come out here," she said. There was a new quietness in her voice, and in it he felt its vulnerability. *And no matter what, I am choosing to believe that she meant at least that.* In a moment that seemed to carry histories within it, he waited for her to look away out toward the darkness of the city. Instead her eyes met his, and he saw that they were again iridescent with tears. *My memory keeps trying to tell me that I wiped one away, but I realize now how fucked up I was, on booze and Oxy and I guess the coke too, and I feel like in the absence of certainty I default in my head to making things as cinematic as possible.*

And so I keep telling myself she kissed me back.

Of the many moments that interweave to comprise this story, some feel closer than others. In archival records or human consensus, tethers exist that let us grasp them as they may have been encountered then. Others lie just beyond their depths; from the closer vantage afforded by the more accessible archaeological base camps, we can discern their content from the cut of their shadows, sonar-like.

And others now belong to the deep. There aren't many of these. You'd be surprised by the complexities of what the more tenacious and ethically compromised journalists or investigators can piece together in the twenty-first century, if they know where to look in the planetary ether of data that metastasizes every hour with our most intimately mundane biographies. (For obvious legal reasons—it already took a good year of lawyering for the saintly editors at ███████████████ to finally let this go to print—I will here plead the Fifth.) And so there is something rare and indeed sad about those moments that have been truly lost to history, and rather than attempting to explicate their content with crude vicarious logics, we might allow ourselves to find their form and magic in the fact of their lostness.

What we do know is that for a brief, impossible moment on a cold night in December 2009, a sixteen-year-old boy named Foster Dade kissed a sixteen-year-old girl named Annabeth Whittaker on a rooftop against the shimmering possibility of Manhattan, this time with a deliberation that had been denied to him in the lake below the mountains four months prior, and that he loved her, for the same reasons that he understood the beauty with which history recedes into distant twilights. We can pretend very briefly, as he did, that she let his lips meet hers, for reasons that eluded him and will elude us. And then we can let it fall away again and tumble almost lazily back down into the silver depths of what we cannot know, and watch the light hit it as it falls.

But we can say with some surety that he did not hear the sliding glass door open.

"Dade, what the fuck."

Jack Albright's face was bisected almost artfully by the darkness of the terrace. His expression defied simple diagnostics, and against its impenetrability Foster felt the thrall of fear with which higher-order mammals anticipate imminent violence. It was only later, without the moment's deluge of adrenaline, that Foster realized that as he'd turned toward the apartment, he'd felt Annabeth not only flinch but wipe the back of her hand against her mouth.

"What the fucking fuck." There was a hollow disbelief to his words, and despite everything Foster heard in it a lucidity he had not heard in Jack's voice in any months.

"Jack, I didn't—it was Foster," Annabeth said desperately, and as she moved to him Foster could see in Jack's face that he believed her honesty.

"Are you—fucking kidding me."

Just beyond Jack in the darkness was Porter. Both of them—Jack and Porter—seemed incapable of complex motion; they stood very still. There was something horrible about Porter's face, which had contorted with an unrecognizable, animalistic emotion. Annabeth now stood with Jack, pulling at his jacket in desperate entreaty. Foster saw then that the others had been moving out to the terrace too when Jack had halted, and they'd almost compulsively done the same, stalling beneath the shadows of the entrance's awning and attempting to comprehend what had happened.

Jack answered this question for them. "He fucking kissed her," he said, his voice louder now. Neither he nor Foster had moved. Foster stood marooned in the terrace's dark corner, keenly aware of the physical stalemate. In what felt like another unconscious evolutionary gambit, he finally stepped toward Jack, hearing himself speak as he did.

"Dude, I'm just really fucked up on these pills and I was just being funny—it wasn't any—"

For whatever coherence his mental presence may have had in those final hours, Foster was still under the anesthetic swell of opioids and alcohol, and despite the rage of Jack's shove and the violence with which he hit stone, he felt his body's impact with the patio only in its dizzying but painless vibrato. The pain would come later. Still it disoriented him, and it took him a moment to look up and see Jack leering over him.

"You fucking faggot," he said. "You fucking loser." And Foster only watched as Jack lifted his foot over his stomach.

"Jack, stop—don't hurt him."

Annabeth's words sounded very far away. Foster did not let his eyes try to find her. The others were around him now, their expressions unreadable. The exception was Mason Pretlow, who was sneering.

Jack paused for a moment, and seemed caught between proceeding to stomp against Foster's stomach and turning his violence to Annabeth. Then he brought his foot back to the stone, and as he did he leaned down toward Foster and let a fat plum of saliva fall to his face. It hit the bridge of his nose, and as he instinctively sat up it slid down to meet his lips. Before the memory of the humiliation grew too excruciating, Foster would try to parse exactly whose laughs he had heard in that moment. Mason's was the loudest and the most violent, Gracie's unmistakably cruel. He would tell himself that the others had been necessary exercises in loyalty, though this would become less comforting over the subsequent months, when those loyalties demonstrated their fortitude and capacity for weaponization. Freddie and Pritchett had laughed; so had Porter.

"You fucking loser," Jack said again. "Get the fuck out of here."

There was something safe about the vastness of Madison Avenue at that hour, wide and silent except for the occasional slide of taxis moving uptown. It was somehow nearly three. Because of the second Oxy he had swallowed on the long descent to the Cohens' lobby, Foster would remember the subsequent hours only in the protracted smudge of these empty, lamplit boulevards as they passed before him. That he had nowhere to go only vaguely bothered him. The next morning, Eduardo, the Pierces' doorman, would tell a very hungover Pritchett that his nice friend had appeared in the lobby shortly after three thirty, explaining with an eloquence that defied his conspicuous intoxication that he needed to get his bag from 12A, and that he had no key, and that he did not want to wake up Mr. and Mrs. Pierce.

He very quickly forced himself to forget those final moments in Sofi's apartment, though later he would still think of the first burn of hateful eyes as Sofi had led him to the elevator.

"Porter was sobbing in Sofi's bedroom, and I think Foster tried to go in there and talk to her," Will Thierry told me. "Freddie and Pritchett wouldn't let him—they were pissed too; everyone was. I think to most people it just seemed so—pointless. Like, why ruin everything?"

Will paused for a moment, and looked thoughtfully out the window of our booth. "We used to always go to the J.G. uptown, when we'd come to the city to get drunk," he said. "It was right by Pritchett's. But yeah." And here he looked strangely sad. "I sincerely really liked Foster, but I guess I was always sort of—scared of him." He smiled. "I was such a straightedge at Kennedy, and when I learned about the whole drug thing—I dunno. The way he sold them, but also the way he did them. Some of my friends were wild, but I never saw anyone get fucked up the way he did. And that night was the first time I really got freaked out by him. It just didn't seem like something a stable or happy person would do. Honestly, I think everyone else kind of felt the same way. Honestly—that might be why Jack and Mason didn't end up beating the shit out of him that night. We didn't know what else he might do. So we just made him leave. And he left."

. . . and I guess I just walked. I remember I kept thinking about the taxis that passed by me: who was inside them; where they were coming from; where they were going. I took half of an Adderall IR which kept me going.

I kept thinking about the night of Sofi's birthday party—when Jack and Annabeth and I walked until we reached the Brooklyn Bridge. I hadn't remembered that Annabeth had taken pictures until she posted them on Facebook early that summer, in a big album with a bunch of pictures from spring term. In them, we're standing there alone on the bridge with the city behind us, and you can tell that we're tired, even though we didn't realize that we were.

I'm kind of embarrassed at how satisfying it was to get the Facebook notification telling me that she'd tagged me in pics. I just remember my first few months at Kennedy, when I'd look at her albums and see them all together. I remember I would sometimes sit there and count how many contacts I'd added to my phone and how few pictures I'd been tagged in since starting school. Sometimes, when I was really lonely, I'd look at the profiles of older kids who'd either graduated or been kicked out, whose names I only knew through the stories that people told about them. I was the most fascinated by the kids who'd been expelled: I know being fucked up shouldn't make you interesting, but . . . it sort of does. I'd look at pictures of them doing the kind of stuff we were doing that night, and I'd wonder about the secrets of the lives they'd had for themselves at Kennedy, and it would all seem sad and profound within my own loneliness.

I keep going back to the pictures, as if staring at them will somehow restore things to how they were that night, when the three of us stood on the Brooklyn Bridge at sunrise and Annabeth wrapped her arms around us just as the city was beginning to wake up. For a few perfect minutes our lives belonged to something wonderful

And I realized then that I just loved them so much.

My phone died pretty much right after I left Sofi's apartment, which in hindsight was a good thing: all I wanted to do was call or text Annabeth or Jack or Porter. It's been five days and I haven't heard from anyone. I've seen them online on iChat, and once or twice their camera icons have been gray at the same time. A few times I've started typing out long messages and then deleted them before sending.

It was basically sunrise when I got to Penn Station. There wasn't really anything else for me to do. The lady at the Amtrak counter could see that I'd been crying, and she was really nice and let me rebook my ticket for free. I must have looked so stupid, standing there in my wrinkled tux. Right before I got on the train, I suddenly wanted to turn around and get a taxi back to Sofi's. I was sort of delirious from the comedown/lack of sleep, and I began to believe that none of it had really happened—that I'd fallen asleep in her guest bedroom and had a bad, vivid dream. And then I remembered that my body hurt.

I guess I should maybe write here that when I was walking downtown from Sofi's, I thought about how easy it would be for me to jump off the Brooklyn Bridge.

XIII.
Foster Dade's MacBook Pro/Music/iTunes/Playlists/january 2010 (Created January 12, 2010)

Name	Time	Artist
Sweet Disposition_RAC_Remix.mp3	6:31	The Temper Trap_YouTubeAudioDwnld
Time After Time	4:01	Cyndi Lauper
With or Without You	4:56	U2
I Think Ur a Contra	4:29	Vampire Weekend
Mr. Brightside	3:43	The Killers
Fake Empire	3:25	The National
All the King's Horses	4:20	Robert Plant
The District Sleeps Alone Tonight	4:44	The Postal Service
We Will Become Silhouettes	5:01	The Postal Service
Clark Gable	4:54	The Postal Service
Take It Easy (Love Nothing)	3:21	Bright Eyes
On Melancholy Hill	3:53	Gorillaz
So Here We Are	3:52	Bloc Party
Fix You	4:56	Coldplay
When You Were Mine	5:07	Cyndi Lauper
Free Fallin' (Live)	4:23	John Mayer
All My Friends	7:42	LCD Soundsystem
White Houses	3:45	Vanessa Carlton
Live to Tell the Tale	5:16	Passion Pit

19 songs, 1.6 hours, 148.4 MB

XIV.

Several times a week during study hall, Donavan House Master Doug Pratt marched from room to room with a clipboarded checklist he printed each Sunday from Microsoft Excel. The document contained each resident's name beneath a list of a dozen hygienic and organizational expectations, none of which could be found in Kennedy's annual Student Handbook. Boys who'd failed to make their bed or put their dirty underwear in a hamper received a demerit; three demerits meant a detention. That a teacher had built himself an extrajudicial deep state within Kennedy's wider polity was less distressing to administrators than it perhaps should have been: in his eighteen years on the Kennedy faculty, which he joined four years after returning from Kuwait and two after his first divorce, the school's varsity crew had won the national secondary school title ten times; and there were certain colleagues who quietly admired what they saw as Pratt's commitment to certain values in an epoch of their institutional softening. His eight-year tenure as House Master had rebranded Donavan House as a very unhappy place to live.

Theresa Daniels had spent nearly two decades alongside Doug Pratt in the Mathematics Department, and by all accounts relished her appointment as Dean of Students as a vacation from what she saw as his obdurate and tacitly misogynistic professional manner. So when she arrived in her office in Alumni Hall that gray morning in January 2010, she did not hide her annoyance with the day's appointment calendar, atop which was a fifteen-minute meeting with PRATT, D (9:00am–9:15am).

But for all his temperamental shortcomings, the military had imparted in Doug Pratt an unsentimentally Talmudic respect for chains of command and his place within them. It was Theresa Daniels who now had the office in Alumni Hall, and so it was Theresa Daniels to whom he brought the Ziploc of colorful pills he'd found wedged behind the cushions of Donavan's common room couch, seeking further instruction. The two capsules in the Ziploc had been flattened beneath the seat; the chalky orange disk had crumbled into oblong thirds. Though the bag lacked any discerning markings, his tour in the Gulf had taught him the merits of trusting his instincts, so before check-in that evening he walked from Donavan House to the infirmary, asking if the nurse practitioner on duty could take a look at something, and with her confirmation he scheduled the following morning's appointment in Alumni Hall.

After contemplating the pills for a moment, Mrs. Daniels told Mr. Pratt that it would be impractical to drug-test every boy in Donavan, as he'd proposed; she explained to him, somewhat guardedly, that the lab in nearby Hopewell only scanned Kennedian urine for marijuana and cocaine. "Those are the primary offenders, Doug, and these tests are expensive," she said, her annoyance returning. "For anything else we'd do a hair follicle test—and talk about expensive."

"But," she said finally, "keep an eye on things. Talk to your prefects and keep your duty team in the loop. If you see fit, bring it up at a House meeting. And Doug," she added as he stood to leave, "I appreciate your telling me about this."

And that night, Mr. Pratt took over check-in, and as each boy came through the common room he studied them quietly, looking for undue intensity in their affects and gait. There were those boys, of course, on whom he subconsciously allowed his scrutiny to falter somewhat. Willem Matheson, a bespectacled and friendless Second Year, returned to Donavan from the Science Olympiad team's weekly meeting just before eight o'clock. He checked in as he always did, presenting himself silently and unobtrusively before retreating. "Evening, Willem," Mr. Pratt said kindly, to a boy whose meekness had confounded and occasionally enraged him since the start of the academic year four months prior. And as Mr. Pratt studied the list of names, as if the neat checkmarks he'd ticked alongside them would somehow elucidate new forensic clues, Willem climbed the stairs to his second-floor single and opened his compact little Toshiba laptop to Facebook. In the eight months since he'd made his account, only three conversations had come to populate his Facebook Chat inbox, one of which was with his grandmother in Kansas City. He clicked on the most recent thread and began to type.

Hi Foster. I lost what I bought from you on Saturday. Can I meet
you in the library this evening?

XV.

"—and I'm personally a big fan of my own constitutional law syllabus,
but I think you should really consider Mrs. Cline's seminar on sub-
Saharan Africa next fall if you're—what the hell was that?"

Foster apathetically observed that it was the first time he'd heard
Mr. McCall swear. His House Master quite literally jumped when
the rock struck the window's glass. With the same apathy Foster
noted that of all the dull thuds of stone aimed in the direction of his
window in the weeks since the Poinsettia Ball, this had sounded like
the cleanest strike yet.

Mr. McCall moved across the room and leaned over Foster's bed to
pull back the drawn blind, cupping his hand to the dark glass. "Jesus
Christ—hold on, Foster," he said, and with a sudden agitation moved
out of the room and down the stairs to Brennan House's back door.
"Pretlow!" Foster heard him bellow. "Mason Pretlow!" Foster had
quickly become adept at forestalling the hot flush of humiliation, and
to that end he returned to his desk and placed his Bose headphones
back over his ears, silencing the sound of discipline below.

The first rock struck the edge of his windowpane on a weekday
afternoon three weeks prior. He'd been sitting at his desk then, too,
immersed in laying twenties and tens in loose stacks atop his Honors
Biology notebook. He had nearly toppled his desk chair backward
when the impact resounded against the glass. He'd quickly looked
out the window, heart pounding, and there on the walkway between
Brennan and Donavan he saw Jack, Freddie, Mason, and the Second
Year lacrosse player Chandler McDermott, laughing. Jack stuck a lazy
middle finger up in the direction of the second floor, and then they
carried on toward the Field House.

Several times a day thereafter, stones of varying size struck the
north face of Brennan House. McDermott and the other Second Years
on the lacrosse team had become sort of auxiliary junior members

of Jack and Mason's cabal, which in the first weeks of 2010 found
a new primary organizing principle in the torment of Foster Dade.
These younger boys were dumber or at least less clever than Jack and
Freddie and even Mason, and the tactics they refined in their desire
to impress the older boys were cruder, more bestial. They lobbed the
biggest rocks when they passed Brennan on the way to the library or
the Dining Center or sports practice. By mid-January, Mr. McCall's
small boys had started collecting the jagged chips of brick that had
fallen from the house's facade. That Foster had pulled his blinds
down in the first week of January and consciously angled his desk
lamp away from the windows made no difference: they threw the
rocks whether he was there or not. Mostly, the blinds were down
so they could not see his face when they did.

On a purely physiological level, the humiliation was more toler-
able than what he understood as an intense and almost implausible
paranoia. By the end of that first weekend back from Christmas break,
the sound of nameless Second Year boys laughing on their way back
to Arsdale House would make him tense up at his desk, bracing for
the short shudder of the rock's strike; by mid-January, he was flinching at the gravelly chafe of winter-stiffened car tires on the driveway
below. The fear spiked in these moments, but with time returned to
a baseline of ambient, uncurable nausea. When he left Brennan, he
would seek less-trodden paths, peering over his shoulder as he moved.
Presumably out of shame, Foster did not delve into the details of this
pain on his Blogspot, referring only vaguely to *the Ames guys* or *the
lacrosse assholes* or *my paranoia these days*.

The problem with "paranoia," however well it connotes his almost
physical misery in that period, is that it usually implies a fear that is
groundless or even irrational. But for all that we can say about the
state of Foster Dade's mental and emotional psychosphere in those
first months of the new decade, he was not delusional. If anything,
he proved adept at denying the precise magnitude of what he found
himself confronting.

Three days after my last conversation with Will Thierry, I received
an Instagram message from the handle @sir_friedrich_1. I hadn't ever

followed Freddie Pieters on social media, and I'd given little thought to
the possibility of reaching out to him: his place in this narrative always
struck me as merely incidental, a circumstance of shared friendships;
little in Foster Dade's extant archives gave me much of a reason to
think otherwise. *I wish I could crack the code of how Freddie gets
away with being so eccentric and still so (ugh) cool,* Foster had written on his Blogspot in his first term at Kennedy. *I also kind of know
that maybe for the same reasons, I'll never really know him—I'm not
sure that anyone does.*

His years at Wesleyan had mellowed him, I'd heard; those who
knew him there recall a boy who spent a great deal of time taking
MDMA alone and watching Kubrick films. His father had secured him
a private equity job in the city thereafter, though his Instagram suggests
he spends much of his time in St. Moritz and Shanghai. After cross-
checking his Instagram story with the timestamp of his message—*Yo
Willy T told me about what ur doing on Dade hmu*—I deduced that
he'd contacted me from a rooftop bar in Bangkok.

We would FaceTime the following day. He was considerably
heavier than he'd been at Kennedy, and I'm still not sure if my rather
startling impression of his amicability had something to do with this.
He chain-smoked Chesterfields as we spoke; he seemed to be in the
cabin of a yacht. Still unconvinced of the stakes, and halfway convinced I was being subjected to a practical joke, I found myself with
the confidence to shirk my normal platitudes.

"Listen, we were cunts," he told me when I turned to the winter
of 2010. "I'm just speaking generally. The way we walked around
campus—cunts. The way we hit on younger girls—cunts. The guys
older than us had been cunts, and we were cunts, and the guys younger
than us then got to be cunts. That was just Kennedy. Rich white kids
being rich white kids. And rich white kids are cunts."

"Is that how Foster would have described it?" I realized that I
rather enjoyed this stridence.

"Nah," he said. "I felt bad for Dade. Always a nice guy—smart as
shit, and fucking hysterical in his weird quiet way. It was just Pretlow,
y'know, and then I guess Albright got somehow twisted too."

"And what about you?"

From his phone's screen, Freddie appraised me. My directness seemed to stoke a sense of some kindred recognition in him; I had the sense that we were playing a friendly but high-combat game of chess.

"Yeah, like I said—cunts." There was something in the default nonchalance of his voice that I heard as sincerity. "Y'know—we were sixteen. Seventeen. Whatever. Sometimes it's easy just to go along for the ride—and I bet this sounds fucked up, but when you don't let yourself think about it, it can even be kinda fun."

It's a wretched cliché that bullies are cowards, but we can note without impugning our credibility as objective observers that Jack Albright and those who took up his cause—Mason Pretlow; Chandler McDermott and the defenseman on the lacrosse team named Thomas Connelly, whose vast neckless head made Foster think of a mugshot, or a thumb; to a lesser extent Pritchett Pierce and Freddie Pieters himself—were evasive and indeed craven in their infliction of cruelty upon Foster Dade. This fact did nothing to mitigate its success. The rock-throwing exercise gives us a tidy little allegory for the broader campaign: they moved in numbers and operated from a vantage that unfairly rendered their target vulnerable; their missiles were violent, but their deployment was calibrated to regulate in the offense's favor both the degree of consequential damage and the plausibility of a defensive counterstrike.

Most important, though, the assaults seemed calibrated to maximize the number of civilian witnesses. By the end of January, Foster realized that his jeans had loosened around his waist, and he found himself incising a new improvised notch in the leather of his Brooks Brothers belt with a nail. He went to the Dining Center late each afternoon for his silent early dinner but found himself avoiding it otherwise. He looked with dread to Mondays, when he had no choice but to show up in Brennan's dining pod for the weekly House lunch. He did his best to stand up from the table and clear his plate as soon as McCall wrapped things up, so he could pass through the front doors into relative freedom before the boys in Ames and the attending females congregated on the fat leather couches along the lobby's high windows. It was on one of these occasions in the last half of the month that he saw a small cluster of Second Year boys standing by the wide bulletin board along the foyer's wall. One of them saw Foster and prodded his friend, and they looked to him and snickered before basically scampering away.

Though its membership would eventually quadruple each year as the decade ticked on, in early 2010 the Kennedy Gay-Straight Alliance was nothing more than a ragtag triumvirate consisting of the Fourth Year Carlton Magdalan and two of his female friends. It was an ad hoc operation: Lorin Parsons, who'd agreed to serve as their required faculty advisor, would forget that the club existed until the one or two times per year that Carlton approached her with a plan for some public invocation of solidarity. That winter, they had colonized the wide bulletin board in the Dining Center's downstairs foyer for what they called a "Tolerance Wall." On a vast rectangle of white poster paper, the KGSA had glued the images they'd printed—nominally depicting representatives of various marginalized identities—next to little blocks of text they'd cut into the shape of speech bubbles, each declaring some pithy little affirmation of pride.

It had been on display for almost a week before that lunchtime, though Foster of course hadn't seen it until then. As the Second Years fled the scene, he paused to study the apparent object of their amusement. The display was minimalist in its design, and so his eyes almost instinctively snagged on the sole aspect that deviated from its simplicity.

The man in the stock photograph was probably around his father's age, maybe a bit younger, standing before a desk in a nondescript corporate office. Given their brevity, the words within his speech bubble were larger than his neighbors', lending a heft to his declaration "I am a proud homosexual!" Foster looked at this, and then back to the upper margin of the printed image, where his eyes had stopped. There, in penciled block letters, someone had written FOSTER DADE.

It was by some rare act of mercy that no one—not least the boys in Ames—had seen him tear the photograph from the wall. It was with the same agitation that he'd recently found himself compulsively checking Facebook several times per hour, looking down below his classrooms' wooden tables to the BlackBerry in his lap. He'd been

staring idly at his phone while crossing campus the previous week
when he saw on its crude Facebook app that he had seventeen notifications. The paranoia was still only incipient then, but something
about this bothered him. As he clicked on the little red numeral, he
saw Jason Stearns and Noah Baum leaving Fenster Hall. In the weeks
since Christmas, he'd found refuge in his *Kennedian* co-writers; if he
knew Jack et al. were at an away game, he'd go with them to Vito's.
They were happily oblivious to his suffering, and he was both grateful
for and miserably envious of their ignorance, of the good-natured
ease with which they'd built a home for themselves at Kennedy with
no regard for the politics to which he himself had succumbed. They
cheerfully stopped for a moment, and as they then made their way
onward to Arsdale House, Foster saw that his phone had died under
the shock of the winter cold. He jogged back toward Brennan, and
after declaring himself checked in to Ms. Chissom he went to his room
and stood before his MacBook.

The notifications were identical in their wording. *Mason Pretlow,*
Chandler McDermott, and three others liked your picture. Mason
Pretlow, Chandler McDermott, and three others commented on your
picture. He felt the nausea intensify in its horrid heat and forced
himself to click.

He had forgotten about the photos in question, which he'd posted
three and a half years earlier to populate the blank shelves of the
Facebook account he'd made that morning. They were old even then:
mundane scenes from seventh- and eighth-grade happenings; scenes of
middle school boys doing the things they do for rebellious thrills before
they discover alcohol. There he was with Max Frieholdt at Chelsea
Rosenbaum's fourteenth birthday party, wearing the bras they'd found
in a downstairs hamper; there they were at the Forever 21 in the Towson
Mall, mugging with a bikini-clad mannequin. Later, against future del-
uges of the same nature, he would find meager solace in the knowledge
that anyone who encountered the comments in their News Feed might
interpret them by default as harmlessly ironic teasing between friends.
But he also knew that many of the people who saw them would know
that they were not that. Below him and Max and the mannequin:

Freddie Pieters: did you hook up with her?!?!?!?

Mason Pretlow: oh wow she's hot . . . i know you've had some issues with getting hard but hopefully that wasn't a problem with her!!!!!!!!!!!!

Below them in Chelsea Rosenbaum's bras:

Thomas R. Connelly II: do you do this in brennan by yourself?

Chandler McDermott: oh wow sexy!!!!! you should model these for **Annabeth Whittaker.** Chandler had tagged Annabeth in this comment.

It took Foster fifteen minutes to delete the photos one by one before finally deleting the entire album to which they belonged, and another hour and a half to go through every image and artifact of content that he had shared or been tagged in over the previous three and a half years. He did this while cringing in humiliation at the disgrace of his own past behaviors; what had once seemed harmlessly silly now seemed to warrant the ridicule he had received. In the weeks that followed, when he'd log on to find that Jack or Mason or occasionally even Pritchett had posted on his wall or found some overlooked photo on which to comment, he considered deleting his profile altogether, or removing them from his list of friends, but the thought of that confession of injury sickened him. Their comments were always written in the same tenor, an effete register of mocking amicability. The prevailing theme was that Foster was gay, though in craftier instances they managed to wed this with opaque allusions to what had happened at Sofi's, or to his sexual history with Porter.

Foster's accumulation of Xanax and other benzodiazepines had spent the first months of the school year in an empty prescription bottle at the bottom of the cabinet in his closet. He'd been proud of how sparing he'd been with them in the fall, and when he finally opened their bottle back at school in January he counted three dozen pills in all, a medley of Xanax and Klonopin and a handful of Valium. By the end of the month he had worked his way through half of the bottle.

Btw, he'd said to Alexei over BBM one evening during Christmas break, *is there any way you could send me more Oxy? I'll pay this time obviously.*

He was frightened of the opioids and the elegance with which they so perfectly removed his anguish, and so when the crush of things became terminal, he forced himself to reach first for the Xanax. He'd spent Christmas break stoned on what remained of Alexei's oxycodone; he had no memory of the Christmas morning he spent with his mother and sister. When Alexei's first shipment of 2010 arrived in the Kennedy mailroom in his second week back at school, he found within it an unopened manufacturer's bottle that was slightly squatter than the others. *OxyContin*, it said in solemn blue letters. *The real thing—not generic!* Alexei had scribbled on the tear of paper taped to it.

It was no small miracle that Foster maintained his commitment to self-control that winter, because what the Oxy did—and to a different and less tactile extent the benzos did too—was itself miraculous: for a short, perfect stretch of hours, it made him not care.

It had been a Tuesday night in the third week of January when he'd been forced to return to the library for the sake of business. He chased the quarter-disk of Oxy and half of the little orange football of Xanax with Vitamin Water as he left Brennan. At nine thirty, when the library's staff moved silently along the stacks to gesture to their watches and then the exits, he realized he had been sitting in his study carrel for two hours, and that in that time he had not once felt afraid.

He'd been stepping out into the cold when he heard Chandler McDermott's violent laugh. Foster had disliked McDermott long before that winter, watching from afar the prior spring as the tall curly-haired boy from Basking Ridge did his best to flatter Jack Albright by emulating his horrible bravado. He saw him standing there beneath the streetlight over the driveway with Thomas Connelly; he wondered if they'd been waiting for him.

But to his delight he found himself indifferent. The flush of the drugs warmed him against the freezing night, and he stared straight at them as he walked. He consciously did not adjust his course as he passed them, and just before his backpack grazed Chandler's he allowed himself to smile with the amused apathy that in that moment seemed real. He wasn't sure if he'd imagined their slight wavering as he passed.

He was already across the driveway when he heard Connelly's voice. "Faggot." But there was a reservation to it, as if he'd realized right as he'd opened his mouth that Foster wasn't yet far enough away for him to attack confidently. And as Foster turned and walked casually back toward them, his smile wider, Connelly seemed to falter.

"Thomas, why do you have a 'Second' after your name on Facebook?" Foster asked evenly. "Are you a yacht?"

Connelly looked confounded.

"Why is—your name . . . Foster Dade," he said finally. "Are you a—gay porn star?"

Foster's eyes bulged almost reflexively at the stupidity of the comment. He felt himself grin.

"You're named after your father, Thomas," he continued. "I know this because I see him commenting dumb fucking things on your dumb fucking lacrosse photos. Is it weird that he's fifty and doesn't know to spell 'hustle'? If you're named after your father, you're a Junior, not a Second. Unless you're a boat. Are you a boat, Thomas?"

"Get the fuck out of here, Dade, you druggie faggot." This was McDermott.

"*Druggie faggot.*" Here Foster assumed an effete, mincing voice, letting his hand go limp at his wrist for effect. "Speaking of weird—Chandler, is it weird for that First Year you're dating that you'd rather be sucking Jack Albright's dick? Lizzie, right? Does Lizzie know about your *crush*?" He said this last word with the same drawl. "I'm asking because I think Jack would probably let you, if you asked. Suck his dick, I mean."

For a moment Foster thought blandly that Chandler was going to punch him.

"At least Jack doesn't think I'm a clingy pathetic loser."

In the days that followed, when the drugs had faded and the nausea had returned, Foster would come back to McDermott's words and wince at their bite. But in that moment he laughed.

"On the contrary, Chan, I think *Jack*"—and here he delivered the effete whine in a baritone that uncannily echoed McDermott's—"probably thinks precisely that."

Another pause. "You're pretty tough when it's just two of us, Dade. Why don't you go back to Brennan and jack off to Annabeth."

Foster looked at them again, and with a happy shrug he turned and went. Only back in his room did he feel the kick of adrenaline, and to preempt it he returned to his closet and picked himself out another crumbled piece of Xanax.

Mr. McCall was gone for several minutes before he returned to Foster's doorway.

"Foolishness," he muttered. "He's a friend of yours, I take it?"

Foster blinked, then shook his head softly. "Not exactly."

"Well," and here Mr. McCall paused, as if finally comprehending the truth within whatever lie Mason Pretlow had told him, and for a moment his face was suddenly awkward. "Anyway. I was saying I think you'd really get a lot out of Mrs. Cline's class next fall. But the real reason I wanted to come by"—and here Foster flinched, and stopped himself from impulsively looking toward the closet—"is because I hadn't had a chance to talk with you about Jae. I know you guys were buddies, and I know how hard it can be when this happens to a friend."

Now Foster paused, as if waiting for Mr. McCall's words to betray a concealed knowledge. "Yeah, Jae was great," he said, holding his voice back from quickening. "You know I went to Hong Kong with him last summer. He didn't really have a lot of friends here, but for some reason we really got a kick out of each other."

Mr. McCall pondered this sympathetically. "Well, know that I'm always around if you want to talk about it—or anything else. It's always such a shame when something like that happens—just such a waste."

In the spring of 2004, following a rash of academic dishonesty cases in the English Department, Kennedy's administration had invested in a plagiarism detection software called CheckOver Plus. The consensus among the student body was that this was a wasted expense. This was a business appraisal, rather than an ethical judgment. CheckOver Plus was almost postmodern in its user-unfriendly complexity; a student who'd spent two hours on a paper then spent two more attempting to navigate the program's submission portal. But while the rest of the faculty had moved on with renewed faith in the stalwart simplicity of Kennedy's Honor Code, Anne-Marie Cline had spent several weeks mastering the counterintuitive technics of the software they'd largely abandoned. Her students did not know that she faithfully ran their submitted work through CheckOver Plus's unsparing dissections before grading it herself. That the software had presented no major infractions in half a decade did not impel her to contemplate either the efficacy of the software program she loved or the Honor Code she doubted.

On the night of the third Thursday in January, Mrs. Cline was on duty in Hewitt House. Both her standard and Honors U.S. History classes had submitted their first papers of the winter term that afternoon. As she always did, she would tackle the drudgery of grading the former first, saving the relative delight of her Honors students' more refined arguments like dessert. Shortly before ten o'clock, she clicked on the document submitted by Jae-hyun An and imported it into CheckOver Plus, which began to whir. She grimaced slightly—the boy, to the best of her knowledge, could not speak English—and then stood up, cracked her knuckles, and allowed herself a bathroom break.

She was washing her hands when she heard her computer begin chiming.

After five years in its standard grayscale, the window on her laptop's screen was red. *Possible Plagiarism Detected*, it read. *Would you like to view the infractions found?* Mrs. Cline did. Her initial and briefly crushing thought was that the software was defective. It hadn't identified singular instances of uncited material or undue paraphrasing; rather, it had highlighted the entirety of the four-page essay. *Original source located*, read a thin bar atop the document. *Would you like to view it?*

The homepage of the website in question contained only many lines of Korean text, some of which were hyperlinked. Mrs. Cline did not read Korean, so she set forth clicking the underscored links arbitrarily. But she could comprehend the text of the pages that followed, which were in English. Each contained a single paragraph—what she recognized intuitively after fifteen years of teaching as respectable if banal five-sentence paragraphs, with a thesis statement and transition, which set up respectable if banal arguments on their topics: *The Catcher in the Rye*; the history of the Electoral College; the pollution of eastern American watersheds. Below each block of text, where the first body paragraph should have been, there was only a string of Korean characters, followed by a rectangular gray icon containing the words *Pay With PayPal®*.

Later, Charlie Obermeier would say that he'd seen Mr. McCall leading Jae from Brennan across the lawn to Alumni Hall just after breakfast. "The dude looked totally unfazed—like he had no idea what was going on."

"He probably didn't," Nic Bergman would snort. "If my English was that bad I would have bought my essays too."

When Jae and McCall emerged from the administration building and returned to Brennan several hours later, the black Suburban was already parked out front, its besuited driver waiting expressionlessly on the front porch. Foster would tell Charlie that he'd been in the library, and that the Suburban and Jae had both been long gone by the time he'd returned.

In the days and weeks after Jae's expulsion, Foster would think about this lie. The truth is that he had been lying awake in bed after midnight the night before when he'd heard McCall's and Chissom's footsteps moving upstairs, and that the following morning he'd woken up to three notifications on BBM.

> **JAE [01:13:01AM]:** Hey Foster ~
> **JAE [01:13:01AM]:** I am in trouble for schoolwork and think will be expeled
> **JAE [01:13:01AM]:** I will not tell

The truth is that Foster had spent the day in a sort of nauseous dream, forcing himself to attend classes only because a sudden infirmary visit may have provoked suspicion. He would keep his distance from Alumni Hall between classes but cast furtive looks in its direction, toward the first-floor windows that looked into the Dean of Students' office. When the day was over, he returned to Brennan and locked himself in his room, and for the hour that followed he sat on his bed and listened to the sound of Jae's trunks moving down the stairs. With a heady sickness he waited for a knock on the door, but it never came.

In the days that followed, he continued to wait, and in a dark kiss of mercy the dread that had burned in him hotter with every successively thrown rock had been replaced by something grimmer and darker but less acerbic. He ignored the Facebook Chats and text messages that pinged upon his screens every afternoon, asking him if he'd be in the library. He moved a stack of Tupperware bins from beneath his bed to the floor of his closet, stonewalling the door to the small chamber within it; he considered disposing of his inventory altogether but couldn't bring himself to do it. It took him several days to finally find the nerve to message Jae, only to find that his Facebook account had disappeared, so he picked up his phone and went to BBM.

> **foster dade [11:10:44PM]:** Hey man. I'm really really sorry I didn't get to say goodbye before you had to go. It's so fucked up what happened. I really appreciate you not saying anything to anyone. I think I may be done with it for good now. I'm really going to miss you, and want to stay in touch. Are you back in Korea?

The check mark next to the message hung there empty for a moment after Foster pressed send, but the D indicating its delivery never appeared. It was still empty when he looked again an hour later. His phone finally hummed the following afternoon. With a lurch of fear and shame he scrolled to BBM, where Jae's name sat atop the list of messages in bold type. He opened it.

Your message could not be sent at this time. (ERR-984:
User does not exist.) Please try again later.

And then, on the second to last day of January, he was sitting at
his desk idly playing FarmVille when a new Facebook Chat dinged
into the bottom of the screen. He thought with brief excitement of
Jae, then looked to the message.

> **Willem Matheson:** Hi Foster. I just wanted to let you know
> that we just had a House meeting in Donavan about drugs.
> Apparently he found the pills I lost the other week.

> **Willem Matheson:** I'm letting you know because he told us
> that the administration thinks it was the Korean boy in Brennan
> who got expelled last week who may have been responsible.
> From the sound of it he thinks the issue is over. Just an FYI in
> case that's why you haven't been responding to my messages.
> Thanks

XVI.
SAT Score Report
Foster H. Dade
The Kennedy School
800 Eastminster Road, Mailbox #263
Eastminster, New Jersey 08615

Test Date: Saturday, January 30, 2010

Section Scores:
Critical Reading: 800 (National Percentile: 99%)
Mathematics: 760 (National Percentile: 96%)
Writing: 800 (National Percentile: 99%)
Essay Score: 11/12
Total Score: 2360

XVII.

ACADEMIC MEMO: WINTER TERM 2009–2010
COURSE: Second Year English
INSTRUCTOR: Mrs. Debra M. Sassoon
STUDENT: Hannah Phelps-Berkowitz
HOUSE: Hewitt
HOUSEMASTER: Mrs. Roberta Cantrell
ACADEMIC ADVISOR: Ms. Pamela Sutt
DATE: 01/26/2010

After her successful performance in my First Year Humanities English section last year, I was delighted to learn over the summer that Hannah had been assigned to my Second Year English section. In light of our history together, her work so far hasn't simply been disappointing— frankly, it's baffled me. Hannah's first paper of the fall quarter, on Macbeth, was strong, if somewhat overwritten (though I tend to be forgiving when it comes to students going beyond the assigned page limit, within reason), and a showcase of her intellectual and argumen- tative strengths.

Around early October, however, I noticed what looked to me—and I speak with twenty years of experience as an educator—like the first symptoms of the complacency that sometimes follows success. I noted this to some degree in my term-end report, but given her strong start to the quarter and what I know about her capacity for academic excellence, I understood my words then as a preemptive note of caution. (She finished the fall quarter with a B.)

I realize now the insufficiency of my expressed concern. Her fall term record now seems exemplary when compared with her performance so far this quarter, which as of this past Friday (1/23) is halfway over. Tardiness is the least of my present concerns. As I write this memo, I am waiting with diminishing patience for Hannah's midterm paper, which was due last Wednesday (1/21).

In Second Year English, each student must submit weekly short response papers on the work we are reading. These are not optional assignments. (I have now rather charitably reviewed my syllabus twice for any possible ambiguity in the relevant phrasing, as I struggle otherwise to comprehend a confusion of which no other students are guilty.) Of the six due thus far, Hannah has submitted two; ultimately, these are more troubling than the missing assignments. For context, we began the quarter with Tom Stoppard's *Rosencrantz and Guildenstern Are Dead* and just finished Arthur Miller's *Death of a Salesman*. Hannah submitted her second short response paper last Thursday. I quote it here in the service of my point:

"JESUS tells me that I believe the Saleman [*sic*] was addicted to sex with death, and which by he didnot sucede [*sic*] at Sales. The garbage disposal was invented in the 1950s (when this book Happens) and so the Salesman could have just put his arm in it and ground it up but there would be to [*sic*] much Blood."

What I think may have happened here: for the course's midterm project, I gave the students the choice of writing a four-to-five-page academic paper or a piece of creative writing in the style of one of the two plays we've read so far this term. It seems that Hannah pursued the latter option; I recognize Stoppard's darkly absurd comedy in the assignment she returned. But this was a weekly short essay, which are meant as exercises in academic writing. It seems Hannah must have confused these assignments, and while I applaud and hope in the future to continue nurturing her creative verve, this instance demonstrates a more general carelessness. It's my intense hope that Hannah will address these lapses, which contrast sharply with the work of the thoughtful, attentive girl I had the pleasure of teaching last year.

XVIII.

VirtualTeenTalk Forums—Puberty 101—Sex
BY: SailorMoonGurl94
February 19, 2010 / 4:01am EST
RE: HELP

> THERE IS A MAN INSIDE ME
> THE FBI IS INSIDE ME
> THEY KNOW I STOLE
> I HAVE BEEN MicroChipped

XIX.

It was one of those things that was almost boring in its inevitability, and when he got the call with the news, Raj Chakravarty's smile there in the library was pleased but mostly sedate, as if he'd been told his flight would be landing on time. "I mean, the guy wrote three articles a week every week since the first week of freshman year," Noah Baum said, swiping a French fry through ketchup. "Honestly, it would have been stunning if he hadn't gotten it, and frankly I think he would have had an aneurysm." He seemed only minorly irritated.

"Yeah, but tell that to Rosalie and Jenny," Jason said, reaching over Foster's pizza to take a fry from Noah's plate. "Both of whom are apparently still crying in Perry, just, like—inconsolable. Two and a half years of obsession for zilch."

Noah sniffed. "I'm taking it like a champ."

"You should be very proud of yourself," Foster said kindly. " 'Executive Editor' honestly has a more powerful ring than 'Editor-in-Chief.' Don't undersell the value of appearances."

"Look at him! Our Opinions Editor!" Jason slid his hand beneath Noah's and swiped up two more fries. "Already spouting opinions! He's a natural!"

The elections for the 130th Editorial Board of the *Kennedian* had concluded three hours earlier. Foster had been sitting in his study carrel on the second floor of the library when his phone began to hum against the table. It was Sasha Burnell. "Dade—you're Opinions," she said brusquely. "Bravo. Get ready to work your ass off. And don't take this news lightly. This year was a bloodbath."

So it had been. The Fourth Years of the 129th Ed Board spent seven hours in total litigating the applications submitted by their prospective replacements, in what Dr. Tierney later described as the most vicious episode of campus politics he'd witnessed in his quarter-century at Kennedy. The final calls historically went out on the night of the second Thursday in February, but by ten o'clock that night, the men and women of the 129th were still in their office in the basement of Fenster Hall, an hour late for check-in, more than a few of them hoarse from shouting. Sasha sighed into her hands finally. "Send them an email. Tell them they'll know tomorrow. Let them go to bed. Let me go to bed."

In the end, Editor-in-Chief went to Raj, with Sasha casting the tie-breaking vote. (Noah Baum privately believed himself to be uniquely suited for the responsibilities of running a weekly high school newspaper—or so he hoped to describe himself in his Yale application essay later that year—and presented himself to the outbound editors as a sort of McCain-like maverick. It was the same victimless but rather grating chutzpah that had led Sasha Burnell to find Noah intensely annoying at his first writers' meeting two and a half years prior; though Andrew Mastoff had tried to assemble an eleventh-hour devil's-advocate campaign on behalf of Noah's candidacy, Sasha's subsequent glower had very quickly taken the wind out of his sails.) Rosalie Haddish and Noah would flank Raj as Executive Editors, and Jenny Xiu got News. "I feel for her, but I dunno why she's so bummed," Jason said. "News is super cool. Digging up administrative corruption and clandestine drug rings and all that." Foster had forced himself to laugh. Jason had been appointed Culture and Features Editor, and when Foster found him on the edge of the Meadow after leaving the library, he was hollering with giddy joy into his iPhone. "Ma, I gotta run," he yelled. "Gotta go celebrate. I'll tell Foster congrats." He grinned and arched his eyebrows at Foster. "My mom says congrats."

In those years, for purely practical reasons that nevertheless held a certain symbolic potency, the Editor-in-Chief of the *Kennedian* was one of three students at Kennedy with the power to send emails to the entire school. (The other two being the Student Council President and the Editor-in-Chief of *Farrago*, Kennedy's yearbook.) Foster had been sitting with Noah and Jason in Vito's when their phone screens illuminated with the all-school email from Sasha Burnell, congratulating the newest members of the *Kennedian*'s Editorial Board. For the remainder of the evening, heads turned in their direction, and classmates stopped at their booth on the way out to extend their congratulations and wish them well.

"We're in the big leagues now, boys," Jason said. "College counseling telling me Stanford's a reach—we'll see who's laughing!"

For the first time in many weeks, Foster felt himself smiling with satisfaction. *This is going to sound profoundly depressing, but: until tonight, I'd forgotten what it feels like to be happy and sober at the same time. For a wonderful hour I didn't let myself think about any of the bullshit.*

It was then that Porter stepped inside. She seemed to have come from ice hockey practice, and her cheeks were pink and full from the cold, her hair pulled back into a wet ponytail. Behind her were Gracie and Sofi, and before he could bring his eyes down to his plate, there was Annabeth, talking animatedly into her phone as she entered.

He'd left three voicemails for Porter over Christmas break. The calls had gone immediately to her voicemail, and finally he'd googled *no ring straight to voicemail iphone call* to realize that she had blocked his number. On the nights thereafter, he'd lie on his bed after smoking a joint on the patio downstairs and call her simply to listen to her mailbox greeting.

I've come to accept that maybe I'm just a bad person. Or at least fatally selfish.

It was on the night of New Year's Day that Annabeth called him. He'd been sitting in the downstairs living room, staring at *School of Rock* on AMC. It was a little after ten, and his mother had fallen asleep on the large armchair by the piano. His breath had snagged in his chest when he saw her name upon his screen, and as he stood up too quickly he briefly thought he was about to faint. He answered it on its ninth ring, closing his bedroom door behind him.

"—Hello?"

He knew from Facebook that Annabeth had spent the last days of 2009 at the Albrights' in Morristown, and that Mason had come up from D.C. and Pritchett down from the city for a New Year's party. There was a pause on the other end of the line, and for a moment he expected to hear Jack's voice.

"Hey, Foster."

Afterward, he would not remember what he had said, only the note of levity he had forced into it and the silence that had followed its failure, and then the words that Annabeth finally spoke.

"I don't really want to make this a conversation—I just want you to listen to what I have to say. Like, really listen."

"..."

"I just wanted to say—I can't think of a shittier thing than what you did that night at Sofi's. I've been really pissed off about it, and I needed some time to calm down, and even now—it was just really fucked up."

"..."

"I'm not even talking about me. Porter is one of my best friends. I think maybe you don't fully realize the—magnitude of what you did. I've spent the last week and a half or whatever thinking that—it's like I never even really knew you. And it was shitty to me, too—not even with Jack." Foster felt himself flinch at the sound of his name in her voice. "I had to convince one of my best friends that I wasn't involved with or didn't have feelings for her boyfriend. And I don't even know if she believes me."

"..."

"And listen—I don't pretend to know what goes on in your head. But I know you have your shit. But that doesn't make anything okay. And I just wanted to say—I just don't think it's good for us to be in each other's lives right now. I'm not trying to make this into a fight or drama or anything. I just think—for my sake, but also for yours. Surely—surely you get it."

In his reclusiveness, he had seen her fewer than five times in the six weeks he'd been back at school. (*It's the first quarter in my time at Kennedy that we don't have English together*, he'd noted on his Blogspot three months earlier, just after Thanksgiving. *She told me it makes her sad.*) It was always from afar, and each time he would find himself rerouting his path in a desperate effort to avoid intercepting her. He always wondered idly where she was going.

With the exception of classes, which he attended with a forlorn passivity, he spent his most prolonged stretches beyond Brennan in his study carrel. It was there that Sofi Cohen found him on a Friday night at the beginning of February.

"May I come in?"

He gestured wordlessly to the seat across from him. She closed the door, and after turning to see who may have been audience to their encounter, she sat and looked at him.

"Hey, Sof," he said quietly.

"It's very unpleasant being mad at you," she said finally. "It kind of feels like you've kicked a puppy. But—look at me," and here he realized that he'd been unable to meet her eyes, "If we're going to talk, you need to learn how to make eye contact. It's bothered me since I've known you, and I'm still pretty pissed off at you, so I get to tell you now."

He felt himself smile.

"It's nice to see you," he said after a moment. His voice was still quiet.

She sighed. "I suppose I've worried about you. For what it's worth," and her gaze softened somewhat, "I am not on board with what the guys have been doing to you. I think you really fucked over a friend who'd been good to you—two friends, actually, and I'm not even talking about Porter yet—but it's not cool how he's responded. And I've told him as much."

"Has Annabeth?"

Sofi exhaled in tired frustration. "Oy. Look—" and she paused, as if contemplating her words. "It's really never been that surprising to me that you and Annabeth got so close. The truth is—and please forgive me—I've never met two people more up their own asses about how fucked up they are. I have no fucking idea what may have happened between you two over the course of your friendship, and frankly I would prefer to not even guess, but if I had to, I'd imagine that what happened at my house was probably not all that insane in light of whatever—thing you guys had." She paused. "I don't mean thing like thing, but like—"

"I know what you mean."

"And because I've known and lived with Annabeth Whittaker for basically three years, I know that it wouldn't come as a total shock if she'd somehow encouraged some of it. But this isn't about Annabeth. It's about Porter."

Foster felt his eyes drop to the table.

"I think you probably don't fully get just what you meant to her. And I don't think you understand what was at stake there. The girl did everything in her God-given power to get over the craziest trust issues I've ever seen. And over the course of an evening you basically let her know that every fear she ever had was completely valid."

"Sof—I really was just super fucked up. And—" He stopped and looked back down to the table. "All I've done since is feel like fucking shit. I feel like fucking shit."

And a tear fell onto the table.

Sofi looked at him for what seemed like close to a minute. He blinked several times and then swallowed.

"The thing is that I believe you," she said finally. "And I didn't come here to give you a free pass for what you did. You fucked up. But," and there was a meager but merciful tenderness in her brown eyes then, "my suspicion is that you've been feeling pretty alone. And sometimes the punishment is a lot worse than the crime and—well, my dad's a lawyer." Her lips betrayed something close to a smile. "So I'm biased toward justice. And I just wanted to tell you that."

"Sofi," he said just before she opened the door. His voice was dry. "Can I fix it?"

She pondered this for a moment. "People move on," she said simply. "The boys will move on. Not Mason, maybe, but Mason's, well—"

"A psychopath."

She snorted softly. "Something like that. But everyone else—we'll see. I will tell you that if you ever try to get close to Porter Roth again, I will personally murder you. But, yeah—people do move on."

She turned to go, but before opening the door she paused again. "But—Foster."

He looked up at her.

"Maybe you shouldn't be surprised if they don't."

"What's eating you, Dade? Perhaps you have—an *opinion*?"

Noah extended his hand to Jason for a high five. Jason dropped his straw's crumpled wrapper into it. "That's Dade's ex-gal."

Foster let himself smile. "It is." He had been staring down at his plate since Porter and Annabeth had entered, hearing but not listening to Noah and Jason as they spoke. "And I—was not very nice to her."

The girls sat at the front booth in the windows, and as they passed him with their plates he forced himself to look with intense interest to Noah, who was sitting against the wall.

"They seem less than thrilled with your presence, Dade, hate to tell ya."

"Which *they?*"

"Well, just Roth, and Gracie Smith, but I'd imagine Gracie Smith will look less than thrilled on her wedding day, so yeah, maybe just Roth."

They finished their fries and Cokes, and as Foster slid his plate into the garbage he heard Sofi's voice behind him at the soda fountain. "Congrats, Dade," she said quietly, concentrating on the stream of Diet Coke filling her cup.

"Thanks, Sof."

A gentle sleet was falling as they returned to campus. Noah and Jason retreated into Talmadge House, and as Foster carried on across the Meadow, his phone hummed with a call from his mother.

"I'm so proud of you, bug," his mother was saying. "You've really made such a wonderful existence for yourself there, and you should feel really good about it. I know it hasn't always been the easiest thing."

"Thanks, Mom," he said, and when he hung up he began to sob.

He was sitting in his carrel finishing his biology homework when he felt his phone vibrate briefly on the seat next to him. He ignored it for a few minutes—the majority of his texts at this point were from customers—before finally putting his pencil down and retrieving it. He blinked at the screen for a moment, staring at Annabeth's display name on BlackBerry Messenger.

> **ALW [09:08:16PM]:** hey. i just saw the all-school email from sasha and i just wanted to say congratulations. i know how huge a deal the kennedian is (to you and to everyone here and also to college admissions officers lol) and you should feel really great about it.

It took him several minutes to bring himself to respond. He found himself thinking about Sofi's words two weeks prior, but they seemed distant and inaccessible, their frequency garbled by the message before him.

> **foster dade [09:17:58PM]:** Hey. Thank you, Annabeth. That really means a lot. I'm super thrilled and still can't really believe it.
> **foster dade [09:18:04PM]:** I really hope you're doing well.

And he sat there, staring at the message as it arrived in Annabeth's inbox. A moment passed, and within the adjoining checkmark, the letter "D" for "Delivered" became an "R," for "Read." He waited for the indication that she was typing. He was still looking at his screen when the librarian rapped on the carrel's door ten minutes later, pointing to her watch.

The sleet had turned to lazy flurries, and he shoved his hands into his North Face's pockets as he walked back to Brennan. He said hello to Miss Chissom, who bowed to him in congratulation. As he climbed the stairs, he did not at first see Jack Albright loitering on the landing just below his bedroom door. There was something unnerving about his standing there, and about the smile on his face as Foster looked up with a start.

"Oh, hi there," Jack sang lightly, and then turned and moved down the stairs. Foster saw that he'd begun typing something into his phone as he rounded the corner.

The departing members of the *Kennedian*'s editorial board would never ascertain why several hundred copies of their final issue had disappeared seemingly overnight from campus. After sending the issue to the printers that Thursday night, Sasha Burnell had at last acquiesced to the complacency that had been beckoning since she'd received her early-admission acceptance to Stanford two months prior; when her co-editors—none of whom were under any delusion about the *Kennedian*'s readership figures—asked her about the curiously empty distribution boxes at the doors to the school's academic buildings, she'd quite literally shrugged them off. "The surplus always gets trashed anyway—who cares," she'd told Andrew Mastoff, before returning to Expedia to find a spring break flight to Cabo.

Foster's door was met with a slight resistance as he pushed it open. When it finally relented, he understood with another flood of nausea why Jack and Mason and the other boys hadn't been at Vito's with the girls. His room was filled knee-high with crumpled copies of the *Kennedian*. He stood in the doorway and blinked as the loose balls of newspaper spilled out past his ankles into the hallway. He stumbled as he stepped through their tide. A single copy had been unfolded upon his bed, and on it in fat black Sharpie was the word *CONGRATS!* written in the same jagged hand in which he'd seen his name in pencil on the Tolerance Board.

He did not let himself cry as he began to push the newspapers out into the hallway. He realized while doing so that small corners of the paper were disintegrating in wet pulpy bits against his wrists and blue jeans. He held one up and instinctively sniffed it, and was met with the unmistakable and acrid smell of urine.

"We thought you might like something nice to celebrate."

Foster looked up to see Jack standing in his doorway, holding his phone up to take a picture.

It would take him an hour and a half to shove the newspapers into the garbage bags he'd taken from the custodial closet, finishing just before Miss Chissom did her end-of-night rounds. There were five minutes until the campus internet would shut off with lights-out, and for a moment Foster considered simply not opening Facebook; when he ultimately did, he prayed for an ephemeral instant that it would not be there, though of course it was. *Mason Pretlow tagged you in a photo.* And there he was, bent down to the urine-mottled newspapers, his hands deep within them, looking up to Jack's camera. The image would survive on Mason Pretlow's Facebook overnight; Foster never ascertained who'd persuaded him to take it down the following morning, or where else it may have circulated thereafter. He would think only of his expression in the photograph. It was a look of dumb, humiliated bewilderment, his mouth slightly agape and his

eyes wide and entreating. It was only after Jack had left and Foster
had been able to clear enough newspaper from the vestibule that he
was able to close his door and cry.

XX.

Third Year English: Winter Term 2010
Dr. Arthur Tierney
Final Paper Prompt
Tuesday, February 17, 2010

Very simple. The stories we've read this quarter are stories about victims
and their injuries. Pick one of those stories and tell me about how victim-
hood and personal injury—physical or emotional or both—contribute to
a character's development over the course of the work.

10–15 pages
Due Thursday, March 18, 2010
BIBLIOGRAPHIES OR DEATH

XXI.

It took the 130th Editorial Board of the *Kennedian* until a little past
one in the morning to submit their inaugural issue to the printers.
Even then it happened only after the third phone call from the printers' night manager, who five miles away was standing before his silent
machinery in the warehouse off Nassau Street, wanting to know why
the press hadn't fired up and why he couldn't go home to bed his wife.
Raj Chakravarty had fielded these calls with mounting agitation before
finally throwing his phone quite violently at Dr. Tierney, who was
sitting on the office's old couch drinking a Dr. Pepper.
    "Charlie, my guy!" he bellowed into Raj's iPhone. "Listen—we've
got first-timers here. *Neophytes.* Rite of passage, though, yeah?" He
looked up at Foster and winked at him. "Eleven o'clock next week
or I'm buying lunch. You're a good man, Charlie, yeah."

Across the room, Rosalie Haddish was smirking in self-satisfaction at Raj, who had slid into the desk chair at the Editor-in-Chief's iMac and brought his face into his hands. "Should have gone with my layout for Sports."

Foster had slept only seven hours over the preceding two nights, returning to Brennan on both occasions shortly after midnight after finally giving up in surrender. He'd told his writers—*my writers: I hate how much I like the way that sounds*—that he'd need their drafts by dinnertime on Tuesday, but it wasn't until halfway through study hall the following evening that Eloise McClatchy had called him breathlessly to tell him about a spilled Diet Coke and a fried Mac-Book, promising him the article by midnight at the latest, six a.m. at the super-latest. In the end this had been stressful but fine, not only because of the supplementary text messages Foster received from Eloise that even he recognized as shameless flirting.

The truth was that he loved the thrill of it all. Foster had no qualms that for Raj and Jenny and Rosalie and Noah the *Kennedian* was understood as a practical and nominal endeavor, pursued less in the spirit of journalistic passion than with an eye to the first drafts of the Common Application they'd begun writing. But he also understood with a certain contentment that, with the possible exception of Jason, no one else on the newspaper's board felt the visceral rush he felt in its frenetic rituals: in hustling to meet editorial deadlines; in dictating the middle paragraphs of the board's first weekly editorial while simultaneously fiddling with the alignment of a pull quote within an article (the body text of which he'd spent twenty minutes kerning with the quietly impassioned intensity of a Genevan watchmaker); in peering over Raj Chakravarty's shoulder to the digital layout of the first edition's masthead and seeing *Foster H. Dade '11* over the words *Opinions Editor. It's nice to be proud of something,* he wrote after that first Thursday night close, *and to feel like I belong to something again. It's a different sort of belonging, a safer sort—and I'm now wondering why I ever feared that safety, and why I instead chose a belonging where I never really belonged.*

Editing the *Kennedian* also meant that he would be spending several extracurricular hours each week in the company of Dr. Tierney. Tierney had served as the *Kennedian*'s faculty advisor since coming to Kennedy in '88, watching the paper's voyage into the digital age from his usual seat on the editorial office's couch, pulling wide slices of Vito's pepperoni from the boxes that arrived at Fenster Hall's doors each Wednesday and Thursday evening and smearing pizza grease on the printed pages he decimated with red pencil and blue pen.

"Atta boy, kid," he'd said to Foster as he looked down through his reading glasses (perched on his nose in front of his usual spectacles) at the long sheet of draft paper Foster had pulled from the office's tomb-like HP LaserJet. "Kiddies, take a look at Dade's page if you're out over your skis."

He felt Tierney watching him sometimes as he sat there at his computer. There was nothing off or inappropriate about the intensity of the teacher's gaze, but it discomfited Foster in the knowledge it seemed somehow to possess. He had sensed it, too, the previous afternoon, at the end of their afternoon English class. Tierney had handed them the prompt for the term's final paper as they closed their notebooks and screwed the caps back on their Snapple bottles. Most had given the printed page a perfunctory glance before tucking it into a binder pocket or laptop case, but Foster had studied it for a moment, or perhaps several. When he looked up, his classmates had exited into the afternoon, and Tierney was sitting atop the edge of his desk, looking contemplatively out to the Meadow and then to Foster.

"See ya, Dr. Tierney," Foster had said, finally folding the prompt and slinging his backpack over his shoulder.

"Hey, Dade." Something in Tierney's voice was quieter, missing its usual manic edge. "You doin' all right, kid?"

Foster paused for a moment and did not look his teacher in the eyes.

"Yeah," he finally lied. "Doing great."

It was on that first deadline-straining Thursday night in the third week of February that he'd felt his BlackBerry hum. It was a little after eight; he'd emailed McCall an hour earlier to tell him he'd be stuck at the *Kennedian*, and that Dr. Tierney would vouch for him if necessary. Shortly thereafter it vibrated again.

It was ten minutes before he pulled himself away. "Bathroom," he called out to the figures hunched before their computers as he headed out into the basement's hallway, pulling his BlackBerry from his pocket.

There on his screen was Annabeth's name.

ALW [08:04:10PM]: are you at the newspaper?

And then, just below that, seven minutes later:

ALW [08:11:33PM]: let me know if you're around and can talk.

It wasn't precisely clear where Annabeth had been, but beneath the spill of the copper streetlight he could see that she'd been crying.

"If I just—introduced myself to you right now, could we just pretend we're meeting for the first time?"

She smiled with a sniffle. "I've heard of crazier tactics."

And for the first time in almost three months, they let their feet take them in no conscious direction out toward the vastness of campus. They crossed before the First Year Houses along the Yard, where in yellow windows fourteen-year-old silhouettes hunched seriously over their homework, and set out toward the football field. It was here, on the cusp of the school's dark pond, that they finally sat.

He wouldn't return to the *Kennedian*'s office until just after nine o'clock, and when he did both Tierney and Rosalie Haddish would take note of the strange smile on his face and study him in two different modes of suspicion.

She told me that she missed me, he wrote that night. She told me that she knew I hadn't meant anything by what happened—that she knew I was fucked up, and that she'd mostly been upset out of loyalty to Porter. She said Porter, not Jack. "We were both really fucked up that night," she said. "And shit happens."

Annabeth, what about when you kissed me in Lake Placid, is what I wanted to say. But I understood the fragility of that moment, of the fact of our being there together, so I didn't.

I didn't.

We talked for a few minutes about life, the way we always talked about life. I had forgotten how good it feels to make her laugh. I told her about the Kennedian; I did not tell her about the rocks hitting my window, etc., or about anything related to the Adderall. She told me she'd been really sad about Jae, and even though she didn't say "Adderall" or "drugs," she told me I really needed to be careful.

She told me she'd felt alone without me, and then she started crying.

Eventually I realized that it was more about Jack than me. In a way, it was the conversation we had been having on Sofi's terrace, except we were both sober, and I didn't ruin it by kissing her. I was more relieved than I should have been to hear that their sex life is apparently . . . underwhelming, even though it clearly manifests/results in Jack being an asshole to her. They'd been together that night before she texted me, out on the House football fields.

We sat there until check-in. She said goodbye to me there, and after looking at me for a moment she hugged me.

(Side note: it feels really weird and kind of pretentious to write out dialogue in quotation marks without paraphrasing it.)

"Porter is still one of my best friends," she said. "And Jack is still my boyfriend. And so it can't be like it used to be. But" (and then she said it again) "I've missed you. And I guess I realize I kind of need you."

There are moments that I look back upon here where I'm kind of knocked over by their beauty. It's corny and sappy but whatever. The night of Lessons and Carols last year; that first blizzard a year ago; those nights late last spring in the Meadow with Annabeth and Jack. But now I realize that Kennedy has never looked as beautiful as it did tonight.

XXII.

Hannah Phelps-Berkowitz had been placed on academic probation at the end of January. By the New Year, Hannah's teachers and advisors had begun corresponding with growing urgency about her work, which seemed to indicate not only academic foundering but a psychological duress well beyond the purview of their training as residential guardians. We know that there were two meetings that January with Dr. Clarissa Bonsavage, the Cranbury psychologist who moonlighted as the in-house therapist of the Kennedy School infirmary. The first had been a group session: Pam Sutt was Hewitt's day student advisor, and she'd sat alongside Roberta Cantrell on the stiff love seat across from Rose Berkowitz, Daniel Phelps, and their only daughter in the pleasant Febreze-candle glow of the infirmary's consultation room. We don't have access to Dr. Bonsavage's records of this meeting, but we do know that that afternoon, she arranged a follow-up session between her and Hannah alone two Tuesdays from then, on January 26.

In the eight days after Jae-hyun An's expulsion, Foster Dade had let his Facebook Chats accumulate unread in their inbox. In most cases, those who'd sent them didn't notice his silence, and thought nothing of it when he replied apologetically a week and a half later. Even those regular customers who'd come to depend on his services had enough back-supply to sustain them; finals were still seven weeks away. His neglect brought him some comfort, and when he finally resumed operations in early February he was too preoccupied by working through the backlog of messages to give much thought to the growing distress conveyed in the twenty-two solicitations left for him by Hannah Phelps-Berkowitz.

It is a testament to the elasticity of the adolescent mind that it would take another month of intensive amphetamine abuse for Hannah to suffer the more pernicious psychological or physical side effects of their withdrawal. Her desperation in those messages—*Hello Foster please respond or I can come find you on campus if that is better I would like to buy more Adderall; Foster???????? Where r u?????*—spoke mostly to what was on an existential physiological level still basically a bad habit, albeit one that had already invoked the earliest symptoms of psychosis. Because for all of her persistence on Facebook over that week and a half, by all accounts Hannah returned during that time to something vaguely approximating her normal, if an acutely sleepy version of it. She showed up to class, where her dumbfounded silence proved significantly less conspicuous than the increasingly bizarre outbursts of the preceding week.

And when she returned to Clarissa Bonsavage's office in the infirmary on the Tuesday in question, the therapist then concluded in a memo to her parents and advisors that Hannah only seemed to be exhibiting what looked to her like a woefully undiagnosed case of medium-to-high-functioning autism, referring her to a colleague down the road in Princeton who specialized in the condition. In a particularly violent splay of irony, Dr. Bonsavage concluded the memo by recommending that Hannah also be tested for ADHD.

Because the money had always been the most incidental component of it all, Foster hadn't really ever stopped to wonder how his clients afforded the pills they bought from him: parental allowances, he figured. The frequency and volume of Hannah Phelps-Berkowitz's purchases hadn't exempted her from this disinterest, and even at their most intensive they'd been more annoying than startling. Her last visit to his study carrel had come three days before her expulsion, and with respect to what would happen soon thereafter, there was nothing narratively interesting about it: she'd placed two hundred dollars on the table and he'd slid her the Ziploc of Vyvanse 70s and IR 15s, deliberately not really looking up from his MacBook to meet what he knew to be her discomfiting, vacuous stare.

Much later, when Hannah's Compaq was finally swept and inventoried, the concluding report would include the ten-page transactional history of an eBay user named SailorMoonGurl94, who between November 2009 and February 2010 had made five thousand dollars in sales. When the authorities found her account, several items remained listed: a pair of Persol women's sunglasses; a red leather Hermès handbag; several dresses from Dior and Prada. Only one piece of inventory was not a high-end fashion item: the 2007–2008 edition of the *Greenleaf*, Greenwich Academy's annual yearbook ($24.99), in which its previous owner had been named Best Dressed.

Jacqueline Franck would not notice until early February that there were vacancies on the shelves of her closet in Hewett House. This spoke to either the myopia of her self-absorption or the indifferent caprice with which she amassed her gilded inventory, or both. Her mother and father had offered to fly her and Sally Pinelli down to join them at the Breakers over Presidents' Day weekend—Bettina would be joining her own parents in Vail, and Jacqueline had quietly delighted in excluding Kaitlyn Sanders and cataloguing her flicker of pain—and she had gone to her closet to locate a Dior tube dress that had sat superfluously in its Neiman Marcus box since she'd bought it. She'd shrugged irritably when she couldn't find it and made a mental note to order another, then reached up to a shelf to retrieve the Manolo Blahniks that had arrived in the mail room the prior week. Those, too, were missing.

"Sal," she said to her roommate, "have you been taking my shit?"

"Don't flatter yourself," Sally had said, not looking up from her chemistry textbook.

Jacqueline Franck would graduate from Kennedy with a transcript of B-minuses, but there are many different kinds of brilliance. Later therapists would observe in this impassive patient an almost doctoral perspicuity when it came to diagnosing and redressing the inequities and abuses of her world; that this world and its crimes were lucid to her alone did not delegitimize the artistry of her narcissism at work. Swiftly and vigorously she had assumed Kaitlyn's guilt: it provided the logical and inevitable conclusion to nineteen months of silent revulsion at a girl she alone knew did not belong; the indictment would account for a multitude of sins that for too long had gone unpunished. "You probably wouldn't be able to afford the dinners and stuff," Jacqueline had said sweetly after letting Kaitlyn overhear her and Sally discuss the logistics of getting to Newark for their flight to Palm Beach; as she saw it, Kaitlyn's wince of humiliated pain was evidence enough.

In the days that followed, Jacqueline delightedly began to catalogue further disappearances: the Cartier bracelet her mother had bought her over Thanksgiving; one of the two Hermès bags she'd brought from her dozen at home; multiple pairs of Hanky Panky thongs (she'd almost salivated at the thought of bringing this up, and made a note to wait for Jack Albright and Pritchett Pierce to be in earshot). She hadn't noticed the missing yearbook. She wouldn't involve Ms. Cantrell or Mrs. Daniels or even her mother, she knew; it wasn't about the theft. She planned her assault for Thursday at lunch.

In her distraction, she had arrived in her European History classroom that morning without either her notes or textbooks, and spent the subsequent walk back to Hewitt dwelling not on Kaitlyn but on fat, slovenly Mrs. Cline, who had dispassionately told her to be back in ten minutes prepared for class. Hewitt was silent when she entered. Flicking irritably through her phone, she had not realized that her and Sally's door was slightly ajar as she reached the top of the stairs.

It was only when the person standing before her closet turned that Jacqueline brought her eyes up from her screen. Had the girl remained motionless, Jacqueline may not have noticed her at all.

Recounting things later, caught up in the deliciousness of her adversity, Jacqueline would claim that her former lab partner had been wearing her trilby, but the banality of this narrative flourish suggests it's not worth verifying. What we do know, though, is that Hannah Phelps-Berkowitz—hatted or not—was standing there before Jacqueline Franck. We can assume that as the scene clarified itself, Jacqueline's face fell into the same rictus of disgust that Hannah may or may not have comprehended as such in the First Year biology lab a year earlier, even before Jacqueline's eyes turned down to the rolling backpack at Hannah's feet. Its handle was retracted and its zipper was open, and inside Jacqueline saw a shapeless sheath of color that she recognized as her Homecoming Dance dress.

Today, Daniel Phelps and Rose Berkowitz both still teach at Princeton; property records indicate that they still reside at the same forlorn ranch home in Princeton Junction in which their daughter grew up. Google Street View last updated its imagery from that zip code last April, and indeed at the address in question you can still see the smudged panoramic composite of Daniel Phelps's brown Econoline van. He did not have a cell phone in 2010—he may not have one now—and it was only after Theresa Daniels managed to reach him through the Princeton Computer Science Department's administrative assistant that the van sputtered through the gates of the Meadow, at this point two hours after Kennedy's administration had decreed to expel his daughter.

I was startled by the promptness with which Dr. Phelps responded to the first and only email I ultimately sent him. It was relatively early in my research, and I only had the most geometrically simple understanding of everything that had happened, and of his daughter's position in it. Hannah Phelps-Berkowitz existed in my notes and in my mind as only a name; even when I began to amass the details of her expulsion and everything preceding it, it would still be months before I learned of her digital complement and the vast archival contrail left behind under the username SailorMoonGurl94. In the interest of brevity, I won't transcribe my initial email to her father here, but I will note that his short reply came within an hour.

No thank you

Hannah remained prolific until the end. I'm not sure if her parents know this or at least its full extent, or if it would matter much if they did. We have no insight into how Hannah Phelps-Berkowitz spent the days after her expulsion, but we assume from what we know about amphetamine withdrawal that she found herself in a crucible of psychological and emotional terror that I suspect very few of us can even approximate in our darkest imaginations. Her disappearance in late February 2010 from the forums where she'd found a home before very publicly living out the grotesque prelude to this horror suggests that she was in a certain sense lost to herself, instead clawing through the darkness at the fun-house walls of her terminal sarcophagus at whatever edge of reality she could grasp.

What we do know is that when Hannah Phelps-Berkowitz was in seventh grade, she and her mother planted a garden. As with many communities built around hobbies whose esotericism incubates an intense, almost filial loyalty among their participants, the forums of

Gardening World Online date back to the earliest iterations of the mass-market internet. Gardening World Online has persisted valiantly into the twenty-first century—and in the first months of the COVID-19 pandemic, its webmasters reported a 400 percent increase in traffic—but graphically and spiritually it remains much as it did a quarter of a century ago. The thirty-five-year-old introverts who joined the forum in the mid-1990s are in middle age now, and in that time their commitment to what's now a decades-long dialogue on the intricacies of mid-Atlantic fertilizers hasn't waned. The inadvertent sincerity of their project is itself a relic of this earlier time.

SailorMoonGurl94 created her account on Gardening World Online on June 5, 2007. This would have been the tail end of her seventh-grade year, when several of Weird Hannah's classmates still hadn't given up on their effort to torment her into speech. But neither her reticence nor any hidden pain manifests in the several dozen posts she wrote on the site's forums that summer, which present to us only a girl who was really excited to be starting a garden with her mom. This excitement alone seems to have motivated much of her chattiness; every now and again she asked more seasoned gardeners for input, but more often than not she just wanted to share. *We have horrible aphids all over our tomatoes—yuck! But we tried the bug-killer that DahliaBlossom1967 recommended, and it seems to be working. I'm ready to take them off the vine and eat them!*

After the initial enthusiasm of that summer, she posted on and off again in the years that followed, with each season her digital voice softening somewhat, maturing. *The frost killed our daffodils. We're pretty disappointed. But that's central Jersey for you.* They were and still are a convivial bunch, and over the years Sailor-MoonGurl94's profile had amassed a small number of followers, who got an email notification whenever she began or responded to a thread on the forum. It had been more than a year since her last contribution when these fourteen accounts awoke to a message from noreply@gardeningworldonline.com, linking to the following thread.

**Gardening World Online Community Forums—Plant-Specific
Issues—All Things Vegetables**
POST: XXXXXXXX
FROM: SailorMoonGurl94
Tuesday, March 2, 2010 | 2:14am EST

XXXXXXXXXXXXXXXXXX XXXXXXXXXXXXXXXXXX
　 XXXXXXXXX XXXXXXXXXXXXXXXXXXXXXXXXXXXX
XXXX XXXXXXX XXXXXXXX XXXXXXXXXXXXXXXXXX
XXXXXXXXXXXXXXXXXXXXXXXXXXXXXXXXXXXXXX
XXXXXXXXXXXXXXXXXXX XXXXXXXXXXXXXXXXX XXXXXXXXXXXXX
XXXXXXXXXXXXXXXXXXXXXXXX

Another followed the next day.

**Gardening World Online Community Forums—Plant-Specific
Issues—All Things Vegetables**
POST: [No Subject]
FROM: SailorMoonGurl94
Wednesday, March 3, 2010 | 11:18pm EST

eBay Sunshine eBay Sunshine eBay Sunshine eBay Sunshine

MICROWAVE Sunshine MIRCROWAVE Sunshine MICRWAOVE Earthquake
Sunhine Sunshine EARTHQUAKE Sunshine

I shave my head SHAVE MY HEAD

WilliaM SUNSHINE

　　March 4 was a Thursday. The cold that had brought that Monday's snowfall had stayed over central Jersey, and the edges of the
parking lot at the train station in Princeton Junction were ridged
with hard lodes of ice, their surfaces pockmarked and brown with
dirt. By mid-afternoon, the sun had started to sift itself through the

dirty cotton of the sky, and though the light was yellow and feeble, those who stood on the platform for the commute home from their jobs at the university had let themselves unzip their jackets down to their chests, turning their heads up toward what warmth might be offered. The southbound Amtrak trains traveling along the Northeast Corridor shared these tracks with New Jersey Transit over the length of Hanover County before leaving Trenton for Philadelphia and then Wilmington, and every so often the Acela would spit by along the center rails between the commuter tracks to and from Penn Station, coming out of nowhere and disappearing just as quickly.

It would be nine o'clock when the last of the commuters on the platform that afternoon finished their cursory interviews with the law enforcement officers who'd been dispatched to the scene just before five, though at that point it was purely perfunctory. The older officers had had similar incidents before, and they knew that the amount of amassable information was narrowly finite: given both the visual obstructions of heavy steel machinery and the woozy amnesia that attends shock, there's only so much that can be seen, let alone recalled accurately.

It was a homebound receptionist from the university art museum who had seen the girl first. She had been standing at the platform's northern edge and returning her *USA Today* to the satchel at her ankles when either her peripheral vision or some monstrous agent of fate had turned her head down the tracks beyond the platform's end fence, in the direction of Manhattan. Her first thought was that it was a man in some sort of costume, and that she was witnessing a performance whose meaning would clarify itself. The person didn't step as much as teeter over and between the rails of the center and southbound tracks. She first thought it was a man because there was no hair on their head, but then she saw that the person was nude, and had breasts.

Others may have seen her before the woman screamed; it's useless to guess. Others joined her then, their shouts less performative appeals for a solution than instinctive expressions of powerlessness. The platform's edge was ten or eleven feet above the fat rocks of gravel below the rails, and those standing upon it would later describe feeling marooned as the girl moved slowly toward them. In their interviews, almost all of those who described this sensation did so before mentioning seeing the far light of the southbound train or hearing the scream of its whistle. Others would describe the expression upon the girl's face, though this, too, would have been an inadvertent fabrication: the police officers tasked with watching the surveillance footage New Jersey Transit had provided them would note with surety that before the train hit her, Hannah Phelps-Berkowitz had turned where she stood to face it. The footage was low-resolution and black-and-white, intended mostly for discerning the big-picture locomotive aberrations that might accompany a derailment, but in it they could see the ghostly grain of the girls' buttocks, turned to face the station platform.

Almost all of those who had stood on the northbound platform at Princeton Junction that day had reflexively looked away as the girl's pale form disappeared into the growing headlight orb of the 4:58 to Hamilton, its last stop. They weren't sure if what they heard was the sound of her body or simply one of the myriad ordinary noises of large-scale machinery mid-kinesis, and when they finally let themselves look up, it was a small blessing that wherever the body or what remained of it had ended up, it was not somewhere where they could see it.

What they did remember—and in the nightmares that bridged the weeks and months that followed, this was no better—were the faces that populated the billious light of the train windows on the other side of the tracks, where the final double-decker carriages in the train's long chain had finally jerked to a stop. Those who occupied those cars would recount similar relationships with those who stood on the platform. Together they played out an improvised duet on the emergence of human horror. Those who sat aboard the train looked around confusedly—it seemed they'd stopped just beyond their penultimate stop's platform—until they saw through their soundproof windows the silent screams of those commuters standing on the concrete promenade. Those who stood on the platform were left to witness the animalistic processes by which we realize the enormity of certain terrors: faces of puzzlement and irritation shifting in silence into rictuses of startling misery. People leaned down and vomited. Despite its almost religious wretchedness, there's a protocol for these things, and the conductor's second-in-command had begun calling New Jersey Transit's emergency dispatch before their locomotive even hit the girl. The train was still slowing when the police arrived.

After Hannah Phelps-Berkowitz died, it would take investigators three months to compile a report of what they'd downloaded to the state's hard drives from her Compaq laptop. This spoke mostly to bureaucratic inefficiency on their end, or more fairly to the nature of the case in question. In their intensive dialogue with the relevant authorities in the immediate aftermath of Hannah's death, Kennedy's administrators would make clear that, unless the circumstances absolutely demanded otherwise, they were hoping to understand what had happened as a tragic and utterly isolated accident. Hannah's parents had dumbly affirmed their lack of interest in initiating any sort of civil action against Kennedy, or whomever at Kennedy may have been determined liable.

So it wasn't until the middle of the summer holiday that Sheila Baxter received the documents that in the most narrow sense ultimately offered no new insight into the circumstances that had culminated in Hannah's demise. It had been nearly two decades since she'd left the *Globe*, but she'd never really lost her journalistic impulses, and there'd been certain aspects of the story that had felt woefully underreported, or at least lacking in sufficient context. With the more urgent anxieties put to bed—having persuaded the most important reporters that the whole imbroglio that spring, and the tragic death that only in a convoluted philosophical sense had resulted directly from it, had really just been a flash in the pan—she allowed herself the bandwidth to read these documents for other details, those that had no bearing on the legal dimension of the matter.

In the years since she'd embarked on her journey with those first jejune visits to VirtualTeenTalk.org, SailorMoonGurl94 had forged a vast and serpentine digital footpath. She had found a safe waystation at her trailhead, and up until the weeks preceding her death she had returned regularly to that first forum, where for the first time in her life Hannah Phelps-Berkowitz had something resembling friends. In those five and a half years, they'd forged their kinship through the uncertainties and concerns they shared, which ranged in Hannah's case from the ludic (*Has anyone been able to reach the crystal castle in Kingdom Hearts VI for PC?*) to the openly physiological (*Is it normal for flatulence to smell worse during menstruation?*) to the heartbreakingly personal (*How do you ask a boy to be your boyfriend? What do you do if he says no?*). For several months after she died, other longtime denizens of VirtualTeenTalk.org with usernames like familyguy_fan _10 and CrazyMouse911 would respond to her last posts with increasingly concerned inquiries into her whereabouts. Daniel Phelps and Rose Berkowitz had not taken out an obituary for their daughter—not because they were ashamed by the circumstances, but because in her death as in her life, they lacked the guiding structures others built through rote sentimental ritual—and by summertime these inquiries began to appear less frequently.

The last post would come early that fall from lonelygirlinindiana. "Wherever u are, SailorMoonGurl94," she wrote in September 2010, "I hope ur happy and are playing a lot of Kingdom Hearts and know that your VTT friends love u ☺ <3 ☺ <3."

XXIII.

I'd been waiting at our empty table for a little over thirty minutes when I finally recognized Eloise McClatchy's eyeglasses over the press of heads that crowded the front of the bar by the doorway. They were the same glasses she was wearing in her Twitter avatar, in which she smiled out with an almost endearing disdain at her thirteen thousand followers: an expensive tortoiseshell pair from Oliver Peoples or Moscot, in which if you looked closely you could catch the reflected glint of the photographer *Vanity Fair* had contracted for staff headshots. She navigated the crowd of the bar without bringing her head up from her phone, and somehow made it effortlessly to our empty table without one upward glance.

"I fucking hate Twitter," she said, looking up from Twitter. She pressed the lock button of the orange case and dropped her phone into her tote bag. "Sorry. My mother backed out of the driveway over our dog and I had to provide emotional counsel." She said this as if her Uber had been stuck in traffic.

Eloise had been a Third Year when I arrived at Kennedy, and I'd known her there only as everyone younger and more impressionable had: as a figment of her own prominence within the closest thing Kennedy has to an intelligentsia, who seemed to exist in our imaginations only behind the halogen-lit podium at School Meeting or as a boldfaced name on (and eventually atop) the *Kennedian*'s masthead. I recall finding her very pretty, though my sense was that her assertiveness scared off the sort of boys who in their twenties would fall hard for similarly cerebral girls as quickly as the second or third Hinge date: drawn then not only to their intellectual intensity but also the new aloofness with which they'd emerged from the uncomfortable chrysalis of adolescent audacity. She was one of six in her class to go on to Yale, where she would become the Weekend Editor of the *Yale Daily News* her junior year, and inevitably ended up among those plucked from the rarefied pool of Ivy League journalists for the media jobs their contemporaries from the Universities of Missouri and South Carolina would spend several postgraduate years working toward with inconsistent success. She'd started at Condé Nast with a *New Yorker* internship in the summer before her senior year, and when she returned to One World Trade Center for the news blogging position with *Vanity Fair*'s website, the 2016 presidential election was just five months away. Her acerbic disillusionment predictably earned her a respectable following among the New York City media class, followed by more mainstream online prominence after a handful of viral tweets on the sclerosis of American democracy. I was among those less interesting Twitter users who out of both jadedness and jealousy tended to find such figures grating, but I'd learned that in 99 percent of those cases the individual behind the online personage is either very lovely or utterly dull.

Eloise McClatchy was the former, to my somewhat delighted surprise. I suppose by that I mean that the woman who arrived very late to the bar on the Bowery—and with whom I ultimately spent two and a half hours—was very different from who she was on Twitter. She brought with her none of the cloying irony that over the course of our early adulthood had become our generation's default style: the vocabulary of shibboleths and grammar of flat detachment in which we found an orthopedic substitute for feeling the things that had become too visceral to feel. Of everyone I ultimately spoke to about Foster Dade, it was Eloise McClatchy who had the most to say: not with respect to historical specificities but rather in the sadness we found ourselves sharing as we explored his story together.

"I'll tell you what's interesting," she said at one point, finishing her first merlot. "I was hung up on Kennedy for so long after I graduated—I actually hated Yale by virtue of comparison; I thought nothing could ever be as special as Kennedy had been, at least in my own experience." She lifted her empty glass to the bartender, signaling another. "But it was a few years before I finally realized that I'd been miserable there. I'd done very well but—I never fit in. I spent four years wondering why Jacqueline Franck and Sally Pinelli and Kaitlyn Sanders had failed to realize that I existed. It's almost like I was too earnest for the place—and I don't say that to congratulate myself or make myself feel better. Earnestness has its merits and its limits." She looked thoughtfully to me. "Though I'd imagine I'm now guilty of something of an overcorrection."

I looked back at her, briefly silenced by the truth her words had carried, which left me with the discomfort of recognition. "But when you realized you'd been unhappy," I said finally, "Did you become any less hung up on the place, or less infatuated with it?"

She smiled as the bartender placed the wine in front of her. "Nah."

She said she didn't remember who had sent her the Word document. It was to my knowledge the one extant copy of the final paper Foster Dade wrote for Dr. Tierney's Third Year English class at the end of his last term at Kennedy. "I guess it was shitty of me to have asked for it when I heard about what was being sent around," she'd said at the bar. "But I can at least say my motives were pure. I was obsessed with him." She grinned wickedly at this. "Like, intensely erotic schoolgirl crush. I was so fucking jealous of Porter Roth. So of course I was curious to hear him bare his soul."

The file itself had survived the many transitions from her successive MacBooks over the preceding decade, but in its transit its metadata had been scuffed and elided, and thus we are unable to discern precisely when Foster Dade sat down and wrote it. We can conclude, however, that it predated his discovery of Hannah Phelps-Berkowitz's death.

For all its ostensible complexities, Adobe InDesign has been the developed world's default desktop publishing software for most of the twenty-first century, and for reasons that defied even himself, Jason Stearns took to the software like a fish to water. Within two weeks of his editorial board's tenure, he was moving from computer to computer, patiently explaining to a seething Noah Baum and a close-to-weeping Jenny Xiu how to adjust the tracking of a subheadline to fill the width of the page. His acumen was considerably less instrumental to the office's collective morale the following week, on the first Thursday in March, when—having finished laying out his own pages by Tuesday afternoon—he spent the subsequent two evenings drafting a mock series of obituaries for each of his fellow editors.

"Foster Harrison Dade, 16," he rhapsodized with his eyes upon his screen, chewing on the gnawed butt end of a ballpoint pen. "Killed by his own very complicated emotional inner life, which you wouldn't understand." Only Tierney and Foster himself had laughed at this. Raj Chakravarty was updating the banner atop that week's front page, which now read March 5, 2010 (Vol. CXXX, No. III).

Jason had carried on before giving up in the face of his audience's mounting irritation. There was a short spell of silent productivity before it broke again with his voice.

"Holy fuck."

They looked to him. There'd been a vacant strangeness in his words that Foster did not recognize.

"Do—do any of you know that Second Year who was expelled? Hannah Phelps"—he narrowed his gaze upon the text message on his screen—"Bartowitz?"

"Berkowitz," Foster quietly corrected him, still looking at his screen, but after flushing at his compulsivity he realized that no one had heard him. There was a pause.

"She—died today. She—she was hit by a train."

"Fuck off, Stearns," Raj Chakravarty muttered, broadening the width of a photo of Pauline Ross on the front page. "This isn't funny anymore."

"Raj"—it was the first time Jason hadn't called him Chakravarty or some abbreviated form thereof—"I'm not joking. Look."

His phone moved from hand to hand around the office. The text had been sent by one of Arsdale House's three prefects, whose known access to otherwise concealed secret knowledge always brought an imprimatur of solemn credibility to the things they disclosed.

"Jeez Louise," Tierney said, who had finally looked at his phone and found the email Theresa Daniels had sent to the faculty an hour before. "Jeez Louise."

Foster returned from the *Kennedian* office that night shortly after nine. Brennan House was silent when Foster came in through the side door. It was only as he reached the landing of the second floor that he heard the stifled laughs coming from inside his room. The door was slightly ajar; the yellow lamp inside was on. Before the nausea he had learned to ignore had a chance to assemble itself, he pushed the door open.

"What the fuck."

His MacBook was where he'd left it on his desk, but it was open now, and in the screen's white pallor he saw the faces of Jack Albright and Mason Pretlow, intense with delighted concentration.

They looked up in unison as Mason smacked the screen closed. His ogling smirk never once flickered. Had Foster allowed himself to look more deliberately at Jack, he would have seen a minor tensing of guilt ultimately overwhelmed by a nihilistic mirth, as if he was delighted to have been caught.

"Oh, hey," Jack said, smiling enigmatically. "We were just—trying to see if we could send a playlist to ourselves, that's all."

He imagined himself grabbing the MacBook and slamming it on Jack Albright's skull.

"We gotta run, buddy," Mason said, his voice rich with the cruelty of its old disingenuousness. He shoved the computer to the side and the two pushed past him out into the hallway, slamming the door behind them with unnecessary velocity. Their laughter was manic in its violence, and it rose through the house as they passed through the rear door and out into the night.

It would be half an hour before Foster found the courage to open his MacBook to see what they had seen, which is to say it would be half an hour before he felt the familiar nod of half an Oxy that he pulled from his sock drawer in a blind strike against the desperation of the moment. As the warmth began to hug him, he sat on the floor of his room with his back against his desk and pulled the laptop down with him.

Foster saw only the smeary purple nebula of his MacBook's default desktop wallpaper. It would be several more minutes before he forced himself to open Safari and click to his browser history. With a spurt of relief he saw that nothing more than several pages of Gmail populated its first page, and allowed himself to close it, and by some drug-assisted force of will he would fall asleep that night having convinced himself more or less persuasively that the earlier incident had been a nonevent, nothing more than his nemeses' best attempt at a paranoia-stoking psyop.

For reasons difficult to comprehend, Foster had not yet learned to distrust what he still understood as the benevolence of the drugs in question. The short answer is that their neurochemical insistences flattered him, and against the loneliness of everything else, he opted to listen when they did. Because of this, he had not thought to inspect the timestamps on the items in question within his browser history, or to look to the bottom-right corner of his screen, where that morning he'd minimized and promptly forgotten about a second Safari window he'd opened to his Blogspot.

XXIV.

There are four technicians who report to the office of the Mercer County Medical Examiner, and all four of them had been dispatched to the station in Princeton Junction the previous afternoon. They hadn't yet found the body when the call came in, and the chief coroner knew from his many years on the job that depending on the nature of the impact, there was a chance that the typical two-man team would still be locating its pieces by sunset. But it was the case photographer who found Hannah Phelps-Berkowitz's trousers. There'd been no concurrent reports of an un- or partially dressed white female anywhere along the quarter-mile between her parents' house and her destination, but they'd retrieved only a pair of pants from the low dune of gravel along the tracks north of the station, around an hour and a half or so after the initial call had come in from the train's second engineer.

As their blue-gloved fingers had lifted the trousers toward a translucent plastic evidence bag, they'd discerned a gentle weight within the pocket, and from it they pulled an orange Velcro wallet. In it was a single Kennedy School student ID card.

Most students were at dinner when the solitary police cruiser pulled in around the Meadow and pulled to a stop in front of Alumni Hall, and those who saw it thought little of it; its siren was quiet and its strobes were unlit. So they wouldn't notice as Roberta Cantrell, Theresa Daniels, and Sheila Baxter got into the latter's Audi and followed the cruiser back out of the driveway in the direction of Princeton Junction. Nor would they see Mrs. Daniels disembark from a taxicab in front of Alumni half an hour or so before check-in, pulling her tote bag from the cab's back seat and returning to her office to finish and then send the all-faculty email she'd spent the ride back to campus drafting on her BlackBerry.

The prefects would be the first students to learn, but not until nine thirty or so, and by the time word began to slowly trickle out among their younger classmates it would be nearly lights-out, and the overnight interlude would stall the rate at which such news normally disseminated across Kennedy. In classes the following morning, there'd be an atmospheric solemnity that wouldn't make sense or indeed assign itself a name until midmorning, when they took their seats in the Manning Arts Center.

Each March, Kennedy hosted the mid-Atlantic regional squash championship; to encourage their classmates to fill the stands, the varsity girls' team spent several weeks late each winter term choreographing a flamboyant, sporadically suggestive skit to be performed at School Meeting. On this Friday morning, the girls on the team left their 10:00 classes earlier for the Manning Arts Center's backstage dressing room, where they prepared themselves accordingly. They had arrived several minutes before Dean of Students Theresa Daniels, who as they dressed had stood herself atop the building's front stairs, repeating the same words every few dozen students or so.

"There will be no student performances today—please go in and take your seats—there will be no student performances—"

Given her fundraising commitments afield and general detachment from the populace over which she nominally presided, Head Master Pauline Ross would appear at two or maybe three School Meetings a year, and they almost always came at the start or end of a term. It was only a rare display of emotional subordination from Theresa Daniels that morning that prompted Head Master Ross to cancel her flight that afternoon to Albuquerque, and just after ten o'clock, the two of them crossed the Manning Arts Center stage to its center podium. There at the side of the foot of the stage stood the twelve members of Kennedy's varsity girls' squash team in neon spandex and tutus, their hair trussed up with gel, far from their assigned seats. They would remain there in catatonic horror over the minutes that followed, as Head Master Ross brought her gracelessly solemn preface to a close and Mrs. Daniels looked to the eight hundred dark faces before her and told them what had taken place the night before.

It would be four to six weeks before the toxicology report would conclude definitively what they had privately ascertained in mid-March, but on the morning of that School Meeting, the circumstances that gave life to this inference were only just beginning to gestate. So when Mrs. Daniels stood at the podium of the Manning Arts Center and described Hannah Phelps-Berkowitz's death as a suicide, it seems safe to say that she had no reason then to believe otherwise.

Those eight hundred teenagers moved out through the front doors of the Manning Arts Center and into the morning in silence. Foster found himself still seated as the auditorium emptied around him, and when he finally stood, his feet took him not through the lobby's wide doors but down the adjacent staircase to the dim bathroom in the Arts

Center's basement. There, after ten weeks of traveling with an ambient but fundamentally psychosomatic nausea, Foster finally threw up. He would do so three more times in the days that followed. Each time he would stand or kneel before the toilet for several minutes thereafter. It was almost purifying in its violence, as if he'd consumed a dram of some ancient religious psychedelic and was expelling exorcised spirits in the form of putrid viscera. The drier heaves tore against his chest and then finally subsided, but he would stay there a bit longer and blink down through the tears of physical stress at the porcelain as the flushing water thrashed against it.

He spent almost all weekend alone in his room. Ames House was hosting Saturday night's dance downstairs in the Dining Center. "What a fucking buzzkill," Foster had heard Freddie, the House's social chair that year, say that afternoon as he passed along Brennan with Mason and Thomas Connelly after lunch. "Couldn't that girl have found a good train next week to've walked in front of?" They'd suddenly become bored of throwing rocks, but Foster still tensed as he heard them approaching, and he'd begun to breathe a bit easier as their steps regressed toward the Meadow when he heard Connelly's voice. "Fuck you, Dade!"

Evening fell, and from across campus he heard the thuds of Swedish House Mafia straining against the Dining Center windows. It seemed that at least a critical mass of students had pushed through the odd collective numbness that had carried across campus after School Meeting on Friday, and the evening was flaked with shouts of distant laughter. Foster ordered himself a pineapple pizza from the Domino's in Hamilton after check-in, but found himself capable of eating three bites of a slice before he thought he might vomit again. Unable to do otherwise, he found himself thinking of the messages he had deleted from his Facebook Chat inbox, the contours of their words insisting themselves through his nausea.

> **Hannah Phelps-Berkowitz:** Hello Can u meet me
> **Hannah Phelps-Berkowitz:** Oh U must
> **Hannah Phelps-Berkowitz:** Spank Spank Sloooo, Yankee Dodle

Hannah Phelps-Berkowitz: Sleep!! When??????? Help Me

Hannah Phelps-Berkowitz: I close My Eyes to Sleep and the Bees Are eating Me

In the days that followed, there were fleeting moments when Foster successfully convinced himself of what Theresa Daniels had told them at School Meeting. *There was something deeply off about her,* he wrote on his Blogspot late that Saturday, March 6. He did not identify anyone by name, but—well. *Some of the stuff I've heard from people suggests that there was something really wrong there even before this. I'm not pretending there aren't very real side effects or impacts or whatever, but the sense I get is that her relationship with Adderall/Vyvanse was a symptom rather than a cause. It's not like drinking, where you black out and crash a car.*

And yet we can also intuit that these moments of self-deception were precisely that. I'm referring to the deceit, but just as crucially to its momentariness.

When he retired in the spring of 2020, thirty years of students in total had sat around Dr. Arthur Tierney's classroom table on the second floor of Memorial Hall. (On the first day of his last year of teaching, he had quite literally fallen over himself upon learning that the mousy girl in his final First Year Humanities section, Margaret Taub '23, was the daughter of Charlie Taub '89, who'd been in his first-ever Fourth Year seminar on Milton three decades prior.) "I should just cart you out to fundraisers as the headliner," Geraldine Miller from the development office had said as she hugged him at his retirement party in the Head Master's Residence, for which several hundred of his former students had traveled from as far as Hong Kong. He'd been told it was a departmental gathering, and when he stepped into the entryway to the manor's ballroom to see a generation and a half of faces beaming at him with the success of their surprise, he had stood there for a moment, wordless for the first time in his life, and then he sat himself on the mahogany floor and wept.

The toasts alone went until ten thirty; the music finally shut off at two. At one point he rounded up a dozen or so men and nearly as many women at the bar beneath the high windows. For a second, he looked mistily upon them, these weedy sixteen-year-olds who'd struggled through Plath and forgotten to bring their *Twelfth Night*s to class and gotten or given their first handjobs in the surreptitious darkness of his classroom five or fifteen or twenty-five years before, who now had gray in their hair and summer places on Nantucket and children with braces. Then with a conspiratorial wink, the man who'd mystified and enchanted these adolescents with his signature soliloquys and digressions and brilliance procured a teetering tower of glasses and a bottle of Patrón and took tequila shots with them. Shortly before midnight, Hardy Kane and Scott McCall had wheeled out an ice luge in what was allegedly the shape of Shakespeare's head. True to her word, Pauline Ross had left Kennedy two years after the Bicentennial Campaign for a Manhattan hedge fund, but she'd come back for the event, and others watched with spellbound wonder as she and Tierney went head-to-head at the Bard's collarbones while Hardy Kane splashed twin handles of Grey Goose into the holes bored into the icy skull. At one point, a rosy-cheeked Theresa Daniels—who had stepped down as the Dean of Students in the aftermath of the 2009–2010 academic year and returned quietly but mercifully to the Math Department—let Tierney sweep her out to the center of the room, and the two waltzed with perfect grace to "Wild Horses." Jason Stearns, whom Tierney had socked in the gut with delight upon learning he'd gotten married to a Bain colleague four months prior, later claimed that he and his former teacher had smoked a joint together in the middle of the Meadow just before three in the morning, but this can't be independently verified.

For all that's changed at Kennedy, the *Kennedian* is still the *Kennedian*, and with the same Calvinistic gravitas with which they and their predecessors had done everything, the members of the 138th editorial board crafted their final issue as farewell tribute to their advisor. By its calculation, Tierney had taught just north of 3,200 students in his three decades at Kennedy. What these individuals will tell you—as they did in the long panegyrics they submitted for the edition, which in their collective weight forced the 138th Editor-in-Chief to call the printer's night manager at midnight that Thursday to say that the eight-page issue would now run at twenty-four—was that Tierney's twitchy peripateticism was something of a red herring. Even in his final years, during which he celebrated his seventieth birthday, no one who'd spent the necessary hour reading the blue ink of his essay-length annotations in the margins of their graded papers had the presumption to scoff at his long-winded free associations as the bumblings of a senile or woolgathering mind. Those with the temerity to send in those papers two days late learned from the marked-down grade circled above their bibliographies that, all appearances to the contrary, his luminosity was not encumbered by the academic's self-absorbed absentmindedness. His students learned this very quickly: though he conceded it might be even faster to figure out how to scan and email the papers he'd marked up in blue pen, which he said seemed like a pain in the ass, none of those 3,200 students could remember submitting an assignment that hadn't been waiting graded in the manila envelope affixed to his classroom door more than twenty-four hours later. (On more than one occasion, a student who'd turned in a final paper just after breakfast had been waiting outside the chapel for the lunchtime shuttle to Newark International when they'd heard Tierney hollering their name as he bounded down Memorial Hall's broad front stairs, brandishing their stapled pages over his head like a winning lottery ticket.)

Of the tens of thousands of pieces of student writing Art Tierney had read in what was then his twenty-two years at Kennedy, the final paper Foster Dade wrote as a student at the school defied every formal, argumentative, and genre-delineating precedent. After early tours of duty as Assistant House Master in Donavan and then House Master to the cluster of cerebral and troublemaking Fourth Years in Haskell, Tierney had decamped to a three-hundred-year-old stone cottage just beyond the far end of the golf course. It had been the private home of Rev. Josiah van Arsdale, who'd founded the Eastminster Classical Academy in 1810 on his family's hundred acres between Princeton and Trenton. Tierney had repurposed the northern bedroom of the two on the second floor as his study, with his desk against the front window and several thousand books on the shelves occupying the three other walls. The PC and Dell printer the administration had given him had sat in their boxes for the better part of two terms before he finally heaved the computer onto his desk and placed the printer on a turned-over milk crate by his feet.

It was there on the night in question that Art Tierney's Outlook account would have chirped with the arrival of Foster Dade's email. By temperament and work ethic he was basically nocturnal, and he would have put down whatever he was reading—for reasons unbeknownst to everyone, he spent three weeks early that spring with the four novels of the *Twilight* series—and clicked to his email, and then he would have downloaded its attachment and let the small printer by his sockless ankles whir to life. By the syrupy lamplight he would have stapled its upper corner and glanced just below it to affirm that the paper's heading adhered to stylistic expectations (even as late as Third Year, they so often did not), and then he would have begun to read.

It seems safe to say, though, that as his eyes flickered down past the first sentences of the fourteen-page document, he understood intuitively that his usual twenty-four-hour return-delivery window would not apply to this case. He always read his students' papers thrice—once for wider macroscopic first impressions of their thesis and voice, then for the more intricate components of their argument, and once more to double-check his own first response—but his experience here defied standard ritual: he would read it in its entirety, unable to pause and make a note to himself even if he'd wanted to, and in the time between then and when Foster Dade stood before his classroom table with his North Face backpack hanging off of one shoulder, Tierney would pick up the printed essay and return to isolated moments or ideas or phrasings, which in that intervening period had started to swim to the top of his conscious mind like cosmic fibers, threatening to entangle themselves there if he didn't let himself hear them again. "It was one of the best pieces of student writing I've—ever read," he would confess to Scott McCall several months later, during their weekly steak dinner at Witherspoon Grill in Princeton.

One of the hardest things about writing about boarding school in the twenty-first century is figuring out how to convey to the unacquainted reader that the world of *Dead Poets Society* is about as familiar to the most recent generations of Kennedians, Exonians, et al. as a German technical college. Given the bleakness of everything else, it's tempting to look to the bond between Foster Dade and Art Tierney as something pure and salvation-bringing and poetic. But the truth is important here. And the truth is that Tierney would hold on to Foster's paper for as long as he did—regardless of the exact chronology, "a couple of days" is descriptively a safe bet—because he did not know what to do with it. This isn't to completely negate the very real connection between the two of them; on the contrary, we can't really comprehend the matter at hand without it.

This is why, after finally sliding the stapled pages into the beaten leather of his attaché case, where it would sit silently until the coming Tuesday, Tierney almost intuitively understood that Foster's was a different sort of case, even if the obligations it demanded of him looked a lot alike. This may have been why he spent several days thereafter preoccupied with the emotional profundity of the self-indicting essay that had arrived in his inbox. Indeed, he thought of little else. He'd later remember his two-year stint as Dean of Students in the mid-1990s as the psychological nadir of his tenure at Kennedy—"Jeez, man, I got a little bit of power and all of a sudden I kind of knew why Mussolini had so much fun"—but it had left him with a fluency in the contradictions and tensions within the Kennedy disciplinary code that was almost Brandeisian in its elegance. He knew that the paper in his attaché case lacked precedent not only scholastically but jurisprudentially. As a legal thinker, he had little appetite for textual originalism, and despite the rigidity of his standards, at the end of the day he understood the law as only as good as the living souls it ensconced. Fourteen pages of what seemed at moments like a purely literary effort would not suffice on their own as anything resembling admissible evidence—and even then it wasn't entirely clear what the crimes to be arbitrated had been—but this was only the crudest of the salient details that burdened him. In quiet but diametric opposition to the spirit and practice of the Ross-Daniels administration, Tierney thought motive mattered.

And this is what confounded him in the days that followed, and when he contemplated the matter, he saw the face of the light-haired boy whose eyes had struck him in their sadness when he'd arrived silently at Kennedy fifteen months prior. In the five academic quarters that had followed, the sadness had never really dissipated, but with time it had availed a certain light: pale and low-wattage in its chiaroscuro, yes, but light all the same. Then one day in that second winter Tierney had looked across his classroom table at Foster and had seen that the light had gone. It wasn't until he read those pages that he began to understand the deeper spiritual arithmetic of why.

What Art Tierney realized for sure, though, was that the confessions in that document weren't exactly confessions, per se. What interwove them wasn't guilt or dull moral obligation but something more honest. Whether or not they incriminated the author seemed incidental—not only to the reader alone past midnight in the light of his study but to the author himself, who after emailing the paper to his teacher that Saturday night pulled on his fleece and stepped silently out into the night, quietly sliding his uneaten Domino's pizza into the garbage can outside Brennan before moving out into the far reaches of the darkness of campus, looking up to the vast universe overhead.

XXV.

And so it was on the following Tuesday afternoon that Foster heard Dr. Tierney call his name as he slung his backpack over his shoulder and turned to leave.

"Stick around for a minute, Dade, would you?"

They'd spent the first English class of the week with William Henley's "Invictus," the final stanza of which Tierney had scrawled in his angled cursive along the chalkboard behind the classroom table. "I am the master of my fate," he'd whispered hoarsely as he turned to his students, who realized that his eyes glistened with wetness. "I am the captain of my soul." In that moment Foster had finally forced himself to look at his teacher. It had seemed momentarily like Tierney was going to turn his head toward him, and Foster had spent the remaining half hour of class thinking about that flinch, the way Tierney's weepy eyes had been spangled with the fluorescent light overhead as he finally turned back to his seat at the end of the table.

Tierney was straightening the chalk into lines within the grooves of the aluminum sill below the blackboard, and only when the final student was gone did he straighten his shoulders, pausing for a moment before going to the door and closing it.

"Have a seat, Foster," Tierney said softly, standing at his desk and pointing to the chair on its other side. It was, Foster realized, the first time his teacher had called him by his first name.

For the first time Foster noticed the small silver frame upon the desk, in which a much younger chestnut-haired Tierney embraced a pale woman with a round face: Tierney's first wife, whose death after cancer many years before had sometimes found a fleeting place in his long arias before receding into the wake of where it took him. Foster blinked at it, his face warmer than he would have liked, and when he looked up he realized that Dr. Tierney had laid Foster's paper on the smooth oak of the desktop.

"You understand," Tierney said, and there was a slower deliberation to his voice that Foster had not heard before, "why this troubles me, don't you?"

Foster sat there for a moment and then nodded. Tierney looked down at the first page and lifted it away to the next, and then spoke.

"I would in fact be remiss," he said, his words still soft, "if I didn't tell you that this is one of the most elegant collections of words I've read in a very long time." He looked at Foster then, and despite the new and frightening solemnity to his face, Foster saw that his eyes betrayed the light he'd known them to hold. "Miss Whittaker, hm?"

Foster nodded again, and then to break the press of the silence that followed as Tierney returned his eyes to the paper, he finally opened his mouth.

"Dr. Tierney—I really don't know what I was thinking. I was just sort of free-associating and wanted to explore certain themes of—you know—darkness. It was stupid of me to send it to you and—I really don't know what I was thinking," he heard himself say again.

"But Dade"—and here Tierney's words weren't unkind, only palpable in their deliberation—"I think you do." He looked at Foster and then fleetingly toward the window. "I think you do." He seemed to be repeating it to himself.

"So, um." Foster heard an almost childlike meekness in his own voice and swallowed. "What happens now."

Tierney's expression was frightening in its inscrutability.

"I'm afraid I'm going to have to spend a little bit more time on that one. There's"—he tapped his long fingers gently against the pages—"a lot going on here. I'd be lying if I said moments of this didn't upset me. And we're both men here, Dade—so I hope you'll respect wherever my thinking ultimately goes on the matter, just as I respect your decision to submit this to me."

And then his face seemed to soften. "And now I would like to speak to you as your teacher, in the most original meaning of the word—not as a member of the Kennedy English Department but as the person who for almost thirty years has spent each night before bed wondering if the teenagers who come into my classroom five times a day think I'm wasting their time." He looked at Foster. "I've been at this for a very long time, and maybe it's unprofessional of me given the circumstances"—he tapped the papers again—"but I've found as I've gotten older that there are fewer and fewer moments where at the end of the day I go to bed knowing that I've done my job, and I know them when I see them, so I would like for you to sit across from me now and let me teach."

Foster nodded, and realized that his throat was warm with the start of tears.

"Do you know what Leonard Cohen said about love songs?"

Foster shook his head.

"He said: 'Children show scars like medals. A scar is what happens when the world is made flesh.'"

Foster stared at him.

"You are a child, Dade. I don't mean that pejoratively, or as a dig at your maturity or your intellect or anything else. It's just a fact. You're a Third Year, so—sixteen? Seventeen?"

"Seventeen next month."

"Seventeen next month. You're a child, and when you're seventeen next month you'll still be a child. You're all children when you come here, and even though when you leave, you can go vote and buy your-selves your spearmint Skoal, you're basically still children—if slightly smarter, more sexually experienced children." He paused. "And that's what we do here. We take children and we do our damndest to give them what we think they need to become older, slightly smarter chil-dren, because not long after that they won't be children anymore. And that's all we can do. After that, it's anyone's game. And the world is fucking garbage."

He reached across the desk and took the silver frame.

"Fucking garbage," he said again. "I was thirty-seven when Sonia died. Sonia was thirty-five. She was pregnant when she got sick, and then she wasn't pregnant anymore, and then she was dead. And I was a child. I wore my scars like the fucking Medal of Honor, let me tell you. For three years I showed the world my broken fucking heart, hoping there'd be someone to fix it, or at least someone who'd tell me how."

The light outside the classroom's high windows was brighter behind the clouds than it had been at lunchtime. Students were moving across the vastness of campus toward the Field House, and Foster could hear the distant bursts of their happy, untroubled shouts. The classroom was dark except for what pressed itself through the windows.

"And I can't sit here and tell you how I finally grew up, because to this day now I don't have a clue. I wrote a lot. And I came here. And the scars don't ever go away, and sometimes they still hurt like an absolute bitch, and it's been twenty years. But somehow you learn how to carry them inside of you. It's how love songs are written, probably. I say 'probably,' because what the hell do I know about writing love songs, but I do know that I hear them differently than I used to. When I was a kid."

Down below the classroom, an Athletic Department bus chafed against the driveway as it pulled around the Meadow toward the gates. It broke the stillness of the afternoon, but then the stillness restored itself, and seemed to hold a multitude of things within it. For a moment Foster sat there.

"Dr. Tierney, why do I do this to myself?"

He did not know how he found these words. He understood intu-itively that they had found their shape in what Dr. Tierney had meant to say to him. In them, he heard the question that had hummed across fourteen pages and several hundred Blogspot posts in their incomplete effort to ask it. It was a adolescent question, but Foster Dade was an adolescent, and in the stillness of the moment, it unfurled for him the clarity of the world he'd spent months wandering. He saw the chapel swollen with candlelight the night before Christmas break, and the impossibility of Manhattan from the bridge in the varied lights of frigid midnight and spring dawn. He saw the celestial trails that still shimmered faintly after many months across the vast banded constellation of the mid-Atlantic, from the sandy cusp of Long Island at Southampton down past the city, across the tired hills of New Jersey and the fields of refinery light that enclosed it to the stillness of North Baltimore when its streets were asleep. It was the question of a child who had learned to stifle his fear of that darkness by imagining the secrets that found harbor in its shadows—a child who heard the vastness of his question and let its simplicity fill those unseen spaces he could not populate.

Tierney looked at him for several moments. His face was taken by the shadows that had spilled into the room's dusty half-light.

"I think," he said finally, "that a child is not supposed to hurt like this." His fingers didn't tap the pages this time so much as come to rest against them. Within the shadows his eyes were cloudy with their sadness. "A child does not deserve this. And—I think that what differentiates children as a species is their unique capacity to compensate for such hurt. There are mechanisms there that atrophy in adulthood." He looked at Foster. "I also think that this capacity I'm describing is an ethically neutral virtue. What it produces—the things it produces in order to cope—might be riveting and as creative endeavors they might even be impressive, but as far as homeostasis goes, they're wired with the short term in mind." He blinked. "And as a result they sometimes have consequences. And I suppose in the service of preempting those consequences, one should take inventory of where these mechanisms end and the rest of themselves begin."

It was only two nights later, a couple of hours before dawn on March 11, that Art Tierney would return to his upstairs study and open Outlook. *If either of you has time to meet today to discuss this . . .* he wrote in the subject line after locating smccall@kennedy

.org and tdaniels@kennedy.org in the recipient drop-down list. And
then he would rise from the desk and move down the old stone house's
narrow stairs, stooping slightly to avoid hitting his head on the low
landing above, and step out into the bright morning with his coffee.

That evening, Theresa Daniels's name would appear with a chime
in his Outlook inbox, and for the second time in as many days, Tierney
found himself reading the standard summative memo the Dean of Students sent to Kennedy's faculty in the immediate aftermath of a major
disciplinary event. Having the administrative sense not to put certain
things in writing, Daniels crafted these emails with a passive-voiced
clerical paucity, withholding extraneous details and auxiliary names.
Her email on the night of March 11 would accordingly refer only to
an "incriminating document written by the student," and Tierney
would find it odd—though perfectly within her jurisprudential rights,
of course—that she had not reached out to him for further dialogue
about the document in question before pursuing disciplinary action.

Tierney did not know, of course, that at the time she sent this terse
report to the constituents of Group_AllFaculty@kennedy.org and
shut off her office lights, the email he'd sent that morning remained
unopened not only in Theresa Daniels's Outlook inbox but Scott
McCall's too. Only later, over the first of their steak dinners in Princeton, would Tierney learn from McCall that his own private ethical
dilemma over the paper he'd received that March weekend had ultimately amounted to an academic exercise. When he sent his predawn
email to the Dean of Students and the student in question's House
Master, Tierney had no way of knowing that several hours earlier,
Scott McCall and his wife had awoken in their bedroom on Brennan
House's second floor to the sound of an insistent knock on the House
Master apartment's door. Tierney did not know, then, that by the time
he'd finished his third cup of coffee on his back porch that morning,
taking in the brightness and warmth of what felt very much like the
start of spring, Scott McCall would already be sitting in Theresa Daniels's office in Alumni Hall. He did not know that both of them were
looking down at printed copies of the same document he'd forwarded
them, sitting across from the dark-haired boy in a Kennedy Lacrosse
jacket who'd gotten there first.

* * *

Annabeth Whittaker was sitting at the foot of the stone steps below when Foster left Memorial Hall. She was reading an old paperback copy of *White Noise*. The cable-knit sweater she wore was the color of sand and hung down against her thighs, and as she sat she'd brought her knees up to her chest and pulled its hem up over them. As he stepped down from the main doors, her eyes moved up from the book's pages to meet his.

"Hi," she said shyly, after a moment.

Foster felt himself smile.

In the weeks since she'd come to him outside the *Kennedian* office, this was how they had found each other: against the quietude of those rare moments when the campus around them was empty, when everyone else was in the Field House or the Dining Center. There'd been maybe three or four of these surreptitious encounters, but their infrequency also seemed to avail the same pensive magic with which they brokered the crystalline stillness of the empty grounds. He understood that this was how it had to be.

I know I shouldn't be celebrating the way things are, he'd written one Sunday night soon after their first quiet walk. But even though it's definitely different between us, I also feel like there's something in the things left unsaid that feels . . . almost more intimate. Not romantic intimate or sexual intimate, just . . . safe.

She and Jack had been fighting. This was the simplest rendition of the truth, at least, and more or less interchangeable with the version she gave Foster in those final weeks. She almost always withheld the specifics. Her reluctance to divulge these details to Foster belonged to what he'd come to recognize as the inscrutable ethical logic by which she privately justified her return to him. In his gratitude for her magnanimity, Foster chose to simply go along with its convoluted mental gymnastics. They did not talk about Jack in the context of his friends, which is to say they did not talk about how they had tormented Foster for close to a quarter of a year. In those moments when their conversations seemed to bring them toward that topic, he let himself believe that her ignorance was genuine. Annabeth's refusal to share the details of her and

Jack's mutual hostility seemed to illuminate the safety of this little two-person kingdom: she brought to it only her pain, ambient and decontextualized and deep. And Foster could allow himself to believe it had something to do with him.

"I've been worried about you," Annabeth said finally as he stepped down to meet her at the foot of the stairs. They found themselves standing immediately before each other, their toes facing, and for a moment they both grinned at the absurdity of it, as if they were emperor penguins preparing to march. But then the softness with which she had spoken returned to her face.

"You say that every time you see me now." Foster let himself smirk at her wryly, and yet she seemed to know that they both felt the salience of her words.

"Hannah Phelps-Berkowitz—you sold Adderall to her, didn't you?"

They'd started to walk along the driveway around the Meadow, and he tried to stop himself from stalling at these words, but the softly probing rise of her eyebrows informed him that she had seen this. The little nuances of her concern seemed somehow miraculous to him.

"I did," he said finally. "But I don't know—"

"I don't either," Annabeth said quickly. "That's not what I was saying. I just—I can imagine it's kind of unnerving to have . . . *that* happen to someone to someone who belonged to your life. Which she did," she continued as he began to speak, "even if you were just her drug dealer."

"Oh, don't use that term. It makes me sound vulgar."

She smiled impulsively at his words, as if she'd forgotten the weight of their cadences. But then her face fell again, and where her smile had been Foster now saw something that looked like fear.

"Foster, you need to stop." They weren't walking anymore. They stood on the driveway's shoulder just below the rise of Brennan's front porch. She looked at him and there was distress in her eyes, anger even, and against the events of the days that followed he would find himself wondering what within her—what clause or corollary or syllogism in her wretched, schizophrenic ethical code—had made her want to seem to care. "I'm, like—profoundly fucking serious. This isn't me saying 'be careful' anymore. This is me saying 'stop.' Tomorrow. Today. Like—don't even fucking walk me home; go inside Brennan and do whatever it is you need to do to bring this all to an end."

"But I want to walk you home." And in this moment he was smiling.

For several seconds what had seemed like anger in her sea-glass eyes now trumped all doubt. It was strange, now, to think about that first evening eighteen months earlier, there on the Brennan porch. I hate thinking about those first months, he'd written over the summer, not long after coming back to Baltimore, when things still hummed with the glow of a goodness made more lovely by the shell of the loneliness through which it had pushed. But as always, I can't ever seem to separate certain songs from memories—meaning that if I listen to a song a lot during a certain period, six months or a year or three years later I'll listen to it and it'll take me back, sometimes in a really vivid way. "Screaming Infidelities" by Dashboard Confessional; "Wake Up" by Arcade Fire: they'll come on shuffle and I'll find myself thinking about those days that fall. About how lonely I was, and how self-conscious, and how I once faked a phone call while crossing paths with Frances Evans and Gracie Smith on campus so they wouldn't see me as this total friendless loser. But sometimes, when this happens, I'm weirdly kind of wistful for it. Because back then Kennedy still seemed like something colossal and profound, and my sadness mostly had to do with how outside of it I felt.

As he stood there with Annabeth, he thought of the girl who'd been standing there in the foyer of Brennan. He thought about the mercy of her kindness, of her interest, and how as he'd stood there in awkward silence out on the porch, the intimidation of the faces around her had seemed to acquiesce to the gravitational pull of her sitting there up along the short wall. I'm uniquely good at finding the faults in people, especially as I get to know them better, he'd written in one of those early posts, but she is perfect.

The anger danced in her eyes and then collapsed. "I have never met someone," she said, "who has a bigger appetite for misery. You're a glutton for punishment, Foster Dade," and his name seemed to spangle the quiet world that existed between them as they stood there, "and I am going to be historically pissed off if you get fucked over for it."

"Sometimes I think it's too late," Foster said simply. He heard the honesty in his own words.

Annabeth blinked at this and then sighed. There was something different between them then. He had felt its shimmer in their quiet meetings over the preceding weeks, after that first walk into the darkness from outside Fenster Hall, but it seemed to realize itself then, there under the cool copper of early March. He had marveled before the profundities that found life between them in the preceding year and a half—on the colossus of the bridges that spilled out from Manhattan, within the freckles of raindrops that fell against Lake Placid before she'd kissed him—and yet this found its profoundness in something different, unstylized by grandeur. It took its spell from the new quietude with which they walked, in the fact of their reconciliation. It didn't lend itself to the same poetry, but it was precisely in this illusion that it felt real.

And as she looked at him—despite the vagaries of everything, despite the capriciousness with which she enchanted him and the abundance of evidence that had amassed to prosecute the fidelity of her affections—he understood that she felt its realness too. It would only be later—not much later, but later—that her reticence in that encounter and others would begin to make sense, but even then, he'd cling to the simple fact that, despite everything he'd learned that had brought her distance into horrible relief, she'd still chosen to wait for him below the steps to Memorial Hall.

They kept walking.

XXVI.
http://www.fhd93.blogspot.com/2010/03/expectations_part_2
(Posted March 8, 2010)

Annabeth was waiting for me outside of Mem today. I don't know if she even knew that I was in there meeting with Tierney, and of course I didn't tell her about the paper, for obvious reasons. It was the first time in the last few days—and honestly, since the Poinsettia Ball— that the world seemed somehow correct in how it sat on its axis. I walked her back to Hewitt. We're in different sections of Honors U.S. this quarter, but it's the same final exam, and she asked me if I want to study in the library tomorrow night. We haven't done anything like that together since everything happened. Maybe I'm being optimistic, but it makes me feel like everything is slowly starting to heal itself and get back to normal. Even Jack et al. seem a little less obsessed with being assholes. In hindsight it's wild how infrequently Jack and I cross paths—he's on the third floor this year so we don't shower in the same bathroom, and I guess I've been spending pretty much all of my time in my room this quarter—but I ran into him in the common room yesterday, and for the first time in three months he didn't sneer or say something shitty or act like he was going to shove me with his shoulder when I passed. Maybe I was imagining it but it seemed like he gave me a nod.

Maybe I am being too optimistic. Sometimes I think about the start of my time at Kennedy, when as my depression got worse I began to think that the universe—or at least this universe—is somehow funda- mentally designed to reject my presence, like I'm some invasive virus that's gotten into a very healthy immune system. Recently I've been thinking that again. But it's not as horrible as it was back then. Maybe I just don't get bothered by the same bullshit that used to make me miserable; maybe with the bullshit of the last few months I've just gotten tougher. Maybe I've grown up. And I do feel older than I did. I've had sex, at least. (Side note: I've been thinking about trying to talk to Porter. It seems like maybe enough time has passed.) I would like to write about all of this someday, down the line. I can't picture myself as a thirty-year-old (or even a twenty-year-old) but I some- times think about how wonderful it will feel when I can look back on these years and know that they're over, and when I focus on them I'll be able to focus on the good stuff. Even on the worst days, I know there's been a lot of good stuff. I think I'm going to call it quits with my . . . business operation. Because I feel different than I did a year ago, I have a hard time remembering what made me want to do it back then, and in hindsight the whole thing just seems so stupid. And then I'll start working on fixing everything else.

(Ed. Note: This was the final entry posted to Foster Dade's Blogspot.)

XXVII.

It was Annabeth Whittaker who reached out to me. I should confess that by that point, I wasn't planning on getting in touch with her. I knew from how several of her friends had responded that the odds of her even replying were next to none, but the embarrassing basic truth is that I was afraid. I was afraid for the same reasons I'd been afraid of her when I was a new Second Year at Kennedy: even then, after everything that happened, she existed on campus as she always had, with the insouciant radiance that at the end of four years at Kennedy had occupied the passive daydreams of no fewer than three dozen starstruck boys. It's a testament to the potency of her magic that she was basically forgiven by those classmates who'd been wounded by the crime that she somewhat miraculously got away with. (That she did get away with it may have spoken at least in part to the same magic, though the official reasons were more pragmatic.) In a nice little allegorical touch, the Terpsichorean Society would do *The Crucible* for the black box production in the winter of her Fourth Year; those who six months prior had found their names in a 236-page PDF document would later find themselves under the spell of her ethereal kindness and allow themselves to believe that, at the time its contents had been written, she had been somehow bewitched.

Because of my own susceptibility to the fluency of her existence, I also found that the prospect of the more complicated truth frightened me in what it threatened to compromise. So for many months I set forth on this project, and as its evidence began to spill in high piles across my kitchen table and accumulate on my laptop desktop, an empty hole remained at the center of what this information had begun to weave into form. Sofi Cohen had been miraculously helpful, but after a dozen hours of phone calls and FaceTimes and coffees with which I tried to stretch a compensatory caul of data over the hole in question, I think I was beginning to annoy her.

I was at my parents' house in North Carolina over Thanksgiving when the fat little Gmail notification brought my phone's screen to light. I'd just ordered a home meteorology station on Amazon and was feeling proudly grown up—after twenty-six Christmases, I'd finally gotten my father something more materially valuable than a recycled piece of school art or the first political biography I'd seen on the discount table of Barnes & Noble on the morning of Christmas Eve—and I assumed it was only the shipping confirmation that had arrived in my inbox, so I returned to watching *The Crown* alongside Gretchen, the squat little corgi–golden retriever mix my mother had rescued from the humane society thirteen years earlier.

It was when I looked away from the television to idly send a Snapchat that I saw Annabeth Whittaker's name. The subject line below it simply read *Kennedy*.

Gretchen glanced indifferently up at me as I leaped from the couch. Only once I'd closed the door to my childhood bedroom behind me did I let myself open the email.

Hey—

We didn't know each other well at Kennedy, but Sofi Cohen has told me a little bit about what you're working on. I'm actually not flattering you when I say it sounds fascinating. I've found that it's easier and more painless in the long run to dispense with bullshit at the start of things, and thus I will tell you candidly that when Sofi told me about your conversations, I was more than a little concerned, for obvious reasons. I don't have anything to hide—which is exactly what someone with something to hide would say—but I was at the very least a supporting player in the story you're interested in. I assume you're an ethically solid journalist and that you were going to reach out to me at some point, but if that's not the case I thought I'd send you an email and tell you that I'd be up for talking. I'll be back in New York this weekend and I'm around through Christmas.

Her hair was shorter than it had been at Kennedy, or at least straighter, and in the warm light of the sushi restaurant's entrance it danced with the snow that had started to fall outside. Even after she'd announced her engagement the previous spring, the boys who continued to fall in love with her each month did so in the way they had since she was fourteen, under the persuasive, starlit lull of their sense that she loved them back. As she stepped into the little restaurant, beaming at the maître d' while pushing a hand through the dazzling snowmelt of her hair, I understood why. With raised eyebrows and big eyes she grinned at me, and in that grin I saw the same glow of wild conspiracy that I realized Foster Dade had seen. It invited you to share in the secret of the absurdity of the world. You understood, looking at her, that this was privileged information, omnipresent but elusive until she in her brilliance had pulled it from the sea in her shimmering silver nets, and that for reasons that made sense in her smile, she'd chosen to share it with you.

"You're lucky I'm too cheap to hire a lawyer for an hour."

The events of the spring of 2010 had danced off her with an elegant glide. Nine months later, she was accepted in early decision to Dartmouth. In a wild, cosmic twist, Blake Mancetti would be admitted in the regular decision round three months later. There's a subgenre of friendship unique to the alumni of schools like Kennedy, who depending on the year will arrive at Duke or Middlebury or Johns Hopkins alongside anywhere from five to twenty of their high school classmates. In those first drunken months, they'll find one another by chance beneath the muggy half-light of college bars or fraternity basements. It doesn't matter that they may have exchanged a total of four words in as many years at Kennedy. What was once the mundane fact of common circumstance becomes something more profound. This is especially true when they're drunk. They'll locate one another in these dark corners, and screaming over the music's thudding bass they'll do their best to get back to what they'd once had. Dartmouth is a small school, and over Annabeth Whittaker and Blake Mancetti's four years there they'd strike up an aloof but very much amicable friendship, sustained in these encounters at bars and parties. He came out as bisexual in their freshman spring and gay the following fall, and despite the friendliness of their interactions, there's no evidence that he ever shared with Annabeth the details of his earliest adolescent sexual explorations, for reasons we could describe as either duplicitous or noble in what was withheld.

She and Jack formally broke up two months into that first year of college, though like most high school relationships forced out of fear to weather the emotional infertility of early undergrad, it had really collapsed after graduation. Several hours after they cross the head of the Yard and receive their little leather-bound diplomas from the Head Master, Kennedy's Fourth Years embark on a weeklong stretch of itinerancy along the mid-Atlantic seaboard in the Volvos and Tahoes on loan from their parents, moving in improvised caravans along I-95 to wherever the night's party has materialized. It's a gorgeous and deeply strange stretch of days, Grad Week, a sort of collective fugue nurtured by the momentousness of leaving Kennedy forever and their increasingly immiserating hangovers. Virginities are lost. (For Jason Stearns and Jenny Xiu it would be with each other, on Jason's parents' bed at the Stearns' beach house in Spring Lake. This had been the venue for the week's first and biggest party, and when the graduates arrived at sundown, they found Jason chomping on a cigar in a silk bathrobe in the front yard, standing before a kiddie pool he and Noah Baum had filled with sixty pounds of ice and more than a hundred bottles of cheap champagne.) Grad Week carried on valiantly into the sixth night that year. On the penultimate hungover morning, Sofi Cohen had gone to the Class of 2011's Facebook group and invited anyone willing to make the seven-hour trek to her parents' house in Southampton to do so, expecting only close friends and maybe a dozen others; by eight o'clock that night, the cars parked outside had spilled out onto the edges of Meadow Lane, and when the Southampton Police came after midnight in response to multiple noise complaints, they documented in their report "at least 150+" underage drinkers. Of these six nights, Annabeth had ended five in tears.

She'd finally broken up with Jack on her third visit to Princeton, just before Thanksgiving, and for three years she was more or less single. There were hookups that rehearsed themselves for a few weekends thereafter, wine-drunk nights of varying tediousness spent in the beds of ice hockey players and Theta Delta Chi brothers, but nothing more substantial. The relative stability and sobriety of life in New York City thereafter would give similar trysts a slightly longer shelf life, but they registered as little more than distractions, fitted unromantically into the pauses in her eighty-hour workweek on the debt capital markets team at J.P.Morgan. She lived in the East Village and then Nolita with two friends from Dartmouth, and forgave the banality of her life in those three years by accepting them as the obligatory first chapter—or second, if you count the junior summer internship at J.P.M.—of the longer professional timetable to which she'd rather cynically joined everyone she knew in subscribing, which was no less banal but a lot more lucrative. In keeping with that agenda, she spent her third autumn in Manhattan applying to business schools. She deemed it an act of fidelity to the intellectual fervor she'd otherwise sacrificed to the gods of capital that she chose Booth at the University of Chicago over Wharton at Penn, ranked fourth and second respectively.

It was in the fall of her first year that she met Elliott Crawford, a second-year M.B.A. student who was concurrently pursuing a J.D. at the law school. He was four years her senior, and had gone to Groton before Brown, where he rowed crew. Between classes in her last two semesters, she'd walk across the grassy width of the Midway Plaisance beneath the university's high Gothic towers to study alongside him in the law library, and at the end of the day they'd get in Elliott's Grand Cherokee and drive up Lake Shore Drive to the apartment they'd decided after seven months to share together in the West Loop. They moved back east together after Annabeth's second year and with the enormity of their combined salaries—Annabeth was starting at McKinsey; Elliott was a first-year associate at Cravath—got a place in the West Village, with high windows and a loft and soon thereafter a Jack Russell terrier. A month before, he'd come with her to the Class of 2011's tenth reunion—their Ten Year, in the parlance—and by all accounts had been a wonderful sport. They'd told each other about their boarding school years, as boarding school people tend to do, marveling at the shared idiosyncrasies of their experiences, and with time he'd learned about Frances Evans and Gracie Smith and her own role in the circumstances around their expulsions. But she never told him about Foster Dade. Two months later, in mid-August, they would drive up from the city to Annabeth's parents' place in Lake Placid for a weeklong respite before starting work. Twelve years to the day after Foster had pulled into their gravel driveway to see Annabeth sprinting barefoot toward him, Elliott would take her on a hike to the summit of Whiteface Mountain, where he bent down on one knee and proposed.

I knew all of this, of course, but I let her tell it to me anyway. We were the only ones in the restaurant, which had been finagled between a sunglasses shop and a neon-lit bakery on Mott Street. *You'll probably think I have no taste, but it's stunningly cheap and honestly the best sushi I've had outside of Japan, swear to god*, she'd texted me with its address after we'd exchanged numbers.

"The tackiest thing about me is how much I love those awful Americanized tempura rolls with, like, sriracha and Yum Yum Sauce on top," she said before we ordered, "but if I order one you don't get to write about it."

It took the better half of an hour for us to get to the topic we'd met there to discuss, and when we finally did I realized that I had very happily spent the preceding stretch letting her take me away from it.

"I suppose you have a job to do here," she said finally, and I let my eyes meet hers.

We spoke for an hour and a half as the snow fell outside. There was something at once superhuman and utterly organic to the specificity with which she returned to events and encounters a decade past: at that point in my research, I did not need her contributions to flesh out the story's precise historical infrastructure, but nothing she said contradicted the narrative I'd laid; if she lied, the lies were inconsequential. But I also realized as she spoke that we'd both turned to the raw sweep of history to divert ourselves from particular localities within it.

We finally got where we were ultimately headed, and almost by accident, thanks to Mason Pretlow.

"The boys are all still close, but he didn't come to our Ten Year—neither did Jack, actually—and Mason sometimes chimes in on the

GroupMe we all have, but it's usually incoherent and at like three in the morning when he's coked up. No love lost. It's just, like—a lot of darkness there. Angry darkness. I know at least two girls at Trinity say Mason raped them, and virtually everyone who's hooked up with him says it's just—kind of a scary experience."

I looked at her. "Why do you think he hated Foster so much?"

She smiled at the directness of the question. "Because Foster was smart," she said, with the same equanimity. "He had a lot of books and loved writing for the newspaper and had a very dry, absurd sense of humor that I don't think Mason had the intellectual bandwidth to even recognize as humor. Plus, Foster didn't really play sports, which is what saved Jack and Pritchett. I mean, tennis, yeah, but he didn't hide behind it the way they did with lacrosse and crew." She seemed to stop for a moment as her mouth twitched briefly into something rueful. "He never thought he'd bother. I guess all of that offended Mason's sensibility of, like, virile masculinity or whatever, or threatened it." She took a sip of the warm sake she'd ordered. "I guess the easier and blunter way of putting it is that he thought Foster was gay."

"Do you think he was?"

She smiled again. "The craziest thing about going back to Kennedy for our Ten Year—fuck, I'm old—was that literally every student seemed to identify as bi or queer. Which goes to show how much things have changed, like, tolerance-wise, but my point is—" She contemplated her words. "You know, who knows. I don't think he was gay, no. But, I dunno—he was never truly happy in his own skin, and that could have had something to do with it."

"Is that why he sold Adderall?"

"I have no idea why he sold Adderall. I think, yeah, maybe he was trying to satisfy a certain idea of himself, and I guess selling drugs fit the bill. But I've always kind of wondered if—I dunno. I've had, like, three different therapists talk to me about quote-unquote self-sabotaging behavior. Sometimes I think something in him made him—I dunno." Her eyes seemed to apologize for the falter in her voice.

"Is that why you think he released the Facebook thread?"

Outside, the snow had begun to rise in thin sheets from the windowsill along the glass. There was a fragility to these gentle accumulations, which in their translucence smeared orange with the glow of the street behind them. I could not discern the meaning in her eyes, but when she finally spoke, there was something in the distance of her voice that seemed at once philosophical and sad.

"No," she said softly. "I think he released the Facebook thread because he was hurt."

"Well, do you blame him?" I was surprised at my own tenacity, but it did not seem to upset her.

"Speaking of things I talk about in therapy." She smiled. "Well— *talked* about, I should say. Maybe it's fucked up, but until Sofi told me about it"—she tilted her sake glass in my direction—"I hadn't really thought about all of this in a while. Maybe deliberately; I dunno." She took a sip. "But you ask if I blame him. I don't know if that's the right question. Blame doesn't matter—what happened happened. The turn of the cosmic wheel and all that. Kismet, et cetera."

She smiled again, as if to apologize for her facetiousness. "The honest, nonbullshitting answer is that I was sometimes a cunt in high school. I always prided myself on being less of a cunt than, I dunno, Gracie, and when I was nice—and I tried to be nice—it wasn't bullshit." She stopped for a moment. "But sometimes you want to be clever, or funny, or—approved of. And in those moments, it's weirdly easy to forget everything else. So do I blame him for what he did? I don't know. Do I understand what he did?" She looked at me. "I don't really know that either. But"—and she didn't cry, but there was a heaviness to her voice—"I imagine it really sucked for him, finding that."

XXVIII.

"I understand that it's supposed to be vicious satire, but I think the billionaire pig-men are actually very adorable."

Annabeth happily turned her history textbook across the table to Foster, who looked down at the cartoon of a porcine Andrew Carnegie, from below whom protruded the legs of impoverished children.

Foster grinned. "Would you hook up with him?"

"With enthusiasm and intense arousal."

"Wow, Whittaker, you're a perv." Foster thought he heard a prurience in his voice, so he looked back to his notebook, where he'd been transcribing the terms on their study guide. "Okay—Jacob Riis. Yellow journalism."

The day had been beautiful in its normalcy. For an undisturbed stretch of hours he'd taken himself to class, feeling himself smile at his teachers as he sat down and volunteered his thoughts in discussion. He would not know why all of it—Hannah, Tierney, everything else—had receded toward some far nebulous horizon of his mind, but he'd opted not to challenge it.

He had been back in Brennan after classes when his BlackBerry had buzzed against his stomach.

> **ALW [04:46:01PM]:** are we still on for the library tonight? i'm so behind on history
>
> **ALW [04:46:57PM]:** btw—i think jack and i are taking a break.

It was still light when he got to the library, and when Annabeth appeared in the glass of his study carrel the sky behind him was purple and red. She grinned at him, and as she did, he saw that her eyes were red.

It had been with an almost maternal smile that the nurse at Planned Parenthood had handed Annabeth the prescription for the postcard-size sleeve of birth control pills in November. She had wept against the brick wall of the clinic at the kindness of it before walking the half-mile to the Hamilton bus station, and the following day, she'd taken the folded slip of paper to the infirmary, where the receptionist had placed it in the folder of student prescriptions that were brought to the pharmacy in Princeton Junction thrice weekly. Every morning in the four months thereafter, she stood before her mirror in Hewitt House and pressed a little green disk through the blister packet, and with a drink from her Nalgene she swallowed it and her Wellbutrin together. It was her commitment to this regularity, Jack told her, that in his mind had justified his decision to surreptitiously pull the condom from his penis. He had been thrusting atop her for several minutes when, reading what looked like boredom on his face, she'd asked him if he wanted to take her from behind. As they rearranged their naked bodies on the cold floor and she turned to face the wall, he'd tugged it off with a quiet snap and slid it into the wastebasket by his knees, and then he brought his penis back inside her.

She wasn't sure how she'd noticed—she supposed it was completely plausible that he'd discarded the condom in the immediate aftermath of his orgasm—but with a pause of intuition she'd held her cupped hand just below her vagina, and as she tensed her abdomen with closed eyes she felt the warm spill of semen dribble against the tips of her fingers. "You're on birth control," Jack had said with irritated confusion as she wept. "And it doesn't fucking feel like anything with a condom on."

She had left him there, and the following afternoon once classes were done, after retrieving the white paper bag of Plan B from the sympathetic nurse at the infirmary, she'd met him outside Hewitt.

"I'm actually not even upset—I'm just so tired from it all," she'd said. "And I cry when I'm tired. But I'm not going to cry."

But she had held herself to her promise with impressive resolve, sitting down across from Foster and turning herself to her textbook and notes, and as night settled in outside the wide windows, those in neighboring carrels could hear the music of her laugh. Foster spent that hour and a half entranced by the fact of it: it was the first time in three months that they had sat together in the library, and the anxiety he was carrying began to soften as the sky became safe in its darkness. He let himself watch her pen move across the pages before her to fill them with her manic, looping scrawl. Her lips moved silently, almost indiscernibly, with the words she wrote, and he listened to their quiet music.

"Haymarket Affair—Haymarket Affair—eighteen eighty—oh!" She looked up at Foster suddenly. "Shit. I was supposed to give my primary sources notes to Evan Siegel. Can I use your computer for a sec? What I get for being a good girl and eliminating distractions."

"Your primary source notes aren't the only thing Evan Siegel wishes you'd bring him," Foster grinned, pulling his MacBook from his backpack and handing it to her. She flicked a paper clip at him. As she took it, he imagined with a brief flash that he'd left some particularly mortifying display of pornography open in his Safari browser, before remembering he'd closed it upon his history study guide in Microsoft Word shortly before she'd arrived.

"I'm logging you out of Facebook," she said as she typed, the silver glow of the screen upon her face. "Sorry not sorry."

Her fingers moved convulsively against the keyboard, and then with a note of finality she pecked the enter key. "Mischief managed," she said, handing the computer back across the table. "All right, baby, Horatio Alger, let's do this."

They left as the library was closing. "Definitely overkill, but I got an A-minus on my midterm and I need to crush this," Annabeth said. The moist air had chilled with nightfall, and Foster felt himself shiver as they stepped out onto the brick terrace. He glanced at Annabeth to see that she was smiling at him.

"Hey," she said. "It's nice to be back."

Foster thought about what it would be like to hold her hand, but there was a comparable warmth in the intensity of her eyes, and he found himself smiling too.

"It's nice that you forgave me for being a horrible juvenile idiot."

"Having fun?"

Jack Albright's voice came through the darkness with a glass-like clarity. Foster flushed with shame at the physicality with which he flinched. He looked up to the sidewalk that carried on toward Brennan and saw Jack standing with Mason Pretlow, Freddie Pieters, Chandler McDermott, and Gracie Smith.

"We were just doing some studying and couldn't help overhear your cute little homework date." The infantilizing mockery in Jack's voice was violent. He stepped toward Foster, Mason and Chandler moving with him, and Foster felt himself tense in frightened agitation.

He thought desperately of the Xanax and Oxy left behind in his sock drawer. Jack was grinning sweetly.

"I think it's so sweet that you two are having a nice time together," he said, towering over them. "Do you think maybe you'll give her another little kiss?" With this last word he brought his hand against Foster's chest. Foster staggered against the force but did not fall.

"Fuck off, Jack, you child," Annabeth said coldly—bravely, Foster thought. "Your insecurity is showing."

Jack sneered at her, and for a moment looked as if he was going to say something to her. But then he turned his eyes back to Foster. "How ya doin', Foster?" The jeering sweetness had curdled in his voice. "Sell many pills tonight?"

"Hey, Dade"—this was Thomas Connelly, who'd materialized behind them—"is it *weird* that a girl had a mental breakdown and walked in front of a train because of you?"

Foster felt something within him seize—an angst that by some evil miracle metastasized into rage. He turned not to Connelly but to Jack.

"Would you be less upset about Annabeth hanging out with me," he said flatly, "if you'd been able to be anything other than a total fucking loser at sex? Yeah, I tried to kiss her—but when I fail at something I own up to it. I don't, y'know, blame Adderall for my inability to achieve orgasm." He said these words vaguely suspecting Jack and Mason would laugh at their hypocrisy, and he blushed with regret, but their suddenness seemed to preempt a retort. Violence spasmed across Jack's face, but it seemed to briefly silence him. The voice he heard next wasn't Jack's but Gracie's.

"I'd watch your step, Foster," she said. "We all got pretty tired of pretending to like you. I know I'm *pathologically incapable of enjoying things*, but I gotta say, you spent a lot of time talking shit about us when we went out of our way to be nice."

"Grace—" This was Annabeth, but her voice seemed unsure of itself. Gracie rolled her eyes. Her words hung there with a meaning that all of them but Foster seemed to intuit.

"Oh, we all know what Foster likes to say about us," Jack said. Something in Gracie's comment had brought an agency back to his gaze. He was smiling. "Seems to me he should be more concerned about his slut father, but hey, what do I know."

"Jack, stop." There was an urgency in Annabeth's voice that Foster had not heard before. He could not look at her, nor did he want to.

"You're a fucking loser, Foster Dade," Mason said, his expression rich with delight at what he'd witnessed. He looked as if he was going to keep going, but as the boys and Gracie laughed, he seemed to decide that he was satisfied.

Foster wasn't sure how he'd finally broken away, or what had occupied his mind along the short stretch of concrete back to Brennan. Their laughter hung there in the night. He could hear it as he climbed the stairs to his room. He shut the door behind him, and in the grasping narrowness of his desperation he found himself reaching for his MacBook, as if the minor dopaminergic press of the screen's glow would rescue him. He sat at his chair and put the computer upon the desk before him.

Annabeth had left Safari open. In the blissful thrall of mindless instinct, he brought the cursor to the Facebook tab along the gray band below the address bar, where it sat between YouTube and KENNEDY EMAIL. And then he realized that Facebook was already open. The screen was white and empty, but at its center was a small box in which Foster saw the commands that Annabeth had failed to click before she'd shut his laptop. *This will log you out of Facebook. Are you sure you want to continue?*

He stared at it for a moment, and as he did, two rocks thrashed against his window, followed by the same barks of laughter that had followed him back from the library. He heard the downstairs door open, and heard the mirth in Jack's clomping footsteps as he climbed the stairs. And in the helplessness of the moment, Foster clicked cancel.

It had always been mundanely strange seeing someone else's News Feed, for the reasons it's mundanely strange to drive someone else's car or sleep in their bed when they're out of town: the perspective it affords is at once intensely familiar and inscrutably not. He looked out at the long band of text and saw his own name: Foster Dade liked *Passion Pit*, *Girl Talk*, and *(500) Days of Summer*. Annabeth had four notifications, and though he hit back against the urge to click the little gray globe upon which the number was stamped in red, he let his eyes move down to the stout ribbons of text along the screen's lower edge, where her most recent messages sat. There were three. The first, still open, was from Evan Siegel, confirming with a little smiling emoticon that he'd meet her outside the Dining Center at breakfast for her notes. The second was from her brother, Charlie. And next to that, against the short column of users' names, was a group conversation with Sofi Cohen, Frances Evans, and Gracie Smith.

We can speculate, I suppose, as to what Foster's mind did in those first moments, as he sat there looking at his screen in the dim light of his room. We can assume that he paused again, as he had when he opened his MacBook to see that Annabeth had failed to log out, but we can also assume that Jack's words and Gracie's had hung over him as he returned to his room, and that the urgency of their unanswered questions almost certainly called out for clarification. But all of this is conjectural. The only thing we know for sure is that he brought his cursor to the four girls' chat and clicked it open.

For all that can be said about the contents of the pages that follow them, there's an incontrovertible quaintness to the earliest exchanges in what is today known as the Kennedy Thread. Legends perpetuate themselves through a process of distillation; with each retelling, their superfluities and waste are clarified away or absorbed into the ever-brightening points of salience. The legend of the Thread would persist long after the lawyers representing its four authors successfully scrubbed the internet of even partial versions of the document itself. What would be lost in the story that carried on thereafter is the fact that the overwhelming majority of its several hundred pages were exceedingly banal. Even the cruelest teenage girls have to figure out when they're meeting for lunch. It was Frances Evans who'd sent that first message on the first day of September 2007, thirty-six hours after she and her fellow members of the Class of 2011 had moved into their rooms. "heloooooooo," she wrote. "does anyone have any idea where on campus i can buy tampons? lawls." The correspondence of those first weeks twinkles with an earnest reticence; in it, we can hear the novelty of their encounters with their new world, with its institutions and rituals and, most crucially, its politics. Even then, though, there was sex, theirs and others.

"brent rivenbark wanted me to suck his dick tonight," Gracie Smith would write before the end of their first month together. "if i do, do i have to swallow his cum?"

There's something charming and sad about these first messages when contrasted with the very last, which had been sent a couple of hours before the thread would be frozen in time forever. They were the first messages Foster saw when he clicked upon their window, and they disclosed the details of Annabeth's decoupling from Jack that she herself had not. He read them with a queasy ache that very soon thereafter would seem comparatively pleasant.

It was easier to scroll up through the thread when he expanded it to occupy the entirety of the Safari window, and with long strokes against his trackpad he moved at random through time. He heard the messages in their senders' voices.

> **Sofi Cohen (April 7, 2009, 8:14pm):** ughhhhh you guys
> **Sofi Cohen (April 7, 2009, 8:14pm):** katie macinerny (sp?) in perry had anal with that fourth year donald something and shat on his dick
> **Sofi Cohen (April 7, 2009, 8:15pm):** how gross is that
> **Frances Evans (April 7, 2009, 8:18pm):** ewwwwwww!!!!!
> **Gracie Smith (April 7, 2009, 8:19pm):** of course she did
> **Gracie Smith (April 7, 2009, 8:20pm):** she's such a skank
> **Gracie Smith (April 7, 2009, 8:20pm):** i hard that back home in eighth grade at a party she got fucked while sucking another guy's dick
> **Gracie Smith (April 7, 2009, 8:20pm):** heard******
> **Annabeth Whittaker (April 7, 2009, 8:27pm):** lol hard
> **Annabeth Whittaker (April 7, 2009, 8:27pm):** don't let gracie's freudian slip fool you—she wishes it had been her

. . .

Annabeth Whittaker (May 31, 2009, 2:14am): interrupting our regularly scheduled programming to inform you that j.t. ricciardelli has quite possibly the weirdest and most diseased dick at kennedy

Annabeth Whittaker (May 31, 2009, 2.15am). it's also really really small but like . . . that's the least of our worries

Sofi Cohen (May 31, 2009, 8:12am): wow good morning

Sofi Cohen (May 31, 2009, 8:12am): say more

Annabeth Whittaker (May 31, 2009, 10:15am): lol sorry i just woke up but i needed to share that last night

Annabeth Whittaker (May 31, 2009, 10:15am): also his semen tastes like . . . mustard?

Gracie Smith (May 31, 2009, 10:18am): is it bad that i always pictured him with a gross dick just because he's poor

. . .

Frances Evans (September 20, 2009, 2:44pm): i'm in the library and i am pretty sure rosalie haddish is wearing a trash bag

Frances Evans (September 20, 2009 2:45pm): jk it's a dress

Foster continued to scroll, down toward the present and then back up again. He would find himself at a long stretch of mundanity **(Gracie Smith [August 1, 2009, 1:33pm]:** wait do we actually have to do the assigned reading if we're in honors u.s.) and then just before flicking elsewhere he'd glance a few lines down and find himself staring at a suddenly visceral exchange. He'd only idly contemplated the fact that Porter was absent from the thread, but with time he began to comprehend why.

Gracie Smith (February 20, 2009, 12:18am): guys i'm so fucking sick of her

Gracie Smith (February 20, 2009, 12:19am): does she know that none of us fucking like her

Sofi Cohen (February 20, 2009, 12:20am): be nice

Annabeth Whittaker (February 20, 2009, 12:25am): i like her!

Annabeth Whittaker (February 20, 2009, 12:25am): but also
yeah lol

Gracie Smith (February 20, 2009, 12:27am): her vag
is hairy

Gracie Smith (February 20, 2009, 12:29am): and per mason
apparently it smells

Frances Evans (February 20, 2009, 8:01am): tbh i feel like
she's really condescending about school stuff

Frances Evans (February 20, 2009, 8:01am): i think she might
just be jealous

. . .

Frances Evans (November 18, 2009, 12:01pm): is it just me
or has porter gained like ten pounds?

Sofi Cohen (November 18, 2009, 12:10pm): it's all that dick
she's getting from foster

Annabeth Whittaker (November 18, 2009, 12:19pm):
~L~M~A~O~

Gracie Smith (November 18, 2009, 12:22pm): I'd very much
appreciate it if u never made me think of foster dade's dick
again lmao

Annabeth Whittaker (November 18, 2009, 12:23pm): she told
me he didn't (couldn't???) finish the frst time they fucked

Sofi Cohen (November 18, 2009, 12:26pm): i understood it as
more of an erectile dysfunction situation

Gracie Smith (November 18, 2009, 12:22pm): lawlzzzzz

He had come across his name at earlier moments in the boundless string of messages. It had been innocuous and in most cases
incidental—**Annabeth Whittaker (February 1, 2009, 3:17pm):** foster and
jack are watching a movie together in brennan tonight but we can do dinner on
sunday—but even in its innocuousness it had made him shift uneasily,
and as he passed through its moments of cruelty he found himself
fighting against his old nausea. It redoubled as he read those messages
from mid-November, and with a new vibrance he heard Gracie's words
outside the library: *We all got pretty tired of pretending to like you.*

It's difficult to say precisely how long Foster Dade spent reading those messages that night before he finally did what he did. I've met a few people who said they ended up reading the thread in its entirety to counter the dullness of study hall or detention; when I did the same, it took me four hours to get from September 2007 to March 2010, though admittedly I probably spent more time than most with its many stretches of banality. It's unclear if Foster gave it the same attention, or if against the suffocation of his nausea he simply opted to do what so many Kennedians would do the following morning and in the days thereafter, which is hit command-F on his keyboard and against every physical lash of better judgment type his own name.

And irrespective of how he got there, we know that as he sat before his MacBook that Wednesday night, he found himself staring numbly at its screen, his throat tightening up, listening to the meaning of Jack's and Gracie's words outside the library disclose itself.

> **Annabeth Whittaker (February 28, 2010, 10:41pm):** holy shit you guys
> **Annabeth Whittaker (February 28, 2010, 10:41pm):** holy shit
> **Annabeth Whittaker (February 28, 2010, 10:41pm):** foster wrote an essay about me
> **Sofi Cohen (February 28, 2010, 10:42pm):** ??????
> **Annabeth Whittaker (February 28, 2010, 10:42pm):** for tierney's class
> **Annabeth Whittaker (February 28, 2010, 10:43pm):** [File: Paper1A10.docx]
> **Annabeth Whittaker (February 28, 2010, 10:43pm):** and about his family, which, yikes
> **Gracie Smith (February 28, 2010, 10:44pm):** omg hahahahahahaha
> **Gracie Smith (February 28, 2010, 10:44pm):** i'm fuckign dying
> **Annabeth Whittaker (February 28, 2010, 10:44pm):** i know
> **Annabeth Whittaker (February 28, 2010, 10:44pm):** like

Annabeth Whittaker (February 28, 2010, 10:45pm): what

Frances Evans (February 28, 2010, 10:46pm): omg how did u get this

Annabeth Whittaker (February 28, 2010, 10:46pm): jack

Annabeth Whittaker (February 28, 2010, 10:46pm): he says he saw it open on foster's comp when foster was at the newspaper

Annabeth Whittaker (February 28, 2010, 10:46pm): sent it to himself

Annabeth Whittaker (February 28, 2010, 10:47pm): which is shitty of him but like

Annabeth Whittaker (February 28, 2010, 10:47pm): this is next level

Gracie Smith (February 28, 2010, 10:49pm): "If one were to look upon my admittedly short romantic resume" omg hbahhahahah

Sofi Cohen (February 28, 2010, 10:50pm): you're evil

Frances Evans (February 28, 2010, 10:51pm): ya i think it's really sweet!

Gracie Smith (February 28, 2010, 10:51pm): who else has this

Annabeth Whittaker (February 28, 2010, 10:51pm): all of ames at least mason and pritchett and chandler m

Annabeth Whittaker (February 28, 2010, 10:52pm): i guess at least now we know he isn't gay

Annabeth Whittaker (February 28, 2010, 10:52pm): wiat

Annabeth Whittaker (February 28, 2010, 10:52pm): wait**

Annabeth Whittaker (February 28, 2010, 10:53pm): they found his blog too lmao

Annabeth Whittaker (February 28, 2010, 10:53pm): jack just sent it to me

Annabeth Whittaker (February 28, 2010, 10:53pm): literally like his diary

Gracie Smith (February 28, 2010, 10:54pm): send. it.

Annabeth Whittaker (February 28, 2010, 10:58pm): http://www.fhd93.blogspot.com

Frances Evans (February 28, 2010, 10:59pm): omg this is so long

Sofi Cohen (February 28, 2010, 10:59pm): can we search for our names

Gracie Smith (February 28, 2010, 10:59pm): already on it

The clouds that had hung over campus that week had been boundless and empty and unchanging, but that night they finally relented against spring's first spills of warmth, which rose to pull them apart. In the patches of dark sky their sundering betrayed, the moon was fat and bright. They stained the light they held into the bands of cloud that had not yet split their seams, and in their illumination Foster could see their westward motion. He watched their tails pass against the smear of white before moving on into the darkness.

He sat there without moving for a very long time. Beyond his door, several nations away, he heard Ms. Chissom move along the stairs, calling to the boys that there were five minutes until lights-out. He wouldn't have cried—not then; quite possibly not thereafter. What he felt in the immediate aftermath of that discovery wasn't quite a panic attack; its physicality was incidental, and unlike those fevers of crisis he'd known months before, it neither found an apogee nor receded after its crescendo. It was quieter than that, though not necessarily gentler. It brought something resembling a torpor: even when those first minutes burned in their humiliation with something like panic, it took him a long time to finally click the word *Blogspot* on the gray band below Safari's address bar, where it sat between *KENNEDY EMAIL* and *mom's netflix*.

Foster had proudly customized his blog's layout and design shortly after he'd opened his Blogspot account two and a half years prior. He'd experimented with a handful of the platform's typeface options before deciding he liked the familiar minimalism of Verdana; he liked the crispness with which its azure lettering met the eggshell-colored vacancy of the page on which it sat. Sometimes, when he couldn't sleep, he would open his blog and read the earliest collections of words that had occupied it, and he'd feel proud of himself for chronicling his emotions so diligently, since after all it seemed to help.

After he went to his Blogspot that Wednesday night, he would let the richness of its sky-colored light spill out onto his desk for many minutes for what would be the last time, before finally clicking on his account settings page. Several more minutes would pass before he finally let himself click the two words that stood in red ink at the bottom. *This action cannot be undone, and your work will be lost.* And then it was gone.

He continued to sit there, and when Ms. Chissom rapped gently on his door upon seeing the thin slice of light below his door, he reached out and turned off his desk lamp and sat there in the darkness. The cosmic bands of his screensaver lashed across his MacBook's screen. It was nearly midnight when he finally ran his finger back against the trackpad to restore its light.

He had bought the flash drive a year and a half earlier, four days before the start of his first year at Kennedy. Since then, the drive had sat forgotten and in its unopened packaging in the pencil case he'd brought from home. "I swear I'll use it," he'd told his mother when she pulled it from the cart in the checkout line.

It took a moment after he plugged it into his MacBook's USB port for UNTITLED to appear in his Finder's sidebar. He clicked back to the Safari window he'd minimized, where the Facebook thread remained open as he'd left it. *holy shit, foster wrote an essay about me.* There was a crudeness to the rendition that *Save As . . .* generated; in the PDF it deposited on his desktop, certain lines of text spilled below the bottom edges of its pages and stout text ads populated its margins. But it fulfilled its purpose.

In its liberation, the moonlight spilled itself in a silver pallor across central Jersey that night, and in it the campus was bright. A tired Buildings and Grounds officer had stalled his regulation Prius along the driveway outside of Upper House, where he sat with his thermos listening to Rush Limbaugh. The radio's blue glow was spectral in the darkness of the car. His shift would be over at two, and he would pass its remaining hour staring but not looking out at the ghostly expanse of the sleeping school. At one point, he thought he saw the figure of a boy slide against the moonlit earth, but then it either passed into a region of shadows or had never been there at all.

And as the guard returned to his Limbaugh, Foster Dade pulled open the southern door of Fenster Hall and stepped into the blackness. "The building's never been locked, ever," Andrew Mastoff had told him when he'd given him the key to the *Kennedian* office.

In the perfect silence of the empty building his footsteps seemed to strain against the stairs down to the basement. He paused there, not breathing, and then he pulled the key from the pocket of his North Face fleece, where it had bounced against the flash drive as he'd crossed the grounds. It was the first time he'd surreptitiously entered the darkness of the office since he'd done so with Porter. He found he was still adept at stumbling through it. He found the high back of the chair in front of the Editor-in-Chief's computer, where Raj Chakravarty sat hunched on Thursday nights.

Raj had left the desktop open to InDesign, and minimized in its bottom corner was a Safari window open to the school's email platform. It was Noah who wrote the summary of each weekly issue every Thursday night, and before he left he logged on to the *Kennedian*'s email account to schedule its dissemination the following morning. For reasons unclear to recent Editors-in-Chief, you had the option to anonymize those outgoing messages under the default handle all-school@kennedy.org, and Noah had apparently done so by mistake that first week, to Raj's great irritation.

"They already regret trusting us with this," he'd moped, gesturing in the direction of Alumni Hall. "Don't fuck it up."

Foster plugged in the thumb drive. He clicked back to the email account. Below a little icon of a postage stamp atop the screen sat the words *New Message*. He clicked it.

XXIX.

Foster Dade's MacBook Pro/Music/iTunes/Playlists/A Musical Education for F. H. Dade on the Occasion of His Sixteenth Birthday, 4/19/2009 (Feat. Erudite Commentary from the Author) (Created April 19, 2009)

Name	Time	Artist
HAPPY_BIRTHDAY_FOSTER _voicenote1.mp3	0:42	AWhittakersMacBook
Superboy and Supergirl	3:04	Tullycraft
My Girls	5:41	Animal Collective
Silly Love Songs	5:54	Wings
So Rich, So Pretty	3:27	Mickey Avalon
This Must Be the Place (Naive Melody)	4:56	Talking Heads
Ocean Breathes Salty	3:44	Modest Mouse
i_just_learned_how_to_do_these _voice_recordings_and_fucking _love_it_lol_voicenote2.mp3	0:22	AWhittakersMacBook
With You (feat. Drake)	3:49	Lil Wayne
Can You Tell	2:43	Ra Ra Riot
Lost Coastlines	5:31	Okkervil River
Escape	3:28	Enrique Iglesias
Simple Song	4:15	The Shins
Apartment Story	3:33	The National
In the Aeroplane over the Sea	3:22	Neutral Milk Hotel
All My Friends	7:42	LCD Soundsystem
in_conclusion_voicenote3.mp3	1:23	AWhittakersMacBook

17 songs, 1.1 hours, 118.3 MB

XXX.

The first sobs were heard from Perry House, shortly before seven o'clock that morning. Katie McInerney had woken up with her phone's alarm for her daily run, and was happily loading a new playlist to her iPod when she glanced idly to the unread message in her school email inbox. Its subject line simply said "read me," so she did.

Years later, when the scandal had otherwise dissipated under the amnesiac winds of history, those who were at Kennedy that day would still sometimes talk about the strangeness of it: the unnerving music of what can accurately be described as collective weeping. The air outside was mild that morning, and the predawn custodial staff had lifted the downstairs windows of the Ellipse Houses to let in the springtime. It was in those Houses where it began, and from these open windows it carried out to the grounds.

It was an act of precocious strength that many of them forced themselves to go to school—though they allowed themselves to forgo breakfast—and they wept as they walked to and between classes, at a certain point no longer pausing to wipe the tears from their eyes. It was mostly but not exclusively girls. Johnson DeWitt, a legendarily kind, very overweight Second Year from the lower-middle-class town of Wayne, was seen sobbing in the Arsdale House common room. He had never spoken to either Gracie Smith or Frances Evans, and so he did not understand why in October they had spent an afternoon discussing which of their bras (Gracie's A cups to Frances's Cs) would be a better fit for him. By the end of the first class period, twenty-five students had checked into the infirmary, where they would remain for the rest of the day and in some cases that night.

Theresa Daniels had arrived at Hewitt House before breakfast. Those who say they saw her escorting the thread's four authors into her Honda Civic would impassively note that three of them had been crying. Frances Evans's sobs were as loud and violent as any of her victims'. Sofi Cohen did her best to choke hers back, though the effect was counterproductive, and Annabeth Whittaker was simply silent, her face stoic but wet. Gracie Smith had been the last to follow them out of Hewitt. Several witnesses report that her face betrayed no emotion at all; if anything, they said, she looked vaguely annoyed to have been woken up.

A frenzied exchange of emails among administrators, House Masters, and teachers on the all-faculty email thread had decided by mid-morning that it would be imprudent to simply cancel classes: it would stoke the appearance of mass emergency that had already begun to spasm across campus in the wails that rose up over the grounds; formalizing it would only give credence to secondary forms and waves of hysteria. They were all only just then beginning to ascertain the magnitude of the ongoing devastation, and in that uncertainty, any move that might have codified it seemed to threaten to intensify its damage, as if it would tacitly affirm the elegance with which these four girls had torn their classmates' souls apart. In the end, classes went on, but they were maybe half-attended, and by the end of the morning, teachers had begun to just let the students who did show up use their classrooms as a private place to cry.

By lunchtime, Gracie Smith and Frances Evans had been expelled. There'd been no other choice, really. The relevant administrators weakly understood this: they understood that the rulebook had been thrown out altogether with this one. Its consequences belonged to a different and more monumental order than disciplinary precedent. They tried to imagine a world in which the two girls remained at Kennedy, and they just couldn't. Watson and Marjorie Evans had already been in the Alumni Hall foyer when they heard their daughter's guttural scream on the other side of the thick door: she had called them before breakfast that morning, hyperventilating before her open MacBook and what was open upon it, and a visit aimed at consoling her very quickly became (for Watson) a sort of aggressive cram session with the Kennedy disciplinary code and a consequently convoluted appeal to the requisite bodies of power on his daughter's behalf, and (for Marjorie) a morning spent crying at her daughter's pain. Gracie's parents arrived in their Mercedes an hour or so after lunch, at which point their daughter had spent an hour sitting unpleasantly within the administrative center of a school she no longer attended.

Those teachers who went on to occupy administrative or residential-supervisory positions at Kennedy down the line still sometimes return to Annabeth Whittaker and Sofi Cohen's common fate as a sort of learning object: as a case study in either instances of necessary lenience or in precisely what not to do, depending on the teacher in question. A lot of them were pissed when they found out that only two of the four had been kicked out—that was in fact the exact word Lorin Parsons used, *pissed*. In the emergency faculty meeting that evening, Theresa Daniels would rehearse three reasons her administration had chosen to only suspend the two others.

The first—and, given the mutiny that threatened itself in Memorial Hall as the meeting wound down, probably the only thing she needed to expound upon—was that Gracie Smith and Frances Evans had been responsible for a disproportionate sum of the Facebook thread's cruelty. Despite their persuasive performance of sage detachment, Kennedy's faculty (and particularly those who served as House Masters) had an acute and indeed preternatural sense of the political taxonomies that took shape every fall with the arrival of the new First Year class. In most cases, those who'd spent time looking in stunned horror at the document that had arrived in their inboxes had been able to read its cruelties and distinguish between the catty internecine tensions of the social brahmin (Annabeth and Sofi) and the far more disturbing sadism that delighted in the arbitrariness of its targets (Gracie and Frances). Having read the Kennedy thread, I can confirm it was indeed Gracie and Frances who seemed to have taken meticulous inventory of the classmates whose existence they had otherwise declined to ever acknowledge. They didn't know, of course, that the year before she died of cancer, Rosalie Haddish's mother had sewn for her daughter the dress they would go out of their way to notice and mock; they probably weren't aware that their classmate Janna Barker had stood before her bedroom mirror in Perry and wept about her thyroid medication's metabolism-slowing properties long before Gracie would lend her the alliterative nickname Jumbo Janna. If Sofi and Annabeth could be held responsible—or so Donald Cohen, who unlike Frances's father was both an actual lawyer and a very generous alumnus, would argue in Theresa Daniels's office that afternoon—it was in their passivity. They withheld their talents for rhetorical savagery in these moments, and indeed Donald could point to several instances where his daughter had told her friends to be nicer.

By virtue of their relative intellects—at least relative to Frances's—Sofi and especially Annabeth could be almost eloquent in their own lapses into cruelty. But they reserved these talents for less helpless or more predictable targets. Those faculty members who'd presided over the girls' Houses of the Ellipse would concede that in their experience they'd overheard their charges say similar if not worse things about both the boys they'd hooked up with and their own friends.

The second was that both Sofi Cohen and Annabeth Whittaker—but especially Annabeth Whittaker—were a demonstrable value-add to the Kennedy community. Both were commendable students—Sofi good; Annabeth excellent—and both had thrust themselves into the domains of athletics and extracurricular activity in their very first weeks as First Years. None of this could be said about Frances Evans or Gracie Smith: the former's grandest designs of ambition had her following her grandfather and father and two older sisters to Trinity College; the latter would invariably be recruited somewhere for squash.

We could cynically parcel the third reason in with the second. The blunt fact of the matter is that both Donald Cohen '75 and Skip Whittaker '80 had been attentive in their generosity to their alma mater. Donald's donations were vaster than Skip's, but Skip traveled in a social circle of fellow Kennedians that in recent decades had come to inhabit the relevant stations of alumni power that allowed the institution to run. We have no choice but to accept the basic utilitarian logic of the circumstances at hand. By nine o'clock on the morning of Wednesday, March 10, Skip Whittaker had gone to his BlackBerry's contacts and called or sent emails to seven of the sixteen members of Kennedy's Board of Trustees, and in the two hours that followed, Theresa Daniels's email inbox and personal phone line began to quiver with the sort of message she always opened promptly, from the sort of sender she knew better than to leave hanging.

"You all know who their fathers are," she'd finally snapped before the increasingly irked sea of faculty in Memorial Hall that night. "You may want to pretend it doesn't matter, Lorin"—she looked to a seething Lorin Parsons—"but it matters."

So Annabeth Whittaker and Sofi Cohen were suspended from Kennedy for six weeks, through Easter weekend. That their classmates fumed privately about this for a day or two and then ultimately let the matter drop spoke mostly to the fact that dwelling on the issue would have required them to allocate additional mental and emotional real estate to something they very badly wanted to forget. The same can arguably be said for their teachers. Two weeks into Annabeth's and Sofi's suspension, Theresa Daniels would sit in Pauline Ross's office and announce her resignation as Dean of Students. Back in her own office across the hall, she had six unread emails from Sheila Baxter in the Communications office. The first of the reporters had begun to call. In this meeting, Daniels, who had come to Kennedy in 1990 as a twenty-six-year-old with an M.S. in mathematics from Rutgers and a newborn baby on her hip, looked at the Head Master and with the deep psychological fatigue of the preceding weeks said that she understood if, given her administrative failings, it was best if she left Kennedy altogether.

"Don't be ridiculous, Theresa," Head Master Ross said briskly. "These are teenagers. With the internet. Something like this was bound to happen sooner or later."

Foster did not go to class on Wednesday, March 10. He'd passively understood that against the magnitude of what he'd done, teachers would have bigger things to worry about than his attendance.

It was a little after two in the morning when he got back to Brennan, and, though he wasn't asleep until four, he awoke with the earliest press of light against his blinds. He inhabited the following hours in a sort of fugue, moving idly from his bedroom to the small study on the first floor of Brennan and then back again. It was as he sat in the armchair by the study's wide windows that he saw Annabeth Whittaker. She was walking alongside Skip and Diane, both of whom were pale and expressionless. It was two o'clock or so, and they had left Alumni Hall against a lull in human motion outside. Those students who weren't in class were in their own bedrooms, or in the infirmary, and in the silence of the grounds things felt vaguely normal.

Annabeth was weeping. She had on an old flannel shirt she'd worn one cold night in Lake Placid, when he rolled them a joint while she stoked the fire pit, sending embers spitting up in braids of light to meet the stars. Her ponytail bounced a bit as she walked. Perhaps because of his sleep deprivation, or because of the shock of what he'd done, and perhaps because after fifteen months he had finally expended the last of his emotional reserves, Foster realized that he felt nothing. He felt nothing when he saw Jack Albright and Mason Pretlow returning from class that afternoon, their faces dark and distressed and upset. He felt nothing when Jack passed through the front doors of Brennan and saw him sitting there at the study's window.

"If I find out," he said slowly, his voice belonging to some distant sea, "that you did this—I swear to fucking God I will kill you. I mean that literally, Foster. I will beat you within an inch of your fucking life."

Foster only stared at him, and then felt himself smile sadly.

XXXI.

Once again we face confusion in the timeline. The constituent events are easy enough to cobble together; the issue is understanding them in their correct alignment with the quiet thoughts and emotions that allowed them to transpire. We've faced this problem before, but the stakes feel higher here. I am talking less about Foster Dade than about Jack Albright. I made the mistake of telling my editors at ███████████████ about the menacingly ambiguous threats he'd lobbed my way, so I can't blame them for then passing it along to their in-house counsel. All of them have a job to do, and it just so happens that it sometimes gets in the way of mine. But we can make it work. My point is that I was told in no uncertain terms that I must here suppress the conjectural impulse I've otherwise indulged throughout this project, and that anything not immediately verifiable as fact is grounds for the legal action I should basically brace myself for regardless.

So I cannot speak with any certainty about the backdrop to what happened on the evening of Wednesday, March 10. I do not know what secret history prefaced it, and I do not know if any knowledge of this history would make the fact of what happened—just around six hours after his girlfriend had been suspended—any less jarring in its timing. Jack and Annabeth were, after all, only "on a break," and indeed when she returned to campus at the end of April they would once again find themselves hopelessly in love. I do not know how or if this history persisted beyond the night in question. I do not know if it ever replicated itself on any other occasion in the years thereafter.

On hot Friday nights in June, Manhattan's summer interns amass in listless packs at the corner of Bowery and East Fourth to press themselves into the claustrophobia of Phebe's and B Bar. It was there in the summer after his freshman year at Yale that Mark Stetson met a boy from London named Adrian Prewitt-Bowles, who had gone from Eton to Princeton. They would date for two years, during which time Mark became a beloved weekend novelty among the kids whose social capital at Deerfield or Collegiate or Harrow had proven fungible in the brick manse of the Ivy Club. Among them was Jack Albright. If you're a certain type of cynical, it's easy to suspect Mark Stetson's trustworthiness: the fluid elegance of his motion through the world seems to evade the laws of gravity that tether the rest of us to a more obligatory physics of belonging. But the simple fact remains that in all those years of their lives' intricate intertwining—at Kennedy, at Princeton, in the years in New York City since—Mark Stetson never told anyone what he had learned when they were both fourteen, when as smooth-faced, bright-eyed children they found themselves living as neighbors on the second floor of the First Year boys' residence. I can't speak to what Blake Mancetti may or may not have said, but it's worth noting again that to the best of my knowledge—however credulous it may be—Annabeth Whittaker has never found out.

Malcolm Pataki had been sitting at his desk in the IT department in the basement of the library when he got Theresa Daniels's email that afternoon. He'd seen the all-school email in his inbox that morning, but as with all student activities emails he still inexplicably received, he deleted it.

It hadn't taken much work to identify its provenance, though it was something of an inconvenient pain in the ass to match up the relevant IP address with its geographical analogue on campus. It was only after scrolling down to the cluster of punctuated eleven-digit numbers under the heading FENST-HALL that he found it. There were thirteen computers registered to room B12, and he was able to tell Theresa Daniels that the email had come from one of them, though of course the number meant nothing to him. He'd done his job, and then he went home, stopping first at the student pizzeria across the street. And as he tapped red pepper flakes onto his cheese slice, back within the gates of campus Theresa Daniels was standing in the basement of Fenster Hall, waiting for a very distressed Raj Chakravarty to fumble with his keys to open the door.

There was no *Kennedian* that week—there never was the week before finals—but when their phones and computers chimed with Raj's email, at around five thirty, a quorum of the members of the 130th Editorial Board were together in the library, studying for Honors U.S. History. Raj hadn't been with them when Daniels called—he studied alone—and Foster had told them that morning that he wouldn't be able to make it. But the rest of them, Jenny and Jason and Noah and Rosalie, had spent their first half-hour debating whether Tierney and Daniels would let them do a story for the first issue after spring break on what had happened. (Rosalie had seen the thread, of course, and she, too, had cried upon discovering her name. But it had been brief and almost perfunctory, and then she wiped her eyes and stood up a bit straighter and decided her priority that day was studying for finals.)

They read Raj's email in silent unison. "Holy fucking shit," Jason said finally.

"None of us could have even possibly guessed it had been him, even then," Jason would tell me a decade later. "My initial thought had been that a psychopath had been stalking one of the girls and that it had been the latest salvo in his effort—like *Fatal Attraction*. Maybe he'd snuck onto campus. I didn't know."

So he'd thought nothing of it when Foster Dade texted him as they sat there, asking if they could meet in the library's downstairs lobby.

Jason Stearns [05:44:13PM] Just come up dude! We're all here talking about this fucking INSANITY. What do you think happened?

Nor had Jason thought it strange that Foster had insisted that they meet discreetly. "I knew he was super close with Whittaker and friends with the others, so I just assumed he was in shock about it. Especially since they talked about him in it."

And there Foster had been, standing in the cool seclusion of the vestibule that led to the back door from the library's grand atrium.

"Dude, how fucking wild is—"

"Jason, I need your key. The key to the tennis closet."

"The—key? Uh—why?"

"Jason," Foster said, turning to stare into his friend's eyes, "I don't think you would possibly understand how grateful I'd be if you did this for me with as few questions as possible. One day, I promise you this, I will explain it to you. In the meantime, you'd be doing the nicest thing anyone's done for me in legitimately many, many years."

Fifteen years earlier, the members of Kennedy's varsity boys' tennis team had colonized a bleak but spacious chamber in a dark wing of the Field House's first floor. It was a foul, almost horrifying space, rank with the accumulation of several decades of athletic detritus and janitorial supplies. For reasons unknown to anyone affiliated with Kennedy's Athletics Department, the room had initially been intended for the disposal of chemicals. Against its far wall, beneath the murky and almost subaquatic light from the industrial bulb overhead, was a wide, dense basin that drained into an even denser pipe that went down into the concrete floor. Black and moist and gnarly, it looked something like a pernicious and prehistorical algae. It became clear that using the tub to dispose of acetates and epoxies would constitute an environmental crime and almost certainly a biohazard, and the room sat forgotten until the cusp of the millennium, when a junior captain on boys' tennis decreed that the team needed a storage facility for their balls and hoppers and wrapped-up nets.

Jason Stearns would succeed this unnamed captain a decade and a half down the line. His grand designs to finally truly renovate what was then known simply as the tennis closet collapsed after spending an hour prodding a broom handle into the chemical basin's drain. It had dislodged the wrecked blockage there, and as he peered down to the depths of the horrible pipe, which carried on twenty feet into the ground before seeping its discharge into the now-desiccated earth, a horrible and utterly foreign smell began to rise from the drain and fill the closet. "Never again," he'd said after unceremoniously vomiting in front of the girls' lacrosse team in the corridor outside. "What I fucking get for trying to do something good." The drain, Foster knew, had never been closed back up.

Jason looked at Foster quizzically, and for a moment Foster waited for him to collate the pieces of the puzzle. But he didn't.

"I need this back, like, yesterday," he said, pulling the fat greenish key from the lanyard in his pocket. "This is the *real* copy. Blake Mancetti's had the spare since, like, September and he still hasn't taken the time to get it back to me, the rotter."

Foster threw his arms around Jason. "I owe you," he murmured. "I owe you more than you know."

It had taken him barely a couple of minutes to empty the contents of the small plastic bins in his closet into a garbage bag. The effortlessness of it was bizarre and even wistful in its anticlimax. He watched each spill of capsules topple down into the black plastic, sometimes stalling for a moment against a crease before sliding away. The blues and reds and whites of the Vyvanses; the chalky pastels of the immediate-release Adderalls. Their collective mass in the corner of the plastic bag was about the size of a football. In its volume it briefly stunned him: the weight and magnitude of it; the way its individual pills slid against his gentle grip. He stared at this accumulation, feeling the palpability of what it seemed to metaphorize, and for a moment he was awestruck.

We don't know if he'd decided to get rid of his pharmaceutical inventory after or before he stared numbly at Raj Chakravarty's email upon his BlackBerry. But to borrow Annabeth Whittaker's words a decade later: *It's the wrong question.* He was smart enough to have known long before that day or even the night before—months before, arguably—that he would eventually find himself sitting where he sat on his bedroom floor, waiting for the inevitability of a knock against his door. *Dr. Tierney, why do I do this to myself?* I think Foster's decision to go to the Field House that night had to do with something less materially consequential, or at least I've chosen to interpret it that way.

We know that after he left the library with Jason Stearns's key, he returned to Brennan to retrieve his backpack, in which he'd placed the plastic bag of pills. We know that he stepped back out into the blue evening a little after seven thirty. The buildings of the campus around him were swollen with yellow light. He walked back along the edge of the library, beneath the window of the high study carrel where he'd spent those many afternoons against the weight of the maples outside as their colors bled and bloomed and returned to earth. The Houses along the Ellipse stood council-like together before the golf course. He carried on to where the service driveway began its long amble through the hidden expanses of the grounds, past the turf stadium and the soccer fields and along the prefab clusters of faculty houses.

The Field House was empty that night as he walked the length of the concrete rise along the track beneath the central atrium, against which the dusk above had darkened the broad tent of clouded glass. His feet carried him silently. The door to the tennis closet was at the end of a dim cinder-block corridor, past the sentinel of vending machines and locked utility rooms of unknown function. He stepped through the translucent glow of the Pepsi machine and into the darkness, reaching in his pocket for the key.

Foster had finally deleted Honesty Box from his Facebook account in mid-February. He'd chosen to assume Jack and Mason and Chandler McDermott were the ones populating his Honesty Box with several messages a day (most of which simply said "faggot"), but he couldn't really know for sure. This assumption had found credence in an unchallenged, until-then-forgotten conviction: that it had been Mason Pretlow who'd sent him the first Honesty Box message he'd ever received, in the winter of his first year at Kennedy. It had arrived in those weeks in January when he began to find himself alone in the Dining Center or Vito's with Annabeth and Jack, the three of them together in their marvelous solitude. Mason had done little to mask his contempt, and though it had stung when Foster clicked on the notification that took him to the waiting anonymous message, he told himself with some success that Mason was simply jealous.

are you into dudes?

He'd deleted it, and until this moment, he hadn't thought about it since. But as his eyes confronted the scene before him in the tennis closet, it returned suddenly and with visceral color, one in a reflexive kaleidoscope of memories that sought to elucidate the meaning of what he saw and did not understand. In those first seconds of silence, Foster felt his mind vacillate between its vivid constituent parts, and he began at last to see the meanings that had stood there in plain sight. He thought of the night Mark Stetson had come out as gay thirteen months earlier, when he'd gone up to Jack's room in Brennan, met by strange, silent vehemence. How he'd taken this personally, one of many wobbles in a temperament that for a year and a half had confounded and entranced him. He thought of the hours following Sofi Cohen's birthday party, when he'd emerged from his blackout to see the thin, pale shape of Tripp Altridge leering at Jack on the couch, and he thought of the palpability of Jack's silence against it. He thought of Jack's disappearance that night at Tripp's house in the Hamptons, suddenly vivid in its incontrovertible truth. *I'm the most gullible person I know*, he'd written on his Blogspot once. *Just completely credulous. I let people tell me what they want to tell me, and I totally accept that it's my own fucking fault if I believe them.*

The tennis closet was a large room, but fifteen years of amassed equipment and flotsam had occupied its vacancy, and there was something claustrophobic and green about the sickly light that flickered from the bulb overhead. Boxes of old uniforms stood in teetering stacks alongside buckets of acrylic court paint and empty bottles of weed killer. Stringless racquets lined the walls.

Jack looked up first. He was against the far wall, and Foster found some comfort in the accumulation of boxes and junk that rose from the floor between them, as if they provided some sort of sentinel. Jack's expression was almost vicious in its surprise, and Foster noted his own meager spasm of schadenfreude before it collapsed into the wider magnitude of the silence spanning the space between them. Through the room's brackish glow Foster saw the paleness of Jack's naked thighs, where his sweatpants hung at his knees. His forehead danced with the sweat that had stuck his dark hair to the sides of his face. The wildness in his eyes spurted with something more salient and indeed more painful than the rage Foster knew. In that moment, Foster instinctively understood that the anger itself had been only incidental, derivative; it took something deeper and nameless. Instead of fury Foster now saw only an older brokenness. What frightened Foster—what his own eyes may or may not have told Jack—was its familiarity.

Beneath Jack there in the closet was a boy.

It took Foster several moments to recognize Blake Mancetti. He was kneeling before Jack, his shoulders hunched, his back arced out toward Foster. The collar of his tattersall shirt had come unbuttoned and turned upward. There was something nearly vulgar in the meaninglessness of his expression, and in it Foster took sudden inventory of a different set of peripheral, forgotten memories: Blake's sedulous stares from across Vito's and the dance floor of Sofi Cohen's sixteenth birthday party; the seeming aimlessness with which he'd lingered outside Brennan House on a Thursday night five months prior; Jack's empty-handed return from the Field House an hour later. Foster looked back to Jack, where for the first time he saw something pleading in his eyes. Later, he would not know if it had been Jack or Blake who had spoken.

"Get the fuck out!"

Foster stood there dumbly for another moment, and then obliged.

XXXII.

The two First Year Houses at Kennedy stand in perfect symmetry along the east and west banks of the recessed, brick-walled lawn of the Yard, which stretches out from the foot of Fenster Hall. Unlike the turreted, gabled residences along the Meadow, there is a geometrical simplicity to the two dormitories: a single long hallway runs the length of each floor; in almost all cases, the rooms along it are identical in both size and configuration.

We do not need to reiterate the precise alchemy by which this group of boys in the Class of 2011 found one another in the first days of their first term at Kennedy. But it's worth acknowledging the import of the relevant circumstances, of geography and serendipity. On the last day of August in the summer of 2007, then-fourteen-year-old Jack Albright arrived at Kennedy to learn that he'd be sharing the First Year triple suite at the end of the second-floor hallway with Pritchett Pierce of Manhattan and Mason Pretlow of northern Virginia. By virtue of its size, the suite occupied almost all of the residence's northern end; only one standard double room abutted it.

The school's residential administrators steel themselves each summer for the bureaucratic and logistical hurricane of move-in day—food allergies require notation; insulin prescriptions require transfer to the infirmary's pharmacy; agitated mothers preparing to part with their teenage firstborns require placating—and the call received that morning from a South Korean country code was, in the wider scheme of things, one of the more minor crises. One Sang-hoo Park of Seoul had been accepted off the wait-list at Exeter at the last possible minute, and the car service carrying him south from Newark International had reversed course and was heading north toward New Hampshire. The name tags on the First Year Houses' doors had been printed and laminated three mornings prior, and over the months that followed, Sang-hoo's name would remain one of the two on the door to the room neighboring the triple suite. The other was Mark Stetson's.

The relevant alchemies transpired; they found one another. No one from Buildings and Grounds had ever come to remove the second barren twin bed against the wall opposite Mark's, and so it was there that they gathered. At night after lights-out, they could congregate far from the House Master's apartment with the knowledge that their laughter and the muffled throb of Kanye West were audible only to those neighbors who'd realized early on that their own invitations would never come.

I would meet Mark Stetson just before midnight in Washington Square Park fourteen years later. I tell this story as he told it then, and will abstain from my own digressions or improvisations. We had walked east from Little Italy into the narrow inlets and canals of Chinatown. There was a phosphorescence to the darkness, though the neon signs in their storefront windows had stopped humming hours before, and I thought of the dead stars whose final spurts of light still transit across the universe to fleck the sky. There was a quiet edge of fissure to his words as he spoke, as if the meanings they assembled had atrophied in their disuse.

"I guess I think I liked the fact that it was my room that we used," Mark said. "I wasn't out yet, obviously, but I knew I was gay, and kinda assumed it was obvious, and plus, like—it felt like everyone there was white except for me. So I guess I felt like I had to find some way to earn my place." He smiled almost ruefully. "Even though ninety-nine percent it wasn't a place I particularly liked."

Resentment finds nourishment in oversimplifications, and those Kennedians who looked upon these friends as monolithic in its impervious arrogance failed to imagine their bloc having its own interior politics. From afar, these students did not know that—for instance—for reasons discernable only to themselves, Annabeth Whittaker and Gracie Smith spent a month that winter privately besmirching each other to their shared companions, or that when Pritchett Pierce left the triple suite for the showers down the hall, Mason Pretlow turned to Jack Albright to mock the fastidiousness of their roommate's wardrobe, organized in his closet by shade of pastel and dispatched twice a month to a dry cleaner in Hopewell Junction. They did not know that one night that January, Mason and Jack themselves would come to blows, when Jack, returning to the third floor from the library, happened to hear Mason and Pritchett on a video chat with Gracie Smith and Frances Evans before opening the door.

"As I understand it—Jack had hooked up with Kendall MacPherson after the dance that weekend, and apparently she went to blow him and—he couldn't get hard," Mark told me. "And she told Dalia Truett, who was hooking up with Mason, and—I guess Mason found it funny, and Pritchett just happened to be there."

For several weeks after this conflict, only one member of the triple suite would quietly step out into the hallway after lights-out and tap gently on the door of the room to the right. "Honestly, I think Mason was happy to have an excuse not to," Mark said. We were continuing east; across the street, two men pulled coolers of seafood from their open truck to the curb before a grocery store, but otherwise the streets were still. "After I came out, pretty much everyone would eventually tell me that it had been obvious in hindsight, but I think Mason was the only one who really seemed to—know. He was always, *always* weird around me—like, I used to get the sense that he'd shift an inch or two away from me if we were sitting next to each other, like I had something he could catch. Or Jack and I would, like, semi-ironically put on Backstreet Boys, and Mason would just, like—shut down. So yeah, he stopped coming by. And Pritchett was always a path-of-least-resistance person, and then his grandpa died and he was back in the city for like two weeks anyway, so, uh—yeah. It was just the two of us. And—I guess that's how it happened."

It is in the fallible nature of memory-making to restore wholeness to necessarily imperfect raw material. It seeks cohesion at the expense of historicity; it assigns its boundaries arbitrarily. So it has been with this story. So it was with Mark Stetson's recollections of the cold early months of 2008, when Jack Albright would return from Mark's room to his own bed in the triple suite in the still hours that precede the first graying light of dawn.

"It was—never talked about," Mark told me, flicking the empty pod from his Juul to the sidewalk and fishing in his pocket for another. "At least not then, when it was happening. I mean—honestly, I think I'd still halfway convinced myself I was bi, which is fucking hilarious." He pressed the new pod into its aluminum reservoir with a click and brought it to his lips. It crackled briefly as he inhaled. "So I was fine with it. And eventually I realized that not talking about it was, like, the necessary precondition of the whole thing. But that didn't come from my end."

It was the silences that denied it any sort of coda. Winter thawed into a gray, wet spring; the earth of campus grew spongy underfoot. "Obviously Jack and Mason were fine—teenage boys can be just as psycho as teenage girls, but boys are idiots, and forget about things," Mark said. "And it's weird, but I always felt like it was the return to normal that scared Jack. We'd all hang out again in my room, all of us, except now Jack was suddenly quieter, and he was always the first to get up to leave. And yeah—things stopped, I guess."

On a Tuesday morning in the first week of May, the residents of the boys' First Year House set out for breakfast to find a stack of printed forms waiting on a table in the common room. The document contained two prompts.

> *PLEASE LIST UP TO THREE (3) MEMBERS OF THE SAME SEX YOU HOPE TO LIVE WITH NEXT YEAR. (IF YOU HAVE A PREFERENCE, PLEASE SPECIFY A PREFERRED MEADOW HOUSE AS WELL.)*

> *RETURN TO MR. DOYLE'S MAILBOX NO LATER THAN THIS FRIDAY, MAY 9, 2008, AT 5 PM.*

"I have no idea why we decided we wanted Ames—I think maybe we thought it would be easier to get away with drinking, just 'cause Mr. Byrd was so checked out," Mark said. "But it was going to be all of us, and then—" He paused for a moment, as if evaluating the validity of his memory. "Then one night that week, maybe literally the night before the forms were due, after everyone'd gone to bed, he knocked on my door again. And I let him in. And"—and here Mark smiled again—"the next afternoon he told everyone that his dad and uncles were really pressuring him to request to live in Brennan, since they'd all been in Brennan, and that we should take his name off our housing forms."

I was silent for a moment and realized that we had stepped back out into the chalky glow of the Bowery. I looked up to see the towers of the bridge rising up before us, as Jack Albright and Foster Dade and Annabeth Whittaker had eleven Aprils prior. *There was something oddly quiet about Jack when we met up with him—maybe it was just his Adderall comedown, or me still under its influence, but I kept thinking I saw a sadness in his eyes that I'd never seen before,* Foster had written.

"So then what," I said finally. "What about the others?"

Mark looked at me and smiled again. "Sofi's told me that you've done your homework. And since we've gotten this far—the honest answer is that I don't know anything for sure. Not about Tripp. I do know that we were at Vito's one night that year, and Jack left his phone on the table when he got up to get his pizza, and I saw Tripp's name in his Facebook Chat notifications. But who the fuck knows."

"And Blake?"

Mark paused again, as if appraising his words. "What about him?" Mark hit his Juul again and exhaled. "Listen, like—I can count on one hand the number of one-on-one conversations Jack and I had after our first year. He found me in the Dining Center after one of our final exams a few weeks after I came out to make sure that our *secret was safe*, but I wasn't privy to his private matters of the heart otherwise." Here I heard the bitterness that seemed to break from the sadness of his earlier smiles. "I dunno. Blake was safer, I guess, from Jack's perspective—he wasn't shitting where he was eating—and he probably went about it the way we all went about it: by sending him an Honesty Box message asking if he liked to suck dick. God only knows what it would have been like if we'd had Grindr."

"And what about Foster?"

"Now *that*, I have no fucking idea. I went up to Dartmouth one weekend my freshman year to see Annabeth and randomly ran into Blake at some frat party, and we ended up having some intense conversation when she went off to buy coke. Nothing happened," he added, seeing my eyebrows twitch upward. "He was absolutely blacked out, so I doubt he remembers any of this, because to my knowledge I'm the only person he's ever told—but yeah." The insouciance of his words betrayed their brittleness, and in them I felt the husk of what had long ago been emotion. "Apparently—or so Blake claimed—Jack and Foster also jerked off together once. And he told me about that night in the Field House. He seemed to like the idea that Foster had been just, like, devastated by jealousy and pain, seeing them."

"What do you think?"

"I think Blake Mancetti is a narcissist and a diva who never got over the fact that Foster got to be friends with the cool kids as a new sophomore and he didn't. Maybe they did jack off together once—

Foster and Jack, I mean—but, like"—and here Mark smirked—"you'd be surprised how many good little straight boys have engaged in secret little experiments."

We'd been walking for an hour when we turned west onto Houston. We were both silent for a moment, and when Mark spoke again, the facetiousness had fallen from his voice. "I dunno—it was my understanding that Foster was very seriously fucked up. And I don't just mean in terms of the drugs or whatever, and I don't just mean that he was crazy. I mean—I assume you've read all the stuff he wrote. It kind of seemed like maybe he'd been just barely holding it all together, and then something about everything that happened suddenly made it too hard to pretend." He hit his Juul again and let out the vapor in a sigh. "But I'm sure the truth is a lot less interesting."

XXXIII.

Foster Dade
English III / Dr. Arthur Tierney
Final Paper
Due March 16, 2010

There were money problems. This is the version of events they put out into the world, and for all I know it may have been true. I know that my father had a very good job at a pretty major regional bank back home in Baltimore, but I suppose there's a chance that, too, had always been illusory. My older sister, Maggie, knows a lot more than I do about certain things, but they're things that I've never found all that interesting or important. In any case, there are things I know—things that ultimately feel more crucial to the big picture—that I know and she doesn't.

I don't know if she knows that I am responsible for our parents' divorce. For everything else I fuck up with my emotions, she and I don't really fight, at least not the way we did when we were kids, so there haven't been any of those moments of anger where she might have otherwise weaponized that fact against me. I know that there are people in Baltimore who know the truth—who don't believe it was a money thing, in other words—but while I've seen them looking at me and muttering in a way they wouldn't mutter if it really was just about money, I don't think they know my role in the whole thing. (It's the one thing I don't really ever write about on the blog I keep in lieu of a journal, if only because writing about it really hurts.) For three years, my mother has insisted that it's not true: that the truth would have come out eventually. But the fact of the matter is that the truth came out because of what I did.

This isn't an essay about tennis, but of course it kind of is. This is an essay about tennis because it's an essay about my father. To this day, I've never learned or figured out why he was so set on me playing, and in the context of everything else it kind of feels like a cliché. Crazy sports dad acting out his rage/insecurity by yelling at his kids from the sideline, etc. I wanted to quit after sixth grade. That was the first year I played on the Gilman middle school team: the first year I realized that I was good but by no means stellar, which I was fine with. I understood even then that I was supposed to be stellar, and I figured it would be in everyone's best interest if I cut my losses and sussed out some other talent my father could scream at me about.

But I didn't quit, and in seventh grade I spent every weekend traveling to play in tournaments with kids who didn't seem to have any emotions on the subject at all: they just played, as if automated, and their equally automated parents stood on the sidelines and just stared at their robot children until the match was over. These were the kids who invariably won.

If one were to look upon my admittedly short romantic résumé, they would probably be underwhelmed. I've started to realize that on a pretty basic biological level, I feel incapable of normal trust or intimacy, physical or romantic. The most interesting thing about me is that for ten months, I have been selling ADHD medication to my classmates and other acquaintances at various private boarding or day schools between Virginia and Maine. Being at Kennedy sometimes feels like living in an autonomous territory within a larger country: there are no federal or state laws; only Major School Rule Violations. As a result, I often forget that what I'm doing is not only illegal but insanely illegal. I've lost count of exactly how much money I've made, but if I do the math in my head, I'd guess it's about as much as a year's tuition at Kennedy. But I couldn't care less about the money. I do this because it's one of the ways that I allow myself to feel remotely valuable to this world. People my year here are starting to get into pretty serious relationships—by this I mean they have sex and tell each other they love each other—and when I look at what they have, I realize that the closest thing I have to it is selling Adderall/Vyvanse: it's the only way I feel sincerely seen by someone other than myself. I realize how pretentious that sounds, but bear with me. I lost my virginity this past fall to a girl I never loved. We dated for roughly three months, and I see now that I was miserable pretty much the entire time: partially because of my inability to find any sort of satisfaction in it, and partially because for the entirety of that time, and for both the twelve months before it and the two and a half months since, I have quietly been in love with a girl named Annabeth. I suppose this paper is about her, in the same way that it's about tennis, and I'll get there.

My dad was in Boston the week before the Radnor Valley Tennis Invitational. It was in September of eighth grade. Gilman makes an annoyingly big deal about the transition to high school: several times a week they tell you that their ninth grade is about as academically challenging as certain universities. As an "early taste of upper school's academic demands," Ms. Hensley assigned us a five-page research paper on an ancient civilization of our choosing. I'd always found China incredibly interesting. I remember being five and having a book called something like This Is the Way We Go to School, which was about thirty pages of illustrations depicting kids of various nationalities doing the thing the title implies. I remember loving the depiction of China in the book, even though I'd guess now that the illustrator had never been anywhere close to China: he'd drawn a girl biking happily along the Great Wall with chopsticks sticking out of her bag. For some reason I was obsessed with it, and in the years that followed I'd take out books from the library about Chinese history and Chinese culture.

Point being: the obvious choice was to write about China. Ms. Hensley made it annoyingly clear that papers lacking cited evidence would suffer come grading time. I was actually very excited about it: for as long as I can remember, I've loved pursuing knowledge for its own sake and then putting it into words. I was thus mildly annoyed when she informed us it would be due the following Monday: immediately after the weekend of the Radnor tournament.

I don't know when I first saw the little Toshiba laptop up on the shelf in my dad's study, but I know that it had been there for a few years at least, and I suppose I'd always assumed that it didn't belong to anyone—that my dad had brought it home from work one day and promptly forgotten about it. My mom was in the kitchen that night when I asked her if I could bring the laptop to the tournament and do my paper on it at the hotel. I used to love it when my dad would go out of town: it was almost like she stopped being our mom and became a pal, all three of us united by being alone at home together. She said it was fine, and so the night before I left for Philly, I stood on the office chair in the study and pulled the laptop down, very proud of myself.

Perry Wilson's mom took us to the tournament that weekend. I neither liked nor disliked Perry, though I suppose he had his moments. He was mostly friendless at school, and I think his mother confused our playing tennis together for something more; because my own mother was (is) a very good person, I'd been forced in seventh grade to begrudgingly attend a handful of very dull sleepovers at Perry's. Perry had been very excited about going to the tournament together, and in the car to Philly I got the sense that he and his mom had reimagined the weekend as a sort of spectacular two-night slumber party, contingent on me basically being held hostage. Still, I like traveling—I like the hotels and the restaurants and the way their monotony is consistent everywhere. Mrs. Wilson took us to the Red Robin near our hotel, and back at the hotel Perry and I watched the first half of American Pie on his portable DVD player.

I lost in the third round the next day; Perry lost in the second. And after dinner that night (P. F. Chang's), I told Perry that I needed to work on my paper.

For as long as I could remember, my dad's password to everything was Barter6262. I never asked him what it meant, and I wasn't sure how I'd even learned it: it's just one of those things I absorbed at an early age, and after everything happened, I'd learn that Maggie and my mom hadn't ever known it. This was how I got into his Toshiba laptop.

The first thing I realized was that it hadn't been sitting forgotten in his study all that time. When I logged on, his calendar opened and began to chime with reminders; emails began appearing in his Outlook inbox. I'd looked over his shoulder at his work laptop before, and later I'd realize the messages didn't look like the emails he got from BB&T. I opened a Word document and Internet Explorer. When I went to Google to search for some material, I noticed how long the recent search history was.

At first I thought that I had missed some sort of crucial piece of data that would explain it all: perhaps he shared the laptop with people at work, or perhaps he'd been hacked, or perhaps he'd been searching the things he was searching for medical reasons. I had hit puberty in the middle of the previous summer, and though I never talked about any of it with him— boners, hair, masturbating, etc.—I always figured both he and Mom had figured it out via their omniscient parenting instincts. It had been thirty years since he'd been in my shoes, after all.

I never shared with anyone the exact details of what I saw that night in that Hilton Garden Inn. I could say what I needed to say without them. I didn't tell them what terms I saw when I began to type "Shang Dynasty": terms like "sexy college girls anal" and "slut takes big black cock husband watching." As if I needed to prove to myself that it was real, I started typing new letters at random. N: "naked teen spanked fucked public"; E: "eighteen yr old slut pegging 3some big black cock"; K: "kinky threesomes boston craigslist." I kept moving to new places in search of information that would prove me wrong. I clicked to the History tab, where I saw a list of websites with names like cuckoldfantasies.net. The most recent item was a Craigslist link, and I clicked it. I do not know why I still remember every word.

CRAIGSLIST / Boston / Personals / Casual Encounters / **m4mf looking for cuck couple**

Fit married mid-40s dad in town traveling looking for slut/bull for discrete fun. BDSM/humiliation play a plus. Help me degrade your girl the way I cant with my wife. Very experienced. Not gay but will suck. Can host at InterContinental. Reply with pics.

Two things were below that. The first was my father's cell phone number. The second was a row of three pictures. In the first one, cut off from the neck up, a naked man stood in front of a hotel mirror. His penis was hard. The second was of a tattooed woman bent over a bed, taken from above by whoever was having sex with her. And the third one I had seen before: our Christmas card from the year before, taken in the Bahamas. It had been cropped, but imperfectly. My father was in a golf shirt, smiling his tight smile, and sitting there to his right was me.

I did not realize until it was too late that Perry was looking over my shoulder.

All I remember about that night is that I threw up, and that Perry didn't talk to me afterward. I never really figured what prompted him to tell the other guys at school what he'd seen. I could end here and say that the moral of the story is that I came to Kennedy. (I could have stuck around at Gilman, I'm sure; maybe people would have forgotten. I spent a lot of time thinking about what made them believe his story, but the point is that they did.) But that's not where the story ends. There's a wonderfully riveting second act, in which a thirteen-year-old boy comes home from a tennis tournament. My dad was coming back from Boston on Wednesday.

It was Tuesday night when I finally told my mom, though my memory of that evening is hazy. I remember that she was humming as she cleaned the kitchen. I started sobbing as I told her, crying so hard she couldn't understand what I was saying, and so I simply gave her the laptop. I remember hearing her cry, and I remember hearing my dad's car pull into the driveway on Wednesday after school. I had gotten an iPod the Christmas before, and I put it on as he came in the front door, and I suppose I lay there for several hours, listening to U2 and Journey and Madonna. I did not let myself take my earphones off.

And then I heard my door open. My dad had broken through the lock, splintering the wood by the knob. I heard my mother screaming as he came in. He pulled me off the bed by my shirt, I remember.

"You fucking asshole," he said. "Do you know what you did? Do you know what you fucking did?"

And then he was gone. That was two and a half years ago. I have not seen him since then. My mother still hugs me better than anyone and tells me it's not my fault, but there are moments when I look at her and something in her eyes tells me she doesn't entirely believe that. I'm writing this paper because for three and a half years I have lived in silence with the knowledge I am sharing with you know. I atone for what I did by withholding myself from the world—by holding back my own brokenness in order to keep it from breaking anything else.

I think that's why I fell for Annabeth Whittaker the way I did. I remember so vividly the first time I saw her, in the light of late August on my first day at

XXXIV.

Foster Dade was expelled from the Kennedy School on the morning of Thursday, March 11, 2010. He had returned to his room in Brennan House just before check-in the prior evening, where he would remain until he heard the knock on his door just before breakfast the following morning. The version of his story that's still told today claims that he'd already started packing up his things into his large Tupperware bins when Scott McCall and Delia Chissom appeared in his doorway, but as a narrative detail it seems a bit too cute to be plausible. In the more immediate days thereafter, students would claim that the garbage bag of pills had been located in the trash cans by the back door to Brennan, but the validity of this is incidental.

Charlie Obermeier and Nic Bergman had gotten special dispensation from Mr. McCall to watch the first night of the ACC tournament, and they'd later recall that they'd been sitting in the common room eating Papa John's when Jack Albright came through the doors from Brennan's porch, twenty minutes late to check-in. There are strange intimacies that emerge in the residential experience of boarding school, and among them is the fluency with which you come to recognize another person's footsteps. Nic Bergman lived across the hall from Foster Dade on the second floor that year, and when Foster was expelled, he waited two days in a sort of shiva-sitting before moving his television and Xbox and beanbag chairs into the newly empty room across from his. He and the other Second Years would hang out there on the year's remaining Saturday nights after check-in, and though he was too embarrassed to share this with his friends, Charlie Obermeier later recalled the strange and unnerving sense of presence that seemed to occupy the room alongside them, and though he realized he was being melodramatic, he'd fall asleep on those nights thinking about Foster Dade in that room, sitting at his desk with his Bose headphones on and nodding along to Passion Pit or the Cure, looking up with arched eyebrows at whomever had tapped on his door in pursuit of grammar advice or Adderall.

By virtue of his proximity to the stairs that year, Nic had come to know the raucous clomp of Jack Albright's feet as he moved up or down through the house. The night before Foster was expelled from Kennedy, Nic had returned to his room at halftime in the UNC–Georgia Tech game to quickly scribble out his Math II homework when he heard Albright descending the stairs outside. There was something subdued to it, he'd noticed indifferently, but even in the reticence of the steps, he knew the way the wood of the old stairs strained beneath Albright's mass. And as the movement ceased just outside his room there on the second floor, Nic idly hoped that Albright would be swinging open his door with his usual yawps of masculine bravado, but it remained closed and the hallway outside stayed silent.

The night before Foster Dade was expelled, Jack Albright appeared in Foster's doorway. "Yeah, I talked to him," he'd tell his friends in the days thereafter with the coy, cocky grin he'd been able to summon. He never expounded upon the nature of this conversation, and Mason and Freddie and the rest of them would be left to imagine Jack defending his girlfriend's honor with rhetoric or violence or both, leaving Foster cowering in a corner or simply pulling out his suitcase right then and there. That the subtextual implication—that Foster's departure had been a voluntary exercise in self-abasement—found credence in this circle spoke to the arrogance of their faith in their own despotic moral order, and to the rather striking degree to which they knew absolutely nothing.

The truth was that it hadn't been a conversation by any normal definition. Jack had simply stood there, struggling against the memory of his humiliation to look Foster in the eyes. And Foster had simply stared back. He was frightened of Jack in that moment, but then again he had always been: even in the grandeur of their spells of closeness, the ferocity with which Jack Albright seemed to throw himself through the world had been explicit in the violence that propelled it. It was only when Foster had finally learned the truth that he saw this violence for what it was, and what frightened him in that moment was the silent pain that lashed within it. He had spent those happy stretches never quite convinced of Jack's affections, which could seem conditional or simply fictitious depending on the affection in question. It was only then, in those silent minutes that night at the very end of everything, that Foster finally came to believe them. More than anyone else, maybe even Annabeth, Jack had felt the flicker of Foster's anguish, and in his own, it had pulled him in. It's in this fact that we can now see the inevitability of what ultimately happened.

"Jack," Foster had said quietly.

And Jack had looked at him a little bit longer, and then without a word he turned and left, closing the door behind him. They would never see each other again, of course, even the following morning, even given Jack's centrality to its events. We do not know when Jack Albright began to amass the contents of the file folder he'd created on his computer, only the incontrovertibility with which it incriminated Foster. He returned to his room and methodically began to print its contents. Foster Dade's final paper for Tierney was really only an aesthetic flourish to a much richer body of forensic evidence, and it and the Blogspot were less compelling to Theresa Daniels than the many dozens of screenshotted text messages, both Jack's and others, in which Foster very meticulously laid out what he had to sell and what he was selling it for. (Jack's decision to include his own correspondence was a calculated gamble, carefully hedged by both his unimpeachable public profile and the accompanying narrative it sustained; in the end, a rather deadened Theresa Daniels would opt to accept that the exemplary student athlete and third-generation Kennedian had indeed been victim to his housemate's psychological predation, and simply thank him for having the courage and maturity to speak out against a close friend.) Nic Bergman would hear Jack's footsteps again that night, after lights-out. From his own room, Foster would watch Mr. McCall's living room window fill with light, and through the gap in its gentle curtains he would see Jack Albright step inside.

* * *

Expulsions are rarely angry affairs. It's a waste of emotional band-width, as far as Theresa Daniels was ever concerned; any punitive damage yelling could inflict has already been felt tenfold. There isn't much available evidence to tell us what happened inside Alumni Hall that day; Foster Dade's was ironically the one student file I couldn't obtain from the administration's database. But I'd imagine that he left Kennedy the way he came, which is simply quietly. No one saw McCall and Chissom bring him to the Dean of Students' office that morning, and only Nic Bergman claims to have seen Charlotte Harrison crying noiselessly as she packed up her son's bedroom in Brennan. It was sometime in the afternoon that the pewter Lexus pulled away toward the Meadow. It slid around the edge of the vast lawn, past Brennan and Donavan across the expanse from the quiet solemnity of Memorial Hall and the chapel's high belfry, and after passing Ames House it moved out the gate and turned south toward I-95.

PART IV

This is the room where we always dreamed
Of grass and splendid evenings

—Passion Pit

I.

My earliest drafts of this project date back to the spring of 2015, submitted then as exercises for an undergraduate creative nonfiction workshop in my sophomore year of college. They were short essays, written with magazines in mind, and in them I tended to begin Foster's story with his expulsion. I understood this to be the poignant thing: in these crude, simplified renditions, I believed that every event leading up to those final hours could be collapsed and condensed into the density of their narrative magnitude, like the ephemeral flashes of light brought into the dark gravitational mass of a dying star. I approached those preliminary events accordingly, recalibrating their details and interpretations to accommodate the magnificent drama of the minute final act, which in my younger mind was nothing more than the entirety of the play itself.

A few things prompted my revisions to this conceit, the final product of which you've just read. The first is that I grew up a bit, I hope. I'm less swayed by the exploitative thuds of tragedy than I used to be. I spent many years too frightened of my own vulnerability to attempt to tell a story that I'd promised myself I'd tell, and for once I'm grateful that my ego got in the way of things. My earliest research sat neglected on my computer for several years before I finally came back to things in earnest; when I did, the story I found in their uncurated mass was different than the one I'd first set out to reconstruct. It found its form in the very chaos of this early archive, and the three and a half years of work that followed were an exercise in its illustration, rather than its curation. What I mean by that is the truest version of Foster Dade's story exists only in the impossibility of its organization into any tidy narrative cabinet. The many gigabytes and pages of research

I accumulated in the service of transmitting that truth only multiplied its disarray. (My roommates know that I mean this very literally, and insofar as these final pages can moonlight as an Acknowledgments section, I'd like to offer them an apology.)

I'm wary of our culture's recent celebration of journalism as a selfless or especially noble enterprise, and in the interest of tempering my own self-regard accordingly, I should admit that something cheaper ultimately motivated me to decenter my approach away from the coda that had initially promised elegance. At the end of the day, the body of data sustaining this narrative began to seem richer and indeed more profound on its own terms than any contrived moral arc I may have produced. It found its errant, kaleidoscopic light in the voices that came to spill across it, voices that were more lucid and less grating than my own: Sofi Cohen's and Jason Stearns's; Mark Stetson's and Eloise McClatchy's; the four dozen others that patiently and eloquently helped illuminate a nineteen-month period otherwise befuddled by lost time. Indeed, Annabeth Whittaker's.

I went back to Kennedy recently, on a Saturday in late fall. I was embarrassed at how self-conscious the idea of driving in through the main gates suddenly made me, but nevertheless I left the Uber outside Vito's. A group of girls sat in the front booth with their long hair against the window, and across from them were boys in baseball caps and quarter-zip sweaters. It occurred to me that they'd been as young as two years old when Foster Dade came to Kennedy.

I hadn't been back since my Five Year. It had been wet and cold for mid-May that weekend, and I'd always preferred the campus in autumn anyway, so with a placidity I hadn't enjoyed then I let myself cross the Meadow. It was the weekend before fall quarter finals, I gathered. Two boys were sitting up on the Brennan porch; one of them was idly tossing a tennis ball into the air and catching it. A boy and a girl were standing by the foot of the chapel, kissing. The place was beautiful and unnervingly unfamiliar. I chose to not spend too much time contemplating the students I passed: I found I could notice only their youth, and it threatened to dislodge something I had for ten years taken for granted about my own time there. I considered stopping in front of Brennan, asking the boys on the porch if they could let me inside, but instead I walked on.

And on the train back to Manhattan that evening, I began to understand the coarser, less personal reality that ultimately disqualified the plausibility of any single elegant conclusion to the story I have tried to tell. The simple truth is that after Foster Dade was expelled from Kennedy, the world spun on.

Jack Albright got engaged two months after Annabeth Whittaker did, to the girl I'd seen him walking with outside J.G. Melon the previous winter. Her name is Hailey Davenport, and she grew up in Richmond; they met at Princeton in her first year and his last. I gather from those who've met her that she's both incredibly kind and incredibly boring. I've looked at her Instagram, and my sense is that she's the sort of person who understands life as an exercise in minimizing one's own imposition upon it. I wish I could tell you that the timing of his proposal with respect to his first girlfriend's engagement was anything other than incidental. I can envision a version of this story in which Jack Albright and Annabeth Whittaker found themselves inextricably and happily connected by the common wistfulness of shared history: their loss of virginity to each other; their early stabs at the emotional demands of romance; the turbulence that spasmed across their high school years, particularly with the sudden arrival of a quiet boy from Baltimore. But that is not this story. The duller, perhaps sadder truth is that he called her a bitch when she broke up with him at a frozen yogurt shop on Nassau Street, and that they exchanged only polite but cursory words when they saw each other years thereafter. Every now and again, a long-extinguished high school flame will flicker back to ephemeral life on the Saturday night of the Five Year—I have a rather sweet if voyeuristic photo on my phone I took of Skye Franklin and Connor Urquhart standing at dusk on the football fields beyond the reunion tent—but that did not happen to them. Their group of friends was irreparably fractured by the twin expulsions of March 2010; Porter Roth never quite forgave the two girls left behind, and spent her Fourth Year happily forging new ground with Jason Stearns and

Noah Baum and the other lighthearted cerebral types who hung out in the evenings on the benches outside Haskell House.

That only six months had passed since Foster Dade's expulsion when I arrived at Kennedy now seems almost laughably paltry when I think about my first encounters with his story. I'm older now, of course; half a year occupies a smaller fraction of my lifetime now than it did a decade ago. This might have had something to do with what seems in retrospect like the suddenness of things: the haste with which his story began to spin itself into the nebulous tendrils of mythology, elongating and shifting in their form with the early litigation of details. I suppose that in those first months, its magic blossomed against the uncanny silence left behind in the truth's otherwise recent wake. I can't pretend I ever exchanged a single word with Annabeth Whittaker or Jack Albright or Porter Roth in our overlapping year at Kennedy, but when I watched them from across the dusk-lit distance I somehow understood that the events of the prior spring belonged to a history that even then was inaccessible, if only by virtue of its constituents' resolve.

I sympathized with the concertedness of this silence, and today I owe it for the luster it helped sustain in a legend that may have otherwise passed by me. But for a very long time, I never quite believed the very conceit responsible for the shimmer than emanates from the story in question. I'm referring to the immutable finality with which that story came to a close: the very coda I've been reluctant to engage as such. What made Foster Dade's story so compelling so soon after his expulsion was its tacit emphasis on his disappearance. That was always the word, sometimes used interchangeably with *vanish*. As in: when Foster Dade was expelled from Kennedy, he simply disappeared, or vanished.

And yet I see now that there is a truth to this, not only in its allegorical music but in the very facts themselves. At some point in the forty-eight hours after Foster Dade deleted his Blogspot, he deleted his Facebook, too. It's not clear precisely when this happened—Jason Stearns remembers seeing him online the evening after Foster borrowed his key to the tennis closet, but can't be sure. We can imagine the cute sort of postmodern argument that when he effaced himself from the internet, he effaced himself, too. There's a certain credence to be found in this: after all, it was the internet that had allowed fifteen-year-old Foster Dade to imagine the refuge he might find at Kennedy, in those anxious summer nights on Facebook before coming to school in the fall of 2008. It was the internet that let him make those futile stabs at bringing those daydreams into the clarity of realization: in the thrill of seeing Annabeth's photos of him and Jack on the Brooklyn Bridge at dawn; in the delightfully inane wall posts he exchanged with Jack Albright and Pritchett Pierce in those fleeting cozy months leading up to the start of Third Year; indeed in the sprawling network its translucent bridges of data equipped him to construct, later known only as the "Kennedy Adderall ring."

But the competing truth is that Foster Harrison Dade—the boy who for a short stretch of time looked upon the world in its analog splendor, and dazzled in it—did survive beyond the internet after he effaced himself from it, if only for a little while. He returned to Baltimore with his mother that day, and at some point in the month thereafter he returned to the Gilman School, though by July the thin spokes of the Sotheby's sign had been stuck into the earth along the edge of their front yard. In a real estate market still emaciated by global crisis, 190 Overland Road sold with an almost suspicious immediacy. By August, the Lexus was gone from the driveway. In its place was a Volvo belonging to the middle-aged psychologist who lived there with her husband, who every morning could walk the half-mile under the lush greens of North Baltimore to his office in the English Department at Johns Hopkins. They did not have children, and so the upstairs bedroom that looked out over the front yard became the husband's study.

Charlotte Harrison remarried that winter, and those neighbors in Baltimore she'd stayed in touch with during those final years understand that her new husband was a tax attorney named Bruce, and that they now lived together lived in Seattle. They'd been introduced by mutual friends who'd known her in Washington, and before he'd returned from a yearlong professional project in New York City, she'd taken the Acela up to Penn Station several times a month, and sometime shortly after going home to the West Coast he had proposed.

We know very little about Foster Dade's life in the year and a half after he left the mid-Atlantic with his mother. A Soundcloud account registered to one fdade93 in February 2011 is mostly barren; we might infer that its creator signed up for the site with an immediate and narrow intention and then promptly forgot about it. Two files populate the account's Liked Tracks page: Avicii's Essential Mix on BBC Radio 1, which was then beginning to be talked about, and the Dream Academy's demo cut of "Life in a Northern Town." The user's profile carries no other identifying data.

Given the attention and care with which I've reproduced the events in it up until this point, I'm obviously tempted to occupy this absence of factual material with a gestural improvisation of what is missing. And given what we ultimately know, and given the abundance of clinical literature on the subjective experience of addiction, I could do this with a certain faith in the veracity of my efforts. We would at least know where to truncate this postlude if I did pursue it.

Though she'd begun to forge a happy existence for herself in Seattle, it was in Baltimore that Charlotte Harrison had built her life, and where her son embarked on his, and for this reason we can find the short obituary in the archives of the April 5, 2012, edition of the Baltimore *Sun*. He had died two days earlier, two weeks before his nineteenth birthday. It was a cursory, almost clerical paragraph; only the names of his mother and father and sister in the final sentence intimate that a life had transpired beyond it. Only the parents who are particularly maudlin in their grief specify overdose as the cause of death in these documents, but public medical records in King County affirm for us that this is what happened. At risk of engaging in the very conjecture we've cautioned against, it seems reasonable to venture that by the time he was expelled from Kennedy, the genetic blueprint of Foster's incipient addiction to opioids—which biologically would have existed long before the first parcel of white pills arrived from Hong Kong—had already reached the point of synaptic nourishment that all but ordained the dependency that followed.

I note this with no somber or winking reference to any specific narrative turn in his story: on the contrary, I wish to suggest only the pure biology of it all. It would be very easy to allegorize things on this front, of course. The Adderall operation, the OxyContin overdose: we could weave together a metaphorical cautionary tale about intoxication and addiction and self-destruction in the service of the same thematic currents that have carried us to where we are now, but to do so would be to both cheapen and complexify something that needs or deserves neither.

I share the details of his death only to preempt your own inevitable discovery of what happened to him. But the simpler fact is that Foster Dade in many respects ceased to exist when he left Kennedy. His disappearance from those networks only lends material form to a quieter elision: when he left, he took with him the world he'd come to illuminate through the twinkling elegance of his attachments to it—a regency of daydreams and dusklight and the infinite promises of old cities seen from high bridges when their tributaries of light whisper into the darkness. What startled me throughout my research for this project was precisely how few people knew that he had died. At a certain point I began to realize that the story they were telling me depended on the illusion of a certain boundlessness: for them, its charge rested in the unspoken but unchallenged idea of the disappeared boy persisting out there somewhere, forever sixteen, looking up to the cosmos with his sad eyes and exploring them. I've chosen not to condemn these tacit interpretations. I realize that each holds its own shimmer for the person who holds it: I think back to my own early months at Kennedy, lying awake in the moonlight that spilled through my window from out over the Meadow, and I remember the strange solace I found in those mythologies we told one another late at night, when we'd sit together in our little kingdoms of darkness, spun together by the electric possibilities of our silence, watching the chalky embers of headlights press down Eastminster Road.

It has been twelve years since I first heard this story; whatever wholeness it may have once possessed has dispersed itself now. What we can do is watch it recede into the stellar mystery of such nighttimes, and hold the wonder of the shadows that remain.

II.

Foster Dade / English III Final Paper / Page 14

. . . though I suppose I'm precisely where I realize I should be. I know subconsciously that I do these things because I think they bring a complexity to life—to myself—that fills the gaps left there by the things that have happened. I'd like to think that the gaps will fill on their own someday. I'm not sure what this'll mean with respect to my dad: I don't think I'll ever not despise myself for what I did, but maybe I'll learn to be philosophical about it. No matter what she might secretly feel sometimes, my mom is still my friend. And so is Annabeth. I know deep down that she and I will never have what she and Jack have, but to be utterly honest, I'm not sure I want that, or at least I'm not sure I'd know what to do with it if I had it. What I cherish is the magic of the connection. Of being understood. And there were moments when I felt it with Jack too.

But I realize now this isn't a paper about Annabeth, or my father, or Adderall, or tennis. It's a paper about me. It's a little after midnight as I write this; I'm listening to "With or Without You" by U2 and feeling like an utter sap as I look out my window at the campus at night. There are moments like this when I allow myself to see the beauty I'd always foreclosed to myself. Part of me thinks that my ability to see it when I do is inseparable from the pain I feel, and when I think that, the pain suddenly isn't so bad. The sun's going to come up in the morning. I really don't like myself a lot of the time, but sometimes I look back over the words I've written on my blog and elsewhere and I kind of smile at my own bullshit. I'll grow up, and then I will come back to them again. It's fine. I will be fine. There is a spastic firelight in everything. The trick is knowing how to find it.

THE END

Author's Note

Any story is only as good as the lives that populate it. In this respect, the paragraphs that follow attempt a sort of metanarrative of the novel you've just read. Earlier drafts were guilty of the sort of masturbatory solipsism you might associate with the word *metanarrative*, but I've realized—in part because my agents and editor are literally always right—that the only version of this book's history worth telling finds its warrant in the names that follow. A narrative is a narrative, of course, and accordingly I'll defer to some pretense to chronology in rendering it. TL;DR: My cup runneth over.

In March 2013, as a twenty-year-old sophomore in the Writing Seminars at Johns Hopkins University, I submitted an assignment to Tristan Davies's fiction workshop titled "How Love Songs Are Written, Probably." The eleven-page story followed a young man from Baltimore in the hours ahead of his expulsion from a boarding school in New Jersey. For reasons still unclear to me, this character had begun appearing on the peripheries of my short fiction half a year earlier. He began as simply a name, one that I typed into a Note on my iPhone in September 2012; soon thereafter, he began populating the background of the parties or high school classes I tended to write about for my undergrad fiction classes. When I began to revisit these documents in the months after finishing this novel, I saw a boy conspicuous only in his silence, described chiefly with respect to the sadness of his eyes.

It would take half a decade of indecision and self-doubt before I finally set out to expand Foster Dade's story into the book you've just read. I still do not know what finally impelled me to begin writing *Foster* in earnest in July 2018, in my final months as *Time*'s congressional correspondent in Washington. What I do know is that I soon thereafter sent the first fifty pages to Stephen Langer. Over the two and a half years that followed, Steve would read multiple iterations of the evolving draft with an enthusiasm that almost single-handedly kept this project alive in its early days. His preternaturally sharp sense of nostalgia and unflinching honesty salvaged the book from existential weaknesses; far more importantly, he told me to keep going. For this I am so stupidly grateful.

It was Steve who encouraged me to share those first chapters with Ruth Landry, who at the time was working in the literary division at ICM. She looked past their early deficiencies and saw the story I sought to tell, and in doing so gave me the confidence and perspective to carry on. If the preceding pages possess anything resembling a coherent formal architecture, it found its primal blueprint in her candor and wisdom. In more ways than one, you are holding this book in your hands because of her.

I have learned with time and ample practice to see that there is an ineffable harmony between disappointment and serendipity. In September 2020, I was a twenty-seven-year-old former journalist whose email inbox had recently welcomed twelve discrete rejections from twelve discrete Ph.D. programs. In a fit of nihilism, I'd spent the summer returning to the novel I'd been writing in sporadic fits over the preceding twenty-six months. By the fall, this book was just over six hundred pages long and just over halfway finished.

I always assumed that Academy Award winners thanked their agents onstage as a matter of ritual. I now understand that no exercise—not a speech, not a written homage, not my firstborn child—can adequately express everything I want to say here to Sloan Harris and Julie Flanagan. It is in the nature of miracles to deny the lucidity of their workings to the beneficiary; I thus won't ever know how or why they looked at that early bloated, digressive mess and saw the book I'd wanted to write since I was fifteen. Over the months that followed, their dynamism, creative brilliance, and general mercy equipped me to finish telling Foster's story; without it, there is a very good chance that I would have simply never done so. For the better part of a year, they lived with this book as intimately as I did; what light it may possess is as much theirs as mine.

What I will really remember of this period is their friendship. I will remember the many hours of happily conspiratorial phone calls in the winter and spring of 2021; I will remember the many cliffs they walked me off of. Sloan's avuncular patience and wisdom became my most palliative talisman. There was a familial thrall to our trio, and in every meaningful respect, Julie became my fourth sister. I sometimes suspect this was not a mutually fulfilling arrangement. Several times a week—often late at night or on Saturdays—her phone would hum with my spastic, self-obsessed versions of *hello*: "do you think the comma on page 384 should be a semicolon"; "would it be better if the manuscript were still nine hundred pages long"; "I think Taylor Swift would like my book." She was and is a wonderful sport about this (and everything else). I owe everything to her, and to Sloan. Since I was in second grade, I have wanted to spend my life writing stories; they have given me the gift of believing that I can.

I trusted Sloan and Julie unfailingly even at the most uncertain moments of this process, and so I trusted them when they told me to take a call in October 2021 with Zack Knoll. My professional life to date has been a sequence of relationships with patient editors, but none has hummed with the serendipitous magic of this one. Zack, too, understood instinctively what this book sought to be, and over the months of revisions that followed, I learned from his trenchant brilliance how we might achieve it. I will forever be in awe of his indefatigable work ethic, the lucidity of his creative and intellectual insight, and his preternatural gift for nudging me from my own stub-born indecisiveness. If there is cohesion or rhythmic elegance to this book, I say with utter certainty that it is Zack's handiwork, and that no other editor could have led us to anything close. His friendship, compassion, and candor kept me sane through many all-night edits and rewrites; each time, he saw what I was often too enervated or nearsighted to see, and encouraged me to trudge onward. You're reading these words because he got me where we needed to go, and I will never not be grateful. (This gratitude extends to the rest of the magnificent team at Overlook, whose commercial, aesthetic, and spiritual investment in my words—to say nothing of their willingness to take a chance on an unknown twenty-eight-year-old kid—would be nothing short of an act of divinity: Lisa Silverman, John McGhee, Sarah Masterson Hally, Eli Mock, Deb Wood, Andrew Gibeley, Kevin Callahan, Jamison Stoltz, and Michael Sand.)

This book owes its existence, too, to so many other acts of love, some less editorially tangible but no less magnificent than others. Jaquelin Perry and Mary-Lynn Moore were among its earliest and most consequential champions; I am forever indebted to their love and advocacy, even on the days when they beat me at Wordle. Here and elsewhere, Hudson Cole's perspicuity and bluntness kept me tethered— more or less—to the humility necessary to finish writing a novel. Alistair Fatheazam had far better things to do during the COVID-19 pandemic than read six hundred pages of an incomplete book, but he did so with a lawyer's rigorous eye; the feedback he offered me on a Nolita rooftop one cold November Saturday indelibly shaped the course of the manuscript and subsequent revisions.

Several hundred pages of this book's first draft took shape in the upstairs study of Lisa Ruddick's house in Hyde Park. I am forever indebted to Lisa's hospitality, and also to her friendship and wisdom, which buoyed me as I navigated a period of transition. I have a predilection for seeing life's more unlikely digressions to their delightfully absurd conclusions; it was in this spirit that I found myself spending much of the pandemic's first year alongside Ferebee, Brook, Bishop, Ford, Clarke, and Caroline Taube in Manhattan, North Carolina, and Costa Rica. Ferebee's and Brook's benevolence allowed me to write this book's final chapters in January 2021 and complete several revisions in the months thereafter; both would generously read and provide invaluable feedback on one of those (much longer) early drafts. On the most arduous days of writing and revising, though, it was the raucous company of Bishop, Ford, Clarke, and Caroline that saved me from myself. This is a book about youth, and when my own recollections seemed to elude me or deny me the necessary richness, the four of them reminded me what it meant to be young.

In August 2008, when I was fifteen years old, I left North Carolina for a boarding school five miles down the road from Princeton University. *Foster Dade Explores the Cosmos* is a work of fiction, but certain facets of Foster's world are indelibly my own. There really is a Memorial Hall at my high school that looks out on a round lawn designed by Olmsted; there really was a rancid old couch in the newspaper's basement office, where virginities were in fact lost. We really did congregate in our housemates' rooms late at night; we really did whisper the folklore that seemed to suffuse our common existence with the codifying shimmer of mystery. These stories really did haunt us long after we left. I could not have written this novel without the friendship of those with whom I cohabitated this world, whose feedback and support allowed me to remember this shimmer. I was a lonely, mostly friendless fifteen-year-old when Kylie Loeffler first asked me to go on a walk on a Saturday afternoon, and for a decade and a half since she has buoyed me with her unconditional warmth and humor. Her faith in me was this book's first sunlight. Nate Reilly and I had arrived on campus as new sophomores, but it wasn't until we found ourselves living together in Haskell House two years later that we discovered our common eye for the little absurdities of our world. Years later, his shrewdness and zeal challenged me to get those absurdities right. It is easy in certain spells of unchecked pretension to shrug off morality in the service of art, but too many times to count, Chris Murphy's candor and wisdom reminded me what really matters. Katherine Jones read and responded to early drafts with the mordant bluntness that has delighted and petrified me since we were fifteen; in art and in life, she keeps me honest. Maggie Salisbury's empathy and wit and the many, many hours of conversations it sustained were an unrivaled joy and comfort to me in the last and hardest months of writing and editing.

I could go on. There are so many others whose knowledge, support, or friendship—and often all three at once—inflects this book's pages or helped erect the earliest scaffolding within which they found form: Gabriel Ojeda-Sague, Thabet Mahayni, Justin Gitlin, Justin Landis, Spencer Perl, my teachers Callie Siskel and Tristan Davies, Dexter

Zimet, Brian Hershey, Jenna Santoro, inter alia. But five names remain that warrant a bit more than this. I will start with three individuals who've known me longer and know me better than anyone else I've named here: my sisters, Sophie, Susanna, and Eugenia. For nearly three decades, their self-confidence, forthrightness, and intelligence have saved me from myself too many times to count; forever and always, family do family. Certain things are learned, of course. My father has never wavered in urging me on along the circuitous paths I've forged for myself; every day I learn from his tenacity and humility. He is who I want to be when I grow up. My mother first read this novel in the summer of 2021 and offered me perhaps some of the smartest, most trenchant feedback I'd receive, but of course this was always going to be the case. For my entire life, she has been my most ruthless editor, my most formidable Scrabble opponent, and my fiercest champion. I am sustained by her advice, humor, and hugs. I am in awe of my stupid good fortune. I dedicate this book to the five of them.

So I'll conclude by quoting Marge Gunderson in *Fargo* (1996): *And here you are. And it's a beautiful day.* In the months after I finished my last revisions on this novel, I began to dream about my high school. In these dreams, it is always move-in day; it is neither 2008 nor 2022 but somehow both at once. I find myself in the first room I occupied there; the late-afternoon sunlight that catches in its cobwebbed window is the same light it was then. Sometimes, I find myself looking for one person in particular, who these days is only ever proximate to me in dreams like these. Normally, though, I look out across the lawn and discern the other faces that comprised the world to which I've returned. Many of them I've seen so many times in the decade since I left, yet in these dreams they appear to me as they did then. I realize that I remember things I'd otherwise forgotten: the fall of certain shadows; the dances of certain lights. I am fifteen again for a moment. I feel the possibility of everything. And then I wake up.

Chicago, Illinois
May 2023

ABOUT THE AUTHOR

NASH JENKINS grew up in Wilmington, North Carolina, and graduated from the Lawrenceville School in 2011. After graduating from Johns Hopkins University, he worked as a correspondent for *Time* in Hong Kong and Washington, DC; his cultural commentary has also been published by the *Atlantic*. He received his M.A. from the University of Chicago in 2019 and is currently a Ph.D. student in the Program in Media, Technology, and Society at Northwestern University. He lives in Chicago.